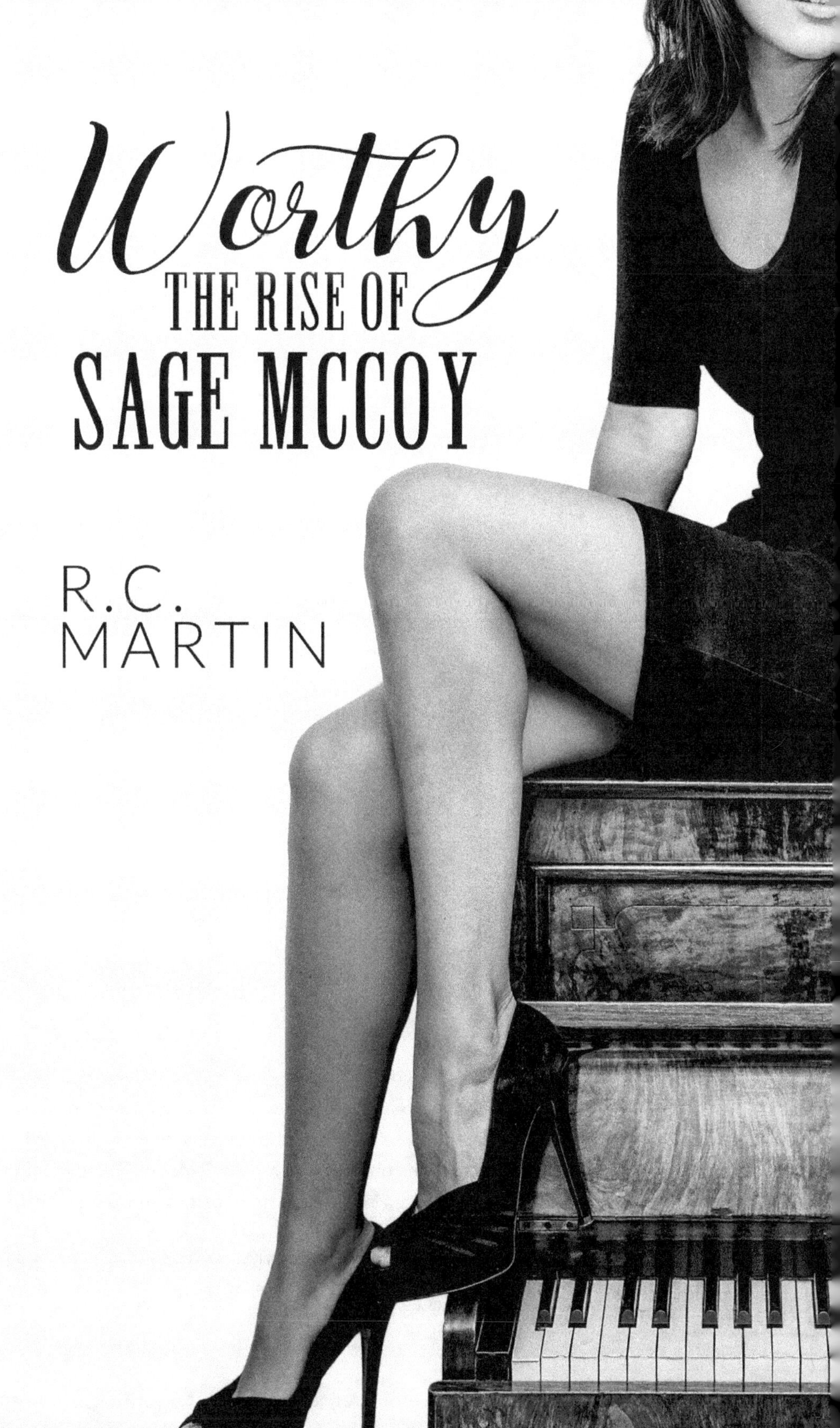
Worthy
THE RISE OF
SAGE MCCOY
R.C.
MARTIN

Cover Design by Cassy Roop at Pink Ink Designs ©2018
www.pinkinkdesigns.com

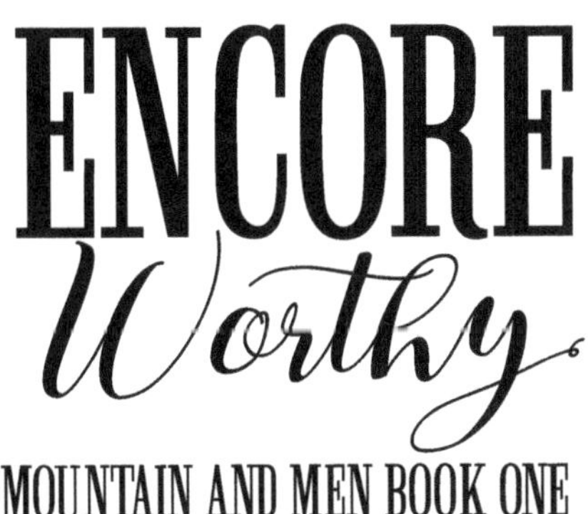
ENCORE
Worthy
MOUNTAIN AND MEN BOOK ONE

PROLOGUE

Sage

I see the demons in your eyes and I want to dance
Can't stop the beat I hear from one haunted glance
Take my hand, baby, don't let go
I'll set you free, baby, won't let go
All night/One song
This room/My home
I'll set you free, baby, don't let go
Tonight/Just give me tonight

I DON'T BELIEVE IN love at first sight. Love is messy. It's complicated. It's fucking *crazy*. How can you tell, with just one look, that you're staring at someone you love? How can you guess, in just one moment, that you'll go through shit and back just to make her smile? Can you seriously guarantee, without even knowing her name, that you're ready to take on her demons? In an instant, are you brave enough to give her yours?

I don't believe in love at first sight. When I saw Millicent for the first time, I wasn't thinking about forever. I remember thinking how gorgeous she was. She looked so fucking hot in that short skirt with those long-ass legs. Then I took one look into her dark green eyes and I felt it—felt her *music*. She barely smiled as we were introduced, so cool and seemingly unimpressed. That's when I knew I had to have her. For just one night, I wanted to feel her burdens, her pain, her heart;

I wanted to get lost in the notes of her melody, and I wanted her to shatter as she screamed my name.

I should have known better; should have known that one night was never going to be enough. I felt her *music* and it permeated through my soul. The second I walked away from her, I couldn't deny that she had left a mark. In an instant, lyrics were pouring into my head. I pulled out my phone without hesitation, recording myself singing the words, the melody coming to me as effortlessly as if it were my next breath.

I finished the phrase, believing that the words could be true. I pocketed the promise of a new song, thinking of how I could get my temporary muse alone and naked. She deserved a damn fine fuck for serving as my inspiration. Little did I know that she was anything but temporary; that one night would never be enough. She was worthy of more than a moment, more than a song.

Millicent Valentine was, and will always be, encore worthy.

ONE

Millicent

I NEED A DRINK.

Sometimes I wonder why I even bother with that woman. My mother is not a *mom*. She hasn't been for a really long time. I moved away—no, *ran* away—after I finished high school, just so that I didn't have to feel obligated to spend any extra time with her. Sure, Colorado is a far cry from New Jersey, and maybe the distance between us is a little dramatic, but I'm happy here. Well, I'm generally happy here. Then she calls me. Like clockwork. Every two weeks, always on a Saturday night—as if she knows I don't have a life.

Every conversation feels the same. She wants to know how work is going. She wants to know if I'm eating enough. Then she proceeds to bitch and moan about her own damn, miserable existence. She does it in such a way that if you were anyone other than me, you'd think she was talking about something as casual as the weather. But I *am* me; I've known the woman since birth. Listening to her talk about her life is like listening to her tell me why I owe her thirty minutes every other Saturday—because she brought me into this world and she sacrificed everything to make sure I stayed in it.

Fuck. I need a drink.

Sometimes, I'll remember having a *real* mom. Sometimes, when I least expect it, I'll be five years old again; I'll picture us playing together at the beach, my father snapping our picture with one hand, his cold brew in the other. Sometimes, I'll remember what it was like to have a family. Then, in the blink of an eye, I'm twenty-six again. Suddenly, I'm a woman who was abandoned by her father at six, a daughter who was left with a lifeless woman for a mother, and I feel just as alone as I always do.

Talking to Natalya Valentine every two weeks is just a sad reminder of where I come from and a horrifying picture of what my life could turn into if I'm not careful.

I take a deep breath before I insert my key and unlock the door to my apartment. I know my roommate, Sarah, is home. I saw her car in the lot on my way in. She's been living with me for a week and I've already managed to alienate her. I don't know her story. I don't know why she moved to Fort Collins or what she does from day to day. It's kind of hard to bond when you're avoiding each other. It's my fault and I know it, but I can't figure out how to fix it.

My last roommate, Jess, was hardly ever home. She was totally dedicated to her studies, which had her on campus all the time. I respected her immensely for her dedication. Our desire for knowledge was something we had in common. Well, just about the only thing we had in common. She also had a boyfriend, another reason she was hardly ever at home. She only brought the guy around a few times. He had shit aim when he pissed drunk and I sure as hell wasn't cleaning up after him. She wasn't a big fan of being on clean up duty when she was nursing her own hangover, so they made a habit of crashing elsewhere on the weekends.

She moved out just after graduation with plans of pursuing her master's degree. A friend of a friend told me about Sarah and it wasn't long before my empty spare room was filled. It just so happened that I was going when she was coming, so our first meeting was pretty pathetic. Our second encounter was even worse.

I'm a little OCD. I can't help it—it's in my nature. So, when I got home last Saturday and found that she had totally destroyed my kitchen and stolen my stash of chocolate chips in order to make cookies, I lost my shit. I'm not a warm and fuzzy person, but even I'll admit that I was a total bitch. It's entirely possible that she was baking with the hopes of sharing with me—I'll never know.

What I *do* know is that she's not as bad as I made her out to be. I think I might have called her a thief and a sloth during my rampage, but she's neither. She replaced all the ingredients that she used the very next day. Sarah's also really quiet and tidy; she just gets a little messy in the middle of her process. I have to remember that not everybody's brain works like mine and not everyone is as damaged as me. She totally seems like the warm and fuzzy type.

Making my way down the hallway to my bedroom, I spot her in the bathroom getting ready. She looks really pretty—her long blonde waves draped down her back, her toned, voluptuous body in a short pink dress with a jean jacket. She's finishing up her makeup, which makes her bright blue eyes pop. For just a moment, I admire her *glow*.

I've been told I'm quite beautiful. I'll admit that I consider myself to be an attractive person, but I most certainly do not *glow.*

"Hey," I say as her eyes meet mine in the mirror.

"Hey."

I stop, willing myself to *try* and make conversation. It's the least I can do, considering the way I've treated her thus far. "You going somewhere?"

"Yeah. Josh, Aria and I are going to The Brew Cycle. There's a band playing tonight that I wanted to check out."

"Oh. Cool." I nod, already unsure of where I could possibly go with this conversation.

It's not that I'm completely inept when it comes to talking to people, but I spend a lot of time in my head. In an instant, I know this conversation can only go one of two ways. Either I make a comment about her plans, which might come across as a desperate desire to receive an invitation; or, I inform her that I plan on staying in and drinking a bottle of wine while I reread Anna Karenina for the billionth time.

And if that doesn't sound pitiful, I don't know what does.

Deciding to quit while I'm ahead, I don't say anything more as I turn to continue my journey to my room. I don't get two steps before she's speaking again.

"Do you want to come?"

I stare at her for second, taken aback by her invitation. I wasn't expecting this chain of events at all. I don't go out much. Every once in a while I'll get together with a few of the professors that I work with and we'll get drinks. It's as close as I've ever been to a clique. I don't have a group of friends that I spend a lot of time with. My work is important to me and it's easy for me to get lost in it. That, or a good piece of literature—*which totally makes me sound like the loser my mother thinks I am.*

Honestly, what mother calls her daughter on a Saturday night?

God dammit—I need a drink.

Sarah lifts her eyebrows at me in question and it's decided. "I can be ready in ten minutes."

"Perfect. We're leaving in fifteen."

"Where the hell is Keith?" I mutter as we finish our set up. We go on in less than twenty minutes and the son of a bitch still hasn't shown up yet.

"He'll be here. Calm down, Sage," mumbles JJ, his attention glued to his Macbook.

"JJ is right," says Maddox, clapping a hand on my back. "Keith's just being a dick because he didn't get his way at rehearsal last night. He'll show."

I shake my head as I look around the stage at the rest of the guys. Derrick, on his throne behind his drum set, shrugs without a word. Knox props up his guitar and then looks out over tonight's crowd. He grimaces at me before he jerks his chin, signaling for me to look over my shoulder. Keith is strolling in with his bass guitar and some chick draped all over him.

Fuck.

"I need a drink. Do me a favor, make sure he's got his shit together," I grumble before exiting the stage.

I don't know what Keith's problem is lately, but he needs to get a fucking grip. Now is *not* the time for playing games. We're finally getting somewhere with the band; our hard work is going to pay off. I can feel it. We sound better now than we ever have before.

Mountains & Men started like all the greats do—in a garage. There weren't always so many of us and we've seen a few guys come and go along the way. Maddox and Knox have been with me since the beginning. We've known each other since we were kids. Their family moved into my neighborhood when I was twelve. Maddox was thirteen and Knox was fifteen. I don't know how I managed to score an *in* with the *Bradley Boys*—maybe they took pity on me, as I had two sisters and no brother to boast of—whatever the case may be, we've been almost inseparable ever since.

Even though I'm the youngest in the group, Mountains & Men has always been my baby and I'm the voice that drives our sound. We all have our role to play and I'm their leader. I've earned the damn title and the guys respect that.

Most of them, anyway.

Keith is really starting to be a pain in my ass. I put up with his shit because we can't afford to lose him. I swear, our bass slot is cursed. We've been through three bass guitarists since our conception. It's fucking ridiculous. Keith has managed to stick around for a while—but he better get his act together before he pushes me too far.

I make my way to the bar, avoiding Keith along the way. I take a deep breath and admire the crowd instead. We're the opening band tonight. It's not the best slot, but we were requested by name when the band who was supposed to perform backed out. We'll never turn down an opportunity to play.

The Brew Cycle is one of our regular gigs. Derrick made sure of that. It's a pretty cool spot, right on the edge of Old Town—just blocks away from campus and all the nightlife that's always buzzing with people in this town. The venue itself is classic Fort Collins—bikes and beer paraphernalia all over the place. While the dream is to play at venues far greater than this, I'll never take nights like this for granted. I love this place.

I order a beer, as I always stay away from the hard stuff before I go on. I don't perform drunk or high or any of that shit. For me, it's all about the music, the energy, the crowd—I don't need anything other than the thrill I get just from being on stage, and I'll never compromise my sound. Most of the guys don't perform drunk, either. They may have a few drinks—and I sure as hell won't stop them; I'm not their fucking mother—but we all know our limits and we don't play sloppy. We play hard and then we party hard.

"Hey, Rockstar." I hear her voice just as she taps my shoulder.

I turn, unabashedly happy to see her face. "Sarah! You made it," I cry as I pull her in for a hug.

I live and breathe Mountains & Men. It's who I am. That said, it doesn't pay the bills just yet. By day, I work a part time gig at Little Bird Cafe, also recently named *Home of Brandon's Bakery*—that's how I met Sarah. She's new, been around for about a week now. It didn't take long for me to decide she's one sweet-ass chick. Case in point, she came to see us play tonight.

I step back, curling my fingers beneath hers as I lift her arm and give her a proper once over. I've seen the way my boss, Brandon, looks at her. She's most certainly off limits, but that doesn't mean that I can't look.

"*Damn,* babe. Remind me *not* to introduce you to the guys. Their girlfriends would *kill* me," I tease.

Truth be told, only two of us have girlfriends. Maddox has Andrea. *Well, today, at least.* They break up about once a week, so they really don't count. Then there's JJ; his woman's name is Violet. *I swear he's going to marry that girl.* The rest of us are just a bunch of single fools playing the field. Knox is the worst. He's about one notch away from being a fucking man-whore.

Sarah laughs at me, shaking her head as she lets go of my hand. "I brought friends," she says, turning her attention over her shoulder. "These are my neighbors, Aria, and her boyfriend, Josh." I shake both of their hands and thank them for coming.

Then all I see is *her.*

Her long legs, tucked into that tight, frayed jean skirt.

Her narrow hips, begging to be guided in a side to side sway.

Her perfect tits, smaller than average and perfect for biting.

Her straight hair, hanging past her shoulders.

Her sweetheart lips, just plump enough to suck on.

Her eyes, green and gorgeous.

Her *eyes,* haunted and mysterious.

There are demons in those eyes . . .

" . . . my roommate, Millie." I nod, hearing only the end of Sarah's introduction.

"Hi," speaks the vision before me. A smirk tugs at the corner of my mouth, pleased to know that the name Sarah just spoke into my ear belongs to this woman.

I can tell as I take her hand that she's completely unfazed by me, but that will change. *I see the demons in her eyes and I know we'll dance.*

My smirk morphs into a smile at her cool touch. She's not convinced, but I am.

Fuck, yes—a challenge.

When I let her go, I feel her melody start to swirl around in my head. My heart rate kicks up a notch, the thrill of this chase—of this composition—amping me up. I don't hear the overhead music, I don't hear the hum of the crowd, I hear her—I hear *Millie.*

I will myself to look away, knowing I've got to get back to the guys. Before I go, I bring my lips to Sarah's ear. "Your roommate is a fox. Put in a good word for me, alright?" I grin at her as I begin to back my way through the crowd. I look at Millie one last time before I turn my back on them, pulling out my phone as I go. I've got to get this out . . .

I hit record and the words tumble from my lips.

I see the demons in your eyes and I want to dance
Can't stop the beat I hear from one haunted glance
Take my hand, baby, don't let go
I'll set you free, baby, won't let go
All night/One song
This room/My home
I'll set you free, baby, don't let go
Tonight/Just give me tonight

"I thought you were going to get a beer?" asks Knox as he jumps from the side of the stage upon my approach. I shake my head and chuckle, pocketing my phone. "What the hell happened to you? Ten minutes ago, you looked about ready to make heads roll," he mutters with a frown.

"I'm getting laid tonight, bro," I state boldly.

His face breaks out into a grin as he laughs. "Why am I not surprised? Point her out to me later and maybe I'll be nice and keep my distance," he adds with a wink. "Come on, the guys are waiting on us."

Two

Millicent

God, he's fucking sexy as sin!

As I wiggle my hips in time to the beat of the music, I close my eyes and run my fingers through my hair, desperate for *touch* as the sound of his voice washes over me. I love to dance, love to move my body in ways that are inexcusable anywhere else—*except the bedroom.* It makes me feel sexy, beautiful, and desirable, like every woman should feel. But dancing to the cadence of *his* voice?

He's an arrogant little shit, I just know it. I saw it in his eyes when we were introduced—those icy blue eyes, framed in those horn-rimmed glasses. *Who the fuck looks sexy in those things?* He does, and he knows it. I felt it in his touch when he squeezed my hand. I saw it in that cocky smirk that tugged at those lickable lips.

To deny my attraction to him would be a lie unworthy of the effort. Especially considering one glance in his direction, with the sound of his tenor voice swirling around me, totally turns me on. He wears his dark brown hair slicked to the side, like he walked straight out of the nineteen-fifties. As their set continues, a few strands fall out of place and he smooths them back. It's an act of convenience, but he takes advantage of it as he throws a wink at the desperate girls in the front. They scream and he grins and I roll my eyes before I close them again, uninterested in watching him flirt with his groupies.

Even in the darkness behind my lids, I see him. I see the way his black t-shirt hugs his sculpted chest. I see the sleeve of tattoos that decorates his left arm. I picture his fitted, dark-washed jeans hanging low around his hips. And those red

Chucks—the shoes he wears as he jumps, struts, and dances across that stage.

Shit. I need another drink and I need to get laid.

It's true that I don't get out much, but I'm no prude. When I have an itch, I know how to find someone to scratch it. I'm sure of two things when it comes to sex: with a little effort, I can coax a cock into my pussy; and when it's all said and done, eventually, he'll leave. They always do.

"Hey, Dancing Queen, we're going to get another drink. Thirsty?" Aria asks, bumping her hip against mine. Aria and I don't know each other very well, but she's always incredibly nice to me. I like that about her. I don't think twice before I answer with a smile and a nod. A drink is exactly what I need, and while I'm at it, I'll scout the room for someone to help quench tonight's thirst.

As we make our way off the dance floor, I notice that Sarah isn't with us. Looking back over my shoulder, I see her dancing with the guy who came in earlier—his eyes glued to her like she was the only person in the entire universe. A pang of jealousy constricts my heart before I look away. It's not *Sarah* that I envy. The look in her eyes when she explained to me that Brandon was her boss, coupled with the way their bodies are adhered to each other just now, I honestly hope it works out for them.

The ache in my chest has little to do with *them* and everything to do with what I can't ever allow myself to believe I can have. I've tried love before and it has failed me every time. That kind of pain, that kind of abandonment, there's only so much a girl can take before she decides her fragile heart just won't survive another break. I know that I'm damaged goods, I know that my disposition isn't soft and cuddly, I know that I'm not perfect—but I'm me. I don't know how to be anyone else and nobody seems to be able to tolerate that truth. *Or me.* At least not for longer than a couple nights.

It is what it is. There's no use crying about it, so I just accept it.

As soon as we arrive at the bar, Josh signals for the bartender. She heads our way, taking Aria's order first, then mine. I ask for a gin and tonic, my drink of choice for the night. The woman behind the bar nods before she starts to prepare our order.

"Gin and tonic, huh? That's a pretty bold drink for a little lady like yourself," drawls the man behind me, who I assume is waiting to be served. I peek at him from over my shoulder, curious to see the face that goes with that country boy accent. He's got a mop of curls on his head, which makes him seem boyish in that charming sort of way. He's tall and bulky with muscle and I can see that his eyes are brown—*brown, not icy blue; not framed by a pair of horn-rimmed glasses.*

I shake the last thought away, wondering why in the hell I'm comparing this man to Sage, that arrogant little shit with a voice that's dangerously alluring. *He doesn't need another admirer, of that I am sure.*

Before I can think of a response, the cute guy with the country drawl reaches around me, clapping a few bills on the counter. "Her drink's on me. I'll have a Jack-n-coke."

The back of my neck grows warm and my stomach tingles, the promise of a future bed fellow making me anxious with anticipation. "Thank you," I murmur, looking up at him before taking my glass.

Aria nudges me gently with her elbow and I turn to meet her gaze. "We're going to head back to our table. Are you alright?" I offer her a slight nod and she smirks at me knowingly in return. "You know where to find us."

As soon as they leave, I turn back to my country boy. He grins at me before he holds out his hand. "I'm Dylan," he tells me.

"Millie," I reply, accepting his gesture.

"Have you been here before?"

I fight the urge to roll my eyes.

Really? Is that really the line he's going to start with?

"Yeah," I reply, hoping to move beyond his cliché icebreaker. "You?"

"A few times," he answers before taking a swallow of his drink. "I like the live music. This band is alright." He shrugs as he looks over his shoulder at the stage.

This time, I *do* roll my eyes. Mountains & Men are a hell of a lot better than *alright.* They're actually *really* amazing. There're six of them up there, and yet they sound so much bigger. I'd say it's a combination of personality and talent. I look beyond Dylan and watch them for a moment.

The drummer plays with his whole body; his hard, sculpted chest, covered in only a tank-top, adding to his appeal. He thrusts his tongue out as his sticks fly across the drumheads and I can't help but smile. The bass player is his contrast; he's totally laid back, just as cool and relaxed as the notes he contributes.

There's the guy on keys—but I know he's bringing so much more. He's the horn line and the electronica sound that adds another dimension of character to their sound. He looks lost in the music, playing on the keys while messing with his computer.

Of course, I can't neglect the two hot fools now in the middle of the stage. Both electric guitar players sound like they're in the middle of a riff battle and *loving it.* They're playing back to back, bobbing their heads in unison.

Then there's Sage.

Every musician on that stage is pouring out an energy that fills the entire room. Anyone with a pulse can feel it. But Sage—he's a streak of light—blue, like the hottest part of a flame. As soon as the guys on their guitars finish their joint solo, they push away from each other and Sage emerges from behind them, sliding his way to the mic stand. He fists it with one hand, shoots his other in the air, and wails his way back into the lyrics.

I'm instantly covered in goosebumps.

"I take it you're a fan?"

I bring my eyes back to the man standing in front of me, appalled at how easily I forgot him. *Christ, what's the matter with me?* Sage isn't even my type, so why on earth do my eyes keep drifting in his direction? He's like those guys who spend hours *flexing* in front of every mirror they pass at the gym. I don't allow men like that in my bed.

Except, Sage can sing like a fucking rockstar *god.*

I wonder if he sings to wet a girl's pussy. It would totally work . . .

Oh, for fuck sake!

I take a swig of my drink, trying to find my words as I focus on Duncan. *Or was it Denis?* "Uh, yeah. This is my first time hearing them, but I think they're kind of great."

"To each his own, I guess," he says with another shrug.

For reasons I can't justify, rationalize, or understand, his dismissal—which doesn't even have anything to do with *me*—rubs me the wrong way. Suddenly, my neck is no longer warm with my wanton anticipation and my insides are far from a flutter as I gape up at him.

"So, are you from around here?"

All of a sudden, I'm bored. I shake my head as I down half of my drink, my eyes seeking out my friends. "New Jersey," I answer after I swallow, the gin warming my insides.

"Wow. What brought you out here?"

I sigh, honestly feeling sorry for the guy. I can't blame him for trying, but he just hit the wrong button. I throw back the rest of my drink and set my glass on the bar. "My mom's a bit of a bitch and we needed some space," I say bluntly. I don't know if it's his choice of conversation or the alcohol in my system that drives my unforgiving rudeness, but I've got to get myself out of this. "It was nice meeting you. I should go find my friends now. Hope the next band is more to your liking."

Fuck me, I think to myself as I walk away. *I'm such a bitch.*

"Awesome set, guys!"

"Yeah—you guys are amazing. When's your next gig?"

"You got any of that shit online? I need it downloaded yesterday!"

We're accosted by our fans as we carry all of our equipment from the stage out to the trailer Derrick's got hitched to the back of his SUV. All six of us field their complements and their questions. Derrick answers inquiries about where we'll be playing over the next few weeks; JJ is quick to hand out a couple of our flyers, telling people where they can go online and download our MP3s. I'm flying high as a fucking kite, the adrenaline from the show still coursing through my veins.

I'm also anxious to get back inside. I've got a fine ass woman I have to hunt down.

I saw her, saw her dancing to our music in the middle of the crowd. It didn't matter that I could barely see two feet from the stage, the lights shining in our faces making it nearly impossible to see beyond them. My eyes sought her out as if her body was calling out to me. *My voice had her swinging those little hips, her eyes closed as she lost herself to our sound.* It was so fucking sexy, I had to look away from fear that I'd get a hard-on in the middle of our set.

"Hey, Dweeb, where the hell are you, man?" asks Derrick, knocking me upside the head. I don't even get mad that he hit me, knowing good and well that if anyone was trying to talk to me just now, I have no clue who or what they said.

"What's up?"

"We're done, dumb-ass. Let's go get shit-faced!" cries Maddox from the side door.

"Drink all you want, but you better keep your fucking dick in your pants. You see a girl who needs some attention, just point her out and I'll take care of her," says Knox, hooking his arm around his brother's neck.

"You got that right," pipes in JJ. "We *do not* need Andrea showing up pissed as hell, kicking our door down after she finds out you messed around with some random chick."

"Hey, in my defense, we were *broken up!*"

Derrick shakes his head as we follow them back inside. "You're such a punk. As long as she lets you fuck her, you're never really broken up. Now shut the hell up—you've got first round."

"*Shots!*" Maddox shouts, leading the way to the bar.

"Wha—Dweeb, where are you going? Bar's this way?" mutters Derrick, looking at me with a confused scowl.

"I, uh," I begin to say, scanning the crowd, looking for my conquest.

"Oh, yeah—Sage is getting laid tonight," Knox calls out with a grin. "He's a lost cause. Come on, Derrick. Good luck, kid."

I return his grin as I flip him off. "Don't need your luck, bro."

He and Derrick laugh before we go our separate ways, the crowd swallowing us up. When I see Brandon, practically attached to Sarah, I start heading their way. Millie comes into view and I smirk victoriously when I see that she doesn't have some guy hanging all over her.

Not that I would have let some sorry ass prick stop me. Tonight, that girl is mine.

I'm stopped by a couple girls before I can reach my destination, their hands pawing at me in an attempt to get my attention. I barely see them as they spout out their praise for Mountains & Men. I thank them for their kind words, because I'm not a dick—anyone who appreciates our music deserves our gratitude—but then I push past them, my eyes locked on tonight's trophy.

"Oh, my gosh, Sage!" cries Sarah as I fill the space between Brandon and Millie. "You guys were *amazing!* I had no idea you could sing like that. I'm so glad I came—you are so good!" I can't help but chuckle at her animated greeting. I can tell she's been drinking and she's too fucking cute.

"Thanks, Sarah, that means a lot," I reply, looking from her to Brandon.

He nods at me before he speaks, "Yeah—that was a great set. Thanks for giving us a reason to dance." I chuckle knowingly, understanding his meaning exactly.

"Right!?" squeals Aria. "You guys killed it! I could listen to you all night."

"Thanks," I repeat before my eyes seek out my target. I can't stop myself from smiling when I see Millie is looking right at me, as if she's been waiting her turn for my attention. I prop my arm against the table and lean closer to her. I can smell her perfume interlaced with the scent of her sweat and I can't wait to taste her milky white skin. "What about you, gorgeous? Were we tolerable?"

She lifts one shoulder demurely, her eyes leaving mine as her focus falls to the ink that covers my arm. "Definitely tolerable," she murmurs, peeking at me from beneath her eyelashes. "I might even be impressed."

"Good," I say, taking a step closer to her. "Now it won't be awkward when I ask you to have a drink with me. You in?" She hesitates, but I'm not taking no for an answer. Before she says a word, I take her hand and start leading her to the bar. She doesn't protest; and when I ask her what she wants, she doesn't even think before she tells me her order.

Gin is her poison.

I order a beer, not in the mood for the hard stuff. When I bag this gorgeous creature beside me, I sure as hell want to remember it.

"You're awfully sure of yourself, you know that?" she asks as I hand her her gin and tonic. I wink at her before taking a swig of my beer. "How do you know I'm not already with someone?"

My mind fills with images of her dancing earlier and I take a step closer to her, lowering my lips to her ear. I have to take a deep breath, willing myself not to kiss the spot just behind her jaw—it's fucking calling to me; I ignore it for the moment, willing myself to speak. "No way in hell would I let my girl dance alone, in a crowd swarming with drunk assholes, if she looked as sexy as you do out on that floor. If you're not here alone, he's a fucking prick and I'm going to dance all night with his woman, showing him how it's fucking done."

When I pull away to peer into her eyes, the look she's giving me makes my dick twitch. Her dark green stare holds a dare and I can't help the smirk that tugs at the corner of my mouth. She has no idea I accepted her challenge the second we met.

I watch as she brings her glass to her lips, tilting her head back as she downs the entire drink all at once. She shakes her head when she's finished, the sting of the liquor making her shudder; then she sets her glass on the bar and hooks a finger through one of my belt loops.

"Come on, then," she purrs. "Let's fucking dance."

I take a long pull of my beer before leaving the half empty bottle on the counter. It doesn't escape me that for the second time tonight, this girl has me forgetting to chase my buzz. I let her tug me through the crowd and into the middle of the dance floor. The next band, *Crazy Blue,* is groovin,' making it easy for us to fall into the beat.

I take back control, gripping Millie's hips and spinning her away from me before snaking my arm around her waist. With her back pressed against my front, I take hold of her wrist and bring her hand up to rest behind my neck. She holds on and I graze my fingers down the length of her arm, then her side, until I reach the hem of her shirt. She fits against me like a puzzle piece, her heels making her just tall enough to rest her head against my shoulder as she leans against me.

She swivels her hips, pressing her ass against my junk, and I feel myself growing hard. We let our bodies do all the talking, the music steering the direction of our conversation. When I can no longer restrain myself, I bury my face in her neck. She smells so fucking incredible, just a whiff of her skin turns me on even more. I press my lips against the warm, fragrant spot just below her ear and I can *feel* her sigh as she tilts her head, granting me easier access. I part my lips to kiss her again, using my tongue this time. She tastes both salty and sweet, and a thrill of anticipation rushes through me, wondering what the rest of her will taste like.

"God, I can't wait to taste your pussy," I mutter thoughtlessly.

She lets me go in an instant, turning around to face me, no doubt so I can get the full effect of her glare. "You really are one arrogant son of a bitch, aren't you?"

"Don't kid yourself, doll face, your body has spoken loud and clear. I know you want me."

She rolls her eyes and takes a step away from me. "Fuck you."

She turns to walk off, but I stop her, sliding my arm around her waist and pulling her against me so that we're chest to chest. "You bet your ass you'll fuck me—right after I've fucked you, gorgeous." I graze my nose along hers, stopping when my mouth is a breath away from her sweetheart lips. "I'll set you free, baby, don't let go. Tonight, just give me tonight," I murmur, the lyrics from earlier pouring out of me as if they belong to her and her alone.

When I stick my tongue out and trace it against her bottom lip, she gasps; but instead of pulling away from me, she grabs hold of my hips and pulls herself closer. "Tonight. You and me, doll face. You in?"

"What's my name?" she asks over the music, her face still only millimeters away from mine.

"Excuse me?"

"My name, asshole. I'm not some nameless, fangirl, slut, Sage—I'm not here to fall at your feet and suck your cock as if it's my privilege. *What is my name?*"

A shit eating grin breaks out across my face. She's a fucking firecracker and I love it. *Her name.* That's the magic word. Like I could forget *her* name—my temporary muse.

I bring a hand up and grip the back of her neck, my fingers lost in her silky, soft hair. I'm about to kiss her smart-ass mouth, and she's not going anywhere. "Millie. Your name, doll face, is Millie." Before she can respond, my tongue is making its first sweep through her mouth. I can feel the vibration of her hum as she relaxes against me, all evidence of her fight vanishing instantly as her lips start to move with mine.

Arrogant son of a bitch, my ass. Tonight, this girl is mine. Now, not even she can deny it.

THREE

Millicent

I'VE NEVER BEEN so annoyed and so turned on all at once. The little shit keeps taking what he wants—*and I keep letting him.* There's just something about him, something I can't quite put my finger on, something that makes me want to shed every bit of self-discipline and willpower onto the dance floor and under my feet. He fed me my name hours ago and we've been inseparable ever since. He literally will not let me go; on the dance floor or at the bar. When Sarah, Aria, and Josh were on their way out, I remember the way his hand gripped my waist when they asked me if I was ready to go.

For reasons that can only be explained by my pussy herself, I told them I wanted to stay with Sage. He promised he'd get me home and—*fuck me*—I can hardly stand the wait any longer. The cocky fucker has a cock I'm dying to fuck. I've been duped. I'm pissed and horny and no one else will do. Not tonight, anyway.

I'm drunk. I know I am. I'm not entirely sure how many drinks I've had, just that Sage hasn't forgotten to ask if I need another as the night progresses. Though, I haven't lost my wits entirely. I've noticed he's hardly had anything to drink; definitely no more than three beers, the last of which was consumed at least an hour ago.

He brought me to the bar ten minutes ago, after I told him I was thirsty. I hardly felt the gin as I put this one away. "If you're not drinking, why are we still here?" I ask, pushing aside my empty glass. I regret the question as soon as I ask it. I sound like I'm whining and I'm most certainly not *that* kind of bitch.

He responds first with a kiss. Just like every other kiss he's bestowed upon me tonight, it catches me off guard. His lips are soft, so incredibly soft, but firm and decisive as they move against mine. He runs his tongue along the slit between my lips, seeking entrance into my mouth as he pins me against the bar. When he sinks his fingers into my hair and presses his pelvis against mine, that's when I feel it—the tingly sensation that spreads from my head to my toes as the back of my neck heats up and my desire pools between my legs.

"You sick of dancing with me? I'm more than happy to take you to bed, doll face."

"Was beginning to think you'd changed your mind . . ."

He takes my hand and presses it against the impressive bulge in his pants. I have to stifle my gasp, knowing his ego doesn't need the boost. "Does it feel like I've changed my mind? Let's get the fuck out of here."

He wraps his fingers around mine and begins leading me out of the bar. I grip his hand tightly, a little surprised at just how much I need him in order to keep my balance. Once in the parking lot, I draw in a deep breath of the night's cool air. It feels amazing out, the absence of too many bodies, loud music, and booze quite refreshing. I'm not paying attention to where we're going until he opens the door to a sleek, black Audi convertible—the top down and the tan leather interior inviting.

I spin around, propping myself against his chest when I lose my footing, and look up into his eyes. "*This* is your car? You're playing gigs at The Brew Cycle and you drive a fucking convertible?"

"Get in, gorgeous," he insists, smacking a kiss against my lips. "*This* isn't the ride I promised you."

A whimper escapes my throat at the prospect of being alone and naked with the man before me. I reach for another kiss, not the least bit concerned that I'm now taking all that I said I didn't want. He cups my ass, pulling me against him while he gives me a generous squeeze. I voice my desire with a moan.

He nibbles on my bottom lip before he pulls away. "In the car, doll face," he demands. This time, I obey. He drops down into the driver's seat just as I'm fastening my seatbelt. "I promised I'd get you home. What's your address?" I rattle out the information he's after and he plugs it into his phone before he starts his car.

As he pulls out of the parking lot and into the street, my hair is whipped around my face. I'm so buzzed, even the damn car is making me want Sage—just another piece of sexy to go along with his pretty package. I run my fingers along the leather of the armrest on the door and the center console, loving the smooth texture and the rich, creamy color in contrast with the stark black of the outside.

"Hey, doll face," he begins to say as he shifts gears. My eyes drift down to his hand on the gear shift; suddenly, watching him drive is all I can think about. "You okay, baby?"

"Hmm?" I ask, my eyes snapping up to meet his.

He smirks at me before turning his eyes back to the road. "You can feel my car up as much as you want, but he won't return the favor. *I* on the other hand . . ."

I lift an eyebrow at him, even though I know he's no longer paying attention to me. His implication that I'm *feeling up* the wrong thing makes me defiant. My annoyance, which has been simmering all evening, coupled with my arousal, which is irritatingly a byproduct of his very presence, collide into a devious idea. I spread my legs, resting one hand on my knee before I slowly begin skimming my fingers up my bare thigh. I make it all the way to the lacy edge of my panties before I hear him whisper a curse under his breath.

"Don't you fucking dare," he mutters, grabbing hold of my wrist. His touch is gentle in spite of the demanding tone behind his voice—husky with lust. He brings my hand to his crotch before he lets me go. I chew on my lip, conflicted as to whether or not I want to pull away.

He's bossy and I don't know how much I like it.

Before I can make up my mind, he shoves two fingers inside of me. I gasp and then moan as my hand reflexively grips his cock—which seems to be growing underneath his jeans.

"Tonight, your orgasms belong to me. Got it, doll?"

My mind grows hazy as he continues to slide in and out of me, his eyes trained on the road. I wonder if he can *really* be trusted to take full responsibility for my orgasms—*orgasms, with an 's'*—or if his peacock feathers are only for show. He's so fucking confident at every turn; it's both infuriating and sexy at the same time. With my hand still on his jean-clad cock, I decide to seek confirmation of just how impressive his *bulge* might be.

I moan again when I follow his erection along his thigh. He's packing more than half a foot, without question.

"That's right, gorgeous, I'll take care of you. Got me?"

"Yes," I whimper, just loud enough to be heard from over the roar of the wind blowing past our ears.

"Good." As he says the words, he pulls his fingers away from me and promptly sticks them in his mouth, sucking away my arousal. "*Fucking hell,*" he groans. I feel him grow harder, trying the seams of his jeans. His phone instructs him to take the next right and he finds his stick shift, barely slowing down as he races around the last corner before we've reached my apartment building.

He parks the car and takes hold of the back of my neck, drawing my face to his as the top of his car stretches over us. I'm too distracted by the feel of his tongue dancing with mine to notice the darkness that shrouds us as the moon is blocked from view. He feels his way up my side, his thumb grazing the underside of my breast before he pulls away.

"Come on, doll face."

I'm out of the car without further encouragement and I don't look back as I make my way to the building, trusting that he'll follow. A giggle I cannot silence bubbles out of me when he wraps his arms around me from behind, pulling me back as we both continue to walk forward. His lips find my neck just as one of his hands cups my breast, and I decide that I'm quite content when he has the freedom to use both hands.

"I'm up one flight," I barely manage, making my way to the stairs.

He spins me around and presses me back into the corner, pushing his hard-on against my hip. "God, you smell fucking amazing, right now. I could take you on these stairs."

I wrap my arms around his neck, my keys dangling from my fingers, and hook my ankle around his calf. "Don't tempt me," I whisper.

He grunts, taking hold of the back of my thighs before he hoists me off the ground. I lock my legs around his hips as he races up the stairs. "Door," he mutters.

"The first one on the left."

"Keys."

I dangle the right one in front of his face and he snatches it, keeping me close as he unlocks the door and carries me inside. He locks us in and then tosses the keys before his lips are adhered to my neck again. I can barely think about anything but the strength of his body in contrast with his tender yet desperate affection, and then he lowers me onto the couch.

"Not here," I insist, pushing him away just slightly. "Sarah." He nods, needing no further explanation, and then I'm airborne again. "At the end of the hall." He gets us there in no time and I reach to swing the door closed once we're inside.

I unlock my legs from around him and slide down his front, unabashedly dragging my hands along his chest, loving the way his muscles feel beneath the thin fabric of his t-shirt. The moonlight and the street lamps shine through my open blinds, and I don't miss the satisfied smirk that tugs at his lips.

He's such a smug asshole, but he's sumptuous. That I cannot deny.

I reach up and gently pull his glasses from his face. He lets me, staring at me the whole time. His eyes are so blue, so beautiful, and the way he's looking at me makes *me* feel gorgeous—just as he's been calling me all night. *That* look makes my surrender to his arrogance totally worth it. I won't get to keep him, I know; but for just a moment, he wants me and I want him and that's all that matters. His intent gaze makes me want to bare myself to him.

I step around him, carefully setting his glasses on my dresser before I reach for the bottom of my shirt.

"Don't," he speaks softly, his lips grazing my ear. I look up, catching our reflection in my vanity mirror just in front of us. "Let me," he murmurs, kissing the space just below my ear.

I'm naked in seconds, my bare back pressed against his fully clothed body. A small voice in the back of my head tells me that I should feel embarrassed, but I'm too busy enjoying the pleasure of his two fingers working my pussy, his other hand gently squeezing my tit as he nibbles on my neck. When his thumb begins to rub my clit, I gasp, my building orgasm just a breath away.

"*Sage*," I mewl, reaching back to grip his neck as my insides clench his fingers, my legs instantly unsteady.

He doesn't pull out until I've ridden the wave of my release and then he brings the digits to his mouth, like he did before. "*Shit.* You're going to ride my face, doll. I want you to come all over my tongue."

Fuck. He wouldn't need to sing to wet a girl's pussy. All he has to do is speak.

I turn to face him, desperate for more, as if I hadn't come for him just a few seconds ago. I reach for the bottom of his shirt and he lets me yank it over his head. My eyes *devour* him. His chiseled chest is covered in tattoos. I run my hands over all of them—across his pecs, down both of his sides, up his arm. He's beautiful.

His muscles tense when my fingers trace his abs and I smile when I hear his breath catch in the back of his throat. It's my turn to take back some control. I open his jeans, sliding my hands under the fabric of his boxers and over his backside as I begin to push both down to his ankles. I descend with his pants, planting myself on my knees in front of his cock. My mouth waters at the sight of him. He's got the longest dick I've ever seen—nine inches, if I had to guess—far more impressive as it stands to attention in front of my face than when I felt it in his pants.

I don't think twice before I take him into my mouth.

"Oh, *fuck*," he sighs, his hands immediately tangled in my hair.

I grip what I can't fit in my mouth with my hand as I begin to work my way up and down his shaft. I relax my jaw, closing my eyes as I concentrate on taking as much of him as I can. I suck, lick, and then swallow; the groan that follows rumbles from his chest and sets my entire body on fire. I hum as I suck him harder, needing to hear that sound again.

"*Jesus, doll face.* You're going to make me come." My heartbeat speeds up as he speaks and I know that's exactly what I want—to taste his release as he's tasted mine. I reach for his balls and he moans. "Is that what you want, baby? You want me to come in your mouth? Your fucking smart-ass, sexy, hot as hell mouth? *Ah—fuck, Millie!*" he cries, his legs going stiff as his cock fills and then empties its contents down the back of my throat. I suck him dry before I pull away, licking my lips in satisfaction.

Before I know what's happening, I'm in his arms, my legs around his waist, his tongue in my mouth as he carries me to the bed. He kisses me hungrily and I reciprocate with fervor, completely uncaring that my dripping wet pussy is smearing my desire across his abdomen.

Let him know how much he turns me on. I want him to know.

His peacock feathers are not just for show.

He rolls us over so that I'm on top of him, and then tears his lips away from mine before grinning up at me. "You're something else, doll face, you know that?" I smirk down at him and he points at his mouth. "Get up here."

I know exactly what he wants and my pussy aches for me to comply, so I do. He pushes himself further up the bed so that I can grab hold of my headboard as I settle myself over his mouth. One swipe of his tongue has me practically panting. He flicks my clit before he thrusts inside of my center. I arch my back and lower my hips, unable to stop myself.

"That's it, gorgeous. Take what you want. Ride my face, baby." I whimper pathetically, any residual rational, logical, or self-conscious thought, spared by my intoxicated state, completely obliterated by his words as I begin to grind against his mouth. He feels incredible and all I want is *more*. I throw my head back, crying out as my orgasm crashes through me. He laps up all that I have to give before he snakes his hands up, grabbing my hips and pulling me down. I fall—my chest pressed firmly against his.

"Do you have any idea how fucking hot you are? How goddamn good you taste?"

"Show me," I whisper before plunging my tongue into his mouth.

He grips his arms around me tighter, grabbing a palm full of ass as he lifts his hips and teases my entrance with his hard cock. "I need a condom, right fucking now."

"Do you have one?"

"Doll face, the question is, do I have enough?" He rolls us over again before he climbs off of me and reaches for his jeans. I watch as he digs out his wallet and pulls out two square packages. "Guess I'll have to make 'em count."

He tosses one onto my nightstand, ripping the other open with his teeth. We stare at each other as he sheathes himself and I grow short of breath at the sight of him—completely on display in all of his glory.

"What?" I ask softly when he doesn't return to the bed.

He's still for a moment longer and then he crawls into the space between my legs, wasting not a second more before he sinks himself inside of me. I suck in a breath, arching my back as he fills me completely. I've never felt so full, so complete. It's like, for the first time in my life, I understand how a man is supposed to fit inside of a woman. Our gazes locked, I know that this is a moment to cherish—a fleeting connection that I'll never forget. He's the best decision I've made all night. Tomorrow he'll be gone, but tonight . . .

"Sage," I beg when he doesn't move. "Sage, please. Please, *move.* I need you to *move.*"

"And in my arms you'll find your ecstasy
When you lose yourself, I'll set you free
Baby, just let go and let it be, let it be
Tonight/ Just give me tonight."

He sings the words softly before he begins to pull out of me and I could die.

Right here. Right now. Without another orgasm—*I. Could. Die.* I don't care what song he's singing or how many times he's sung the same lines to the countless women I'm sure he's taken to bed. All I can think about is the sound of his voice as it washes over me and the look in his eyes as he stares at me, making me feel like it's just him and me in the whole world. Then he rolls his hips and glides back inside of me and I free fall into his sweet oblivion.

"You feel incredible, baby. Abso-fucking-lutely incredible."

I open my mouth to respond, but he steals my words with a kiss. Soon, we're both covered in a thin layer of sweat as we pant and moan for one another. When I plant my feet on the bed in order to push my pelvis up to meet him thrust for thrust, he stops me, wrapping one leg around his hip and then the other.

"Your orgasm is mine, baby doll, remember?"

"I need it—I need it now! I need more! Sage—more!"

"Who do your orgasms belong to tonight, doll face?"

"You," I moan.

"Who?" he asks, pumping in and out of me faster, *harder.*

"Oh—god—*you, Sage, you!*"

He brings his hand between us and presses on my clit and I know I'm about to come so fucking hard. When it hits me, my nails dig into his biceps as I free an uninhibited cry. He groans as my center squeezes around him, pulling forth his own release.

"Fuck, yes, Millie—strangle my cock, baby!"

He collapses on top of me when we're both finished and we work for a moment to catch our breath. When I sigh wistfully, feeling sated and sleepy, I close my eyes. He lifts his head almost immediately, smacking a kiss against my lips.

"Don't you fucking dare. Open your eyes, gorgeous," he insists. I obey, lifting an eyebrow at him. He smirks as he shakes his head. "We've got another condom left."

"Seriously?" I murmur in disbelief.

"You bet your sweet, little ass." I giggle when he pulls my bottom lip between his teeth. He releases me, dragging his lips along the length of my jaw. "Sleep tomorrow."

"It *is* tomorrow."

He shakes his head at me once more. "God, this mouth," he mutters before he presses his against mine. "You'll sleep when we're done, doll face. Got it?"

"Got it."

An hour later, at god knows what time, he lets me close my eyes and I fall asleep tucked under one of his arms, my cheek against his chest.

FOUR

Sage

My eyelids are heavy when I try and open them, and it takes me a second to remember where I am.

Only a second.

When I catch a glimpse of her ashy brown hair, a complete and utter mess after riding in the convertible and then riding me, my dick twitches. Then my bladder sends an urgent message to my other head and I'm reminded of why I've been called out of sleep.

I ease my way from the bed, careful not to wake Millie, and then search for my boxers. I slip them on and find myself stealing one more glimpse of her naked back, the sheets only covering her from the waist down. I can't even count how many times I've snuck out of a woman's bed after a night of sex, leaving before she woke up—sometimes with a note, sometimes not. I can count on *one hand* how many times I've wanted to climb back under the sheets with the sleeping beauty. I turn away from her in need of the bathroom, but with every intention of returning.

Millie and I were a little busy last night, so I wasn't given the grand tour, but it doesn't take a genius to figure out that one of the two doors in the hallway leads to my source of relief. I peek my head into the room on my right and I know straight away that I'm looking into Sarah's room. It's empty, leading me to assume she's behind door number two. I knock, hoping I can interrupt whatever girl routine she's in the middle of.

"Sarah?" She swings the door open and I offer her a tired, lopsided smile. "Hey, Sarah. I've really got to piss. Are you almost done in there?" I wait, somewhat impatiently, as she gapes at me. "I usually don't mind an audience, but in this case—"

"Right! Yeah. Um. Yeah—go," she stutters, switching spots with me. I'm quick to shut myself inside.

As I pull my dick out to relieve myself, I close my eyes and tilt my head back. Immediately, my mind is filled with memories from early this morning. Being with Millie . . . it was nothing like I thought it would be. I figured she'd be a fun and wild ride, but *fuck me*—she's unbelievable. Last night was, hands down—*dick up*—the best lay I've ever had. *Ever.* It had all the excitement and wonder that comes with a good fresh fuck buddy, but it also felt natural and relaxed, as if our bodies had met before. It wasn't just the sex, though. It was Millie.

I remember it, when I buried myself deep inside her tight, warm pussy. I remember hearing the music—*her music*—just like earlier in the night, when we had met. I couldn't explain it—*can't* explain it—but I wrote the words that fell from my lips in that very moment. I looked down into her eyes and, *shit*, it was like magic. They were there.

I swear, that woman is more than a muse. I've never sung to a woman in bed before. Certainly not like that. I have no fucking clue what it means, if anything, but I sure as hell know that I need another night with her. Another *dozen* nights. One night of purely, unadulterated, passionate sex will never do.

After I finish my business, I open the door to find Sarah exactly where I left her. I'm so fucking tired, I can't bring myself to offer up any sort of morning conversation. Instead, I compliment her dress before heading back to Millie's room. I close the door, drop my boxers, and climb back into bed.

I'm instantly overwhelmed by the scent of her—she smells like sex, sweat, and something sweet and feminine. *Vanilla.* I decide that she's too far away and I scoot closer, pulling her into my arms. She sighs as she rolls toward me, resting her cheek on my chest. A small smile tugs at the corner of my mouth as I close my eyes, falling back asleep within seconds.

When I wake for the second time, we're spooning. I'm not sure how we managed to sleep our way into this position, but I won't complain. I like holding her.

Fuck. I sound like a damn pussy.

I know by staying I'm acting out of character, but I can't make myself move. I don't want to. I remember her dark green eyes—her haunted, mysterious eyes—and that mouth—she's such a smart-ass; but the way she looked at me when I sang to her, and the way she called my name when I made her come for the fourth time. . .

I think she may be just as out of her element as I am, but she wants me just the same—no way in hell am I walking away now.

I'm impressed that she's still sleeping. I can only guess by the sunshine pouring into the room that we've slumbered through the entire morning. I smile when she groans and arches her back, pushing herself even closer to me. I trace lazy circles on her stomach with my thumb and she gasps before she turns around. I can tell she regrets the quick movement immediately as she groans once more and buries her face in my chest.

"Morning," I say with a chuckle.

"You're still here," she grumbles, her morning voice raspy and sexy as fuck. My dick twitches.

"Disappointed?" I ask, now tracing circles against the small of her back.

"Surprised." She yawns and curls even closer to me. She's like a fucking cat; and I'll be damned, but I like it. "I feel like shit."

"You put a few back last night," I remind her, reaching up to smooth her hair away from her face. She tilts her head up and opens her eyes to look at me, and I'm instantly hard.

She's so fucking gorgeous.

Her makeup has faded, her eyes are bloodshot from her hangover, and her hair is a mess, but she's still the most beautiful woman I've ever held in my arms.

"Fuck . . . I wish I had a condom right now. Bet I could make you feel better, doll face."

She studies me for a moment, not saying a word. I'm beginning to think I've pissed her off before she tells me, "Behind you. Nightstand. Top drawer."

I arch an eyebrow before I lean away from her, reaching behind me to open the drawer. Sure enough, there's a small stash of condoms inside. I grab one, holding it between two fingers as I scowl at her. "You mean to tell me that these were here the whole time?"

She rolls her eyes at me and then lays on her back. "Are you going to bitch or fuck?" she sighs.

A slow grin tugs at my mouth until a laugh bursts out of me. When she looks my way, her eyes light up and a small smile plays at the corners of her mouth. "You're kind of a bitch, did you know that?" The light from her eyes vanishes and she starts to roll away from me. I stop her, climbing on top of her and caging her between my arms. "Don't you fucking dare." She pinches her eyebrows together when she looks up at me. "That wasn't an insult."

"*Right*. Because a girl *loves it* when a guy calls her a bitch."

"Okay, I'm sorry. I didn't mean it like that. I just—you're a no nonsense, no bullshit kind of girl. I like it," I tell her, lowering my lips to the softest spot on her neck, just behind her ear. She sighs when I open my mouth for a taste. "What do you say, doll face?" I whisper, sliding my hand down her side. I take my time, reacquainting myself with her petite curves, changing directions when I reach her knee. I trace my fingers up the inside of her thigh and then I dip a finger into her heat. My dick throbs when I find that she's already aroused. I leave a wet trail of kisses all the way to her lips and then I stop, my mouth hovering over hers. "Forgive me?"

"Just shut up and kiss me," she moans.

I don't waste another second, crashing my mouth against hers as I push two fingers into her wet pussy. She thrusts her hips up and I pull away from her. I smirk when she whines.

"Fuck! I'm sorry—don't stop! Make me come, Sage."

I rip open the condom package with my teeth before rolling the rubber over my rock hard dick and sinking myself into her core. "I'll take care of you, gorgeous." She spreads her legs wider and I slip in just a little deeper with a groan. "Sweet Jesus, you feel so good. So tight around my cock. I could fuck you all day."

"I think I'd let you," she mutters, breathless.

I smile down at her before I bring my mouth to hers once more. She circles her arms around my neck, keeping me close as my tongue sweeps through her mouth and my dick pumps in and out of her pussy. When I slide a hand underneath her hips, lifting her so that I can take her from a different angle, she rips her lips from mine with a gasp.

"*Oh, my god! Sage—shit—right there, right there—don't stop!*" Completely captivated by the way she's beginning to unravel beneath me, I'm spurred on by the sound of her voice. My thrusts come faster and harder. "*I'm going to—Sage!*"

Her words are swallowed by her cry as her orgasm explodes, making her whole body tremble. Her pussy tightens around me and I grunt as she beckons my release, milking me dry. My spine tingles as pleasure floods my veins and I feel sated and high. I collapse on top of her, short of breath. I don't know how long I lay, my arms and legs tangled with hers, my dick still buried deep inside of her, before I pull out and remove the condom.

"I think you broke my vag," she mutters, propping herself up on her elbows.

My eyes trail up and down her naked body, appreciating her long, toned legs, her narrow hips, her tight waist, and her perfect tits—perky and round and just big enough to be considered larger than too small. "I'd be more than happy to fix it," I reply, finally bringing my eyes to meet hers.

"Christ. You're a machine," she mumbles, slowly making her way off the bed.

"Hey, where are you going?"

"I need to drink about a gallon of water and I need to eat something."

"You mean I didn't make you feel better?"

She smirks at me from over her shoulder and I can't keep the grin off my face. Instead of speaking, she makes her way to her dresser and pulls out some clothes. I watch as she steps into a pair of sweatpants—commando. *Fuck, that's hot.* Then she pulls on one of those workout tops girls wear, leaving her shoulders bare. She curses under her breath when she gets a look at herself in the mirror and quickly pulls her hair into a knot on the top of her head.

"Hungry?" she asks, looking back at me as she makes her way to the door.

"Right behind you, doll face."

Millicent

I SMILE WHEN HE joins me in the kitchen, annoyingly satisfied that he put on his pants but neglected to don his t-shirt. His glasses have also made a comeback, his hair a dark, beautiful, disheveled mess atop his head. My stomach tingles in excitement as he walks right for me, placing his hand over mine on the refrigerator door before stopping behind me. He kisses the space just behind my ear before he speaks.

"You're staring." I can *hear* the smile in his voice and I barely manage to stifle a groan. "What's for breakfast?" He wraps his other arm around my waist, pulling me back against him, and all my inhibitions seem to go into hiding.

Here, now, in the light of day—even sober and irritatingly hungover—I'm drawn to him. I know that this feeling will go away—that *he* will go away; I know that relaxing against him is a stupid idea and that making him breakfast is a mistake; worst of all, entertaining the idea that I could spend the rest of the day in bed with him . . .

"Millie?" he chuckles, his lips pressed against the nape of my neck.

"Grilled cheese," I answer, shaking my head to clear my thoughts. I regret the movement instantly, my headache suddenly returning. "And, technically, I think this would be lunch." I reach into the fridge for butter and cheese just as his phone begins to ring. He lets me go, reaching into his pocket for the device as he leans against the counter beside the stove. When he silences the call, I raise an eyebrow at him. "You're not going to get that?"

"It's just my sister. I can call her back later. Oh, but while I'm thinking about it . . ." his voice trails off as he unlocks his screen and pushes a few buttons. "What's your number, gorgeous?"

I open my mouth to speak but no words come out. I wasn't expecting him to ask. It's been a few months since I've had a one night stand, but I get the distinct impression we're breaking all the rules.

"Out with it, doll face. No fuckin' way I'm leaving here without it." I squint at him and he grins at me. "You're killin' me. What, am I supposed to leave our next meeting to chance? I don't think so."

I remind myself that another night in bed with him won't break my heart—not if I don't let it. *Which I won't!* Giving him my number is hardly a big deal. It's not any worse than making him grilled cheese. I rattle off the numbers and then pull out the bread.

"Millie—do you spell that *i-e* or *y*?"

I giggle, amused, surprised, and impressed that he cares. "Well, aren't you meticulous."

"My baby sis, Rosemary, lets me call her Rosy. She's pretty emphatic about how I spell it, though. Always with a *y*—I made the mistake of tacking on an *i-e* just once."

"I see," I murmur, sneaking a peek at him in my periphery as I smear the butter across four slices of bread. "Well, I spell it *i-e*."

"Is it short for something?" he asks, pocketing his phone.

"Millicent," I reply without pause.

"*Millicent*." He speaks my name as if he's *tasting* it. "I like that. Millicent, what?"

"I'm sorry," I mutter, setting the first sandwich on the skillet. "Did I miss the part where this turned into an interview?"

"Come on," he insists, nudging me with his foot. "Is it too much to ask for your last name? I've seen you naked."

"I've seen *you* naked and I don't know—"

"Sage Lawrence McCoy. Now I've told you mine, you tell me yours."

"Fine," I comply, looking straight into his warm, icy blue eyes. "Millicent Tatiana Valentine." He shakes his head as a knowing smirk tugs at the corner of his mouth; only, I'm not sure what's amusing. "What?" I ask self-consciously.

"Figures," he says softly, leaning toward me. He doesn't stop until his lips are a breath away from mine. "Even your name is sexy."

Before he can kiss me, his phone starts to ring again. He sighs as he pulls away from me and I cover up my disappointment, flipping the sandwich in the skillet.

"I should take this," he mutters apologetically.

"You're fine."

"Bet your ass, I am." He taps my backside and I roll my eyes. "Rosy," he speaks into the phone. I can't make out what is being spoken on the other end, but the woman doesn't sound happy. Sage, on the other hand, can't contain his laughter.

"Pep—Pep . . . Pepper! Chill a minute, would you? Damn! I wasn't screening my calls." He laughs again and the sound makes my stomach flutter. "I'm sorry, I'm sorry—I swear, I didn't mean anything by it. You know I love you, Pep. I'm kind of busy, sis, what do you need?" I flip the sandwich again, checking to see if both sides are the perfect golden brown. Noting that the top is lighter than the bottom, I flip it once more. "Count me in for dinner. Okay—I've got to go. Tell Rosy I said hi." He chuckles once more and then ends the call.

"I swear, Pepper is the most anal-retentive twenty-five-year-old I know. I'd blame her maternal status, but I think she's always been a little intense."

I look away from the sandwich in front of me, confused by what he's just said. "Wait—*who* is Pepper?"

"My big sis."

My stomach drops. "She's twenty-five?" Considering numbers are essentially what I *do* for a living, it takes me a fraction of a second to realize that there is *no way* Sage is older than twenty-four, making him no less than two years my junior. "How old is Rosy?"

"Nineteen," he replies with a shrug. "Why?"

Shit. It takes me another second to figure out that if his parents spaced out their children equally, Sage can be no older than twenty-two, making him *four* years my junior. Then again, he could be as young as twenty.

Fuck!

"How old are *you?*"

"Um—twenty-one. *Why?*"

"Oh, *shit.*"

He scrunches his brow at me and then his eyes flicker elsewhere. "Baby doll, I think you're on the verge of charing that grilled cheese."

I gasp, thoughtlessly using my hand to snatch the sandwich from out of the pan. It's really hot, causing me to burn my fingers, and I drop it on a cool burner before sticking my fingers in my mouth. Then his words register in my head—*baby doll.* He called me *baby doll.* Sage—the twenty-one-year-old who fucked me all morning—is calling *me* baby.

Oh, my god.

I make my way out of the kitchen, moving as fast as my sore body and pounding head will allow. I hear Sage calling after me, but I ignore him as I gather the rest of his things from my room. Picking up his red Converse and his t-shirt, I spot the three abandoned condom wrappers scattered around the bed and I'm suddenly short of breath.

I'm older than his big sister, for fuck sake!

"Millie, I—What are you doing?" he asks when I turn and find him in my doorway.

"You need to go. Now. You need to go now."

"Whoa, baby, slow down—what'd I miss?"

"*Stop* calling me baby!" I insist, shoving his things into his arms. "*You're* the baby. Fuck—I can't believe I slept with you. I'm like a cougar or a pedo or something."

"What?" he scoffs with a grin. "What are you talking about?"

"You're twenty-one! Oh, dear god, you're barely legal," I mutter, shoving him down the hallway. "You need to leave. Now. I mean it."

"Millie, stop. Wait! How old are you?"

I feel it as my cheeks blossom with a blush and I curse my face. "Older than twenty-one, Sage." I walk around him, unlocking the door and holding it open for him.

"Come on, you can't be old enough for it to matter."

I press my fingers against my temple, my headache amplified by my humiliation. "Do you know how old a twenty-one year old guy is in *girl* years? Like, fifteen. *Maybe* seventeen. *Shit.* I'm definitely a pedophile."

"Hang on one fucking second—I resent that, first of all," he argues, his face scrunching up in offense. "Second, unless you're, like, thirty or something, I don't understand why you're freaking the fuck out."

"Thirty? You think I look *thirty?*"

"Dammit, doll face, that's *not* what I said. You're being irrational. Let's just go back into the kitchen, eat some grilled cheese, and talk about this."

"Grilled cheese? Is that what's got you so adamant about staying?" I hurry back to the kitchen, grab the half burnt sandwich, and return to the door. "Here. I've fed you. You can go now."

"Millicent." My breath catches in my throat at the way he says my name. For a second, I regret having told him. "You're being ridiculous. How old are you?"

"I'm twenty-six. I'm older than your anal-retentive *big sis.* I'm also probably more OCD than she is, by the way. I'm sorry, but you have to go. We can't do this." I give him one more shove, forcing him on the other side of the threshold, and then I shut him out.

"Millie. Millicent! Are you being serious right now?"

I close my eyes, resting my forehead against the door. Images of Sage and his naked body flood my mind and I can't stifle the whine that flees from my throat. I wasn't ready to say goodbye—but fuck! Five years? Worse, *twenty-one?* He's a baby!

A part of me wants to argue that he certainly owned my body like a man, but—

"Millicent—doll face, come on, let me in."

"You need to go, Sage."

I hear him huff out a sigh and then take a bite of his burnt sandwich. "I'll be back, gorgeous," he says, his mouth full. "You can count on it."

Listening to him pad his way down the stairs in his bare feet, I'm not sure whether I feel hope or dread at the prospect of seeing him again. I draw in a deep breath and make my way back to the kitchen. As I begin to make another grilled cheese, a new wave of exhaustion hits. Now, the only thing I want to do is crawl back into bed and hide under the covers for the rest of the day.

A few minutes later, after I've plated my sandwich and filled up a glass of water to take back to my room, Sarah walks in—*glowing*, of course.

"Hey," she practically chirps. I offer her a feeble nod. "So. You and Sage."

For reasons I can't quite explain, my heart sinks hearing his name. "Mm-mm," I murmur. "We're not doing this now. We're not talking about it." I have no doubt in my mind that Sarah knows how old Sage is, considering they call each other friends. I don't even want to know what she's thinking right now. To my relief, she doesn't push the conversation. When she heads to her room, I make my way to mine, fully prepared to sleep for the rest of the day.

FIVE

Sage

BY THE TIME I get to my car, I'm halfway done with the grilled cheese sandwich Millie practically threw at me as she shoved me out the door. I hold it in my mouth as I throw my shirt over my head and tuck my feet into my shoes, finishing it as I sit perplexed in the driver's seat.

I can't believe, after the night we had, that she gives two shits about how old I am. I sure as hell don't care. Our five year age gap is *not* that big of a deal. If we're going to talk numbers, she should count the five orgasms I gave her—the five times she called out my name as she came apart at my touch.

Fuck. This is not over. It can't be.

I start my car and back out of the parking space, reluctantly leaving her apartment complex. I should probably stop at the house and shower, but I still smell like her and the thought of washing her away is far from appealing right now. Instead of heading home, I drive straight to Pepper's. She lives with her husband, Dr. Harold Montgomery, on the south side of town. He gave my big sis a pretty pompous name, but Harry is a cool guy—wicked smart, totally down to earth and laid back, exactly what my sister needs. I wonder if he'll be working today or if he'll be around for dinner.

They've just about got a full house now. Their two boys, Henley and Carter, got a sister, Sophia, a few weeks ago. Pepper swears she's done popping out kids now that Harry has made himself a girl, but I wouldn't put it past them to have at least one more. Pep is an outstanding mother. She impresses me every day.

Rosy's old, red, VW Bug sits parked on the side of the street in front of the house when I arrive. I shake my head as I pull into the space in front of her. That thing really is a piece of shit, but she loves it. She'll drive it until it leaves her stranded on the side of the road somewhere and I have to pick her ass up. I can't blame her for hanging onto it. She worked like hell to buy it after she graduated high school. Stubborn determination—that's something she and I have in common.

I hear Henley and Carter before I even make it to the front door. I let myself in without knocking and see the two of them running around, their little bare feet clapping against the hardwood floor as they squeal with excitement. I can't tell if Maestro is chasing them or if they're chasing Maestro, but they all look happy. They don't even notice me as I walk inside and find my way to the kitchen. Pepper is standing with her back to me, leaning against the counter as she watches them.

"You really should get them a dog," I tell her before pressing a kiss on top of her head.

She jumps and then turns around to smack me playfully in the middle of my chest. "God, Sage, don't sneak up on me like that!" She wraps her arms around me and I return her embrace before she pulls away. "And no. They don't need a dog. They have Maestro."

"Maestro is *my* dog," I say with a chuckle, looking over at my black, french bulldog as he slides across the floor.

"And therein lies the beauty. He visits, they play, and then you take him home and take care of him. The *last* thing I need is someone else to take care of."

"Can't argue with you there." It's then that Maestro hears my voice. His head pops up and he barks once before he comes racing toward me. Henley and Carter follow and then catch on to who he's after when they see me.

"Uncle Sage!" cries Henley.

"Unka Sage!" mimics Carter. At two, he's still struggling to get his *l's* out. Even I have to admit, it's pretty damn cute.

I drop to my knees to greet all three of them. "Hey, guys, what's happenin'?"

Henley speaks first, giving me the rundown of just about everything that his four-year-old brain can remember since I last saw him yesterday afternoon. I pet Maestro absentmindedly as I listen. It's not hard to admit, my nephews are a couple of my favorite people.

"Where's Sophia?" I ask them.

Carter's eyes grow big as he brings a finger to his mouth and shushes me. "Aunt Wose has Sophia."

Pepper chuckles from behind me and I look up at her with a grin. "She's in the living room. Good luck prying Sophia away from her."

I give her my best *oh, please* expression as I stand and head into the next room.

Pepper has done a damn fine job of making their house extra homey, and the living room is everyone's favorite place to chill. Rosy is being swallowed by one of their big, over-stuffed, brown armchairs. She's got a textbook open in her lap and Sophia is nestled in her arms. Guessing by the small smile that lights her face, I'd say she's not getting very much studying done. She looks up when she hears me approach.

"Hey, big bro. When did you get here?" she asks before puckering her lips.

I lean down and she kisses my cheek. "Just got here," I murmur, admiring my niece. She's sleeping, as if she knows the raucous her brothers are making is her reality and there's nothing she can do about it. Rosy sniffs and I jerk my head back to look at her.

"You smell like a bar. And sex. And—" She sniffs once more. "Vanilla."

"How the fuck do you know what sex smells like?" I ask, scowling at her.

She returns my scowl with one of her own before she smacks her little hand against the top of my head. "Language, Sage!"

"Answer my question, *Rosemary*."

She rolls her eyes, which makes me think of Millie, and then she speaks. "I've smelled it on you and the guys enough to know, dummy."

I look into her eyes for a moment, searching for the reassurance that that's the *only* reason she knows. I nod when I'm sure she's telling the truth.

"You're *such* a hypocrite."

"Wrong. I'm the guy any douche has to get through before he's allowed between my sister's legs."

She groans, lifting Sophia away from her and towards me. "You're the biggest pain in my a-s-s. Here. Take your niece." Before I can reach for her, Rosy changes her mind, hugs Sophia close, kisses her cheek, and whispers, "You're so screwed, baby girl. With your dad, and your brothers, and your uncle—you'll never get laid. Don't worry, though. You've got me, too." She kisses Sophia's soft, chubby cheek once more. "And ignore the smell. Uncle Sage is the best, I promise."

I playfully rub my knuckles against the top of Rosy's head and she ducks away from me before I gently scoop Sophia into my arms and make my way to the couch. Pepper catches my eye as she enters the room and shakes her head in disbelief. I chuckle, amused that she's surprised.

The three of us are pretty close, always have been. Granted, it didn't always look that way, what with all our bickering and arguing growing up, but we wouldn't trade each other for anything. That said, Rosy and I have always been really tight. Besides the fact that we're closer in age, Pepper was out of the house and married by the time I was sixteen. Pep is the sensible, wise, motherly one—she's our rock; but Rosy is my best friend, and I hers.

That is, when I'm not trying to keep guys out of her pants.

It's a fucking hard job to do, but someone's got to do it.

"So, who was the unlucky lady who had the misfortune of waking up after being ditched by the likes of you?" Rosy asks as I stretch out on the couch with Sophia.

I let out a long sigh, gazing down at the sweet little girl bundled in pink against my chest, and then mentally replay my morning. I remember the way it felt to hold Millie in my arms; how she wrapped herself around me when I kissed her; the sound of my name on her lips . . .

I'm yanked from my thoughts when I look down and see Pepper pulling my shoes from my feet. "I can only imagine where these things have been; they *do not* need to be on my couch," she tells me before she sits and drops my feet into her lap. "Also, judging by the look on your face, Rosemary's question requires an answer. What groupie has your head so foggy the afternoon after?"

"*Not* a groupie, sis. Not even close." I free another sigh, propping my head against the back of the couch. "God—she was amazing. I have to see her again."

"*What?*" gasps Rosy, tossing her textbook onto the floor as she curls her legs up underneath her. "Now I've *got* to know! What's her name? What does she look like? Did you get her number? Are you going to call her? You hardly ever call!" She gasps again, cutting me off before I can even utter a single syllable. "Is she why you didn't answer Pepper's call? Were you still with her when you told Pep you were busy? Is that why you still smell like last night in the middle of the afternoon?"

"*Jesus*, Rosy—take a breath!"

Pepper pinches my ankle and I jerk my foot out of reach with a frown. "*Language*," she mutters.

"Sorry," I grumble.

"Do you *not* remember how long it took me to get Henley to stop saying s-h-i-t every other minute? That was totally *your* fault."

I chuckle and she smacks my leg. "Alright, alright, stop with the abuse."

"Stop *stalling!*" Rosy insists. "I want to know about this girl. She came to your show, right? Is she going to be at the next one? Can I meet her?"

I sit silently as I stare at her, a blank expression on my face, waiting for her to stop. "Are you done?" She gestures with her hand that she's zipping her mouth closed, and I wait another second before I continue. "Her name is Millicent."

"*Millicent?*" Rosy scrunches her nose. "She sounds . . . *interesting*."

I shake my head at her, irritated that she's already formed a negative opinion about Millie based solely off of her *name*. "Yeah, *interesting*. She's interesting. You guessed it. Nothing left to tell."

"What?! No! I didn't—" She stops stuttering when Pepper starts laughing. "What's funny?" she pouts, folding her arms across her chest.

"Nothing," Pepper says with a smile. She turns to look at me as she continues. "She knocked you on your a-s-s. I can tell. I've *never* seen you shut down over a girl so fast in my life."

I shrug, sure there's no reason to deny it. Truth is, *she doesn't know the half of it.*

"*No,*" Rosy whines, jumping out of the chair as she crawls across the floor to kneel beside me. "I'm sorry I got judgy. Millicent—that's a—it's a very pretty name." I arch an eyebrow at her and she huffs out a sigh. "Okay. So it makes me think of an old lady who works at a library and is constantly telling everyone to be quiet, I can't help it! I'm *sure* anyone who could knock you on your a-s-s is far more interesting than that. *Please?* Tell us everything."

Knowing that I won't be able to keep my mouth shut if Rosy keeps begging, I concede. "I met her last night at The Brew Cycle. She's—she's got these eyes. And her lips—even her nose . . . she's gorgeous; flawless, like one of those glass dolls mom collects?" I cough out a laugh, remembering when she asked me what her name was out on that dance floor. "Her mouth, *god—*"

"Okay, don't get gross," Pepper interrupts.

"No, I don't mean it like that. I mean, *yeah,*" I say with a smirk. "But it's more than that. She's such a smart-aaaa—*a-s-s.* She's different. She didn't watch me perform and then go on and on about the band and how good she thought we were. She didn't throw herself at me or anything like that. *Definitely* not a groupie."

"So, what happened? Did you ask her out?"

"Well," I begin to say, reaching up to run my fingers through my messy hair. "Not exactly. She didn't really give me a chance before she kicked me out of her apartment."

"*She* kicked *you* out?" Rosy asks, her eyes wide with shock.

"She freaked when she found out I was only twenty-one."

"*Only?* How old is she? Did you bag a cougar?"

I furrow my brow at my baby sister, then shake my head once. "Rosy—don't talk like that. And *no,* I didn't. She's only twenty-six."

"That's not so bad," Pepper says with a shrug.

"Yes! *Thank you.* My thoughts exactly."

"Then again, I married a man seven years older than me. My opinion is a bit bias."

"Okay, yeah, my opinion is a bit bias, too—*obviously,* because you're my big bro, but honestly? She just doesn't know you," says Rosy, resting her hand over mine. "It doesn't take long for anyone to figure out that you're not the average twenty-one year old male. Sure, you can get a little wild—but you're also really driven, goal oriented, smart, and responsible. Mountains & Men wouldn't be half of what it is and what it's going to be without you."

"Thanks for the highlight reel of my resume," I tease.

"Hey, I'm serious," she says with a little laugh. "If she's really worth it, you just have to make her see how great you are. *If* she's worth it. Maybe take into consideration she spread her legs for you already," she tacks on softly.

"Don't talk about her that way," I reply, feeling surprisingly defensive. "She's worth it."

"There you go again," Rosy huffs. "*Hyp-o-crite.* But fine—I'll take your word for it."

"She's different, Rosy," I say, ignoring her dig. "I can't explain it, I just—" I try and find the words, *any* words that won't make me sound like such a fucking pansy. Then I remember—"The second I met her, I had these lyrics in my head. When I walked away from her, I heard the melody—it happened so fast."

"A muse," hums Pepper.

I nod, but I don't tell them that I think she's more than that. I don't tell them that I had this undeniable urge to sing to her the moment I was inside of her. I don't tell them how badly I wish I could call her *right now*. Instead, I close my eyes and sigh before I assure them, "I'm definitely going to see her again."

"Well, I'll be d-a-m-n-e-d. My big bro is falling for a girl."

A smirk curls at my lips but I don't open my eyes or confirm her statement. "Right now, your big bro is going to fall asleep. Wake me when it's time to eat."

"I'm sure Sophia will wake you when *she's* ready to eat."

"Fair enough," I say, holding her closer. "Now leave us be. We're bonding."

"Dweeb, we're going out after JJ gets home from work; you comin'?" asks Derrick, plopping down on the couch beside me. Maestro follows him into the room and paws at my legs. With one arm, I scoop him up and he circles my lap a couple times before laying down between my legs, his head propped on my thigh.

I look away from my phone, still unsure whether or not I want to call. *Again.*

It's been two days since Millie kicked me out of her apartment. The first time I called, it was Sunday night after I left Pepper's place. She answered, but I soon found out it was only because she didn't recognize my number. The conversation didn't last long. When I called her yesterday, she ignored me. Today, I'll admit it—I'm going fucking crazy.

I haven't been able to finish her song. I don't know how to end it. The last verse has been eluding me, as if it knows that our story isn't over—that Millie and I don't end after one night. I have to see her again. I'm dying to taste her, to feel her come apart beneath me, to hear my name on her lips as she shatters.

"Sage, seriously?" mutters Derrick, elbowing my ribs to get my attention. "Since when has a little pussy left you so distracted? It was *one night,* dude. Come out with us. There are plenty of fish in the sea."

The thought of bagging another girl has never felt so unappealing. If I needed any more confirmation that I'm on the verge of losing my mind, that was it. "I need to get her out of my system. One night wasn't enough. I just need—I need more."

"Maybe it's not the girl. Maybe it's just the chase. I know in *Sage World,* girls jump at the chance to hook up with you, but this chick doesn't seem all that interested. Why don't you just skip the hard part and *come out* with us?"

"She wants me, D," I mutter, remembering the look on her face just before she slammed her door in my face. I said her name and her eyes . . ."She wants me, she's just too fucking stubborn to admit it."

"*Or,*" he pauses as he leans forward, resting his elbows on his knees as he looks back at me. "This could just be a classic case of rejection. I know you haven't fallen victim to it in a while, maybe you forgot what it looks like, but when a girl doesn't answer your calls—*she's not that into you.*"

I shake my head, knowing he's wrong. I haven't told the guys about how things ended Sunday afternoon. They don't know why Millie refuses to take my calls. They don't understand that her reluctance is based on her bullshit idea that I have the maturity level of a *fifteen* year old. They don't even know about the half-ass song that's been playing on repeat in my head for the last three days.

Fuck it, I think before I scroll through my contacts and make another call.

"I'm studying; but since you're you, you've got two minutes. Hit me," Rosy says in greeting.

"I've got to bring Maestro by. You good with that?"

She gasps before she speaks. "Did she call you back?"

"Not exactly. Listen, you might only have him for an hour—but it could be all night."

"Yeah, no problem. I have class at nine, but you have a key. Or I might be able to drop him by the house in the morning on my way."

"Doesn't matter to me. Let me know what you decide. I'll be there in thirty."

"Does this mean you're coming out with us?" asks Derrick as I end the call and urge Maestro out of my lap and onto the floor.

"No. I'm going to see her."

"Wait—what?" he mutters in shock. "This chick got a magic pussy? You're entering into stalker territory, man."

"Her name is Millie, asshole, and don't fucking talk about her pussy." He just laughs, throwing himself back on the couch. "Come on, Maestro. We're out."

SIX

Millicent

I'VE BEEN TO THE GYM FOUR times in the last two days. I was hoping that a second hour of cardio after work would wear me out enough that I'd forget what I've been craving since I woke up late Sunday night.

Sage.

I reach for the knob in the shower, turning off the hot water, allowing an icy chill to wash over me for a few seconds. Thinking about Sage while I'm naked and wet is just downright masochistic. I groan in frustration as I kill the tap, step out of the tub, and wrap a towel around my shivering body. I wish I could forget him. Forget his soft lips, his greedy hands, his huge dick.

Fuck. It's been two days, for crying out loud!

Granted, it doesn't help that he's already called me a half a dozen times this week. It's kind of hard to forget the man when his voice keeps filling up my voicemail.

God, his voice.

As I stand in front of my vanity mirror, my hands poised and ready to open up my dresser drawer, I look right through my reflection. My mind clouds with the memory of him filling me as I've never been filled before; his sexy voice singing to me as he stared at me with those blue eyes.

I huff out a sigh and tug open my drawer, a little more aggressive than necessary, before I begin digging for clothes. I have no business dreaming about him. His body might be infuriatingly irresistible, but that little arrogant shit is just a kid. He's twenty-one. He's a lead singer of a great band. He's cocky and confident and, honestly, I can't blame him. I know he's got girls falling at his feet. It's no wonder that he gets what he wants—the world hasn't told him *no* yet. Five years might not seem like a lot, but I remember being twenty-one. I was still in school and—and I'm just not that person anymore. I'm older and, *shit*, I teach calculus to kids like him! Day dreaming about him is like fantasizing about a professor-student relationship and *that* is unacceptable.

Knowing I'm in the for night, I skip any underwear and slip into a pair of sweatpants and a spaghetti strap tank top with a built in bra. After towel drying my hair, I return it to the bathroom and then head for the kitchen. I'm sure the only way I'm going to get any work done tonight is if I have a glass of wine to help relax me. I feel wired, even after a long day, and I know a simple cup of tea will not do the trick.

The school year has barely just begun. So far, the few courses that I teach have started mostly with review. I like to get a grip on what my students know before I plan out the rest of the semester. The assignments I look over tonight aren't for a grade, even though they'll get points for simply turning it in. I won't deny that I can be a hard-ass in the classroom. There's so much for me to teach in just a matter of weeks; I expect my students to keep up, but I'm not cold-hearted. I'm a resource. I want to be able to help them—figuring out what they already know enables me to do my job to the best of my ability.

I'm sitting on the floor, papers piled neatly across the coffee table, my first glass of wine half gone, when a knock sounds at my door. I'm not expecting anyone, so I'm not sure who I'll find when I get up to answer. For a moment, I wonder if Sarah has forgotten her key or something. Then I look through the peephole. I gasp, my neck heating up and my stomach fluttering at the sight of him. I take a step back, cursing my body for reacting to the tiny, distorted image of him standing on the other side of my door.

"Millicent, I know you're in there. Open the door."

I take a deep breath, squeezing my legs together, wishing for the ache he causes just by *speaking* to go away.

"Sage, what are you doing here?"

"Open the door, doll face." I shake my head, even though I know he can't see me. "Millicent—just open the door."

My hand reaches out to slide back the deadbolt and twist the knob, as if it's actively rebelling against my mind. When the barrier between us is no longer separating us, I can't help but drink him in. Black Converse. Fitted blue jeans. Black graphic t-shirt—each scrap of fabric hugging that body worthy of admiration. When my eyes meet his, I want to flip him off for being so damn alluring.

"*The truth is in the lie of just one night,*" he sings softly. My breath catches in my throat and he tilts his head, narrowing his eyes as if he's studying me from behind his glasses. He takes a step toward me before he continues, and my heartbeat picks up speed.

"Can't stop the beat, can't stop my feet, just want to dance
I'll set you free, but will you let me go?
You cage me in and now I can't let go.
All night/One song
This room/My home
Set me free but, baby, don't let go
Tonight/ Just give me tonight."

My feet, my arms, my lips—they *all* conspire against me and in *one* step, my body is in reaching distance of his; in *one* second, my arms are circled around his neck; in *one* breath, my mouth is pressed against his—and before I can make sense of what in the hell I'm doing, he's crushing me against him as his tongue invades my mouth in the most delicious way.

I'm instantly burning with a fierce desire for him, my craving for this man bursting free from all my efforts to squelch any and all interest in what he has to offer. I want him. I want him so badly, I can't even think straight. I'm so excited and turned on, my body feels like it's vibrating with anticipation—or is that the rumble of his deep groan that rattles his chest? Whatever it is, it fuels my hunger and I don't stop him when he backs me into the living room, or when he closes the door behind him, or when he slides his hand under the waist band of my sweatpants, squeezing my bare ass as he presses me against the erection hardly concealed in his pants. He groans again and I tighten my grip around him, lifting myself onto my tiptoes in an attempt to somehow get him even closer.

"Shit, I can't stop," I whisper against his lips.

"Good. I need my cock inside your pussy, baby doll. I want you right now."

"I'm not wearing any panties," I murmur, daring him with one glance. "What are you waiting for?"

"Sarah?" he practically growls.

"Not home."

I barely get the words out before he's got me turned around and bent over the the back of my couch. I practically whine in impatient desperation when he yanks my pants down around my ankles. My chest feels tight as I grow short of breath, listening as he loosens his belt and unzips his jeans. I hear him rip open the condom just as his pants drop, the thud of his buckle hitting the floor making my pussy ache.

I suck in a breath when he rubs his cock across my entrance and over my clit, wetting himself with my arousal. I arch my back in a silent plea and he grabs my hips in a tight grip. "Hold on, doll face. This is going to be fast and hard."

"Fuck," I cry when he thrusts into me, stretching me open and filling me to full capacity. His warning was not for nothing and he doesn't pause for even a moment before he begins to pound in and out of me. The sound of his skin slapping against mine is unfathomably sexy, and I mewl at the pleasure he's forcing upon my body.

"You like that, baby? Did you miss my dick like I missed your pussy?" he grounds out as he releases one of his hands from my hip and grabs a fistful of my damp hair. He pulls hard enough to get me to arch my back a little more, but gentle enough that the whimper I let loose is one of pure enjoyment.

"Oh, god, yes," I mutter honestly, too distracted to lie or even come back with a smart remark. My body did miss him and no amount of physical exertion would allow me to forget it. Now, as he takes me like he hasn't taken me before, I'm afraid I'll never be able to forget him. Not ever. "Sage—Sage—Sage," I chant mindlessly as I feel my orgasm start to build; it's warm and enticing and all I want is to be consumed by it.

When the pressure from his fingers around my hip disappears, the last thing I expect is for his hand to slap across my ass. The moan his palm elicits surprises me just as much. "That's for saying I have the maturity level of a fifteen year old." He spanks my other cheek as he continues to pummel in and out of me and a shock of pleasure rushes up my spine. "That's for ignoring my calls." Then, without warning, his fingers are squeezing my throbbing clit and my orgasm hits me like a fucking tornado. "And *that,*" he begins to say, speaking loudly so that he might be heard over my cries, "is for opening the door."

His declaration is followed immediately by a growl, his response to the ecstasy of his own climax. He rides out his release, thrusting into me once, then twice before he releases my hair and lays across my back. He kisses the side of my neck as he continues to rock his hips lazily; and I sigh, feeling sated at last.

Sage

AFTER I PULL OUT, I remove the condom and bring my pants up around my waist. I head to the bathroom to dispose of our protection, but I don't bother buttoning my jeans closed. I have every intention of a repeat performance. When I make my way back out into the main room, I find Millie dressed and standing with one hand on her hip, the other holding an empty wine glass. She sighs when she sees me and then heads for the kitchen. I follow, right on her heels.

"Sage—what are you doing here?" she asks, planting her hands on the counter as she leans against them, her back to me. Her shoulders are rigid in her current posture, but she's still exceptionally delicate, her skin creamy and soft. All I can think about is how I want to drag my lips against every inch of her back. "Sage," she moans, dropping her head.

"I think you know why I'm here," I reply, sliding my hands around her hips. Unlike before, when I was fucking her, my grip is firm but gentle. The last thing I want is for her to bolt—not now that I've finally got her attention again.

"We . . . we can't—"

"I think we can, doll face. I think we just *did*."

"Okay, so this is about sex," she states. When she turns around and folds her arms across her chest, I'm sure to maintain my grip, sliding my hands up around her waist. "You owned another orgasm. *Thank you*. You can go now."

I smirk before I lean in and rest my forehead against hers. "Go out with me."

"What?" she breathes, dropping her arms.

"You heard me. A date—I want to take you out. Say yes."

She leans away from me and pierces me straight through with her dark green eyes. "Don't be ridiculous. Did you not hear anything I said on Sunday? You picked me up at a bar. We had great sex. You don't know anything about me. You do not want to take me on a date and I—"

"Enough," I interrupt her, placing both hands on the counter so that I've got her caged between my arms. "I'm not some punk kid. I'm a fucking man who knows exactly what he wants. I might be younger than you, but that doesn't mean *shit*. Don't trick yourself into thinking you know anything about me, either. Getting to know each other is what a date's all about, doll face. I know enough about you to know that I want more. So say yes."

She hesitates and I know already I'll get what I want. She won't make it easy, but the truth is in her eyes.

I bring my mouth to hers and press a soft kiss against her lips. "Sage," she sighs when I pull away.

"Say yes."

"No."

"Wrong answer," I insist. I tug her bottom lip between my teeth and she whimpers, bringing her hands up to my chest. I smile when she doesn't push me away and then suck her lip further into my mouth before letting her go. "Say yes."

"It would never work. *We* would never amount to anything and so—what's the point?" she asks with a shrug.

I groan in frustration, bringing my lips to her neck. Her hair is still damp from a shower and she smells sensational. I flick my tongue out, sneaking a taste of her skin, and she grips my t-shirt. I chuckle before I whisper into her ear. "Give it up, doll face. You know you want me."

This time, when her hands press against my chest, she tries to push me away. I don't budge. Instead, I lift an eyebrow at her and fight a smile at the indignant look on her face. "See? That right there? *That's* why I'm saying no."

"Excuse me?" I scoff. "You're saying no because I'm telling you the truth? Don't kid yourself, Millicent. *You want me.*" When she tries to shove me again, I circle my arms around her and lower my face so that the tip of my nose touches the tip of hers. "Don't you fucking dare, doll face. You want me and I sure as hell want you, so stop being so damn stubborn and say *yes!*"

She hesitates again and I shake my head at her before I grab the back of her thighs and hoist her up around my waist. She squeals in surprise but then wraps herself around me, studying my face as I carry her down the hallway. "What are you doing?" she asks when I kick her bedroom door closed behind us.

"I'm about to fuck some sense into you. Unless, of course, you'd rather I just leave." I palm one of her tits as I say the words and I can feel her hardened nipple through the cotton of her tank top. When she doesn't object, I grin at her before tossing her onto the bed. "Yeah. That's what I thought."

Neither of us has spoken in a few minutes and I wonder if she's sleeping, her leg hooked around mine, her cheek on my chest. I know I should be tired, we've been at it for I don't know how long, but I can't bring myself to close my eyes. She hasn't said yes yet. She's so goddamn stubborn.

Sarah told me that she thought Millie seemed like the kind of person who has a lot of walls up—more like a fortress. I guess I can't say I'm surprised. *I see the demons in her eyes.* What I haven't been able to pound into her is that I'm not afraid of her demons. I've got my own scaring the shit out of me.

I'm pulled from my thoughts when I feel her fingers glide over the lyrics scrolled across my ribs on the right side of my chest. I wait for her to say something, but she doesn't. Instead, she props herself up on her elbow as she begins to study the artwork that spans across my chest. She touches the skin inked with a cassette labeled *mixed tape* on my right pec, the string of tape unraveling in a coil that turns into the chord connecting to the blue headphones in the middle of my sternum. She traces the two lines that mark a heartbeat between the speakers and then continues to follow them when they stretch across my chest to my heart. Each line turns into script—the top reading *Pepper* the bottom *Rosemary.*

She pauses for a moment, bringing her eyes to meet mine. I want to kiss her. She's so fucking beautiful. There's not even a hint of makeup on her face and it makes me wonder why she wears it at all. Before I can move or speak, she continues her exploration of my ink. My arm is still wrapped around her waist, leaving my left side exposed. Under what looks like the charred away flesh is a sheet of music that goes from just under my arm, all the way down my waist.

When she sits up, her naked breasts practically begging for my attention, it takes just about all my willpower to keep my hands to myself. I let her take my hand from around her and bring it into her lap. She twists my arm so that she can see the inside of my forearm where I got my first tattoo. Like my side, it looks as though my skin has been ripped away and underneath are the keys of a piano, weathered and worn. She twists my arm again and exposes the red, Fender Stratocaster that's propped up against an amp. The guitar takes up my entire forearm, the strings turning into a music staff at my elbow. The staff, riddled with notes, wraps around my arm and the stand of the old school microphone that covers my shoulder.

She looks at me again when she gently nudges me, this time a request in her dark green eyes. Knowing what she wants, I roll onto my side so she can see my back piece. The mountain-scape that spans from my left to my right shoulder takes up a good quarter of the length of my back. The mountain itself is outlined and shaded in black; but the sky above it is filled with the colors of dawn. Just when I begin to wonder if she'll spot the small figure of the man standing at the base of the mountain, I feel her find him with her fingers.

"Are you staying?" she asks, her voice soft and low.

I look at her from over my shoulder, curious to know what she's thinking, but smart enough to know that now might not be the time to ask. Besides, there's another question still on the table. "Are you saying yes?"

She stares into my eyes for a moment before she replies, "I don't know."

It's the first time tonight that she hasn't said no and I don't even try to hide my smirk.

"Then I'm not going anywhere, doll face."

She nods once and then lays down, turning her back to me. "I have to get some sleep. I have work in the morning. Would you mind shutting off the light?"

I reach for her bedside lamp and click it off before turning towards her. I don't even think twice about pulling her into my arms. When her back makes contact with my chest, I feel her exhalation as she relaxes against me. I don't know what her deal is, but after tonight, my guess is that our age difference isn't the only thing that's making her so resistant. It's something bigger. Something scarier. But holding her in my arms right now—I know whatever is holding her back is not as daunting as what I feel in this moment.

I want her. More than I've wanted anyone in a long time.

Her alarm clock sounds at a quarter after six. She groans before she reaches over me to smack the snooze button. I chuckle, still half asleep, when she plops down on top of me.

"I don't know why you're laughing," she grumbles. "This day is going to suck ass and it's all your fault."

Holy shit. I love the way her voice sounds when she wakes up.

"I didn't hear you complaining last night."

"Shut up," she mutters. She tries to roll away from me but I lock her in my arms and she gives up before falling back asleep.

Ten minutes later, when her alarm goes off again, she doesn't move. Deciding another ten minutes of sleep won't hurt, I hit the snooze button. The last thing I want to do is get up, but now that my body has registered that it's morning, I've got to piss. I slide out from underneath Millie, careful not to wake her, and then jump into my boxers before heading to the bathroom. Before I even notice that the door is shut, it's being opened and all I see is Sarah wrapped in a towel.

"Fuck—sorry!" I mumble, holding up my hand to shield my eyes. "Brandon'll have my balls if he finds out I saw his girl naked."

"I'm not naked!" she gasps.

"And I didn't see you," I insist. "What are you doing here, anyway?"

"Uh—what are *you* doing here? I *live* here!" she sputters.

My shoulders lift and then fall in a shrug. "I thought you weren't home."

"I thought Millie wasn't returning your calls."

I peek around my hand at her with a smile. "I told you—she digs this," I remind her, gesturing to my body.

She smiles at me before speaking again. "Well, good for you."

"Now I just have to get her to go out with me. On a *real* date. Sure you can't be of any help?" I ask, remembering Brandon telling me that I wasn't going to use Sarah as bait to win Millie over.

"I'll see what I can do," she agrees with a nod.

"Yes! Thank you!" I hold up my hand and she gives me a high five. I have no idea whether or not Sarah will be able to sway Millie, but at this point, I could use all the help I can get.

"Sage?" she asks, pulling me from my thoughts.

"Yeah?"

"I'm not making any promises, but I definitely can't do anything as long as I'm standing here wrapped in my towel."

"Right. Sorry," I mutter, stepping aside so that she can pass.

"And I'm not done in there, so make it snappy."

"Yes, ma'am."

I notice Millie still has five more minutes to snooze by the time I make it back into her room, quietly shutting the door behind me. Knowing she'll probably kick me out when she finally wakes up, I don't bother getting naked or crawling back under the sheets with her. Instead, I sit on the side of the bed and watch her sleep.

After the shortest five minutes of my life, her alarm clock sounds again. She whines, rolling onto her back and throwing her arms over her face. I reach over to silence it, my eyes glued to her body as I blindly search and find the off switch. She inhales deeply and exhales slowly, the rise and fall of her tits making my mouth water.

Without stopping to think, I crawl over her, propping myself up on my hands and knees before I lower my mouth and close my lips around her nipple. She moans as I suck and my dick starts to harden. I bite down on her tight bud and she gasps, arching her back and pushing her chest up. I run my tongue around her nipple before I pull away and blow on it.

"I have work," she mutters feebly as I begin to show her other breast the same attention.

"Skip breakfast. I'll be your caffeine fix."

"Sage," she breathes in pathetic protest as I kiss my way down her stomach. I smell her arousal before I settle my face between her legs and I know already that I'll be taking an extra long shower when I get home, remembering this exact moment when I'm stroking my dick. "*Oh, my god,*" she whimpers with the first swipe of my tongue. It's not long before she's panting, tugging at my hair, her legs trembling as she comes in my mouth.

"Millicent," I murmur, biting and then kissing the inside of her thigh. "Say yes."

She looks down at me with a sleepy, satisfied, sexy as fuck smile and says, "Maybe."

I bite her again before I roll out of bed. I'm getting the hell out of here while she's still riding the high of her orgasm, her head too hazy to realize she pretty much just agreed to go out with me.

SEVEN

Millicent

As my students file out of the classroom, my phone starts to ring. *Again.* I silence it as I drop it in my purse and gather the rest of my things so that I can head back to my office. Staying up all night with Sage instead of working has definitely put me behind. I intend to spend the next couple of hours locked away, looking over assignments before I go to the gym.

Sage might not be good for my heart, but he sure as hell has done a number on my body. I've probably burned a million extra calories this week in an attempt to rid myself of my sexual frustration. Out of bed . . . and, more recently, in it.

It only takes me a few minutes to walk over to the next building where the offices for the math department are housed. Just as I set my things down on my desk, I hear my phone chirp in my bag, alerting me to a text. I sit before I dig it out and shake my head when I see that I have three missed calls and a text message, all from the same man.

I'm a fucking man who knows exactly what he wants.

His words replay in my head for the dozenth time since he said them, and I do my best to stifle the little bit of hope that is seriously starting to irk me. I slide my finger across the screen on my device and open his text. A blush creeps into my cheeks and my breath catches in my throat when I read what he's sent.

Sage: Have you already forgotten what happens when you don't answer my calls? Or are you just begging for me to smack that ass again?

Just as I'm about to begin typing a reply, he calls. I roll my eyes and then answer. "Hello?"

"You're one hard woman to get ahold of, doll face."

"I'm at work, Sage. I can't exactly answer a call in the middle of class."

"Class? You're a teacher?"

I chew on my bottom lip a moment, reality smacking me across the face. I've spent hours in bed with him and there are a million things we don't know about each other. *Do I want us to know each other?*

"I'm a professor," I answer, deciding that my occupation is a safe piece of intel to share. "I teach at Front Range Community College."

"A professor?" he deadpans before he groans. "You're killing me, baby doll. That's so fucking hot." His response catches me off guard and I don't know what to say. My silence doesn't seem to deter him. "If I'd have thought my professors could have been as gorgeous as you, I might've endured a couple more years of college."

I furrow my brow, trying to make sense of his words. "You're not in school?"

"Nope."

"You . . . you didn't go to college?"

"Hey, don't judge. College isn't for everybody. I did a couple years, took the courses I thought I needed, and I got out. My dreams don't require a degree."

I cross my legs and drape my arm across my knee as I think about what he's said. He's talking to someone who has a bachelor's, a master's, and a belief that higher education is valuable.

What am I doing? Every time I learn something new about him, it's only further confirmation that pursuing anything with him is not a good idea. I should have showed him to the door as soon as I woke up Sunday morning. I should have never offered him a grilled cheese.

"What if your dreams don't come true?" I mutter. As soon as the words pass through my lips, I know I'm being a bitch. Pushing him away is one thing, but what I just said? It was an awful thing to say. Anyone who has the optimism and strength to hold onto a dream deserves the chance to go after it without people like me tearing them down.

"They will," he assures me, interrupting my thoughts. "Even if I die trying."

"I'm sorry," I sigh. "I didn't mean—you know what? I should go."

"Not so fast. I haven't even asked you when you're free for our date, yet."

My eyebrows shoot up in surprise. "I wasn't aware that I agreed to go out with you."

"But you will. Are you free Friday night?"

"No," I reply, not even stopping to think about it.

"You're lying."

"Sage—"

"What are you so afraid of, Millie?"

"Why are you so adamant, Sage?"

"I'm more than you give me credit for, baby. You can't deny there's something between us."

I fidget with my fingers as I try and find the words to say. He's not *entirely* wrong. However, it's purely physical and I can't help but wonder, how long before that fades? How long before he gets bored and moves on to the next pretty girl who throws herself at him? And when that day comes, because it always does, will it hurt? Am I strong enough to stick around and test my limits? Can I date him without falling for him?

Something tells me the answer is *no.* I'm not that strong. Deep down, I know that too much attention from one man will only shed light on the truth that I'm usually so careful to keep under wraps. The truth is, I get lonely. I'm human. It's easy to cover it up with work and books and the occasional one night stand. But—dating? It's just a recipe for disaster and I know it.

"Millicent . . ."

My stomach flutters at the tone of his voice and I close my eyes as I draw in a slow breath. "I'm just a woman. There are others." Saying the words fills me with disappointment. I know, in this moment, that there's already a small part of me that is aching to latch onto him, which is exactly why I need to say goodbye.

"One date, gorgeous. Just say yes. I won't take no for an answer."

"Sage—"

"*Jesus,* you're so fucking impossible, did you know that? I don't know what asshat made you so guarded, but it's like I said. I won't take no for an answer. I want you, doll face, and I know you want me, too. I'm taking you on a date. Until then, I've got a show this Saturday. We're headlining at The Wash Bar. I hope you'll come."

"I'll think about it," I mutter, not sure if I mean it or if I'm simply hoping it'll get him off the phone.

"You're playing hard to get—but I'm not afraid of a little challenge. I'll catch you later, doll face."

He disconnects the call without another word.

I'M AT THE OFFICE longer than usual, content to drown myself in work for a few hours. I catch up on all that I fell behind on last night; then I get ahead on my lesson plans for the next couple of weeks, making sure that I stay close to the syllabi that I created to plot out the course of the semester. When I finally make my way to my car, I think about just going home. I'm exhausted. But then I think about climbing in my bed and I know that the pillow on the right side of the mattress will smell like Sage. Thinking of Sage reminds me of the way he woke me up this morning, and remembering his tongue awakens the desire that emanates between my legs, and I know I won't get any sleep until after I've managed to exhaust myself completely.

Fucking bastard. Fucking arrogant little shit with a fucking unbelievably talented mouth. And don't even get me started on that dick . . . Fuck!

By the time I get to the gym, I'm so irritated at myself for turning into *exactly* who I told him I wasn't—a nameless, fangirl, slut who would fall to my knees and suck his cock as if it were my privilege. Well, I suppose the nameless part isn't accurate . . .

Oh, but the sound he makes when he comes, it just might be a damn privilege to suck that out of him.

When I pull into the parking lot, I turn off my car and press my head back against the headrest. I inhale deeply and exhale slowly, combating my desire to call him. Something tells me that if I told him I had an itch that I needed him to scratch, he would do it. All night long. I'm so tempted that I leave my phone in the glove compartment when I get out of the car and make my way inside.

Just as I'm about to step foot into the locker rooms to change, Aria and Sarah are on their way out. They stop when they see me, both of them looking energized after an invigorating workout.

"You're here late," says Aria. "Too bad you weren't a little earlier, you could have joined us for Josh's class."

"Yeah, I didn't plan on being here so late, but I got caught up at work and . . ." I trail off, deciding that *why* I'm here at this hour isn't something I need to divulge. "Are you two headed home?"

"Yup," Aria replies with a nod.

"Actually, Millie, do you mind if I talk to you for a second?" asks Sarah, tightening her long ponytail.

"Um, okay."

"I'm going to bother Josh," Aria says with a wink. "Just come grab me when you're done. Good seeing you, Millie. Enjoy your workout." She bounces off and I give my attention to Sarah, completely unsuspecting of what she might want to speak to me about.

"I ran into Sage this morning at the apartment," she tells me with a small smile.

When she doesn't continue, I shrug and shake my head in confusion. "Okay. And?"

"Aaaaaand, I don't know," she laughs, in that way that tells me she's not sure how to respond. "He seems to be really interested in you."

"Yeah," I mutter, still uncertain where this conversation is supposed to be going.

"Look, I know it's none of my business, but I really think you should give him a chance. He's a good guy, from what I can tell. And, actually, I was thinking that maybe we could all go on a triple date or something. I can't this weekend, because I already have plans, but maybe next weekend? You, Sage, Aria, Josh, Brandon and I—we could all go to The Brew Cycle and hang out. It could be fun. I mean, we had a great time the other night, right?"

"Um," I begin to say, adjusting the strap of my gym bag against my shoulder. "I'm not really sure what I'll be up to next weekend."

She smiles at me knowingly. "Just think about it, okay? I know you and I got off to a rough start, but I hope we can be friends. Spending a night out with everyone would be totally low key. No pressure."

"Sure. Okay, yeah. I'll think about it," I concede, appreciating her olive branch.

"Great. Well, I'll let you get to your workout. See you."

"Bye."

We part ways and I don't waste any time changing into my shorts and tank top. I really don't want to spend the next hour thinking about Sage or Sarah or The Brew Cycle—I just need to clear my head. I'm pulling my hair up into a ponytail as I make my way out onto the gym floor. It's then that I realize that by leaving my phone in my car, I've left my collection of audiobooks, too. Knowing I'll have to find another way to occupy my thoughts, I opt to exhaust my body with a run on the treadmill. The line of machines face the half of the gym dedicated to the free weights and there's always plenty of eye candy to keep a bitch in heat distracted.

Five minutes into my run, someone catches my eye. He's tall with a mop of blonde hair on his head. He's not wearing a shirt, only a pair of shorts with his tennis shoes. He looks like . . . *Hercules*, and that observation makes me smile. I watch him do a rep with a set of heavy weights, working his biceps, before he drops them onto the mat. I roll my eyes when he pulls out his phone and snaps a shot of himself in the mirror. I look away, immediately uninterested, but not before he catches me staring. For a second, I think I'm in the clear; but when I look back in his direction to insure he's not concerned with me, I spot him headed directly toward me.

I stifle a groan and up the speed on my machine. When he's closed the distance between us, he doesn't speak to me right away. Instead, he hops onto the treadmill next to mine and starts to jog. It's not long before his pace matches my own. I can tell, looking out of the corner of my eye, that he keeps glancing in my direction. Finally, the inevitable break in silence occurs.

"Do you want to race?" he asks, speaking loud enough to be heard over the hum of the moving belt and the *thump, thump, thump* of my footfalls.

I look over at him, caught off guard by his question. "Excuse me?"

He grins and the dimple in his cheek makes me want to smile in return, but I fight the urge. "Do you want to race?" he repeats.

"Um, no . . ." I mutter.

"Oh, come on. First one to three miles wins. You've already got a head start."

"Just what would we be racing for?" I ask, a little short of breath.

"If I win, I get to take you out. If *you* win, you get to choose where we go."

My mouth falls open and I clamp it shut when he winks at me.

What the fuck? Do I have a stamp on my forehead that says, 'Looking for a good lay—cocky bastards wanted'? Because that's what it's starting to feel like.

"Lighten up," he says with a chuckle, pulling me from my thoughts. "I'm a good time, guaranteed."

"Good for you," I mumble.

"*Kidding!* Well—sort of. I am a good time. My name is Keith, what's yours?"

I look away from him, wondering how long I'd have to ignore him before he caught a clue.

"If you don't tell me, I'll just have to call you beautiful. I'm certainly not opposed if you aren't. It's true."

His compliment softens me up just a little and I decide I don't have to be so rude. The least I can offer him is my name. "My name is Millie."

"Ah, see? Now we're getting somewhere. Though, if you won't race me for a date, I guess I'll have to go about it the old fashioned way. So how about it? You, me, dinner, Friday night?"

"Uh, I don't think so," I tell him, looking straight ahead.

"What about if we just happened to be in the same place at the same time?" This time, when I look over at him, he's not on his treadmill. Instead, he's standing right beside mine. "Saturday night. There are a few bands playing at The Wash Bar. I'll be there. I'd love to buy you a drink."

I stare at him for a moment, struggling to decide if his persistence is annoying or brave. I can't decide and I'm soon distracted as I'm reminded of the first invitation that I received to attend The Wash Bar this weekend—from Sage.

"Beautiful?" he asks, pulling me from my thoughts.

"I'll think about it," I reply, for what feels like the tenth time today.

"I hope you do," he says with a wink.

As I watch him leave, I think about my Saturday night plans and any attempts to shove Sage into the recesses of my mind are eradicated. It seems as if I can't escape him. I increase the speed on my machine one more time, running for another fifteen minutes before I get off to head home.

The next two days fly by and without a word from Sage. Much to my chagrin, I find myself checking my phone repeatedly, only to realize that I've missed not a single call or text. Friday night, when I go to sleep, I rest my head on the pillow that holds the remnants of his scent, and I admit that I miss him. Not just the way he owns my body and the pleasure he all but demands, but the way he pulls me into his arms and holds me before we fall asleep. I miss his smirk and the confidence that shines in his icy blue eyes.

I'm a fucking man who knows exactly what he wants.

I've told him *no* so many times that I can't be surprised by his silence. Nevertheless, I can't help but wonder if he's given up already. His sudden disappearing act has my entire body wondering if I'll ever feel his touch again. He wanted me and I said I didn't want the same thing. I'm beginning to see that that was a lie. In spite of all the reasons that tell me he's a bad idea, I have to admit that he was right. I want him, too.

EIGHT

Sage

Keeping my cool and avoiding my phone has me going fucking insane. I haven't stopped thinking about Millicent since the moment I hung up on her Wednesday afternoon. It was then that I decided that the only way to prove to her stubborn ass that she wants me was to pull away. I remember the look in her eyes when she opened the door and saw me Tuesday night. '*Shit. I can't* stop,' she said after she threw herself into my arms. I made her come again and again and again. And when I was done, she let me pull her into my arms and hold her all night.

Chasing after her is a fucking shit show. It's so damn obvious that she wants me and yet she won't give in. So, I decided to change my tactics. I sure as hell hope it works. One more night, I just need one more night to convince her to go out with me. I know it. If she doesn't come to The Wash tonight, I don't know what will stop me from showing up at her doorstep as soon as our set is over. I miss her and I want her too much to deny it.

Saturday afternoon. Two o'clock. As soon as I get off work. That's when my silence ends. I've been waiting all damn day for this.

Me: Hey, gorgeous. Tonight. We go on at 10. I'll see you?

I stare at my phone as I walk from Little Bird to my car. I wait as I put the top down and then decide that a few more minutes of silence won't kill me. I need to take my fucking tampon out and get home. When I arrive, I see Rosy's car in the drive. She's sitting out on the front porch playing with Maestro. JJ and Maddox are on the lawn, throwing a frisbee back and forth.

"'Sup, Sage?" Maddox asks with a nod. JJ waves and Rosy giggles as Maestro sprints towards me.

"Hey," I mutter as a blanket greeting. I scoop up my dog and kiss the top of his head, arching my neck back when he tries to lick my face. "I love you, too, buddy, but you know how I feel about your tongue on my face. I've seen where it's been. I like my junk, too, but damn." When I sit beside Rosy, he wiggles out of my arms and I let him go.

"How was work?" Rosy asks, bumping her shoulder against mine. I shrug, trying hard not to think about my phone. It feels like it's burning a hole in my pocket. "Did you do what you said you were going to do?"

"Yeah."

"And? Has she replied? Is she coming?"

"I don't know."

She frowns and then throws her arm around me. My baby sis is pretty small in comparison to me, so her fingers barely reach across the width of my back.

"She won't be the last girl to knock my big bro on his ass. You just need to keep your eyes open for the next—"

"I'm not going hunting tonight, sis."

She opens her mouth to speak and then closes her lips as she stares at me contemplatively. A couple seconds go by and then she sucks in a breath and tries again. "I don't get it, Sage. Don't get *you*. We know how often *that* happens, so explain it to me. You've known her for a week. And I use the term *known* loosely. What is it about her that has you acting . . ."

"Like a fucking pussy?" I finish for her. "Go ahead, say it."

"Okay, I will," she says mockingly. "What is it about her that has you acting like a *fucking pussy?*"

"Don't talk like that," I state with a smirk.

"Ugh! Come on!" She moves her arm from around me and elbows me in the ribs. "I will not have you chasing after some snobby, stuck up, wench who doesn't appreciate you and your awesomeness. You've bagged some pretty questionable girls in your day, all of which I overlook—with the exception of that Chelsea chick. I still have no idea what you were thinking when you took her home. I mean—gross. But this Millie woman? Just give me one reason why I should allow you to spend another night pining over her."

"She's like a song, Rosy. I'm just not done listening."

I look over and watch as her expression softens. She then kisses my cheek and rests her head on my shoulder, hugging my arm. "That's it. I've got to meet her. She's turning my brother into a big ole sap and I *love* it. She better come tonight. That's all I'm saying."

Just then, my phone buzzes in my pocket. We both jump before I reach to pull it out. When Rosy squeals and squeezes my arm, I know she's peeked and read my new message. I don't mind, though. It's good news.

Millie: I'll see you.

Game on, baby doll.

Millicent

I CHANGE MY OUTFIT three times. It's stupid, I know, but I feel like wearing something bold and sexy and it takes me three attempts before I'm satisfied. I decide on a plunging neck, navy blue, drawstring dress. The material is light and drapes comfortably over my body, the hem cut high on my thigh. The spaghetti straps criss-cross over my back and the drawstring around the middle is pulled tight, accentuating my waist. With my back and my shoulders bare, my lack of bra is what makes this dress daring, my minimal cleavage on full display. My hair is pulled into a loosely knotted bun at the nape of my neck, drawing even more attention to the crazy amount of skin I'm showing. I finish the ensemble with a pair of yellow stiletto pumps and my hot pink envelop clutch.

I arrive at The Wash Bar a little after nine. There's a crazy line to get in and I know that inside will be packed. Sage told me earlier that there was going to be a cover charge but that he would make sure my name was on some list. His text instructed me to bypass the line and give the bouncer my name. It's exactly what I do and I'm allowed in with no fuss.

This place is at least twice the size of The Brew Cycle and buzzing with energy and activity. It's quite apparent that school is back in session and the students that fill this college town are back and ready to party. There's a band on stage, in the middle of their set, and a mob of people on the dance floor. The bar is busy, filled with patrons waiting to put in their drink order, and I wonder how I'll ever find Sage. With less than forty minutes before Mountains & Men take the stage, I decide to wait in line for a drink and worry about finding him after he's performed.

Fifteen minutes later, my gin and tonic in hand, I'm standing on the outskirts of the dance floor, watching the performing band. I'm startled when a pair of hands take hold of my waist and pull me back against the body behind me.

"You made it," he whispers in my ear. I jump, spinning around to find *Hercules, the selfie guy* from the gym, smiling at me. "I think I was supposed to buy you that drink, though."

"Don't mention it, it's fine," I say, lifting my glass before taking a sip.

"You look hot as shit, beautiful," he says, taking a step toward me, his hands finding my waist once more. I can tell that he's already had a few drinks and I wonder how hard it'll be to shake him. I totally forgot he was going to be here.

"Look, I'm kind of—"

"Hey, I can't stay, I go on in a few minutes and the guys'll bitch if I don't meet up with them soon. But don't leave, sexy. I'm buying you that drink, later."

Before I can register all that he's saying, he leans in and kisses my neck. I recoil, but he doesn't notice; then I watch him wade through the crowd until I lose him in the darkness.

Sage

Our ninety minute set is sick as shit. By the time we take the stage, the venue is *packed*. Knowing Millie is somewhere out there, lost in the crowd, only fuels the adrenaline coursing through my veins. Quite a few of our local fans are in the audience and we have them singing their asses off during our crowd favorites. The guys and I are tight, our sound even better than our last rehearsal. I swear, I don't remember the last time I had so much fun performing.

I fucking love nights like this. When we murder it, like we just did, I feel it in my gut. *This is just the beginning. Mountains & Men are fucking going places. It's only a matter of time.*

"Let's get this shit out of here," grumbles Keith, loading his arms with gear. "There's a girl out there whose ass is mine and my dick is thirsty."

"Fuck. Nobody gives a shit about your dick, Keith," mutters JJ.

"Got that right," pipes in Knox with a laugh. "Maybe you should give me her name, no sense in her wasting her time with the likes of you."

"Shut the fuck up. Even if I knew her name, I wouldn't tell you. You'll have to find your own skank."

"Wow, Keith—really classy. You don't even know her name?" Rosy scoffs as all six of us climb down the stairs and head toward the back entrance with our first load.

"Hey, babe, you look hot," says Maddox, tapping my sister's ass with his guitar case.

"Thanks, Maddox," she hums, forgetting all about Keith.

I roll my eyes and ignore him. I know he does that shit to get a rise out of me; but I also know that Andrea's around here somewhere and they're still together this week—not to mention Maddox is almost as much of a brother to Rosy as I am. *Almost.*

"Hey, what are you doing back here?" I ask her as she follows us. I glance at her outfit, noting that she's in a pair of tight jeans, a barely there tank top, and heels. Suddenly, I'm glad she's with us and not out there with the mob of assholes I'm sure have been staring at her all night.

"The roomie brought some friends and they wanted to meet M&Ms *totally hot* lead singer." She laughs when Derrick grunts. "Be nice. I told them I could do better than just Sage. So will you come?"

"I've got to find Millie, Rose. I—"

"Dweeb—help me out, here. *Five minutes!* We don't all have a hot chick out there waiting for us."

"Yeah, please, big bro? Help me score some cool points. What good is it being related to you if I can't show you off like a shiny new toy every once and a while?"

I laugh, shaking my head at the both of them before I reluctantly agree. "Fine. *Five minutes.*"

Millicent

Up there on that stage, he's sexier than I remember. Knowing what he can do to my body, remembering every dip and curve of the physique that hides beneath his clothes, imagining what it feels like when he rolls his hips against mine while I watch him up there seducing the crowd—needless to say, I'm hot and wet and aching to see him as soon as his set is over.

I don't take my eyes off the stage as I watch them empty it of their equipment. When I catch sight of *Hercules* making his way back across the platform to gather another load, I still can't believe that he's part of the band. Though, why I didn't recognize him before doesn't take much guess work. I'm sure it'll come as a surprise to him when he finds out that I wasn't here for him, but for Sage.

After they're finished with their tear down, I can't help but smile when I spot Sage making his way from the back and into the crowd. Perched on the periphery of the dance floor, I can't decide whether or not I should go to him or stay put and allow him to find me. Before I can make up my mind, I watch as a girl sidles up beside him and takes his hand. The petite brunette smiles up at him and he lets her drag him toward a bunch of girls who seem to gush with excitement at the sight of him. He laughs and flirts with them, posing for selfies, and my stomach drops.

As if I've been drenched with a bucket of cold water, I stand in horrified shock. It only takes me a second to realize that I'm not shocked by *his* behavior, but by *mine!* I can't believe I came tonight with the expectation that he still wanted me—wanted us.

Fuck. There's no us! What was I thinking?

I'm completely irritated with myself knowing that *this* was why I knew pursuing anything with him was a bad idea; and yet, I'm here. For every woman that says no to him, there are a dozen more waiting in the wings to say yes. I'm obviously not the only one who looks at him and melts with lust. He's sex on a stick with a fucking voice that would make any girl drop her panties on demand.

Of course, I would know. I've done it. More than once.

I feel like an idiot. He went two days without speaking to me and I was stupid enough to think that it didn't erase everything he said about wanting me. I let myself get caught up in him and I let my guard slip just a fraction of an inch, and now I'm paying for it.

I'm sure of two things when it comes to sex: with a little effort, I can coax a cock into my pussy; and when it's all said and done, eventually, he'll leave. They always do. I don't know why I thought that Sage would be different. I don't know how I could have let two nights of incredible sex bring me to this place where I now feel rejected. Honestly, I have no one to blame but myself.

"Surprised?"

For the second time tonight, I jump at the sound of his voice. Thanks to Sage's introductions during the show, I now remember that his name is Keith. I shake my head in a failed attempt to shake off my disappointment from a moment ago and peer up at the tall, blonde figure in front of me. "I'm sorry, what?"

"The show—did I surprise you?"

"Yeah," I mutter honestly.

"You can tell me what you thought over that drink," he says, throwing his arm around my shoulders.

"Um, you know, I don't think so," I say, sliding out from underneath him. "I was just leaving."

"No way," he insists, gripping his arm around my waist as he ushers me to the bar. "One drink, beautiful. One drink with me and I bet *home* is the last place you'll want to be."

"Keith, I appreciate the gesture, but—"

"Come on," I whines, spinning around to face me. "You can't leave, not now that I can appreciate your attention. One drink."

I sigh, unable to deny that a drink does sound appealing, regardless of the company. "Fine. *One* drink."

Sage

Five minutes with my sister and her new friends turns into *ten* and I'm beyond relieved when Rosy links her arm through mine and helps me escape. After I thank her for getting me out of there, she tells me that the only *thank you* she'll accept is an introduction to the girl who has me completely on edge at the moment. I concede to her demand, anxious for any excuse to find Millie.

The crowd that I was thrilled about a half an hour ago is the bane of my existence now. After fifteen minutes, we still haven't found her. I have no idea how in the hell I'm supposed to spot her in the sea of people that fills this place. I try calling her phone, but she doesn't answer—not that I'm surprised. *It's loud as fuck in here.*

"I could help if I knew what she looked like!" Rosy yells up at me over the noise.

"I told you—light brown hair, dark green eyes, legs for days."

"*Right*," she mutters dubiously. "That's *so* helpful."

"Shit, Rosy, I don't know what she's wearing—it's the best I can do."

"Okay—calm down, Sage. We'll find her," she says, squeezing my arm. "Let's try the bar again?"

"Yeah, okay."

As I search for Millicent's face, I begin to question if she's even here. She said she'd come, but what if she changed her mind? It's entirely possible that I pissed her off with my two days of silence and she decided I wasn't worth the effort. Our set ended forty minutes ago—if she was looking for me like I'm looking for her, wouldn't we have found each other by now?

"Whoa—Sage!"

"What?" I ask, looking down at Rosy who is now tugging on my arm.

"I'm sorry. I know you're looking for Millie, but that girl with Keith? At the end of the bar? She looks totally fucked up. Given that I think Keith is a bit of a dick—can we just go check on her really quick?"

She points to what she's looking at and, for a second, I can't move. Millie is at the very end of the bar, sitting on a stool next to Keith. She's propped up against the wall, her head tilted lazily to the side. She's not even looking at him as he leans toward her, his hand skimming up the side of her thigh and under her short dress.

My blood starts to boil at the sight of *his* hands on *my* woman and all I want to do is shove my elbow into the fucker's face. I shrug Rosy off, leaving her behind as I let my long legs carry me to the end of the bar. As soon as I've reached them, I grab Keith's wrist and yank his hand away from her.

"What the hell?" he grumbles, scowling at me.

"What *the fuck* is going on here?" I growl.

"Sage?" Millie's voice is small and I whirl around to face her.

"Doll face, I've been looking all over for you!"

"You have?" she asks, sounding surprised. She lifts her eyes to look at me and then groans before she closes them. "I'm *so* dizzy."

Before I even know what's happening, I've got two fistfuls of Keith's shirt in my hands, my face inches away from his. "*What. Did. You. Do?*" I grind out, my rage causing me to see red.

"Get the fuck off me! I didn't do anything," he bites back, shoving at my hands.

My grip tightens as I shake him. "The fuck you didn't! What is wrong with her?"

"So she can't hold her liquor. That's not my fault, asshole. Let me go!"

"You fucking piece of shit—you're *lying!*"

"Sage! *Sage—calm down!* What is going on?" I hear Rosy only after she touches my elbow. When I whip my head around to look at her, she gasps and takes a step away from me.

"Call Knox. Get him over here," I demand. I don't wait to see if she does as I ask, my attention back on Keith in a second. "I'm going to ask you *one more time*. What the fuck did you do to her?"

"Ask anyone," he dares me. "I just bought her a drink."

He sees my fist before it connects with his face, but he's too slow to dodge it. The blow leaves him stunned, giving me the opportunity to hit him again. And again. And again. I hear Rosemary behind me, screaming for me to stop, but I don't. I can't. It isn't until Knox's arms pull me away that I lift my hands in surrender.

"Let's go, Sage. We're done for the night," he mutters in my ear.

I shrug him off, leaning over Keith as he lays staring at me from the floor. "I don't ever want to see your sorry ass again, you hear me? We're *done!*"

I don't realize that I'm out of breath until I turn around in search of Millie. Rosy, who's got to be at least a half a foot shorter than Millicent, is helping to hold her up. She looks just about unconscious and it makes me sick. Without a word, I take her arm and wrap it around my neck before I scoop her up and cradle her against my chest.

"Oh, my god," Rosy murmurs, understanding relaxing her face. "This is Millie?" I nod once, unable to find my words. "Get out of here, Sage."

"Yeah, you need to go, man. I'm sure they called the cops. We'll take care of this. Just go."

I offer them both another nod and then head for the door.

NINE

Millicent

My eyelids feel unbelievably heavy. It takes me a great deal of effort and concentration to get them open. My head is pounding and my neck is stiff. I feel like I can't move, which makes me panic, but all I can manage is a pathetic whimper. As soon as the sound escapes my lips, I hear a jingling noise before I feel a wet nose sniffing at my face. It startles me and I gasp, closing my eyes once more. When the dog barks, my fear escalates.

I have no idea where I am. Furthermore, I can barely remember last night. I feel unbearably sluggish, like I'm suffering from the worst hangover known to man. I try and recollect any clue that might tell me where I am, but the only thing I see is the blackness behind my eyelids.

I feel the weight of the dog as two paws press against my side and another bark fills the room. Then I hear a door open and a small ounce of relief washes over me at the sound of his hushed voice.

"Maestro, stop it!" He lifts the dog off of me and sets him on the floor. Maestro whines but Sage ignores him and the bed dips when he sits beside me.

His fingers gently tuck a few strands of hair behind my ear and his touch encourages a second attempt to open my eyes. I can only see a part of him, enough to notice that he's wearing a pair of sweatpants and nothing else. It's then that I realize, underneath the sheets that cover me, I'm not wearing the dress I picked out last night. Instead, the worn, soft cotton of a t-shirt has been pulled over me.

When did I take my dress off? Or did Sage take it off? Did we . . . ?

"Sage?" I croak.

"*Jesus,*" he murmurs, cupping his hand around the back of my head. "I'm so relieved that you're awake."

"Where am I? What happened?" I wonder aloud. I don't recall even *speaking* to Sage last night; the fact that he's here has me completely confused. The only reason I'm not totally freaking out is because it's Sage. Somehow I know that he would never hurt me. Still, I feel worse than shit, and the fact that I can't explain why makes me nervous.

"You're at my house, doll face," he murmurs, running his hand over my hair. "I brought you home with me from The Wash Bar."

The Wash Bar—that's something I remember. I remember changing three times before I left; I remember Sage and the band and then . . . nothing.

I want to see his face so I try to sit up. My muscles feel almost nonexistent.

"Baby, don't try to move. Just rest, okay?"

The concern in his voice heightens my confusion and I manage to tilt my head back so that I can look up at him. He looks like he hasn't slept at all. Suddenly, lying down makes me feel entirely too vulnerable. I try sitting up again. This time, instead of encouraging me to lie still, he helps prop me up against the headboard.

"You're one hardhead woman, did you know that?" he teases with a smile that doesn't reach his eyes.

My head. Now that I'm up, it hurts even more. Sage was right; sitting up was a bad idea. Nevertheless, I can't relax when there are so many unanswered questions whirling around up there.

"What happened? Did I—? Did we—?" None of the possibilities that come to mind right now make sense.

"You don't remember anything? Keith? The bar? Nothing?"

Try as I might, I can't recall a single moment after Mountains & Men finished their set. I back track, in a desperate attempt to retrace my steps, and then I remember the blonde—*Hercules.* Keith. "I—I talked to Keith before. I met him at the gym," I ramble, reaching up to press my fingers against my aching temple. "I didn't know . . . I didn't know that he was one of your guys. But—what does he have to do with anything?"

I watch as his eyebrows tug together and his jaw tenses. Then he relaxes, drawing in a deep breath and shaking off the anger that darkened his features just a second ago. "I'm so sorry, Millicent. I'm sorry I didn't find you sooner. I was with my sister and—"

"Your sister?" The words fall out of my mouth just as a memory flashes before my eyes. *Sage. In the crowd. Surrounded by a flock of girls.*

"She wanted to introduce me to some of her friends. This all could have been avoided if I just came looking for you right away. I'm so fucking sorry, baby doll."

"I was . . . I was leaving." I look *through* him, bits and pieces of the night coming back to me. The details are hazy at best, but they're something. "Keith—he wouldn't leave me alone. He insisted on buying me a drink. How much did I have? How did I end up here with you? Shit—why can't I remember?"

"Millicent, he slipped you something. You had *one* drink. When I found you, you were almost unconscious."

"He . . . he *what?*" My heartbeat speeds up as my panic returns. I try one more time to remember more, *anything* more, but there's nothing there! And my head—it feels like it's going to explode! "Fuck!" I cry, annoyed when my eyes fill with tears of complete and utter frustration. I know crying won't help me remember shit, but I can't stop. "Who the fuck roofies anyone anymore?"

"Christ, I'm so sorry, baby," he mutters, pulling me into his arms. My head tucks perfectly between his neck and his shoulder and my body leans into him without my permission. He feels too good. "I always knew Keith was a dick, but I had no idea . . . I'm so sorry."

My frustration over my memory loss soon morphs into a terrifying realization of what *could* have happened. Where would I be waking up this morning if not for Sage? What would Keith have done to me before I woke? Just thinking about how close I was to being abused and then abandoned makes it hard for me to breathe.

"Hey, it's okay, Millie. I've got you."

I slip my arms around his neck and hold him as tight as I can. I feel like I can't get close enough. "What if—what if you hadn't found me? What if—?"

"I'd never let anything happen to you, doll face." He scoops his arm under my legs and pulls me into his lap. "I would have beat the living shit out of that fucker if Knox hadn't pulled me off of him."

"You—you hit him?" I hiccup, pulling away just enough to look through his glasses and into his eyes.

"You bet your sweet, little ass, I did." When he reaches up to dry my cheeks with the backs of his fingers, I see his bruised knuckles and pull away a little more, taking his hand in mine.

"Sage . . ."

"That piece of shit better hope we don't cross paths again any time soon," he says in reply.

I study his hand for another moment before I bring my eyes back up to meet his. The words *thank you* are perched on the tip of my tongue, but I can't bring myself to say them. Those two little words don't even come close to the gratitude I feel towards him right now.

"I don't know what to say," I finally manage.

He leans forward and touches his forehead to mine. "Say you'll go out with me."

I hesitate for just a moment, a memory from the night before reminding me of a doubt I can't quite wrap my head around anymore. He groans and I giggle and it feels out of this world amazing to be in his arms, giggling after everything that we've been through in the last twelve hours. When I nod, he pulls away from me, his tired eyes brighter than they were just seconds ago.

"Was that a yes?"

"Sarah invited us to The Brew Cycle next Saturday night."

"*Us?*" he asks with a smirk.

"Yeah. A triple date."

"*Thank you, Sarah,*" he sighs as he gently takes my face between his hands. "Your ass is mine, baby doll. You just wait." He presses his lips to mine in a kiss so soft, so sweet, and so tender, I almost swoon. "I hope you know I'm not waiting until Saturday to spend some time with you. Today, it's you and me, in this bed, no exceptions. You need some serious rest and I'm going to make sure you get it."

"Okay," I agree without argument.

"Good. Now, how's your head?"

"Killing me," I answer honestly.

"Stay put. I'll get you some water and a couple pain killers."

He lifts me from his lap and sets me back down on the bed before he gets up and heads for the door. I watch him go before slipping down between the sheets. I woke up confused and afraid, this bed unfamiliar; now, as sleep begins to pull me under once more, I know that I don't want to be anywhere else.

WHEN I WAKE FOR the second time today, I feel completely different. My head still aches a bit, my mouth is dry, and my stomach is empty, but I feel more like myself. I look around in search of a clock and I see that Sage has one hanging on the wall. It's after two in the afternoon, but I barely register the time. His room is not what I expected. As I sit up, I take in my surroundings.

The walls are surprisingly bare. There are no half naked women hung or anything like that. Instead, just beside me, above his desk, there's a bulletin board filled with scraps of paper and sheets of music. On either side, the only two posters in the room are of two different bands, which I assume are his favorite.

He has a big window that takes up most of one wall, but the curtains are drawn, hiding the sun and his view. On the wall directly in front of us, he's got a TV mounted above his dresser beside his closet. The closet door is open and I can see that he's got clothes and Converse shoes strewn all over the floor, but the rest of his room is surprisingly neat.

The nightstand on the other side of Sage holds a glass of water, a bottle of pain meds, and a new toothbrush. I look down at Sage, his face relaxed as he sleeps, and I wonder when he thought to bring me a toothbrush. Grateful for the chance of a fresh mouth, I quietly slip out of bed and walk around to retrieve all three items.

Maestro snores softly from his doggy bed in the corner and I do my best not to make a sound as I slip out of the room in search of the bathroom. There are three more doors in the hallway, two of which are closed, and I wonder who occupies them. With a flip of a light switch, my desired destination is confirmed and I close myself inside. After I use the bathroom, I wash my hands, wipe away the mascara that has accumulated underneath my eyes, and then brush my teeth. Almost all of my hair has fallen out of my bun from the night before. I'm surprised the hair-tie is still holding onto anything at all. I shake it out, slip it around my wrist, and finger comb my hair, opting to just leave it down.

I swallow a couple ibuprofens, sucking the water from the glass until it is gone. Thirsty for more, I decide to venture out in search of the kitchen. I slowly wander my way down the hall and find the stairs. I hear voices down below, but my thirst far outweighs my hesitancy to meet Sage's housemates. At the foot of the stairs, I find myself in the entryway of the house, the front door to my left. Just beyond that is the living room. I spot all of them before they notice me.

On one couch, his legs stretched out with his feet hanging over the side, I recognize one of the guitar players. His dark hair is cropped short, his face sporting the evidence of a morning without a shave, and he's wearing only a pair of gym shorts. He laughs and his whole face lights up, making him even more handsome.

On the adjacent couch, there are three more people—two guys and a girl. The guy on the far end I recognize as the second guitar player. He looks like the other one, only with a little less muscle mass and shaggy hair. There's no question that they are brothers. The man beside him is their keyboard player. His head full of spiral curls, grown out over his forehead, is unquestionably recognizable; his light brown skin on display, as he sits shirtless like his friends, making his smile stand out as he laughs with the others. Their attention is glued to the TV as they play a video game of some sort.

The girl, who has short dirty blonde hair, her bangs swept elegantly across her forehead, is the only one who is fully dressed, wearing jeans and a tank top. I don't know why, considering her company, but she makes me feel severely underdressed. I feel the heat of a blush creep up my neck when she looks over and sees me. She smiles kindly, making me feel slightly less embarrassed before she speaks.

"Hey," she says softly. "It's really good to see you up. How are you feeling?"

"Um, I'm okay. Thanks," I murmur, tugging at the hem of Sage's t-shirt.

"Did you want some water?" says the guitar player with the short hair, pointing at my empty glass. "Here, I'll get you some." He jumps up off the couch, abandoning his game control as he makes his way toward me. "I'm Knox, by the way," he says, offering me his hand as he takes my glass.

"Millie," I reply with a small smile. It's not every day that I meet people in little more than my underwear, and they theirs.

"Shit, I'm sorry," he says, looking down at himself and then back into the other room. "We usually wear clothes when people are over." My eyes flicker to the blonde and she laughs.

"I don't count. I'm with JJ. I'm Violet, by the way. And that's Maddox," she tells me.

It takes me just a second longer to realize that over half of the band *lives* in this house. I fold my arms across my chest, suddenly feeling even more uncomfortable. "Do—do all of you live here?"

"Hell no," cries Maddox. "Just us and Derrick. You're good, babe. Fuck-tard's not here."

"Oh. Okay."

"I'll be right back. Let me fill this up for you," says Knox before turning to head for the kitchen. I watch him disappear down the hall before looking back in the living room, unsure whether I should join them or stay put.

"Wow. Sage really likes you," says Violet, nudging JJ as she nods in my direction.

He smirks, eyeing me over. "Yeah, he does." My confusion must show on my face because he's quick to clarify their meaning. "He put our name on you."

I look down and take a good look at the shirt I've got on. I hadn't really paid much attention to it before, other than how soft it was from so much use. Now, as I stare down at it, I see that the logo for Mountains & Men is etched across my chest. Before I can say a word in reply, I feel a hand sneak up underneath the hem of the shirt before grabbing my ass and giving me a squeeze. I gasp, my eyes widening in shock, my blush coloring my cheeks.

"What are you doing walking around in nothing but my t-shirt, doll face?" Sage whispers into my ear.

"I was thirsty. I came to get some water."

"I live with a bunch of guys, Millicent. They're my friends. I'd hate for that to change when I find them staring at your legs."

His possessiveness makes me scoff and my embarrassment is forgotten. I'm suddenly feeling defiant, considering my bare legs are really no one's concern but my own. I turn to face him, giving him my best annoyed expression. "They're walking around without shirts on and you're worried about my legs?"

He wraps his arm around my waist, pulling me against him tightly, and I suck in a breath. I can feel his hard cock pressed against my hip and my own desire is made evident by the pulsing ache between my legs in an instant.

"Your legs are hot as hell," he mutters just loud enough for me to hear, grazing his nose along mine. "I'm not going to let you walk around this house getting a bunch of dicks hard and filling their heads with ammo for their fucking spank-banks. Got me?"

I nod, unable to conjure a single word.

"Get your ass upstairs, doll face. I'll bring you some water and something to eat." When I start to pull away from him, ready and willing to do exactly as he says, he doesn't let me go. I look at him, an unspoken question in my eyes, and he smirks at me before pressing his lips to mine. "You're so goddamn gorgeous." He kisses me again before I push my way out of his arms and take a breath.

"Keep that up and they'll see a lot more than my legs."

He laughs, which makes me smile, and I wink at him as I turn for the stairs. He smacks my ass before I'm out of reach, eliciting a small yelp. When I look over my shoulder at our audience, I see Violet wearing the biggest grin. She waves and I wave back, feeling slightly awkward, then disappear up the stairs.

TEN

Sage

EARLIER, WHEN I CAME back to the room to find Millie asleep, I decided to head out to pick up a couple of things. I didn't want to leave her before, not until I was sure she was okay; after I had the chance to speak to her, I was levelheaded enough to leave the house. I didn't go far, stopping at the nearest corner store outside of our neighborhood. I got her a toothbrush and picked up the necessary food items for grilled cheese. As I stand at the stove now, making one for her and two for me, Knox hops up onto the counter next to me.

"You better be glad you saw her first, kid, that's all I'm gonna say."

I flip him off, not even bothering to look over at him, and he laughs.

"*Sage,*" says Violet in a singsongy voice. I turn and look over my shoulder, spotting her as she mimics Knox, sitting across from him on the island counter. "She seems nice."

"She spoke, like, two words," huffs Maddox, making his way into the kitchen and directly to the pantry. He pulls out a bag of pretzels and sits next to Violet. JJ stands in front of Vi and she wraps her arms and legs around him, resting her chin on his shoulder.

"Uh, no," I mutter, shaking my head as I look back to the skillet. "We're not going to do this. We're not going to *pow-wow* over Millicent."

"She's pretty," Violet says, ignoring me. I don't say a word, flipping the sandwiches to reveal two perfectly golden tops. "So what's the deal? Are you two dating, now?"

"How'd she end up with *Fuck-tard?*" asks Maddox, his mouth full.

I shrug. "They met at the gym. Guess he was bugging her about buying her a drink. The details are sketchy. Look, I don't want to talk about that asshole."

"We'll have to talk about him eventually. We're short a bass player, now."

"No shit, Maddox," I grumble, putting the two finished sandwiches on a plate and starting another.

"Sage is right," pipes in JJ. "We don't have to talk about this now. Your girl, she's really alright?"

"Yeah. I think so. She was upset earlier, but I think she's okay."

"And is she?" Violet probes. "Yours, I mean. Is she *your girl?*"

"Vi . . ." JJ mutters.

"What? I'm just saying, it would be *nice.* One less revolving door around here. Not to mention, a concert companion."

"What about Andrea?" Maddox asks, seemingly offended.

"*Please,*" we all grumble in unison.

"Fuck all of you," he laughs, knowing we have a point.

"Anyway—back to Millie."

"Vi, I told you, we're not doing this. There's nothing to tell."

"Like hell, there isn't! Was I the only one here watching that flirt-fest?" she asks, lifting her hand. "You, Sage McCoy, *do not* flirt in the entryway of this house. It should be called an *exitway.* That is where you kick girls out—*if* they're lucky enough to make it through the door! I haven't seen you like this in *years.* So, level with me here—give me *something.*"

I finish the last sandwich, adding it to my stack; then I grab Millie's glass of water and face my friends. "I want her. For now, that's all there is. That's all you get." I leave the room without a backwards glance, heading directly to my bedroom.

When I open the door, Maestro strolls out into the hallway. I look down at him and he looks up at me. "You in or you out, buddy?" He listens to the hum of conversation downstairs before he goes hunting for a new crowd. I shake my head at his indifference and then close the door behind me.

"Grilled cheese sound good?"

Millie is standing at my desk, admiring my clutter. When I sit on the bed, she comes and joins me. "Grilled cheese always sounds good. Thank you."

"What is it with you and these things, anyway?" I ask as she takes her first bite.

She shrugs, finishing what's in her mouth before she answers. "It's my comfort food. Always has been." She doesn't look at me when she speaks, making me think there's more to her answer than she's telling me, but I don't press. "So, that looks like the mess of a genius," she says, nodding back over her shoulder.

"Is it killing you? Do you want to go stack it in neat, even piles?"

"A little," she replies with a grin that makes my dick stir.

"Well, I wouldn't call myself a genius, but sometimes shit that doesn't suck happens over there."

"How long have you guys been here—or, I guess, how long have you been *Mountains & Men?*"

"I met Maddox and Knox when I was twelve, when they moved into my neighborhood. We'd all dabbled in music one way or another on our own. We started fooling around with the idea of a band a few years later. By the time I was eighteen, we'd roped in JJ and Derrick. At some point, rooming together became an act of convenience, one of life's blessings in disguise. We found this spot with the perfect garage and moved in. Been here ever since."

She hums, signaling that she's listening, and picks at her sandwich. "And Keith?"

"He's only been with us for a year. It's not exactly a loss."

She sighs, looking away from me again. "I'm sorry this happened, that it's screwing with your band. I can see how important they are to you."

"Don't you fucking dare," I insist, reaching out to tip up her chin. Her dark green eyes meet mine and I shake my head at her. "Don't apologize for *anything*. He's not worthy of another thought. We'll find someone new. Someone better. We'll be fine—we always are. Got it?"

"Yeah. I got it."

"Good. How's your sandwich? Do you need another one?"

"No. It's perfect."

"Do you want to watch a movie or something? I'll let you pick," I tease, in an attempt to lighten the mood.

"Okay. What have you got?"

Ten minutes later, we're watching the opening credits to *Ferris Bueller's Day Off*. Needless to say, her quick and easy choice just gives me one more reason to like her. When I push the pillows against the headboard and prop myself up, I lift my arm in a silent request for Millie to tuck herself against me. She does, and it doesn't take long for her lithe, warm body to distract me. After another ten minutes, the last thing on my mind is Ferris Bueller.

"Hey," I murmur, looking down at her. When she looks up at me, I don't hesitate before I press my lips to hers. Each time I deliver a light kiss, I'm reminded of how long it's been since I've tasted the inside of her mouth. When she opens up for me, I dive in, reaching up to sink my fingers in her hair. She twists her tongue with mine and all I want is more. I kiss her deeper and she moans, the sound awakening my dick. When she leans into me, one of her legs hooking over one of mine, I grab her hips and bring her to my lap. She straddles me, her hands turning needy as she feels her way across my shoulders and down my chest. She rocks her hips, pressing her pussy against the bulge in my pants, and we both free a sigh.

"You miss me, baby doll?"

She nods, closing her mouth around mine as she rocks her hips once more. I groan as she teases me, my cock undeniably hard for her. I slip a hand into her panties and swipe my finger over her entrance. She gasps, her hands finding their way into my hair.

"Make me come, Sage. I want you," she breathes.

I toss my glasses onto the nightstand before I open the top drawer and reach for a condom. It takes me longer than it should, the feel of her lips on my neck and her teeth tugging on my earlobe distracting me.

"Fuck, doll face."

"Yes, please," she says with a grin.

I strip her out of my shirt and her hard nipples stand out as if they are screaming for my attention. I suck one into my mouth and she whimpers as she grinds against me again, clearly impatient.

"Sage, don't make me beg—I will. I swear, I will," she mutters.

I chuckle as I pull away from her, lifting my hips off the bed. "A little help?" She wastes no time pulling my pants to my knees. My dick stands to attention in between us and I can hear it as her breathing turns ragged with desperation. I rip open the condom and suit up before shoving her panties aside. She doesn't need permission to ease her way over me, so she takes what she wants.

She's feeling greedy and it's sexy as fuck.

"That's it, doll face, take my cock—all of it, baby."

When she's fully seated, she reaches back to grip my thighs, offering her the leverage she needs to glide up and down my shaft. Watching her take control turns me on even more, and I can't help but stare, my hands roaming up her legs, across her stomach, around her tits, then back down.

"Oh, Sage, you feel so good—so fucking good," she groans.

"Just good, huh?" I question, taking hold of her hips.

It's my turn to drive.

Using the power of my legs, I thrust my hips up *hard*, hammering into her over and over. "Who fills your pussy like I do? Tell me."

Her hands grope their way up my body and around the back of my neck, her eyes focused on mine, her mouth open as she whimpers and sighs. Each sound uttered is like a note sung and it's the sexist fucking song I have ever heard in my life. I know listening to her will only make me come faster.

"Answer me, doll face," I demand. "Who fills your pussy like I do?"

"No one—*oh, shit*—Sage! No one!"

"Are you going to come for me, baby doll?" I mutter, my thumb finding her clit as my balls start to tighten.

"Please," she hardly manages. Her grip tightens around my shoulders as she throws her head back. "Sage—*fuck! Yes!*"

Her pussy clenches my dick and my groans mingle with hers as I spill my release. "Millie—baby—!" She frees a sated sigh as she rests her forehead against mine, her hands falling to my chest as we both come down from our moment of bliss. "Every time, doll face—fuck, I can't get enough of you."

"Me neither," she breathes.

She kisses me, her mouth hungry for more, and I don't refuse her. I hold her against me with one hand and squeeze her ass with my other. She hums when I roll us over, pinning her beneath me. I pull away just long enough to take my dick out of her heat and toss the used condom aside. We kiss until I'm hard again and then she has only one request.

"Again."

LATER THAT SUNDAY evening, after a couple hours of worshipping each other's bodies, we finally watched the movie. As soon as it was over, Millie told me that she needed to get home, so I took her to her car and then followed her back to her apartment. I went with the excuse of wanting to make sure she got in alright, but I'm still not sorry about the twenty minutes we spent making out in front of her door before she forced herself out of my arms. I could tell it was hard for her to say goodbye, which I'll admit felt pretty damn awesome.

Monday came and brought hell with it. Dealing with the aftermath of beating the shit out of our bass player and kicking him out of the band fucking sucked. Derrick and I spent a good amount of time going over all the gigs we have for the next few weeks, trying to line up a couple guys to fill in until we can find a replacement. JJ started blasting want ads all over social media, and we hope to get some hits and start the audition process soon.

It's been a little tense around the house. Nobody blames me for my actions or my decision, but the timing sucks ass. We've got some really big shows coming up, so we've all been a little on edge. It certainly doesn't help that by Thursday, relieving a little stress by hitting the gym isn't cutting it anymore. I need some fucking pussy and the only pussy I want has been temporarily unattainable. If she's not working, I am—either with the guys or at Little Bird. Even still, I've called her every day. There's something about hearing her voice that calms me down and pulls me into a creative space.

I finally finished writing her song and JJ and I have been collaborating on the composition. It's going to be some pretty sick shit. I haven't told her about it, though. I want it to be a surprise.

Fuck. Rosy was right. This chick is turning me into a sap . . .

I want her, anyway. She's worth it. I just know it.

Friday night, as I stand behind the coffee bar with Brandon, the evening rush long forgotten, I wonder what Millie is doing. I can think of a few things I *wish* we were doing right now, but I know I won't see her until tomorrow night. The Brew Cycle with everyone should be fun. I appreciate Sarah putting the whole thing together and triggering Millicent's *yes*. It's a start, and I'll take what I can get.

When I look over at Brandon, his focus zeroed in on his phone, I can't help but laugh. I know, without even having to ask, who he's texting. It's written all over his face.

"Did that hurt?"

He looks up from his phone with a scowl."What?" he asks, sliding his mobile into his pocket.

"That tat on your forehead. You know, the one that says, *Pussy-Whipped,*" I tease, pointing at his head.

He flips me off, which makes me laugh again, and he joins in before he mutters, "Shut up."

"Seriously, you should see what you look like when you're texting her. She's got your balls."

"No shit! I sure as hell am not complaining, though."

I study him, folding my arms across my chest as I lean up against the front counter."Fuck, man. You're not kidding around. You're for real about her."

"You're not seriously just now figuring that out, are you?" he asks with a smirk.

I shake my head at him, knowing that he doesn't get what I'm saying. Everybody knows how they feel about each other. It's the most obvious shit in the world. But this . . ."No, I mean, like—you love her and shit." He doesn't say a word, which is all the confirmation I need."Part of me wants to give you a hard time," I say with a smirk."But I can't. You're one lucky dude. Sarah's the shit."

"I can't argue with that."

"I owe her big time for getting Millie to go out with me."

"You really like this one. I've never seen you try so hard."

"It's like I said, man—she's insane," I tell him, rubbing my chin."She's wicked smart and sexy as fuck." I shake my head, thinking over the past week. I'm getting to know her, but she's different than other girls. I know that there's so much more to her than she's letting me see."Sarah was right, though. She's got her guard up all the time. I've got my work cut out for me. But I know she's worth it. I just have to get her to see that I am, too."

"Good luck with that, man. Seriously. I hope it works out for you."

"Thanks."

We chat for another few minutes and then he heads to the back to finish up a few things before we close. I clean up a little bit, my thoughts continuously drifting back to Millie. I was giving Brandon shit about Sarah, but I don't really have room to speak. I can't even remember the last time I thought about a girl this much. This isn't about the chase. It's about *her.*

Her long-ass legs.

Her narrow hips.

Her perfect tits.

Her straight hair.

Her sweetheart lips.

Her eyes, green and gorgeous.

Her *eyes,* haunted and mysterious.

There are demons in her eyes and I can't look away.

I can't let go.

ELEVEN

Millicent

When my mother calls, I ignore her.

For the first time in forever, I have a date with a guy that I can't wait to see. He's made it nearly impossible for me to go two minutes without thinking about him. It's as if he's managed to find a way to manipulate time to his advantage; every moment, every hour, every day that goes by that we don't get to see each other—he *uses* that as a tool. A weapon. I've been fighting it all week—futilely battling my thoughts, longing for the control that he seems to have taken from me.

My life now *excepts* him. *Anticipates* him. What used to be a physical longing, an ache that could only be soothed by his touch, has morphed into this mental struggle. I find myself *daydreaming* about him when I should be grading assignments. I'm *dreaming* of him instead of sleeping with no memory of my subconscious activity. I except his call every day; I anticipate his texts when he's thinking of me. He's relentless.

I'm a fucking man who knows what he wants.

He's not a liar. He knows what he wants and what he wants is *me*. For reasons I haven't defined with words yet, I want him, too. I'm still not convinced that this is smart. I'm not convinced that this is safe. I'm not convinced that either of us will make it out of this unscathed but . . . for the first time in forever, I have a date with a guy I can't wait to see. That *feeling* is not one that I can tuck away and ignore. Even if I wanted to, he wouldn't let me. So, when my mother calls, I ignore her.

The last thing I want to do, just hours before Sage gets here, is listen to my mother bitch and moan like she always does. I don't need to hear how miserable she is and how much of that is my fault. Not that she would ever say so explicitly, but I'm not an idiot and both of us know it. While she might choose not to care, I care.

Tonight, I care.

The third time she calls, I pour myself a glass of wine before I swipe my screen to answer, ever so begrudgingly. "Hello?" I answer.

"Where were you? I've called three times? Why didn't you answer your phone?"

I take a deep breath and then a sip of wine before I reply. "I just answered, mother."

"Tati, don't get smart with me," she demands, referring to me by the nickname only she ever uses. *Millicent* was apparently my father's idea. *Tatiana* was hers—she's called me Tati for twenty years, now.

"I have plans tonight. Can we do this another time?"

"Plans? Tatiana, I don't ask you for much. One phone call every two weeks. You should know better than to make plans."

I roll my eyes and then guzzle down the rest of my drink. "God, mother—*heaven forbid* I make plans on a Saturday night." I regret the words as soon as they pass through my lips. Not because I don't mean them, but because it sets the woman off. I'm only half listening to her rant when a knock sounds at the door.

Happy for any excuse to end this call, I hurry to see who is in the hallway. I barely get the door open before he's coming toward me, grabbing the back of my thighs to hoist me up around his waist. I squeak out my surprise, my reflexes beckoning me to lock my ankles behind his back, my free hand gripping his shoulder. He grins at me before kissing the side of my jaw.

"Hey, doll face."

"Um—mother, I have to go. Something just came up. I'll talk to you in a couple weeks, okay?" I end the call before she has a chance to respond and let the device slip from my fingers onto the floor. "What are you doing here?" I ask Sage, ignoring my phone when it starts ringing. "It's only seven thirty."

"Wanted to see you," he says, reaching up to grip the back of my neck. He draws me down for a kiss and I don't fight him. "Wanted to taste you," he mutters before slipping his tongue into my mouth. He reaches up to squeeze my ass, a habit of his that I find myself growing fond of, and I can't help but curl my lips into a smile against his.

"Your timing is perfect."

When my phone starts to ring again, he looks down at the floor and then back at me. "Are you sure about that?"

"Shut the door and kiss me, Sage."

"How about I shut the door and you take off all your clothes?"

For a moment, I wonder if he's joking. Then I get a good look at his face and it hits me as if it's an absolute truth—Sage never jokes about sex.

I unhook my legs from around him and slide my way down his chest until my feet are on the floor. I take one step back, and then another, my eyes locked with his as I reach for the hem of my tank top and begin pulling it over my head. He closes the door just as my bra is revealed, and my neck warms when I see the lust in his eyes.

He watches me without moving a muscle as I push my cotton shorts down my legs. My bra goes next. Then my panties. I'm hardly surprised with how much he can turn me on just by *watching* me. Knowing that his gaze holds the unspoken promise of a level of pleasure only he can provide, I revel in his slow perusal of my nakedness.

"Do you know how fucking beautiful you are? Every inch of you, baby." He takes his time closing the distance between us and then slowly slides his hands up my sides, his thumbs tracing the underside of my breasts. "I don't want to share you, Millicent. Not even a little. Let's do this. Just you and me. No one else. You in?"

My mouth falls open of its own accord. I certainly was not expecting him to say what I *think* he just said. "You want—you want to be *exclusive?*" I ask.

"Call it what you will, doll face. I don't want anyone else's lips on yours," he says, brushing a soft kiss against my mouth. "I don't want anyone else's hands on your tits," he continues, his fingers pinching one of my nipples. "And I sure as *fuck* don't want anyone else's dick near this pussy." I suck in a sharp breath when he cups his free hand between my legs.

"Sage—we haven't even been on a date yet."

"Is that an excuse? Or do you really think one night, or even a dozen nights out will change either of our minds?" As he speaks, he dips one finger into my core. I pull my lip between my teeth when he adds another. "Are you really going to make me ask again later? We both know how this will play out. We've done this before. You want me, Millicent."

I stifle a whimper as his fingers continue to slide in and out of me. When I unfasten the top of his jeans and slide my hand down his boxers and around his hard cock, he licks his lips.

"You're such an arrogant little shit."

He lifts an accusing eyebrow at me. "That feel little to you, baby?"

I press my lips together, suppressing a grin. A smirk tugs at the corner of his mouth as he rests his forehead against mine. "There's a fine line between *arrogance* and *confidence*. I toe the line, baby doll, but I never cross it. If there's one thing I'm confident about right here, right now, it's that *your* pussy is wet for me and *my* dick is hard for you, and when you say *yes*, I'm going to make you come against the wall—so cut the shit and tell me you won't fuck anyone else. *You and me,* doll face. Just you and me."

I think about it for another second, knowing that he's right; knowing that any reservations I have, any reason I might come up with that would justify my hesitancy, it's all bullshit. My body is sure of the answer already. I can't argue that he satisfies me in a way that no one ever has before. He is the master of my orgasms—I come at the command of his body, and his body unravels me often.

I don't know how to protect my heart against him, but I can't stop us from moving forward. So I don't fight it. Instead, I let go of his cock and I reach into his back pocket for his wallet. He pulls his fingers out of me and sucks on them as I hunt for the condom I know I'll find. When I take out what I'm looking for, he strips out of his shirt and I push down his pants. I rip open the package and roll the rubber over his long, hardened length before he bends down and picks me up, guiding my legs around him.

I breathe out a sigh saturated with longing when he presses my back against the wall and fills me with every glorious inch he has to offer. Once he is all the way inside of me, he pauses and stares at me—his icy blue eyes piercing my green ones. I want him to move, I *need* him to move, but he doesn't.

"Sage—"

"Say it. I want you to say it."

"Yes," I obey.

"Yes, what, baby?"

"Just you and me. No one else."

"Who owns your orgasm, baby doll?" he asks as he begins to pump in and out of me.

"You," I mewl, instantly lost in the pleasure of his friction. "Only you."

"You bet your sweet, little ass."

When he leans forward to kiss me, I meet him halfway. It's not a tame kiss, but a greedy one—we suck, we bite, we lick and then repeat. As he pulls away, he repositions me—slipping one arm, then the other, under my legs, so that my knees are hooked over the crook of his elbows. He spreads my legs wider, opening up my hips, causing him to go even deeper. The deep, guttural groan that slips out of me will not be silenced.

"Shit, Millie—you're so goddamn sexy. Come all over my cock, baby."

"Faster," I moan, so close to finding my release that I can utter no other words.

He pounds into me faster *and* harder. Heat spreads throughout my body from my core as my insides constrict with my orgasm. He continues to move in and out of me, his own climax following on the heels of mine. His thrusts turn lazy as we both come down from our heightened state of pleasure, and then he smacks a kiss against my lips before he pulls out and eases me down to my feet. I grab onto his biceps to steady myself, my legs feeling unreliable, and he grins.

"You okay, doll face?" I nod and he kisses me again—only slower this time. *Deeper.* The way he caresses my tongue with his does *nothing* to strengthen my legs. "Hate to hit and run, but I've got to go," he says when he pulls away.

"What?" I mutter, still breathless from that kiss.

"Yeah, I have to run home," he tells me as he removes the condom, ties it up, then pulls his pants around his hips. "I've got a hot date tonight." He winks at me before he disappears into the bathroom. He's only gone for a second, but when he reemerges, his eyes take me in from head to toe as if he hasn't seen me in a while. "Think she'll put out after one night?"

"Maybe," I say with a laugh. "If you play your cards right."

He grins as he scoops up his shirt and tugs it over his head. "I better not be late, then." With one more kiss, he heads for the door. "See you in an hour, doll."

He slips out and the smile on my face lingers. I ignore the small voice in the back of my head that's trying to grab my attention, trying to *warn* me that I'm entering into dangerous territory. I don't want to remember the past. Not right now. Not tonight. Tonight, I want to get dressed and go dancing with that twenty-one year old man; that man who seems to want no one but me. I want to embrace every little thing he makes me feel—all of which far exceeds anything I've felt in so long.

So I ignore the small voice in the back of my head as I pick up my clothes from off of the floor and head for my closet. I rifle through my hangers, searching for the perfect dress for tonight. I decide on a sleeveless, mini tunic dress. The rose floral pattern is bold and colorful, the belt that goes with it will go perfectly with my nude wedge heels. The dress *and* the shoes will both do wonders for my legs. I hope it drives Sage crazy.

I hop in the shower, washing away my day and the sex I just got finished having. I smile, knowing that it won't be long before I'm covered in a new, thin layer of sweat from a night of dancing. No doubt followed by the delicious musk that will coat my skin after hours in bed with Sage. I shake the thought away, knowing that now is not the time to get distracted.

When I'm finished in the shower, I blow dry my hair, opting to leave it down, and apply a bit of make up. I slip into my dress and I'm fastening the buckle on my shoe when a knock sounds at the door. I feel a ridiculous amount of excitement as I grab my clutch and head down the hallway.

I saw the man an hour ago, for Christ sake.

Yet, despite all reason, when I twist the knob and pull back the barrier that separates us, my stomach flutters at the sight of him. Red Converse. Black jeans. Charcoal gray t-shirt, *Mountains & Men* scrolled across his chest. His sleeve of tattoos covering his left arm on display. And those horn-rimmed glasses . . .

Who the fuck looks sexy in those things?

He does. He knows it. And now I know it, too.

"Hey, gorgeous," he says, giving me a once over. Tingles rush down my spine when he brushes my hair over my shoulder and then presses a kiss against the sensitive spot just behind my ear. "Good thing I claimed your pussy earlier," he whispers before pulling away, holding out his elbow. "Let's get out of here."

EPILOGUE

One Week Later

Millicent

"Love . . .
Why I don't like the word is that it means too much to me,
far more than you can understand."

—Anna Karenina [Leo Tolstoy]

"ENCORE! ENCORE! ENCORE!"

The room is buzzing, the crowd begging for more. I look around from where I stand, just a few feet away from the stage. Mountains & Men just finished their set. They were *amazing*, which doesn't surprise me in the least. I know Sage and the guys must be going wild off stage, listening to the roar of their fans—new and old.

We're in the next town over at a place called Moxi Theater. The band was offered a headlining spot by chance. *Literally*. They entered a lottery with dozens of other bands and won the coveted spot. The energy in the room, the excitement that seems to be overflowing—that's not chance in the slightest. That's all them. They killed it tonight.

"This is fucking *insane!*" cries Violet, gripping my wrist to get my attention. "I bet they're flipping their shit back there!"

The shouting in the room grows louder as Derrick walks back out onto the stage, sticking his tongue out to rile up the crowd even more. Knox and Maddox are close behind, followed by Wren—their bass guitar stand-in. When JJ comes back out, Violet cups her hands around her mouth and yells, "*Get it, baby!*" I'm sure he can't hear her, but she doesn't seem to mind, pleased to add to the cacophony of cheers.

Derrick drops the beat and then Maddox begins to pluck out a solo. I know right away that he's playing the beginning of a song I've not heard before. Knox joins in, then Wren, then JJ, and then out he comes . . .

He oozes sex appeal. It's not something I can simply see, but something I *feel*—me along with every other female in the room. I know this by the change in pitch of the cries that battle against the sound of their music. I'm sure he could hop off the stage right now, take his pick of girl by the hand, and she would follow him into any dark corner he wished to occupy. I know the immense amount of pleasure he could bring her, and I'm sure he would leave her begging for a different sort of encore.

I know because it's exactly how I feel.

"I've got to be honest with you," Sage speaks into the microphone, quieting the crowd, the band still playing behind him. "I was *really* hoping you'd want just *one more* song." The patrons yell and the grin that splices his face makes my stomach flutter. "We've got a new one for you tonight. Something special we've been working on." Violet grips my wrist again, but I can't tear my eyes away from Sage. "There's a girl out there who inspired me to write this," he continues to say, his eyes finding mine, as if I'm the *only* person in the room. "It's called, *Just Tonight*. This one's for you, doll face."

I see the demons in your eyes and I want to dance
Can't stop the beat I hear from one haunted glance
Take my hand, baby, don't let go
I'll set you free, baby, won't let go
All night/One song
This room/My home
I'll set you free, baby, don't let go
Tonight/Just give me tonight
Can't stop the beat, can't stop my feet, just want to dance
I'll set you free, but will you let me go?
You cage me in and now I can't let go.
All night/One song
This room/My home
Set me free but, baby, don't let go
Tonight/ Just give me tonight.
And in my arms you'll find your ecstasy
When you lose yourself, I'll set you free
Baby, just let go and let it be, let it be

Tonight/ Just give me tonight.
I see the demons in your eyes and I want to dance
Can't stop the beat I hear from one haunted glance
Take my hand, baby, don't let go
Set me free, baby, won't let go
All night/One song
This room/My home
I'll set you free, baby, let it be, let it be
Tonight/Just give me tonight

Love. It's not something I've allowed myself to feel in so long. Love is messy. It's complicated. It's fucking *crazy*. In my experience, it sweeps you up and then spits you out, taking with it pieces of yourself that you can never get back. I vowed that I would never become its victim again. Now, here, in a room filled with people, one pair of icy blue eyes is threatening to knock down every barrier I've worked so hard to maintain in order to keep my heart safe.

Sage McCoy may just be my undoing—and it scares the shit out of me.

Worthy of the HARMONY

MOUNTAIN AND MEN BOOK TWO

If your dreams do not scare you, they are not big enough.
Ellen Johnson Sirleaf

ONE

Sage

As the crowd goes wild, screaming for more, we're acting like a bunch of fucked up clowns offstage. Derrick jumps up and down, as if he'll explode unless he releases some of the adrenaline that courses through his veins. JJ is pacing back and forth, clapping his hands in excitement every time he gets a peek at the audience that can't seem to get enough of us. Knox has Maddox in a headlock, the both of them laughing as they mess around, so hyped up they don't know what to do with themselves.

Then there's me, with the biggest fucking shit-eating grin on my face. I run my hand over my mouth in an attempt to wipe it away, knowing I need to find some semblance of cool before we go back out there to give them what they want. My lips refuse to cooperate. I laugh like a lunatic as I let the music of the crowd's plea seep into my pores.

"Encore! Encore! Encore!"

This is, by far, the best fucking night of my life.

Luck of the draw has us closing out the show at The Moxi Theater, a packed concert hall in the next town over from home. Best damn lottery win I could ever imagine. A night on stage with a crowd like this is worth more than money can buy. There were some great bands here tonight, some of which could have filled the coveted closing act just fine, but the win was ours. Despite being down a bass player, we managed to play one hell of a show. Wren, our stand-in who is watching the rest of us flip out, did a damn fine job. Too bad we can't convince him to join our ranks. We always sound great with him on stage with us.

Tonight, we owned that motherfucking stage.

"Time to give them what they want, eh, Dweeb?" calls out Derrick, clapping a hand against my back.

My stomach flips in excitement when we make eye contact. I've been hoping for this moment all night long. This crowd is the *perfect* audience to unleash our latest song. We've been working on it all week, but I swore that we wouldn't play it unless it felt right. Now, our fans are *begging* for it and they don't even know it.

"Let's do this!" he says before he makes his way out on stage.

The patrons go wild when he sticks his tongue out at them, riling them up before he goes to sit on his throne behind his set. Knox lets go of his brother and then elbows me with a grin before the two of them make their way out as well. Wren follows closely behind and then it's just JJ and me.

"Kill it, man," he says, holding up a fist. I knock my knuckles against his with a nod and then he's gone, too. I hang back and take a deep breath, willing myself to find the focus I need to deliver the best damn encore this crowd could ever hope for.

Derrick drops the beat before Maddox jumps in on his guitar. His brother, Knox, adds another layer of guitar before Wren joins in on the bass. When JJ rounds out the mix on the keys, I take one more deep breath and then make my grand entrance. The screams coming from the crowd battle against the music coming from the guys, and I've never felt more alive in my life.

This—this is living.

I head straight for the microphone, gripping it with both hands where it rests in the stand. "I've got to be honest with you. I was *really* hoping you'd want just *one more* song." When the audience cheers at me in response, my grin is back. I fucking love this shit and I can't even pretend that it doesn't faze me. Moments like this are what dreams are made of, and I know that this is merely the beginning of Mountains & Men.

"We've got a new one for you tonight. Something special we've been working on," I begin to say, my eyes drifting to the one spot they've been drawn to all night. I spot Millicent standing beside Violet and my heartbeat speeds up. I embrace the desperate desire that claws at my insides at the sight of her—another reaction to which I can't feign indifference.

It's been exactly three weeks since we've met. A part of me thinks what I'm about to do is crazy. I'm not that guy—I haven't been for a long time—the sap dedicating songs to a woman. I can't help it, though. She does something to me. Even in a crowd of hundreds of people, her beauty makes my heart race and my dick twitch, like she's the only one in the room.

Fuck it, I think when her eyes lock with mine.

"There's a girl out there who inspired me to write this. It's called, *Just Tonight.* This one's for you, doll face."

One verse into the song, and I can tell it's just as sick as I hoped it was. The crowd is dancing and the band is rockin', and as the words pour out of me, I can't help but smile when I think about that first night. That woman, with her long-ass legs, her sexy, swaying hips, her perfect tits, and that mouth—god, that smart-ass mouth.

I do my best to engage the crowd, throwing a couple winks and reaching out my hand to touch the outstretched fingers of the ladies closest to the stage. It's fucking hot as hell under the spotlight, but I couldn't care less. I'm exactly where I want to be, doing exactly what I want to be doing. When my eyes find Millie's once more, a smirk tugs at my lips at the sight of her. She's just standing—*staring.* I'm used to looking out there and seeing her dance. Doll face likes to move that smokin' hot body of hers, but it's obvious that I've surprised her.

Fuck. Yes.

This song is for her. It's a reminder that just one night was never going to be enough for her and me, no matter how much she wanted to fight it. Right now, I sing for her. Tonight, she's here for me. And the first chance I get, I'll give her a hell of a lot more than a song.

Millicent

"COME ON!" VIOLET insists, tugging at my wrist.

My focus snaps in her direction, but all I see is the back of her head—her dirty blonde hair styled in a pixie cut that leaves her slender neck fully exposed. I open my mouth to protest but no words come out. Furthermore, my feet seem to be in agreement with her command, even though I'm not sure where she's taking me. I look back to the stage, now empty as the overhead lights illuminate the once darkened venue, and I realize that Violet is dragging me *against* the crowd.

"Where are we going?"

"Backstage," she says, as if it's the most obvious answer in the world. "Hurry."

My brain finally gains control of my feet and I stop walking, pulling my arm away from Violet. She halts, turning back to look at me with her dark blue eyes. She doesn't wear much makeup, but her expertly applied cat-eye eyeliner and her generous amount of mascara make her irises pop. When she tugs her eyebrows together, it's concern and not frustration that is clearly etched across her face. "Come on. What's wrong?"

"Nothing. I—" I look back to the stage, my mind instantly replaying the last seven minutes.

This one's for you, doll face.

My breath catches in my throat and my heart beats wildly in my chest. I resist the urge to bring my fingers to my neck to actually *feel* my racing pulse. I don't think it's slowed down since Sage's eyes locked with mine from up there behind that microphone. He said that I inspired him to write that song. *Me*. It's a truth I am still trying to wrap my head around.

I remember our first night together as if it were yesterday. It practically *was* yesterday. I only met the man three weeks ago. In any case, it's not a night I'll soon forget; I was sure of that fact long before now. Just thinking about the way he's able to own my body makes the back of my neck warm and stirs the longing that resides in the pit of my stomach. I remember how he sang to me as he filled me with his glorious cock. I remember thinking that I didn't care how many times he had sung those lyrics to however many women he had taken to bed before me. In that moment, he owned more than my orgasm—more than my body.

In that moment, he owned *me*.

Resist as I might, that first night is the reason I'm here. My body craves him and my mind can't stop thinking about him and my heart…well, that's a different matter. My heart is not meant to be given away. Not anymore. Not since the last time I managed to pick up all the pieces I could find and paste it back together. Sage can't have it. I'm not even sure that's what he's after, which is perfectly alright with me. Then again, after that song, I suppose I have no idea what he wants from me—other than exclusive access to my lady bits.

"Millie," Violet chuckles, interrupting my thoughts as she reaches for my hand. "Come on! The guys are waiting."

"Shouldn't we stay out here?" I argue, not sure if I am ready to see Sage.

"What? No way!"

I can't blame her for being excited. Mountains & Men just put on a phenomenal show. I'm sure she's *more* than anxious to meet up with her boyfriend, JJ. I, on the other hand, could use a minute.

"Why don't you go ahead? I think I'll just step outside for a second. I could use some air," I tell her, fanning my face.

I'm not exactly overheating, but fresh air sounds like a welcomed refreshment. I'm not sure I've breathed very much in the last ten minutes. The air I did manage to suck in was heavy with the smell of too many bodies crammed into one place with a not-so-subtle hint of marijuana. I imagine this is quite normal, though I can't say for sure. Concerts, parties and the like have never really been my thing—nevertheless, I can't deny that tonight has been fun.

"You're *crazy* if you think I'm letting you out of my sight." Violet grabs my hand, gripping my fingers fiercely as she lifts an eyebrow at me. "It's only been two weeks since the incident with that dickwad, Keith." I open my mouth to argue but she shakes her head and continues speaking before I can. "I get it. Different time, different place, but Sage asked me to keep an eye on you. He told me as soon as they were done that we should meet up with the guys backstage."

Again, I open my mouth to protest and her eyes soften with understanding—*solidarity*. "I know you're a big girl and can take care of yourself. Trust me, I believe you, but you are *not* making me go back there without you. Sage will lose his shit."

"Violet—"

"He swears if he had found you as soon as the show was over, nothing bad would have happened to you. His overprotectiveness will wear off eventually, but for now, let's not push it." My heart speeds up even more, unsure what to think of the fact that he feels so protective over me. No one has ever seemed to care so much about my whereabouts. Well, aside from my mother—but that is for entirely different and purely selfish reasons.

"Besides," she continues, a grin lighting up her pretty face. "I bet he'll kiss you. I *promise* you, *that's* something you don't want to miss. You haven't been *kissed* until you've gotten yourself a post-performance smooch. They're my favorite, and you're keeping me from mine. So come on! Let's go."

This time, when she tugs me toward the heavy curtain that blocks off the backstage area, I don't resist. There's no one standing there to prevent us from heading back, and she doesn't hesitate to push aside the barrier that stands in our way. As soon as the curtain falls behind us, she is swept up into a pair of arms. She squeals and giggles, letting go of me as JJ spins her around in a circle before crushing his lips against hers. She wilts against him as he works her mouth, and I avert my gaze, not wishing to intrude upon their moment.

Just when I start to look around in hopes of spotting Sage, I feel a pair of arms slide around me from behind. I peer down at the strong limbs that have me caged in, one arm covered in tats, the other bare, both beautiful and sturdy. He pulls me back against his chest, hot and damp with sweat; my body acts of its own accord, relaxing against him as I breathe him in. He smells good enough to eat, and the thought of licking him distracts me.

"Hey, baby doll," her murmurs into my ear.

"Hey," I reply, my voice more airy than I anticipated.

He kisses the space just behind my jaw before he speaks again. "Did you like your song?"

And there it is...

Your song.

Mine.

The words he sang to me in bed—as well as the ones he sang to me when he showed up to my apartment, completely unannounced, before he ravaged me over the side of my couch—yeah, they weren't just pieces of songs he'd sung before. He'd written them for me. They are mine—a terrifying truth he's just admitted to me. I'd be lying if I said that it didn't also give me a thrill that made my insides flutter. When he squeezes me tighter against him, as if beckoning my reply, I decide that the truth won't hurt me. At least not yet.

"Yes. It's really great. You guys sounded awesome up there."

Before I can take my next breath, he has me turned so that I'm facing him. When his lips crash against mine, I gasp, gripping hold of his shirt in order to keep my balance. With my mouth parted open, nothing stops him from sliding his tongue between my lips. I sigh, loving the way his warm, wet tongue dances with mine. He sucks my bottom lip, biting me gently before he dives in for another taste. One of his hands slides around the back of my neck, supporting my head as he deepens the kiss; his other hand drops to the small of my back, and I'm pulled closer. I swallow his moan when his erection rubs up against my hip through his jeans.

"Been thinking about this mouth all night, doll face," he mutters as he kisses his way along my jaw before nibbling on my ear. "You're coming home with me tonight."

I offer him a nod and nothing more because, *hello*, who could be capable of speech after a kiss like that? He smirks at me, the arrogant little shit, and then continues to devour my mouth. I know we're not alone, but I don't even care. He feels so undeniably good. I wrap my arms around his neck, pressing myself against him in earnest. After watching him up on that stage, I won't refuse my body what it wants.

"Good God, man—enough dry humping," calls out one of the guys. I don't know which one; partly because Sage has my head in a fog, partly because I haven't spent enough time with the band to know them by voice only.

"Can it, D," Sage mumbles against my mouth.

"I mean it, Dweeb. We've got business. Get your ass over here."

He pulls away from my mouth but keeps his arms wrapped around me as his icy blue eyes stare through his horn-rimmed glasses and down into my eyes. For a second, neither of us says a word as we work to catch our breath.

"You're one hell of a muse, gorgeous." He reaches down and squeezes my ass and I can't fight my grin. I sort of appreciate how much he adores my ass. "Stay with Violet, yeah? I'll be right back."

He smacks a quick kiss against my lips before he lets me go. I watch as he struts his way toward Derrick, their drummer, who stands shaking his head with an amused look on his face. They exchange a few words and then Derrick leads him to a man who seems to be waiting to speak to them.

"What'd I tell you?" says Violet, playfully jabbing me with her elbow. "Some kiss, huh?"

I breathe a halfhearted laugh as I look over at her, unsure if I've got any words to spare.

"He really likes you. It's looks good on him. *You* look good on him," she says with a grin.

"Oh," I mutter, feeling slightly uncomfortable with the direction this conversation is taking.

"It's okay to admit it, you know?"

"Admit what?"

"That you like him," she says with a laugh. "I promise you, no matter what he may or may not be saying, you're not a fling."

"He's not—he's not my boyfriend," I stutter, folding my arms across my chest. I don't know why I tell her that, or why I'm suddenly feeling defensive. Truth be told, I'm not really sure what we are. We agreed to be monogamous, but that's just sex. Outside of that, we barely know each other.

"I hear you," she says with a knowing smile. "I'm not sure your face agrees, though. Come on, let's go help Wren. The sooner they're packed up, the sooner we can get out of here."

I follow her lead, heading up on stage to join Wren. As we climb the short set of stairs, I look over at the rest of the guys while they huddle around some stranger who seems to hold their attention. My eyes linger for a moment on Sage and my stomach tingles. I force myself to look away, appalled by the realization that Violet is right. Whatever she just saw on my face is now spreading awareness to the rest of my body. Sage McCoy has managed to steal a little piece of my heart. I *do* like him.

Fuck.

I know I should probably quit while I'm ahead; cut my losses and all that shit. What's one more piece of my heart gone? I probably won't miss it. Yet, the thought of giving him up now? It's totally ridiculous, but I can't seem to stomach the idea of being without him. I tried. Granted, it was only for a couple of days, but I put in a solid effort. All it got me was a few restless nights, a lot more cardio clocked at the gym, and the realization that I am not ready to give him up yet.

I shake my worry away, knowing that this will work itself out. Eventually, the novelty of all that is new between us will wear off and he'll get bored. They always do. Then they always leave. As long as I guard what's left of my heart, I'll survive. There is absolutely nothing wrong with indulging my body for a while, so long as I keep my heart out of it. The moment I start falling for him, I'll reevaluate my options. For now, my heart is fine. He can have what he's managed to steal but nothing more. It's not like he's giving me his heart.

He isn't. At least, I don't think he is.

TWO

Sage

WHEN DERRICK TOLD ME that there was someone he wanted me to meet, I never in my wildest dreams imagined *this*. Apparently, Travis Pratt caught D just as he was coming off stage, asking to speak to our band manager. Currently, Derrick's it. He's good with the business side of things, plus he's the most organized, so we've always trusted him to take on that role. When Travis told him who he was, D insisted that I needed to be in on the conversation. Now, all five of us guys are circled around one Mr. Travis Pratt—road manager for Lawful Sinners.

Fuck me.

After praising our performance, he tells us that he's been keeping an ear out for an opening act for Lawful Sinners' next tour. They're headlining with a couple of other bands, but the opener slot is still vacant. Lawful Sinners is a group based out of Denver. They've been around for a couple of years, paying their dues, making a pretty good name for themselves. This will be their second U.S. tour.

"This is the deal—take my card. You cats need some representation. No offense, kid," he says, tipping his chin at Derrick, "but you need someone handling the business while you're up there beating the shit out of those drums. I've got a gal, real sharp, works down in D-town. I'll make sure she's at your next gig."

"Two weeks from today," JJ announces. "FoCo. The Brew Cycle"

"I'll tell her she's missing out on a good thing if she doesn't get her ass up there. She likes what she hears, she'll call me—we'll see if we can't work something out."

"Thank you," I manage, offering my hand. He gives me a firm shake before doing the same with the guys, and then he's gone.

"Holy. Shit. What the fuck just happened?" asks Maddox, burying his fingers in his hair.

"I think we might have just got our first big break, lil'bro," says Knox, clapping his hand against his brother's back.

I stare down at the card in my hands, my mind racing, my palms sweating. "We need to find a bass player. Like, yesterday," I mutter, shaking my head in disbelief. I look up and glance around at my second family and the closest I've ever had to brothers. My adrenaline from before is now amped up even more. "All hands on deck, guys. This is it. We can't have some fucking rookie up on stage with us two weeks from now screwing up our shit."

"We got it, boss," says Derrick, bumping me with his shoulder. "Tonight, we drink. Tomorrow, we hunt."

"For the record, when you guys make it big, if I'm still rolling up cords and packing up equipment, I want a t-shirt that says *'M&M's Hottest Roadie'*. I also expect a paycheck, and there better be *lots* of zeroes in it."

We all look over and see Violet, Millie, and Wren making their way off stage. Wren's bass is closed in its case in one hand, and he's got an amp in the other. Millie's got the case that houses Knox's pedals and Violet appears to have all of JJ's electronics packed up, too.

"If your t-shirt says anything, it'll say *'JJ's Hottest Groupie,'*" he says, making his way toward his girlfriend.

"Pfft," she scoffs with an eye roll. "I'm no groupie, baby. I'm your girl and you best not forget it."

"Never." He kisses the tip of her nose, taking the gear from her hands, and she smiles at him before she hurries back on stage to gather another load.

I slide Travis's card into my back pocket just as Maddox reaches for the case in Millie's grasp. "Thanks, babe. I've got this."

"Watch who you're calling babe, *Maddy,*" I warn as I approach, draping my arm around Millicent's shoulders.

He curls his lip in a half-hearted snarl and flips me off.

He hates it when we call him Maddy.

"Try not to get your panties in a bunch, I just call 'em like I see 'em." He wiggles his eyebrows before he turns, heading for the back door that leads to the alley where Derrick's SUV and the band trailer are parked.

I ignore him, sliding my arm down around Millie's waist as I hold her against me tightly. "You my roadie now? I could get used to you coming to all our shows. You don't really have to help with our equipment, though."

She shrugs, looking over her shoulder at the others. "It's not a big deal. Violet seems to know what she's doing and I thought I could lend a hand."

"Violet *definitely* knows what she's doing. She knows our set up almost better than we do. She could set us up and tear us down by herself," I say with a chuckle.

"She also said the sooner we pack up, the sooner we can get out of here."

The look in Millie's eyes when she says that makes my dick twitch. Suddenly, getting out of here as quickly as possible is a fantastic idea. "Does someone want to get naked?" I jibe, only half teasing. I can hardly wait to strip her down and have my way with her—all night long.

"Enough eye-fucking," Maddox yells as he passes us on his way to the stage. "Let's get our shit out of here."

"Someone's raggin'," I reply, pulling away from Millie only to take her hand as I make my way toward the stage.

"Shut up!"

"Uh-oh," sings Violet as she helps JJ pack up his keys. "Sounds like *someone* is single tonight! Andrea wasn't here, was she?"

"Please. Like I care. I've put up with her long enough. We're done."

"Mmmhmm," Violet hums, exchanging a mischievous look with JJ.

Knox looks at his brother and then smirks at me. I fight to contain my laughter. The drama between Maddox and Andrea never ends. Guaranteed, she'll be at the house later tonight—bitching at Maddy and then filling the basement with her annoying as hell, squeaky sex noises. I *do not* envy Derrick. He might have the biggest room in the house, but he shares a wall with the youngest Bradley brother. He's a good sport and he doesn't complain. Much.

A half an hour later, we're packed up and ready to head out. The guys feel like drinking and, after a night like tonight, I don't disagree. Knox suggests picking up some beer and just heading back to the house. When our resident man-whore suggests a night in, we all lift an eyebrow in curiosity. After he tells us to screw ourselves, he explains that he thought we could kick back and scour YouTube to see if we could scope out any local talent. Mixing business with pleasure is agreed upon by all of us and we're en route right away.

JJ and Violet ride with Millie and me and we spend the ride back home talking about the show and filling the girls in on our exchange with Travis. I would kill for a chance to tour for six weeks with Lawful Sinners. The exposure alone would be insane. It's just what the band needs right now.

First, we need to find a fucking bass player that'll actually stick.

When I pull into the drive and turn off the car, I look over at Millie. She hasn't been to the house since the night I brought her over, passed out after Keith drugged her drink. She looks over at me and catches me staring. I smirk at her in response. I decide that tonight, I'm not going to stress over a bass player. Tonight, we're celebrating. When I get her alone, I'll be sure that by the time she finally passes out in my bed, it'll be for entirely different reasons.

Millicent

Sometime after one in the morning, we're all well on our way to being drunk as we lounge around the guys' living room. For a while, Knox and JJ had their laptops out and the five band members were drinking and surfing the web for musicians. Violet had her phone and she tugged me down onto the couch with her as we did the same. After a while, she got distracted and she's been exposing me to all sorts of random videos on the web, most of which she finds wildly hilarious.

I'm not really much of a beer girl, but every time I finish one, Maddox or Sage seems to be putting another in my hand. Same for Violet. Now, I'm not sure if I'm laughing at the ridiculous shorts that fill the screen of her mobile because they're funny, because I'm tipsy, or both. Either way, I don't mind. I've never done this before and it feels…*good.*

I don't really know much about the the members of the band or Violet; I don't know how old they are, who's in college and who's not; what they do for a living or how they all came to know each other; and yet, I get the feeling that nights like this are what it feels like to be a normal twenty-something on a Saturday night. I don't know that I belong here, but something about this night makes me want to stay.

Or, rather, *someone.*

I wouldn't go so far as to say that I have *no* friends, but I don't have many. It's the way I like it. I'm better by myself. Or, at least, that's what I thought growing up. Now, my isolation seems like more of a habit than anything else. I've always felt like the odd man out in social settings such as this one. Even after I escaped from New Jersey and moved to Colorado, starting fresh at a college where no one knew me, I still felt like *outcast* was a sort of skin that I couldn't shed. I made a few friends over the years in various classes. I even dated a couple of guys and was silly enough to fall in love, but they didn't stick around. I've learned that men usually don't. It's better not to get too attached. Not to anyone.

I go out enough to keep the label of *Shut In* off of my back. I know better. I can't shut out the world or I'll end up like *her.* The woman I ran from. I won't let anyone, not even myself, take me to that place—change me into that person. I have boundaries, carefully constructed boundaries that I trust will keep me *Millie.*

When I was in college, homework and literature were my escape—my excuses. Now that I'm older, it seems my excuses haven't changed. Nevertheless, I put in the necessary effort. Happy hour with my fellow professors, clubbing with Aria and Josh—now, occasionally, with Sarah and Brandon—it's enough. I'm not afraid of being by myself. On nights when I feel lonely, if I wear the right dress and sit at the right bar, I can chase away the feeling. I've been told I'm beautiful; and if my success rate at snagging a one-night stand says anything, I'm assuming it proves I can be quite appealing when I want to be.

But this—sitting around, drinking beer and goofing off with Violet on the couch, the boys abandoning their hunt in favor of video games—it feels…different. *Good.* There's something about Violet that makes me feel welcome. I don't fit in with these people, which is normal for me, but none of them seem to care.

My attention is pulled away from Violet's screen at the sound of Maestro's barking. Sage's little French bulldog, covered in black fur with a white belly, paws his way into his owner's lap. Sage ignores him for only a moment, his focus glued to the television screen in front of him.

"Outside?" he asks, his thumbs still busy as they press furiously at the control in his hands. Maestro barks his affirmation and Sage pauses the game, tossing the device in his hand to Maddox. "Kick ass, Mad Lips."

"Don't I always?" he mutters, starting the game as Sage stands to his feet. Maestro barks again, racing in circles, clearly excited for the chance to relieve himself.

Sage catches me staring and winks at me before he leans down and taps the side of my thigh. "Come on, doll face."

I look to Violet, who wiggles her fingers in a little wave, and then reach my hand out for Sage to help me uncurl myself from the place I've been nestled for a while. He doesn't let me go as we make our way to the front door. As soon as it's cracked open, Maestro goes racing down the front porch. I assume, due to Sage's lack of concern, that he's not worried about the little guy running away.

"Wait, I have to find my shoes," I mutter, sweeping my hair out of my face as I look down at the pile just beside the door.

"You don't need them. It's nice out. Come on," he tells me, wrapping an arm around my waist as he steps out in his bare feet.

I acquiesce, only because I'm a tad bit intoxicated. That, and he smells way too delectable for me to argue. He closes the door behind us and leads me to the top of the first step. He peers into the darkness, checking on Maestro, then focuses his attention on me. I suck in a breath when he circles both his arms around me, pulling me against his chest.

"Hey."

He speaks and the sound of his voice in conjunction with the the warmth of his body against mine makes my knees week. Suddenly, I'm reminded why I'm here—why being in a room full of people I barely know, drinking beer I'd never think to purchase on my own, is all worth it. My body is suddenly wide awake and buzzing with want.

"Hey," I manage.

"I've kind of been neglecting you," he murmurs, dipping his head to kiss the side of my neck. "Got carried away with the guys." He licks my skin and I feel my nipples pebble in response. "Sorry, baby."

I clear my throat, hoping that when I speak, my voice will work. "It's fine," I say, and mean it. "I'm not as needy as you might think."

He pulls away from me, flashing me his signature smirk before looking down at his chest. My gaze follows his and I find my fists are both gripping onto his t-shirt, my ten fingers making me a liar. He chuckles and then seals his lips against mine. Now fully aware of my hands, my grip tightens, pulling him even closer. He palms both hands around my ass, pressing me against him with purpose, and I moan into his mouth.

"Seriously?" Sage and I pull away from each other at the sound of her nasally, high pitched voice. "If you're going to go all *she Hulk* on his ass, you probably should take it indoors. A little tact goes a long way."

I look at the voluptuous blonde standing in her too high heels and too short dress, her purse hanging from the crook of her elbow.

Okay, to be fair, I suppose I own heels that high and dresses that short—but this bitch just called me a she Hulk!

I shift my focus back to Sage when he scoffs, sliding his hands from over my ass to around my waist before he speaks. "Really? You're here for a booty call after one in the morning and you're going to school us on tact? Fuck off, Andrea."

She rolls her eyes and waves her hand, as if batting away the legitimacy of his point. "Is he in there?"

"He does live here," Sage replies dryly. That, apparently, is all the invitation she needs. Without another word, she walks around us, heading for the door. As soon as she's out of earshot, Sage shakes his head and smacks a kiss against my lips. "That's officially our cue to hit the sack, baby doll."

I furrow my brow in confusion. "I thought Maddox said they were done?"

He shrugs and whistles for Maestro before he says, "They fight and then they fuck. It's annoying as hell. One day he'll realize her pussy just isn't worth it. She treats him like shit. Anyway—" He swats at my backside just as Maestro joins us on the porch. "Enough about them. Let's get naked."

THREE

Millicent

WE DON'T SAY A word to the others when we re-enter the house and make our way to the stairs. I can hear the faint traces of an argument as the sound of Maddox and Andrea's voices scale the walls of the staircase that leads to the basement. I'm impressed with the volume at which they are screaming at each other and in awe of how everyone else seems to think nothing of it. As soon as Sage and I make it to the landing of the second level, his hands are under my shirt. He splays his long fingers across my stomach, pulling me back against him as we both stagger to his bedroom.

He kisses the hair that's draped over my ear just as we pass over the threshold. When he starts humming to me, a shiver races down my spine. And then—

"I'll set you free, but will you let me go?
You cage me in and now I can't let go.
All night/One song
This room/My home
Set me free but, baby, don't let go
Tonight/ Just give me tonight."

As he sings, his rich, tenor voice so smooth, his breath against my ear enticingly hot, his words meant for me—*only me*—it's as if my entire body is suddenly aflame. I spin around to face him, my lips seeking out any piece of him that I can find. My mouth grazes his chin as my arms wrap around his neck. I follow the length of his jaw, kissing and licking, desperate to taste him.

I hear the door slam shut and then, in the blink of an eye, my back is pressed against it and I'm no longer the one delivering kisses. I don't complain. Instead, I follow his lead, allowing him to undress me. My shirt hits the floor. Then my bra. My back bows away from the surface behind me as he takes one of my nipples into his mouth. His tongue swirls around the hardened bud and I sigh deeply as I reach up to run my fingers through his hair. He sucks hard and then lets me go with a pop. My small boob shakes and I watch as he smiles before pressing a kiss in the middle of my sternum.

"Such perfect tits, baby doll," he murmurs before he showers the opposite nipple with the same attention. By the time he's finished with my breasts, I'd imagine he could blow on my swollen clit and I'd come for him. I'm so wet, you'd think my pussy was desperate.

Then again, maybe it is. It's been a couple days since this man has been inside of me. I don't usually feel so needy after seventy-two hours. Hell, I've gone months without getting laid before; but ever since that first night with Sage, I feel like I can't get enough. My body is always hungry for him. Despite my best efforts, there's not an inch of skin on me that will ever forget him, as he's seen fit to explore every part of me. Resistance was futile and my pride has long since surrendered to my lust.

Sage kisses his way up my chest, along my neck, and toward my lips. I pull away from him, reaching for his glasses, ready to take my turn undressing him. As I fold his horn-rimmed frames closed, he takes them from me and gently tosses them the short distance to his dresser. Much like our first night in my room, his space is lit only from the light of the moon and the street lamps that shine through his open curtains. Nevertheless, I can make out the blue of his beautiful eyes, and his hooded gaze makes me feel absolutely gorgeous. I want to crawl all over him—I want to feel the heat of his skin pressed against the heat of mine—I want his hands and his mouth everywhere—and I want it all *now*.

I reach for the bottom of his shirt and he helps me take it off. When I start to unfasten the top of his jeans, he tugs at mine. His hand slips down the front, his fingers cupping my soaked thong, and I respond in kind—reaching for his hardened length inside of his boxers. He grunts, his long, thick appendage twitching at my touch.

"Want to eat your pussy," he mutters, pressing his forehead against mine.

"Want to suck your cock," I reply, giving him a squeeze.

He grunts once more before he frees his hand and takes hold of each side of my jeans. "You first." He sinks to his knees and then strips my legs bare, guiding my ankles out of my pants and then my thong. He tosses both garments aside before he places his hands on my hips and turns me around. "Brace yourself, doll face."

He nudges my legs apart, widening my stance. I clap my hands against the door just as his tongue slides along my slit. "Oh, god," I moan, tilting my head back. He sucks my throbbing clit between his lips and my fingers curl, trying to find purchase on a surface that will give me nothing.

"Fuck, you taste good," he mumbles against my sex. Even just the kiss of his breath makes my legs tremble. "I'm hungry, baby doll." He licks at my entrance, teasing me, and I whimper, pressing my flushed cheek against the cool door. "Gonna need you to come all over my tongue." I nod, even though I know he can't see me, and then he plunges inside of me.

I can barely breathe, his mouth making it hard for me to think about anything besides the pleasure he's giving me. He molds his hands around my backside as he flicks the tip of his tongue across my clit, and his name falls from my lips.

"Sage, oh, Sage," I moan, and then I pull my bottom lip between my teeth.

I can feel it as every muscle in my body tenses, bracing for my release. When he pushes two fingers inside of me, curling the tips as he smothers my incredibly sensitive sweet spot with his firm, hot tongue, I can't be silenced. I come and he doesn't stop his ministrations until he's satisfied with the extent of my orgasm.

He laps up my release and then I hear it as he sucks on his fingers, humming with satisfaction. I'm still pressed against the door working to catch my breath when I feel him nip at my ass with his teeth. A grin plays at my lips as a giggle bubbles out of me, and then I sigh as he kisses his way up my back.

"I'm going to write a song about your pussy, baby. So damn delicious, I could eat you for every meal."

"You better not," I laugh, turning to face him. "I most certainly don't need a room full of people singing about what's between my legs."

"Mmm, cities full of people," he growls, pressing his erection against my hip. "*Countries* full of people, doll face. Everyone will love it—only I'll get to taste it."

"You're disgusting."

"But you don't deny it," he whispers, tracing his nose along mine. "The whole world will sing of your magnificent pussy."

I cup my hands around his face and peer into his eyes. He's serious. Perhaps not about the song describing his intimate relationship with my vagina—god, I hope that's the beer talking—but the rest of it? For a moment, I think about our car ride here after the concert. Listening to him talk about the possibility of being invited on this tour, hearing his excitement—this is his dream. It's *all* of their dreams. I don't know if I've ever held a dream with such enthusiasm. Or maybe I did. Once.

I shake the thought away, irritated by the alcohol induced walk down memory lane. I don't wish to go there. I want to be here. Now. With *him*. The dreamer.

For his sake, for the light that shines in his icy blue eyes, I want for his dreams to never know darkness.

"I hope the whole world will sing with you, Sage," I finally manage. "Just *not* about my pussy."

A wicked grin curls his lips and then he grips me around my waist and lifts my feet from the floor. I hook my ankles behind his thighs and he carries me across the room, not so gently depositing me on his bed. I open my mouth to grumble but then he rubs his jean clad bulge against my wet pussy and my complaint disappears.

"Hey, it's your turn," I breathe.

He shakes his head at me as he lifts himself onto his feet. He drops his pants and boxers, kicking them aside as he reaches for his nightstand drawer. "Need to be inside you, gorgeous," he mutters, ripping open the condom.

I don't argue.

He crawls back on top of me, weighing me down just enough so that I feel him from head to toe, supporting what he thinks I can't handle on his elbows. "I like you here," he whispers against my lips, rubbing his heavy cock against my swollen center. "In my bed."

"Oh, yeah?"

Reaching down between us, he positions himself at my entrance and slowly invites himself inside me. "Yeah," he breathes, blowing out what I suck in.

All thoughts of his confession are eradicated by the feeling of his cock as he pumps in and out of me. Sage stretches me open and fills me up like no one ever has before. I'm not sure I'll ever get enough of him. It's a truth I simply cannot deny. Every time we're together, it gets better. He's learning my body and I'm learning his.

"Who owns your orgasm, baby?"

"You," I admit without hesitation. It's true. I won't even pretend otherwise. He always leaves me sated and exhausted in the most blissful way.

"You bet your sweet, little ass," he mutters, pulling out of me. I gasp, surprised and disappointed, and then he smirks at me before sitting up on his knees and flipping me over. He tugs up on my hips and I prop myself up on my hands and knees, my belly anxious and my pussy longing for his return. He slides back in with ease, one hand gripping my hip, the other caressing one side of my ass. His fingers squeeze and I close my eyes, wanting nothing more than to get lost in him.

"Oh, god," I mewl when he hits some magical spot.

That's new.

My insides spark, my skin tingles, and I break out into a sweat all at once.

He hits it again.

"Oh, shit, Sage—yes! Right there, right there, right there!" I gasp, my fingers clawing at his sheets. I moan and it's loud. I should be embarrassed, but he feels too good. I can't shut up. I won't.

"God, Millie—can't get enough of this pussy," his voice rumbles as he thrusts into me faster. "Need you to come, doll face."

My whole body is trembling. I can't speak. I can't breathe. I'm overwhelmed. Surely, he must know—he must know that I'm about to explode. When my orgasm bursts, euphoria flooding my veins, my voice claws its way from my throat. "Sage! Yes! Fuck—yes!"

He grunts a string of expletives, pounding into me even harder. I feel it as he grows larger and then spills his own cum. He groans as he rides out his release and then we both collapse. This time, he doesn't brace himself, but buries me into the mattress as he weighs me down.

His skin is slick with sweat and he smells of sex and his own natural musk. It's marvelous and I never want him to move.

"Damn, baby doll."

"Mmmm," I hum, offering him all I have to give.

He presses his lips into my hair and then rolls off of me and onto his back. After a couple deep breaths, I roll over as well, resting my cheek against the bed as I look over at him. I watch as he pulls the condom off, knotting it before carelessly tossing it onto the floor. I roll my eyes, too spent to offer any other protest.

When he looks over at me, he tips his chin and says, "Come 'ere." I roll onto my side, closing the distance between us, and he shakes his head, patting his chest. "Here." Before I can interpret what he means, he rolls toward me, gripping me around the waist before flopping back onto his back, settling me on top of him. My hair falls around my face as well as his, my ends brushing the bed, and he reaches up to sweep the strands behind my ears. "Not done touching you, yet," he tells me

I nod, press a kiss against his lips, and then rest my head on his shoulder. He traces his finger tips up and down my back and along my sides. I free a sigh, closing my eyes.

"Don't you fucking dare," he murmurs, playfully smacking my ass. "We're not finished, doll face."

I move positions, folding my arms across his sternum and propping my chin on my hands. "If you don't stop touching me like that, sleep is *exactly* what will happen." He grunts, resting his hands around my backside with a smirk. "You should probably talk to me, too."

"About what?"

I shrug and blurt out the first thing that comes to mind. "Did you guys find anyone you're interested in to replace Keith?" I know that Sage and the rest of the guys don't blame me for what happened a couple weeks ago at The Wash Bar. Keith is most certainly responsible for his own horrible actions, but that doesn't mean I don't feel like I played a part in their loss. Just like Sage is sure he could have prevented me ending up in harm's way that night had he found me sooner, I'm convinced they'd still have a bass player had I not shown up that night at all.

Then again, if it wasn't me, it would have been someone else. I suppose what Sage said is true. Judging by Keith's character, it wasn't really much of a loss.

"Maybe," he says, interrupting my thoughts. "We'll see who turns up for auditions this week."

"What about Wren? Why can't he stay?"

"He used to play with us, back when we first started," he begins to explain, his fingers starting up again. "Wren was in the same class as Derrick, that's how we got hooked up. He played with us for about a year or so and then he got his girl knocked up." Sage shrugs, as if to imply that it's no big deal. "He split on account of it was time for him to settle down. The guy got a full-time gig, got married; he does the dad thing more than anything else now. Obviously, he's still got it. Wren'll fill in for us when we're in a pinch. It's happened a couple of times—fucking curse of the bass slot. Anyway, he's good people, but he won't stay."

"Mmmmm," I hum my understanding and then rest my head on his shoulder once more. "So he went to school with Derrick?"

"College, yeah."

"CSU? Did they graduate?" I ask, genuinely curious.

"Yeah. What of it? You judging me again, doll face?" He doesn't sound like he's joking, but his fingers don't stop tracing across my skin and his voice is still warm and soft. His lack of education isn't so much a fault as much as it is something that makes us drastically different. Being a college professor makes me kind of a big advocate for higher learning. I think I'll always be a student at heart.

"*No*," I exaggerate. "Just making conversation."

"Hmm. Well, believe it or not, I'm the only one who never finished college. I was sixteen when we started the band. Knox was in his first year at CSU and he's how we picked up Derrick. I met JJ when I started taking my music comp classes. D graduated first. Then JJ. Then Knox. Maddox is supposed to graduate next spring."

"Wow," I murmur.

"What? You thought we were all just a bunch of punks playing music for a dime?"

I lift my head and attempt to stare through the darkness and into his eyes. I don't know if I'm imagining the slight hint of defensiveness in his tone or not, but I suddenly wonder if my initial reaction to finding out that he's not a student offended him more than he let on. When he told me, it had come as a surprise. Dealing with our age difference had been enough as it was—I'm still not convinced the five years between us won't play into the demise of whatever it is that's going on between us. In any case, I certainly don't think less of him as a *person* just because he doesn't have an interest in college.

"Hey," I begin, pausing to make sure I have his full attention. For some reason,

I feel particularly adamant that he understands how I see him. "I heard you when you said college wasn't your thing. I *hear* you up on that stage. You are amazing. All of you. I've never thought anything less. You've got a great voice. I really do hope the world will sing with you."

For a moment, he doesn't say anything. His fingers come to a halt as he presses one palm against the small of my back, bringing his other hand up to cup around the back of my neck. He lifts his face and touches his nose to mine, and I bite my lip when I feel him growing hard beneath me.

"And we shall sing, gorgeous, of your perfect pussy."

I manage to groan and giggle before he presses his lips against mine. "Sing about my pussy and you will pay dearly," I mutter, my mouth still adhered to his.

He grunts, lifting his hips and rubbing his length against my stomach. "How about, for now, I just fuck it?"

"Mmm," I hum with a smile. "Yes, please."

FOUR

Sage

I DRAW IN A DEEP breath as sleep slips out of my grasp and then blow it all out as I peek open one eye. The sun, which is already high in the sky, is pouring through the curtain of my window. I usually close the blinds before I go to bed to prevent this kind of morning greeting; but when I open my other eye and look at the reason I forgot, I could give a fuck.

Millie's on her side facing me, her arms curled up against her chest, her legs tangled with mine. Her long, ashy brown hair is fanned out across my pillows, leaving her face on display for me to admire. She's so damn beautiful, I could stare at her all morning. Or, rather, all afternoon. I like how she'll sleep well past noon on a Sunday, as if that's what Sundays were intended for.

It's been a long time since I've had a repeat guest in my bed. Most of my hookups don't happen here at all, but I meant what I said last night. I like having her here. I also liked having her at the show last night. When she came backstage with Violet after our set, it was like my whole body was abuzz with the reminder that I want this girl. This *woman*. I haven't yet taken her out on a real date, just the two of us. She still seems reluctant to go there with me. But this is a battle I intend to win. And soon. I want more of her—more of her smart-ass mouth, more of her sexy giggle, more of her drop dead gorgeous face. Fuck, I sound like a pussy.

I don't even give a shit.

I drape my arm around her and draw her closer, wishing to feel her warm skin pressed against mine. I sure as hell want more of this body all over me. She's hands down, dick up, the best lay I've ever had. Every damn time.

I lean over and press a kiss against her bare shoulder and she sighs, stirring up my dick. A smirk pulls at the corner of my mouth as I kiss her again, making my way toward her neck. She squirms, nestling herself closer to me, her thigh brushing against my cock. I pull her even closer and nibble on the soft, fragrant skin just below her jaw. She tastes both salty and sweet, her skin still sticky from our tumble in the sheets early this morning. I can smell the lingering trace of vanilla that she wears, too.

"If you leave a mark, I'll kick your ass," she mumbles, her lips grazing my throat. The sound of her morning voice, raspy from sleep, has my cock's full attention.

"Oh, yeah?"

"Mmm," she hums.

"And if I do it where no one will see it?"

As soon as the words pass through my lips, I duck my head and latch onto the side of her boob. I bite while I suck and she gasps, her hands finding their way into my hair. I pull away and admire the pink mark I've left, then smile when I look up at her. Her lips are parted, her breathing slightly ragged, and her eyes are barely open. I know right away that it's lust I see in her hooded gaze and not exhaustion. I decide to take it upon myself to change that.

I close my lips around her nipple, sucking hard as I swirl my tongue around the tip. She utters my name with a moan, turning me on even more. My hands are everywhere as I latch onto her opposite nipple. I feel my way across the soft skin of her flat stomach, along the delicate curves of her side and over her hip. When I bite and suck her creamy skin, marking her tit as mine, she arches her back and I trail my fingers around and down, grabbing a palm full of ass.

Fucking love her sweet, little ass.

By the time I'm finished with her, her breasts are splattered with hickeys. I nibble and lick my way up her chest and along her neck until my lips find hers. She grabs hold of my face, keeping me close as my tongue seeks entrance into her mouth. Then she wraps her legs around me and I groan when her warm, wet pussy makes contact with my dick.

"You still want a taste?" I mutter against her mouth. She opens her eyes, her gaze instantly locking with mine before she nods. A smirk tugs at my lips before I smack a kiss against hers and then roll us over so that she's on top of me. "Have at it, doll face."

I fold my arms behind my head and watch as she kisses her way down my chest, across my abs, licking the indented curve of my hips. I pull my lip between my teeth, biting down hard when she fists my dick and sucks one of my balls into her mouth.

"Fu-uck," I mutter when she moves on to the other. Then she flattens her tongue against me, licking her way from base to tip before she wraps her lips around my head. "Fuck, baby doll. Just—*fuck!* You feel so good."

She takes as much of me into her mouth as she can, stroking the rest of me with her tight fingers. As her head bobs up and down, she hums, giving voice to her own enjoyment. I reach down, sweeping her hair out of her face so that I can see her. She's the finest little thing my cock has ever seen. She sucks harder, taking me deeper, and it takes everything in me to keep my shit together. When I feel my balls start to tighten, I sit up and lift her off of me. She sits back on her heels, lifting an eyebrow at me in question.

I reach over into my nightstand and pull out a condom. I hold it up between my fingers as I explain, "If you're going to make me come, you might as well get yourself off too, yeah?"

She leans toward me and snatches up the condom just as I wrap a hand around the back of her neck, drawing her lips to mine. She moans into my mouth and I reach down between her legs, dipping one finger and then another into her wet center.

"Want this pussy on my cock, baby."

"Then stop kissing me so I can get the damn condom open."

"Easier said than done," I reply with a chuckle. I pull my fingers away from her and immediately place them on my tongue as she rips open the condom and then rolls the rubber over my hard length.

She gives me a gentle shove and I acquiesce to her silent insistence, laying down on my back. Her eyes lock with mine as she crawls on top of me, taking hold of my dick and lining us up. She eases herself over me and I grow even harder as I watch the expression on her face change. Her mouth falls open, her eyelids droop, and her cheeks hint at a blush. She rests her hands against my chest, breathing deeply as she remains still, allowing her body to adjust to this position.

When she starts to move, pushing herself up and then sliding back down, riding me, I can't keep my hands to myself. My fingers stroke and squeeze her thighs before I feel my way up her sides. I palm her tits, then pinch her nipples; she moans and speeds up her pace.

"Sage," she breathes.

I pinch her nipples again, loving the way my name falls from her lips.

"Can't get enough of you—you fill me up," she mutters, arching her back as she begins to bounce her ass, her wet cunt coating my dick. "God, you feel amazing. I want you—I want your cock so much."

"You got it, baby doll," I assure her with a groan, reaching around to squeeze her tight cheeks. "This cock is yours to ride whenever you want."

"Mmmm," she hums, tilting her head back as she closes her eyes.

I barely hear it when my door opens—too lost in the beautiful woman wrapped around me to even register that we've got company. Then a voice breaks me out of my trance.

"Sage, I—" Her voice is cut off by her own shriek.

In a fraction of a second, Millie freezes, her eyes wide as she stares down at me. I'm up, my arms pulling her tightly against my chest as I look over her shoulder at my sister, who stands slack-jawed in the doorway.

"The *fuck?*" I cry, scowling at her. Maestro, who has been quiet until now, starts barking and pawing at her ankles, which seems to fluster her even more.

"Sorry! Shit—I'm sorry! I—I didn't—I mean—I—"

"Get the fuck out, Rosy!" I demand, wondering why in hell she's still here.

"Yeah. Yes, of course. I'm sorry! I, um, yeah..." She turns on her heel, Maestro following her out before she slams the door shut, making Millie jump.

"Rosy?" she murmurs. "That was your *sister?*"

"Yeah," I tell her, pulling away just enough to see her face. "I don't know what the fuck she was thinking just barging in here."

"Christ," she bites as she tries to pull away from me.

"Whoa—no, no, no! You're not going anywhere, doll face."

"What?" she cries incredulously. "You can't be serious! I need to go. Now. You need to take me home."

"I'll take you wherever you want just as soon as we're done."

"Sage—"

"You feel that?" I ask as I grind her hips against mine, reminding her just how hard she makes me. "You're not leaving me with that shit. I'm not a big fan of blue-balls, baby, and you're the only pussy I'm doing these days."

She scowls at me in disbelief. "Your sister has seen me twice. The first time, I was drugged and unconscious. Now, I'm all over your dick—*naked!* You'll have to excuse me if I'm suddenly *not* in the mood."

"About the part where you're all over my dick, I—"

"Forget it, Sage. I—"

"No. Fuck no," I insist as I slide one hand down around her ass, the other around her neck, holding her against me as I lift to my knees. She opens her mouth in protest, but I press my lips against hers before she can utter a word. She makes one final attempt to pull away from me, but her efforts are half-hearted. When I sweep my tongue over hers, she sighs in sweet resignation.

Yeah. That's what I thought.

"Lean back, baby," I say, easing her head and shoulders onto the bed. "I'll take care of you, just like I always do. This ain't over until I hear you scream."

"God, I'm surprised there's room for me in this bed with you and your ego," she quips.

"What was that?" I ask, turning my ear toward her as I begin to rock my pelvis against hers. She hums a sigh on my first stroke and a smirk tugs at my lips as I guide her legs around my back. "Mmmhmm. Your orgasm is *mine*, gorgeous." I grip her hips tightly as I ram my cock in and out of her. From this angle, it's not long before she starts to unravel.

"Oh, god," she groans, reaching behind her to grab hold of anything she can find. Her fingers extend to the end of the bed, and she latches on as she arches her back, spurring me on. "Shit—*Sage!*"

"You still want me to stop?" I grunt, knowing full well nothing—not even the fucking apocalypse—could make me pull out of her now.

"Stop and I'll kill you!" she manages, her breaths coming in shallow, ragged inhalations. "*Sage*—" She gasps and then makes the sexiest noise. I can't even call it a moan—it's deeper, more melodic, and it pushes me closer to my own release.

"Come, Millie," I demand, my jaw clenched as I force my body to hold on just a little bit longer. "Come, baby!"

"I'm—I'm—coming! Fuck!" she cries out, her body trembling around mine. "Oh, my god—Sage!"

"Jesus," I groan, her pussy clenching tightly around my cock, coaxing my release. "Hell, yeah, baby doll." I thrust into her once, then once more before my body stills, my pleasure robbing me of mobility. I heave in a few deep breaths as I smile down at Millie and then I bring my body down to rest on top of hers. "What'd I tell you?" I pant. "I got you, gorgeous. Don't doubt."

"Mmm," she hums, reaching up to kiss my lips. "Won't happen again."

"Damn straight." I punctuate my declaration with another kiss. When I open my mouth around hers, she traces her fingers up my neck and sinks them into my hair, keeping me close. I kiss her deeper, transfixed by the way just her lips make my heart race. She sighs contentedly, causing my dick to twitch; then she groans, pulling at my hair as she severs our kiss.

"No. You can't get hard again."

"Wanna bet?" I chuckle.

"I'm serious, Sage," she says, cupping her hand around my mouth when I lean down for more. I can tell she's fighting a smile. She's so goddamn stubborn. "It's time for you to take me home."

I stick my tongue out, licking her fingers, and she gasps, pulling her hand away. I laugh softly, immediately dipping my head to pepper her neck with kisses. "You sure you can't stay? Rosemary really has been dying to meet you."

"Absolutely not," she sighs, absentmindedly tilting her head to grant me full access to what I want. "I have every intention of sneaking right through the front door."

I pull away from her, grinning when her eyes meet mine. "You're planning on *sneaking* out?" She nods and I bite back a laugh. "Remind me again which one of us is the immature one?"

"Hey," she protests, giving me a shove. "There's no way in hell I'm meeting *anyone* looking like some groupie sex kitten." With that, I burst out laughing, rolling away from her and onto my back. She sits up, shaking her head at me before she climbs out of bed.

"Come on, doll face. Give yourself some credit. You're far from a groupie."

She looks back at me from over her shoulder and rolls her eyes before she steps into her thong. "Anyway—meeting family was never part of our deal."

"It's not *not* part of our deal, either," I counter, standing to my feet as I remove the condom. I knot it and then toss it into the wastebasket next to my desk.

"Not happening," she tells me, slipping her arms into her bra straps before she pulls her shirt over her head. "At least not today."

"Fine. Not today." I accept the fact that Rosy's chances at an introduction would have been a lot higher had she *not* intruded on us while we were in such a compromising position. She'll whine about how much she wants to meet the girl who's turning me into a sap, but really, she brought this on herself. I've got more important things to discuss with the beauty whose scent now coats my skin. "Let's talk about our date."

"What date?"

"The date I'm taking you on," I reply nonchalantly, heading for my dresser. I don a pair of boxers and cutoff sweats before pulling a tank over my head. "Just you and me, doll face. How does Wednesday sound?" I ask, slipping on my glasses.

"Wednesday is the middle of the week."

A smirk graces my lips as I close the distance between us, circling my arms around her waist. I don't mention how impressed I am that she's more concerned about the day of the week I've chosen than the fact that I'm insisting we go out just the two of us. "Can't do Friday, baby doll, and Saturday is too far away."

"It's a school night," she protests.

"Come on, Professor Valentine. Break some rules. Live a little! You know I'll make it worth your while," I say, wiggling my eyebrows at her. She pauses and I can read hesitation in her eyes. I press my mouth against hers and then tug her bottom lip between my teeth before kissing her once more. "Millicent..." Her eyes widen and she sucks in a quiet breath at the sound of her name. Her reaction is so minute, if I wasn't paying attention, I'd miss it—but I'm always paying attention. At least, I am as far as she's concerned. "You know there's no use in arguing. So just say yes."

"Yes," she breathes.

"Wednesday," I murmur, cupping my hands around her ass.

"Wednesday."

"That's my girl." I slap her backside and smack a kiss against her lips before I pull away from her. "Alright. Let's sneak you out of here." I hold my hand out and her palm meets mine before I lace my fingers between hers. Then it hits me like a tidal wave.

> *"If I sneak you out the back, will you let me come?*
> *Take a chance, just one glance, and we'll both be gone.*
> *Let's run real fast, drive real slow where you wanna go.*
> *We'll blow through perfect towns/ We'll leave a mess behind.*
> *Forget the girl you were/ I'm not the boy I was*
> *You turn me upside down/ I'll make your world go 'round."*

The words stop just as quickly as they came. Without even thinking about it, I hum the melody once more, committing it to memory while I stare into Millie's dark green eyes. As the workings of a new song fade away, my muse is all I see. I kiss her—hard—in awe of the unexplainable way she inspires me. I've got it so fucking bad. I know I'm in way over my head—but when she kisses me back, gripping hold of my shirt as I part her lips with my tongue, I know she's who I want and I'm not sorry.

I pull away from her, resting my forehead against hers as I drag in a couple deep breaths. "Come on, doll face, before I forget I'm not allowed to get hard again."

She laughs and the sound makes my dick jerk.

Suddenly, Wednesday seems too far away.

FIVE

Sage

MILLIE DOESN'T LET me linger long after I drop her off. I'm back home within the hour, hungry as a motherfucker. When I walk inside the house, I head straight for the kitchen. Having spotted Rosy's old, red VW Bug still parked outside, I'm not at all surprised to hear her calling my name as I bypass the living room.

"Hey! Where have you been?" she asks, hurrying after me.

"Um, out," I grumble, unappreciative of her tone—as if I owe her an explanation of my whereabouts. If she thinks she deserves a damn thing after what happened earlier, baby sister has another thing coming.

"I went out to take Maestro for a walk and when I got back, you were gone. Where's Millie?"

I cough out a laugh as I step into the pantry, reaching for a box of cereal. When I turn around, my little sister is right behind me. Barefoot, she stands at the short height of five-two. Like me, the little bit of Italian blood we inherited from our mother is the reason behind her light olive tone skin and her deep, dark brown hair. Hers hangs long and thick halfway down her back. Her eyes are blue, too, just a few shades darker than mine. That's our Scottish blood's doing. I'd be an idiot to ignore the fact that she's a knockout. She's my sister, yeah, but I see it—as does every other dick who crosses her path. Keeping all douche bags out of her pants is a priority of mine.

Right now, however, she's just in my way.

"I took Millie home," I reply, gently but assertively pushing her to the side so that I can get to the refrigerator.

"Dammit. I freaked her out, didn't I?"

"No shit, Sherlock. What were you thinking, anyway? Don't you knock?" I ask, pulling the milk from the fridge.

Rosemary snatches the half empty gallon away from me, earning a frown. "It's almost three in the afternoon, Sage. You are not eating cereal."

"Back off, *mom*, I'm hungry," I protest, taking back the milk.

"Ha. Ha," she deadpans, turning to open the fridge once more. "You know mom would disapprove. Cereal is not a meal."

Ignoring her, I fill up a bowl, pouring too much milk, causing the colorful, fruity circles to spill over the top and onto the counter. As I shovel my first spoonful into my mouth, I watch Rosemary pull out lunch meat, cheese, mayo and mustard. A small smile tugs at my lips. She's such a caretaker, just like our older sister Pepper; and she's always trying to feed people, just like mom.

"How about you stop bitching about my food preferences and we get back to why you thought it was okay to invite yourself into my room without so much as a single knock?"

She grimaces, pausing as she sets out the bread. I lift my eyebrows in question, consuming another spoonful of my *non-meal*. I refuse to ease up on her, no matter how big her puppy dog eyes.

"'Sup, bro," greets Maddox, entering the room with his fingers wrapped around four empty beer bottles that he deposits in the trash. No one would guess it by the looks of him, but he likes to keep a clean house. The rest of us aren't slobs, but Mad Lips is always the first to start cleaning up from the night before. "Heard Baby McCoy walked in on you and Millie bumping uglies," he says with a sly grin.

I drop my spoon into my bowl and glare at Rosy.

"I'm sorry! I was a little flustered after, well, you know…I ran into Maddox on my way out with Maestro. It slipped."

I reach up and rake my fingers through my hair before I look over at Maddox. "For the record, there's nothing ugly about her pussy." He laughs, hopping up to sit on the counter top across from where I'm standing at the kitchen island. Rosy groans as she assembles my sandwich. "I'm still waiting, *Rosemary*."

"How was I supposed to know that you weren't alone?" she cries defensively. "You hardly ever bring girls over. I figured, since your car was parked outside and it was so late in the day, that you'd be alone. I said I was sorry!"

"Could have been worse," says Maddox with a shrug. "She could have caught you rubbin' one out."

"First of all," I pause, stick my hand in my pocket and then pull it out, flashing him my middle finger. "I don't have to rub out shit."

"Stop lying," he scoffs. "You're telling me she got you off even after Baby McCoy—"

I wink at him, reaching for my spoon in order to devour another huge bite. He barks out a laugh and sticks out his fist, clearly impressed. I knock my knuckles against his and Rosy reaches over to smack my arm.

"Don't be gross!"

"Hey," I begin to say with my mouth still full. "We wouldn't be having this conversation at all if it wasn't for you. Which brings me to point number two—I'm a one woman show now, which means you *knock*. Got it?"

"Believe me—I got it," she mutters, setting my sandwich beside my bowl.

"Hey."

"What?"

I wrap my arm around her shoulders and pull her into my side, pressing a quick kiss on the top of her head. She might be a pain in my ass sometimes, but she's still my best friend.

"Thanks for the sandwich."

She circles her arms around my waist as she looks up at me. "So, is she your girlfriend, then?" I shrug, not sure what label to put on *us* while, at the same time, not caring one way or the other that we seem to be undefined. I know she's not dropping her panties for anyone else and, for now, that's enough for me. "I want to meet her."

"Yeah," I reply, choking out a laugh as I reach for my bowl. With my arm still wrapped around her shoulders, her head is locked against my chest. She grunts and attempts to push away from me, but I'm stronger than she is. "Next time, you might want to make sure she's wearing *clothes*."

"Make sure who's wearing clothes?" Derrick asks as he joins us. He's in a pair of running shorts and tennis shoes, his iPod strapped to one of his bulky arms. Fresh from a run, he's still working to catch his breath as he brings his water bottle to his lips.

"Rose, here, walked in on Sage and Millie doing the dirty," Maddox is quick to clarify, pointing his chin in our direction.

Derrick scrunches his face at Rosemary and I can tell he's trying not to laugh. "Yikes. Bet seeing his naked ass was a bit traumatizing."

"Actually, now that you mention it," she mumbles, still smushed against my side.

"Whatever. I'm a fucking piece of art. Don't hate."

"Ew! God, Sage, let me go!" She pushes against me again, but I pretend not to notice as I take another bite. "You stink, by the way. I'm surprised she wanted to be anywhere *near* you."

"Rosy, Rosy, Rosy—don't you know she smelled the same way walking out of here? Scent of the Magic O, baby girl."

"Oh, dear god! Get the fuck off, Sage!"

Derrick and Maddox both laugh as I set her free. I reach over and palm the top of her head, turning her face toward me. "Don't talk like that," I teasingly chastise. She just rolls her eyes.

"You're gross. Now I feel like *I* need a shower. I'm getting out of here. But before I go, I have to tell you what I *originally* came over for."

"Shoot."

"I met this guy last night." I frown at her, already not liking where this is going. "Chill out, would you? This isn't about me, this is about *you*. Well, Mountains & Men. He plays the bass and he's looking for a group. I told him I'd put you in touch."

"Nice work, sis."

"We're doing auditions Tuesday," pipes in Derrick. "That is, if we can line up a few more guys."

"Guess we better get to it, huh?" asks Maddox, jumping down from the counter. "Just need to shower."

"Me, too." I abandon my now empty bowl and grab my sandwich as I begin backing out of the kitchen. "Garage in twenty?" The guys voice their agreement and then I look to Rosy. "You out of here?"

"Yup. Do your band thing. I'll catch you later. Oh—and the next time you talk to Millie, will you apologize for me?"

I offer her a nod and a smile, knowing she'll probably feel bad about this far longer than Millie or I will remember to care. "I got you, little lady."

Millicent

After Sage drops me at home, I head straight for the shower. With plans to spend the rest of my afternoon catching up on some grading, I know I need to rid myself of the scent of him. I ignore any and all meaning behind the truth that he's able to distract me even when we're not together.

The apartment is quiet and feels a bit empty with just me home, especially after spending the night at Sage's house. Not that Sarah and I make a habit of frequenting the same room. In the brief time that we've been living together, I usually only see her in passing. Her mornings start before the sun and, with Brandon in the picture, she's gone more times than not. Recently, she's even stopped coming home to sleep, except for a night here or there. I'm certainly not complaining. What she does with her time is her business. Furthermore, if she's happy, then she should keep doing whatever it is that she's doing.

I suppose, for some women, not all men leave.

Now, though, with her being out of town, the silence is different. Her parents were in a horrific car accident and she's gone to care for them. I have no idea when she'll be back, only that she left from work in a panic yesterday afternoon. Our neighbor, Aria, was kind enough to relay as much information as she could after she and Sarah arrived at the hospital where her parents were taken. Fresh from a shower, I decide to send Sarah a quick text, asking how Mr. and Mrs. Prescott are doing.

I suppose, for some people, not all moms and dads make you want to run away.

I know that it makes me sound like a god-awful person, but I cringe at the thought of what I'd be expected to do, as my mother's only child, if she were to ever get into an accident that left her in need of my help. When I left New Jersey eight years ago, it was with the intention to never go back. Not for holidays, not for birthdays, not for a random weekend visit. There's nothing about that place that I miss.

Growing up, it was just my mother and me. Grandparents, aunts, uncles, cousins—to me, they are simply a myth. After my dad left, even my *childhood* became more of a concept than a reality. I didn't leave behind anything that I wish to get back. Truth be told, if it weren't for my mother's phone calls—every other Saturday evening, like clockwork—I'd have absolutely nothing tying me to my past.

To a lot of people, loving one's mother is natural. It's not something they think about, it's just something they do. Even mothers far worse than mine are loved, sometimes to a fault. But my relationship with my own mother is more of an obligation than anything else. It's hard to love someone who stopped taking the time to show you love, even if she did give birth to you. No, my awareness of love is derived from the loss of it. I know the pain of love more than I know or understand its joy.

A text from Sarah pulls me from my thoughts. I shake them away, raking my fingers through my damp hair, unsure how long I was wandering around in my head. Drawing in a deep breath, I check my phone. Apparently, both of Sarah's parents are in better condition today than they were yesterday, which is definitely good news. I tell her as much before I grab my school bags and head to the living room.

I spread out on the coffee table, stacking each pile of assignments in order of priority. Once I'm all set, I head to the kitchen to grab a quick bite to eat. I'm certainly not a chef, even less so when I feel pressed for time, so I settle for a yogurt and a granola bar. Once finished, I make myself comfortable on the couch and lose myself in work.

I have a bit of a thing for numbers. I always have. They are constant. Reliable. I can trust them—trust that they won't ever change; trust that, no matter what ugly equation you put them in, they will always serve as your tool to solve the problem.

Math has been my strongest subject since I learned addition, and calculus is my favorite level. I enjoy teaching it. To me, it's fun to interact with the students who truly get it—whose minds are carefully, brilliantly sculpted calculators. It's also incredibly rewarding getting to help those who don't always understand. Chasing after that light switch, working to explain it in such a way that it all clicks in their mind—it's one of the best parts of my job.

I'm not like Sage. I've never really been a dreamer. I didn't dream of becoming a college professor. I didn't exactly chase after it, either. It just made sense. I earned my bachelor's, then my master's and then found my way back to the classroom—just on the opposite side of the desk. I've only been teaching for a couple of years, but as far as jobs go, I got lucky.

Thinking of Sage pulls me out of my numerical trance. Temporarily distracted, I notice that I've been working for hours. Having put a significant dent in my tasks, I decide to break for the rest of the night. Sage still lingers in my thoughts, and I can't help but wonder what he's doing. I haven't heard from him since he dropped me off hours ago. Not that he owes me a call or a text. He doesn't. We have plans to see each other in a couple days and that's enough.

Or at least, that's what I tell myself when I check my phone and spot not one new notification.

After I put away my things in preparation for the beginning of a new week, I opt for take-out and order Chinese. While I wait for it to arrive, I pluck a book from my shelf. Tonight, it's *War and Peace*. I read until there's a knock on my door and then I break only long enough to answer, pay the delivery man, and plate my food.

When I start to nod off, I clean up and then get ready for bed. I try not to think of Sage; try not to remember waking up in his arms this morning; try not to think of his lips all over my breasts; try not to think of the taste of his cock—I try not to miss him. I long for him. He's stolen a tiny fraction of my heart and I can't deny that I *do* long for him—but to miss him is dangerous. To miss him is something deeper than longing. So, as I crawl between the sheets, setting my phone on my nightstand, I try to push him out of my mind.

It's when I close my eyes that my mobile alerts me to a text.

I ignore the tingling sensation in my stomach when I see who sent me a message.

Sage: Hey, doll face. You up?

Me: Just heading to bed.

Sage: Too bad I'm not with you.

I press my lips together, fighting a smile as I try and combat the memory of his hands all over my body.

Me: I could use the sleep…it's probably better that you aren't.

Sage: I'm the perfect lullaby, baby. Didn't you know?

I pull my lip between my teeth as a chuckle forces itself from my chest, then roll my eyes.

Me: Goodnight, Sage.

Sage: Sweet dreams, gorgeous.

SIX

Sage

LITTLE BIRD CAFE IS, hands down, the greatest job I've ever had.

That is, unless you count the band. But to me, that's never been a job...more like a privilege.

Two years ago, after I quit the student life, I started working at my favorite coffee shop. Truth be told, when I first heard about the place, it wasn't because of their coffee. A couple times a month, they host an open mic night. The guys and I used to do an acoustic set when we could. That was back when we didn't have a regular spot at The Brew. In any case, the first few times I came here, it was all about the music. Then, when I needed a job, one conversation with Lori and I was in.

Lori used to own the joint before she sold it to Brandon. She was a really great boss, totally supportive of my music. I never got any grief about the times I needed off in order to play a gig. She understood, being the dream chaser that she is. Brandon's the same way. He's big on making sure he doesn't hinder his employee's abilities to have a life outside of work and, in some cases, school. My part time hours and wages aren't going to have me retiring any time soon, but they keep a roof over my head and food in the fridge. With five of us guys living in the house, rent is dirt cheap. Plus, with the money we earn from gigs, we do alright.

"Oh, shit," I mutter, spinning around on the stool I occupy behind the counter. I face Brandon, who has a pad of paper in his hands where he's scribbling something down as he takes inventory of what supplies we've got at the bar. I probably shouldn't bug him, but considering the topic I've got on my mind, I'm sure he won't be bothered. "I haven't asked about Sarah's parents. How are they?"

Just as I suspected, he stops what he's doing to address my inquiry. "They're a little better," he says, sliding his pen behind his ear. "They moved her dad out of the ICU this morning. Hopefully it's not too long before they'll both be released from the hospital."

"That's good. Any idea when she'll be back?"

"No," he answers simply, folding his arms across his chest. "I'm sure it'll be a few weeks, at least."

"That's rough."

I'll admit, I feel for the guy. He's got it bad for that girl. I'm talking head-over-heels-pussy-whipped in love. I know it's only been a couple days since he's seen her, but I can tell he misses her.

"Yeah. You're telling me," he says with a halfhearted chuckle. "But she's where she needs to be. I'll go down and see her Saturday night." He draws in a deep breath, as if steeling himself for the reality of the next four days. "What about you? What's going on with you and Millie?"

I can feel it as a grin spreads across my face and I can't even try and play it cool. No matter; Millie's definitely worth a smile. "Actually, I'm taking her out on a date tomorrow. A *real* one. Just the two of us."

"Nice. Where are you taking her?"

I open my mouth to respond and then frown when I realize I have no idea. We didn't talk about it. Granted, I could pick a place and call it good—but what if she doesn't like the restaurant I choose? I definitely don't want our first date to be a dud.

"Good thing I asked," Brandon says with a laugh, interrupting my thoughts.

"Damn. You're right. I don't usually do the dating thing. Feeding them isn't really my M.O., if you know what I mean."

"*Yeeeaah*," he replies with an amused scowl. "Look, it's not rocket science. What does she like?"

"Uh..." I reach up to scratch the back of my head. "Grilled cheese."

"Seriously?"

"What? It's true!" I say with a shrug.

"Right. Well, if you want a second date, I wouldn't advise taking her out for grilled cheese."

"No shit. Any recommendations?"

"Honestly, with the foodies around this town, you could go anywhere. Just find out what she likes. You won't lose your man-card for asking."

I nod at him, grateful for his advice. "Good call."

"Got your back, young blood," he says, clapping his hand on my shoulder before he heads to his office.

I pull out my phone with every intention of shooting Millie a text, but then I see the time. Noting that I'm off in twenty minutes, I wonder if it would be better if I called her. I haven't heard her voice since Sunday. I'm not too proud to admit that I miss it. Just like I miss her face. Her lips…

I slide my phone back into my pocket, a smirk tugging at the corner of my mouth. I just got an even better idea. At two o'clock on the dot, I bag up two cinnamon swirl coffee cakes, baked this morning by Brandon himself, and then head around to the opposite side of the counter so that Rachael can ring me up.

"Two, huh?" she asks, taking my cash. "Either someone's feeling hungry, or…" She let's her sentence hang unfinished, clearly seeking for me to finish it for her.

"Yup," I say with a wink.

"That's for a girl, isn't it?"

"I'll see you later, Rach," I reply, backing my way through the lobby.

"Sage!"

I offer her a wave, chuckling as I make my exit.

Millicent

"Millie, wait up!"

I stop walking, adjusting the straps of my tote over my shoulder at the sound of her voice. Lindsey Clark is a fellow math professor. Her office is located just across the hall from mine. As I look back at her while she hurries to catch up, I assume we're both headed for the same place.

I'm the youngest professor in the entire math department, but Lindsey isn't too much older than I am. At thirty-two, she exudes both maturity and youth—or, at least, the *glow* of youth. Much like my roommate, Sarah, there's something bright and timeless about the woman. Today, her rich brunette locks are contained in a chignon at the nape of her neck—a few curls hanging loose around her face. The purple dress she has on seems to make her brown eyes even darker, while the cut accentuates her admirable bust, thin waist, and curvy hips. She's taller than me, even when I'm in heels and she's in flats; so today, as we're both in heels, she towers over me.

It's her smile that makes her so eye catching. It lights up her whole face. She's the closest thing I have to a friend on campus and when she stops me, always genuinely happy to see me, I'm not bothered in the slightest.

"Good afternoon," I greet her as she closes the distance between us.

"Hey. Heading to your office?" she asks, pointing to the building just across the way.

"Yeah. You?"

"Mmhmm," she hums. We both resume walking at once. "I didn't really get a chance to chat with you yesterday. How was your weekend?"

Immediately, my mind is filled with thoughts of Sage. Up until now, I'd had a pretty good handle on my craving for him. Other than a few texts here and there, I haven't had any significant interaction with him since Sunday. I embraced the distance, knowing it was necessary; but, truth be told, a part of me…*dislikes* it. Now, it's as if the floodgates have opened and my entire body yearns for him. His touch. His kiss. His voice.

"Um, it was good," I finally manage. "Yours?"

"Totally boring," she says with a groan and a laugh. "Errands. Chores. Work. I haven't been on a date in weeks, which is really starting to kill me. I'm going to need to fix that soon, before I become a cat lady or something. Tell me your *good* weekend was more eventful than mine."

"I went out," I reply evasively. I haven't told her about Sage. In fact, I haven't mentioned him to a single soul that he doesn't know. I can't really explain why, but it doesn't seem like a very safe idea.

"Oh, yeah? Where'd you go?"

"Uh," I stall as we make our way through the doors of our building.

The sound of our heels echo through the quiet halls, amplifying instead of drowning out my silence. I take a breath and decide that telling her about Mountains & Men is not the same as telling her about Sage. I can share at least that much.

"I went to a concert, actually. A bunch of local bands were playing at The Moxi in Greeley."

"See? Now *that* sounds like a good time. Look at you, living it up! I'm impressed, Millie."

I laugh, not because what she's said is particularly funny, but because she has every right to be impressed. Me at a concert on a Saturday night is definitely a new, recently developed, and reoccurring habit.

"Millie, aren't your office hours in the morning?" she asks as we round the corner to our destination.

"Yes. Why?"

She smiles at me as she points in the direction of my door. There, sitting with his knees propped up and his focus glued to his phone, is Sage. As per usual, he's wearing a pair of jeans, a graphic t-shirt, and a pair of Chucks. My breath catches in my throat at the sight of him. Or maybe my sudden inability to breathe correctly has more to do with the erratic beat of my heart?

"Student of yours?" Lindsey whispers softly as we approach.

Before I can answer, Sage looks our way. When his eyes meet mine, his signature smirk curls his lips and he winks at me.

"Or an admirer?" Lindsey hums, elbowing me.

I look up at her, unsure what to say, and then back at Sage. He's standing now, looking devilishly handsome. I swear, I don't know how he manages to make *jeans* and a *t-shirt* so incredibly sexy. And don't even get me started on those glasses.

Lindsey giggles, pulling me from my thoughts and beckoning my attention. "Whoever he is, he's freaking hot! I expect an explanation later. Details, my friend. *Lots* of details." I say nothing in reply, which she seems not to mind. She waves at me and then slips into her office.

"Hey, doll face," Sage murmurs, leaning against the wall just beside my door.

"Hi. What are you doing here? How did you find me?" I ask as I unlock my office and step inside. He follows me in, shutting the door behind him.

"I'm a pretty smart guy, Millicent." I discard my things on the floor beside my desk and turn to face him. He's right behind me, holding open a small paper bag. "Take a whiff, baby doll."

I arch an eyebrow at him, feeling slightly suspicious, and he encourages me with a nod. I lean closer to him and then draw in a deep breath through my nose. I smell cinnamon and sugar and I know whatever is inside must be delicious. "What is it?" I ask, bringing my eyes up to meet his icy blue stare.

"Brandon's cinnamon swirl coffee cake. It's my favorite. He only makes it on Tuesdays. I thought you might like one."

"That was thoughtful," I murmur with a small smile.

"I have my moments," he says before tossing the pastries onto my desk. I blink and then his hands are cradling my head, titling my face up so that he might reach my lips. I stifle a moan when his mouth meets mine, my body leaning into his instinctively. Without thinking, I open up for him. When his tongue grazes mine, *he* moans, dropping a hand to the small of my back to draw me even closer.

Somewhere, in the back of my head, I remember that there is a narrow window just beside my door—a window anyone could look through and see us right now as we suck, lick, *taste*. Somewhere, in the back of my head, I know that this isn't professional in the slightest—but I don't care. I *can't* care. I've missed him.

Fuck. I've missed him?

When I reach up and circle my arms around his neck, I accept the fact that he's managed to steal another fraction of my heart. Him being here, going out of his way to search for me and find me, to bring me his favorite pastry, it's the kindest thing any man has done for me in a very long time.

And this kiss—*Jesus*, this kiss!

The small voice in the back of my head reminds me that I'm not allowed to fall for him—not anymore than I already have. I can't keep him. He won't stay. When he finally leaves, I have to be able to keep my shit together, which means he can't have my heart.

With all my might, I latch onto that truth and force myself to pull my face away from his. I gasp, surprised by how breathless I feel, and watch as he runs his tongue along his bottom lip as he attempts to catch his own breath.

"Have I told you, yet, how fucking hot you look right now?" he murmurs, his hands sliding down until they rest against the top of my backside. "I wouldn't learn shit in your class." I grin at him as I shake my head. "Do you always wear pants to work, doll face?"

"No," I mutter, scrunching my brow in confusion. "Why?"

"Because," he speaks softly, dipping his head to kiss my neck. "Your pants make it kind of hard to do what I wish to do to you right now. Maybe next time I drop by, I'll be in luck." He licks his way to my ear and then nibbles on my earlobe, making me shutter. Laughter rumbles from his chest as he gives my ass a squeeze and then pulls away from me completely.

I clear my throat, running my fingers through my hair as I try and get control of my damn pussy. I can't believe he just said that. Now I'm wet and wanting and he's—he's sitting on my desk, eating a cinnamon swirl coffee cake. He smirks at me when I look over at him and holds out the bag with the remaining treat inside. I snatch it away from him and plop down in my chair. Reaching inside, I pinch off a bite and drop it on my tongue as I look back over at him.

This time, I don't even try holding back my moan. It tastes even better than it smells.

"Good, huh?" I nod, breaking off another bite. "I knew you'd like it. And—speaking of food, I thought I'd let you pick where you wanted me to take you to dinner tomorrow night."

"Is that so?"

"Yeah," he says with a cool shrug. "I don't really know what you like. What's your favorite restaurant?"

I pause for only a moment, but it doesn't take me long to come up with my answer. "Giuseppe's."

His eyebrows shoot up in surprise and he chokes on his bite of cake at the sound of my answer.

"What? You have something against Italian cuisine?"

He pounds his chest and clears his throat as he shakes his head at me. "Italian blood runs in my veins, baby. I practically grew up on Italian cuisine. I just—I don't know. I didn't expect for you to say that."

"I grew up in Jersey. There was this one Italian restaurant I would go to a lot. It's one thing I actually miss about home. Giuseppe's is a close second."

The words are out before I can think through my admission. I don't know why I told him that. I don't talk about my life back in Jersey—not with anyone.

"Alright," he says with another shrug. "You sure that's your favorite place?"

"Yes, Sage, I'm sure," I reply, both amused and confused by his reaction.

"Okay, then. That's where I'll take you. I'll pick you up at seven."

"Okay."

He pops the last bite of his cake into his mouth as he checks the time and then stands to his feet. "I've got to jet. The guys and I are auditioning a couple bass players this afternoon. Wish me luck?"

"Good luck," I say, and mean it.

He leans down and presses a quick kiss against my lips. "Thanks, doll face." He kisses me one more time before he heads for the door. "Don't work too hard."

"Oh, I will," I chuckle. He looks back over his shoulder as he steps back into the hallway and offers me a wink. "Wait, Sage?" I ask, standing from my chair. He stops and leans into the room, bracing his hands on either side of the doorframe. "Thank you—for the coffee cake."

"Any time, gorgeous."

SEVEN

Sage

I WAKE WITH A START, sitting bolt upright as I search for my clock. I squint, in need of my glasses as I look to the wall to see what time it is. I barely make out that it's a quarter after nine. "Shit," I mutter, jumping out of bed. I must have forgotten to set my phone alarm before I was knocked out. It was a rough night.

I breathe a sigh of relief when I open my bedroom door and spot that no one is in the bathroom. Then, I waste no time before hopping in the shower. I make sure to grab my toothbrush along the way. As I wash my junk, I scrub my teeth—*who says men can't multitask?* I'm headed back to my room, a towel around my waist, when I run into Violet. In little more than one of JJ's t-shirts, she emerges from his bedroom, rubbing her eyes. Her short, blonde hair is a mess from sleep and I can't help but chuckle. She's kind of cute first thing in the morning.

"Hey," she grumbles. I know that she didn't have nearly as much to drink last night as the rest of us, in her attempts to stay sober enough to mediate the fucking Mountains & Men pity party, but I can tell she feels the effects of last night, too. "Oh, good. You're up." She yawns. "I wanted to check. I know you said you had someplace important to be this morning."

"I do. Thanks for checking. I have to move my ass if I don't want to be late, though."

"Mmm. Yeah. Don't let me keep you," she mumbles, shooing me away with her hand before she closes herself in the bathroom.

God. Sometimes, I don't know what we'd do without that girl. She belongs to JJ, but she looks out for all of us. Shit—she's one of us.

It takes me two minutes to throw on some clothes. I slide my glasses on my face and, not even bothering with my hair, I scoop up Maestro and head downstairs. I let him out back, giving him the chance to do his business while I fill a bag with some food for him and grab his leash. When I call him inside, he's obedient and comes running. He follows me through the house and out the front door to my car, jumping in when I open up the passenger side for him. I know I'm running late, but I decide to make a quick pit stop. I'm sure she'll forgive my tardiness if I bring her a peace offering.

Ten minutes later, I'm jogging into Little Bird, begging the powers that be that there isn't a line a mile long. Just my luck, Tabitha and Brandon are both behind the counter. By the looks of the full lobby, I just missed the craziness.

"Hey, Sage. What's up?" asks Tabbi.

"I need a sixteen-ounce soy, caramel latte—extra hot and as fast as possible. I'm late." I rattle off my order and then offer her a pleading grin.

"Coming right up," she hums, returning my smile with a flirty one of her own.

The girl has it bad. Not to sound like a prick, but it's completely true. I try not to encourage her. She's cute and all, but I don't bag my co-workers. I thought about it once. Then, for a split second, I imagined having to work with her day after day and the awkwardness of her wanting more and me wanting nothing. Until recently, I liked to keep my options open. I preferred my hook ups to be simple with no strings attached. Tabbi's nice, but I knew she'd come with one big ball of string.

"You're not a soy man," says Brandon as he rings me up. "You going to see your sister?"

"Yeah. Sophia has a doctor's appointment this morning. I think she needs to get shots or some shit like that. Anyway, Harry's at work and she didn't want to have to take the boys, so I told her I'd watch 'em."

He lifts his eyebrows at me and then turns to grab a cup. He fills it with black coffee, slaps on a lid, then slides it to me across the counter. "No offense, but you look like you could use that."

I chuckle, immediately grabbing his offering, prepared just the way I like it. "Thanks, man. Rough night."

"Millie?"

I shake my head once. "Whiskey. Auditions didn't go as well as we'd hoped. If we don't find someone by the end of the week, we're up a fucking creek. We need someone who knows his shit backwards, someone committed, someone who fits."

"You know…" he pauses, folding his arms across his chest as he strokes his chin. "I might know someone."

"Don't mess with me man," I mutter before taking a sip of my coffee.

"No, I'm serious."

"And you're just telling me about this now?"

"Sorry," he laughs. "It *just* clicked. Name's Alex."

"Well, give *Alex* my number. That is, if this *Alex* character has what it takes."

"Trust me. You won't be disappointed. I can't believe I didn't think of connecting you two before. I'll pass along your number for sure."

"Thanks, man."

"Who's Millie?" asks Tabbi, sliding my sister's finished drink across the counter.

I look to Brandon and I can tell he's biting back a laugh. "A friend," I answer simply.

"Oh, did you decide where you're taking her tonight?" Brandon asks.

"She wants to go to Giuseppe's."

"Wait—what? Isn't that—?"

"Yeah," I say with a shrug, backing my way to the door. "I know. But what the lady wants, the lady gets."

"Good luck, kid," he calls out with a laugh.

Even though my hands are full, I still manage to flip him off—with both middle fingers—as I join in his laughter. "I'll see ya."

Fifteen minutes later, when I pull up to the Montgomery residence, already feeling the rejuvenating power of my cup of Joe, I hurry to the front door. I ring the bell and wait with Maestro on the porch, preparing myself for Pepper's wrath in response to my tardiness. Instead, I'm caught off guard when I'm greeted with a smile.

"Somehow, I just knew ten a.m. on your day off would be a bit of a struggle for you. Oh, is that for me?" She opens the door, handing me my beautiful niece as she takes the latte. "Mmmm," she hums after her first sip. "You love me." She sighs and then nods for me to follow her inside.

"Um, what's going on?" I ask, confused. I step into the house and watch as Maestro goes charging for the noise. The boys are obviously in the next room playing.

"I don't have to leave until ten-thirty. So you're not fifteen minutes late, you're fifteen minutes early."

I gape at her for a moment as she turns to smirk at me in the entryway of her home. "Christ, Pep. I busted my ass getting here."

"I appreciate it. Now you have a few minutes to chat with your big sis. And watch your language, for crying out loud. My precious girl can hear, you know?"

I smile down at my niece, barely over a month old, who looks up at me with her pretty brown eyes. I press a gentle kiss against her forehead, amazed at how much she looks like Pepper. "Sorry, Soph."

"Kitchen," says Pepper with another nod. "Don't let the boys see you."

We sneak by the living room, where the boys are busy with Maestro, and head into the kitchen. They love my French bulldog; so much so, they haven't connected the dots that if *he's* here, so am I. Once we're out of sight, Pepper leans against the counter and looks at me intently from over the rim of her cup.

Unlike Rosy and me, she inherited more of our father's features. Her skin is milky white, and her shoulder length hair, worn back in a ponytail more times than not these days, is a dark reddish brown color. While Rosy and I both have blue eyes, Pepper got mom's brown eyes. When we were younger, she used to complain about how different she looked from her younger siblings, but she got over it. She's beautiful, even now—soft around the edges after giving birth to her third child. She amazes me, really. Except, at the moment, that look in her eye has me feeling more suspicious than anything else.

"Why are you looking at me like that?"

"So, I talked to Rose yesterday. She had quite the interesting story to tell me."

"Oh, good god!" I groan, rolling my eyes.

Pepper laughs, her amusement lighting a twinkle in her eye. "We won't talk about it," she assures me, for which I am grateful. "But as a fair trade, you have to tell me *something*. One girl—four weekends. That's pretty impressive."

"I told you. I want her."

"So it's going well? She's over the age thing?"

"We're working on it. I'm taking her out tonight."

"Oh, yeah?" she asks, lifting her eyebrows at me. "Where?"

I clear my throat once before I respond. "Giuseppe's."

She immediately covers her mouth with her hand, but it does nothing to silence her gasp. "You *are not* taking her there."

"It's where she wants to go. It's her favorite place. What was I supposed to say, *no?*"

"Oh, Sage. You *do* want her, don't you?"

We're interrupted by a high pitched scream followed by crying. Pepper sets her coffee down, all thoughts of Millie and Giuseppe's fleeing her mind as she starts for the next room.

"Wait—no, no," I insist, handing her Sophia. "I got it. You get her ready to go."

"You're sure?"

I give her my best, *oh, please,* expression. "I'm Uncle Sage. *I got this.*"

As soon as I walk into the room, Carter, my two-year-old nephew, looks over at me and instantly stops crying. I can't help but chuckle as I drop to my hands and knees and crawl toward him and Henley, my four-year-old buddy. I reach out to wipe away Carter's alligator tears and he smiles at me before he starts chatting. Whatever was bothering him before, it's certainly not bothering him now.

Like I said. I'm Uncle Sage. I got this.

Millicent

By some miracle, I manage to get through my entire work day without being cornered in a room by Lindsey. I know the day is coming. I know she'll have endless questions about Sage—my *admirer.* I haven't dated anyone since I started working at the college. The last guy I was silly enough to fall in love with left me just before my very first class.

Literally. Right. Before.

Needless to say, I haven't had anyone to talk about. Neither am I a woman who kisses and tells, so it's not as if she's heard about every single one-night stand I've had over the past two years. I'm sure seeing Sage waiting for me at my office speaks *volumes* in her mind.

Then again, to say that it doesn't speak volumes in my own mind is a lie unworthy of the effort. The same goes for denying the anxious anticipation that has my stomach tingling as I finish my makeup. I'm excited to see him. There's no point in lying about it. No one would believe me, not even myself. He texted me earlier, warning me what would happen if I backed out at the last minute. When I assured him I wouldn't, he told me he'd spank me anyway, if I so desired.

I have to take a deep breath, pushing aside all thoughts of him bending me over the couch…

My tongue glides across my glossed lips as I close my eyes, losing the battle against my memory.

Smack!

"That's for saying I have the maturity level of a fifteen-year-old."

Smack!

"That's for ignoring my calls."

A shiver races down my spine as my eyes flash open. Looking at myself in the mirror, I notice my cheeks are flushed, as if he fucked me five minutes ago.

"Fucking hell," I cry out, cupping my hands around my face. "What is happening to me?"

Just then, a knock sounds at the door, making my heart race—and therein lies my answer.

Sage. Fucking Sage McCoy is happening to me.

For a moment, I don't move. My reflection is like a bright neon sign, warning me that I'm doomed. With every day that goes by, I want him a little more. Right here, right now, I could cut my losses. I could tell him that I can't do this. That I can't be exclusive. That I can't be his *doll face.* But in truth, I can feel my body rebelling against the thought. I can feel his pull from beyond the barrier that's keeping him out of my apartment right now. I practically came, *just seconds ago*, remembering how good it feels to be owned by that man—that twenty-one-year-old man with a voice of a rock star and a body of a god.

I *am* his *doll face*, his *baby doll*, his *gorgeous girl…*

I am Millicent, the woman with the fractured heart, never to be whole again; and that bastard is chipping away at me, piece by piece.

"Doll face?" he calls through the door, banging a little harder.

I take another deep breath, nodding at my reflection—silently assuring myself that I will survive this fall. *I will.* Then, without looking back, I hurry to meet him. When I open the door, his face goes from flustered to relieved to stunned. I watch as his eyes travel from my head to my toes and then back up again. I can feel the heat that spreads across my chest and up my neck, and I curse my body for being so damn transparent.

"You look—*amazing*," he murmurs.

Giuseppe's isn't the fanciest Italian restaurant in town. In fact, that's part of the appeal. It has more of a homey feel, a lot like the place where I ate growing up. Nevertheless, I figured a date with Sage called for a dress, at the very least. I chose my dark green bandage dress with the capped sleeves and the zipper that goes down the front. I paired it with my nude stilettos; and even with the extra height, Sage still has at least three inches on me.

He's wearing black Chucks and black jeans—which is not the least bit surprising—but he's completed his ensemble with a gray button-up shirt, the sleeves rolled and pushed up over his elbows, exposing the generous amount of ink on his left arm.

God, he's sexy.

"You look nice, too," I say, feigning a sense of calm I have yet to grab hold of since he first knocked at the door.

He smirks at me as he takes a step in my direction. Then he reaches around my waist, pulling me against him tightly. "You feel that?" I can hear it as my breathing grows shallow in response to my awareness of him. My lips part in an attempt to suck down more air. "Do you feel that, doll face?" he asks again, sliding his hand a little lower, pulling me a little closer. I manage a nod and his smirk grows wider. "With you in that dress, this will be a very long and uncomfortable meal. I think you've earned yourself a little punishment, baby doll."

I reach up, gripping my hands around the back of his neck. "Just shut up and kiss me."

His chuckle is lost in my mouth as I free a sigh into his. One of his hands rests securely just below the small of my back and the other slides up and around my neck, his fingers buried in my hair. He kisses me long and hard and I know my lips are starting to swell, but I don't give a single shit.

"Fuck. Me. Millie," he breathes against my lips. He rests his forehead against mine and I can tell he's staring at the small amount of cleavage I'm able to manage in this dress. He shakes his head and then backs away from me. "If we don't leave now, we'll never leave. And I promised you a date, gorgeous." He holds out his hand, wiggling his fingers. "Let's jet."

I nod, turning to grab my clutch from off of the coffee table, and then wrap my fingers around his. He gives them a squeeze as I shut and lock the door behind us, and I swear, another piece of my heart goes missing.

EIGHT

Millicent

HE WALKS ME TO his car—his *black Audi convertible*—and opens the passenger side door for me. I remember the first time he made the same gesture. I was drunk and desperate with desire, anxious to leave The Brew Cycle so that we could be alone; but I wasn't so out of it that I didn't take note that his vehicle didn't seem to make sense in regards to what I knew about him. Three and a half weeks later, it *still* doesn't make sense.

How does a twenty-one-year old college drop out—part time rocker, part time barista—own such a sleek, modern, sexy sports car?

As he slides into the driver's seat and starts the engine, I decide that I've endured the mystery for as long as I can. "Sage?"

"*Millicent?*"

I fight the urge to press my hand against my chest, but I so desperately want to. It's stupid, of course, but the irrational part of my brain assumes that if I cover up the place where my heart resides, then he'll stop stealing bits and pieces of it.

For reasons I cannot explain, I adore the way he says my name. My *full* name. No one calls me Millicent. Since I was a child, I've introduced myself as *Millie*. It's not that I don't like *Millicent*, it was just easier to use my nickname. Then, of course, there's my mother, who hasn't called me by either of those names since I was six years old. To her, I am *Tatiana*, or *Tati*. After my father left us, she refused to refer to me by the name that he had chosen. My middle name had been her choosing. Only *she* calls me Tatiana, and I don't respond to it fondly.

But when my name falls from Sage's lips—his rich, manly voice caressing it—it steals my breath. Every time. I'm sure he knows, which is why he does it, but I couldn't stifle my reaction even if I tried.

"Doll face?" he says with a chuckle, reaching for me. His warm palm covers the top of my hand before he laces his fingers between mine, holding my hand upside-down. For a second, I wonder why he's positioned our hands this way, and then it clicks as he moves them over the gearshift. I wrap my fingers around the smooth surface and he clutches mine effortlessly as he accelerates down the road, shifting to a higher gear.

Now, I'm feeling oddly turned on.

He chuckles again, pulling me from my thoughts, and it dawns on me that I haven't said a word since I spoke his name.

"Um—I've been meaning to ask you about this car."

"What about it?"

I furrow my brow when I realize that every version of my question sounds horribly rude. As if he can read my thoughts, he speaks before I can.

"You want to know how I can afford it." He doesn't phrase it as a question, but as a statement. I look at him hesitantly and he peeks over at me with a knowing smirk. All I can offer in return is a nod. "It was a gift from the good *Dr. Harold Montgomery*," he says, exaggerating his emphasis on the name I've never heard.

"Who is that?"

"My brother-in-law," he says with a grin.

I shift in my seat, turning toward him as much as my seatbelt will allow. His answer only sparks more questions. "I'm confused," I admit. "Your brother-in-law gave you a sports car and Rosemary drives an old, beat up, VW Bug?"

Sage laughs. "Better not ever let her hear you talk about her baby in that tone. She loves that thing."

"Sage," I mumble, wishing for a straight answer.

He sighs, giving my fingers a squeeze before he concedes. "When Pepper turned sixteen, my parents bought her a car. When I turned sixteen, they bought me one, too. When I turned *eighteen*, I pissed them off and they took it away and gave it to Rosy on her sixteenth birthday."

"So you used to—"

"No," he cuts me off with a shake of his head, sure that he knows what I was about to say. "Rosy only drove my old car until she graduated high school, at which point she had saved up enough money to buy the car she drives now. It was her way of asserting her independence.

"Anyway, I went about a year without a car. It wasn't a big deal. I'd moved into the house with the guys by then and they helped me out when I needed it. Plus, we weren't so far from campus that I couldn't bike when the weather was nice. Then, for my nineteenth birthday, Harry and Pepper decided to gift me with this. It was Harry's. Carter had just been born and, with two kids in car-seats, he needed something more practical."

"That's very generous."

He nods and I watch as a small smile pulls at the corners of his mouth. "Yeah. You're right. It was sort of their way of showing their support."

"What did you do to piss your parents off?"

"I didn't choose the college they wanted," he replies with a shrug. "And when I told them I wasn't going to leave the band for school, they told me I was free to do whatever I wanted—just not on their dime."

Again, his answer floods my mind with more questions; but this time, I keep my mouth shut. I know, eventually, my curiosity will get me into trouble. I certainly don't want to talk about my parental issues, so I won't badger him to talk about his.

"What about you? How'd you end up in Fort Collins when you grew up in Jersey?"

"Oh, well…" I pause, completely aware that his broaching the topic of my relocation is entirely my fault. If not for me starting the conversation with my nosey questions, then for me agreeing to go on this date in the first place. It's just as he told me weeks ago—getting to know each other is what dating is all about.

I decide that avoiding the topic of my mother is paramount, and I come up with the most vague explanation possible. "I just wanted to go somewhere different—be somewhere far away. I only applied to universities in the west, and Colorado State appealed to me the most. So—here I am."

"You never thought about going home after graduation? You don't miss it?"

"No. I don't miss it at all," I answer, the words coming out faster and harsher than I intended.

He gives my fingers a squeeze and I look over at him when he lifts my hand to his lips, kissing my palm as he smiles over at me. "You just miss your favorite Italian restaurant."

Grateful for the segue, and for his awareness that the topic of *home* is an uncomfortable one, I smile and nod at him. "Precisely."

Given that it's the middle of the week, Old Town Fort Collins isn't crazy busy. There are definitely enough people out, seeing as the weather on this fine September evening encourages an outing, but it's not so crowded that we can't find parking. As we exit the car, crossing the street to head the short distance to Giuseppe's, Sage takes my hand. I can't help but notice that it's becoming another habit of his—one that I kind of like, which worries and thrills me at the same time.

The Italian restaurant is located just a couple doors down from the corner, in a long stretch of food places that line the street. When we step inside, the hostess looks up at us and *immediately* her eyes brighten at the sight of Sage. I don't think much of it at first, as I've seen the way women respond to him—myself included—but then the glint in her eye turns mischievous before she speaks.

"Hey, *stranger*," she practically purrs. "Long time, no see." She props her arms against the hostess stand and leans forward, exposing a generous amount of cleavage that puts mine to shame. Suddenly, I wonder if I'm invisible.

"Hi, Kathy," Sage replies, his tone seemingly indifferent. "Table for *two*, please," he says, lifting our joined hands.

Finally, she looks my way. Feeling suddenly visible again, I smirk at her, boasting with my eyes that while she mans the door, I'll be enjoying a meal with the delicious man whose fingers are wrapped affectionately around mine.

I'm being quite the silent bitch, but I don't care.

I won't bother reading into *why* I feel the need to stake any sort of claim over him, either. He's not my boyfriend.

Kathy clears her throat, standing upright as she picks up two menus. "Right this way."

We're seated on the edge of the room, at a table for two, and she leaves us with not another word.

"Friend of yours?" I ask, arching an eyebrow at him.

"Not really." He nods to the narrow menu in the middle of the table. "You like wine, right?"

"Yes."

"Pick one. I'll have whatever you have."

"Okay." I pick up the menu and scan the list before it occurs to me—"I assume you'll be having pasta?" He nods once, smirking at me. He hasn't even bothered to look at the food options. "What kind of sauce?"

"I like a mix of marinara and alfredo."

"Hmmm," I hum, perusing the list once more. When I've decided what wine I think would pair well with my usual order and, apparently, his usual, I fold the menu closed and set it down. Before Sage can ask me what I'm ordering, our waiter arrives. He starts to introduce himself, but then pauses when he recognizes Sage.

"Hey! What's up, man? Surprised to see you here. Oh, I was at The Wash last time you and the guys performed. You sounded pretty damn sick!"

Sage looks from the yet-to-be-named waiter, to me. It's only a quick glance, but I can tell by the regret in his eyes that when he thinks about that night, it's not the show that immediately comes to mind, but what happened after.

"Thanks, Jacob."

"Does Rosemary know you're here?" he asks, craning his neck as he looks around the room.

"Shit," Sage murmurs under his breath.

I sit up straighter, remembering the last time I had a run in with Sage's younger sister. To say that I'm not really prepared to meet the woman who saw me naked just a few days ago would be an understatement. When Sage starts looking around the room as well, I step on his foot underneath the table, demanding his attention. His eyes are on me in an instant.

"Your *sister* works here?"

Jacob snorts. "His whole—"

"Can it, Jake," Sage mutters, his gaze still locked with mine. "And get us some water while you're at it, will you?"

Jacob leaves without a word. Considering Sage's rude dismissal, I'm sure the expression on his face is doing all the talking, but I don't see it. I refuse to take my eyes off of the icy blue ones they are focused on now.

"*Sage?*"

"*Millicent?*"

"No. Don't. Don't do that." I narrow my eyes at him, and all at once, I begin to piece a few suspicious clues together. His initial reaction to my suggestion of this place. His familiarity with the staff. His awareness of the menu. "You're hiding something. Something bigger than the fact that your sister works here. What is it?"

He doesn't answer me at first. Just when he opens his mouth to speak, a pair of arms fling around his chest and an absolutely stunning face appears on his shoulder. I know who she is without an introduction. I've never actually *seen* Rosemary, a completely humiliating thought, but you could spot the family resemblance between her and her brother in the blink of an eye.

"Holy shit! I *cannot* believe you're here! Mom and dad—"

Sage twists around just enough to clap a hand over her mouth. "Tell them I'm here, and I won't speak to you for a month. Do you hear me, Rosy? *A month.*"

"What the *fuck?*" The words tumble from my lips of their own accord. I didn't mean to say them, but I'm having a hard time keeping myself together. If I'm understanding them correctly—"Your *parents* work here?"

"What the hell, Sage," Rosemary blurts out, pulling his hand away from her face. "You didn't tell her?" Again, he opens his mouth to speak, but she looks at me and steals his chance to explain. "Our parents own this place. Mom's the executive chef. Giuseppe was our great-grandfather's name."

Sage groans, tilting his head back as he looks up at the ceiling. "*Fuck*—Rosemary, *stop talking!*"

"What?" she asks innocently. "There's no need to be shy about it. I'm Rosemary, by the way," she says, offering me her hand. "You can call me Rose. I've heard so much about you." Her cheeks fill with color and I have a guess where her mind just went. "Anyway, I've been looking forward to meeting you."

I feel like I can't breathe. My eyes dart from Rosemary's outstretched hand, to her face, to Sage's face, then back to Rosemary. I don't know what triggers my brain to shake her hand, but I do. She beams at me, but all I can think about is the fact that Sage's parents are somewhere in this restaurant and I can't do this! I can't meet his parents. I'm the woman their son is sleeping with, not the woman he's meant to bring home.

Home. God, I barely even understand what that word means to me, *let alone what it means to Sage and his family.*

And don't even get me started on the concept of family.

"Why did you bring me here?" I ask him, dropping his sister's hand.

"Hey." He leans across the table and brushes his knuckles down my cheek. "Breathe, baby doll." I bat his hand away, but he catches my fingers and holds onto them. "I'm sorry I didn't tell you. I wouldn't have brought you here if you hadn't told me it was your favorite. I didn't know Rosy would be here. I thought we could be in and out without anyone even knowing."

"I won't tell them that you're here," Rosemary promises. "But..."

"But what?" asks Sage. Just like earlier with Jacob, he doesn't look at Rosemary as he addresses her. Instead, his focus stays locked on me.

"Well, if you order your usual, mom will know."

"Sage," I barely manage, shaking my head as I try pulling my fingers out of his grasp.

"Don't you fucking dare, doll face." He laces his fingers with mine and then stands to his feet. "How do you feel about burgers? There's this place down the block—"

I'm on my feet in an instant, willing to go anywhere that will get me out of here.

"You're really leaving?" asks Rosemary, obviously disappointed.

"I haven't stepped foot in this place in almost two years. I'm only here because of Millie, and if she doesn't want to stay, I'm not staying."

"Yeah. Okay."

I watch her shoulders sag and I see the compassion in her eyes as she stares up at her brother. Somehow I know that the love they share is deep and wide, their bond thick and impenetrable. I'll never know a sister's love like that. Hell—not even my mother loves me like that.

"Call me later?"

"Tomorrow," he assures her, playfully placing a hand on top of her head and messing up her hair before he leads me out.

He doesn't say a word as he guides me down the sidewalk, heading to grab a burger, I suppose. At first, I'm not sure what to say. I can't tell if I'm angry, irritated, or curious. This is not at all how I thought our evening would transpire. A couple minutes ago, I felt completely blindsided; but the more distance that is put between us and Giuseppe's, the more my anxiety dissipates. After another moment of silence, it's my curiosity that begs me to speak.

"If you didn't want to go there, why didn't you tell me?"

He coughs out a humorless laugh as he looks over at me. "Do you realize how long I've been trying to get you to go on a date with me? I wasn't going to argue with you about where you wanted to go."

"But your family's restaurant? You could have said something."

"I know. God, I know," he groans. He stops walking and pulls me into his arms. "I'm sorry. I fucked up, okay? Can we *please* just forget the last fifteen minutes and start over? You look hot and there's no way in hell I'm taking you home without feeding you." He arches a brow at me suggestively. "You'll need the sustenance for energy."

I bite my lip in an attempt to hide my smile, appreciative of the fact that the flirty, arrogant little shit is back. Am I ready to meet his parents? *Fuck no.* But that wasn't his intent. If what he said to Rosemary is true, then he was making a sacrifice for me tonight. Just like the surprise visit and the cinnamon swirl coffee cake, this is gesture that I cannot overlook. With his arms wrapped around me, keeping me close, I realize that I'm not ready for him to take me home, either. Being here with him is the only place I want to be right now.

"Do these burgers come with fries?" I ask, gripping a fist full of his shirt in order to pull him even closer. "Because I *love* fries."

"I'll buy you all the fries you can eat, baby doll," he assures me, sealing his word with a kiss.

NINE

Sage

MILLICENT WASN'T KIDDING about her love for fries. I finish my burger before my fries and she finishes her fries before her burger. When I spot her eyeing my basket, I chuckle and then switch them. She smiles at me from across the table and I offer her a smirk as I pick up her half eaten sandwich.

Words can't express how relieved I am to see the light in her pretty, dark green eyes. After what happened at Giuseppe's, I thought for sure I'd be in deep shit. The look on her face when Rosy told her that not only did our parents own her favorite restaurant, but they were also in the building, it about put me in straight up panic mode. Thank fuck I got her out of there and, as far as I can tell, she's having a good time.

We steer clear of any heavy topics of conversation as we talk about a bunch of random shit. She tells me more about her job and I tell her more about the band. We talk about the places we've been and, surprisingly, neither of us are very well traveled. Of course, I dream of seeing the world—singing at venues in every country. She admits that she aspires to visit Russia; that she longs to see the land in which some of her favorite novels are set, even if it's a more modern representation than what she's read. I'm not at all surprised to learn that she's a fan of classic literature, just as she's not surprised that I am not.

When we've finished with our meal, I dispose of our trash and meet her at the door. I approach slowly, taking her in for the dozenth time since she answered her door at the beginning of the night. Her dress reminds me of every delicate curve on her body and accentuates her long-ass legs and her perfect ass. I know mine isn't the only cock that stirs at the sight of her. Every guy in this joint has checked her out, but I can tell she hasn't noticed.

She has no idea how fucking gorgeous she is.

"Let's get out of here," I tell her, securing my arm around her waist.

As we start our walk back to my car, she grows quiet. I wonder what she's thinking, and I'm about to ask when she finally speaks.

"Can I ask you a question?"

"Yeah," I reply with a shrug.

She looks at me as she reaches up to tuck a few strands of hair behind her ear. "You said that you hadn't been to Giuseppe's in almost two years. Does that mean you haven't seen your parents in just as long?"

"Nah," I reply. "We see each other. I have my pride, but I'm not an asshole. I show up for holidays and birthdays."

She nods and I can tell she wants to know more, but she doesn't ask. After the way she shut down on me in the car when I asked her about New Jersey, I'm smart enough to figure out that she has no desire to talk about whatever beef exists between her and her parents—but I have no issue with being honest. Truth is, the rocky relationship I have with my mom and dad is just further proof that I'm chasing after a dream and I'm not going to let anyone or anything stop me.

"Remember how I told you my sisters and I all got cars for our sixteenth birthdays?" She hums her affirmation, the look in her eyes communicating that I've got her full attention. "Well, that's also when we had to start working at Giuseppe's. They wanted to teach us about the value of a dollar and all that; plus, they weren't about to pay for our gas to drive everywhere. Anyway, Pepper worked there until her sophomore year of college, until she found an internship in her field of study. I dipped as soon as I graduated high school. Moved out and everything.

"Our relationship was a little strained after that, but I still hung around. Then a year and a half later, when I decided I was done with college, they lost their shit." I shake my head, remembering that conversation—if you could even call it that. It was mostly them yelling at me and telling me I was ruining my future. "To this day, they still believe I'm wasting my talent."

"I don't understand. Haven't they seen you perform?"

"No, not really. I mean, they used to listen to Knox, Maddox and me mess around, but they hoped I was going through a phase."

"If they've never heard Mountains & Men, then how can they argue that you're wasting your talent?"

I look at her, studying her expression as I try to think of how to explain. I can tell by the way she's staring at me that she's genuinely interested in my answer. Her question implies that she believes I'm not wasting my talent at all. She's told me before how much she loves the band, how much she enjoys seeing us perform; but just like the other night—when she told me that she hoped the whole world would sing with me—I can feel her belief in *me*. It makes me want to kiss her.

I press my lips to hers softly. She leans into me, just slightly, and I kiss her again before I turn us around, leading us back in the direction we came.

"What—where are we going?"

"I want to show you something," I tell her with a sly grin. "We passed it, though. Come on."

We don't have to walk very far before I see it—the alley I've been to more times than I can count. As far as alleys go, it's about as dangerous as a well lit room. It's wide, the walls covered in paintings with lights strung up along the way. It leads to The Square, where small shops and more restaurants are located. What I'm looking for, though, is at the mouth of the entryway. The piano painted yellow with pink polka-dots.

Scattered throughout Old Town, there are about a half a dozen painted pianos. I know the location of every single one. I've spent many a drunken night, after hours at the bar, wandering around in search of the out of tune contraptions.

I pull out the bench and sit. When I look up at Millie, she's eyeing me suspiciously. "Come 'ere, gorgeous," I insist, holding out my hand.

She wraps her fingers around mine and follows my tug. I guide her down into my lap so she's sitting on my right thigh, her body turned so that I can still see her face. "What are we doing?"

"I told you," I murmur before kissing her cheek. "I want to show you something."

I poise my hands on top of the ivory and ebony keys in front of me and pause for a moment, clearing my head as I search for the notes I'm looking for. When I find them, I begin to play. Millie sucks in a breath as she sits up taller and gapes at me. I catch her eye and offer her a wink before I focus my attention back on my hands. Soon, all I feel is the music pulling me under. I close my eyes and surrender to the unstoppable force that is my passion. My fingers don't stop and I don't miss a single note or phrase; it always comes back when I sit in front of the instrument that I know as intimately as I've ever known any woman.

When I'm finished, I take a deep breath and then open my eyes. At the sound of a quiet applause, I look around and see that a few pedestrians have stopped to listen. I wave, dipping my head in thanks before I direct my focus back to the woman in my lap.

"Oh, my god, Sage," she mutters, her eyes wide in wonder. "What was that?"

"*That* was Beethoven. *That* was the piece that got me into Juilliard."

She jerks away from me, her lips parting as her mouth falls open. "Holy shit."

I shrug, reaching up to run my fingers through my hair. "When I was two, my mom brought home this toy piano. Apparently, I wouldn't play with anything else for weeks. When I was three, they started paying for my lessons. My parents are totally into the college thing, if you hadn't guessed, so I applied to all the schools they told me to. I knew I wasn't leaving, but a part of me just wanted to prove that I could get in anywhere. I got in everywhere—scholarships included. But that wasn't the dream. That's never been the dream."

I stop talking and wait for her to say something. And wait. And wait. I frown when she doesn't speak, her eyes just searching my face for I don't know what. Suddenly, I wonder if playing for her was a mistake; I wonder if, now that she's seen this part of me, if she thinks the same thing my parents do. She's a damn college professor, for crying out loud. No matter what she says, I know college matters to her.

"You think I'm wasting my talent too, don't you?"

She blinks and shakes her head, as if to clear her mind of whatever thoughts were keeping her silent. Then, she shakes her head again; only this time, at me. She surprises me when she places a hand to my chest with a small smile. "No," she speaks softly. "I mean, you're amazing. That—that was incredible. But, I've also seen you up on that stage. I see the way you love it, the way the crowd loves *you*. You were born to perform, there's no question about that. But, Sage, you were meant to grace the stage in jeans and a t-shirt—not a penguin suit."

I laugh as I wrap my arms around her, pulling her against me. She gets it. She *sees* me. I thought she was something special before. Now? Now, I want her even more.

I slide a hand up her back, into her hair, and around the nape of her neck, drawing her in for a kiss. With a single flick of my tongue, she opens up for me and frees a sigh. She shivers when I lick the roof of her mouth and then suck on her top lip. I grow stiff in my jeans when she wraps her arms around my neck, crushing her mouth against mine. She gives and I take, then we switch—both of us clinging to the other as we explore one another's mouths.

"Sage," she breathes, her lips still grazing mine. "Take me home. Get me out of this dress."

"You got it, doll face."

I CLOSE HER front door behind me, spinning the deadbolt before my heated gaze scours her from top to bottom. She hisses a breath in through her teeth, lifting her hair off of her neck and back, as if she's burning up under my perusal.

"Too hot in that dress, doll face?" I ask, my voice low and my speech slow.

She whimpers, biting her lip as she tilts her head to the side. Pulling one of her hands from out of her hair, she slides her palm down her neck and along the exposed skin of her chest. She traces her fingers along the top of her dress, toying with the zipper between her breasts before she slowly starts to slide it down. My eyes widen and my breathing grows ragged when I see that she's not wearing a bra. She stops the zipper's descent halfway, then traces her fingertips from the middle of her stomach, all the way up between her tits.

When I catch a glimpse of a small bruise on her smooth, flawless skin—a reminder of the last time I was inside of her—every bit of restraint in me *vanishes*.

In one, long stride, I close the distance between us, griping her hips as I pull her against me. I drag my lips along her neck, kissing her, tasting her, *needing* her. She moans as I lick the path she just made with her fingers, increasing my hunger.

I reach for the zipper, yanking it down without mercy. She's quick to shrug her arms free of the garment, and I growl when I notice that she's completely bared to me. I can't say whether or not the noise that rumbles from my chest speaks of my irritation that there's only been one degree of separation between her body and my mouth all damn night, or if I'm in awe of the fine ass woman who stands before me now—in nothing but a pair of fucking heels. Either way, it doesn't matter; I'm all over her in seconds.

I crash my lips against hers, kissing her hard and sloppy as my hands roam over her breasts, down her sides, around her ass. I squeeze her taut, yet malleable flesh, pressing her against the raging erection barely constrained by my pants. I can focus on only one thing right now—my mission to make her come over and over and over again. I want her to fucking *beg* me for more before she *pleads* for me to stop, her body too exhausted to endure one more moment of pleasure.

I pull away from her abruptly and she gasps, her eyes raking my face for an explanation. I look past her, down the hallway and through her open door, spotting her bed. I tip my chin, giving her one more squeeze before I step away from her. "Bed. Now. On your hands and knees, baby doll."

Slowly, she begins to back her way down the hall. When she reaches the halfway point, she kicks off one heel and then the other before she turns and saunters her way to the bed. I don't take my eyes off of her as she crawls into position, sticking her pretty ass up in the air. A grin spreads across my face, knowing she's completely aware of what she's doing—knowing she's completely aware of how much I love her ass.

I toe my way out of my shoes as I unbutton my shirt. Once the last button is loose, I shrug my arms free and begin to follow in her footsteps. By the time I've reached her door, I'm in nothing but my boxers, the condoms from my wallet held between my fingers. I can hear her rapid breathing as she waits for me and I'm sure her patience is wearing thin. I remove my last item of clothing, discarding my glasses on her dresser before tossing the rubbers beside her on the bed.

I bend down and kiss the small of her back, causing her to suck in a breath. Then I bite her ass and she whimpers. My dick jumps at the sound and I wonder just how long I'll be able to survive without being inside of her.

"Did I tell you to take off your heels?" I demand to know, rubbing her backside with my hands. She doesn't respond, so I smack her left side. Her back bows and I ask her again. "Millicent—did I tell you to take off your heels?"

"No," she barely manages as I rub small circles around the light red mark I've created on her skin.

"Do you think there should be consequences for taking them off?"

"Yes..."

She hardly gets the word out before I smack her right cheek, eliciting another pathetically sexy sound. I wouldn't consider myself a particularly kinky lover—but when a woman enjoys a good spanking, it turns me on to no—fucking—end. I smack her again and this time, it's my name that falls from her lips.

"What do you need, baby?"

"Oh, god—touch me. Please, Sage—make me come."

Smack.

"You want me, doll face? Are you *wet* for me?"

Smack.

"Yes. Yes—touch me."

I slide a hand down her back as I crawl up behind her, leaning over her as I sweep her hair to one shoulder. I lick her exposed ear and she whines when I suck on her earlobe. "Where do you want my touch, Millicent?"

"Don't tease me," she insists, her voice husky and dripping with lust. "I'm so close—so wet—just touch my fucking pussy and make me come, Sage."

Hearing her say that she's already close spurs me on and my arms are wrapped around her in an instant. With one hand gripping her tit and the other sliding its way to her sweet spot, I bury my face in her neck and breathe her in. Almost seconds after my fingers make contact with her clit, she's trembling beneath me.

"Goddamn!" I mutter, rubbing faster—harder.

She reaches back and grabs a fistful of my hair as she mewls, my name on her lips like she's chanting her favorite mantra. The scent of her arousal now fills the room, making my mouth water. I flip her over and spread her legs, dropping my head before she can protest. The second my tongue makes contact, she bucks her hips and cries out. I hold her down, devouring her sweetness, humming into the space between her slick flesh.

She's my favorite fucking candy
I'll always lick, lick, lick
'til the center of her tootsie pop
And if I bite/just know I might
She'll taste just right, all night
'Cause she's my favorite fucking candy

The words come to me as I lick, suck, and nibble. I repeat them in my head, committing them to memory, and then grin up at her. She's both totally unsuspecting of the lyrics she just inspired, and totally lost in her own moment of ecstasy as her hooded gaze locks with mine. When I graze my teeth over her clit, her head falls back and she comes again.

And if I bite/just know I might
She'll taste just right, all night
'Cause she's my favorite fucking candy.

TEN

Millicent

HE ALWAYS STAYS. Deep down in my soul, I'm sure that one day he'll grow tired of me; he'll leave and he won't look back—and yet, ever since that very first night, after he's done owning every single one of my orgasms, and after he's come as many times as the night will allow, he wraps me in his arms and *he stays*.

He's better at mornings than I am, and he's usually awake before me, holding me, waiting to greet me with kisses—some sweet and tender, some passionate and ravenous. Either way, I can't think of a better way to wake up. Seeing his beautiful, icy blue eyes admiring me first thing in the morning makes me want to stay in bed all day.

It also scares the shit out of me.

I draw in a deep breath and shake the thought away, my eyes scanning the assignments I have laid out on my desk—the assignments I'm supposed to be grading. I managed to find my focus to teach my first class of the day, and my second and third are in just a couple of hours. I should certainly be trying to get something done, instead of daydreaming about the pianist who played me and pleasured me just as well as he did that piano last night.

I run the back end of my green grading pen across my lips as I remember the end of our date—me in his lap as he played me *Beethoven*. Christ—he had blown my mind. I hadn't been expecting that sort of performance. He really is brilliant. I can see why his parents would be upset with him for choosing another path, even if I don't exactly agree with them. At the very least, he most certainly has skills to fall back on if he ever decides that it's time to move on from Mountains & Men. I knew he was good with his fingers—but watching them create music?

"Knock, knock!"

I'm startled out of my thoughts at the sound of her voice. Lindsey grins at me as she invites herself into my office and plops down into one of the chairs in front of my desk.

"Hi, Lindsey," I manage, trying desperately to clear my mind of anything and everything that reminds me of Sage.

"I know you know why I'm here, Mill." She wiggles her eyebrows at me playfully and I stifle a groan. "You managed to escape me yesterday, but I haven't forgotten that dark haired, blue-eyed Adonis of a man who was lurking around your office Tuesday."

"Oh," I mutter, wishing I could claim ignorance. "He's—" My conscious prevents me from assigning him the title of *nobody*. Every part of my body, *every part*, knows that would be a huge-ass lie. He's not *nobody...*

I fear he's becoming the exact opposite.

"He's...what?" asks Lindsey with a devious smile. "Hot? Sexy? Lickable?"

Yes. Yes. And absolutely, yes, I think to myself, still unsure what to tell her. He's not my boyfriend. We've only really been on one *real* date, in spite of the fact that over the last three, almost four weeks, he's made me come more times than I can remember. He's the only man I'm sleeping with, sure, but he's *not* my boyfriend.

He's also not a *friend*. I'm certain I've never had any friends who bite my—

"Millie!" she cries with a laugh. "Spit it out already. The suspense is killing me, over here."

"His name is Sage," I spit out with a self-conscious shrug.

"And you're...?"

"Undefined." I let the word hang in the air for a moment before I nod, sure that that's the best answer I can provide. "We're undefined."

"Hmm," she hums, narrowing her eyes at me. "And what does one *do* with Sage in the realm of *undefined?*"

We have sex. A lot. Earth-shatteringly, amazing sex.

I don't say the words aloud, but I can tell by the look on Lindsey's face that my silence eradicates my need for words. Then I feel the blush that fills my cheeks and I know I couldn't be anymore obvious even if I tried.

Fuck.

"I don't want to talk about it," I murmur, averting my gaze as I look into my lap.

"Why, Millie Valentine—I do believe you're *smitten*."

I flinch at the word, my heartbeat picking up speed as I bring my eyes back up to meet hers. I shake my head, but I can't find my voice. Now, I really wish that she would leave. I can't have this conversation. I won't.

Just then, there's a light knock on my open door and we both look back to see one of my students standing in the hallway. "Professor Valentine? Am I interrupting? I had a few questions about our last assignment."

I breathe a sigh of relief and Lindsey looks at me with a raised eyebrow. "We're not finished," she whispers, and I believe her. For now, though, I've been saved, yet again, by my love of numbers. They've never let me down and for that, I'm eternally grateful.

"Hi, Saundra. Come on in. Professor Clark was just leaving."

Sage

It's been another long ass afternoon. I look around the garage at the guys and the weight of our dilemma weighs on me even more. We just said good riddance to yet another wannabe bass player. It's the fifth one this week and I'm really starting to stress the fuck out. We all are. With this agent coming to see us play next weekend, now is our time. We need to have our shit together or we could miss our chance. Who knows when the next one will come around? These things don't just happen.

I slump down into one of the worn, comfortable couches we keep out here and tilt my head back. This place is home. And I don't just mean that in the sense that the garage is attached to our house. Never once have we parked a car in here. It's like our sacred place—meant only for the creation of music. We keep most of our shit out here, except for in the winter months when we store the instruments inside, where it's insulated and the cold won't get to them. But we'll practice out here no matter what the temperature.

Violet was the one who suggested we pick up a couple second hand couches and make the place a little more cozy. Sometimes, when any of us want to get away, we'll come out here and chill. Lately, it hasn't so much felt like an escape out here—more like a marooned ship. As time passes, we drift farther and farther away from civilization—farther away from any chance of finding a decent guy to make our band complete again.

"Is this Alex guy still coming?" asks Knox. He's sitting across the room on the other couch, his feet propped up on a small table as he absentmindedly plucks at his guitar.

"Yeah," I mutter, reaching into my pocket for my phone. Brandon had followed through, giving my number to Alex, who reached out to me yesterday. "He said he'd be here at four-thirty."

"It's four-twenty-nine," Maddox grumbles. "Fucker better show."

"Hey," pipes in Derrick.

We all look in his direction, where he sits behind his set. He tips his chin, signaling for us to look out of the open garage door. We watch a car pull up across the street. When the driver side door opens, I furrow my brow in confusion.

"Who's that?" Derrick asks.

I shrug, not even bothering to look back to see if he noticed the gesture. I'm too focused on the pretty girl reaching into her backseat to pull out—*Fuck. Me*—her bass guitar.

She straps the instrument across her back and then looks both ways, making sure there's no traffic before she crosses the street. The closer she gets, the more details I notice. She's got long dark hair, the curled ends died a rich purple, the front held back with a rolled up, yellow bandana. She's a tiny little thing, too; can't be more than an inch taller than Rosy, and probably weighs one-twenty soaking wet. In grey combat boots, jeans, and two tank tops—white over teal—she appears completely casual. I can tell, as she walks between the cars parked in the driveway, that she doesn't dress to draw attention to her body—but that doesn't mean she doesn't have a body worth looking at.

"Hey," she says hesitantly, offering all of us a small wave. "I'm guessing you're Mountains & Men?"

"Yeah," Maddox answers. "Who the hell are you?"

"I'm Alex. I talked to Sage about an audition? Sorry—I don't know which one of you is Sage."

"That'd be me," I say, raising a finger.

"Right," she mutters, lightly tapping her fingers on her forehead, as if to express her thoughtlessness. "Brandon did describe you—dark hair, tats, glasses...I should have known."

I look at the guys, each of them studying Alex with a different dubious expression, and then meet her gaze once more. "Uh, funny you should say that. Brandon didn't tell me too much about you. Actually, he didn't tell me *anything* about you. Like, that you're a girl."

"Oh." She coughs out an embarrassed laugh and then shrugs. "Is that some sort of problem?"

"Look, Alexandra? Alexandria? Whatever your name is—no offense, but we're a bunch of dudes called Mountains & *Men*," Knox explains.

"Huh," she scoffs, propping her fists against her hips. She looks around at every one of us before she speaks. "Are you sure you're not just a bunch of sexists *jerks* called Mountains & Men? And my name is Alex, by the way. *Just* Alex."

"Hold on," I say, standing to my feet. I lift my hands up slightly, hoping to stop the sudden rise of tension in the room. "Look, we're just surprised, okay? All Brandon told me is that you could play. How do you know him, anyway?"

"We go to the same church. I play in the worship band."

"Oh, *fuck* no," Maddox replies emphatically. "You brought us a fucking *church girl?* This is not going to work."

I sigh, reaching up to run my fingers through my hair. I'll be the first to admit, Brandon left out quite a few important details about *Alex,* but we're kind of desperate. I told Brandon not to fucking mess with me and he assured me that he wasn't. I trust him. The least we could do is see if she can play. I open my mouth to say as much, but Alex speaks before I can.

"Goodness, I don't know why I'm about to defend myself. Lord knows you've insulted me enough that I should turn around and leave you high and dry, but here I go." She pauses, claps her hands together, and weaves her fingers as she lets her arms drop in front of her. "The way I heard it, you need a bass player. I get it that you're all *dudes,* but this is about music, is it not? You might be taller, bigger, stronger, with an extra appendage that I don't have, but none of you have what the one with the *boobs* has—" She points at her tits and my eyebrows shoot up in shocked amusement. I also can't help but look. "And that is," she continues, drawing my focus back to her eyes, "the ability to play the bass like a badass.

"I've done my research. Granted, I might not be able to put names to faces, but I've listened to everything you have online. I'm ready for this audition. I'm looking for a band—*you're* a band. I can play anything you want. Now, are we going to do this or not?"

For a moment, none of us says a word.

"You've listened to our shit?" Derrick asks, appearing intrigued.

"Pretty much non-stop for the last twenty-four hours. And don't call it shit. You know it's not. It's really good. *Great,* even. But you know *Contortion* wouldn't sound half as sick without that bass."

"Wait a second," JJ says, speaking for the first time since Alex arrived. "You're telling us you learned *Contortion?* In the last twenty-four hours?"

A small smile pulls at her lips as she nods once. "Remember the part about me playing like a badass? I don't boast about much. In fact, I suck at a lot of things; but playing the bass is the one thing I'm most proud of. It's my gift. I practically live to play. So..."

"She says she can play *Contortion,* I want to hear it." JJ stands from the couch and makes his way over to his keys.

I look to the rest of the guys, hoping to feel them out. Derrick spins his sticks between his fingers and tips his chin at me. Maddox shakes his head, but gets up and plugs into his amp anyway. Knox shrugs and then does the same. I turn my focus back to Alex and gesture with a sweeping motion of my hands for her to come on in. She takes her bass out, straps up, and plugs in. Once everyone is set, I step to the mic.

"You sure you're ready for this?"

She takes a deep breath and squares her shoulders before she responds. "Yes. Let's do it."

"Okay," I say with a smirk.

The song starts with just vocals and keys. JJ and I kick things off simultaneously. When I begin to sing, the words come as effortlessly as my next breath. Then, after I finish the opening phrase, Derrick clicks the beat and everyone joins in at once. Alex falls into the mix as if she's been here all along. Suddenly, I actually have to think about the words to the song as I continue to sing; all the while, Knox, Maddox, JJ, Derrick and I are exchanging glances. She wasn't lying. She's a fucking badass.

When we get to the middle of the song, there's a bass solo. While she plays, her focus glued to her fingers as they glide along her fret, I watch her intently—the way she moves with the beat, her right shoulder marking time—and the way she seems to get lost in the notes. When she nails it, the garage erupts with our roar of astonishment. We don't even finish the song. JJ pulls his headphones from over his ears then reaches over to clap her on the shoulder. I think in his excitement, he nudges her harder than he intended, and she stumbles forward a step. She catches herself and laughs it off just as Knox comes over and offers her his hand.

"You can rock my world any time you want, little mama."

"Um, thank you?" she says warily, reaching out to accept his gesture.

"Someone's got the shakes," he says, pulling her closer. "Do I make you nervous?"

She laughs again, pulling her hand out of his grasp. "You in all of your giant glory?" she asks, motioning to their height difference. "*No*. You and all of your *talent?* Yes. You *all* make me nervous."

"Better get used to us, Alex," says Derrick, pointing at her with a drumstick.

"Wait just one fucking minute," calls out Maddox. "That's it? She's in without any discussion whatsoever?"

"Maddy—she just played circles around all the losers we've heard so far! What more do you want?" asks Knox.

"Cut the *Maddy* shit, I'm serious. It's about more than just playing. We're not so desperate that we'll take any hot little number off the street without doing our due diligence."

"Mad Lips is right," I admit.

The five of us guys have been through a lot together. We've been Mountains & Men for years, pouring our sweat, tears, and blood into our name. We can't adopt someone who won't be willing to go through the ups *and* the downs with us. It's obvious that Alex knows her shit backwards, but can she be family?

"Take the floor, man," I tell him, folding my arms across my chest. "Ask what you want."

"First of all, we're a fucking rock band. We play, we drink, we swear, we party, then repeat. We don't need a little church mouse coming in here trying to *clean us up* or some shit."

"Is that what you're worried about?" Alex murmurs. "Look, I'm a Christian, yeah. But that doesn't mean I'm going to come in here and hit you over the head with my bible. It's like I said before, this is about the music. I won't judge you if you won't judge me. Even if you *do* judge me. I play, I drink, I swear, and I party, too. Maybe not as much as you, but to each his own."

"Yeah. To each his own, *douche*. Damn. Show some respect," mutters Derrick, throwing his stick. It hits Maddox square in the chest. He scowls back at the drummer, but one look is all it takes for Maddox to fold. We all know Derrick believes in the Big Man Upstairs, too.

"Is there anything else you want to know about me?"

"Look," I begin. "Here's the thing. We can't afford to lose another bass player again. Not now. We're trying to get some things moving and we need someone who is going to be in this—rehearsals, gigs, all of it. Can you commit? Like, *really* commit?"

"I'm a full-time student. I have worship band practice on Wednesdays and church on Sundays. Outside of that, I'm in."

"And if we start expanding our reach? Hitting the road and all that shit—you'll be missing school. What then?" asks Maddox.

"Taking a semester or two off never hurt anyone. You only live once, right?"

"With the way you play, why aren't you in a band now? Why us?" JJ asks.

"Honestly?" She looks down at her feet and then up at all of us. "I get a little stage fright. It's something I've been working on, though. I just—I'm getting too old to hide and I don't want to anymore. I want to play as much as I can and as often as I can—I just want to play."

We all fall silent, and for a moment, I give everyone a chance to process everything that's happened in the last few minutes. I wait, leaving the floor open for anyone else to say what they need to before we put this discussion to bed.

"Alright. Let's take a vote, yeah?" I say, ready and willing to give this girl a shot. "All in favor of giving the broad a chance, say aye."

All at once, we each agree.

"*Aye.*"

ELEVEN

Millicent

I WORK INTO THE EVENING, in need of a little catch up time after last night with Sage—and I won't even mention the level of distracted he's had my thoughts all day. Regardless of the reason why, I don't leave campus until six-thirty before I head to the gym. I'll admit, every time I walk into the building, I wonder if I'll see Keith. This is where I met him, after all. I'm not sure what I'd do, given the chance to confront the bastard who tried to date rape me. As my eyes scan the floor on my way to the locker rooms, I'm not sure I'll be finding out tonight, either.

I change into my snug, black sports bra and matching yoga running shorts, throwing on a pale blue, loose fitting, racer-back tank top. I lace up my tennis shoes and stow away my bag before I start heading back out to the floor. Slipping my phone into my bra, I reach up to pull my hair into a ponytail. Just as I'm finished, my phone starts to ring. I pull it out and my stomach tingles when I see his name light up the screen.

"Hello?" I answer.

"Come over, doll face." I hear laughter in the background and I wonder what he's up to.

"Come over where?"

"The house. We're celebrating! Mountains & Men has a bass player, baby."

"Oh, wow. Congratulations," I reply.

"Yeah. You've got to meet Alex. You comin'?"

I look around me, remembering where I am and why I'm here. "I'm at the gym. I just got here."

"Fuck the gym. I'll give you a workout later. Violet just got off work and she's bringing us pizza. We sent Mad Lips and Knox on a beer run—*I told them to pick up a bottle of wine...*" He sings the last part in a coaxing manner that causes an ache between my legs. For a moment, my rational thought decides it's on hiatus. "Millicent, come over. I want to see you. Want to *taste* you." He whispers the last sentence and I about face, heading straight for the locker room.

"Okay. I'm coming. I just need to change and—"

"Don't bother. Get that sexy, little ass over here. See you soon."

He ends the call without another word. I stare at the phone for a minute before I reach for my bag, securing the strap over my shoulder. On my way to my car, it occurs to me that all he had to do was call for me to come running. The truth has my stomach in knots, but my feet don't stop my forward progression. I want to see him. Touch him. *Taste* him.

I will survive this fall. I will.

Or so I keep telling myself.

When I pull up to the house, parking in the street, I notice that everyone is in the garage. As I walk up the drive, I see Violet standing with her back to me, two pizza boxes poised against her hip as she listens to the band play. Sage's voice makes my stomach flutter and my pussy pulse. When he sees me, he grins around his words, making my heart race.

Fuck.

Violet must have seen it too, because she turns to look over her shoulder at me as I approach. "Millie!" she calls out with a wide smile of her own.

"Hi, Violet."

As soon as I'm in reaching distance, she loops her arm through mine and tugs me to her side. "I told them they had to play for their supper," she tells me with a giggle. It's then that I notice the *Jo-Jo's* t-shirt she's wearing, the logo matching the print on the boxes she's brought. "Alex is the shit. She had my respect the instant JJ told me that they voted her in. I mean—to add a girl to their mix? That's just downright impressive. Then I heard her play—oh, my gosh, Millie. She's perfect!"

Violet's words don't fully register until I scan the room and find her. *Alex.* Standing with the five guys that I know to be the heart of Mountains & Men, she looks tiny. Nevertheless, as she plays, she exudes a confidence that all but demands my attention. It's more than that, though. She's beautiful, in that cute and innocent sort of way, but with a hint of a rebellious streak. Her hair is so dark it's almost black; it fades into a deep purple at the ends, which, after a long day, appear to have lost her attempt at curling them. Her eyes are dark, too; but even from here, I can see that they are full of light—full of *life* and energy and passion. And when she smiles…

My eyes follow the direction of her gaze and my heart stings when I see Sage smile back at her. Violet was right. Alex is perfect. It's as if she's the element their concoction was missing. They've got chemistry. Suddenly, I'm all too aware that while I should be happy for them—while I *am* happy for them—I feel disappointed.

She's been here for all of a day and she fits. I, on the other hand, don't. I never have, which I understood. It was just Sage that I wanted. Yet, reality causes me to question how long that will matter—how long will that mean anything? Sage is going to go wherever his music takes him, as he should. But Alex is the last bit of proof I need that Sage—hell—*all* of them are constantly surrounded by pretty, young things that will fit into his world far better than I ever will.

I'm so lost in my thoughts, I don't realize that the song is over, until Sage comes charging for me. Violet pulls away from me just as he bends, gripping the back of my thighs before hoisting me up off my feet. I squeal in surprise, wrapping my arms and legs around him. He grins at me, giving the bare skin of my thighs a squeeze.

"If I had known this is what you wear to the gym, I would have insisted you change," he murmurs. "You know how I feel about the guys seeing these legs."

"I—"

"Kiss me," he demands, cutting off my rebuttal. "Need your lips, doll face."

When I look into his eyes, his blue gaze echoing his words, I can't refuse him. I brush my mouth against his and his grip around me tightens, making me want more. I kiss him assuredly and he responds in kind. He teases me, flicking just the tip of his tongue against mine, and in this moment—nothing else matters. Just this. Just him. Just Sage.

One of the guys plucks the opening chords to Marvin Gaye's *Let's Get It On*, and Derrick jumps in with the beat. Sage laughs before humming the words into my mouth. Then he smacks one more kiss against my lips before he sets me down. "Come on, baby doll. Got someone I want you to meet." He takes my hand and, as he leads me into the heart of the garage, all the guys greet me with their version of *hello*.

"Millie," Sage begins to say as we come to a stop in front of their newest member. "Alex. Alex, Millie."

"Hi," she says, offering her hand.

"Hello." I have to let go of Sage in order to return the gesture; but immediately after, Sage has his fingers wrapped around mine.

"I think I'm going to call you Zip," he tells her. She lifts an eyebrow at him in question. When he responds, he's speaking to me. "She's like a fucking zip-drive, I swear. We've been downloading shit into her for hours. She picks it up so quick. We've already planned our set for next weekend."

"Wow. That's great."

Alex makes a small sound and I can tell she's embarrassed by his praise. She catches my eye and shrugs. "I have perfect pitch. It helps. Anyway—" She looks around me at Violet. "Have we earned our pizza? I'm *starving*."

"Fuck, yeah," calls out Maddox. "Let's eat."

Sage

It's not long before we're all sitting around a couple empty boxes of pizza, drinking and shooting the shit after the intense hours of work that we put in today. We take the time to get to know Alex a little bit more. We learn that she's the same age as Maddox and in her last year of college, as well. She's studying psychology, simply because it interests her; she has no idea what she wants to do with her degree when she's finished. She's a Colorado native, like most of us, and her parents live in Longmont. She's got an older brother who lives out in California, and they are three years apart. *Exactly* three years; they share the same birthday and everything.

When Alex is sick of being in the spotlight, she turns her questions toward us. We end up telling her about how we all met, about the curse of the bass slot, and a whole bunch of other random stories that make us who we are. At some point, Knox heads inside to grab his acoustic guitar. Maestro, who has been in and out all day, decides to grace us with his presence when Knox returns. He paws at my legs and I pick him up, setting him in my lap. He quickly saunters into Millie's lap before making himself comfortable. She lifts her hands in surprise, looking down at Maestro before glancing over at me. I just smirk at her—*pup knows what's up*. She relaxes, lowering her hands until they cover his fur.

It's then that Knox starts messing around on his guitar. He starts plucking the melody to The Beatles *Blackbird* and a lazy smile stretches across my face. Hearing this song always reminds me of high school—the Bradley boys and me sitting around, just chillin', playing music. When I start to sing, the conversation in the room stops. I look to Millie, who's been pretty quiet since she arrived, and offer her a wink. I'm glad she's here. I'll have to show her just how much later.

I hear a voice humming along with me, and my eyes search the room. It only takes me a second to find Alex, sitting between Derrick and Knox on the couch opposite me. They hear her, too. Derrick nudges her, then signals that she should sing with me. A slight blush heats her cheeks, but she complies. My eyes grow wide in astonishment at the sound that comes out of her. I drop out, leaving only her timid but pure vocal tone.

"Whoa, whoa, whoa—stop!" I stand to my feet, squinting as I point a finger at her. "You can fucking *sing*, too?"

"Uh," she chuckles. "I guess."

"You guess?" asks Derrick incredulously, stealing the words right out of my mouth.

She shrugs. "I mean, I rock the bass. That's my thing. But I've been singing just about my whole life. My dad is a pastor and my mom heads the music department at his church. My involvement was practically a birthright."

"Can you sing and play at the same time?" When she nods, I march over to her and grab her hand, pulling her up off of the sofa and taking her to JJ's keys. "Fucking hell, Zip. You're a goldmine. *You* are *totally* backing me up on a few songs. None of these guys can sing for shit."

Violet laughs as the guys grumble in response. In all fairness, Derrick isn't too bad—but he refuses to sing and play. I guess I don't blame him. He's a kick-ass drummer and I wouldn't want to mess with his sound; but I've been jonesin' for some back up vocals for a while now.

I pick the first one of our songs that comes to mind before I start playing the notes to my vocal lead, then I add in the harmonic notes. I play the chorus once, singing along as I look to Alex, who is studying my fingers on the keys. The second time through, she hums along with me; the third time through, she's singing. I couldn't keep the wild grin off my face even if I tried.

I owe Brandon. Big time.

Then I hear Maestro's paws hit the ground. When I look over at Millie, she's shaking her head at Violet, who is saying something I can't hear. Then she stands and looks over at me. I don't know what to make of the expression in her eyes, but when she waves at me and starts to leave, my stomach drops.

What the fuck?

I look to Violet but she only shrugs, giving me a sympathetic glance before she, too, watches my girl leave. I call her name, but she doesn't stop her retreat. I abandon the keys and go chasing after her. She's halfway down the drive when I catch her around the waist.

"Doll face, what the fuck? Where are you going?"

"Home," she states, not even bothering to look at me.

"Why? It's still early. And didn't I promise you a workout?" I add teasingly.

Her eyes finally meet mine, but she's not amused. "I can't do this. I don't belong here. I'm going home."

My heart rate speeds up at her words. I can't tell if she's talking about *tonight*—just being here with the band—or *us*. "You can't do what?"

"*This. You,*" she replies, pressing her hands against my chest as she attempts to push herself out of my arms.

"Don't you *fucking* dare," I mutter, gripping her hips with both hands and pulling her flush against me. "What are you talking about?"

"This is not my world. It's *yours*. I don't know why I'm here, especially considering you've got a shiny new toy to play with."

"What—*Alex?*" I scoff. I furrow my brow at her in confusion. "Are you... *jealous?*"

"What?!" She pushes my chest again in a failed attempt to get away from me. "No, I'm not *jealous*." The words that come out of her mouth say something different than the rosy tint in her cheeks, and I can't help but laugh. She gasps at my reaction, and then glares at me. "Fuck you, Sage."

"You are, aren't you? You're jealous!"

"Let me go. I'm going home," she seethes.

"Think again, Millicent." Before she can argue any further, I smack a kiss against her lips and then grab one of her hands. I pull her back up the drive and through the garage, not bothering to acknowledge my mates as I lead her into the house.

The laundry room is inside to the right. I close us in and then my mouth is on hers, my tongue invading her mouth as I back her up against the dryer. She whimpers and tries to push me away, but her attempts are halfhearted—she's too busy kissing me back. I slide my hands underneath her tank top, cupping her tits. I can feel her nipples through her bra and it arouses my cock. I press my hardening length against her and she moans, her fingers now gripping my t-shirt in her fists.

"The band is my life," I tell her, removing her tank top, then her bra. "Music is who I am." I wrap my lips around one of her nipples, sucking as I shove down her shorts and panties. They fall to her ankles and she's quick to step out of them, along with her tennis shoes. "Alex is a godsend. She's just what we needed. *More* even." I reach behind my head and rip off my shirt, needing to feel her bared flesh against mine. I bring my lips to her neck, kissing her as I reach for my wallet. I pull away from her long enough to find a condom and she wastes no time helping me out of my jeans.

My baby doll was jealous—I don't care what she says—and that truth does something to me. It turns me on, yeah, but it's so much more than that. She's mine. *She doesn't know it yet—'cause she's so damn stubborn she can hardly see straight—but she belongs to me. She has no reason to be jealous. I don't want anyone else.*

Once I roll the condom over my rock hard dick, I lift Millie up onto the dryer, and plunge into her core. The sound she makes at my invasion only makes me harder.

"You feel that? You feel me?" I mutter, pumping in and out of her.

She nods, gripping her fingers in my hair as she stares into my eyes—her breaths ragged and sexy as fuck. God—who knew *breathing* could be sexy?

"You can't be jealous of my first love, baby. Me and music go together. But I'm yours when you want me. You hear me, Millicent?" I squeeze her ass, pounding into her harder. "I'm *yours*."

She moans and then closes her mouth around mine. She feels so incredible—her pussy tight and wet, her skin soft, her body warm. I swear, I'll never get enough of her. A groan spills from her mouth as she pulls her lips from mine, allowing her head to fall back as she surrenders herself to me.

"God, Sage—why can't I just quit you?" she breathes. "I don't—I don't fit."

"Stop. Just feel me, gorgeous. Feel my cock, Millie. This is you and me. Who owns your orgasm? Hmm? Who fills this pussy like I do?"

She whimpers, squeezing her legs around me, and I know she's getting close.

"Answer me, Millie."

"Fuck. Only you! Sage—I'm—oh, *god*—" She cries out, holding back nothing as her whole body tightens around mine.

"Hell yes," I grunt. "Strangle my dick. Shit, you feel so goddamn good."

With a sigh, she sags against me, descending from her orgasmic high. I lift her off of the dryer and turn us around, pressing her back up against the wall as I ram into her as deep as I can go. I'm not even close to being done with her. She leans toward me and, knowing what she wants, I meet her in the middle, kissing her hungrily. Her tongue dances with mine and I know she's not close to being done with me either. When she pulls my lip between her teeth, I free a growl, pumping into her faster.

"Yes, yes—more, Sage, more!"

"You gonna come again for me, doll face? Huh? Come with me," I tell her, slipping my hand between us.

I graze her clit with my thumb and she digs her fingers into my shoulders. She props her forehead against mine, every thrust eliciting a small murmur from her sweet mouth. My balls tighten at the sound and I apply more pressure with my thumb, desperate to get her where I want her. Her breath hitches and she seals her eyes shut tight. Just as I get ready to lose my load, she clamps down around me, pulling forth my release.

I'm senseless with pleasure, the words coming out of my mouth both foul and incomprehensible. A moment later, after we're sated for the time being, I pull out of her and lower her to her feet. I make quick work of disposing of the condom and then bring my focus back to her. Her long ponytail is now coming loose, the skin that covers her chest and neck are flushed, and she looks a beautiful, disheveled mess.

I did that to her.

"Sage, I need to—"

"If you're about to spout some bullshit about going home, save your breath." I snatch my discarded shirt from off of the floor and pull it over her head. "Put this on," I instruct, helping her find the arm holes. "Go to my room. I'll be up in a sec."

She opens her mouth to speak but then closes it when I lift an eyebrow at her. Then she huffs a sigh and grabs her panties, sliding them on before she leaves the room. A triumphant smirk tugs at my lips and I put my jeans back on before I pick up the rest of her clothes and head to the garage. Everyone turns to look at me—the guys laugh, Violet raises her eyebrows, and Alex blushes. That's when I remember that as the newbie, she's never seen me without a shirt on before.

I shrug it off. She'll have to get used to it. Like Knox warned her upon her arrival—we're a bunch of dudes.

"Tell me you fixed it," Violet demands, speaking before I can. "Whatever *it* is."

"I'm working on it."

"Not from out here, you aren't. Don't screw things up with her. I'm serious, Sage. I really like her."

I nod, running my fingers through my hair. "Me too, Vi."

"We're good, Dweeb. No need to be polite," says Derrick with a lopsided grin.

"Right," I mumble with a chuckle. I look to Alex, tipping my chin at her. "See you tomorrow?"

"I'll be here."

"Alright, I'll catch you losers later. And don't give Maestro any beer, got it? That shit's not cool."

They all laugh, but I'm dead serious. I think about calling him off of the couch, where he's settled next to JJ, but Violet shoos me away. Knowing I can trust her, I head back inside where my girl is waiting.

TWELVE

Millicent

HIS BODY IS WARM and heavy, wrapped around me while he sleeps. I'm not sure what time it is; though, I assume it's well after midnight. I'm also unaware of how long I've been lying awake while he slumbers peacefully. His relaxed face, void of his glasses, makes him look younger—*softer*. As I peer through the shadows, broken by only the small amount of light that shines through his open curtains, I imagine that *this* is the true face of my dreamer; that in his sleep, he goes to that place where wishes are granted and the impossible is always the opposite; that in his dreams, the harsh reality of the world is softened and he is rejuvenated so that when he wakes, he has the strength to fight another day.

My dreamer.

I think back over this night. The hours he spent ravaging my body. That moment we stood bickering in the driveway. The jealousy that spurred my decision to leave. I hate that he saw right through me, understanding my feelings even better than I could. I denied it to his face, but we both knew I was lying. I was jealous. Jealous of Alex—the way she seemed to fit in perfectly without even trying, as if it were as effortless as breathing. She *belongs*. But it was one moment in particular that pushed me over the edge.

Her. Standing next to Sage. His fingers gliding across the keys of JJ's keyboard.

For reasons I can't explain, it took me back to the moment we had shared on our date—when he played for me. *Me*. That moment had been mine. *Ours*. I didn't know how fiercely I was holding onto it until I saw him playing for someone else.

Granted, it wasn't the same. He was merely plucking out the notes he wanted her to sing. He wasn't showing off with Beethoven, but my brain hadn't been able to untangle his intentions from the jealousy that wrapped around my heart. It was then that I realized…

I'm not falling anymore. I have fallen.

I adore him. Every little thing about him that I've come to know, I like. More than that, I *want*. His passion for music. His talent, both hidden and on full display. His optimism. His spontaneity. His confidence. His *dominance*. His affection. His foul mouth. All of him—wrapped up in the beautiful, tattooed package that holds me now—I want it all. I want it so much that as I carefully roll away from him and crawl out of bed, I know that I'm not just leaving pieces of my heart behind—I'm leaving an entire chunk of it in his possession.

My eyes well up with tears as I get dressed as quickly and as quietly as possible. I can hardly think straight, the pain in my chest more intense than it was a few hours ago, when I first tried to leave.

I'm yours when you want me. You hear me, Millicent? I'm yours.

His words cling to me now. As they play on repeat in my head, I feel them pulling me back toward him—back into his bed—back into his arms. I search for my shoes instead. I know the pain I feel now is nothing in comparison to how it'll feel if I stay long enough to watch *him* walk away. I didn't mean for it to get this far between us, but here I am. I gave him more of my heart than he was ever meant to have. I don't have much left. If he takes anymore, he'll ruin me. I've been left too many times and I know he would be the end of me. I know because he's more than I ever thought I wanted.

I blindly reach for my shoes, my tears making it impossible for me to see. I remember that I dropped my phone and my keys in the laundry room earlier and I'll have to go grab them; but then, when I try putting on my second shoe, I find them inside. Sage grabbed them, along with all of my clothes. For whatever reason, that just makes me want to cry harder. I have to get out of here. Now.

When I slowly crack open the door, I startle Maestro, who is laying in the hallway. I close my eyes, hoping with everything that is in me that he won't bark. He doesn't. Instead, he trots past me, into the room. I free a quivering sigh and shut the door behind me. I don't even have the strength to give Sage one more look.

I tiptoe my way down the stairs, relieved that I've made it this far, and then stop dead in my tracks when I reach the entryway of the house. Derrick is awake, sitting on the couch in front of the television. Whatever he's watching is turned down so low, I can't image how he can hear it at all. For a fraction of a second, I wonder why he's up at this time of night, but it's a fleeting thought.

"You okay?" he mumbles.

I don't know what I was expecting him to say, but it wasn't that. Caught off guard, I find myself telling the truth. Well, not so much *telling* as *showing*. I shake my head, taking another step toward the door.

"He'll come running. You do realize that, don't you?" I speak not a word as I simply stare at him from where I stand. "He doesn't fall often. The last girl he was with did a number on him. He doesn't trust chicks easily. He sure as hell doesn't commit; hasn't for years. But he wants *you*.

"He'll come after you. He'll come running. He'll fight for you. It's just in his nature. He's a chaser."

"And what happens when he catches me?" I murmur. "How long until he feels the need to chase after someone else?"

Derrick shrugs. "No one can predict those things, Millie. That's life. The thrill of the unknown is why the dive is worth taking. What's the point of living if you aren't going to jump?"

I blink and a tear spills down my cheek. I fear that the dam is about to break and I don't have it in me to think about what he's just said. I need to get out of here. I need to go home.

"Please don't wake him."

He offers me a single nod and then I'm gone.

Sage

I'm not a light sleeper—but when more than one thing disrupts my slumber at the same time, I've been known to crawl my way into consciousness for a minute before settling back into sleep. I hear Maestro's dog tags first. It's a faint noise, more like a tickle of my senses, and I think nothing of it. Then my hands run over cool sheets and I realize my arms are empty. I open my eyes, sure that I fell asleep with Millicent wrapped around me. When I look and notice that I'm in my bed alone, I sit up and reach for my glasses. I survey the room, finding not a trace of my girl. Then I hear it.

A car door.

I jump out of bed and hurry to the window, buck-ass-naked. I don't give a shit who sees me, all I care about is the fact that Millie just left me. Without a word, she got up and left me. How could she? Did I not make it perfectly clear that I'm in this? That she has no reason to run? Didn't I fuck that truth into her all night long? She's got me. She's fucking *got me*.

Now wide awake, the blood coursing through my veins as my adrenaline kicks into high gear, I rummage through my dresser for some clothes. Sweatpants and a t-shirt cover my body in seconds. I don't even bother with socks before sliding my feet into a pair of Chucks. I'm out the door, keys in hand, without a second thought. I wouldn't have even noticed Derrick had I not heard him chuckle from the living room.

"What the fuck, man? You let her leave?" I ask thoughtlessly.

"Hey, she's not my woman. But she knows you're coming," he says with a tired grin. "I warned her you would. She'll be pissed you're right on her heels, though."

"Well, she's got another thing coming if she thinks I'm waiting until dawn."

He chuckles again, but I know he's not laughing *at* me. He's laughing because every word that I've spoken to him is a word he's probably anticipated since he watched Millie leave. He knows me well. "Why are you still here talking to me? Go get her, Dweeb."

I don't waste another second, not even bothering to say goodbye before I fly out the door to my car. I'm pissed that she left, but that's not what drives me. More than anything, I'm afraid she's slipping through my fingers. I can't lose her. I won't. She's pushing me away. I don't know why, but I'm going to find out. She's mine and I won't have it any other way.

Millicent

It takes me longer than usual to drive home. I cry the whole way. The one good thing about driving around at two in the morning is that there really isn't any traffic. That's about the only thing I have going for me right now. I pull into a parking spot in front of my building and wipe my cheeks clean as I take a deep breath. I have to be up for work in just a few hours. I'm going to look like shit. No. Worse. I'll be the fucking walking dead.

I shouldn't complain. I have no one to blame but myself.

Knowing that the sun will be up before I'm ready, I step out of my car and head inside. I'm exhausted, but something tells me I won't actually be able to fall asleep. Not even for a little while. I have to try, though. Calculus equations are kinder when I've gotten some rest, even if only a laughable amount.

I make my way into the kitchen first, flipping on the light before grabbing a glass. I'm reaching for the faucet when I hear footsteps pounding up the stairs. I brace myself, hoping it isn't anyone other than a neighbor who could care less about waking the entire hallway, knowing all along it can only be one man.

Sage.

My dreamer.

My chaser.

My suspicions are proven correct when there's a banging on my door. "Open up, doll face," he yells.

Fuck. Forget waking the whole hallway, he'll wake the whole damn building!

I hurry to the door, swinging it open with a scowl on my face. "*Jesus!* Could you be any louder?"

He's breathing fast, like he ran the whole distance here, and there's a scowl tugging at his brow, too—that is, until his eyes notice the state of my face. I curse my pale complexion, my broken heart, and his timing, all of which contribute to his ability to see just how hard it was for me to walk away. He reaches up to cup my cheek, but I jerk away from him. I know if he touches me, I'll either start crying again, or I'll fall into his arms. Or both.

"I had my dick inside of you less then two hours ago, and now I can't touch you?" he asks, his scowl returning. I don't respond, the knot in my throat preventing me from being able to do so without triggering the waterworks. "Millicent, talk to me!"

I press my hand over my heart as my eyes well up again. "Don't call me that," I barely manage, my voice hardly above a whisper.

"Why not?" he asks, stepping closer to me. "You love it."

"I know." My voice breaks at my admission.

"Baby," he murmurs, slipping his arms around my waist.

He smells like Sage. And sweat. And sex. And me. And just as I had feared, his touch is my undoing. When I start to cry, he shuts the door behind him and then cradles my head against his shoulder, his hard body keeping me upright. A part of me cannot believe I'm having a meltdown in front of him. Though, another part of me—the bigger part of me—needs this just as much as I need him.

"Talk to me, baby doll. What in the hell were you thinking, leaving in the middle of the night like that?"

"I can't, Sage. I'm sorry, we can't do this."

"But we are. It's done. This is you and me."

"Yeah, today, maybe," I argue, pulling my face away from his chest so that I can look into his eyes. My pride has vanished, so I don't even bother hiding my tears. "How long could this possibly last? You're twenty-one years old and—"

"You've got to be fucking kidding me. How are we back to that? Millie," he pauses, gently cupping his hands around my cheeks, wiping my tears with the pads of his thumbs. "What? What do I have to do to prove to you that I'm not messing around with you? I'm here. I'm right fucking here, telling you that I want you. You. Only you!"

"You want me now because it's all about the chase. You'll fight for me now because you don't have me. It's only a matter of time before I'm yours; it's only a matter of time before you decide you want to chase someone else. That's how the game is played, Sage, and I don't want to play with you anymore."

He groans, pulling his hands away from me before he runs his fingers through his hair. "There are so many things wrong with what you just said, I can hardly even untangle it." I open my mouth to speak, but he presses a finger against my lips and shakes his head. "No. I'm done listening to your bullshit, baby. I'm sorry, but I'm just done.

"As long as you keep running from me, you bet your sweet, little ass I'm going to be chasing after you. As long as you keep pushing me away, I'm sure as hell going to fight for you. I want you, Millicent—*just you*. This isn't a game. I'm not playing you—I'm fucking falling for you. I'm not going anywhere. I think I've made that fact abundantly clear. *You're* the one who left me tonight, remember? Which was pretty dumb, by the way. Know why?" He rests his forehead against mine and I watch as his eyes fall closed.

"Why?" I whisper.

"Because, you're already mine, gorgeous. You're my girl and I'm your guy. Simple as that."

"But Sage—"

He silences my feeble attempt at a counterargument, pressing his lips against mine. He kisses me firmly, but gently—slowly—and it's in this moment that I claim defeat. I'll never win this battle—not against Sage. Not against these lips. These hands. This body. *His heart*. He's won.

I'm his.

I lift myself onto my tiptoes and wrap my arms around his neck, needing him closer. He bends down and grips the back of my thighs, hoisting me up. Instinctively, my legs lock at my ankles behind his back. As he begins to carry me down the hallway, I feel it when his cock grows hard—his erection nudging the bottom of my ass with every step he takes. In spite of the hour and the many rounds we had in bed earlier in the night, I want him so much. My rapid pulse pounds in my ears, echoing what my heart wants. What my heart needs.

Sage.

He lies me on my bed and neither of us says a word, knowing that our need for one another supersedes anything that could possibly be said. We're done talking for the night. Instead, I watch as he discards his glasses and then pulls off his shirt, revealing his chiseled torso and the extensive amount of artwork that decorates his upper body. When he drops his pants and steps out of his shoes, I learn that he's not wearing any underwear—his cock springing free in all of its glorious splendor. My stomach tingles and the ache between my legs overwhelms me.

Before he gets in bed with me, he opens one of my nightstand drawers and reaches for a condom. He slides it underneath the pillow where my head rests and then he proceeds to cover my face with the sweetest kisses—his lips tracing the tracks of my tears. It makes me want to cry some more, but I don't. I close my eyes as I seek to enjoy every kiss, every touch, every caress. He takes his time peeling away my clothes, all the while showering my body with a tenderness the likes of which it has never seen. By the time he rolls the condom on, I'm so incredibly wet, I can feel my arousal dripping out of me.

He slips inside of me with ease, his eyes locked with mine. When he's fully seated, he pauses for a moment, pressing a light kiss against my lips. He pulls out slowly and returns in the same fashion. Then, his lips still grazing mine—

"And in my arms you'll find your ecstasy
When you lose yourself, I'll set you free
Baby, just let go and let it be, let it be
Tonight/ Just give me tonight."

As he sings to me—my song—*our song*—I understand that this was inevitable, him and me. He knew it all along. Just one night was never going to be enough. It was never going to be our story. It was never going to be our song. He's been fighting for me this whole time. Now, whether I'm ready or not, I surrender.

"You're mine," he groans as he rolls his hips against mine. "Say it, baby."

"I'm yours," I breathe, feeling my way down his chest and then up again; gripping onto his shoulders as the slow burn within me intensifies.

"Damn straight. And I'm yours, doll face."

"You're mine," I echo.

A knowing smirk tugs at his lips and I arch my back, pressing my chest against his. I want to feel every bit of him. My man. My dreamer. My chaser. He kisses me, sweeping his tongue through my mouth as he tastes me. He rides me nice and slow until we're both panting, calling out each other's names. We come together and it's positively euphoric. I cling to him, wanting nothing more than to be in his arms as my body begins to relax. When I fall asleep, he's still inside of me, and it feels like we're exactly where we're meant to be.

THIRTEEN

Sage

HER ALARM CLOCK SOUNDS and a groan rumbles from my chest—only, it's not my voice that vibrates across my skin. I don't open my eyes to look at her. I don't need to. I just *feel* her—the sexy ass woman whose leg is hooked over mine, her arm slung around me as she uses my chest as her pillow.

"Shit. Shit, shit, shit," she whines. I chuckle lazily, flinging my arm out to blindly reach for the alarm. I silence it, but she continues to whine. "I can't move. Shit."

"Go back to sleep, baby," I murmur, pressing my lips against her forehead.

"I can't. I have work."

I peek open one eye and look down at her. Both of her eyes are still closed. I know she's exhausted, because I am too. We got less than three hours of sleep. I know my girl—she needs a whole lot more rest than that to function, especially after a night with me. "Call in."

"I shouldn't," she mutters, snuggling closer to me.

God, she feels amazing.

"Millie, it's Friday. Call in. Have you *ever* called in before?" Something tells me the goody-two-shoes hasn't. Her silence makes me grin. "Bet your students would love to find out class was canceled today." She grunts but doesn't move. I can't tell if I've convinced her or not, so I try a different tactic. "Stay in bed with me, Millicent. Don't make me get up. Don't make me let you go. I'm not ready."

When she whimpers and pulls away from me, I frown at her. She notices and brushes her lips against mine in an act that can barely be called a kiss. "I'll be right back." I watch as she crawls out of bed, picking up my t-shirt from the floor before she leaves the room. She comes back a moment later, her fingers busy as she types something out on her phone. She's still going when she sits beside me, propping herself up against the headboard.

"What are you doing?"

"Posting an announcement through Blackboard to each of my classes. They might be getting a little break from me today, but I still need them to study."

"Does this mean you're spending the day in bed with me?" I ask with a smirk, skimming my fingers up the length of her leg. She doesn't answer me at first, too distracted with her task; so I slide my hand up the inside of her thigh.

She gasps and then bats my hand away, finally setting down her phone. "Sleep, Sage. I need to go back to sleep."

I laugh, gripping hold of her leg once more before yanking her down and onto her back. I kiss her and then reach for the hem of my shirt. When she protests, I kiss her again. "Need you naked, baby doll." Her eyes lock with mine as she lifts her arms, allowing me to strip her bare. I toss the shirt back onto the floor and then guide her onto her side, pulling her back against my front. I cup her tit in my hand and bury my nose in her neck as I close my eyes. "Fuck you when we wake up."

"Mmmm," she hums dreamily, sleep already pulling her under. "Is that a promise?"

"You bet your sweet, little ass."

We sleep through the morning. I wake up half past noon, but I don't wake her. She looks so peaceful and content—more relaxed than I've ever seen her. I remember her face when she opened the door to me early this morning. It about brought me to my knees. Seeing her so broken and exhausted was gut wrenching. Now, the bags under her eyes have faded and the color in her cheeks has returned. She's beautiful. She's gorgeous. *She's mine.*

I watch her sleep for a half an hour. I know that might make me sound like a total creeper, but I could give a fuck. I just don't want to take my eyes off of her. When she wakes up and smiles at me, all I want to do is kiss her. She returns my affection only until my hands start to wander, then she pushes me away.

I lift an eyebrow, challenging her dismissal. "I'm pretty sure I promised—"

"I need a shower first," she tells me, sitting up.

"How about a shower *after?*"

"Sage, all we've done in the last fifteen hours is sleep and fuck. I feel gross. I won't let you touch me while I feel like this."

She starts to slide out of bed but I sit up and wrap my arms around her waist, pulling her back and into my lap. She squeals, giggling when I nuzzle her neck with my nose. *Shit—if I could bottle that sound…* I reach up and tuck her hair behind her ear before leaning in to whisper, "I'll wash your back, you wash mine?"

"Okay."

I chuckle as I kiss her cheek. "You see there? Compromise. Look how good at this we are already."

We're in the shower for almost forty minutes. By the time we get out, we're pruney—but it's the best damn shower I've ever had. Now, the last thing I want to do is leave for work; but I've gotta jet, and I definitely need to make a pit stop. No way I'm showing up to Little Bird commando, in a pair of sweatpants. My dick print is for one woman only. If I could manage to pull away from her, I might have a chance at being on time for my shift.

"Fuck. I have to go," I sigh, separating my lips from hers. We're standing just beside her front door, where we've been for the last fifteen minutes.

"You better go, then," she murmurs, looking up at me with her pretty green eyes.

"I don't want to," I tell her, leaning in for another kiss. She responds instantly, tightening her arms around my neck as she lifts herself onto her tiptoes and presses her body flush against mine. My dick twitches and I feel bewitched. I've never wanted to hold onto any woman as much as I want to hold onto her.

"When will I see you again?" she asks, pulling away for a breath.

"I work 'til close and then the band's practicing tonight. We'll probably be at it pretty late. You could come hang, though."

She shakes her head, looking down her cheeks. "I don't think so. I—I don't know. After last night—I… What about tomorrow?"

It's obvious, as she looks back up at me, that she's embarrassed about our little scene in the driveway, followed by our disappearing act. The guys and I aren't a bunch of gossips and I know none of them cared, since we were done practicing anyway. Violet was the most interested, but she'll think nothing of it once she hears that Millie's not going anywhere. In any case, I don't press the issue with Millie. I'll give her a couple days and then I'm sure she'll be over it.

"I work in the morning. Depending on how things go tonight, we might try and squeeze in another jam session tomorrow afternoon. Next Saturday will be here before we know it, and we've got to have our shit down." She nods, fidgeting with the neck of my shirt. "Hey."

"Yeah?"

I smack a kiss against her lips. "I'll take you out tomorrow night."

"Sounds nice."

I chuckle, a smirk tugging at my lips as I slide my hands down, my fingers sneaking beneath the waistband of her little cotton shorts. She's not wearing any underwear, her sexiest habit, and I get a semi as my palms glide over her ass, pulling her even closer. "I can assure you, it'll be anything but *nice*. We'll have a good time, though."

"I look forward to it," she says, eyeing my lips.

"Dammit, doll face," I mutter, tracing her nose with mine. "I'm going to be late."

"Then get out of here," she says with a little laugh.

"I am," I assure her, angling my mouth so that it's lined up with hers. "I'm leaving now," I murmur, inching closer. "Any second now."

"*Sage*," she hums.

I kiss her hungrily, growling when she slips her tongue into my mouth. For a minute, I think about blowing off work; but then I remember I owe Brandon a solid and I can't play hooky on him. When I finally manage to pull away from Millie, her lips are red and swollen. She looks so fucking hot, I can hardly stand it. I have to force myself to say goodbye and then sprint out of there.

I'm home just long enough to put on some clothes, let Maestro out to do his business, and fill his dishes with food and water. When I walk into Little Bird, I'm only ten minutes late. I consider that to be a definite win. Joey, who appears to be ready for me to tap him out, sighs in relief at the sight of me. Before I can even get behind the counter, he's hurrying for the door.

"I'll catch you later, man. Brandon's in the back. Eryn's on break, should be back in a few. I have to—"

"Yeah," I say with a laugh and a wave. "Get out of here."

The first twenty minutes of my shift seem to drag. After I restock supplies behind the espresso bar, I help a few flirty girls who come in to *study;* if by study they really mean, sit at a table directly in my line of sight as they proceed to talk loudly and giggle incessantly.

Truth be told, it's not the first or even the second time that's happened to me. *This week*. As the front man of Mountains & Men, I get recognized every once and a while, as long as I'm someplace local. I've been known to attract a fan-girl or two. I've bagged a few of them, too. A month ago, I might have flirted with the table-o-blondes who are about as obvious as can be; not because I was looking for a lay in the middle of the day, but just because I could. Girls have often been an easy way to pass the time. But I'm not interested in girls these days.

I've got a woman—and she isn't blonde.

Holy shit. I let that thought circle its way around my brain once more. *I've got a woman.*

Last night, I made Millie mine. She said it herself. Thinking back on the last four weeks, I know I worked my ass off to get her to a place where she can admit what she really wants. What we *both* want. But until this moment, I hadn't really thought about how big of a deal this is for me. I was too busy trying to win my girl. It is, though—it is a huge fucking deal. I haven't had a girlfriend in three years, not since the last girl I once loved tore my heart out and beat it to a bloody pulp.

God. What a bitch.

After her, I lost all interest in the concept of commitment. I trusted no one, outside of the guys and my sisters. They were the only ones who really understood me; the only ones who believed in me. Nora was the last outsider I trusted with my dream. When that all went to shit, I said—*fuck 'em*. Literally. Fuck 'em and leave 'em. That's what most of them wanted, anyway. No one cared about where I was going or why. Not really. Not if it didn't have anything to do with them. But my dream is *mine*—it has nothing to do with anyone else. The guys are a part of it, yeah, but they each bring their own dream to the table. We're all accountable to fight for what we want, and yet we're in this together—loyal to the aspiration that binds us. That's what makes us *Mountains & Men*.

But Millicent…

She sees me. She gets me. She *believes* in me. Even more, she hopes in favor of my dream. I can hardly express what that means to me. She told me last night that she didn't think she *fit* into my world, but I disagree. She fits with me, which means she's now along for the ride.

I wonder what her dreams are. I wonder what drives her, my gorgeous girl. She's never told me, but I sure as hell intend to find out. I want to know everything about her. I want to see her like she sees me.

"What are you daydreaming about up here?" asks Brandon as he appears from the back, a tray full of pastries in his hand.

I watch as he restocks the case, shaking my head clear. "Uh, nothing. Just thinking," I reply with a shrug.

"I heard you met Alex yesterday. Also heard you got a new bass player."

I smirk at him as he looks over at me and shake my head. "You're an asshole for not telling me that *Alex* is a chick. You know that, right? The guys were practically shitting bricks when she walked in and introduced herself." He laughs, setting aside the now empty tray and folding his arms across his chest. "But she's a little spitfire. She held her ground and got us to listen. She's a badass. For real. Thank you, thank you, thank you." I press my hands together in the center of my chest and give him a little bow.

"Hey, I'm just glad I could help. I don't know too much about her, but we chat every once in a while. I remember her saying she was hoping to find some people to play with outside of church. Sounds like you both win."

"Definitely. Next Saturday. You'll have to come to The Brew and hear us play. I've got a good feeling. We're going to rock the house."

"I won't miss it. Maybe I can get Sarah to drive up for a bit, too, before I head down her way."

"Have Sarah drive up for what?" asks Eryn as she rejoins us after her break, tying on her apron.

"Mountains & Men. Next Saturday. The Brew. Bring all your friends."

She grins at me, shrugging her shoulders. "Duh. Of course we'll be there."

I hold my hand up for a high five and she claps her palm against mine. The bigger the turn out, the better. We need this Stefany chick to be impressed. If she notices we've already got a pretty healthy local fan-base, that's a good first step. The rest is up to us—and I feel it in my gut, we're going to play one hell of a show.

FOURTEEN

Millicent

PLAYING HOOKY ON FRIDAY ended up being a fabulous idea. After sleeping through the morning with Sage, taking the world's longest shower with him, and enjoying our half-hour-long goodbye, I spent the rest of the afternoon lounging. I picked up *War and Peace* and read, completely oblivious to the time. Every part of my body appreciated my attempt at relaxation after the emotional and physical night I had had with *my dreamer*.

It was eight o'clock before I realized I hadn't eaten more than a cup of yogurt since Sage left. Pulling myself away from my novel, I made myself a salad and a half sandwich. When I was finished eating, I got a text from Sage. We exchanged messages sporadically until after midnight, when my eyes were too heavy for me to keep open. I know I fell asleep before I had a chance to say goodnight because when I woke up, I had an unread text that simply said: *Sweet dreams, gorgeous.*

Even upon waking, it made my stomach flutter.

I spent what was left of my morning cleaning and straightening up before I headed out to run some errands. When I got back from the grocery store, I put away my stock, made a quick lunch, and then tried to distract myself with work for the rest of the afternoon.

I missed Sage.

A week ago, it would have been extraordinarily difficult for me to admit such a truth, but it's too all encompassing now to even try to deny it. I miss him. After twenty-four hours of no physical contact, my infatuation with him has made me miss him like some pathetic woman who has nothing better to do with herself. I can't help it, though; and the small voice in the back of my head has been warning me over and over that this—what I feel for Sage—it's a lot more than infatuation.

My enamored state of being with him is both foreign and familiar. It's been a long time since I've allowed myself to feel anything for anyone that even *resembled* love. I don't trust love. The feeling has been known to rip me apart, leaving me with a heart missing bits and pieces I can never get back. I don't trust *myself* in love, knowing just how much it means to me—just how much I crave it. I'm afraid to fall deeper into Sage, and yet, I feel his tug and I am powerless to stop it.

There's also something different about the way he makes me feel—something I've never felt before—something that seems both dangerously alluring and inexplicably comforting. I don't know what to make of it. All I know is that I'm done running from it. I left the majority of my heart in his bed Thursday night, sure that I'd never get it back. Then he came after me, bringing it with him, begging for the rest. Now he has it. He has my heart. There is no turning back now. He has all that I swore I wouldn't give him, which is why I spend all afternoon combating my desire to see him, touch him, *taste* him as I grade homework assignments and tweak syllabi.

It isn't until he texts me, telling me he'll be done with rehearsal around six and he can get me shortly after, that I remember that this is an *other* Saturday. My mother calls me every other Saturday at seven-thirty. It's a dreaded phone call I *never* look forward to. I answer mostly because if I don't, she'll just keep calling. That, and I suppose it's not a horrible idea to give her the satisfaction of knowing that I'm still alive—that's her greatest accomplishment, my existence. Most children would be proud to hear their parents say such a thing. My mother makes me feel guilty about the sacrifices she had to make in order to keep me in this world.

She's told me, repeatedly, that I've no concept of the word *sacrifice*. She's a fucking basket-case for thinking that bullshit. And when I tell Sage that I won't be free until eight o'clock, I can't help the resentment that heats up my body in a wave that rushes from my head to my toes. The sacrifice of the hour I could be spending with Sage is a hell of a lot more than she deserves.

I hop in the shower at six thirty, anxious to ready myself for a night out with Sage. I intend to be fully dressed and ready to go by the time my mother calls. As soon as our obligatory exchange is complete, I'm leaving. I take my time under the water, washing my hair, lathering my body, shaving, all the while thinking of the last time I was in this shower. By the time I get out, my skin is flushed from the memory and my longing for Sage is even more intense than it was before.

With the first of October just around the corner, the evening temperature has been dipping more and more with every passing day. Knowing that it'll be somewhat cool, but still wishing to show a daring amount of leg around the man who feels quite possessive over them, I opt for my cream colored sweater dress. The neck is wide, draping off of my left shoulder, the sleeves long, stretching to my wrists. The material clings to my minimal curves, stopping just above mid-thigh, and I pair it with my above-the-knee, grey suede, heeled boots.

Once dressed, I blow dry my long hair and then style it. I pull half of it back, and let the rest fall well past my shoulders. Just as soon as I'm done with my makeup, my phone rings. I sigh, content with the way I look and grateful that I just have one thirty-minute call to endure before Sage arrives.

I click the light out in the bathroom as I slide my finger across my screen to answer the call. "Hello?"

"Tatiana," she replies, her tone cold. I close my eyes and take a deep breath, knowing I'm in for an earful. "The last time I called you, you hung up on me. You better not pull that shit again today, Tatiana. Do you understand? I ask you for nothing, *nothing*, and you can't give me a few minutes of your time?"

"Mother—I'm not going to hang up on you."

"Good. I've had a disaster of a day."

I plop down onto the couch, half listening to her tell me about her *disaster of a day*. I swear, the woman bitches about her job as if that *is* her job. When my father was around, she had been a stay-at-home mom. They were married pretty young, and had me shortly after, so she never went to college. When he left, she didn't have any education or experience to fall back on. Though, it wasn't long before she was able to get a job working as a clerk at the local grocery store. Twenty years later, she still works at the same store. She's bounced around over time, working in almost every department; but now, she's the customer service manager. She hates it, *has* hated it for as long as I can remember, but I don't feel sorry for her. I *can't* feel sorry for her.

There was a time when I tried to convince her that she could do more—be more—*have* more. I encouraged her to go back to school, to get a degree in a field that actually interested her, to learn the skills that she needed in order to find a job that she loved. After months of her bitching at me for robbing her of her youth and any and all chances of her making more of herself, after months of listening to her tell me all the reasons why she *couldn't* do more—be more—*have* more, I just gave up. You can't help someone who doesn't want to help herself.

I guess I shouldn't have been surprised. In a way, I suppose I wasn't. She thrives off of her misery, like it is her life source or something. It sure as hell is the only thing tying us to one another. She gave birth to me, which had been horrible; and she "*mothered*" me by herself after my father walked out on us, which had sucked the life out of her; and she had "*allowed*" me to leave the state of New Jersey, which left her completely alone—because, obviously, everything is always my fault.

"Tati—*Tati,* are you even listening to me?"

"Yes, of course, mother," I lie. I had definitely zoned out there for a while. Checking the time, I see that we've been on the phone for twenty minutes already.

"I asked you how work was going for you?"

"It's fine, mother."

"It's fine? That's all you give me?"

"Yes. It is—it's fine. There's not much else to tell. In fact, I should probably go. I'm going out soon and—"

"Oh, for the love of god," she grumbles. "You're seeing someone, aren'tcha?"

For a moment, I don't know what to say. The answer is certainly yes, but it's not the truth that makes me pause. No, what catches me off guard is my desire to admit that she's right; my desire to tell her even the most minute detail about Sage.

"Tatiana!"

"Yes. Yes, mother, I'm seeing someone."

"Are you just fucking or what?"

I flinch at her crude question. I'd forgotten what it was like to talk to my mother about the men in my life. "No. He's important to me. It's about more than sex or I wouldn't have told you."

"You're making a mistake. You realize this, don't you? Have you learned *nothing* from me? Have you learned nothing from your own past? How many times have I had to say *I told you so,* huh?"

"This is different," I tell her, shaking my head even though she can't see me do it. "S—" I start to speak his name and then stop, my heart warning me that even his name is too intimate a detail to share with my mother. "He's just different, okay?"

"That's bullshit and you know it, Tatiana. How many times must history repeat itself before you learn? Huh? He will leave you. They always leave you. There is no *different.*"

Her words hit me like a slap across the face. My mother has tried and failed to teach me her version of reality in many areas of life. I know what her darkness looks like. From the time that I was six years old, I have done everything I could to escape it—to make my own way, to discover my own reality. But men…she's always been right about men. She's warned me over and over that they always leave and—and she's always right.

"I don't want to talk about him," I say stubbornly. I stand, pacing back and forth in front of the coffee table. The sting of her words has made me anxious and I resent her a little bit more for making me feel this way.

"Just don't let me hear you cry when he discards you. You don't listen to me. You never listen to me. I feel no sympathy for your heart with all that hopeless romantic nonsense," she bites.

When my eyes begin to well up with tears, I try and convince myself that she's not hurting my feelings. I try and remind myself that she's a bitter woman who doesn't have an ounce of love left in her. I try to hold onto the fact that she's my mother by name only—that she hasn't been my *mom* for a long time; she hasn't been someone who I confide in and, therefore, her unsolicited advice means nothing.

Nevertheless, her warning makes my chest sting. Then, when a knock sounds at the door, my excitement from before suddenly feels different—guarded.

I hate her. I hate her for making me feel this way.

"I have to go. I'll talk to you in a couple weeks."

"Tati—"

"I have to go, mother. Goodbye."

I told her I wouldn't hang up on her, but that was obviously a lie. I can't listen to another word she has to say. When Sage knocks again, I blink away my tears and paste on a smile as I open the door for him. The sight of him leaning casually against the doorjamb takes my breath away, and my heart rate spikes when he smirks at me.

He is different, I assure myself. *My mother is wrong. She's wrong. She has to be wrong.*

"Hey," he scowls at me, stepping closer as he reaches up to brush his fingers along the side of my cheek. I lean into his touch, surprisingly desperate for it. "What's wrong, baby doll?"

"Nothing."

"You don't think I'm falling for that, right?" he asks, circling his arms around my waist. "Something's wrong. I can see it in your eyes, Millicent. What is it?"

I grip hold of his dark, plaid button up shirt, allowing the sound of my name to wash over me. *Millicent. Millicent,* not *Tatiana.* I bask in the truth that I am his, a declaration we made to each other just a day ago, and I shove aside my fear. He's not leaving. He's right here. I'm wrapped in his arms and he's not leaving.

"Baby? You're kind of freaking me out, here."

I reach up and press a kiss against his lips, our contact making my whole body tingle with delight. "I'm fine. Really. Just got off the phone with my mother. It's not my favorite thing, that's all. I'm good." I kiss him again, relaxing against his chest as he holds me closer.

When I open my eyes to look at him, I find him studying me—his icy blue eyes dancing around my face. "Doll face, you look like you need to fucking cuddle. I would say let's stay in and order take out, but you look way too fine for all that. We're going out. I know the perfect place. You ready?"

I nod, smiling up at him. "Just need to grab my purse."

"Alright," he says, smacking my ass. I squeak in surprise and he winks at me. "Hurry, baby. I need to cheer my girl up."

FIFTEEN

Sage

Our drive into Old Town is a quiet one. Millie spends most of it looking out the window. I'm curious to know what she's thinking, what's got her upset and distracted, but I don't pry. Knowing it has something to do with her mom, a topic I know she's reluctant to discuss, I decide to let it lie for a bit. She'll tell me what she wants to when she's ready. For now, I just need to focus on putting a smile back on those sweetheart lips.

As per usual, finding parking downtown on a Saturday night is a chore. I end up sliding into a spot about a block and a half away from our destination. Once we're out of the car, I wrap my arm around her waist and pull her into my side, planting a kiss on her temple. She slips her arms around me, her contact putting me at ease a bit.

"You ever play darts?" I ask.

"No," she answers quietly.

I chuckle, amused by the fact that I'm not the least bit surprised. "Baby doll, what did you do for fun when you were an undergrad? Tell me you've at least been to Cooper's Pub."

"I've been," she mutters defensively. She pinches my side and I look down to see her playful glare. "And I went dancing. The Brew, The Wash—I even went to that Cowboy bar once. Line dancing isn't my thing, though."

I laugh, admiring her as we continue our trek to the Pub. It's in this moment that I realize just how freaking adorable she is. She might have me by five years, but

I guarantee she spent more time with her books than she did going out growing up. Me—not so much. School was easy for me; and while music took up a lot of my focus, I never neglected to seek out a good time. The guys can attest to that.

"Stick with me, baby. You've got a lot to learn."

"Is that so?" she asks. I can hear the smile in her voice before I see it on her face. I nod at her in response before pressing a kiss against her lips. We stop walking for just a second as I kiss her again, and then I smirk at her before I continue to lead her to our destination.

Inside, Cooper's is just as busy as I guessed it would be. The bar area is full of a bunch of twenty-somethings all out to indulge in a bit of booze and a bit of fun. Most of the pool tables and foosball tables are occupied, but I spot an empty table near one of the dart boards that isn't in use. I lead her straight there and we sit just as our waitress walks by.

"Oh, hey," she says, back tracking. Her ponytail swishes from side to side when she comes to a stop, and she flashes me a sly smile. "I'm just on my way to the bar. Can I get you something, handsome?"

I offer her a closed lip smile, resisting the urge to roll my eyes. I get it that she may be working an angle for a good tip, but her flirting isn't necessary. "I'll have a Blue Moon. Doll face?"

I watch as her eyes drift from the waitress to me, as if she's noticed the extra attention I'm being given and she wants to see how I'll respond. A smirk tugs at my lips. I'm amused that she hasn't figured it out yet—that as long as she's in the room, and even when she's not, she's the only woman I'm thinking about.

"I'll have a gin and tonic," she says a second later.

We're carded and then the waitress hurries off to get our order, promising to return with menus. I'd bet anything that she only asked for our IDs because she was annoyed that I wasn't giving her the time of day, but I don't care.

"How are things going with Alex?" Millie asks sheepishly.

"Good. Great, actually. She fits in like a champ. I mean, she's not afraid to dig in and work. I think Maddox is finally starting to warm up to her, now that he's seen her level of commitment, and we're all clicking."

"I'm glad it's working out."

Our drinks arrive along with our menus, but it only takes me a second to decide what I want. They serve a wicked Italian Club sandwich and I get it almost every time, unless I'm here splitting a pizza with the guys. Millie takes a little longer to decide. She ends up ordering the house salad. I can't help but cock my eyebrow in surprise, but she only shrugs before sipping at her drink.

"So, are you going to show me your skills or what?" she asks, nodding to the dart board that's still unmanned.

"I didn't say I was any good. Honestly, I never keep score or anything," I tell her with a laugh, standing to collect three darts. "It is a good way to blow off some steam, though." I stand a few feet back and launch each dart one right after the other. Two of them land within the confines of the triple circle, and one hits the triple circle itself. I'm quick to pluck them off the board before I turn to her and ask, "Do you want to try?"

"Um—"

"Come on, gorgeous. I'll help you."

I hold out my hand and she takes it, allowing me to help her off of her stool. I line her up in front of the board, showing her how to angle her body, and hand her a dart. Her first attempt doesn't even make it across the short distance, and falls to the floor. The pathetic expression on her face when she looks at me in defeat makes me laugh. She sighs and rolls her eyes; but before she can head back to her seat, I circle my arm around her waist and hold her against me.

"Hey, no quitting. You just have to put a little force behind your throw. We're blowing off some steam, remember?" I hand her another dart. "Now, throw it like you mean it."

I kiss her bare shoulder as I pull away from her and she shivers, making my cock pulse. I ignore it, watching as she takes a deep breath and chucks her second dart. It sticks at the bottom of the board, in the double ring, and she gasps as it makes contact. When she smiles at me, her face alight with her surprise, it makes me want to kiss her.

"That's my girl," I say proudly, smacking a quick kiss against her lips before handing her the last dart. "Let's see you do it again."

She hits her mark once more, only this time a little higher than before. When I ask her if she wants to play another round, she nods without hesitation and I collect the darts. We play until our food arrives—her tossing, me fetching and rewarding her with kisses—and I can see it as whatever was bothering her before starts to melt away. She only picks at her salad, claiming she's not all that hungry; but when I finish my sandwich and push my plate across the table, offering her my untouched fries, she can't resist.

After another round of drinks and a couple more games of darts, I decide I'm ready to get out of the busy Pub. The night is a cool one, but it's not cold, and I get another idea—something else I like to do when I want to get my mind off of things. I reach for my wallet, pulling out enough cash to cover our bill and a tip, and then I stand, reaching for her hand.

"Let's go for a drive, doll face."

Millicent

Before we pull out of the parking spot, Sage puts the top down. When I ask him if we'll get too cold, he hands me a zip-up hoodie from the back seat and makes me promise to tell him if I want him to put the top back on. Now, as he drives us away from the city, I could care less how cold I am. I like the wind in my face and the night air blowing through my hair. I like being wrapped in Sage's scent, and I'm content to ride in his company.

I don't know where he's taking me, and I don't care. All that matters is that I'm with him. He makes me happy and right now, I just want to be wherever he is, doing whatever he thinks we should do. He told me earlier that he wanted to cheer me up, and he's done more than that already.

He drives for at least a half an hour, neither of us speaking a word. It's a comfortable sort of silence, one we both seem to enjoy. The farther he drives, the darker the night gets. With the city lights behind us, the stars shine brighter, and I admire them—reminding myself that the world is so much bigger than me. It's bigger than the environment in which I was raised. It's just *bigger.* And in all of its grandeur, life can be different. *My life* can be different. I am not bound to live in the past. Just like the night sky that seems to stretch on forever and ever, I can live beyond the limits of what I've seen—of what I've known.

I'm pulled from my thoughts when Sage veers off the main road onto a dirt path. We ride through a thicket of trees that leads to a large clearing. When he stops, I swear we're in the middle of an empty field, nothing but sky above us.

"Where are we?" I murmur, looking over at him. He's lit only by the moon and the stars, but I can still make out the glint in his eye when he smiles at me.

"We're in a field."

"Yes," I say with a small laugh. "I gathered that much. Are we trespassing?"

"Not exactly." I raise an eyebrow at him, signaling that I'm not satisfied with his answer, and he chuckles. "Come on, get out and push your seat up—we'll climb in the back."

He acts without a moment's hesitation, and unsure of what else to do, I follow suit. "Sage—"

"Get that sexy, little ass back here," he demands, reaching for my hips as I do as he says. I close the door behind me and settle in beside him, snuggling into his side when he wraps his arm around my shoulders. "This land belongs to Derrick. It's kind of a long story, but we come out here sometimes. The view is insane. When we catch a sunrise?" He shakes his head, clearly looking for the right word and failing. "You'd just have to see it to understand."

"Hmm. Do you bring all the girls here?" I say, half teasing. I really don't get why Derrick has so much unoccupied land and what a group of guys would do here, besides bring girls and alcohol to get rowdy.

"No," he murmurs, his lips grazing my forehead, effectively silencing my thoughts. "I've never brought any girl here."

I shift so that I can look into his eyes. "Why me?"

He looks back at me for a moment, not speaking, and I wonder if I asked the wrong question. But then he speaks. "He comes out here to find peace. We all do. Sometimes, we just need to get away from all the bullshit, you know? Tonight, I wanted to rescue you from all the bullshit. Is it working?"

His declaration steals my breath. If he hadn't already stolen my heart, he'd have had that, too. I don't know what to say, overwhelmed by this man who sought to rescue me from my own personal *bullshit*. No questions asked. It amazes me that this is who he is. Then again, it makes sense. He's my dreamer. No way could he hold onto his optimism, his hope, without learning to seek and find an escape—a place to grasp hold of *peace*.

"Tell me something," he murmurs, leaning down to brush his lips against mine in a feather soft kiss.

"Tell you what?"

"Anything. Something...*real*. Something honest."

"I despise my mother." The words come out as I exhale—no filter, no second thought—they just fall right out of my mouth, as if they've been there all night, waiting to be called.

Once I realize what I've said, I search Sage's face for some sort of response. He simply looks at me like he's waiting to hear more. I'm amazed at the calm that I feel. I've never actually said the words out loud. I sigh and then rest my cheek against his chest, surprised that I have more truths waiting on the tip of my tongue to be spoken. Maybe it's this place; maybe it's the darkness and the endless sky. Or maybe it's just him. Sage—the heat of his body wrapped around mine; the warmth of his gaze; the comfort of his presence.

"I don't remember when I stopped loving her. All I know is that it was long after she stopped loving me. She always provided for me, but she never really took care of me. I had to learn how to do that on my own. But she needed me. She's always needed me. In her little, miserable world, I'm *his* scapegoat. Since I was six, she's needed me as her target. I'm to blame for everything that went wrong in her marriage. I'm the reason he left. And I hate her...I hate her for so many reasons."

I don't realize that I've got a fist-full of Sage's shirt until he places his hand over mine. I suck in a deep breath, lifting my head to look at him. He doesn't say anything, though. Neither does he try and pry my fingers away from him. He simply stares down at me, his eyes roaming over my face as if he's trying to memorize me in this very moment.

There's something about his silence that puts me at ease. Like—like he understands there are no words to be said. I've shared with him a piece of my reality, a piece of my bullshit, and nothing either of us can say or do will change it. But here, now, under the stars, he's brought me to a place for me to let it go—even if just for tonight.

"Kiss me," I whisper, suddenly needing his lips on mine more than my next breath.

He responds in kind, kissing me decisively. I free a soft moan, the feel of his mouth satisfying me in a way words could not express. I let go of his shirt, sliding my hand up and around his neck, begging him to stay close. He traces his tongue across my lip, seeking entrance, and I grant him full access as I open up for him. When he deepens the kiss, I feel it as my desire dampens the thin fabric of my thong. I'm no longer close enough—I want more. I *need* more.

Without breaking our kiss, I move to straddle his lap, my sweater dress riding the short distance up my thighs as I settle myself against him. He sits up straighter, pulling me tighter against his chest. I can feel his growing erection beneath me and the instant I grind my center over it, my whole body is aflame—the night not so cool any longer. When I start to shrug my way out of his hoodie, he helps push it over my shoulders and onto the floor before I grip both sides of his face, kissing him even deeper.

Deeper. Deeper. I need him as deep as he can go.

"Baby, tell me you have a condom," I plead, rubbing against his bulge in a desperate attempt to relieve the ache he's caused between my legs.

"Need me inside of you?"

"All of you," I whisper, my lips grazing his. "I need you now. Right now. Do you?"

"Mmmhmm," he hums. As he lifts his hips to reach for his wallet, he simultaneously makes contact with my swollen clit and I bite my lip as a wave of pleasure washes over me. While he fumbles for protection, I make quick work of his jeans, pulling out his throbbing cock. My mouth waters at the feel of him pulsing in my hand. I unwrap my fingers only to make way for the condom and then I'm up on my knees, poising myself above him.

"Sage, baby," I sigh, his fingers sliding along the length of my slick slit, moving aside my thong. "Don't tease me—please, don't tease me."

"Need your lips, doll face," he tells me, coating his head in my arousal. I kiss him, hard, anxious for what will follow. As I sweep my tongue through his mouth, he penetrates my entrance and then takes hold of my hips, guiding me over him until every last inch of him is buried inside of me. "Fuck, baby. Can't get enough of this pussy."

I manage no more than a groan as I begin to ride him, his cock filling me up just right, giving me exactly what I need. One of his hands lets go of my hip and reaches to cup around my boob. He gives it a squeeze, spurring me on even more, and I wish I was naked—completely bare for him to touch, taste, and savor. I know, no matter how hot it gets between us, it's entirely too reckless to remove any more clothing—in the middle of nowhere or not. Nevertheless, I crave more of his touch.

"Touch me, baby," I murmur, slipping my hands underneath his shirt as I seek to explore every dip of every muscle on his chest.

He growls, dropping his other hand down and around my bare ass, gripping me as he helps guide my movement up and down over his shaft. He kisses and licks his way along my exposed shoulder and up my neck, nibbling on my ear before his husky voice demands—"Say that again."

"Touch me, baby."

"Shit, Millie—" he grinds out. Before I know it, both of his hands are underneath my sweater, gripping my sides as he lifts his hips and takes control. He bucks into me fast and hard, making me gasp in delight. I tuck my face into his neck as my fingers dig into his lower back. I can't silence the senseless noises that pour out of my mouth as he takes possession of my body—my pleasure climbing higher and higher as we both ascend closer and closer to our release.

"Oh—Sage, baby, right there, right—ahh—*yes*. Don't stop!"

"I'm gonna—Fuck—come, baby doll. Need you to come." As he says the words, he smacks a hand against my ass and then holds on. That pushes me over the edge and I lose myself in him, screaming his name into the night. I feel it as I squeeze around him, just as he swells and then spills his own release. He grunts in my ear, thrusting until he is spent, and I'll be damned if that's not the hottest sound I've heard all day.

Both of us damp with sweat, we hold onto each other as we catch our breath. A part of me can't believe I just had sex in the backseat of his car. It's been *years* since I've done such a thing—but it certainly wasn't as satisfying as all of that. *Not even close.*

"Hey," Sage mutters, running a hand up and down my back. I pull away to peer at him through the darkness and he kisses me soundly. "Stay with me tonight."

I nod, not even stopping to think about it. There's nowhere else I'd rather be.

SIXTEEN

Millicent

"Hey, you."

I look over at the doorway just as Lindsey makes her way into the classroom, effortlessly dodging the students who have just been dismissed. I'm sure they're all aching to get out of here after the pop quiz I just doled out.

"Hi, Lindsey."

"I'm headed back to the office. You?"

"Yeah," I reply, tucking away the rest of my things into my tote. I swear, I don't know what I'd do without this thing. I throw the strap over my shoulder and hook my purse over my arm before I offer her a smile and a nod, signaling that I'm ready.

"How are your classes going?"

"Pretty good. I'm just about on schedule, looking to start mid-term prep week after next. How about you?"

"The same. Though, how we're even *thinking* about mid-terms already, I have no idea. I'm not ready to spend hours of my weekend grading exams!"

"Well, you've got a little time," I say with a small chuckle.

"*Speaking* of weekends, thank god it's Friday. Do you have any plans for the next couple of days?"

A small smile plays at my lips as my thoughts drift back to last night. Sage came over after band rehearsal and stayed the night with me. After he owned my three incredible orgasms, he held me while he chatted excitedly about the show tomorrow night. He's feeling pretty confident—they all are, after the week of hard work they've put in. They've worked with the understanding that they are preparing for what could be their best chance at finding real representation and getting them out of the local music scene and onto a national one.

"I'll take that smile on your face as a *yes*," says Lindsey, nudging me with her elbow as we turn down another hallway. "I'd even wager a guess that this has something to do with a certain *male friend* of yours."

I choke out a laugh, shaking my head in an attempt to bring my thoughts back to the here and now. "Um, yeah. His band is playing at The Brew tomorrow night. I plan on being there."

"Shut up. Sexy McHottington is in a *band*? You didn't tell me that."

I laugh at her nickname for my dreamer, adjusting the heavy tote on my shoulder. "Yeah. He's the lead singer for a band called Mountains & Men."

"Oh, my god, Millie! You've been holding out on me. I've heard of them! I mean, I haven't actually *heard* them, but I've heard people talk about them. I hear they're amazing."

"Yeah. They're really great. And—" I lose my words when we round the corner to the corridor that houses our offices. There—leaning his shoulder against the wall beside my door, his legs crossed at his ankles, one hand in his pocket, the other holding his phone—is Sage. He looks up as he hears us coming and my stomach flutters when his gaze collides with mine.

"Speak of the devil," Lindsey whispers.

"Hey, doll face," he says in greeting, pushing off the wall as he closes the distance between us. He surprises me when he slips his fingers under the strap of my tote bag, easing it off of my shoulder and into his grasp.

"Hi," I manage.

"Millie, aren't you going to introduce us?" asks Lindsey.

"Oh. Yeah, sure. Sorry." Sage smirks at me, clearly amused by the way he's able to shift the axis of my world just by showing up where I least expect him. "Lindsey, this is Sage. Sage, this is Lindsey—or, Professor Clark."

"Definitely just Lindsey," she tells him, holding out her hand.

"Nice to meet you," says Sage, accepting her gesture.

"Tell me, how do you know our Millie?"

My head snaps in her direction and I watch as she playfully bats her eyelashes at Sage. She and I haven't really had too many opportunities to talk recently, both of us busy and distracted. Sage hasn't been a real topic of conversation since last week, before our relationship was defined. *Clearly* she's hoping for a definition right now. She's also smart enough to know that it'll slip right out of Sage's mouth far easier than it'll come from mine.

Sage's smirk turns into a knowing grin and he winks at me before he answers. "I'm her boyfriend."

Boyfriend.

Hearing the word makes my skin breakout in goose bumps.

"Boyfriend, huh? I was hoping you'd say that," she replies animatedly, nudging me with her elbow once more. "Professor Valentine, girlfriend to the lead singer of Mountains & Men. I'm so proud." She places a hand over her heart and I roll my eyes at her, irritated when I feel a blush start to heat my cheeks.

"She told you that, did she?" Sage asks, reaching for my hand. He laces his fingers with mine and my stomach flutters, yet again. Suddenly, I want to be anywhere other than this hallway. I'm feeling overwhelmed with the level of *sharing* that's going on right now. "Are you going to come out to the show this weekend?"

"You're playing at The Brew Cycle?"

"Yup."

"I think I just might," she says, smiling at me as she begins to make her way to her office. "Talk to you later, Millie. Nice meeting you, Sage." She waggles her fingers at the both of us and then disappears behind her closed door. I let out a breath I didn't know I was holding and then pull my hand away from Sage's in order to reach for my keys.

"So, my girl was braggin' on me, huh?" he mutters—my arrogant little shit.

I roll my eyes at him as I unlock my door and step inside. "You surprised me. What are you doing here?"

I barely take two steps into the room before he has me by the waist. He pulls me back, pressing me up against the door as he pushes it shut, dropping my tote at our feet. My heart races and my lungs feel like they are shrinking as his hands slowly travel up my sides, stopping at my ribs. His thumbs graze the underside of my breasts and it's all I can do not to moan. Even fully clothed, his delicate touch provokes my desire for him. *Only* him.

"Needed a taste," he finally speaks in answer to my question.

When he leans in, I think he's going to kiss me, but then he ducks his head and presses his lips against the sensitive spot just below my ear. With a flick of his tongue across my skin, I'm instantly wet. I'm no longer surprised with how quickly he's able to turn me on. I know the pleasure he's capable of manipulating. Even now, as he licks, nibbles, and sucks along the curve of my neck, he's got me right where he wants me—and he knows it.

I reach up and cup my hands around the back of his neck, slowly feeling my way up into his hair. It's just long enough for me to grip hold of and I love the feel of its thick, soft texture between my fingers. I close my eyes and breathe in the scent of Sage—spicy and fresh, manly and delicious. I'm completely lost in him and, in this moment, I wonder how I ever thought I could fight this. I thought the fall would break me, but I was wrong. The fall has saved me. I wouldn't have survived walking away from him. Thankfully, he knew that.

His tongue swirls around the dip at the center of my collarbone and the moan I was holding back before breaks free. I gasp when he reaches up and tugs at the collar of my knit top, pulling it down far enough to reveal the small swell of my breast. I bite my lip when he pinches the skin between his teeth, sucking at the same time. He's leaving his mark on me and the knowledge of that, coupled with the painfully sweet sensation, makes me so hot—inside and out.

"*Sage,*" I murmur. My aching core can't take much more teasing. Knowing I won't be finding a release in my office, I need him to stop—but his name is all I can seem to muster the will to say.

"Mmm," he groans, kissing the spot he just marked as he slides his hands down and around my ass. He pulls me against him tightly and I can *feel* what he's trying to say. "So fucking good," he says softly, kissing his way up the other side of my neck. "Every inch of you, baby doll, tastes so—fucking—good."

When his lips finally crash against mine, I'm so fired up that I can feel my inhibitions melting away. I need him closer, and my body acts without seeking my brain's permission. I hook my leg up around his thigh, hoping to satisfy my throbbing pussy with just a hint of him. He presses into my center and I whimper—his act only making me want more.

"Dammit, Millie," he breathes, cupping the bottom of my ass and lifting me from my feet. It's just enough for me to wrap my ankles around the back of his calves, but he lines us up just right, eliciting a gasp of pleasure. "Stop wearing pants to work, doll face. This would be so much better if I could be inside of you right now."

"Mmm, Sage, we can't have sex in here," I manage, looking into his heated gaze as he rubs his hard-on against me—each stroke sending a wave of pleasure across every inch of my skin.

"Oh, no? Well, I sure as hell plan on getting you off right now."

I open my mouth, but no words come out. I certainly won't argue. He's gotten me halfway there already. I know, despite how inappropriate this might be, I'm just seconds away from relief. I don't know how this became my life—collecting pop quizzes one minute, dry humping my boyfriend against my office door the next—but here I am. And all I can say is—

"Baby, I'm gonna come."

"You bet your sexy, little ass, you are."

He kisses me, and the second his tongue grazes mine, my orgasm washes over me like a tidal wave. I groan into his mouth, wrapping my arms around his shoulders as I kiss him deeper, my body draping over his as my muscles begin to relax.

"Love hearing you come, baby doll," he mutters against my lips, giving my ass a squeeze before he sets me down.

"What about you?" I question, my eyes drifting down to get a glimpse of the impressive bulge in his jeans that just drenched my panties.

"I'll be alright," he says, reaching down to adjust himself. "Besides," he pauses, winking at me before he goes to sit behind my desk. "You can make it up to me later tonight."

"Yeah? You're free tonight?" I straighten my clothes and run my fingers through my hair, bringing the long strands to one shoulder, all the while keeping my gaze trained on him—*Sexy McHottington.*

"I'm free for *you.*"

"Oh. I just thought you'd be with the band."

He shakes his head and holds his hands out, signaling me toward him. Once in reach, I let him pull me down into his lap, his arms around my waist and our hands clasped together. "Tonight, it's just you and me. And Maestro, if it's cool for him to come over."

"Sure," I say with a nod. "As long as he doesn't eat my shoes."

"Nah. Shoes were never his thing."

"And you're *sure* you don't need to be with the band?" I search his face, hoping that his words will match his expression. I remember the last time I hung out with Mountains & Men—it's hard to forget the first jealous fit I've had over a man in, well, maybe *ever*. While I don't feel like I fit in his world anymore than I did before, I've come to accept that, knowing he's chosen me anyway. That being said, I don't want him to have to choose me or them. "I know tomorrow is a big deal," I tell him. "If you want me to come over instead..."

"What'd I say, Millicent?" He kisses my lips softly before he continues. "Tonight, it's just you and me. You're my girl, not my leftovers. I know it's been a crazy week and we haven't really had a chance to hang out, but I'm yours when you want me, doll face. Don't forget it."

"Okay," I murmur with a nod. "I should be home by five."

"I'll see you at five fifteen, then."

"Okay," I say once more.

"Alright." He lets go of my hands and taps my legs, beckoning me up. "I really did just drop by for a taste. I've gotta jet—but I'll see you tonight." He jogs to the door and grabs my tote, bringing it over to my desk before delivering one more quick kiss. "Bye, baby."

"Bye." I sit, watching him leave, feeling both a little sad and a great deal more anxious. It's silly that I miss him even before he crosses the threshold into the hallway, but I do. To deny it would be a lie unworthy of the effort. Instead, I embrace the feeling—giving fuel to the anxious anticipation that stirs in the pit of my stomach. I get him all night long, all to myself, and I can't help but feel a little spoiled.

"So!" Lindsey pops her head into my office, a mischievous smirk on her lips. "What time shall I join you for the show tomorrow? I'm *so* there."

Baby, I'm gonna come.

As I walk out of the building into the cool afternoon, I pull at my jeans while I try and fail to stow away that moment for future use. I lick my lips, remembering what her face looked like as she stared into my eyes—her dark green irises dilated with desire. I almost *feel* her groan as I remember her breathing it into my mouth while she came undone against that door.

Fucking hell, she's so goddamn gorgeous.

For a brief minute, I wonder if I'll be able to wait until tonight before I get mine. She makes me so hard, it's like I'm carrying around a fucking brick dick. I've never wanted a woman as much as I want her.

I've never been so desperate to make a woman come as many times and as often as I wish to make Millicent unravel at my touch.

I meant to come say hi. I hadn't been planning on humping her like a fucking animal, but I couldn't stop. She tasted amazing. She felt even better. I just couldn't stop.

I'm pulled from my reverie at the sound of my phone, ringing from inside of my pocket. I reach for it and check the caller ID. *Pepper* lights up the screen and I'm actually relieved when my hard-on starts to go soft at the sight.

"Hey, Pep," I answer, continuing my journey to my car.

"Hey! I just called to tell you that I have *news!*" she exclaims. I can hear the smile in her voice and it makes me smile, too.

"Yeah?"

"Mom's coming over tomorrow night to watch my little Montgomeries. Harold and I actually get a night to ourselves. He's going to take me to dinner and then we're going to come see you perform."

I pump my fist in the air, unashamed of who might see me in my celebratory moment. Tomorrow night is a huge fucking deal—it's our one chance to make an impression on this Stefany chick. I love my sisters dearly. Their names are tattooed over my heart, for Christ's sake. Knowing that both of them are going to be at The Brew tomorrow night makes me feel that much more confident that we're going to play one sick-as-shit set.

"That's awesome, Pepper. God, I'm so glad you'll be there. It's been a while since you've seen us play. You'll get to meet our new bassist, Alex."

"Oh, yeah. Rose told me about her; says she's pretty sweet and a beast on the bass."

I chuckle at that description. Rosy was right in calling Alex sweet, she really is; but she's definitely got a bit of fire in her she'll never let us guys forget. "Yeah, that about sums her up."

"Well, I look forward to meeting her. Actually, um, I was hoping I might get to meet…your *girlfriend?*" Her voice goes up an octave as she says the word *girlfriend* in question.

I grin, staring down at my feet as I fight my amusement. I've been pretty tight-lipped about what's been going on between Millie and me around my sisters. The guys know, and I've gotten just as much playful grief as I have encouragement from all of them. They're happy for me, but they can't help but mess with me, too.

My sisters, on the other hand? I know they'll lose their shit when they find out Millie and I are officially together. Hell, Rosy was begging to meet her the first time I ever mentioned her. I know my girl doesn't really come from a lot of family and the thought of meeting mine is a bit daunting—she doesn't have to say it; just remembering our Giuseppe's fiasco is enough to remind me we have to take this slow. But with the show tomorrow night, there really is no getting around it. I suppose it's time they knew.

"Yeah. She'll be there."

Pepper gasps. "Your *girlfriend* will be there? Really? *Girlfriend?*"

"Yes, Pepper," I say with a laugh. "My girlfriend will be at The Brew."

"*Yes!* Oh, my god! Sage!"

My smile is so wide, my face actually hurts. It feels good hearing her excitement. When I hear her sniffle on the other end of the line, I shake my head at her. "Pep, are you *crying?*"

"Oh, shut up. It's been a really long time since you've had a girl in your life that you've cared about. I'm just really happy for you. I know how much you wanted her to work out."

"Thanks, sis. That means a lot," I tell her, every word sincere.

"Alright, I should go. Sophia will be waking up any minute and I'll need to feed her, but I'll see you tomorrow night."

"Bands start at eight, we're on at ten. Text me when you get there if you can't find me."

"I will. Love you!"

"Love you, too."

SEVENTEEN

Millicent

It's just after nine when I arrive at the bar and it is *packed*. There's a band up on stage and the dance floor is overflowing with bodies, not to mention all the tables full of drinking patrons. It feels like the entire place is alive and my awareness of the energy makes me nervous. I can't explain why, but it all seems so overwhelming.

As I make my way further into the establishment, my eyes are everywhere, looking for anyone that I know. I'm halfway to the bar when I feel a small hand clasp around my elbow. I look over my shoulder and see that it's Violet who is trying to snag my attention. She grins at me when our eyes meet. She looks amazing. She's wearing a faded gray Mountains & Men t-shirt that appears to have been altered, the neck wide and more flattering to her feminine physique. The fitted blue blazer she wears over it is rolled up at the sleeves, and her legs are tucked into a pair of leather leggings. Her red Toms round out her ensemble and I'll admit, she looks to be one, hot, M&M roadie.

"Knew it was you," she says. "Don't tell Sage I said this, but I'd recognize your long legs anywhere, girl."

I chuckle, looking down at myself. I've got on a fitted, short-sleeved, plain white collared shirt—buttoned only high enough to keep my boobs covered. The shirt is tucked into my black, high-waisted shorts, and my legs are adorned with sheer, black, polka-dot tights. My feet are tucked into a pair of red, stiletto, ankle boots for a little splash of color. I'm not roadie chic, but it'll have to do.

"We haven't been here long," she explains, talking loudly over the music. "We just got finished unloading the trailer a minute ago. Harry, Pepper, and Rose have a table. The guys are getting drinks. Come on."

Before I can utter a single word, she starts tugging me into one of the far corners of the room. Her tug is strong and I can't resist, even though everything in me wants to. Realizing that I'm getting ready to meet Sage's older sister—*his older sister who is younger than me*—along with her husband, freaks me the fuck out. Add Rosemary to the equation and I feel as though my sweaty palms are pretty self-explanatory. I've yet to have an encounter with Rose that *isn't* drenched in awkward. Not having Sage here with me as a buffer just makes it all worse.

"Wait!" I manage, pulling my arm away from Violet. She stops and looks back at me, her blue eyes expressing her curious confusion. "Maybe I should find Sage first."

When she smiles at me kindly, I curse her for being so damn warm and understanding all the time. She links her arm through mine and hip-checks me. "You've met Rose before, haven't you? And Pepper is probably the nicest person I've ever met. You have nothing to worry about, I swear."

I open my mouth to protest some more, but I lose my words when she starts guiding me through the crowd again. I spot Rosemary first. She's in jeans and a sequined top—her long hair pulled up into a high, curly ponytail. She's sitting beside an attractive woman who looks almost nothing like her, the two of them caught up in conversation. Watching them smile and laugh together sends an unidentifiable pang through my chest. The nerves I felt upon entering The Brew now shift into full-on anxiety.

There are so many parts of Sage's world in which I don't belong, and his family—the relationship he has with his sisters—it's just one more place that I don't fit. Though, it's not that knowledge that has me starting to panic; it's the knowledge that I know they'll invite me in, anyway—just like Violet and the guys have. I'm still wrapping my head around the fact that I've fallen for Sage, still getting used to the reality of my girlfriend status, and the possibility of being welcomed by his family is just too much.

If he ever leaves—they'll all leave with him.

I feel my body acting before I can catch up to my thoughts. I plant my feet at the exact moment that I hear someone call my name.

Thank fuck!

Violet and I both turn in the direction of the voice and I see Sarah, Brandon, Aria, and Josh headed our way.

"Hey. I wasn't sure if you'd be here. It's good to see you," Sarah says in greeting. She looks tired, which isn't at all surprising. I'm sure taking care of her parents post-accident is exhausting; plus, her drive up here probably didn't help. Yet, in spite of all of the above, she's still *glowing*. There is a happiness inside of Sarah that is endearing, charming, and sweet all at once. It's kind of disgusting, but I cannot deny that I appreciate it. Especially now. Her timing is perfect.

"Sarah, hi. How are your parents doing?"

"They're on the mend," she replies with a nod. "Thank you for asking. I'm excited to have a night off, though. I'll be heading back down tomorrow morning."

"I'm glad you were able to get away for a bit."

"Is Sage with you?" asks Brandon.

"No. Uh," I pause, scanning the crowd for his face. It only takes me a second to come to the conclusion that the bar is far too crowded to be able to spot him at a glance. "He's around here somewhere. I haven't seen him yet."

"We have a table if your crew wants to join us," pipes in Violet.

"Oh. Sorry—guys, this is Violet. Violet—Sarah, Brandon, Aria, and Josh."

"Hey," she says with a blanket wave. "Any friends of Millie are friends of mine."

I fight the urge to grumble. I wouldn't exactly call this group my *friends*. I'm far from a social butterfly, and it's only been a few weeks since Sarah and I have been on speaking terms. We didn't exactly get off on the right foot. Nevertheless, none of them protest the title.

"Are you with the band?" asks Aria, pointing to Violet's shirt.

"I am. Well, *sort of*. JJ—on the keys—he's my guy," she replies with a shrug and a proud grin.

"Oh, my god, Millie! I found you!" cries Lindsey. She comes up from behind me, joining our growing circle. "I tried texting you, but it's so crazy in here, I figured you wouldn't hear your phone." I start to say hello but, in true *Lindsey* fashion, she takes it upon herself to introduce herself around the group. Once she's met everyone, she focuses her attention back on me. "So, where's that hot boyfriend of yours?"

"Boyfriend?" asks Sarah with a growing smile. "You and Sage?"

"Uh—" Just as I begin to answer her, I *feel* him.

Without a word, he slips his tattooed arm around my waist, pulling me back against his chest. Violet lets me go as he dips his head, nuzzling my neck with his nose before he presses his cool lips against my warm skin. Immediately, I begin to relax. I lean into him, needing him to give me more of whatever it is about him that makes me feel calm in the midst of this crowd of people who seem to be directing all of their attention on me.

"Hey, gorgeous," he mutters in my ear.

I tilt my head back, my eyes seeking out his, and smile when his icy blue irises dance around my face. "Hi."

He presses a kiss to my lips and smirks at me before kissing me one more time. "Have you been here long?"

"No," I say, shaking my head slightly.

"Good. Have some people I want you to meet." I inhale deeply and exhale slowly, trying to mentally prepare myself to meet some of the most important people in his life. With him by my side, it doesn't feel so daunting; but that doesn't mean I'm not nervous.

As if he can read my thoughts, he kisses me once more before he shifts his focus to our quiet audience. He greets everyone enthusiastically, thanking them for coming out to support him and the band. He seems completely unfazed by the fact that our entire exchange was being watched, and it dawns on me that he's used to the spotlight in ways that I never will be.

The nerves I felt upon entering tonight, they were for him. In that moment, I wondered how he would fair up on that stage, in front of the packed bar. It was silly of me to worry. The energy in the room? The massive amount of people that makes this place feel alive? It's like *fuel* for him. This is Sage in his element. He was meant to be the center of attention.

"Come on," he tells everyone with a nod. "We've got a table." He takes my hand, lacing his fingers with mine, and offers me a wink as he leads the way. "Come 'ere, doll face. It's time I show you off."

Sage

Millicent about squeezes the life out of my hand as we approach the table. JJ and Derrick are shootin' the shit with my sisters and Harry, and I know the Bradley brothers opted to hang at the bar until it's time to head backstage. Pepper's eyes drift in our direction, and when she see's Millie, I can tell she's no longer listening to what Rosy is saying. Instead, I watch as she discreetly taps Harry's leg underneath the table, catching his attention. He looks to my sister before he looks our way. A sly smirk tugs at my lips as he raises his eyebrows at me, seemingly impressed.

Damn straight. My girl is a fox.

I introduce Millie to Pepper first, and then Harry. She seems to relax a little bit upon making his acquaintance. I never told her how much older than us he is, and I think it surprises and satisfies her that she's not the oldest one in our bunch. Not that Harry is old. At thirty-two, he's got that *boy-next-door, good-guy-jock* thing going for him. I'm sure his blonde hair, blue eyes, and chronic five o'clock shadow make all the ladies that walk into his office want to drop their panties.

Then again—that's part of the job, being an OBGYN and all.

Too bad for them, he's been officially off the market for the past five years. He's a good guy, my brother-in-law, and I couldn't ask for a better man to love my big sis.

Since the bar is loud and our table is full, Millie is spared from too much conversation with my siblings. After a few general questions, Rosy excuses herself to the bathroom and Pepper pulls out her phone, apologetic but insistent that she send mom a text to check on her *little Montgomeries.*

As soon as she's no longer the topic of discussion, Millie grabs my beer and chugs half of it. I chuckle when she pulls the bottle away from her lips and draws in a few deep breaths. "I thought you didn't like beer, baby," I say, wrapping my arm around her waist as I pull her close.

"It'll do for now." She takes another sip and then looks at me guiltily. "Shit—I didn't think—you're going on soon. Was this to help calm your nerves?"

"Nah," I assure her, shaking my head to emphasize my answer. "I'm not nervous, baby doll."

"You're not? Not even a little bit?" she asks, lifting her eyebrows in question.

"No. Why should I be? Tonight, I'm playing with my boys, like always. My sisters are here. My girl is here. The crowd is primed and ready—I've got everything I need. No matter what happens after our last jam, we're going to kick ass, and I'm going to enjoy every fucking second of it."

She stares at me for a second, not uttering a word. Then she grabs a fist-full of my shirt and pulls me closer before crashing her lips against mine. My hands immediately slide down her sides before resting on her ass as I kiss her back. She pulls away just as abruptly as she leaned in, and my eyes go straight for her lips as she speaks.

"I can't wait."

I offer her a grin, giving her ass a squeeze, and she giggles. Too soon, the moment is broken when I feel a tap on my shoulder.

"Hey," Rosy begins hesitantly. "Sorry to interrupt, but I thought you'd like to know…well, you go on in a half an hour and Alex was just in the bathroom puking her guts out."

"Shit."

"She shrugged it off, saying it was just nerves, and then scurried backstage before I could really talk to her. I think she might need a bit of a pep-talk."

I look from Rosy to Millie, my mind tracing its way back to the day we met Alex. JJ asked her why she wasn't in a band already and she said she struggled with stage fright. *Fuck.* We never brought it up again. The last thing we need is for her to lose her shit up there—*hell, if we can get her up there at all.*

"I gotta go, doll." I kiss Millicent once. Twice. Three times. "Stay with Vi. I'll see you after, yeah?" She nods and I smack her ass before I let her go and kiss the top of Rosy's head. I make my way through the crowd, not bothering to tell the guys where I'm going. Hopefully, I can squash this shit before it becomes a problem.

Backstage, the sound of the music and the full bar die down just a bit. It's not a big space, the area doubling as a place for storing extra stock, and it doesn't take me long to spot Alex. She's sitting on the ground, her back against the wall in the hallway leading to the back exit. As I approach, I notice that her hands are clasped together in her lap and her lips are moving. I pause, wondering if I'm intruding on some sort of meditation ritual or some shit, but she hears me and looks up.

"Hey."

"Hey. Am I interrupting?"

"No. Not really." She sighs heavily and gestures to the space beside her. I accept her invitation, sliding down the wall until I'm seated next to her. "Praying really only works if you believe what you're saying, you know?"

"Uh," I mutter with a chuckle. "Not big on prayer."

"Right. Well, in the event that you ever want to try it, it works best with a little faith. I can ask God for courage all I want, but if I don't believe He'll give it to me—my pleas are counterproductive. Right now, I'm not feeling very confident."

"Yeah," I begin with a small nod. "Heard you lost your cookies."

"More like the peanut butter and honey sandwich and Doritos I had for dinner, but yeah."

"That's gross."

"Sorry," she says with a little laugh. She sighs again and I nudge her with my shoulder.

"You're ready for this, Zip. Trust me, there's no way in hell you'd be here tonight if I thought any different."

"Yeah. I believe you. Really, I do. Honestly, earlier today, I felt great. I felt excited. It means so much to me that I get to do this with you guys. But then we got here and…I don't know."

"The crowd freak you out?"

"No, actually. I can handle the people. My stage fright is more like…my own personal demon. It's a lie that lives inside of me, preventing me from doing exactly what I've always dreamed of. It sucks."

I nod, replaying her words in my mind. I understand what it's like to battle the demon within. We all have them, they just manifest themselves in different ways. I've been putting up one hell of a fight for years. Most days, I feel like the fucking king of the world—conquering that shit. But every once and a while, I go to war with my own inadequacy and the question that drives me to work my ass off, even when I'm unsure of the answer…

"You know, we're not called *Mountains & Men* for nothing." She looks at me, raking her fingers through her hair as she waits for me to continue. "This is our dream. Playing music, *sharing* music, *that's* the dream. But for all of us, behind that dream is an obstacle—something that feels insurmountable—*a mountain*. The dream, though…it's worth the climb—worth the struggle, the effort, and the fight.

"You're not the only one with demons. You're not the only one with insecurities. You just have to play through that shit. If you're going to be one of us, Alex, you have to be willing to climb your fucking mountain. It's what makes the dream worthy of the title. So—are you one of us?"

She studies me for a moment, as if she's really considering the question. I respect her for respecting the question and I stare back at her, willing her to grab her demon by the balls and own that motherfucker. Finally, she offers me one curt nod.

"I'm one of you."

"Alright," I say with a grin. I stand to my feet and offer her a hand. She takes it, standing with me. "Let's do it, then."

Before she lets go of my hand, she squeezes my fingers and takes a step closer to me. "Thank you, Sage. Really."

"You got it."

"I'm going to run to the bathroom before we go on." I lift an eyebrow at her and she giggles. "I promise not to puke. I just have to pee."

"Get out of here, then," I say, shooing her away.

I watch her go as the rest of the guys file into the staging area. Knox looks at me, then over his shoulder where Alex just disappeared, and then back at me. "You got a chick. You know you can't tap that, right?"

I scoff, giving him the finger. "I'm not trying to tap that."

"Tap who? Tap *Alex?*" asks JJ.

"No. *Fuck*, no!" cries Maddox. "Band-fucking-rule! Nobody taps the fuckin' church mouse! We *do not* need that kind of drama. Can we agree?"

Knox, JJ, Derrick and I all exchange a look—more amused by Maddy's outburst than anything else. He's right, though, and we all know it. We only pause a second before we all chime—

"*Aye*."

EIGHTEEN

Millicent

As soon as Derrick and JJ leave to meet up with the others, Rosemary and Violet insist that it's time to head to the dance floor. The band on stage wraps up their set and the lull between bands is everyone else's cue to head to the bar for refills.

"Front and center—just the way I like it," says Rose with a grin.

"I wonder what this *Stefany* looks like," Violet says as she scans the room. "She better be here, that's for sure."

"I bet she is, and she's in for one hell of a treat!" Rose beams.

"What are they talking about?" asks Lindsey, leaning down to mock-whisper in my ear.

I explain to her about the band meeting the tour manager for Lawful Sinners and expressing interest in having Mountains & Men come along as an opening act. This *Travis* guy never said it was absolutely certain that Stefany would be in attendance tonight, but he did say that he'd tell her she'd be missing out if she wasn't. I know how excited they are for the possibility to go on their first national tour, and I really hope their hard work pays off tonight.

While we wait for the guys to set up on stage, the house speaker plays the latest radio hits. I can't help but notice Pepper and Harry as they sway to the beat, wrapped in each other's arms. They look so in love, and a pang of longing fills my chest. There's a part of me that still refuses to hope for that—that kind of commitment and affection. I know I have Sage, but I'm already in way over my head with him. To wish for any more seems stupid.

I'm pulled from my thoughts when a group of giggling girls comes to fill the space on the other side of Lindsey. They're obviously enjoying themselves, and their drinks, and I decide to pay them no mind—that is, until I catch wind of their conversation.

"Remind me again why we're up here?" asks one of them.

"*Hello!* This is the whole reason we're here. I *told* you, M&M is the shit. And Sage, O-M-G, totally fuckable."

"Bitch—hands off," her friend says with a wide smile. "The fine ass man on the mic is mine. *God,* have you seen the way he moves his hips?" She frees an exaggerated groan and I pull my lip between my teeth.

He certainly does have a way with his hips. It's fucking magical.

"Whatever—while you two fight over Sage, I'll be taking Derrick home with *me*. That tongue—mmm. I just want to suck it."

Lindsey laughs, catching my attention, and I can't help but chuckle with her. "Seems we're hanging out with some groupies! I *love* it!"

I shake my head at her just as the overhead music fades and the lights dim.

"Seriously, though—does that bother you?" she asks, nodding to the girls beside her.

I shrug as I try and figure out the answer to her question. The truth is, they aren't wrong. He is *totally fuckable*. I can't fault them for thinking the same exact thing that I did a month ago. Besides, he's chosen me. I'm right here, right now, and he's chosen *me*.

"You don't call him *Sexy McHottington* for nothing," I reply with a lopsided smile.

Lindsey laughs, nudging me with her elbow, and then we both direct our attention to the stage. The guys file out with no introduction; but when the room fills with cheers, it's obvious that they don't need one. As Derrick settles behind his drum set and Knox, Maddox, and Alex strap on their instruments, Sage steps up to the mic and scans the crowd with a smirk. When he spots his sisters, they both cry, "*We love you!*" He points down at them, his smirk turning into a grin. Then his eyes find mine and he offers me a wink.

A wink.

That's all it takes to make my stomach flutter.

He looks back over his shoulder, I assume to make sure that everyone is ready. When he turns to look over his right side, I notice as he nods to Alex. He then curls his arms in front of him, flexing his muscles, making her laugh. She bobs her head with excitement and then curls her arms up and flexes in return. I have no idea what that's about, but it seems to be his cue to start.

"Hey, hey," he says, speaking into the mic. The crowd roars and a devilish grin spreads across Sage's impossibly handsome face. "We thought we'd play a little while. You good with that?" His question is met with more cheers. "Hmm, I couldn't quite hear you." Their fans scream louder and he nods his approval. Derrick clicks the tempo and then starts pounding out the beat as Sage says, "Well, we're Mountains & Men—and I don't know about you, but I think it's time to fuckin' dance."

The rest of the band begins to play and Sage jumps up in the air, waving his hands to pump the crowd up even more. Just before he starts to sing, he pulls the mic from out of its stand. My heart races when he hits that first note—his rich, smooth, *sexy* tenor voice washing over me. I sway my hips back and forth, my entire body under the spell of the man on that stage. My eyes devour him as the natural performer in him shines through. He's so hot up there—every show, it's the same—he burns blue, like the hottest part of a flame.

When he gets to the chorus, he sings it one time through before he holds out the mic, instructing us to sing along. He sings the next line and then holds the mic out once more, cupping his hand around his ear as he eggs on the bar full of fans. I find myself singing along with everyone else at the top of my lungs. I can't help it. He's got me. I'm a fan-girl and there's no sense in denying it.

For the next forty minutes, Mountains & Men rock the house. By the time they are finished, they're all coated in sweat. We're *all* covered in sweat—the room buzzing with the energy their music has left behind. Now, there's only one thing I want. One thing I *need*. And when Violet grabs my hand, I don't fight her as she drags me through the crowd.

My lips are *more* than ready—my body aching from the inside out in anticipation of what I know is coming...

Sage.

My dreamer.

My fucking rock star.

Sage

The adrenaline that's coursing through my veins is the most welcome high I've ever felt. As I say goodnight to the crowd, I bid farewell to another great show. Big venue or small, large crowd or intimate, it doesn't matter—it's all about the music. Singing it. Playing it. Sharing it. Reveling in it. *Living* it. This is the dream, and tonight, we fought for it. Tonight, we live to see another day.

"Thatta girl!" cries Knox. I turn just in time to see him bend down and throw Alex over his shoulder. She grunts as she bends, her long, dark, purple hair hanging to Knox's knees. "Way to rock, Zip," he says, slapping her ass. "You're officially one of us."

"Yeah. You killed it," says Derrick with a grin, clapping a hand against the same cheek as he heads off stage.

"Fuck yeah, church mouse. You're a badass," Maddox pipes in. I chuckle when he gives her a smack in passing, too.

"Um, am I the only one who thinks this is an extraordinarily sexist pat on the back?" She squeaks when JJ answers with a slap and a laugh. "Seriously, guys! What the hell? Put me down, Knox."

"Aww, we're just messin'," I assure her, lifting her hair to look into her eyes. Her face is red from all the blood that has rushed to her head, which only makes me chuckle more. "We're a bunch of dudes, remember?"

"*Right*—so, you guys smack each other's asses after a great show. Is that it?" Both Derrick and JJ look back over their shoulders and the four of us share a smirk, knowing good and well we don't go near each other's asses.

"You got a pussy, babe, we get it," says Mad Lips. "If you *really* want to be treated like the fellas and you'd rather a titty-twist—"

"My ass is yours, guys. Have at it!" she says, throwing her hands out in surrender.

We all burst into laughter, Alex included, as we make our way backstage. As soon as I reach the top of the stairs, I see her. I know right away, and without an introduction, who she is. She's a slim little thing; but if her clothing says anything about her, she's got an edge about her and she knows how to use it.

Her leopard print slacks are tight, stopping just above her ankle, highlighting her red Converse. *I like her already*... She's got on a form-fitting white T underneath her snug, black leather jacket, and her blonde hair is piled on top of her head in a messy bun. She's busy typing away on her phone as we come off the stage, but when she hears us, she looks up and smiles.

"Hey, guys. *Great* show. Travis told me I needed to get my ass up here, but *damn*."

"You must be Stefany," I say, stepping forward and offering her my hand.

She returns the gesture with a firm shake. "Yeah. And *you* are my new favorite up-and-coming band. Seriously, you guys are phenomenal. The atmosphere you create—*electric*. How has no one picked you up, yet?"

"Timing is everything," says Derrick, coming up beside me to shake her hand as well.

We all introduce ourselves, and as every second ticks by, my patience chips away little by little. I'm dying to know what all of her compliments mean—I'm more than anxious to get confirmation that our big break is finally fucking here.

"Speaking of timing," she says, letting go of Alex's hand. "This tour with Lawful

Sinners is right around the corner. Busses roll out in a little over a month. I've got an in and I sure as shit want to take you with me. How does that sound?"

"Are you fucking kidding me?" cries Maddox.

Knox smacks him against the chest, a knowing smile tugging at his lips before he says, "We want in. No doubt about it."

"Fantastic," she says, clapping her hands together. "I really think you guys have the potential to make a name for yourselves. It's time to get you out there. There are a few logistical things that we need to work out on the business side—I'd like to sit down with you guys and talk contracts. Plus, I want to get you boys—and girl," she adds with a wink toward Alex, "into the studio."

"Sounds good. When and where?" I ask.

"Monday. Ten a.m. Denver. My office—here's my card," she pauses, handing it to me. "I know it's short notice, but I'm not one to just sit on a gold mine. Can you make that happen?"

"We'll be there," Derrick promises.

"I look forward to it. Thanks again for a good show—I'll see you Monday." She offers us a wave, pulling out her phone as she disappears into the bar. For a moment, we all just stare at her as she departs.

That just happened.

Holy. Fucking. Hell—we're going on tour.

With Lawful Sinners.

"We're going on tour with Lawful Sinners," I mutter under my breath. Saying the words out loud makes it feel a little bit more real, so I decide to say it again. "We're going on tour with Lawful Sinners." I look around at the guys, my brothers, the men who have been with me through thick and thin, playing from the heart, rockin' from the soul. "We're fucking going on tour with Lawful Sinners!" I cry.

Maddox lets out a roar before he pounces on me. Derrick tackles the both of us next. Soon, all of us are laughing and yelling as we jump around—pushing, hugging, slapping. When I look over and see Alex standing alone, laughing at us, I reach out my hand.

"Get the fuck over here, Alex." The guys pause, making a space for her, and then we all huddle up around our little badass bass player. "We did it, guys. This is it. I can feel it."

"Hell, yeah!" cries JJ.

"It's time to fucking party!" says Maddox.

We all chime in a hearty agreement.

"Um, *hello!* What's going on back here?" Each of us turns at the sound of Violet's voice.

I barely notice her before my eyes find Millie. My girl. My sexy as shit woman.

For the first time in a very long time, I have someone other than the guys to share this moment with; I have someone I actually *want* to share this moment with. I want to tell her everything, and I plan to. I know she'll listen; she'll *hear* me because she *sees* me.

But first—*I need a taste.*

I don't hear the guys as they address Violet. As soon as my gaze aligns with Millicent's, I can only think of one thing. I close the distance between us and then bend down to wrap my arms just below her hips, pinning her against my chest as I lift her off of her feet. She circles her arms around my shoulders as she smiles down at me, and I feel like the luckiest motherfucker on the planet.

"We did it, baby," I murmur.

"Seriously? Sage!"

"Kiss me. Need a taste, doll face."

Her smile stretches a little wider before she leans down and presses her lips against mine. I immediately open my mouth, running my tongue along the seam of hers. As she allows my tongue entrance, she cups her hands around the back of my neck, slipping her fingers into the hair at the nape of my neck.

God, she feels so good. Anywhere she touches me, every time, it only makes me want more.

She kisses me long and slow, and in spite of my amped up state, I like her tempo. It doesn't calm me down in the slightest. Instead, it sends my blood rushing to its favorite place. When I pull her bottom lip between my teeth and suck, she whimpers. The sound makes my dick twitch and I squeeze her tighter. I kiss her one more time before I tell myself to pull away. "We're going to celebrate and then I'm taking you home and fucking you every which way until Sunday."

"Sunday is in less than an hour," she says with a giggle, resting her forehead against mine.

"Then I guess I'll just have to keep you in bed all day." When she doesn't protest, a smirk pulls at the side of my mouth before I reach for another quick kiss. By the time I set her down on her feet, we're alone backstage. I take her hand, locking my fingers between hers, and lead the way out front.

Two steps into the main room, a familiar body smashes into mine. Pepper wraps her arms around me in a tight embrace and I can't help but laugh as I let go of Millie in order to return her affection. "You were so great. God, Sage, it's been too long since I've seen you perform. I love you so much! You're my favorite rocker!" She pulls away just enough to beam up at me. "Well, you and Adam Levine. His voice..." She shivers and I cock an eyebrow at her. "Seriously, though," she continues, reaching up to cup her hands around my cheeks. "I'm so damn proud of you, it hurts."

"Thanks, Pepper. It means a lot to me that you're here."

"Any time, baby bro," she promises with a wink.

"Are you sticking around?"

"No, we've got to go. I'm *exhausted* and I've taken all the excitement I can for one night."

"Alright," I say with a chuckle.

"You're a real talent, Sage. You kicked ass up there tonight," says Harry, shaking my hand before pulling me in for a hug. We pat each other on the back and then say our goodbyes.

As they turn to leave, my baby sister steps in front of me with a huge grin on her face. I open my arms and she throws herself at me. "Tell me I'll be staying and playing DD tonight because you're gonna get shit-faced as you celebrate good news!"

"Rosy, we'll *definitely* need a ride home."

"She loved you, didn't she?"

I smirk down at her, offering her a nonchalant shrug. She smacks my chest as she pulls away from me. "I want to know every *single* detail!"

"Can I get a drink, first?"

She rolls her eyes teasingly. "I *guess*."

When I look back at Millie, I find her watching our exchange. I can't tell what the expression on her face means, but I know I'd rather see her smile. I snake my arm around her waist and pull her against me, pressing a kiss to her temple. "Hey, gorgeous. How 'bout I buy you a drink?"

The smile I was hoping for pulls at her lips as she nods her agreement. We're halfway to the bar when we're stopped again, this time by our friends. Brandon and Josh both shake my hand and Aria gushes about how much she loved our set. I'll never tire of hearing our fans sing our praises. I sure as hell will never take it for granted, either.

Sarah catches my attention, tapping my arm before opening hers. I accept her invitation and give her a quick hug. She congratulates me on a great night and I offer my thanks. Just as I begin to pull away, she tightens her grip.

"She's different," she speaks softly—loud enough to be heard over the music and hum of conversation that fills the room, soft enough that no one else can make out what she's saying. "With you, she's different. It's good. Really good. Don't hurt her, Sage. Okay?"

I bob my head in acknowledgement as I pull away from her. Our eyes lock and her warning is reiterated in her stare. I don't respond with words. Instead, I reach for Millie's hand and bring it to my lips.

If only Sarah really knew.

There's no way I'd ever intentionally hurt my girl.
I worked my ass off to get her.
I'll work my ass off to keep her.
She's the harmony to my melody, and our song has just begun.

NINETEEN

Sage

SHE WON'T LET ME touch her.

I'm horny as *fuck*, and she won't let me touch her.

I rode to The Brew with Derrick, JJ, and Violet; but after a night of drinks on the house, not any of us are in any shape to drive—save Alex and Rosy. Took some convincing, but Derrick handed Alex his keys and the Bradley brothers squeezed into my original ride home. Rosy volunteered to play chauffeur for Millie and me, promising to take Alex back to her car as soon as their DD duties were complete.

I thought the plan was all fine and good until I realized Millie wouldn't let me touch her with my sister in the car. I squeezed into the backseat of Rosy's prized piece of shit just to have an excuse to be close to my girl. I thought at least she'd let me cop a feel—but she keeps refusing my advances.

I'm no quitter, though.

I take Millie's chin between my fingers and gently turn her face so that she's looking at me. I press a soft kiss against her lips, pulling away before she can. Then I kiss along her jaw. As my lips descend, so does my hand. I trace my fingertips down her neck and along the exposed skin of her chest. As soon as I reach for her boob, she grabs my hand and pulls it away, squeezing as tight as she can in pathetic warning.

"*Baby,* come on," I murmur. I bite my lip in restraint and peer through the darkness into her eyes, pleading with her.

"Don't. Don't look at me like that," she says airily.

"Like what, baby doll? Like I want you? *Fuck*," I bring my mouth to her ear, flicking her lobe with my tongue. "I want you so bad."

"Sage," she breathes.

I free my fingers from her grasp and force my hand in between her closed thighs. She doesn't stop me as I slide closer and closer to the warmth of her center. I cup her pussy, wishing it wasn't covered in so much clothing, and she gasps, her eyes darting toward the front seat.

"I want in," I whisper. "I want to feel how wet I make you. Want to feel you come all over my cock. Want to hear you scream my name, Millicent."

"Stop," she begs. As she utters the word, she rests her forehead against mine and lines up our lips. I can feel the warm puffs of her shallow breaths, proof that she wants me just as much as I want her.

"You sure that's what you want?" I slowly drag my hand out from between her legs, feeling my way around to her side. "You want me to stop touching you?" I graze the underside of her tit with my thumb and her lips draw closer to mine. I smirk as I use my thumb once more, gently rubbing it over her nipple—I can feel the hardened bud through her bra. "You know I'll take care of you, doll face. You know I'll make you feel so fucking good."

"Sage…"

"Gonna fuck you 'til the sun comes up, baby."

"Ugh! I'm going to barf up here!" Rosy yells. I jerk my head in her direction, but I don't move my hand. "You're drunk, big bro. Know what that means? Your little *whisper* isn't exactly a *whisper* at all. Please—can you *please* just wait two fucking minutes before you eat her out or whatever? I've already seen you two go at it once. None of us needs to relive that."

"*Shit*. Now? *Now* will you stop?" Millie hisses, shoving me away from her.

I scowl at her dismissal, knowing good and damn well that I almost had her. Then, I shift my focus to my sister, leaning forward so that my face is next to hers. "Thanks for bringing that up, twerp. That was *really* necessary."

"Don't call me names, Sage. I'm doing you a freaking solid, here. The *least* you could do is keep your damn clothes on."

A low growl rumbles from my throat as I lean back in my seat. There are so many things I want to say to her right now, but I'm in no mood to pick a fight. Instead, I keep my mouth shut and reach for Millie's hand. I think about sliding it over my erection so that she can feel just how fucking hard she makes me, but I know she'd lose her shit.

The two minutes Rosy promised feels more like five, and it's the longest five minutes ever. As soon as she pulls into the driveway, I bust my ass to get out of her car. I reach my hand back inside to help Millie climb out, and then I slam the door behind her before leading her to the front door.

"Hey, dickhead!" Rosy yells, jumping out of her car. "You're fucking *welcome!*"

"Sage, baby—"

Millie's voice stops me dead in my tracks. I spin around to face her, sliding my arm around her waist and pulling her against me. Fuck if hearing her call me *baby* doesn't make my chest swell with pride. *Damn straight, I'm her baby. And she's my gorgeous girl.*

"What is it, doll face?"

"Be nice to Rosemary. Thank her for bringing us home," she murmurs

"Waited longer than two minutes, baby. Need you out of these clothes right this second."

"Say thank you," she insists, pressing her tits against my chest, "and you shall have me."

I absentmindedly run my tongue across my lower lip while I stare at hers.

"Sage?"

I smack a kiss against her cheek before I look over her shoulder at my sister, who stands with her hands on her hips watching us. "I love you. I'll call you later."

Rosy tips her chin up in response and I know that she's still pissed. I also know that she'll forgive me by the time I get inside the house. Staying angry at each other is almost impossible.

With my implied apology and appreciation all mixed up into one, I bend down and throw Millie over my shoulder. She grunts out a breath of surprise and then grabs the top of my jeans to steady herself. I grip a handful of her ass, wasting no time before I get us inside and up the flight of stairs that leads to my room. After I shut us in, I deposit her onto the bed, turning on the bedside lamp before I seal her mouth with mine.

She moans, reaching up to sink her fingers into my hair. Unlike earlier, just after the show, this kiss is full of desperation. I want her—*bad*—and I can tell by the way she wraps her legs around me, forcing me closer, that she's just as hungry for me as I am for her. I kiss and nibble my way down her neck, every sigh that passes from her lips making me that much harder.

I swear to fucking god, I need to be inside of her now.

I reach for the button of her shorts, unfastening them before I stand to my feet and do the same for myself. I shove my jeans down, just far enough to free my throbbing dick, and then I grab her hips and flip her over, pulling her up so that she's on her knees. She gasps but doesn't protest as I pull her shorts, tights, and panties down her thighs. I'm so lost in lust, I can hardly even think straight.

I run the head of my dick between her slick folds and free a groan. The warmth of her skin feels incredible. I'm just about to sink inside of her when she stops me, looking over her shoulder and into my eyes.

"Condom."

"*Fuck*," I mutter, only a little surprised I forgot. I'm pretty good about remembering—but she's my girl. Neither of us are getting naked for anyone else. "Aren't you on the pill?" Suddenly, the thought of suiting up seems disappointing. I want in *now*. I want to feel all of her wrapped around all of me.

"Sage—*condom*."

I can tell she's not going to change her mind easily. I don't know what's up with that shit, but I also don't have time to argue. My balls are going to turn blue if I don't do something about my raging hard-on, pronto. I reach into my nightstand and grab what I need, ripping it open and sheathing myself before I plunge into her center. I thrust in hard and without warning—her warmth providing just the relief I need.

"Oh, god—*yes!*" she mewls.

My grip around her tightens as I pound into her over and over, my pace unforgiving. She feels perfect—so goddamn perfect. I free one of my hands to reach for her hair. I grip a fistful and pull just slightly, causing her to whimper as she arches her back for me. Then she moans loudly and I know I've found her money spot.

"You like that, baby? Huh? You need my cock like I need your pussy?"

"Yes, yes—Sage—*fuck, right there!*"

I slow down, easing my way out before shoving myself back in, *hard*. She cries out and I do it again. After the third time, I can tell by her trembling limbs that she's getting close.

"Baby—I can't—I can't! Sage, fuck me—please, just fuck me."

A smirk tugs at my lips as I oblige, my balls smacking her clit, each thrust filling the room with the sound of our hot, wet friction. Her fingers ball up around two fistfuls of comforter when her pussy squeezes my dick.

"*Holy sh—*" Her words get cut off with a gasp followed by a cry that's so sexy, it's a song in and of itself. I pull out as soon as the walls of her core relax.

I need a taste.

Need to devour the sweet evidence of her climax.

I turn her over onto her back with ease, and she watches me as I pull her shorts, tights, and panties to her ankles. I discard her shoes, one right after another, and then drop the rest of her clothes to the floor. I'm on my knees a second later, spreading her legs wide before sweeping my tongue along the length of her slit.

"Sage, baby," she murmurs, bucking her hips. I lick her once more before she grabs a fistful of my hair and pulls my face away from her. When our eyes lock, she drags her teeth over her bottom lip before she tells me, "I want a taste, too."

Fuck. Me.

I stand to my feet, tossing my glasses onto the nightstand before reaching behind my head to pull off my shirt. As I shove my boxers and jeans down my legs, I watch as she hurriedly unfastens the buttons on her shirt before discarding it. I toe off my shoes and socks, freeing my ankles as she frees her tits, and then I crawl into the bed with her.

I lie back, resting my head on my pillows, and then point at my mouth. "On my face, baby doll."

She doesn't hesitate, flipping around to give me the perfect view of her pretty, little ass as she straddles my head. I suck on her clit as she removes my condom and then swallows my dick.

Jesus—I may have just died and gone to heaven.

When I plunge my tongue inside of her, lapping up her arousal, she hums. The vibration of her voice makes me moan my own pleasure. She sucks and licks, her adoration of my dick a thing of sheer fucking beauty. For a few blissful minutes, we satisfy our cravings, savoring every last drop.

"Mmm, Sage," she breathes, her hand giving me a squeeze. "I'm gonna come baby, I'm gonna come again."

"Ride my face, baby. Take all you need. Love the taste of your sweet cunt, Millie."

She does exactly as I say, grinding against my mouth until she comes undone, my name on her lips as she cries out. It's so fucking hot. So fucking sexy.

After she rides out her release, she flops onto her back—her chest rising and falling with her rapid breaths. "You're still hard," she sighs, looking from my crotch to my face. I prop myself up on my elbows and offer her a smirk. She giggles as she sits up and reaches for my bedside drawer. "Guess we need another one of these, huh?"

"You bet your sweet, little ass."

Millicent

I've lost count of how many orgasms I've had. Partly because I'm exhausted, partly because there were definitely more than I've ever had in one night. His whiskey dick would *not quit*. My sated body is actually a bit relieved that he finally came. I'm sure I can't take anymore. I'm even more positive that tomorrow—or, rather, *today*—his dick is not allowed anywhere *near* my lady bits.

"Hey," he murmurs, his lips grazing my shoulder. "You good?"

"Mmm," I manage, reaching back to run my fingers through his hair.

"I'm going to get up for a minute. I should let Maestro out before we crash."

"Okay."

"Will you be awake when I get back?" he asks, delivering more sweet kisses.

I cough out a tired laugh, too worn out to even turn back to look at him. The only reason I'm still awake now is because he couldn't keep his hands off of me—or his dick out of me. I'm certainly not complaining, but the second he leaves my body alone, I'm a goner.

"Try. I'll bring you some water. You'll thank me later." He brushes my hair away from my sticky neck and peppers my skin with kisses before he gets out of bed. I watch as he slips into his boxers and then leaves the room, in search of his pup.

He's been all over me for hours. *Hours*. From the moment he saw me backstage, to just now, I've had his touch. I'd imagine that the absence of him now wouldn't hurt a bit. But there's something about him—something about *my dreamer* that's different; something that makes *me* different. I miss him. It's stupid. He'll be back. But I miss him. After a night of sex, he always holds me as we fall asleep. As exhausted as I am, I don't want to miss that. I don't want to miss the moment when he climbs into bed with me and pulls me into his arms. It's one of my favorite things.

A sign that he's staying.

I grab a fistful of his sheets and pull them up around my chest, holding them beneath my chin. It hits me anew that tonight, my man's hard work paid off. Mountains & Men is going to be going on tour in just over a month for just over a month. A part of me is thrilled for him. He deserves it. They all do. Yet, the selfish part of me, the weakest part of me, the most vulnerable part of me—she's afraid of those six weeks.

I'm an independent woman. I can survive without him. But I gave him my heart. Where he goes, it goes. It's a flaw of mine—part of the reason the pieces of me that he holds are just that—*pieces*. Trusting him while he's on the road is my only option. Trusting that, when he gets back, I'll still be the woman he wants. Trusting that, when he gets back, he'll still have my fractured heart in his hand.

And yet, even *trusting* him isn't what scares me the most.

What scares me the most is just how much I'll miss him when he's gone.

My dreamer.

My rock star.

My twenty-one-year old boyfriend whom I fought so hard to resist.

Fuck. Am I a fool?

I'm pulled from my thoughts when I hear the door open, followed by the sound of little paws and a pair of feet. Sage closes the door behind him, a smirk tugging at his lips when he sees that I'm still awake. He sits on the edge of the bed and I push myself up to accept the water he promised. I drink it until it's all gone and then hand him the glass. He sets it aside and then kisses my swollen lips softly before turning out the bedside lamp.

I lay back down, closing my eyes as I listen to him discard his boxers once more. When he slips under the sheets behind me, he wraps his arm around my waist and pulls me back against him. He buries his nose between my shoulder and my neck, breathing me in before he relaxes and surrenders to sleep.

As I begin to drift off, I answer my own question.

Whether this is foolish or not, this—right here, right now—makes him worth the risk.

TWENTY

Sage

MONDAY MORNING, we all pile into Derrick's SUV to make our trip down to Denver. Maddox, who rivals Millicent when it comes to waking up grumpy in the morning, sleeps the entire trip. Knox, JJ, Derrick and I chat idly, tossing around ideas and questions about what we should expect at this meeting with Stefany. D is the most levelheaded; then again, he always is. He spent most of Sunday afternoon doing research on management contracts, scouring the web for anything and everything he could find on one Ms. Stefany Jordan.

Apparently, she's been around the industry for a couple of years. She's worked with a few local bands, but nobody really big. She's twenty-seven, single, and a graduate from DU. Upon hearing the information that D was able to find, Knox has his doubts—but none of us are crazy enough to back out of an opportunity to go on our first national tour. This is Lawful Sinners' last *hoorah* for the year, and they'll be hitting twenty cities in six weeks. No way in hell can we pass that up.

It isn't until we pull up to our destination that I realize Alex hasn't said a word since we left. It's ten minutes until our scheduled meeting. As we head inside, I hang toward the back, reaching for her arm as the others walk ahead.

"Hey, you're quiet. What's up?"

She shrugs and shakes her head, sliding her hands into her back pockets.

"Not falling for that, Zip. Out with it."

She stops and frees a sigh as she looks up at me. I fold my arms across my chest and arch an eyebrow expectantly.

"You guys have been together for years. You've worked your asses off for this very moment. I wasn't here to see it, but I can feel it. I can feel it when I play with you guys. I can *hear* it in the way you guys talk. This deal with Stefany is *huge*. And you know what? You deserve it. I really believe that. It's just like Stefany said the other night. You have the potential to make a name for yourselves. You're *that good.*"

"We," I correct her with a furrowed brow. "*We* are that good. You're part of this band, too, Alex."

She coughs out a self-deprecating laugh. "See, that's where this gets a little messed up. I've played *one* show with you. Just one." She holds up a finger, as if I need a visual. "I don't deserve any of this. I don't deserve to be a part of your greatness. Who am I? Seriously, I'm just the new kid who got lucky. Right place, right time. And maybe I should be flipping out with excitement, but it just doesn't feel right."

"Bullshit," I deadpan.

"Excuse me?"

"*Bull-fucking-shit.*" I enunciate each syllable very carefully to ensure that she hears me loud and clear. "So you're new, who cares? You killed it at The Brew. You were every bit the badass that you promised. We wouldn't be here if we didn't have you. A band without a bass is not a band at all.

"None of those guys in there gives a damn about your *tenure*. We voted you in, so you're in, Zip. If you don't feel like you deserve what's coming, stick around long enough to earn your place. But remember, you're the only one who thinks you don't deserve this. You joined the band a week ago, but you picked up that bass *years* ago. So, yeah, I'm calling bullshit."

She stares at me for a moment, her eyes wide in surprise. Then, slowly, I watch as her face relaxes, her mouth turning up in a lopsided smile. She folds her arms across her chest, mimicking me, and I can tell the wheels in her head are turning. "Ever think about going into motivational speaking? I swear, you have a knack for it."

I bark out a laugh and shake my head at her. "Just call it like I see it. Now come on." I walk behind her, placing a hand on each of her shoulders before guiding her after the others. "We've got a future to discuss."

We catch up with the rest of the band at the elevators. They all look from me to Alex, an unspoken question in their eyes.

"Stage fright," I tell them, squeezing Alex's shoulders before I let her go.

"Babe, we really have to shake that shit," says Maddox, tipping his chin at her.

"Yeah, Zip—we only go up from here," Knox adds, playfully nudging her with his elbow.

"You're a badass, remember?" asks Derrick.

"I'm working on it, boys. I'm working on it," she insists with a grin.

"We're only as strong as our weakest member," JJ begins to say, his tone serious. "Don't go stealing Maddy's title, you hear?"

"*Fuck off*, you douche!" cries Maddox, flipping JJ the finger.

JJ bats at his hand, all of us laughing—Maddox included. Alex just shakes her head at us, amused and seemly more at ease than she was a minute ago.

The elevator dings and we all step in. As we ride to the third floor, I feel my nerves in my stomach zing with anxious anticipation. This is all about to get *real*. Suddenly, every negative thing anyone has ever said about me—about my goals, my dreams—it fuels my assurance that I'm doing *exactly* what I was meant to do. Too many people who claimed to love me, who promised they would believe in me no matter what, have broken their word. My parents, Nora, a bunch of losers I've met along the way, they never understood how much this all meant and how hard I intended to fight for it. I'm about to prove every single one of them wrong.

This is just the beginning. I can feel it. Mountains & Men is going places.

Or we'll fuckin' die trying.

Once we find the suite number that matches the one on Alex's card, we're met with a receptionist who looks like she hates the world. I don't think any of us are overly enthusiastic about approaching her, which turns out to be okay. Stefany rounds the corner, her focus glued to the phone in her hand, and we're spared the unpleasant exchange with the woman behind the front desk.

Stefany looks much like she did the other day—dressed down and looking totally chill. She's got on boots that remind me of Alex's, dark jeans, a *Guns and Roses* t-shirt, and a scarf wrapped loosely around her neck. Her hair is up and out of her face, and I realize I kind of like her style.

"Stefany, hey," I speak up, catching her attention.

"Ah, perfect! You're here. And right on time. I *love* that." She holds up one finger and finishes typing whatever she's working on before she pockets her phone and greets us properly. I'm impressed that she remembers all of our names as she says hello, shaking each one of our hands. "Okay—I work in a little shit-hole-in-the-wall they like to call an office, so we're going to take our meeting to the conference room. Right this way, fellas." She starts walking and then stops abruptly, turning on her heel to face us once more. "Shit. I'm sorry. Alex, you're so fucking outnumbered, here."

"It's okay," she says with a chuckle.

"Church mouse is one of us, right, babe?" Maddox drapes his arm around her shoulders, earning him an amused smirk from Alex.

"Yeah," she says with a nod.

"Thing is, Stefany, her pussy is off limits to any of us, which essentially makes her one of the guys. So, you're good."

"Good *Lord.* Maddox, don't talk about my—*kitty cat,*" she insists, shoving her way out of Maddox's grasp.

We all bust out laughing and I can tell that Stefany is fighting her amusement like a champ. She clears her throat, twice, and then nods over her shoulder. "God, this is going to be fun. Come on, guys."

When we enter the conference room, there is already someone inside. He's an older guy—I'd guess in his late forties, early fifties—and he's wearing slacks, a dress shirt, and a tie. Our residual laughter dies down when we spot him standing upon our entrance.

"Mountains & Men, this is Brooks—Brooks, Mountains & Men." He offers us a nod and then Stefany invites us all to take a seat. "Here's the deal, before we talk shop, we have to do the legally binding stuff. Brooks here is an old family friend. He's a lawyer I like to bring in sometimes when negotiating a contract. Believe me when I tell you, this is for *your* benefit, not mine. He's here to answer any question that you might have.

"Something I want you to know about me—I'm sure, if you did your homework, you know I'm not the most experienced manager in the industry. I've been around the block, but only a couple times. Here's what's up, though—the *last* thing I want to do is cut corners to get to the level I aspire to reach. My integrity is about all I've got and I want us to be able to trust each other. As long as we don't have to worry about our relationship, then we can handle all the other bullshit as it comes.

"This contract," she continues, pointing to the stack of papers in front of Brooks, "is to be beneficial for all parties involved. I will *bust my ass* for you, and I want you to know that up front. I'm good at this. I'm not afraid to approach the big guns, nor am I above hounding the people who have what I need. I'll do that for you guys. In return, I expect you to hold up your end of the bargain. Your integrity matters, too. This is about *music.* It's why I got into this business and, no matter what, it's all I care about. The money will come if you guys keep rockin' the way you do. It's my job to put you in front of the right audience; it's your job to keep their attention. If we both give it our all, we both win. That being said, shall we dive into the fine print?"

I look around at my mates, replaying her words in my head.

This is about music.

I'm greener than fucking spring grass when it comes to the big leagues of music, but I know I like what she's about. At the end of the day, she's our guide, but it's our music that brought us here and it's our music that will keep us going. Sounds to me like she gets that. I, for one, am ready to sign this shit now, but I know we have to be smarter than that.

When Knox offers me a shrug and a nod, I know that means his reservations are waning. Derrick murmurs that he's in, followed by JJ, Maddox, and then Alex.

Stefany looks to me, a hopeful expression on her face, and a smirk tugs at my lips.

"Let's do this."

Millicent

I've read the same page four times. At this point, I'm not even sure why I'm reading it. *Clearly*, I'm far too distracted to digest a single word. I should just call him…

I haven't heard from Sage since this morning, when he and the band left for Denver. I know that he's probably had a lot going on today, but I expected to hear from him by now. It's almost nine o'clock. Up until about an hour ago, I was doing a pretty good job of distracting myself from his silence. I worked late. I threw something edible together for dinner. I cleaned the kitchen. I got ready for bed. I even braided my hair, a rarity for me, just to give my hands something to do *other* than check my phone.

It's not that I'm worried. Not exactly. Something tells me that if he wasn't alright, I would have heard from Violet by now, and I haven't. It's just that he *always* sends me texts or calls me throughout the day. Even in the very beginning, when I swore we couldn't see each other, he was annoyingly good at letting me know whenever I was on his mind. I didn't think that I was the kind of woman who needed that. Perhaps I'm still not—but his break in routine has me feeling restless.

I cannot say why I haven't just called him myself. Honestly, I'm not sure that I'm that kind of girlfriend—the kind that checks in on her boyfriend's whereabouts. Then again, it's been a long time since I've been with anyone. I suppose I have no idea what kind of woman I am in situations such as these.

I pick up my phone, turning it over in my hands as I ponder my next move. I don't know why I'm thinking about this so much. I need to get out of my head. I know the longer I wander around in my thoughts, the closer I'll get to the possibility that this may in fact be my reality in a few weeks. Perhaps being on the road will make it difficult for us to catch each other at a time when we're both available. What if we go days without speaking? What if—

"*Fucking hell*," I mutter, tossing my phone onto the coffee table.

What is wrong with me?

What is happening to me?

One day? I can't go one day without speaking to him?

For Christ's sake, I need to get my shit together.

I jump, startled when a knock sounds at my door. I look down at myself, wondering if I'm in any state to answer. I'm in a pair of sweatpants that hang low on my hips, and a spaghetti-strap tank top. I'm not wearing any underthings, but my nipples aren't hard—a bonus, seeing as how the hair that hangs down my chest is twisted up and useless in the event that I need to hide anything.

My quick assessment ends with me standing to peer through the peephole, and my stomach flutters at the sight of him, relief making me far more happy than it should. When I open the door, Sage is leaning on his shoulder, propped up against the doorframe. He lifts his head, bringing his eyes to meet mine, and a tired smirk tugs at his lips.

"Hey, doll face."

My nipples turn into hard peaks at the sound of his voice. In this moment, I understand *exactly* what kind of woman I am—I'm the kind of woman who needs to hear the rich, alluring, sexy tone of my man's voice. It's what drew me to him in the first place. It's part of who *we* are.

I sigh softly, my shoulders relaxing for the first time in hours as I rest my head against the door.

"What's wrong, Millicent?" he asks, reaching up to run the backs of his fingers down my cheek.

"I missed your voice, today." The words come out automatically, but I know as soon as I've said them that I don't regret my honesty.

"Yeah?" I nod my response and he takes a step closer to me. "Is that all you missed?" He slides his arm around my waist and gently pulls me against him. I go willingly, circling my arms around his neck.

"No," I answer as I exhale.

"What else d'you miss, baby?"

I lift myself up on my tiptoes, amused but not surprised that he's fishing for the details of my longing. *My arrogant little shit.* "Just shut up and kiss me, Sage."

He grins at me before he presses his lips against mine. The second our mouths touch, every cell in my body comes alive. I hold him tighter, needing him closer, and I tell him all he could wish to know with my tongue. He reciprocates my affection in kind, keeping himself in control as he kisses me slowly, deeply, *lovingly*.

I adore him.

I pull away from him with a start when I hear a door slam shut. I recognize the sound, knowing that someone just entered the building, and I'm reminded that we're still half in, half out of my apartment. The interruption was probably for the best. My body is still on hiatus after yesterday and I don't want it, or him, getting any ideas.

"Will you come in? Tell me about your day?"

"Mmmhmmm," he answers with a hum before he scoops me off of my feet and into his arms, cradling me against his chest. "Get the door, baby doll. Hit the lights."

I do as he says, locking us in and shrouding us in darkness. He then carries me all the way to my room, depositing me into my bed. I watch as he turns on my lamp and begins stripping off his clothing. I start to question him, but the words don't make it past my lips—I'm too entranced by the sight of him. I don't have a single tattoo, but I love each one of his. He wears them well; so well, that I have to remind my body that *his* body is off limits tonight.

"Sage—"

"I'm not here for sex, Millie," he interrupts me as he kicks off his shoes and steps out of his jeans. "But I am staying. Though, you probably should keep those clothes on so I don't go breaking any promises."

I giggle, because apparently he makes me do that, and then pull back the covers and slip between the sheets. He joins me, stretching out on his side and propping his head up with his fist as he wraps his arm around me and pulls me close. I prop my head up, too, and he leans in for a quick kiss before he speaks.

"Baby, today was incredible. *Absolutely* incredible. Stefany is great. I think she's exactly who the band needs. I mean, she saw us *Saturday* and today, after we worked out the terms of our partnership, she told us that she'd been on the phone since she left The Brew, trying to get us studio time. She wants us to record an EP before we go on tour. Can you believe that?"

"That's amazing," I tell him, my eyes dancing around his face. He's lit up with excitement and it makes me want to get lost in him. I've never been in awe of someone as much as I'm in awe of him right now. His dream is everything to him and it's on the precipice of coming true. I have no idea what that feels like—no idea what it's like to hold onto a dream, to fight for it, to bask in the possibilities of it.

I rest my hand against his chest, wishing to be closer to him, closer to this *joy*. As if he can read my mind, he hooks his leg over mine, smirking at me as we tangle our legs together.

"She managed to get us a few hours on Saturday for our first session. We have to leave at the ass crack of dawn, but I don't care. I seriously cannot wait to hear what we sound like when we're professionally mixed. I mean, JJ is pretty damn good, but equipment is everything."

"How long will you have in the studio?"

"A couple hours. Do you want to come?"

I balk at his idea, surprised that he would even ask me. "Is that—is that allowed?"

"I'm sure JJ will bring Vi," he replies with a shrug. "I want you there. Say you'll come."

"Okay," I say with a nod. "I'll come."

He smirks at me before he presses his lips against mine. I follow his lead when he doesn't pull away, but instead pins me beneath him. My fingers find their way into his hair as his tongue seeks entrance into my mouth. The weight of him on top of me is welcome, and when I feel him grow hard between my legs, I can't silence the soft moan that escapes my throat.

"*Fuck*," he murmurs against my lips. He rubs himself against me and it's like my sweatpants don't exist. I gasp, my grip tightening in his hair. "Damn, Millie, you're something else, you know that?"

"Hmm?" I manage. I can hardly think as he rubs himself against me once more.

"You *see* me," he whispers. I stare into his eyes, searching for meaning and coming up short. "I've never been with someone who gets me like you do. I've never been with someone who believes in me like you do. You're my best girl, Millicent." He grinds against me again and I can no longer resist.

"Sage, baby, I want you," I murmur.

"I promised—"

"Take me slow. Make me come like only you can. Please?"

"For you?" he mutters, kissing his way down my neck. "Anything."

TWENTY-ONE

Millicent

"MILLIE. MILLIE, WAKE UP, baby doll." I groan, appreciative of the sound of my wake-up call, and totally unappreciative of its intent. "Up, Millicent!" He throws back his covers and smacks my ass. I furrow my brow, my eyes still closed as I whine in protest. "If you want to shower, it's now or never. I waited until everyone else was finished. So, see, you can't be a grump."

"Oh, god. Remind me why I agreed to go with you today?"

"Because you were looking to take advantage of your girlfriend privileges. Behind the scenes with Mountains & Men—lesser women might bitch slap a chick for your coveted invitation."

I roll my eyes, but he can't see me do it behind my lids. I don't remember what time we went to bed last night, but it wasn't nearly early enough to condone waking up before the sun is in the sky on a Saturday morning.

"Dammit, Millie," he begins to say when I don't move a muscle. "I just want you to know, when you have only ten minutes to shower, that you brought this on yourself."

For a second I imagine that my grumbling has rewarded me the equivalent of a nine-minute snooze, but then I feel the bed dip at my feet. Before I know it, I'm on my back, my legs are spread, and his warm, wet tongue is being drug along my slit. When he reaches my sensitive nub, he gently grazes his teeth over the bud, and my body responds instantly, making me slick with arousal.

"Oh, fuck," I breathe, my eyes shooting open as I look down at the man working diligently to rouse me from my slumber with an orgasm.

He grunts, curling his arms around my thighs as he thrusts his tongue inside of me. He feels sensational—the heat of his breath, the firmness of his tongue, the perfection of his calculated movements as he travels between my entrance and my sweet spot. He sucks. He licks. He nibbles. He repeats.

I reach down and grip a fistful of his damp hair, unable to stop myself from bucking my hips. "Sage—Sage, *shit*, Sage." My need to speak supersedes my ability to find any words. I call his name repeatedly, unable to conjure up anything else as the fog of sleep dissipates and haze of lust takes its place.

When he shoves two fingers inside of my center, hooking the tips as he pumps in and out of me, kissing the inside of my thigh, my back bows away from the bed.

"Come for me, baby," he hums against my skin.

"Mmhmm," I sigh, grabbing at his sheets, nodding my understanding. "Don't stop! I'm almost—" Before I can finish my sentence, a wave of euphoric pleasure spreads all over my body. I can feel it as my pussy tightens around his fingers and he wraps his lips around my clit once more, sucking until my orgasm has subsided.

When he pulls away from me, he dips his fingers into his mouth as he stares into my eyes. He's not wearing his glasses at the moment, and my view of his beautiful, icy blue irises on his dangerously handsome face makes it nearly impossible to catch my breath.

"Now?" he asks, leaning over me. "*Now* will you get in the shower?"

A lazy smile tugs at my lips. "Yes," I whisper.

"Good," he smacks a kiss against my mouth before he stands. "We gotta jet in half an hour. Move that sexy, little ass, doll face. We can't be late and I'm not leaving you behind."

Sage

It's five minutes 'til eight when I turn off the Audi and hop out of the driver's seat. Millie—decidedly more awake and fully aware of my hyped-up mood—doesn't waste a second before stepping out after me.

Earlier, after I devoured her sweet pussy, she had only thirty minutes to get showered and dressed. I know girls who have spent a lot longer getting ready and none of them look as gorgeous as my woman does right now. Her long, damp, light brown hair is pilled in a knot on top of her head, leaving her positively kissable neck on display. She's got on a pair of flats; tight, well-worn, dark-wash jeans that hug her long-ass legs; a plain white T that reminds me of her bitable tits and her petite waist; and an oversized, maroon cardigan that hangs down to her knees. Even though I swear she doesn't need it, she managed to find time to put on a little makeup, too. Watching her walk toward me makes me want to pull her into my arms and never let her go. She's sexy as fuck, and she's all mine.

Pussy whipped. That's what I am—totally pussy whipped.

"What? Why are you looking at me like that?" she murmurs, her dark green eyes peering up at me.

I shake my head as I lean down and press a soft kiss against her lips. "Just glad you're here, baby doll."

She reaches for my hand and I lace my fingers with hers. "Me too," she tells me. Her response makes me want to kiss her again—so I do. "Are you nervous?" she asks as I lead her inside. The others arrived just a couple minutes before us and I'm anxious to join them.

"Nah," I answer. "This is going to be fun."

"Do you *ever* get nervous?"

"Sometimes," I say with a shrug. "Usually when we're playing someplace new, in front of a crowd I'm unsure of. There's always this moment, right before I walk out on stage; it's like I'm about to lose my nerve. But then, when I get out there, when I get the mic in my hand…" I shake my head, my mind imagining exactly what it feels like to shed my stage anxiety.

When we enter the little lobby of the studio, and I see the guys all standing around, a smirk tugs at my mouth before I continue.

"No matter what, I've got my crew behind me. As cheesy as it may sound, knowing we have each other's backs, knowing that it takes all of us to be any good, I just know when to man up and do my part. Can't let my nerves get the best of me."

"Well, you are far braver than I, Sage McCoy."

I wink down at her just as Stefany appears from behind a closed door, a big, burley dude with a long beard and a graying ponytail following behind her.

"Morning boys, Alex, and…two chicks I don't know," she says, running her fingers through her blonde locks. It's the first time I've ever seen it down. It's wavy and hangs just above her shoulders. When she folds her arms across her chest, lifting her eyebrows expectantly, a dubious, lopsided smile on her face, I realize that she's expecting an introduction.

"Oh, yeah—Stefany, this is Millie—my girlfriend—and that's Violet."

"My girlfriend," says JJ.

"Ah. Girlfriends. Girlfriends in the studio are cool *only* if they inspire you to work harder."

"Don't worry. I'll kick his ass if you need me to," says Violet with a nonchalant shrug.

"I like you already," Stefany says with a laugh. "Okay, we've only got three hours, so I want to get you in there. *This*," she turns and motions with her hands to the man standing behind her, "is Tank. Tank is one of my favorite sound engineers, isn't that right, Tank?"

He rolls his eyes and shakes his head but doesn't say a word. Stefany laughs, patting him on the arm.

"Tank, this is Sage, Derrick, Knox, Maddox, JJ, and Alex—otherwise known as Mountains & Men. Now," she claps her hands before rubbing them together. "Let's get in there."

"You guys ever been in a state of the art studio before?" asks Tank, his voice gruff and low. We all answer with a *no* of some sort and he nods before motioning us to follow him. "I'll give you the lay of the land before we start."

Millicent

Sage holds my hand through the duration of the tour. Every time he sees something that excites him, or any time Tank says something that fascinates him, he gives my hand a squeeze. He does it unintentionally, which makes it even better. Tank has his undivided attention—rather, he has *everyone's* undivided attention—except mine. Mine is definitely divided. To me, what everyone finds so enthralling is just a bunch of really expensive equipment that does a bunch of fancy things that I know not how to appreciate. What I appreciate more is how in awe everyone else is.

Every time Sage squeezes my hand, a jolt of electricity shoots up my arm, heading straight to my stomach, igniting a burst of tingles. There's something about being here with him, about experiencing this *first* with him, about bearing witness to the beginning of something amazing—there's just something about it that's incredibly overwhelming, but in the most wonderful way. Now that I'm here, I take back my flippant response to his earlier quip about girls *bitch slapping* a chick to be in my place.

I can't lie. I'd act undignified if he expressed any desire to share this with any other girl who wasn't me.

Right here, right now, I know I'm falling for him a little bit more.

It still scares me, but I won't run from it anymore. It's too late to escape my reality. I accept the importance of him in my life. The lingering trepidation that he may one day leave me, just like they always do, is temporarily in the shadow of his presence. I'm not naive or stupid. I know by letting my guard down, I've left myself entirely unprotected against the possibility of losing him, but he makes it nearly impossible for me to bask in the worry of anything beyond now. Beyond the promise of our relationship. Beyond his constant affection.

I am his and he is mine. I hold fast to that truth as I hold his hand, all of us making our way into the sound proofed room filled with instruments.

"Who's the drummer?" asks Tank, pulling me from my thoughts. Derrick lifts a hand, stepping forward, and Tank nods. "You can play on the house kit. Get comfortable. Let's get the rest of you set up and we'll do a sound check."

"Come on, ladies," says Stefany as she begins to back her way out of the room. "You can hang with me in the booth."

I start to pull away from Sage, but he pulls me back.

"Aren't you going to kiss me for luck?"

I smile up at him, resting my freehand against his chest. I know as well as anyone that his raw talent has brought him this far, and nothing I say or do will make it stop now. "You don't need luck," I murmur.

"You ain't lying, doll face," he says, leaning down to line up our lips. He stops just a breath away. "Need a taste anyway."

I grip a fistful of his shirt before pushing up on my tiptoes, eliminating the space between his mouth and mine. We kiss only for a moment, but it's enough to stir a hint of longing. He pulls away with a smile and then taps my ass. I shake my head, unable to wipe the grin off my face as I turn and follow Violet and Stefany out of the room.

"*God*, I *love* you two," Violet gushes when I catch up to them. She links her arm with mine as we make our way to the big, worn, comfy couch squeezed into the room behind the glass partition. "He's totally squishy about you."

"*Squishy?*" I question, lifting an eyebrow at her.

"Yeah," she says with a giggle. "The guy can barely keep his hands or lips off of you. He makes this totally endearing face when you two are texting. His whole demeanor changes when you walk into a room. And he's been writing songs like a *mad man* since you got together. It's like I told you a few weeks ago—you look good on him."

"So, you're his muse, huh?" Stefany asks, leaning up against the sound board as she looks at me. She seems more fascinated than judgmental, but I still don't really know how to answer her.

"Absolutely," Violet insists, nodding enthusiastically. She tosses her head, causing her bangs to flop out of her eyes and across her forehead as she addresses Stefany. "JJ told me you picked the song they are recording today."

"Yeah, I did," she says with a smile. She looks back over her shoulder into the next room as she continues to speak. "I don't know why, but this one felt right." She shrugs, turning back to us. "I love their stuff—but this one is different, somehow. I think it could be their break-out hit."

"Well, *Just Tonight* is about Millie," Violet replies.

Stefany's lips turn down into an impressed frown as she pushes herself upright. "Hope he keeps you around, then." She winks and then turns to check on their progress. When her phone rings, she excuses herself to answer it. She leaves, but her words remain.

Hope he keeps you around.

I wonder what that means. I wonder what it is she's experienced in the world of music. How many girlfriends has she met who have turned into bitter ex-groupies? How many relationships has she watched fall apart while she's on the road? How many boyfriends has she seen cheat or lie while they were away?

Sage has never lied to me before, but what will six weeks apart do to us?

I draw in a deep breath as I shift my focus into the next room. Sage is laughing with Maddox and Knox as Tank helps JJ finish his set up. When they all leave, he'll have his best friends by his side—the men who have been a part of his life, who have shared and invested into his passion for *years*. He'll be busy doing exactly what he's always wanted—exactly what he was meant to do. I'll be left here. Alone.

I'll miss him terribly, but will he miss me just as much? Or will I be a casualty of his dream?

Hope he keeps you around.

Am I allowed to be surprised if he doesn't?

Dare I dream that he will?

Sage

"Okay, let's do a dry run. I'll adjust some levels and then we'll get crackin'," says Tank as he heads for the door. Just as he opens it, Stefany bursts in. "About to get started, Stef."

"Fantastic! I'll only be a second, I swear." He offers her a curt nod before she jogs the rest of the way into the room and bounces on her toes in front of us. "I just got off the phone with Heath." She pauses, as if that name is supposed to mean something to us, and we look at each other in confusion. A sly smile pulls at her lips as she props her fists against her hips. "Lawful Sinners' manager."

"Goddamn. Out with it, woman, you're killin' us!" cries Maddox.

She laughs. "Okay, okay, okay! They caught wind that you'll be part of their tour and they want to see you in action before we leave. Not to worry," she says, holding her hands out in front of her as if to brace herself. "Even if you suck ass—*which you won't*—this isn't an audition. But, they want to get a feel for you guys. *So*, they've invited you to play with them. Three weeks from now. At The Fillmore."

"The Fillmore? Are you serious?" mutters JJ.

"Yup. Welcome to the A-list of up and comers, boys and girl."

"Holy shit," I manage. We've never played at a venue as big as The Fillmore. It's located in the art district of Denver. It's the hottest spot for bands like Lawful Sinners. It's just one step away from the fucking Pepsi Center.

"Wipe up your drool, guys—Tank'll kill you if you ruin his equipment. Besides, The Fillmore will soon be child's play, if I have anything to do about it. Now, let's record some music, shall we?" She hurries out of the room just as fast as she came, and a slow smile makes its way onto my face.

This is fucking awesome!

"Lawful Sinners...we're—we're going to meet Lawful Sinners in three weeks?" Alex squeaks.

"Babe—lookin' a little green over there. You alright?" asks Maddox with a frown.

"Yeah. I just..." Her words trail off as she starts gathering her hair up into a ponytail and away from her neck and back. "Is it suddenly hot in here?"

"Zip, why are you freaking out? You've known all along that we were going to be touring with them," I remind her.

"Mmmhmm, yeah," she sighs before drawing in a deep breath. "I'm not freaking out. I'm fine. I'm great. Three weeks? Yeah. That's—that's awesome."

"Alex—Alex, look at me," I insist. She does as I say, her brown eyes wide and filled with obvious worry. I shake my head and smirk as I take a couple steps toward her. "Mad Lips is right; you really are our church mouse—petrified until the beat drops, at which point you turn into a badass. It's actually kind of cute—but we're not cute, Zip."

"That's for damn sure," Knox grunts.

"Mountains & Men, babe. Mountains & *Men*," says Maddox.

"Their shit is sick, but I bet you could play circles around their bass player," Derrick adds with a shrug.

"That's the truth." I point at Derrick but keep my eyes trained on Alex. Her cheeks turn rosy as a slight smile plays at her lips. "But that's not even the point. You're just as worthy of an introduction as they are. They're people, we're people—we *all* have one thing in common. Music. Just do your thing, Zip. And don't puke. We're about to go on a wild ride and it's going to be one hell of a time." She smiles at me, more confidently this time, and I arch my brow in question. "You good?"

"I will be. Let's drop the beat."

I chuckle and offer her a nod before taking the headphones from around my neck and putting them over my ears. Everyone else follows suit as I step in front of the mic.

"Go for it," Tank says, his voice filling our ears.

That's all Derrick needs to hear before he does exactly as Alex requests and drops the beat.

Millicent

I CAN HEAR EVERY word that passes between them as I watch Sage calm Alex down. He's sweet to her. That, in and of itself, doesn't particularly surprise me. I've seen it before. I've gotten jealous of it before. I'd like to think that everything that passes between them is about the music, just as he said. Just like he told me a couple weeks ago, on the night he owned my body in his laundry room. Twice.

But today—it's different. Today, I'm not so much taken by his behavior as I am worried about *hers*. When he turns back to his mic, sliding his headphones over his ears, her eyes follow him. Furthermore, the smile on her lips has me questioning just how much his encouragement means to her.

Hope he keeps you around.

After six weeks away, every day and night spent with that doe-eyed look trained on him, will he? She's a part of his world in a way that I never will be. He thinks that I *see* him, but every single person in this studio understands his passion in a way that I do not. Of course I know how much it means to him; I'm aware that *my dreamer* is so much more than the arrogant little shit I was sure I was meeting that first night at The Brew; I'm positive that the blood that runs through his veins is fueled with his drive to share his music—to *sing with the world*. But it's not something we share. It'll never be something we share. Will our separation open his eyes to that fact? And with his eyes open, will he see the look on Alex's face that I just saw?

"Hey," Violet catches my attention, snapping her fingers in front of my face. "What are you thinking so hard about, missy?" She narrows her eyes at me, as if she already knows the answer.

"Nothing. It's nothing," I mutter, leaning back against the couch.

"Come on," she insists, shifting her body sideways so that she's facing me. "We're friends, right?" She lowers her voice so that only I can hear her over the boys and Alex's playing. "You can tell me."

For a moment, I'm speechless. The number of people I've had in my life who I could confide in are so few, I could count them on one hand. These days, the amount of people who seem to boast of a friendship with me is actually quite appalling. I'm not sure how I got here, but Violet is right. I do consider her a friend. She's made it kind of hard not to. However, I'm not sure if I'm ready to open up about my insecurities.

"I saw it too, you know," she murmurs, looking through the glass partition before looking back at me. "He's an easy guy to crush on. Believe me. I've seen many a girl fall victim to those blue eyes and that sexy smile. But I also know him. I know him well. He'd never do anything to betray you."

I suck in a breath and let it out slowly. Violet smiles at me kindly, obviously taking that as the confirmation she was after.

"His ex..." She shakes her head and lifts a single shoulder in a shrug. "I just know he would never betray you. Not with anyone. Not ever."

I study her for a moment, wondering if she'll give me more. She doesn't. Just like Derrick, she only makes it clear how much this other woman hurt him. Though, what that has to do with *me*, I'm not so sure.

Violet may be sure that Sage would never betray me, but leaving me and betraying me are not necessarily the same thing. I can't deny that deep down in my soul, the truth is inescapable—no matter how hard I try. It's just like my mother told me, what she's *always* taught me—what *life* has taught me.

They always leave.

TWENTY-TWO

Sage

By the time we're headed out, Tank is pretty happy about the tracks we've laid down. He says it'll take him a couple hours to get it just the way he wants it, but he gives us a little taste of what he's got. We sound so fucking amazing that I can hardly believe it's us. Stefany is beaming as we make our way out of the studio, and she all but demands we go grab a bite to eat to celebrate.

"Burgers. Burgers and milkshakes—that's how it's done. I know this place not too far from here. Just follow me!"

We all oblige, with no reason to argue, and our amped up, rowdy bunch fills the joint with conversation and laughter for the next hour. The more time we spend with Stefany, the more obvious it becomes that fate brought us together. She's the shit—totally down to earth, but also completely professional and determined to see us succeed.

We win—she wins.

It isn't until the bill comes that I realize Millie's been really quiet. I also notice that she didn't eat all of her French fries. I know how much my girl loves her French fries, so I know something is up. On our way out, I take her hand in mine and give her fingers a squeeze. I ask her what's wrong and she tells me that she's just tired.

Bullshit.

When we're alone in my car, on the way back up to Fort Collins, she speaks to me for the first ten minutes. We discuss the recording session and the next time we'll be down to work on a couple more songs. She'll be teaching, mostly, so she won't be able to come, but she doesn't seem too bothered or disappointed by that. I wonder if she got bored today, listening to us play the same thing over and over again.

I turn on a little music, wondering if maybe she'll crash on the drive back, but she doesn't. She doesn't sleep, she doesn't talk, and I don't like it one fucking bit. Given that she blew me off the last time I asked her what was wrong, I don't ask again. Instead, I let the silence rule as an idea comes to mind.

I hop off the interstate three exits early, taking the back roads to Derrick's plot of land. When I pull off the main street and park in the middle of the field, she finally speaks.

"What are we doing here?"

I press a button, looking over at her as the convertible top retracts. "You got some bullshit to let go of, baby doll. Not takin' it home with me."

I climb out of the car, push my seat up, and crawl into the back. For a minute, she doesn't move; then I watch as she follows suit. When she sits as far away from me as possible, I wonder what the hell I've done wrong.

"Millicent?"

She grips her fingers and squares her shoulders before she looks me dead in the eye. "I'd like you to tell me about your ex-girlfriend. I suppose, to be more specific, the one before you started seeing me."

I narrow my eyes at her, even more confused than I was a second ago. "The fuck? Where did that come from?"

"She's been mentioned to me, more than once. Apparently, whatever happened between you two is supposed to be some sort of proof that I can trust you—trust *us*."

I blow out a breath, reaching up to run my fingers through my hair. "Millie—I don't know who has mentioned that bitch to you, or *why* for that matter, but she's got nothing to do with *us*. You should trust me because I care about you. You should trust me because you know I'd never want to see you hurt. You should trust *us* because we're fucking amazing, baby doll. *Nora* should have no bearing on any of that."

She stares at me for a moment, nodding her head slightly. Then, just when I think we're on the same page, she asks, "So—her name was Nora?"

"*Christ*," I mutter, scraping my hand over my mouth and along my chin. "I don't talk about this shit, Millie. Not anymore. You want answers, you get your pretty, little ass over here—this is a conversation that requires fucking cuddles."

A hint of a smile dances across her lips, but I'm one-hundred-percent serious, a fact she picks up on when I open my arms. Her amusement wanes as she crawls into my lap and wraps her arms around my shoulders. I take a deep breath, knowing if it were anyone else asking me to come clean about this, I would refuse them. But Millicent isn't anyone else. Not even close.

"When I was in high school, I had a little side paying gig. I'd play piano for this dance company. Wasn't really a big deal, mostly recitals and stuff. Anyway, that's how I met Nora. She was a ballerina in one of the advanced classes. She was really good. Really passionate. Dance was her life like music is mine.

"Anyway, we hit it off. The summer after I turned seventeen, we started dating. We were together for all of senior year. I fell in love with her. Thought she loved me, too. She said as much. We were together all the time. I mean, we didn't go to the same school, but that just fed our desire to see each other everywhere else.

"At the time, the band was just starting to be something. At least, we thought so. We hadn't met JJ yet, but we had found Derrick and Wren. We were playing at parties and shit, which was getting us out of the Bradley's garage. Nora led me to believe she was supportive of everything I did; though, like my parents, she was partial to my more classical training.

"She wanted to go to school in New York some fancy dance academy. When I got into Juilliard, she practically had our whole future sorted out. She knew from the start that I wasn't planning on leaving town, but she thought she could change my mind. When I finally got her to understand no one was changing my mind, she got it into her head that my decision had something to do with her. It didn't. It had absolutely *nothing* to do with her. I loved her. I wanted her to go and do her thing, but I wasn't going to sacrifice my dream for hers.

"I was willing to give long distance a try, but she was so pissed at me. When she left, I wasn't really sure what we were. I called her every day for a month before I just decided to get on a damn plane and go out there to fix us. The guys helped me scrounge up the money to go fight for her."

For the first time since I started talking, I look at Millie. She's staring at me, her curiosity on full display in her gorgeous green eyes. She's so different than Nora. She's so different than any woman I've ever met. I don't know why she's so hell bent on hearing these details, but I know I'll give them to her without regret. I'll give her whatever she wants if it means I get to keep her.

That's exactly what I want—to keep her. To know her. To know the demons in her haunted eyes… Perhaps if I share some of mine, she'll share some of hers.

"Then what happened? Did you find her?" she murmurs, tracing her fingers up and down the back of my neck.

"Finding her was the easy part. I got her address from her parents. I knew she was shacking up with three other girls in Brooklyn. When I showed up at her place, one of her roommates opened the door. I should have known by the look on her face that something was wrong."

I remember it like it was yesterday. I'd never met the girl before in my life, and yet her eyes spoke of recognition. They also spoke of her fear. She knew the fight from hell was about to go down.

"She tried to tell me Nora wasn't home, but it was a lie. Just as I was asking if I could stick around until she got back, I heard her voice. I'd recognize the noise she made *anywhere*—but I only knew it to be a sound she made when we were having sex." I shake my head, surprised the memory still makes me so damn angry. "I followed her voice, ignoring her roommate's protests, and found her behind door number one with her legs spread for some scrawny-ass dick.

"Four weeks. We'd been apart from each other for *four weeks.* We hadn't even really broken up. I was furious, so I pulled him off of her and punched the motherfucker in the face. The pansy didn't even fight back. Nora did, though. And you know what she said to me?" I pause, locking my gaze with Millie's. "She told me that she'd already wasted a year with me and she wasn't about to waste another day. She said she used to think I was going to be somebody, that I was better than Mountains & Men, better than CSU, better than the kid who played recitals for a little extra cash. But she didn't think that anymore. She said I was never going to be anybody and my decision to stay in Colorado proved that.

"Apparently, a month in the city opened her eyes to how much of a loser I was. Well, *one night* in the city opened my eyes to how much of a bitch she was. Still hurt, though. Swear to god, that was the lowest night of my life. But it was also the start of something."

"The start of what?" Millie practically whispers as she gently brings a hand to my cheek.

"A new life. I vowed from that day forward that nothing—*no one*—was going to stop me from being all that I knew I could be. I promised myself that I would prove everyone who didn't believe in me wrong, and that I would make everyone who *did* more than proud, or I'd die trying."

I offer her a feeble shrug, my story done. She simply stares at me for a couple seconds before she leans in slowly and presses her lips against mine. It's not the response I was expecting; then again, nothing that's happened since I climbed into the backseat of my car has been what I was expecting. I kiss her in return, reaching up to hold the back of her neck. When she pulls away, she rests her forehead against mine and sighs.

"*My dream chaser...*" she murmurs.

"What?" I ask with a smirk.

"You really are remarkable, Sage. I hope you know that. I hope you know that I mean that. I've never met anyone like you. I've never known someone with such fierce determination and drive. You astound me."

This time, it's my turn to respond with a kiss. Hearing her say those words does something to me—makes me feel bigger, badder, bolder. Now, as she kisses me back, her tongue twisting with mine, it hits me all over again. The truth. The truth I've known since that night I woke up without her—since the moment I knew what it felt like to have lost her.

I'm going to love this woman.

I'm going to love her hard.

I know it's coming, and I'm ready.

"What's your dream, baby?" I ask, my lips grazing hers.

"I don't know," she breathes, her fingers gripping hold of my shirt.

"Everyone has a dream." I pull away from her, just enough to be able to look into her eyes.

Her eyes, green and gorgeous.

Her eyes, haunted and mysterious.

There are demons in those eyes…

"Maybe I did, once. I don't wear my resilience as well as you do."

I furrow my brow at her. No way in hell I'm letting that bullshit lie—not here. Not in the field where bullshit is left behind.

"Who was he? Or she? Shit—who was it?"

"Who was who?" she asks, shaking her head in confusion.

"The fuckface who broke your heart—the one who made you so guarded, so scared. Baby, who was it?"

I watch as her eyes turn glassy, filling with tears I can tell she's reluctant to shed. She takes a deep breath and looks away from me, blowing out the air that fills her lungs before she responds. "My father." She coughs out a humorless laugh and shakes her head once more. "I can't blame him for how I am, though. It's not his fault. It's mine. It's my fault for believing that he would come back; for believing that he loved me enough to not abandon me; for wishing that I was important enough not to be left behind, never to be thought of again.

"I was only six. I didn't know better. I still believed in Santa Claus, so how could I not believe in love? I didn't know that without him, my world would be cold and void of any love or magic. So, you see, I admire you for your resilience and your optimism." She forces a smile as she brings her eyes to meet mine. "I hope all your dreams come true. I believe they will. But my dreams—I let them go. It hurt too much to hold onto them."

Suddenly, all her shit makes sense. She was never running from me because she thought I was in this for the chase. It was always bigger than that—bigger than me just leaving when I'd had my fill. She's not afraid of being alone. She's afraid of being broken. Every time she has run, it has been because she was trying to let me go before I had a chance to hurt her. Now I get it—I understand why she needed to hear about Nora. She's still hesitant to trust me, hesitant about letting me all the way in.

Fuck. Is that why she still makes me wrap it up?

I'm not going anywhere. Never was.

"Everyone dreams of something. You'll find yours, again. Until then, hold onto me, doll face," I tell her softly, holding her tighter.

She sighs, curling up against me as she rests her head on my shoulder. "I'm trying."

We both fall silent, and for a while, she just rests in my arms. Unlike before, our lack of verbal communication isn't uncomfortable or tense. I don't know how we got here, what triggered the chain of events that led us here, confiding in one another, but I hope being here brings her peace. I need her to be sure of me. I'm sure as hell sure of her.

TWENTY-THREE

Millicent

It's late in the afternoon by the time we get back to the boys' house. When Sage and I walk inside, we discover that Derrick and Violet headed into work, Alex headed home to study, and JJ, Knox, and Maddox are all in the living room watching a movie. We're invited to join them and Sage leaves the decision up to me. I agree, happy for any excuse to cuddle with him some more. JJ is quick to hop up off his couch, making himself comfortable between the Bradley brothers and giving Sage and me plenty of room to stretch out.

He lays across the length of the couch, leaving barely enough room for me, and I smile as I squeeze into the space between his body and the back cushions. I'm half on top of him, my leg hooked around his, my arm flung across him, and my cheek pressed against his chest. As he kisses my forehead and rests his hand on top of my ass, I'm sure this is exactly how he wanted it.

Violet was right. He can hardly keep his hands or lips off of me, and I'm sure that I love it.

I'm asleep in minutes, hardly even aware of what the movie is about. I don't know how long I'm out, only that when I wake, I smell pizza. I breathe in a deep breath and my stomach growls. I didn't eat much at lunch and the promise of food has me opening my eyes.

"Look who's awake?" Violet says in a hushed voice. I lift my head and look around, hoping I don't look as groggy as I feel. My eyes stop on Violet, who is sitting on the floor, leaning back against the couch between JJ's legs. "You sound hungry.

I brought some grub. Help yourself." She tips her chin at the coffee table and I see the two opened boxes.

"Thank you," I manage, sitting up. When I look down at Sage, I see that he's still sleeping. For a moment, I can't help but stare. He really is one hopelessly sexy man—even in slumber. It makes me want to kiss him. I don't, wishing not to disturb him, but the thought still crosses my mind.

Just as I'm starting to untangle myself from his grasp, my phone starts to ring from inside of my pocket. I stifle a groan, knowing immediately who it is. Now, there is no question as to what time it is.

It's seven-thirty, and my mother is calling.

I know that if I don't answer, she'll just call back until I do. After the day I've had, I'm not sure I have the mental or emotional capacity to stay on the phone with her for long, but the least I can do is acknowledge her existence.

I slide the device out of my pocket, swipe my thumb across the screen, and bring it to my ear. "Mother, could you hold on a minute?"

"Hello, Tatiana. I will hold."

I take a deep breath, wishing I didn't have to pull myself away from Sage—the warmth of his body and the assurance of his affection—and then I crawl to my feet. "I'm just going to take this outside," I announce.

"Sure," says Violet with a kind smile.

When I make my way to the front door, Maestro follows me. I let him come outside with me, knowing that he won't run away, and I take a seat on the top porch step as I watch him wander around the lawn.

"Mother?"

"Yes, I am here."

"I can't talk for long. I'm not at home."

"What do you mean, you are not at home? You know the drill, Tatiana. I ask for—"

"Very little. Yes, mother, I know," I interrupt. My temper is short tonight and I'm already having a hard time reigning myself in. Today, I don't want to deal with this. I don't want to deal with my mother. I just want to be with my friends. Admitting that I desire the company of the people inside of this house makes me feel good. Knowing that I'm welcome warms my heart. But the sound of my mother's voice—

"Tatiana—"

"I'm sorry, mother, but could we please do this another time? I'm with friends and—"

"You're with that bastard boy, aren't you?"

I sit up straighter, offended by the way in which she's referring to the man who holds my heart. She knows nothing about him—nothing except for that he has chosen me—and yet, she's so quick to call him names. It's not outside of her character by any means, but just once I wish she'd keep her opinions to herself.

"Don't call him that," I murmur—my tone even and calm.

"How many times will you blow me off for him? Until he discards you and you suddenly have time for me again? Is that how this is going to go?"

"Nobody is discarding anyone. I'm sorry that I lost track of time and I'm not in a place to speak with you right now, but—"

"You're right," she bites. "You are sorry. Sorry and weak. How did I raise such a stupid child? When will you learn, Tatiana? How many times must we go over this? Out of all the things that I taught you—"

"Enough!" I cry. My heart is racing and I can feel my chest growing tight as I combat my tears—tears that I wish not to cry—tears that she does not deserve. "Let's be honest here, shall we? You didn't teach me anything. All you've ever done is show me what my life would look like if I ever let myself become as bitter as you! And you know what, mother? I don't want to be anything like you! I don't want to be alone. I don't want to be *angry* all the time. I don't want to look at every man I see and resent him simply because he has a fucking dick."

"What did you say to me?" Her voice is low and soft and I know that I've kicked the hornets nest.

It's been a long time since my mother and I have stood toe to toe. I ran away from her for this very reason. If I had stayed, we would have destroyed each other. Somehow, over the past eight years, a telephone call every other Saturday for a half an hour has been enough to keep us linked to a relationship that can barely be called as such, all the while preventing us from killing each other slowly. There is no depth to our connection. There is no affection in our repetitive exchange. There is no *love* between us. Not anymore. Not for a long time. And we've skirted around that truth for so long that I have lost touch with how much I hate it. How much I hate *her*.

Today, after spending my afternoon in Sage's arms—in the embrace of a man who has done nothing but try to convince me that I belong with him—I know for certain that I do not belong to Natalya Valentine. It's not even *her name* that I carry.

"Tatiana, I—"

"For the love of god! Millicent. I go by Millicent, mother."

"You disrespectful little brat. How *dare* you utter that name to me."

"It's who I am! For fuck sake—would you just let it go? It's been twenty years. How is it possible that you can't even hear my name without freaking out? Millicent. Just say it. *Millicent!*"

"Shut your mouth!" she yells. "I have had *enough*. You disrespect me. Your own mother. I brought you into this damn world. I sacrificed everything for you, and this is how you treat me? And all because of some boy who will break you—snapping you in half like the twig you are. You know nothing of this life. You know nothing of the hardship of sacrifice. You know nothing of the price of love. You refuse to see that it is not worth it."

"Bullshit!" I cry, standing to my feet. "Don't talk to me about sacrifice, as if I never had to give anything up to accommodate you. I sacrificed most of my childhood accommodating you—doing whatever it was that I had to do so that we could live in some type of *order*. You put all of that responsibility on me when you decided that the entire fucking world was against you, and your only response was going to be to *give up* and succumb to your bitterness."

"You ungrateful little bitch!"

I cough out a laugh, my only remaining defense against my tears. I know she can't see me when I shake my head at her, but I do it anyway. "If it helps you sleep at night, keep telling yourself that. But I can't do this anymore, mother. I can't—"

"Tati, you listen to—"

"Mother, I'm—"

"No! This time you will not hang up on me, I will hang up on you. I am the one who is done. You think your life will be so much better without me in it? You will see how wrong you are, you naive little girl. I am washing my hands of you. Soon, you will know what it's like to be in this world all alone. Then, I will not be here to pick up the pieces of your remains."

I huff out a harsh breath, appalled by her speech. "Fine!" I cry, calling her bluff. I'm all the woman has and we both know it.

"Fine."

The line goes dead and I gasp, pulling my phone away from my ear to look at the display.

She wasn't bluffing.

Immediately, my thumb hovers over her name, poised and ready to get her back on the line—but I pause, allowing myself a moment to wrap my head around what's just happened. I sink back down onto the porch step and take a breath.

We're done.

Just like that, my mother and I are...*over.*

A part of me feels like I should be elated. I'm finally free. The woman I ran from, the woman I've hardly tolerated for all of my adult life, she's severed ties with me. And yet, I don't feel an ounce of happiness. Neither do I feel sad. Instead, I feel nothing. Nothing at all.

"Millie? You okay?"

The sound of Sage's voice breaks me out of my trance. I don't turn to look back at him, taking a second to try and answer his question. When he comes and sits next to me, placing his hand on the small of my back, a sense of relief washes over me.

"Yeah," I answer honestly. "Yeah, I think I am."

"Was that your mom?"

I nod, seeking out his gaze. Looking through his glasses and into his eyes, I think back on our afternoon and how much we shared with each other. He trusted me, showed me an old scar, and I did the same. Now, I don't want to keep this from him either.

"I think we just…" I pause, trying to find the right words. "Broke up with each other."

He lifts an eyebrow at me, showcasing his confusion. "You *broke up* with your mom?"

"Yes."

He studies me for a moment before he hesitantly asks, "Do you want to talk about it?"

"No," I sigh, laying my head on his shoulder.

"Okay. Well, what do you need, baby doll?"

"Nothing." I wrap my arms around him, burying my face in his neck. I brush a kiss against his warm skin and suddenly I know that my answer is a lie. "You," I whisper, kissing him once more. "I just need you."

I turn my head as he dips his chin, and when our lips meet, a rush of happiness spreads from my head to my toes. I reach up and cup my hand around his cheek, expressing my desire to keep him close. My hunger for him is made evident in our ongoing kiss, and when he traces his tongue around the inside of my lips, I can feel my arousal making itself known between my legs as my panties grow damp. When I moan, he kisses me harder. Then, without warning, he pulls away abruptly. I open my mouth to question him, but he speaks before I can.

"If we don't stop, I'll take you upstairs and we won't be back down for the rest of the night. Let's eat first. I'm hungry, and you must be, too. You hardly touched your lunch."

I'll admit, I'm a little disappointed that he's making me wait, but he's right. "Sustenance," I mumble.

"You got it, doll," he says with a grin and a chuckle. "We're going to need it."

He presses a quick kiss against my lips before he calls for Maestro and stands to his feet. He offers me his hand and helps me up, holding onto me as we make our way inside, Maestro on our heels. We eat and drink with the others, talking over the movie that's playing. Everyone is still pretty excited about their time in the studio and the news of their next big show.

When an hour passes, I realize that my impatience from before has been kept at bay. I may be an outsider when it comes to their world of music, but so long as we are in this house—a place that grows more and more familiar every day—I feel as though I can at least pretend to be one of them. Nevertheless, when Sage leans toward me and gently nibbles on my earlobe, my desire to abandon their company is overwhelming.

"I think it's time for us to get naked," Sage whispers. "Feel like kissing every inch of my girl."

I shiver at the thought and he laughs softly as he gets up and reaches for my hand. I oblige, clinging to him as he leads me out of the room and up the stairs. Neither of us say a word to the others, but they don't seem to mind. They let us go without a bit of protest, for which I am grateful. The promise of his lips all over my body makes me ache with longing.

He shuts us into his room and lets go of my hand before leaning back against the door. "Strip, doll face. Then let your hair down and lay on the bed."

I back away from him, inching my way closer to the bed, my gaze locked with his as he stands perfectly still. His eyes rake over me and, even fully clothed, just his gaze makes my neck warm and my stomach flutter. Slowly, I shrug my way out of my sweater, letting it fall to the floor. My shirt goes next, then my jeans, my bra, and finally my panties. When I let my hair down, running my fingers through it as it falls down my back—messy as hell, I'm sure—I watch as he reaches down to adjust himself in his jeans. Knowing he's hard for me already makes my skin break out in goose bumps.

Obediently, I stretch out on his bed and then I run my hands down my bare body—desperate for *touch* as I wait for him.

"Play with your clit, baby. I want to see you touch yourself."

I don't even hesitate before I bend my knees and spread my legs, reaching down to do as he says. Across the room, he still sets me on fire, and I'm dripping wet in seconds. He watches me as he strips himself bare. When his cock springs free—long, thick, and fully erect—I slide two fingers inside of me, aching for him.

"Fuck," he mutters, reaching for himself.

With my freehand, I grab my breast and pinch my nipple. I'm so turned on, watching him stroke himself, I can hardly stand it. "Sage," I whimper, spreading my legs wider, working my pussy harder.

"Fuck yes—fuck that gorgeous cunt. Make yourself come, Millicent."

I moan, the sound of my name passing from his lips and the feel of my hands on and in my body beckoning me closer to my release. He takes a step toward me, then another, and another, and I want to touch him so badly.

"Sage…"

"You like what you see, baby doll? Does it turn you on to see me stroke my dick?" I nod, a pathetic sound freeing itself from my throat. "Are you thinking about how good I can make you feel with this dick? Are you pretending your fingers are me?"

"Oh, god," I mewl, suddenly needing more. I push three fingers inside of me, soaking them in my arousal. The slick sound of me fucking myself should be enough to leave me embarrassed, but I don't give a single shit—I want him to know how hot he makes me.

"Who owns your orgasm, baby?"

"You," I breathe. "Always, you."

"Then come for me."

I want nothing more.

I side my hand away from my breast and down my body, rubbing my clit as I continue to pump my fingers in and out of me. My eyes never leave his. When he licks his lip and then pulls it between his teeth, I lose it.

"Oh, fuck, Sage—baby!" I throw my head back as my orgasm hits me. I've never made myself come so hard in my life, proving his statement true—*Sage McCoy owns my orgasm, every damn time.*

My eyes fly open when he grips my wrist and lifts my fingers to his mouth. He sucks them hard, making my own mouth water. I manage to scramble onto my knees, my arm still in his grasp as I swallow his cock. He grunts, bucking his hips as he tangles his fingers in my hair, gripping the strands so tightly it burns. For a moment, we both suck. Then, when I swirl my tongue around his head, he groans and frees my hand, burying the rest of his fingers in my hair. I grab his ass and squeeze, sealing my eyes shut as I try and take him deeper. He gasps and then pulls his cock free.

With his fingers still twisted in my hair, he yanks my head back. My neck arches as I look up at him, and then he crashes his lips against mine. We moan together when our tongues meet and I lift up on my knees, longing to be closer to him.

"Need your pussy, Millie," he mumbles against my lips.

"It's yours," I whisper.

He pulls away from me, tossing his glasses on the nightstand before reaching into the drawer for a condom. I lay back, anxious to have him on top of me—inside of me—owning me. He rips the package open with his teeth, sheathing himself quickly before crawling in between my legs. He sinks into me with ease, staring down at me as he takes his time. When he's all the way in, he holds still for just a moment, kissing me tenderly.

"You're my best girl, Millicent," he whispers, pulling out slowly. "You're my best girl."

He rolls his hips, plunging back in, and I mewl. He feels so fucking good. Every time. He fills me up like no one ever has before and I'm sure no one else will ever compare. My mother swears that love isn't worth the trouble, but right here—right now—as he takes me slowly, gently, adoringly, I know that she is wrong. Sage is worth it. He's worth everything.

We take our time. My enjoyment seems to last for hours and I soak up every bit of it—every bit of him. He kisses me over and over again, whispering to me, singing to me, pleasuring me like only he can. When we come, we come together; and as we descend from our first euphoric high of the night, all I want is to be wrapped up in his strong arms—my safe place.

He rolls us over, his cock still buried deep, and holds me against his chest. For the first time in my life, I wonder if this is what *home* feels like.

TWENTY-FOUR

Sage

LOOKING DOWN AT the beautiful girl in my arms, I wonder what she'll be like after the six weeks that I'll be away. Babies change constantly. She's almost three months now, and looking more and more like her mother every day.

"Uncle Sage! Watch this," says Henley from across the kitchen table. He tosses a pea and tries to catch it in his mouth. He misses, sending the vegetable onto the floor.

"Henley, I don't think so, bud," says Harry from the head of the table. He shakes his head at his son, fixing him with a stern look. "We do not throw our food, do you understand?"

"Yes, daddy."

I smirk at my nephew as his shoulders sag in defeat. I'm going to miss the little dude, and his brother, too. I cannot believe how fast this month has flown by and how, in just ten days, we'll be hitting the road. I'm leaving a lot behind, but I won't deny that I can't fucking wait. If the last three weeks are just a taste of what it's going to be like to finally get Mountains & Men off the ground, I'm starving for more.

We finished our EP just this week. The guys and I are really proud of the way it turned out. Stefany is pretty hyped about it, too. She's been shopping for labels with our single *Just Tonight,* on top of tour prep and finalizing the details of our merchandise. I don't know who she knows or how she does it, but she's managed to find a couple sponsors to help back us financially for all the costs we've incurred that aren't covered from our cut from the tour. She wasn't lying when she said she'd work her ass off for us. So far, she's blown our minds.

We were able to cut a few costs by hiring our own graphic designer. Pepper came up with our logo ages ago. Graphic design is what she studied in school. She doesn't use it much these days, but that doesn't mean she can't. She most certainly can and *did*. Our new website is already up and running and it looks sick as shit. We're ready for the nation to know who we are.

I'm ready for them to sing with us.

"Rose told me you *finally* talked to mom and dad," says Pepper, lifting an accusatory eyebrow at me.

Admittedly, I'd been procrastinating on filling them in about the tour. We leave the thirtieth of October and we won't be back until the tenth of December, which means I'll be missing a major holiday. Dad's *favorite* holiday. Needless to say, considering their overwhelming amount of support for my career with Mountains & Men, coupled with me picking up and leaving everything for six whole weeks, I thought they'd be less than enthusiastic.

I was right.

"Look, it's done. I told them, they know, and that's all I'm going to say."

"Heard there was a pretty big argument," she murmurs, clearly ignoring the bit about me not wanting to talk about it anymore.

"There always is, Pep. That's why I waited so long to say something. They'll get over it."

"What about you and Millie? Are you good? I mean—six weeks on the road..." Her voice trails off, leaving me to fill in the blanks.

I shake my head at her, annoyed that she even thinks it's necessary to ask. "Not worried, sis."

"Give him a break, sweetheart," Harry interjects. "You know how much this means to him. We all do. It's exactly why we'll send him off with our support and why we'll all be here when he gets back."

"I know." She sighs, absentmindedly reaching over to adjust Carter's bib. He pays her no mind as he continues to happily consume his serving of macaroni and cheese. Pepper takes a deep breath before looking at me once more. "I'm just going to miss you."

"I'll be back before you know it," I reply with a chuckle.

"But this could be it. This could be the start of...*everything*. I mean, you never know. Then you'll be traveling all the time and I'll hardly ever see you."

"Pepper," I laugh. "Let's just get through this first tour, all right?" She nods and I offer her a smile. "I'll miss you, too, by the way."

"You better."

"What about me? Will you miss me, Uncle Sage?" asks Henley.

"You bet I will!"

"And me, too, Unka Sage?" Carter pipes in, not to be forgotten.

"You too, buddy."

"And daddy?" he asks, pointing his cheesy finger down the table.

Harry and I both chuckle before I assure my nephew, "Yeah. Your dad, too." I blow out a sigh, more than ready to change the subject. "D-a-m-n—this is not a farewell dinner. This is just dinner. Could we lighten up already?"

"You're right. You're right," Pepper concedes, holding her hands up as if waving the proverbial white flag. "Oh, speaking of farewell dinner," she begins, a twinkle in her eyes. "You know Rose and I won't let you leave without one. We'll do it the night before."

I shrug and nod, nonchalantly expressing my agreement to her plan. Really, there is no point in arguing. I'd lose.

"Maybe you could bring Millie? I mean—you guys have been together, *officially* together, for almost a month. I've met her *once*, and I hardly got to talk to her at all."

"I know. We've just been busy. She's had mid-terms and I've had band stuff and—"

"I don't want to hear it, baby brother. Just bring her. Got it?"

"Yes, ma'am."

"Good. Now, who wants dessert?"

Millicent

"KNOCK, KNOCK." LINDSEY announces herself at my office door without a single *actual* knock. I smile at her, slightly amused, and continue packing up for the weekend. "You're heading out early this afternoon."

"Yeah. Tonight's the big show. I have to get home and changed before we leave for Denver."

"Oh, my gosh, *right!*" she gasps, plopping down into one of the chairs in front of my desk. "You get to meet Lawful Sinners tonight."

"I do," I reply with a shrug. Truth be told, I know very little about Lawful Sinners. The only music of theirs that I've heard has been what Sage has insisted I listen to. I know that tonight means a lot to all of them. I understand why, even if I can't relate.

Nevertheless, if the privilege of meeting Lawful Sinners is a bit lost on me, having a backstage pass is not. I've never seen Mountains & Men perform from any vantage point that isn't in the middle of a crowd. Tonight, Violet and I will be just off stage. I imagine that the energy will be completely different—that it'll be more palpable—that Sage will be even more irresistible. *That* is something to look forward to.

"This is their last show before they hit the road, right?"

"It is," I reply with a nod. My enthusiasm for gathering my things suddenly wanes and I prop my hip against my desk, giving Lindsey my undivided attention. "They leave in nine days."

"Wow. I'm still trying to wrap my head around the fact that we survived midterms. Where does the time go?"

"Excellent question."

She smiles at me then crosses her legs and props her elbows atop her knee. "Millie Valentine, that boy wonder has done a number on you—I swear."

I rake my fingers through my hair as I look down at my feet. I'm not sure how to respond to her comment. I certainly can't deny it. It would be a lie unworthy of the effort. Sage has been my undoing, just as I predicted. I fall for him a little bit more every moment that we're together; and every day, one by one, the walls that I constructed long ago to shield me from the pain that I know comes with love, he's managed to tear them down.

I don't want to love him. Right now, what we have is good. I'm afraid of what love would do to us—what it would do to *me*. I don't know how to trust love. It's betrayed me more times than I'd like to remember. Trusting Sage, though—it's paramount. I won't get through our separation if I don't trust him.

Six weeks seems like nothing, in the grand scheme of things. Then again, one might say the same about nine weeks—yet, nine weeks with him in my life has changed everything. From the moment we met, I just knew that I couldn't keep him—that I didn't *want* to. The arrogant little shit. Even when I could fully admit that my body craved the man like I've never craved anything, I still knew that resistance was necessary. Now, I have no fight. Now, he's all I want.

"Six weeks will come and go before you know it," says Lindsey, pulling me from my thoughts.

I nod, a part of me hoping that she's right. However, there's another part of me that hopes that she's wrong. I know what this tour means to him. What it means to all of them. I hope they soak it up for all that it's worth and that it doesn't go by so fast that they miss it.

"Have you guys talked about you meeting up with him while he's gone? I mean, we have fall break around Thanksgiving. You totally could."

"You're right," I mutter, appalled that the thought never crossed my mind before. "I think they'll be on the West Coast by then. I'd have to double check."

"See? That would be perfect! You weren't planning on going back to New Jersey for the holiday, were you?"

"No. Definitely not." Hearing her speak of New Jersey makes me think of my mother. Suddenly in need of a distraction, I resume gathering my belongings.

I haven't heard from my mother for three weeks. Every Saturday, I wonder if she'll call. I wonder if I should. Every Saturday, she doesn't and I don't. I really thought that she would recant her threat of being done with me. After all she's said and done to get it through my head that she is my only constant—that every man in the world is unworthy of affection because he will end up breaking my heart—it's hard to believe that *she* would discard me.

Most days, I don't consider it a loss.

"Well, now that I've planted that little idea into your head, I suppose I should let you go. You have a night out to prepare for. I'll be expecting details on Monday. And if you *happen* to come back with anything signed by the lead guitarist from Lawful Sinners, I would be willing to accept it as an early Christmas present," she says with a wink.

"Noted," I chuckle.

"Have fun, Millie." She parts with a wave and I watch her leave before gathering the rest of my things and heading for home.

I arrive just after four with enough time for a quick clothing change and a moment to retouch my face. Thankfully, I picked my outfit earlier this morning before leaving for work. With November right around the corner, the air is starting to smell like chimney fire. I expect we'll get our first little snow any day now. That being said, I've had to come up with more subtle ways to show off the legs that Sage admires so much. Tonight, I'll be wearing a pair of black sequin leggings, along with a clingy, long-sleeved, black midriff sweater. The small bit of skin that's left on display between the two items is just enough to tease my dreamer. I finish the ensemble with my yellow envelope purse and a pair of electric blue heels.

I choose the heels as a sort of *good luck* for Sage. He doesn't know it, but I do and that's enough. He doesn't need luck. Not with his talent. But the blue of the shoe reminds me of the first time I ever heard him sing. He burns so hot up on that stage…

I shake the thought away, knowing I don't have time to be distracted by my daydreams. Instead, I rush to the bathroom and apply a fresh coat of mascara before running a brush through my hair. I gather it to one shoulder, allowing it to drape down my chest, and decide that for tonight—it'll have to do. I take one step into the hallway just as a knock sounds at my door. Knowing who it is, I don't waste a moment closing the distance between me and him.

The second I open the door, my mouth begins to water.

He's sexier than any man I've ever seen on the front of any magazine.

He's in his favorite pair of Converse—the red ones. He's got on dark wash jeans, and a white graphic t-shirt under a black leather jacket. The black beanie that slouches off the back of his head hides most of his hair, but leaves just enough out that I want to run my fingers through it.

And of course, he's wearing those glasses.

Fuck, those stupid things turn me on.

"Hey, doll face. You look hot," he says, stepping toward me.

"You, too," I manage before his lips are pressed firmly against mine. I reach up and grab a fistful of his t-shirt, needing air but too desperate for this kiss to take a breath.

He slides his hand over my backside, drawing me close as he pulls his mouth from mine. "You ready to jet? We have to go."

"I'm ready."

"Good." He kisses me once more. "Lock up."

We step into the hallway and I turn to close and lock the door. As I do so, his hand doesn't leave my body. He slips a finger under the hem of my sweater, tracing his way from my side to my back. I take a breath, reminding myself that I don't want to love him, and then I turn and offer him a smile.

"Let's go."

TWENTY-FIVE

Millicent

Fighting our way through rush hour on a Friday night is a bitch. It takes us two hours to get to The Fillmore, making us twenty minutes late. When we pull into the parking lot, the guys are more frazzled than I've ever seen them. Violet and JJ rode with Sage and me, the rest of their crew riding with Derrick and all of their equipment.

We pile out of our respective vehicles and immediately make our way to the trailer. Derrick opens it up and we each grab something before hurrying our way through the back entrance. Sage is greeted by a big, burly guy with a bright yellow t-shirt on. He's obviously a member of the security staff and he eyes each and every one of us warily.

"You playin' tonight?" he asks.

"Yeah. We're Mountains & Men. Our manager, Stefany, should be inside. She has our passes."

I notice as his face softens at the name *Stefany*, and he nods before waving us inside. Just as the door shuts behind us, Stefany bursts into the hallway.

"Thank *fucking* god you're here!" she cries, clearly relieved.

"Sorry we're late," Derrick mutters. "Traffic was a fucking nightmare."

"It's okay, it's okay." She waves off his explanation and reaches for the bags in Sage's hands. "Let's just get you all set up and then I'll introduce you around. Doors open in a half an hour—show starts an hour after. You know you're opening up tonight. By the looks of the line that's already wrapped around the building, I'd wager that's certainly not a bad thing."

"We're playing at The Fillmore, Stef," Knox begins with a laugh. "We'd be happy playing for the staff."

"Aww. Aren't you guys just the cutest," she teases before leading us backstage.

The place is swarming with activity. There are roadies and technicians all over the place, getting things ready and putting the final touches on the stage for the show. After one more trip to the trailer, the guys have everything they need and they busy themselves on stage, setting up their stuff with the help of the staff. Of course, Violet is in the thick of it, as usual, while I stand to the side watching like the useless girlfriend that I am.

"A chick with an ass like yours should not be left unattended."

I turn at the sound of his strange, deep, sultry voice and my eyes widen at the sight of him. He's a little shorter than Sage, but still taller than me. He's got wavy jet black hair that falls to his shoulders, and big, brilliant brown eyes full of mischief. He's sporting a bit of scruff, along with a sly grin, and I have to stop myself from perusing the rest of him. Though, it doesn't take a genius to know that he's ripped—I can tell just by the way his shirt hugs his broad shoulders.

"Fuck me, beautiful," he says, bringing a hand up to his chest. "And yeah—I mean that literally."

A small smile tugs at the corner of my mouth as I shake my head at him. Two months ago, if I was on the hunt for a bed fellow, he would definitely have had a chance. Now, he's just some hot guy wasting his time. I'm not looking for a piece of ass tonight, and I'm not interesting in *being* a piece of ass, either.

"No, thank you."

His eyebrows shoot up in surprise. "No, thank you?"

"I'm sorry—are you having a hard time hearing me? Or do you just find yourself so tempting that you can't fathom a single reason why I would say no?"

He chuckles, folding his bulging arms across his chest as he stares at me. "Feisty, just the way I like 'em. I might have you singing a different tune after our set."

"I doubt it," I say with a shrug.

He narrows his eyes, studying me as if I fascinate him. Though, for the life of me, I can't understand why. Smarter men would have gotten the hint and left me alone by now.

"Do you know who I am?"

"Should I?"

He barks out a laugh. "Fuck me," he says with a grin. "And I still mean that literally." I lift an eyebrow at him, but he's not discouraged. "You must not be much of a Lawful Sinners fan."

"They're pretty good," I say with a shrug. "But no, I'm not here for them." As soon as the words come out of my mouth, it dawns on me that—"Oh, shit. You're one of them, aren't you?"

"Guilty. And if you're not here for the headlining band, it means you're here for one of the newbies. So who do I need to outplay for you? Twisted Tuesday or Mountains & Men?"

"Sorry, you don't stand a chance. I'd like to think of myself as a big Mountains & Men fan. And the lead singer happens to be a big fan of my ass. So, while I may lend you my ear tonight, the only man I'll be fucking is *him*."

"Ahhh, I see," he mutters, his grin still firmly in place. "You must be the girlfriend." I affirm his assumption with a nod and he coughs out a laugh. "Look me up after the tour if you're in need of a good revenge fuck."

I stare at him for a moment, appalled by his statement. Suddenly, this conversation is neither fun nor amusing. "What in the hell is that supposed to mean?"

He leans toward me, the mischievous look in his eyes intensified with his close proximity. "It *means*, six weeks is a long time to keep his dick in his pants, especially with more than a few asses as fine as yours hanging out backstage, like you are now."

"I trust him," I murmur. Though, why I feel the need to inform him is beyond me. I don't know him. Neither do I care to know him.

"You might trust him, sweetheart—but it's the musician inside of all of us that can't be tamed." He winks at me as he turns to walk away. "Remember what I said. My offer doesn't expire, beautiful."

Sage

With the help of the crew, it only takes us twenty minutes to set up. Perfect timing. We're headed backstage just minutes before the doors open. I walk straight to my girl, who only seconds ago was talking with Clay—the lead guitarist of Lawful Sinners. I could tell by the look on her face that she wasn't impressed. A smirk curls my lips as to *why* I recognize the face. It's how she looked at me the first time we met. Unfortunately for Clay, he won't have a chance to change her mind. Fortunately for *me*, I've managed to win her over so as never to see that look directed at me again.

"Hey, baby," I say, slipping my arm around her waist. "Over here making friends without me?"

She leans into my side as she shakes her head. "Not really."

"Do you even know who that was?"

"Didn't catch his name."

I can't help but chuckle before leaning down to kiss her lips. "You're something else, baby doll."

"So you keep telling me."

"Dweeb, come on!" calls out Derrick.

I look over Millie and spot him with the rest of our group, waiting on us. I tip my chin in acknowledgement and then take Millie's hand.

"Time to meet the guys we'll be touring with. Come on, doll face."

We follow Stefany down a couple narrow hallways until we're standing in front of a closed door. The sound of music and laughter wafts from the cracks between the hinges and she knocks before inviting herself inside.

"Stefany. Hey, what's up—these your boys?"

Some guy with short curly hair, in slacks and a button up shirt he wears untucked, crosses the large room and reaches for her hand. She accepts his gesture, giving him a firm handshake before she answers his question.

"Yeah, my boys and *girl*. Heath, this is Mountains & Men. Mountains & Men, this is Heath. He's a sucker for Skittles and any book by James Patterson—keep that in mind for if you ever piss him off."

"Or just don't piss me off," he says with a shrug.

"I like that plan. I'm Sage, by the way."

We all take our turns introducing ourselves and then he nods, indicating that he'd like to introduce us to his guys. Clay, Nate, Gabe and Adrian are chillin' on a couple couches in the corner, each of them with a beer in hand. Gabe, their lead singer, and Nate, their drummer, each have a girl on their lap, while Adrian, their bassist, seems to be eyeing the chick refilling the beer cooler. Clay doesn't seem to be interested in any of the available ass in the room, his gaze trained on Millicent.

Jealous fucker. Better keep his hands to himself. I've thrown punches for her before, and I'll do it again in a heartbeat.

Millie hugs my arm, sending a message of her own, and my irritation subsides.

For now.

"Have a seat. Grab a beer. We've got some time to kill," says Gabe, motioning at the empty chairs scattered around the room. "We heard your EP. You guys are good. Looking forward to hearing more."

We all reply with a thank you of sorts, and I know I'm not the only one of us flattered beyond words. I know what I told Alex a couple weeks ago about all of us just being people—and we are, musicians, every one of us. Nevertheless, a compliment from the lead singer of a band with their level of success, it's certainly nothing to scoff at.

"Which one of you is on bass?" asks Adrian.

We all turn and look at Alex whose cheeks burn bright red as she lifts her hand.

Adrian's face falls and then the room erupts.

"Noooo!" Clay cries before he starts laughing, clapping Adrian on the back.

"Daaaaaaamn!" Nate adds, bringing a fist up to cover his grin.

"Clearly, we're missing something here," JJ says, giving voice to what I'm sure we're all thinking.

"You should have heard this guy," Gabe laughs, hooking his thumb at Adrian. "Would not shut up about that wicked bass solo in—what was it?"

"*Contortion*," Adrian mutters, shaking his head in disbelief. "*Fuck!* That was *you?*"

Alex shrugs and Derrick reaches over and smacks her arm. "Ow!" she yelps.

"Stop being such a pussy, Ali."

"Yeah," I pipe in. "Where's the badass who laid us out the day of her audition?"

She rolls her eyes but then smiles at me before she squares her shoulders and looks back at Adrian. "Is it my stature or my boobs that make it hard for you to believe I can rock the bass?"

His shocked expression slowly transforms into one of amusement as a sly smile shifts the features of his face. "Definitely not your stature. Maybe your boobs. But I'll give you mad props either way. We'll have to jam while we're on the road."

Her blush returns and she offers him a nod. "Definitely."

Twisted Tuesday enters the room—four more guys and a few girls I'd imagine are groupies. They don't exactly look like the types of girls you'd want to keep, more like glorified bed warmers—but I'm not one to judge.

More introductions are made and then we spend the next hour shootin' the shit. We talk music, we swap band stories, and they tell us about life on the road. Twisted Tuesday has toured before—never with Lawful Sinners, and not with a bunch of large venues, but it's definitely a one up from what we've got. When the stage manager pops his head in and announces that we're on, we waste no time heading out—a few of the guys following behind to watch from the wings.

I hear the chatter of the crowd before I even get a peek, and my stomach clenches in anxious anticipation. For just a second, I allow myself to get nervous. When I crane my neck in an attempt to get a look at the packed venue, all the air in my lungs rushes out, as if they've suddenly collapsed.

"Holy fucking shit."

"We got this, bro," says Knox. He claps his hands on my shoulders and gives me a squeeze before letting me go. "We're going to rock the hell out of this set."

"Yeah. Yeah—we got this," I mutter, willing my bravery to resurface.

"This is it, man," Maddox cries, smacking his fingers against my cheeks.

I laugh, because I can't help myself, and jerk away from his abuse. He's getting hyped and this is his way of trying to get me there with him. I throw a playful jab to his side and he catches me off guard, pulling me in for a hug.

"I mean it. This is it, Sage. This is what we've been working for since we were a couple of fucking kids who barely knew which way was up. We made it."

I hug him back, soaking in the significance of this show. He's right. It's been Knox, Maddox, and me since the very beginning—and we're finally here.

I pull away from him just as Derrick pats me on the back. When I look at him, he smiles at me knowingly.

"Time to give them one hell of a show, eh, Dweeb?"

"You got it, D."

The house lights go out and the crowd goes wild, now fully aware that the show's about to start. Knowing that's our cue, Derrick, Maddox, and Knox start to take their places. JJ grabs my shoulder and I peer through the darkness, knowing I'll find his fist waiting for mine. I pound his knuckles against his.

"Kill it," he yells over the noise as he goes to join the others.

I almost jump when I feel a small hand slide into mine. I'm surprised to look over and see Alex. She looks back at me, giving my fingers a squeeze as she says, "Tell me something good. I need to hear something good."

I shake my head, understanding that her stage fright has kicked in, but surprised—after the last month—that she still has reason to doubt what she's capable of. "Hey," I lean down so that I can ensure that she hears every word I'm about to say. "Did you see the look on Adrian's face an hour ago? We told you you could play circles around that guy. Now get your ass out there and show him how it's done, Zip."

She squeezes my fingers once more and then lets me go. "Thank you," she says before she disappears into the darkness.

Derrick clicks the beat and then Knox starts plucking out his solo. The stage lights come up and the crowd gets even louder. I know I only have a few more seconds before I have to be out there, but there's one more person I want to share this moment with.

I turn and see Millie staring straight at me, and my heart skips a beat.

Fucking hell. She's turned me into a damn pussy.

I won't complain, though. She's totally worth it.

I slip out of my leather jacket and hang it around her shoulders. "Hold onto this for me," I murmur into her ear. She nods and I flash a quick smirk before smacking a kiss against her lips. "Gotta go, doll face."

Millicent

He walks away from me, and the second he steps into the spotlight and onto that stage, I feel completely and utterly empty. I try shaking off the sensation; I try shoving it into the back of my mind; but the funny thing about *emptiness* is—you can't just *get rid* of it. It's not an emotion that can be ignored or a pain that can be placated. It's a feeling that leaves you hollow, and the only way to reverse the condition is to replace or refill what was taken.

Only, Sage is irreplaceable.

"We're Mountains & Men—and we're about to get *Wild!*"

His introduction is brief, but when he belts out the first note of *Wild,* the band perfectly in sync, the roar of the audience sends a very clear and enthusiastic message: they might not have known who Mountains & Men were a few minutes ago, but they sure as shit know who they are now—and they want more.

Violet throws her arms in the air, yelling her encouragement, her voice lost in the cacophony of sounds that fill the entire building. When she starts singing along, every word memorized, a pang of despair hits me square in the chest—resounding off of the walls of my hollow insides.

I'm losing him.

Right here. Right now.

I'm losing him.

He doesn't belong to me. He belongs to *them.*

He belongs to the crowd, to the countless number of people who will sing with him.

Without my permission, my *emptiness* starts filling up with unwelcome memories.

I think of Clay…

Six weeks is a long time to keep his dick in his pants…

I think of the green room…

Beer. Booze. Boobs.

The amount of scantily clad women hanging out with the bands backstage is probably nothing to any of them. But that was *before* the show; *before* the after-party; *before* the copious amounts of alcohol that I know will be consumed before the rising of the sun.

I think of that embrace…

Maddox held onto Sage like a lifeline, and isn't that what they are to each other? All of them—they are more than family, bound together by something more meaningful than blood—by the very thing that gives life *to their blood—their dream!*

I think of Alex…

I saw it. Even in the darkness, I saw the way she reached for his hand. She's one of them now…one of the men *he'd go to war for. In her moment of need, he'll be there for her, too. It may be true that he would never betray me, but leaving me and betraying me are not the same thing.*

Now—as I look out onto the stage, I see the man who holds my heart and know that I will never get it back. And as he struts before the fans like the peacock that he is, his rich, smooth, tenor voice making my insides quiver, I know that where he goes, I will not go. Tonight is his beginning. His future is even brighter than he is—I can sense it. Yet, in spite of how I feel about the man, I know that we will not last; that the grandeur of all that awaits him will rip him away from me.

I can't keep him.

I fooled myself into believing that I could.

Nine days.

He'll be gone in nine days. Right here, right now, I'm wise enough to know that whatever promises he makes will be made in vain, even if he thinks he means them now.

The truth—the fucking god's honest truth—is that they *always* leave.

Always.

I feel the heat of a body behind me and a chill runs down my spine.

"Should have known, with a catch like you, he's the heartthrob—the fan-favorite type," Clay speaks into my ear. "Like I said—you need me, you look me up, baby."

I clench my teeth together, willing myself to stay calm.

Nine days.

I slip my arms into Sage's jacket. The weight of it wrapped around me and his scent holding me brings me comfort.

I won't get to keep him, I know, but for just this moment—I want him and he wants me and that's all that matters.

Right?

Just then, he looks over at me and winks.

I don't want to love him, I remind myself. *It would kill me to love him.*

TWENTY-SIX

Sage

It's been four days since our show at The Fillmore and the residue of my stage high still lingers. Being up there in front of all those people—the crowd so expansive that I couldn't even see where it ended—it was one of those life changing moments that I'll never forget. And the best part is, I'm about to do that over and over and over again. In five days, we load up and head out for our first leg of the tour. A week from today, I'll be playing for a Texas crowd.

Fucking Texas!

It's time that big ass state knew our name.

"You're doing it again," says Sarah with a laugh.

I look over at her, from where I sit on the stool behind the front counter at Little Bird, and watch as she restocks the pastry case. I know I'm not the only one around here who's glad to have little miss blondie back. Brandon's been in an exceptionally good mood since she's been home, and it doesn't take a genius to figure out why. Millie says that Sarah hasn't slept at the apartment since her return.

Though, she can't really say for sure. I've been keeping her quite busy.

"Hello! Earth to Sage."

"Sorry, what?" I ask, shaking my head as I focus on what Sarah is saying.

"You're going to be like this all week, aren't you? Here but *not* really here before you're gone for good."

"What are you talking about? I'll be back."

She stops what she's doing and looks right at me, resting her hand on her popped out hip. "Do you really believe that? I mean, don't get me wrong, your job will still be here when you get back, but do you honestly think you'll need it?"

I chuckle nervously, shrugging my shoulders as I shake my head. "Sarah—I have no clue. But I sure as hell hope not. I guess we'll just have to wait and see."

"Hey, kid, what are you still doing here?" asks Brandon as he comes from the back. He passes me and heads straight for Sarah, kissing her forehead before he starts timing espresso shots.

I look at the clock on the register and hop off the stool. "Shit. What *am* I still doing here?" I pull off my apron, tossing it under the counter before grabbing my jacket as I walk around to the other side. "Two cinnamon swirl coffee cakes, please."

"Two, huh?" Sarah says with a grin as she bags up my order. "Might one of these be for your *girlfriend?*" she asks, grossly exaggerating the word.

"This is the last Tuesday we'll have for a while," I mutter with a shrug. "Just want her to know I'm not gone yet."

"You know what? You're not too bad at this boyfriend thing."

She rings me up and I hand over the bills I owe her before snatching up my sack of goodies.

"Sarah," I begin to say, backing my way out of the lobby. "I'm the best she's ever had." She laughs and I wink before turning to make my exit.

It takes me twenty minutes to get to campus, and when I arrive at Millie's office, I find it locked. I'm not surprised or bothered. I know she'll be making her way around the corner any minute now. While I wait, I hop on Facebook and scroll through my feed. The guys and I acquired a few more friends on the social media network after having met Twisted Tuesday and Lawful Sinners. Everyone's been talking about the tour, posting clips from our last show, and creating the necessary hype for our first few stops.

I hear the echo of a pair of heels as someone makes her way down the hallway. I pocket my phone, hoping it's my girl. Sure enough, she comes into view and the sight of her makes my dick jerk. She's got on a dress. It's navy blue and covered in a subtle pattern that you'd miss if you weren't paying attention. The top is cut like a blazer, closed halfway down her chest—only she's not wearing a shirt underneath. The long sleeves are folded up her forearm, the gold belt around her waist reminds me of what lies underneath, and the skirt hangs just above her knees—her bare knees.

"You're wearing a dress," I murmur, a devious smile curling my lips.

She approaches me with a straight face, pressing her freehand against my chest as she pushes herself up on her tiptoes. She puckers her lips and I lean down, giving her what she wants. When I pull away, she whispers, "I am. What are you going to do about it?"

"Well, doll face, I would take you against the wall if you'd let me, but since you have *rules*—"

"Fuck my rules, Sage," she breathes.

The feel of her breath against my lips, coupled with the promise of her words, sends a rush of blood to my dick. I kiss her again, this time reaching for her ass and pulling her against me. "Open the goddamn door, Millicent, and stop teasing me before I take you in this hallway."

"You have a condom?"

I arch an eyebrow at her ridiculous question. When I get back, I fully intend on convincing her that we don't need the rubbers. For now, I'm too turned on to argue. "Have you seen my girlfriend?" I ask, giving her ass a squeeze. "I don't leave home without one."

A small smile plays at her lips and she pulls away from me, reaching for her keys before unlocking the door. I follow her inside and she shuts us in before twisting the lock, not even bothering with the lights. The second she drops her bag, I drop mine into the nearest chair and my hands are around her hips, guiding her back against the wall and out of sight of the narrow window beside the door.

My mouth goes straight for her neck. Her hair is pulled back into a long ponytail, giving me full access to what I want. I lick and suck from her jaw, all the way down her chest, until my lips meet the fabric of her dress. She smells amazing and she tastes delicious, and when I press my hard-on against her stomach, the sound of her whimper is my undoing.

I reach for my wallet and she tugs at the button of my jeans. She frees my cock just as I get the condom open, and her greedy hands slide underneath my shirt as I roll it on.

"Are you ready for me, Millie?" I ask, reaching up her dress. I yank off her thong, pulling it from around her ankles before throwing it over my shoulder. As I stand up, I dip a finger between her slick folds.

"I'm ready, baby," she insists, grabbing hold of the back of my neck. "I need your cock. Right now, Sage. I need—"

She gasps as I lift her up and penetrate her entrance in one swift motion. Her legs lock behind my back and I palm her bare ass. The warmth of her skin in my hands and her hot pussy around my dick takes my breath away.

"Oh, Sage—yes," she mewls. "Fuck me, baby. Harder!"

A growl crawls its way up my throat and I pound into her. It's not long before I feel a bead of sweat trickle down my back. It's hot as hell in my jacket, but I can't stop. Not for anything. She feels so fucking incredible.

"God, Millie. I can't get enough of you, doll face."

"Kiss me," she mutters.

I'm quick to obey, tangling my tongue with hers as I rock in and out of her. She sighs into my mouth before she sucks on my lip. When she lets me go, I nip along the length of her jaw and she grips my hair. Her legs tighten around me, causing her heels to dig into my backside. Every sound that escapes her lips pulls me closer and closer to my release. When she tilts her head back, closing her eyes as she frees a long moan, my balls start to tighten.

Love it when she sings to me.

Knowing that I'm not going to last much longer, I slide one of my hands around until I find her clit with my thumb. As I begin to massage her sweet spot, her mouth falls open and her eyes find mine.

"Baby, I'm going to come! I'm going to—*fuck*, Sage! God, *yes*!"

Her pussy squeezes my dick and I pump into her once more before my own release immobilizes me. I groan, pressing my forehead against hers as my orgasm sends a shock of pleasure up my spine. For a moment, I wonder how the fuck I'm supposed to be without this woman for six whole weeks.

"I've wanted to do that since the day you told me you were a professor, before I even knew where your office was," I mutter, still short of breath. She giggles and a smirk tugs at my lips. "Mean it, baby doll."

"I know you do."

I bring my mouth to hers and kiss her slowly, *deeply*. I go soft inside of her, but I'm not ready to pull out yet; and when she kisses me back, clinging to my neck affectionately, I know she's in no hurry, either.

"I brought you something," I tell her, forcing myself to end our kiss before I get hard again.

"Oh, yeah? Something cinnamon?"

"You bet your sweet, little ass." I give her backside a light smack before I set her down on her feet. "You hungry?"

"Mmmhmm. I could go for a treat. Will you help me find my panties, first?"

I chuckle, slipping the condom off and tucking myself back in my pants. "Sure thing, doll."

Millicent

After we straighten up, he sits behind my desk, as he so often does, and pulls me into his lap. As is becoming our custom, we each enjoy our slice of cinnamon swirl coffee cake together.

Custom. I don't even know why I use the word. We won't do this again…

I cherish every single moment, knowing that it is one of our last. I can barely take my eyes off of him, wishing to memorize every single detail of his sinfully handsome face. I never want to forget how *cool* and *beautiful* his icy blue eyes are, or the way his horn-rimmed glasses make him look sexier than they should. I know that it is no use. I know that time will force me to forget; but for now, this hope is all I have.

"What are you up to tonight?" he asks me, pulling me from my thoughts.

"I was going to go to the gym before I head home. I've got some grading I need to get done, too."

"I have a shit ton of laundry I need to do if I plan on packing for this trip. But I could come over after, if you want. It might be late."

"I'll wait up," I assure him with a nod.

I'm running out of time. I'm running out of opportunities to fall asleep in his arms and wake up with his kisses. I used to think it was awful to be blindsided by the end of a relationship—but to see it coming is so much worse.

"Alright. I'm gonna jet, then. I'll call you later, okay?"

"Yeah." I stand from his lap and he vacates my chair, gathering our trash before he kisses me goodbye.

As I watch him leave, the reminder that I'm the one who will have to end this hits me square in the chest. I'm the one who will have to walk away. I can't hold onto his promises with the shadow of the inevitable cast over them. It'll be better to do this now rather than later—cut our losses and all that shit. It'll hurt like a *fucking bitch*, but what other option do we have? None. His destiny has made this decision for us.

I know he'll fight me. I know he'll try and convince me that I'm wrong. He's got an optimistic heart. It's one of the things that I adore about him. It's also the truth I cling to as I selfishly hold onto him for a few more days. I haven't said a word about my decision. He knows nothing of my doubts and what I intend to do with them—and he won't. Not until just before he leaves. Not until he has no choice but to leave me behind.

For the next four days, I am his. I will indulge every desire that I have and I will say yes to whatever he wants. It's why I wore a dress today—why I was prepared to wear a goddamn dress every single day this week, in hopes that he'd drop by with that look of lust in his gaze. If these are the last memories that I will have with him, then I need to make them count. I *will* make them count; because when he is gone, there will be nothing else for me to hold on to.

I know by waiting I'm being a complete bitch, but it's the only way. I won't be able to resist him if he stays to fight for me. He's fought for me before, more than once, and he has won every single fucking time. This time, I won't allow it. I can't. We have to say goodbye. This is about self-preservation. If I end this, I will carry around the pain and our memories until I'm too numb to feel a thing. If *he* ends it… if I *wait* for him to end it, I know it'll destroy me.

I can't operate under the schedule of his heart. It could be *months* before he realizes that what he wants isn't me; before he realizes that I mean nothing in comparison to his dream. By the time he figures it out, I'll surely be in love with him. And it would be a dangerous kind of love. I know this because I know I've never felt about anyone the way I feel about him.

I don't want to love him, I remind myself, *and so my mind is made up.*

I just can't—I can't let him end it. I won't. It has to be me.

Sage

"SAGE!"

I shake my head at the sound of her voice, amused that such a large noise can came from such a small body.

"In here, little lady," I call back from the laundry room. After I finish swapping the clothes in the washer to the dryer, I load a new pile of dirty clothes into the washer. Rosy enters the room just as I start the machine. "Hey, what's up? Didn't know you were dropping by."

"Yeah, I know," she says with a sigh and a shrug. "It hit me today—like *really* hit me…"

Her voice trails off and I scowl at her in confusion, reaching for the basket full of clean clothes. "What hit you?" I ask.

"My bestie is about to leave me for the next six weeks. I only have a couple more days to bug you before you're out of reach."

"Come on, Rosy," I hum, throwing an arm around her shoulders and pulling her into my side. "You know distance will never stop you from bugging me."

"Hey!" She slaps my chest as she laughs and we both make our way out of the laundry room, her still tucked against me. I kiss the top of her head and she wraps her arms around me the best that she can, giving me a squeeze. "You know you'll miss me too, so don't even pretend otherwise."

"Who's pretending?" I ask with a smirk. "Help me fold, yeah?"

"Fine," she says with a sigh of resignation, following me up to my room. "But only because I know this is your way of saying, *I love you so much, Rosy, and these next six weeks are going to suck ass without you*—even if you are having the time of your life."

"Hurry up and graduate, twerp, and maybe next time you can come with us."

We both sit together on my bed and she smiles at me before she picks up a t-shirt and starts to fold.

"You really mean that?"

I offer her a shrug as I chuckle. I wish I could tell the future, but I know that I can't. Even still, I'm not the only McCoy with big dreams. Hers have been on course to crash into mine for a while, now. "That was always the plan, right? Mountains & Men makes it big and my kid sister comes along for the ride."

"More like your wickedly smart and talented kid sister comes along and handles any and all of your financial needs—because *one of us* had to get an actual education."

"In theory," I laugh.

"Seriously, Sage," she begins to say, nudging me with her shoulder. "You know this is the start of something. This tour—no matter where it leads you—it's still a huge fucking deal. I'm so incredibly proud of you! And—shit." I toss aside a pair of socks when I hear her sniffle.

"None of that, baby girl," I insist, palming the top of her head and directing her gaze to line up with mine.

"No, just listen," she murmurs. "You know you've always been more than my brother. You've taught me so much just by being you—by chasing after what you want and never giving up. I admire you more than words can say, Sage, and the fact that you guys are making moves…I'm just really proud of you. I'm proud to be able to call you my brother, and even more so to call you my best friend. I'm going to miss you like crazy."

I pull her toward me, pressing a kiss against her forehead before I let her go. "Me, too, Rosemary. Me, too."

"Okay!" she exclaims, running her fingers through her hair. "Enough of that. I don't even know where that came from."

"You raggin'?" I tease.

"Ew, Sage! Fuck you." She throws a pair of jeans at me, but I only laugh.

Times like these, I'm reminded why she's always been more than a sister to me, too. Our friendship is easy and fun. The fact that we're related to each other and she can't get rid of me is kind of just a bonus.

"Don't talk like that, Rosy. You're a lady—and don't you dare forget that while I'm gone, either."

"Please," she says, rolling her eyes. "Like I need you to remind me that I'm a lady. I'm a badass, big bro—with fucking *class*."

"Yeah, whatever."

"Speaking of *ladies*—Pepper said Millie is coming to dinner Saturday."

"Yup. Four of my favorite girls at my favorite table."

She grins at me and I toss her a wink.

"I like you like this."

"Like what?"

She shakes her head as her eyes rake over me, as if she can't find the right words to express what *this* means.

"I don't know. Like *this*—boyfriend, brother, musician—all of it. You seem really, truly happy."

I nod, thinking about everything I've got going on in my life right now. I have not one thing to complain about. The exact opposite, as a matter of fact. I don't know how I got so lucky. I feel like I turned twenty-one and hit the jackpot. I plan on savoring every bit of my winnings, and working my ass off to keep 'em coming.

"I *am* happy, Rosy. Happier than I've ever been."

Crawling closer to me, she leans in and kisses my cheek. "Good!" she proclaims.

I chuckle and shake my head at her. I don't know why she's gotten sentimental all of a sudden. I'd be willing to bet she's *totally* raggin'. The thought crosses my mind to tease her about it some more, but then I think better of it. If I'm right—it's better just to let her have her day.

"Get to work, twerp. These clothes aren't going to fold themselves."

She sticks her tongue out at me before plucking another t-shirt from the basket. "You're such a brat."

TWENTY-SEVEN

Millicent

I WAKE TO THE FEEL of his lips brushing across my shoulders. When he reaches the middle of my back, he sweeps away my hair so as to continue his journey to my other side. I don't open my eyes. I don't move a muscle. I'm not ready for him to know I'm awake yet. I'm not ready for this day to begin.

How the fuck did Saturday get here so quickly? How can this be the beginning of the end? How am I going to let him just walk away *with my heart?*

I have no answers to my questions. Only this moment. Only his warm, wet lips on my skin. I simply enjoy his sweet kisses and will myself *not* to cry.

After he has kissed his way from one shoulder to the next, he returns to the center of my back and kisses his way down my spine. When he reaches my ass, he bites me, making me giggle, and the low treble of his chuckle can be felt through his lips as he presses them where he just bit me.

"Thought that might get you up, sleepy head."

I groan, turning my head so that I might see him from over my shoulder.

"Come on, gorgeous, wake up. Take a shower with me."

"What time is it?" I grumble.

"Just after ten. I'm supposed to meet up with Rosy at eleven thirty. She's coming by the house to pick up a key and gather up a bunch of Maestro's stuff."

I nod, aware of the arrangement he has made with his sister. Since all of the guys will be gone for the next six weeks, Rose and Violet have been left to look after the house, and Maestro will be staying with Rose. These are last minute details—

the little things that need to be taken care of before the boys and Alex hop on a bus headed for Texas.

"Baby, come on," he urges me, leaning down to kiss my lips. "Please?"

"Well—since you said *please*," I quip, forcing myself up.

"That's my girl," he says with a grin. "I'll go start the shower."

He jumps out of bed and heads for my bedroom door, stark naked. As I watch him go, staring at the tattooed mountain-scape that spans across his broad shoulders, I hope Sarah isn't home. We've gotten far too comfortable in her absence. Not that it will matter much after today.

I'm just climbing out of bed when I hear him call my name, urging me to join him. I assume, given the lack of commotion, that we're alone and I don't need to worry about Sarah. I don't bother with any clothing, either, before I follow after him. When I reach the bathroom, I see that he's already in the tub, and I waste not another second before I join him. He smirks at me when I do and wraps his arms around my waist, pulling me against him.

"Fuck. I'm going to miss you, baby."

The tears his words provoke catch me off guard, and my breath catches in my throat, hindering my ability to speak.

"Hey, now," he murmurs, pressing his lips to my forehead. "No crying."

I nod, pushing myself up onto my tiptoes so that I can wrap my arms tightly around his neck. He's right. I'll have plenty of opportunity to cry later—but not here. Not now. Not when I still have him in my arms.

I try my best to tamp down my emotions and then turn my head to kiss his cheek. I kiss him again and again until he turns his head as well, lining up our lips, giving me exactly what I want—what I *need*. When the tip of his tongue slides across the seam of my lips, gently seeking entrance into my mouth, I immediately open up for him. My stomach tingles and my pussy aches as I kiss him deeper. He reaches up and buries his fingers in my hair, tilting my head back as he takes full control of my mouth, and I moan in surrender.

He might not belong to me, but I belong to him, and I'm not afraid to show him.

He kisses me until my lips are swollen and my pussy is primed and ready, and then he goes down on me. He makes me come twice—once with his tongue, then immediately after with his fingers. I'm more than happy to return the favor, dropping to my knees.

The sound he makes when he spills his release down the back of my throat reminds me of our first night together. I loved to hear him groan then, and I love it even more now.

We wash each other clean, taking our time and using our hands. When we finally get out, he has just enough time to get dressed before he has to leave.

"I'll be back to get you around six," he tells me, sweeping my damp hair behind my ears.

I nod, knowing full well that tonight will not go as planned. It can't. I won't let it.

"Okay, I have to go. Rosy will hound me if I'm late."

"Yeah, go," I hardly manage.

He brushes a kiss against my lips, smiles at me, and then kisses me once more. "Bye, baby."

My *goodbye* gets stuck in my throat, but he doesn't seem to notice as he leaves me alone in my apartment. As soon as the door latches closed behind him, the tears I was holding back before come forth in full force.

I cry knowing that I've just said goodbye to his sexy smile.

I cry knowing that we'll never have another morning covered in kisses again.

Knowing that his beautiful blue eyes will not look at me the same after tonight.

Knowing that I am a fool.

That it's too late.

That I'm in love with him…

And the depth of my love doesn't change a damn thing.

Sage

THE LIVING ROOM in our house is a picture of our future. All of our bags are packed, piled together and ready to be loaded up. I gather Maestro up in my arms and kiss the top of his head as I look around, a knowing smile on my face. The five of us guys moved into this house with hopes of making music and making a name for ourselves. Now, we're well on our way to doing just that. We can hardly wait to get the hell out of here.

I leave through the front door, headed back to Millie's. I got a bunch of last minute shit done today, including getting Rosy all set up to keep my little guy while I'm away. I couldn't really bear spending the day without him, though, so he's been with me all day. The boys'll be happy to have his company at dinner tonight, anyway. In fact, they'll probably be just as happy to see him as Pepper is to see Millie. Maybe with my girl there, Pepper will be less emotional about my leaving. Though, I suppose I'm not holding my breath on that one.

I pull into Millie's apartment complex right at six o'clock. I leave Maestro in the car, intending to be inside for only a moment. However, after I knock and Millie opens the door, I know right away that something is off—*way the fuck off*. My stomach drops at the sight of her—dressed in the same pair of sweatpants and long-sleeved t-shirt she was wearing when I left this morning. Her hair is a beautiful mess, draped down her chest and swept behind her ears, leaving her red puffy eyes fully on display.

"Millicent, baby, what's wrong?" I ask, reaching for her.

She takes a step back from me, shaking her head, and I frown in response.

"Millicent?"

"I can't go with you tonight. I'm not going to Pepper's."

"Why? What happened? What's going on, doll face?"

I watch as she readies herself, taking a deep breath and straightening her spine before she looks right at me with her dark green eyes. "I'm breaking up with you, Sage," she barely manages.

Fuck. She's running.

I know this without any explanation. I know this because I've been introduced to her fears—I've met the demons in her eyes. Only, I'm not afraid of them like she is. No way in hell will I let this happen.

"Don't you fucking dare," I mutter, taking a step toward her.

"Sage—" she starts to say, holding her hand up to stop me.

"No, Millicent—I'm not letting you do this." My heart rate picks up speed, my whole body gearing up for a fight.

"You don't get a say." Her voice cracks as fresh tears spill down her cheeks, and all I want to do is pull her into my arms and promise her that she doesn't need to be afraid.

I take a deep breath, trying to calm down so that I can talk some sense into her. "Millie—doll face—we're going to be fine. I promise, baby, we'll get through this. It's only six weeks. That's nothing. You *know* it's nothing." I reach for her cheek, and this time, she doesn't pull away from me. Instead, she leans her face into my palm and closes her eyes.

Too soon, she cups her hand around mine, gripping my fingers before pulling them away from her face. "I can't do this," she tells me. "I can't be your girlfriend. I thought I could, but I can't. We just don't fit together, Sage. Don't you see that?"

"Dammit, Millie—don't do this. Don't do this again, baby. You want me and I want you, so we fucking fit. That's it! It's not complicated."

"No. You're wrong. It *is* complicated. You're destined for greatness and I—I'm not."

"Mill—" I reach for her once more but she shoves her hands against my chest, silencing me.

"This is not up for discussion. You need to leave."

"Like *fuck!*" I cry. "I'm not losing you, Millicent. Enough with this bullshit. Let me in."

"No," she insists, shaking her head before she tries slamming the door in my face.

I'm quicker and stronger than she is and I smack my palm against the door, pushing it back as I reach for her with my free hand. She gasps when I pull her flush against me, leaning down to press my forehead against hers.

"Millicent—I'm begging you. Don't do this. You *can't* do this. It's not what you want. It's not what *either* of us wants."

"But—"

"Baby," I whisper, tracing my nose down the length of hers. "Stop fighting me."

She grips two fistfuls of my shirt before a sob spills from her mouth. "I can't! Don't you get it? I can't wait for you to open your eyes and see that this won't last—*we* won't last. You're leaving tomorrow and I bet it won't take but six *days* for you to see just how much bigger you are than this town, than *me*. You won't want to come back. You won't want me. And I get it, Sage—I get it. But—"

I scoff, cutting her off as I reach up and hold her face in my hands, wiping away her stream of tears. "*Bull-fucking-shit*, Millie. That's all bullshit. Don't stand here and tell me what I will and will not want when you apparently have *no fucking idea* what you mean to me."

She growls in frustration, batting my hands away from her as she stands her ground. "*You* don't tell *me* what you will and will not want when *you* have *no idea* how this tour will change you! And it will change you, Sage—don't tell me you're so naive that you think it won't."

I growl back at her, running my fingers through my hair in frustration. She's so goddamn stubborn. If there's one thing I know about this tour, it's that she's just as naive about it as I am. If she only knew what she did to me—my no-nonsense girl. She's always argued that she doesn't fit into my world, that she's too different, but that's what I like the most about her. She sees the world in ways that I don't; and I don't get how she does it, but she grounds me and lifts me up all at once. She makes my heart sing. When I'm with her, when I hold her in my arms, I know that I don't want anyone else—that no matter what, I'll fight for her. Somehow I know that if I don't, if I give up, if I walk away, I'll lose a love worthy of its own melody.

I need that—I need her. I need the promise of my girl being here when I get back. She knows me. She sees me—*now*. She sees me *now* as *just Sage*—the pianist who dreams of singing rock music all over the world. I'm *her dream chaser*. She said that—I own that. And if she thinks for one second that the idea of being on the road bagging a groupie night after night—*hell*, bagging *ten* groupies night after night—if she thinks that I want that more than I want her, she's not nearly as smart as I thought she was.

Millicent

I WATCH HIM AS he rakes his fingers through his hair, looking at me with a desperation that mirrors my own. I knew this would happen—knew he would fight—but I thought I could be stronger than this.

I need to be stronger than this.

"Sage, please, just go," I whimper. "Let's just do this now instead of later when it'll hurt so much more."

"Or we could *not* do this! Millie—you're writing our future as if you see it so clearly. Baby, don't write our ending when we've barely scratched the surface of our beginning."

I bring a hand to my chest, pressing down hard in an attempt to relieve some of the pressure that seems to be building there. Every time he speaks, a surge of panic rushes through me, making it difficult for me to even *think* about breathing. I wonder if I can still be me if I push away the one person who matters the most to me. I wonder if I can still be *Millicent* without my heart.

"Millicent," he whispers, reaching for me.

I don't fight him when he slips his arms around me, or when he lines his lips up with mine, or when he kisses me gently. I don't fight him because I'm just as weak as my mother said I was. I *can't* fight him because I belong to him—I have since that very first night when he sang to me in bed.

You know nothing of the price of love.

My mother's words reverberate through my head, pulling me from this intimate moment, thrusting me toward the unwelcome memory that only reminds me of my pain. Pain that I've known for what feels like my whole life. Pain that I've carried with me in the name of love. *Pain* that I know will *pale* in comparison to the damage that will come from loving Sage.

My mother was wrong. I know *exactly* how much love costs. I know because I'm in love with Sage—truly, madly, stupidly in love with him. Yet, in the same breath, I know that I cannot deviate from my plan.

I push him away, shoving my hands against his chest as I step out of his arms. I draw in a deep breath, needing the air to help clear my head. I cannot forget why this is the best way—the only way. I open my mouth to speak, but Sage beats me to it.

"I'll stand here all night and you know it. We're not breaking up unless you can convince me it's because you want nothing to do with me, and after that kiss—you've got a long way to go before I believe that shit."

"This is not about how I feel," I say, shaking my head at him. "This is bigger than that."

"*No,* it's not. This is stupid and you know it. I'm your guy and you're my girl, remember?" He takes my hands in his, lacing our fingers together as he takes a step closer to me. "We agreed."

I try shaking out of his grasp, but he grips me tighter. "Sage—let me go."

"No."

"You're not going to change my mind. We're over. And you can stand here all night if you want, but we *both* know you have someplace to be in the morning. You won't stand up the guys for me."

His grip suddenly loosens and his head jerks back in surprise. "Is that what you want? Are you telling me to choose?"

I cough out a sigh of frustration, my eyes filling with fresh tears as my chest fills with an ache I cannot describe. "*Never!* I would never ask you to choose and you *know* that!"

"Then what? What the fuck, Millie? What do you want from me?"

"I want to know that you won't break my heart into a million little pieces!" I yell, unable to control myself. "But you can't promise me that you won't. Or maybe you *think* you can, but—"

"Millie—do you hear yourself right now? I can't promise that I'll never hurt you anymore than you can promise that you'll never hurt me. Relationships don't work that way. Nobody is perfect. But I'm here, baby. I've always been *right here*."

I sigh, reaching up to bury my fingers in my hair. "That's just it, Sage. You're leaving. You're not going to be *here* anymore."

"It's only six weeks—"

"No, that's not what I mean." I let my arms drop as I begin pacing back and forth in front of him, wishing that this wasn't so hard. Wishing that he would just put me out of my misery and *leave*. "You say you're my guy, but you aren't. I saw it, baby—" The term of endearment falls from my lips without a second thought, sending a pang of longing through my hollow chest. "I saw it, at The Fillmore. I saw you in a whole new light. It was like watching you perform—seeing the audience from your vantage point—it all made sense. *They* are who you've been fighting for. *They* are who you've been chasing after. *They* are who you belong to."

"Baby doll." He stops me from pacing, pulling me into his arms once more. He holds me close, staring into my eyes with a fierceness the likes of which I have never seen. It makes my knees weak and my stomach flutter and I'm powerless against him. "I sing *to* them. I sing *with* them. But I sing *about* you. I sing *for* you. They don't own me. They'll never own me. That's not why I do what I do and I never want it to be. The second it becomes all about them is when I lose my integrity—when I lose *myself*, my *music*. I don't belong to them anymore than they belong to me.

"But *you*...I *belong* to you. Do you know how I know that?"

"How?" I breathe.

"Because I love you, Millicent—I'm in love with you."

His declaration is like a bucket of ice water poured over my head. In an instant, the spell he casts with his icy blue eyes is broken and my strength is renewed. I shove him *hard*. I know he's not expecting it because he stumbles away from me, stepping back into the hallway. The look on his face speaks of his bewilderment, but I don't give a shit.

"You don't get to say those words to me," I tell him, pointing an accusatory finger at his chest. "Not today. Not now. Not because you think it'll change my mind. Not when you'll be leaving in fourteen hours. You don't get to say those words to me!" Every word that falls from my lips comes out louder and louder until I'm yelling, infuriated with him for using those words against me.

"Millicent—that's not a fucking line. I mean it," he argues.

"I don't believe you."

"Then I'll say it again. I—"

I reach up and press my fingers against his mouth before I mutter, "Don't you fucking dare." He narrows his eyes at me, whether it's because I've silenced him or because I've silenced him with his own phrase, I don't know. I don't care, either. I don't want to hear it. Not again. Not now.

Not like this!

It kills me that he's chosen now to say the words that are poised on the tip of my tongue. It kills me that I cannot repeat them back to him. It kills me that he might mean them and he might not and I don't know which to believe. It just *kills* me.

"You need to go. Now. Please, leave."

"Millie—"

"I mean it, Sage. I can't do this anymore."

Before I change my mind, and before he can act to stop me, I step back and slam the door in his face.

"The fuck!" he cries, clapping his hand against the barrier that now stands between us. "Millicent, open the damn door."

"No!" I cry in return, locking the deadbolt for good measure.

"Baby, I lo—"

"Don't say it!" I yell, stomping my foot like an enraged child.

He goes silent and I listen closely so that I might hear his next move. He doesn't leave. Instead, I hear the *thump* of his head as he presses it against the door. For a moment, neither of us says another word. Knowing he's so close, yet so far away, makes the longing in my chest almost unbearable. I reach up, placing both palms against the door, knowing this is as close as I can get.

"Millie," he murmurs.

I think back to a few minutes ago, when he told me he'd stand here all night fighting for me. *That* I believe. *That* is a declaration I can hold onto—but his love? To believe that right here, right now, on the eve of his departure…

"Six weeks," I say softly.

"What?"

"If you mean those words in six weeks—" I pause, sure that he won't. I pause, knowing that I'm stupid for believing that there may be the tiniest possibility… "If you mean those words in six weeks," I continue, "then I want to hear them. But if you don't—I don't want to speak to you again."

"Millicent—"

"Go, Sage," I barely manage as a knot fills my throat. "Just—please. Go."

I don't know how long we stand on opposite sides of the door, neither of us moving, before I feel a *thud* that makes me jump. Then, in a low voice I can hardly hear, he says, "This isn't over, doll face."

His voice is followed by the sound of his footsteps as they descend the stairs. When I hear the front door of the building slam shut, I know he's gone.

Epilogue

Millicent

I love you, Millicent.

I want so badly to go back. Suddenly, I want to hear him say the words again. I want to be in that moment when the words that mean too much to me fell from his lips. I want to live in that pocket of time when he was sure that those were the only words that would save him. Most of all, I want to believe him.

Instead, I'm here. Alone. Curled up on the couch, shedding silent tears. I'm here, afraid that I will never speak to him again. It is what I told him—it was my desperate plea when I knew not what to believe. *Repeat the words or utter no others.* Now, as I drown in the silence of his absence, all I can think about is the reality that led me here in the first place.

I gave him my heart when he wasn't supposed to have it. I fell in love with him, knowing that it would destroy me. They always leave—that is my truth, that is my story, and Sage would have been no different. He thinks he is the exception to my rule. My *dreamer*. But I live in a world he does not know—a world that he does not understand—a reality where dreams don't come true and love doesn't fix anything because love doesn't last.

He took my heart, but I don't wish for him to return it. I'm probably better off without it. Now, there is no fear that I will fall in love again, having sacrificed every last piece to his name. There is only one Sage Lawrence McCoy and I don't want another. I made him leave. I forced his hand. It was going to happen anyway, I just made it happen sooner. Now, I don't have to watch the man I love slip away. I don't have to worry about what the next six weeks will mean for us, because there is no us. Not anymore. He will go where his music takes him, just as he was meant to, and I will watch from afar.

I don't move when I hear the front door open and close. I don't have it in me to hide my tears from Sarah. Not today, anyway.

"Millie?" she coos, inching her way around the couch. "Millie, what happened? Why aren't you with Sage? I thought—"

"I think…we broke up." I say the words with uncertainty, as if I've somehow wandered into denial over what I've just done.

"Wait, what do you mean, *you think?*"

"I mean—" I'm cut off when my phone starts to ring. *Again.* I know without even looking that it's Sage. He's been calling every ten minutes for the last hour and a half.

Sarah turns and spots my phone on the coffee table. She picks it up and kneels in front of me, holding it so that I can see the display. "Millie, you should answer." I shake my head no, but she doesn't give up. "Millie—" She looks from me to the phone and then nervously bites her lip. "Oh, shit. Please forgive me."

Before I can interpret what she means, she slides her finger across the screen and answers the call. "Sage? It's Sarah."

I gasp, shooting upright in a seated position as I gape at her. I ignore the pounding in my head as she stares back at me with wide eyes, almost as if she's just as shocked as I am that she actually answered the phone against my wishes.

"Hold on, I'll try, okay?" He says something that I cannot hear and then Sarah pulls the device away from her ear, holding it out for me to take it. "If you were me, if you saw your face right now, you would do the same thing." She pushes the mobile into my hand and, reluctantly, I curl my fingers around it and bring it to my ear before she leaves the room.

"Hello?" I whisper.

"*Baby*—fuck, hi."

Hearing his voice fills me with a dangerous amount of hope. I try to ignore it, but then I speak, wishing to hear more of it. "What do you want, Sage?"

"You, doll face. You know that."

"I don't—"

"No. No more *don't* or *can't* or *won't* or anything that resembles a *no.* Only one of us is allowed to say *no* and that's me. Millicent, I'm telling you no. We're not breaking up; do you hear me?"

I seal my eyes shut, causing another couple tears to leak down my salted cheeks. Just like earlier, when he wrapped me in his arms, his voice weakens my resolve. I've done my best to fight this love, but I'm afraid I'm not strong enough to win the war.

I've picked my battles—but I've gone in with a disadvantage. He holds my heart. How am I supposed to beat that?

"I hear you," I say softly.

He sighs before he mutters, "Thank *fuck,*" but I don't let him get another word in before I continue.

"Sage, wait. I hear you—but I meant what I said. Maybe we should just…I don't know, maybe we could take a time out. You could figure out what it is that you really feel and—"

"Millie, I *know* how I feel."

"*Now.* You know how you feel *now.* But after six weeks of being apart?" I blow out a breath, reaching up to tangle my fingers in my messy hair. "Look, I can't stay here and watch and wait for you to change your mind. So, please—for me—can we just hit the pause button? Then, we'll talk when you get back."

I hate myself for asking him to do this. I despise myself for being so weak, for giving him this small victory, for giving either of us hope. I want him so badly; but at the same time, I'm too afraid to hold onto him. So, instead, my solution is to torture both of us—to hang onto him without actually hanging onto him. I've given us *hope* when I was determined to let us go…and this hurts more. But the sound of his voice in my ear—

"Baby—"

"Sage, *please?*"

"Fine," he grumbles. "But this doesn't change anything, Millie."

I nod, afraid to believe that he's right. "I guess we'll see."

"Yeah. I guess we will."

Sage

I CAN'T FEEL my ears. I wonder how cold you have to be before you get frostbite. I wonder, but I don't worry. I don't have the capacity to worry; and right now, I don't give a shit about my ears. If it weren't for Maestro, I wouldn't have even bothered digging out the blanket I keep in my trunk, but it's my choice to be out here. Not his. He shouldn't have to suffer. He's asleep on my chest, covered with a blanket and my hands. Tonight, out here in the dark field, stretched out in the backseat of my car, the top down and my feet propped up, he's my only solace.

Though, I suppose the night passed long ago. Morning should bring the dawn, soon.

I have no idea what time it is anymore. I could give a fuck. I *should* give a fuck, but I've been numb for hours now. My phone died sometime around midnight. I wore the battery down calling Millicent over and over and over again. I sat in front of her apartment for at least two hours, hoping that if I was relentless enough, that she would pick up. She didn't—but Sarah did. I swear, that girl is like my fucking fairy godmother or some shit. She's got my back when it comes to Millie. Always has. Even still, talking to my girl didn't fix a fucking thing.

Pepper and Rosemary blew up my phone. I knew, without listening to a single voicemail or reading a single text message, that they were anxiously waiting for me to show up, but I couldn't go. Not without my girl. My last night was supposed to be spent with all my girls—not just my sisters and my niece. If I went to Pepper's house, if I sat at the Montgomery table, I'd have to give voice to the events that transpired and…I just couldn't. So I came here instead.

At nine, they started to really worry. I know because one by one, the guys started calling and texting. In an attempt to shut them up, I sent Rosy a text, ensuring her that I was still alive. Of course, that didn't silence my phone, but I ignored it until it died.

Tonight, under the stars, in the freezing cold, I've wandered around in my thoughts. In the quiet of this place, this place where bullshit is shed and peace resides, I think back to what Millie said about me *belonging* to the crowd I sing to. She's got it all mixed up. It's never really been about the crowd, but about the music. Even then, my music isn't everything. It's who I am, who I've been, and who I will be—it's my passion, it's my heart, it's my dream, it's my first love—but it isn't everything. It doesn't keep me warm at night. I can't hold it or touch it or *taste* it. It will never bring me the physical ecstasy that I crave. It doesn't look at me and make me feel like more of a man than I've ever felt I could be. It isn't Millicent.

Tonight, under the stars, in the freezing cold, I've explored my heart. In the quiet of this place, I've heard the depths of my longing and I'm sure that I am in love with Millicent Tatiana Valentine. I knew that it would happen. I could sense it coming like an unstoppable force that would take me by storm. I never imagined that admitting it would hurt this much.

Tonight, under the stars, in the freezing cold, I've searched my soul. In this peaceful place where my bullshit must remain, I wait for answers. I know why she's done this. I know why she waited until tonight. She knew that I would fight. She was afraid that I would win—and maybe I would have, had she believed me when I told her that I love her. But *fuck*, now we're here—or rather, I'm here and she's there and my love means nothing to her as it stands.

Somehow, over the course of the next six weeks, I'm supposed to prove to her that my feelings are true. I'm supposed to prove to a woman who won't answer my calls, to a woman who will be out of reach, that I love her. The question that only breeds more questions and no answers is—how do I fight for her while I fight to keep my dream alive at the same time?

In the dead of night, the sound of the approaching vehicle cannot be ignored. I'm not surprised that I have company. I knew that they would come, that someone would think to find me here eventually. When I hear a car door open and shut, the sound of someone's footfalls as they walk toward me across the frozen ground, I don't move to greet them.

"*Christ*, I ought to beat the shit out of you," Rosy mumbles, peering down at me. "We've been worried sick, asshole!"

"Now you see me. I'm fine," I deadpan.

"No. You're not fine." She opens the car door and squeezes into the small space between me and the seat. She cups her mitten covered hands around my cheeks in an attempt to warm my face as she looks me in the eye. "Something's going on between you and Millie. I don't know what—none of us can figure it out, but we haven't been able to get ahold of either of you and you aren't there. You're here, which means you're hurting."

Hearing the words from her mouth guts me. My throat starts to close and it's all I can do to manage a swallow. Was it just a few days ago when I thought I had it all? And now I see that what's here today could be gone tomorrow—and maybe I don't have shit.

"Sage, honey, I'm so sorry. I don't know what to say. But you can't stay here. You have to come home. You'll be leaving with the guys in a few hours."

I sigh, knowing she's right, wishing she wasn't—wishing I had more time.

"I love her," I whisper.

She nods. "I thought you might."

I draw in a deep breath when I hear two more car doors open. Rosy didn't come alone and, guessing by the number of feet I hear, I know it's time to go.

"Sage—you're fucking insane. It's freezing out here, man," cries Maddox.

"Yeah, dude, forget this shit. We've got some beers back at the house. Let's get out of here," says Knox.

I look up and find everyone is here—my band of brothers. Even Alex and Violet showed up.

"Sage, whatever's going on, you aren't going to beat it out here," Derrick states. "You can't live to fight another day if you freeze your fucking ass off. Let's go."

He's right. They all are. It's time to leave.

I have no answers. I don't know how I'm going to get my girl back, not with this tour standing in my way—but staying out here won't help. It's time to face the music—*my* music.

This isn't over.

Our song isn't finished.

It can't be.

Worthy of the DISSONANCE

MOUNTAIN AND MEN BOOK THREE

The ache for home lives in all of us,
the safe place where we can go as we are and not be questioned.
Maya Angelou

ONE

Sage

THE HEAVY DOOR SLAMS shut behind me, and the melodic roar of the crowd fades away, leaving nothing but the muffled sound of Twisted Tuesday as their music blares on in the packed venue. Outside, in the dimly lit parking lot, packed full of tour busses and empty trailers, the buzz of another lively city on a cold night is barely heard. I'm still numb. Nineteen fucking days, and it still feels like I'm out in that goddamned field, staring up into the star-studded sky, freezing my ass off.

I pull my phone out of my pocket, not at all surprised to see I've got four unread text messages. Three from Rosemary. One from Pepper. None from the woman I was forced to leave behind—my balls in her fucking vice grip, my heart in the palm of her hand.

Would rather hear you scream
Would rather see you fight
Would rather taste your tears
Would rather/Would rather
Would rather anything but This

The silence of This
Not ignorance, not bliss
Would rather/Would rather
Baby, anything but This

I shake off the words my mind won't let me forget, ignoring the unread messages as I pull up the phone app and tap on the last number dialed. Holding the device to my ear, I listen as the line rings. And rings. And rings. When it finally stops ringing and the sound of her voicemail recording fills my ear, my head drops to my chest as I shake it from side to side. I'm not surprised. I'm not disappointed. I'm numb.

The silence of This
Not ignorance, not bliss
Would rather/Would rather
Baby, anything but This

I listen until the sound of the beep, needing to hear it, wishing not to forget it—the sound of her voice. I don't leave a message. I stopped doing that shit a while ago. I was just saying the same thing over and over again, my audience of one completely unresponsive. I no longer care to speak to dead air, but I sure as shit won't stop calling. It's the only weapon I've got in my arsenal, miles away from home. Hours away from my girl.

Fuck.

My gorgeous girl—my balls in her fucking vice grip, my heart in the palm of her hand.

I hear the loud creaking noise of the heavy side door, but I don't turn to see who's come out to join me as I slide my phone back into my pocket.

"Shit, it's cold," Derrick mutters.

He's not wrong. The Seattle night air is frigid, November showing no mercy. I won't complain, though. The bite of the wind as it brushes against my bare arms is a shock to the system. It's exactly what I need.

"What gives?" he asks, coming to stand beside me.

I turn my head just slightly, noting that he's thrown on a hooded sweatshirt, his arms folded tightly across his chest to protect himself from the brutal chill.

"Nothin'," I mumble. "Needed a minute."

"Sage—man, we go on in ten. You've got to get your shit together."

"Fuck, D, lay off."

"Sage—"

"Name *one* gig I didn't have my shit together," I demand, turning to face him. "Just one!"

He stares at me but doesn't say a word.

"Exactly," I state, knowing that I'm right.

The look in his eyes tells me that his silence wasn't an answer. He's holding himself back, trying to avoid a fight. My gut tells me to follow his lead, but I won't deny a part of me wants to stir up trouble. It's been brewing. Came *this* close just two days ago—Mad Lips and me. D broke it up before it could start. Our resident peacemaker. Nevertheless, I'm pushing his limits too. Just now, I wouldn't mind throwing a few punches for the hell of it—to ignite a shock to the system.

"You're a pain in the ass," he grunts before he turns and walks away from me.

I let him go without argument.

He's not wrong.

"Ten minutes," he growls before I hear the side door slam shut behind him.

Millicent

I STARE AT MY phone as it lights up, ringing on the coffee table. I can see from where I sit, curled up on the couch with a stack of assignments in my lap, that it's Sage calling. My heart beats wildly, and I feel my hope rising. I don't know why I let it. Why I let myself even *dare* to hope. It's a dangerous emotion to embrace, but I can't help it.

I won't answer. I never answer. I *can't* answer, knowing good and damn well that if I heard the sound of his voice, I'd go running—running to him, my *need* for him being too much to bear. I'm hanging on by the skin of my teeth as it is. Nineteen days. He's been gone for nineteen days, and he'll be gone for twenty-two more.

He insisted that we weren't over—that I was still his girl and he was still my guy—but I gave him an out. In twenty-two days, if he doesn't want me, then that's that. While he's adamant it won't happen, I can't deny that I'm still afraid it will. It doesn't make sense that he'd want to come back to me. His world is changing, and he will change with it. Sage Lawrence McCoy is meant to be a bright and shining star; he's meant to be greater than the likes of me.

I don't fit in his world. I never have. While that didn't stop me from falling in love with him, it's all I have to hang onto now. It's the reality that keeps me grounded—the reality that keeps me sitting, curled up on the couch, watching my phone as it lights up, ringing on the coffee table.

I won't answer. I never answer. I *can't* answer, knowing good and damn well that if I heard the sound of his voice, it would be the very end of me. If I let him back in now, I wouldn't be able to turn back. I put up all the fight I had just before he left. I have no more fight in me. Even if all he said was my name, I'd be forced to surrender; I'd be at his mercy. That's how weak I am. That's how weak he makes me.

That's how much I love him.

I look up into the mouth of the hallway when I feel Sarah's presence. She's dressed in a pair of maroon skinny jeans and a pretty, fitted, cream-colored, cowl neck sweater. Standing with one foot still in the bathroom and one foot out, she's holding a flat iron, her long, blonde hair half straightened and half wavy. She's got plans to spend her Friday night out with her boyfriend, Brandon. By the looks of her, she'll be another thirty minutes in front of the mirror.

"Millie…" she says softly, eyeing me intentionally, and yet so very carefully, in that way that only Sarah can seem to manage.

I don't reply. I sweep my ashy brown hair behind my ears and direct my attention back to the sloppy sheet of math problems I'm meant to decipher.

"Millie, I know you want to talk to him. I know how much you miss him—just pick up the phone."

By the time she has finished speaking, the device has stopped ringing. I look back over at it, wondering if it'll alert me to a voicemail message, knowing deep down that it won't; knowing I wouldn't listen if it did. I've got twelve unheard messages stored up for—for I don't know when.

"He's gone now. Too late," I mutter, looking back over at Sarah.

"Millie—"

"I don't want to talk about it."

"Right. Of course not. Why on earth would we want to talk about the elephant that has moved into our apartment?" she mumbles, disappearing into the bathroom.

I stare at the empty space she's just vacated before looking back at my phone. Against my better judgment, I cling tighter to the hope that still has my heart racing. I force in a deep breath and let it out slowly, willing my thoughts to shift away from Sage and back to work. All the while, I let it sink in that he's been gone nineteen days—and he's called me every single one.

Sage

When we started this tour, ten cities and two and a half weeks ago, Mountains & Men was the opening act for Lawful Sinners' headlining gig. That lasted two weeks. We outplayed Twisted Tuesday fair and square, which got us bumped. Travis Pratt, the tour manager that found us and hooked us up with Stefany Jordan, our new band manager, made the call—said we had a sound worthy of the second slot. We accepted graciously and have been rockin' our fucking asses off ever since.

Tonight will be no different.

With a sigh, I readjust my glasses and turn back toward the building. Once inside, I'm struck by the warmth that sends a small shock through my system. It's not just the heat in the building. It's the sound of the crowd. It's the reverberating thump of Twisted Tuesday's bass line. It's the activity of the roadies and the techs, gearing up to swap out equipment for the band change. It's the energy of a live performance that electrifies the entire space.

It's not enough to eradicate the *numbness* that consumes me, but I'll hit that stage soon enough. That's when I'll feel it. The fucking *music*—pumping my veins full of the adrenaline I'm so desperate for.

A hand claps on my shoulder, giving me a squeeze, and I look over to see JJ at my side. He shakes his head, tossing his curly locks out of his eyes before fixing his gaze on me. He lifts his brow, his silent inquiry heard loud and clear over the sound of Lee—the lead singer of Twisted Tuesday—bidding the crowd farewell. As the crowd's cheers grow louder, I offer him no more than a chin lift.

I can tell by the look in his eyes that he wants more, but he doesn't press. Instead, he holds out his fist and I pound my knuckles against his before he joins the rest of the band in the wings. I watch from afar, observing the men I call my brothers as they rile each other up—shaking their nerves before we head out on that stage. It's our first time in front of a Seattle audience. We're making moves, and we intend to leave an impression. I know I should be right there with them—in the huddle, clownin' out, basking in the moment.

I should be, but I'm not.

I could be pissed about it, but I'm not that, either.

I'm just numb.

So fucking numb.

"Hey," greets Alex as she approaches. Adrian, the bass player from Lawful Sinners, trails behind her, offering me a chin lift as they both come to a stop. "You good?" Alex asks, regaining my attention as she playfully tugs at my t-shirt.

"I'm good," I state simply.

"Then tell me something good," she insists, now reaching for my hand.

It's our ritual, one she won't let me forget. *Something good* from my lips is meant to help chase away her stage fright. Yet I won't deny that some nights, I don't think she asks for her sake, but for mine.

I pause, staring down at her. Her long, dark hair is twisted into two braids, each resting against her chest—the ends died a deep, rich, purple. She's got a pink bandana wrapped around her head, and the long-sleeved, low-cut, white t-shirt she has on clings to her torso, sculpting her tits and her waist. The thin fabric stops just over the top of her tight, bright green jeans, which she wears tucked into her gray combat boots. She doesn't dress to draw attention to herself, but that doesn't mean she doesn't have a body worth admiring.

"You look hot, Zip."

She rolls her eyes at me, dropping my hand to smack my arm. "You're so full of shit. That's the best you can do?"

"He's not lying, Lex. Just sayin'," Adrian chimes in with a smirk.

My eyes drift between the two of them, not missing the way Alex's cheeks turn rosy just before the lights go out and the crowd starts to get wild.

"That's our cue," I announce.

Alex follows after me, shouting something back at Adrian that I don't hear. Something tells me I should keep an eye on that shit, but I could give a fuck. She's a big girl who can handle her own. If nothing else, being on the road for the last three weeks with a bunch of dudes has proven that.

JJ, Derrick, Knox, and Alex make their way out onto the dark stage. I take a breath and stretch my neck, preparing to do the same.

"Hey—" Maddox shouts over the noise of the crowd. I peer at him through the darkness as he says, "We all want to kick your ass, but we won't 'cause we get it. You're down and out. But now we're here—fuckin' Seattle, Washington, Sage! Live it the fuck up! She's your mountain, man—face that shit, right out there. That's who we are, and don't fuckin' forget it. Kill it, bro."

He straps on his guitar as he joins the others, and I let his words sink in as I take my place behind the mic.

She's your mountain, man—face that shit. That's who we are…

Derrick drops the beat and the lights go up, the sound of the audience's cry crashing over me like a tidal wave pulling me under. As I drown in the cacophony of screams the likes of which can only be found in this single spot—under the stage lights, in front of an audience, standing with my mates—I know that Maddox is right. The discordance that exists between my girl and me is the mountain I face.

Right here, right now, it's time to face the music—*my* music.

"Hey, Seattle," I drawl into the mic.

The cry I get in response goes up an octave—and I fucking *love* it.

Now, speaking through a grin, I reply, "We're Mountains & Men, and we're going to jam a little bit. You good with that?"

Maddox starts plucking out a guitar solo, kicking off our first song. The tingling sensation of my adrenaline spreads, chasing away the *nothingness* that surges through my limbs.

This is what I live for.

Playin' from the heart; rockin' from the soul.

TWO

Millicent

HAVING SPENT THE whole of Friday night grading calculus assignments, I wake up with no work to do on Saturday morning—the first day of my fall break. After I clean the apartment from top to bottom and make a grocery run, I look around and see the error of my ways. I've been so busy distracting myself with work for the last three weeks that I'm completely caught up in all five of my classes. Now I face a week with no one to teach, no homework to dole out, no syllabi to tweak, and no idea what I'm going to do to distract myself from the ache of loneliness in my chest.

I decide to head to the gym in order to hit the treadmill for a few miles. While I'm there, I get lost in an audio book, enjoying the exertion of my muscles as I push myself to put in a couple more miles than usual. After I've exhausted myself, I head home and clean up only to leave the apartment again, headed to the bookstore. I take my time, browsing through almost half of the store, picking up more than a few titles to indulge in over the next eight days.

On my drive home, I note how quiet the streets are for a Saturday afternoon. The city is far from dead, but the absence of the student population is always felt. Fort Collins, Colorado is most certainly a college town, CSU bringing in thousands of students to the area—thousands of students who have recently fled from campus. Even the kids at the community college where I teach have been anxiously waiting to head out of town for the Thanksgiving holiday. I try not to think about how insignificant the holiday is to me—or any holiday, for that matter.

I plant myself on the couch as soon as I get home, cracking open one of my new purchases in an attempt to wile away the hours. The apartment is quiet and I'm here alone, Sarah never having come back after she left with Brandon last night. I don't think about the many nights I used to fall asleep in a bed across town, in a house full of activity. I don't think about the people who were becoming my friends, or how good it felt to be welcomed into their home—into their world. I don't think about the way they accepted me, regardless of the fact that I didn't belong. I don't think about it.

Or at least, I try not to.

It's six-thirty when a knock sounds at my door, startling me as I shift my attention away from my book. I'm not expecting anyone, and it's extremely rare that someone mixes up my address for another's. When I don't move right away, a second round of knocking sounds followed by, "Millie, it's me! Open up. I come bearing goodies!"

Hearing Violet's voice has me on my feet in an instant, hurrying for the door. When I open it, despite having heard her announce her presence a second ago, I'm surprised to see her standing there. I didn't even know she knew where I lived.

"What—what are you doing here?" I ask, my manners obviously misplaced.

She smiles at me, and the joy in her pretty blue eyes somehow soothes the dull pain that has been somewhat of a permanent fixture in my chest for the last three weeks. It's been a while since I've seen her, but she looks just as gorgeous as ever—her blonde hair cut into a pixie style that suits her small frame and stature; her makeup light but flawless. She's wearing a leather jacket, an oversized sweater with a pattern across the front only she could pull off, and a pair of jeans tucked into black, wedge-heeled boots. She's also got a box of pizza in one hand and a grocery bag in the other.

"Well, you see, I was thinking maybe you'd get around to calling me—you know, Violet? Your friend? When you didn't, I decided that I needed to take matters into my own hands. And, since word on the street is that you're not too great about answering your phone, I thought showing up demanding a girl's night, with a kick-ass pizza, a bottle of wine, and a couple movies, would be my best option. So, can I come in?"

She doesn't wait for me to answer before she squeezes by me and into my unit, heading straight for the coffee table with her Jo-Jo's pizza. She pulls out the bottle of wine and movies she mentioned, and then I watch as she stops and heads for the couch, picking up my discarded book.

"*Portrait of a Lady?*" she asks, arching an eyebrow as she studies the cover.

"Millie," she mutters, looking at me from where I stand at my still-opened door. "This looks boring and old."

"It's a classic," I reply lamely.

"I repeat—boring and old. Not to worry, we'll work on that." She sets the book back down and slides out of her jacket, draping it over the arm of the couch before she asks, "Corkscrew?"

I study her for a second, still surprised that she's here. Regardless, I can't dismiss the fact that I'm relieved to see her. Violet and I have spent a lot of time together, just the two of us. Every time we would go see Mountains & Men perform, or when we hung out with them while they were in the recording studio, she was by my side. I've laughed with her and conversed with her plenty, getting to know her over drinks and music. She's right. We *are* friends.

"I should have called," I murmur, suddenly feeling badly.

"Yeah," she says with a crooked smile and a shrug. "I forgive you. Or, at least, I *will* after a slice of pizza and a glass of wine."

"Right," I reply with a small smile of my own. "I'll be right back."

Sage

When we come to a stop, I look out the window situated just beside the kitchen table. The afternoon sky is overcast, fueling my mood. I drop my pen on top of the notebook in front of me just as JJ taps the table, signaling with a head nod that he's stepping out. I offer him a chin lift, knowing I could use a bit of fresh air. Maddox and Knox stand from where they were camped out in front of the little TV, playing video games for the last hour. Knox grunts as he stretches and then frees a long belch.

"Charming," teases Alex as she makes her way out from the back of the bus, her coat in her arms.

It was decided on day one that our newbie got dibs on the bus's one and only room. Being the gentlemen we are, we thought it only fair that our church mouse was allotted the appropriate amount of privacy—tits before dicks or whatever. Knox, Maddox, Derrick and I claimed the four bunks, and JJ volunteered to crash on the couch at the front of the bus. It's a tight fit, but we know better than to complain.

"Don't act like you don't know how to let one rip," says Derrick with a chuckle, draping an arm around her shoulders as they make their way to the door.

"I cannot be held responsible for my lack of decorum when challenged to a burping contest at three in the morning."

"Whatever you say, babe," Maddox laughs. "I can still see the look on JJ's face when you beat his ass."

JJ grins, shaking his head as he follows everyone out into the lot, shrugging on his coat as he goes. He says something I don't catch, but I'm pulled from the conversation when I step off the bus and see the fans beyond the barricades that have us blocked in. There's probably only about a hundred of them, most of which are screaming girls antsy to meet Lawful Sinners, but it's still pretty sick to see them standing out in the cold just to snag a few autographs. I watch as Clay, Gabe, Adrian, and Nate jog over to their fans, signing whatever is thrust at them and posing for selfies. When I hear *my* name, I stop dead in my tracks.

"Sage!" a group of girls cry in unison.

I lock eyes with Derrick as he smirks at me from over his shoulder, obviously having heard them, too.

"*Sage!*" they call out once more, louder this time. "Over here!"

As I turn in the direction of their voices, I see them right away. They're jumping up and down with a handmade poster, the Mountains & Men logo drawn out across the top. I start heading in their direction, shocked as shit that I've got fans in fucking Portland, Oregon, and that's when I hear it—they're calling *all* of our names. I look back at my crew, watching as they split up to greet our fans, and the surreal nature of this moment is another shock to the system.

"Oh, my god—*Sage!* We *love* your music. Eeep!"

"You are so much hotter in person! Will you take a picture with me?"

"Me too! And could you sign my notebook?"

"Uh, hey," I mutter, reaching for said notebook. "What's your name?"

"Connie," she beams.

A lopsided grin tugs at the corner of my mouth as I scribble her name on the blank page.

"Connie, how'd you hear about M&M all the way out here?"

"Are you kidding?" she squeals. "You're like *all* over Instagram!"

"My sister goes to CSU," someone shouts from over Connie's shoulder. "She said she's seen you guys play a million times! Gah—I'm so fucking jealous!" She shoves her arm through a small opening, holding out a sharpie before she pleads, "Will you sign my shirt?"

"Yeah, sure," I reply with a chuckle. I give Connie her notebook, reaching for her phone before I turn it around and snap a picture of us. She thanks me with a blush before stepping aside. "What's your name, beautiful?" I ask, reaching for the sharpie as the blonde with a sister at CSU steps forward.

"Marla," she practically purrs, unzipping her coat, exposing the plain white T that clings to her chest underneath. "But you can call me *beautiful*. I don't mind." I regard her with amusement as she pulls her bottom lip between her teeth before pointing at a spot on her left breast, indicating where she'd like me to sign.

I shake my head, laughing to myself as I pinch at the fabric clinging to her waist, pulling her shirt away from her chest before I scribble my name exactly where she pointed. She giggles and then holds out her phone for a picture.

For the next fifteen minutes, I sign autographs and interact with the crowd. I even run into people who have no idea who I am but want my attention anyway. I indulge them, knowing that they're the reason I'm here. They're the reason we get to do what we love. The dream isn't *the dream* without every last one of them.

"Yo—*Sage!* We're grabbin' some grub," Lee yells from across the lot. He's standing with Stefany, who's busy with something on her phone, along with Heath, Lawful Sinners' manager, Gabe, Knox, Alex, JJ, and Derrick. Rider and Easton, another couple of guys from Twisted Tuesday, are already piling into one of the SUVs with Nate.

I turn back to a guy who asked for an autograph, handing him the tour flyer before waving goodbye. As I begin to make my way to the group, Clay catches up to me, nudging me with his elbow. I glance over at him and find him grinning as he runs his fingers through his shoulder-length, long hair.

"See you're getting a taste."

"Yeah, I guess I am."

"Fuck—it's even better when you bag a couple of 'em while you're in town. Love 'em and leave 'em with a big ass smile on their face—like you did *them* a favor," he chuckles.

"Not really my thing, Clay."

"Yeah," he scoffs, as if I'm joking. "Nate used to spout that shit, too. You just haven't come across a sweet pussy that can't be denied."

"Whatever, man," I grumble, not wishing to listen to anymore of his bullshit.

The truth is, he's wrong. I *have* come across a sweet pussy that can't be denied. Haven't tasted her in weeks, but I sure as hell haven't forgotten that she's the only one I crave.

Fuck.

"Damn—I forgot," says Clay, pulling me from my thoughts with a snap of his fingers. "That fine piece of ass you got. Promised her a revenge fuck if you couldn't keep your dick zipped up. I'm beginning to think my chances are slim, eh?"

I stop walking, narrowing my eyes at him as I mutter, "What the fuck did you just say?"

"Sage, man—lighten up," he laughs, glancing at me from over his shoulder.

"Lighten up?" I snap, my body begging for a fight as my adrenaline begins to course through my veins. "You promised my girl your little dick? Are you fuckin' kidding me?"

"Come again?" he snarls, turning to face me. We stand toe to toe before he declares, "Mention my dick again and see what happens. I'll be forced to coax my way into that cunt to let *her* tell you you don't even compare. Bet that shit's tight, too—fits like a glove."

I let out a roar, my body moving before I have a chance to think better of it. I shove both of my hands against his broad chest, pushing him away from me with everything I've got. He stumbles backwards before barreling toward me, lifting his arms to retaliate without a moment's hesitation. Then, in an instant, the distance between us grows wider as I'm pulled one way and he's pulled the other.

"Let me go!" I yell, fighting against the resistance around my waist. I know it's Knox without even looking behind me. He's pulled me away from enough fights for me to recognize his unyielding hold.

"Calm down, McCoy—*goddamn!*"

"What on earth is going on here?" asks Stefany. She's now standing between Clay and me, her arms folded across her chest; her gaze flicking back and forth between us.

Clay sneers at me and I glare at him, wishing Knox would let me go so I could unleash every ounce of fury that burns through me on that fuck face.

"Really? Two seconds ago you were willing to throw down in front of all your fans—fans with smartphones that would make your little cat-fight go viral in minutes—and now, what, you've got nothing to say?" she asks with an irritated shrug.

Neither one of us speaks and she throws her arms up in surrender before she starts to walk away.

"Break it up, boys, we're rolling out to grab some food before the show."

I shrug out of Knox's grasp. He doesn't let me go at first, but when he does, I waste no time heading back to the bus.

"Sage—Sage, where are you going?" he calls out after me.

"Not fucking hungry," I insist before I climb inside, slamming the door shut behind me.

I pace the length of the bus, indecisive about whether I want to calm down or hold tight to my anger. Five minutes later, when no one comes knocking on the door and I know I'm alone, the numbness begins to trickle through me once more—eradicating my fury against my will.

After another five minutes, I'm slouched down on the couch, my phone in my hand, my thumb guiding me to the number I wish to call. I hit *dial* and bring the device to my ear just as the line begins to ring. And ring. And ring.

It clicks over to voicemail and I hang up and try again. When the familiar phrase of her recording fills my ear, I sigh in defeat before chucking my phone across the floor.

Fuck!

Millicent

THE FIRST TIME IT rings, Violet doesn't say a word. Instead, she takes a careful bite of her pizza, peeks over at me from where she's sitting—barefoot and cross-legged on the floor, her back propped up against the couch—and then she chews her bite slowly as she directs her attention back to the television, where one of the movies she brought is playing.

The second time it rings, she reaches for the remote and pauses the movie. With the room draped in silence, save the sound of my simple ringtone, she doesn't speak. Neither do I. Pulling my bottom lip between my teeth, I stare down at the device on the coffee table, my heart clenching as I think of the man on the other side of that call. He usually doesn't phone two times in a row. He used to, the first couple of days, but not anymore.

"Millie," Violet murmurs, pulling me from my thoughts.

I clear my throat in response before reaching for my glass of wine.

"Millie, do you want to talk about it? We can talk about it if you want."

"No," I whisper, my voice temporarily disabled. I clear my throat another time before I try again. "No," I manage more clearly.

"Okay," she starts to say as she turns toward me. "But, you know I'm here? When you're ready to talk, you know I'm here, right?"

I nod, unable to offer her more as a knot forms in my throat.

I know what she's saying. I can *hear* all that she's kind enough *not* to say. She knows how he is. She's got eyes and ears on the other side, and I'm sure she talks to her boyfriend, JJ, everyday. Now she's *here*. She's officially in the middle, ready and willing to play mediator. Only, I'm not ready. I can't feed my sense of hope like that.

Twenty-one.

Twenty-one more days until he's home.

Twenty-one more days until I know whether or not the love he spoke of is real.

Violet places a gentle hand on my arm and gives me a light squeeze before she reaches for the remote and resumes the movie. I take another sip of wine and ignore my racing heart.

THREE

Sage

"Play that one more time?" I ask Maddox. He nods before playing a lick on his brother's acoustic guitar.

"Wait, do that again," insists JJ. He turns to his iPad, plucking out his own string of notes on the piano app he's got pulled up.

"What if you ended that on a minor chord?" I ask once they've completed the phrase.

"Like this?" asks JJ before he plays, the last note clashing against the rest just the way I imagined.

"Yeah. Yeah—exactly like that."

"That's sick," pipes in Knox. "Do it again."

Derrick taps out the beat with his sticks before he begins to drum against his thighs. While Mad Lips strums out the guitar part, JJ fills in the gap with the keys. Once they've reached the end of the phrase, they start it up again without pause. I jump in, singing the words I scribbled down just this morning. Alex comes up and stands behind me as we play through the phrase again, humming out a harmony to my melody. JJ smiles over at her as she tries to figure it out. When she's found the notes that fit, she reads the words and sings with me on our final time through.

None of us realize that we've come to a stop, all of us lost in the composition of our newest song. It isn't until there's a knock at the door that we're pulled from our concentration. Stefany invites herself inside and grins at us when she's sees what we're up to.

"Can I hear it?" she asks, bouncing on her toes.

A smirk plays at my lips at the excitement in her eyes. Stefany really is the shit—a tiny little thing with an edge that doesn't go unnoticed. She's all about the music, full of drive and determination, and just as anxious to see us succeed as we are. Over the last few weeks, she's really proven that she's in this with us and we made the right choice when we signed on the dotted line with her.

She runs her fingers through her shoulder-length, wavy, blonde hair, tossing it to the side before folding her arms across her chest, as if she's arming herself for what she insists she's about to hear. I would tell her no, that we aren't finished yet, but I can't deny that what we've got so far is sounding really good.

I look at Derrick and find him already staring me down, waiting for my signal. I offer him a nod and he clicks out the beat before Maddox and JJ start playing. When it's my cue, I sing the words without hesitation.

"Goodbye was never meant to feel like This?"
The dissonance so loud/ The distance too far
Goodbye was never meant to feel like this
Moving in the dark/ Hiding in the light
Would rather you just hold on
Would rather you just give in
Would rather, baby, anything but This."

When we're finished, Stefany studies me for a moment, her eyes telling me something she doesn't give voice to before she nods and says, "I like that. Sounds *great*. Can't wait to hear it when it's finished."

"We'll bust it out," JJ replies with a shrug. "We've got some chill time, yeah?"

"From now until tomorrow night. Welcome to Sacramento, boys and girl! You're stuck on the bus until we get to L.A., but we'll get you beds for a couple nights when we move on. We'll do a grocery run tomorrow and restock the fridge, and there's a laundromat not too far from here if you're interested. And something tells me, after three weeks, you should be *really* interested."

Maddox pulls at his t-shirt, bringing it up to his nose before he inhales loudly. He then shrugs and mutters, "Eh. I'm good."

"Boys are gross," Alex tells Stefany.

"That's the God's honest truth," she replies with a laugh.

"My girl's meeting up with us in L.A. If I don't do laundry, she'll be all over my ass when she gets here. I'm in."

"Vi's coming?" I mutter, pleasantly surprised by the news.

"Hell, yeah—M&Ms original roadie!" cries Maddox.

"You know that means we all have to do laundry, right?" Knox asks with a laugh.

"I *knew* I liked that girl," says Stefany with a grin. "Anyway, I know you've been cooped up for a bit, but I've got an offer you don't want to refuse."

"Lay it on us."

"There's this seedy little bar close by. I can't explain why, but it's a *must* whenever I'm in town. We're all heading over now to shoot the shit before we hit the sack."

"I'm game," says Derrick as he stands, tossing his sticks into his vacated chair.

Just then, the door opens and Gabe pops his head in. "Come on, fuckers, what's the hold up?"

"We're coming. Shit," Knox mutters as he grabs his jacket and makes his exit.

I watch as everyone files out of the bus, not at all interested in joining them. I grab JJ's tablet, intent on working on the hook of the song they've all abandoned for the night.

"Sage? Aren't you coming?" asks Alex.

"Nah," I reply, offering her a half smile. "Don't feel like drinking right now. Besides, I'd probably just get pissed and try throwing a swing or two at Clay. Asshole."

She forces a smile, takes a reluctant step to the door, and then turns back. "I know you're sad—but you're missing half the fun, Sage."

I stare at her, knowing that she's right—too numb to give a shit.

"Lex, babe, you comin'?" asks Adrian, climbing through the door.

I look between the two of them before my gaze settles on *Lex*. "Better go."

She nods as she turns to leave, pausing once more on the last step leading out. "Call if you need anything, okay?"

I offer her no more than a chin lift, certain that I won't call, and then they're gone.

Millicent

MONDAY AFTERNOON, after a restless morning spent reading, I decide to indulge in a grilled cheese sandwich. I don't read into *why* I'm craving my go-to comfort food. I also actively combat memories of the last time I had one *and* the man who made it for me.

I've pulled out all the necessary ingredients and I'm getting ready to turn the stove top on when a knock at the door interrupts me. I scowl, wondering how this could be happening to me *again*. I'm not a woman who attracts the kind of friends who just *drop by* to say hello; and knowing that Sarah left for her all day shift at Little Bird, I can't even blame the intrusion on the possibility that she's forgotten her keys.

I turn off the stove before making my way to the door, feeling oddly *un*surprised to see Violet standing at the threshold, and flat-out startled to see *Rosemary* in her company. She looks so much like her brother—piercing blue eyes, gorgeous, long, dark hair, and the perfect light olive tone skin—it pains me a little to look at her.

"You were totally right," she says resolutely, eyeing me sympathetically.

I know without even asking that she's not speaking to *me*, and I look to Violet for some sort of explanation.

"I know, right?"

"I don't even know you that well, and I can see it in just one glance."

This time Rose *is* speaking to me, and yet I have no idea what she's talking about.

"Excuse me? I don't—I don't understand. What are you doing here?"

"Okay, here's the deal," says Violet, walking around me and inviting herself into my unit.

Rose smiles at me apprehensively, clearly less certain as to whether or not she should come inside uninvited. Nevertheless, as Violet continues speaking, Rosemary gently turns me around and eases me in before shutting the door behind us.

"I wasn't going to say anything. I was going to wait until you were ready to talk about it—but then I got to thinking, that's just bullshit," she says with a shrug.

I open my mouth to respond—with what words? I'm not sure—but she continues speaking before I can.

"*You* are miserable. *He* is miserable. Actually, the way I heard it, he's a pain in the ass. Brooding and short tempered and a total stick in the mud." She removes her coat, throwing it over the back of my couch, revealing her Jo-Jo's Pizza t-shirt. For a moment, I wonder if she's just coming from work; but then she starts up again, regaining my attention. "I guess, on the bright side—which is very dimly lit, might I add—he's writing some pretty sick shit. However, *you* aren't writing sick shit. You aren't even *reading* sick shit. You're just reading *old* shit, which I'm sure is doing little to improve the state of your heart. So, it's been decided."

I reach up and bury my fingers in my hair, completely lost and a bit overwhelmed by her monologue.

"Violet—*what* are you talking about?"

"We're staging an intervention," says Rose. She flashes me a knowing grin as she stands beside Violet.

"An *intervention?*" I mutter, my hands dropping to my sides.

"Violet and I were going to fly out to L.A. to meet up with the band. They know about Vi's visit, but I was going to surprise Sage and bring Maestro. Now there's been a change of plans."

"Okay," I reply, shaking my head at them, still unsure what this has to do with me.

"I'm giving you my plane ticket, Millie. You're going to L.A. tomorrow."

"No I'm not," I state declaratively.

"Yes—yes, you are."

"*No,*" I repeat, folding my arms across my chest, ignoring the way my heart races at the thought of seeing Sage so soon. "Sage and I are—we're on a break."

"You've got really great posture, did you know that?" asks Rosemary, throwing me for a loop.

"What?"

"The first time I saw you, well, the first time I *sort of* saw you, you were in an unfortunate state. The second time—well, um—" She pauses for a moment, a blush heating her cheeks, and I seal my eyes closed until she continues. "I mean, the third time I saw you and actually met you—I remember thinking that you were really pretty, and it wasn't just your face and your hair and that killer dress. You had an air about you, and I took one look at you and thought—*wow*, now I know what my brother has been talking about. And *you* have really great posture."

I think the polite thing to do in this moment would be to thank her, but I can't find my voice. I'm too distracted trying to figure out what the fuck she's talking about!

"Right now, you've got horrible posture," she says, pointing at me. "You look like you're carrying the weight of the world on your shoulders. You look like a vague recollection of the woman I met all those weeks ago, in that kick-ass green dress I still haven't forgotten. *That's* why you're getting on a plane tomorrow. *That's* why you're going to surprise my brother—because you miss him so much, you can't even stand up straight. I know Sage feels the *exact* same way, and this time and space between the two of you is all bullshit—just like Violet said."

I draw in a deep breath and try rolling back my shoulders, but it's useless. She's right, and hearing her call me out only makes me feel worse. Nevertheless, I can't go through with their plan. It's not as simple as they're making it out to be. Nineteen more days—we still have *nineteen* more days until he gets home. He still has three weeks to figure out what he really wants and how he really feels.

"Rose, I appreciate what you're trying to do," I begin softly. "But it's more complicated than all of that. You should go with Maestro, like you planned."

"Do you love him?" Violet asks.

"He loves *you,*" Rose says before I can speak. I suck in a sharp breath involuntarily, and she takes a step toward me. "He told me. He loves you, Millie. And if you love him and he loves you, it's *not* complicated."

I shake my head at them, my heart aching at the mention of his love. Since the moment I shut him out, begging him to leave, I've wanted to hear him say the words again. I wish that we could go back, that such declarations could be shared in a moment that wasn't marred with *goodbye*. But there is no going back, and we agreed—"We agreed," I whisper, my throat clogged with the desperation I feel to resist the hope that's been building in me since the night he left. "Six weeks," I continue, taking a step away from the two of them. "If he meant it, I wanted to hear it again—in *six weeks*."

"Honey, he calls you every day," Violet coos, closing the distance between us. When she rests a hand on my shoulder, my vision grows blurry with tears.

"He burns blue," I manage to squeak out, still combating my cry.

"What?" she asks softly.

"On stage—he burns blue, like the hottest part of a flame. He is *destined* for a life far greater than the one I live."

"*That's* why he loves you," Rose says, smiling at me as if I've just let her in on a secret. "You believe in him."

"Of course I do."

"Okay," she proclaims, reaching inside of her purse and pulling out a printed boarding pass. "I've known Sage my whole life—I guarantee you this is going to go one of two ways. Either you're going to throw away this ticket and wait another three weeks for him to come pound on your door until you let him in, and you *will* be his first stop, Millie; *or*, you'll take this ticket, you'll get your ass on that plane, and you'll put each other out of your misery. It's up to you—but I'm not going to California tomorrow. I've already decided. This ticket is yours."

She turns and drops the boarding pass onto the couch before facing me once more.

"We'll get out of here, give you some time to think about it," Violet tells me, slipping into her coat. "Our flight leaves tomorrow at two. Oh, and Millie?" she asks, pausing as she opens the door. "You're right. Mountains & Men is about to become a household name. I can feel it in my gut. My man is destined for bright lights and packed stadiums, and I'm just a girl who works at Jo-Jo's Pizza. But guess what? He loves me, anyway. Give Sage a chance to love you anyway, too."

They both leave without another word. The moment the door latches closed behind me, I can no longer hold back my tears. I press my back against the door—the very spot where Sage tried his damnedest to fight for me, speaking words I so desperately want to cling to—and I cry.

FOUR

Millicent

BY THE TIME I MAKE it to the gate, they're already boarding the plane. I don't know whether to feel relieved or disappointed that I'm not too late. I'm still not convinced that this is a good idea. I've changed my mind more times than I thought possible in the last twenty-four hours. I almost turned around twice on my drive to the airport. I'm sick with worry, my appetite non-existent since yesterday, but now I'm here—my hopes so high they're out of reach.

The truth is, I miss Sage more than I even know how to express. It's not just the sound of his voice, or the feel of his touch, or those icy blue eyes behind his sexy, horn-rimmed glasses. It's deeper than that; it's heavier than that. He has my heart. Every last piece is wherever he is. I tried to hold back, I tried to preserve the remains of all that I had left to give, but he won the fight I wasn't strong enough to win. The love I have for him is greater than any love I've ever felt. Over the last few weeks, I've come to realize that I'll never feel for another man the way I feel for him—and I don't want to! There is only one Sage Lawrence McCoy. He's earned my heart, and I don't want it back.

All my life, I've lived with the truth that men always leave. It's entirely possible that Sage still might. Nothing in life is guaranteed. And yet, I cannot deny that he's different. He's *always* been different. From the very beginning, he's fought for me in a ways no one ever has before. It scares the shit out of me. I don't know how to trust love. I don't know how to trust his word. I don't know how to trust *myself* when I'm with him. I know, in the deepest recesses of my very being, I want to give him everything—it's *reckless* and *stupid* and so fucking *insane!* There's so much we don't know about each other. And the future, *his* future, *our* future feels so fragile—teetering on the axis of *everything* or *nothing*.

He is my dreamer. It's one of the things that I adore and admire about him. It's been so long since I've grasped a dream. The last one I had hurt too much to hold onto. Now, I'm not sure I remember even *how* to dream. Sage believes that everyone dreams of something; he believes that I'll find mine—and in the mean time, he told me to hold onto him. It scares me beyond comprehension to allow myself to surrender wholly to him, and yet here I am. I know without a doubt that when I get on that plane, this will be it. This will be the end of my fight. This will be my ultimate surrender. He'll *own* me.

"*Millie!*" I barely catch sight of her before Violet crashes into me, wrapping her arms around me in a tight embrace. "You made it! Oh, my god—I'm so glad to see you." She takes a deep breath, pulling away from me in order to showcase her grin. "He is going to be *so happy* when he sees you. I swear to god; he'll probably lose his shit." She squeals as she readjusts her duffle over her shoulder and then reaches for my hand. "Come on, sunny California awaits!"

Sage

I PULL MY GAZE away from the window at the sound of my phone ringing. I look down at it from where it sits on the little kitchen table, and a half smile pulls at my lips at the sight of my sister's name lit up on the display.

"Hello?" I answer, pressing the device to my ear.

"Hey! Oh, my god, I can't believe I actually caught you. I haven't heard from you in *dayssss*. Glad to know you're still alive."

"Yeah," I mumble, pushing my glasses up my face to pinch the bridge of my nose. Truth be told, I've been a real shit—barely calling my family to check in over the last few weeks. I know I need to do better, though I'm not sure I actually will. "Sorry, Rosy. It's been crazy. How are you? How's Maestro?" I ask, readjusting my glasses.

"We miss you," she answers simply.

"Miss you, too, little lady. Hurry up and finish that degree and—"

"Yeah, yeah. I'm working on it. You just keep M&M's lead accountant spot open for me, and I'll be sure to pack a bag for your world tour. *That's* the one I really want in on."

"I hear you," I reply with a soft chuckle.

"So, where are you now? Have you made it to L.A. yet?"

"Not yet. We had a late start. We won't be there for another couple of hours, I don't think."

"You have a show tonight, right?"

"Yeah. We're playing at The Wiltern."

"*Yeah. We're playing at The Wiltern,*" she says mockingly. "Sage! You're playing a show in L.A.! Mountains & Men is hitting freaking Los Angeles, California!"

I hum a small laugh, wishing she was here with me. She's my best friend and one of my biggest supporters; I know she'd get a kick out of every moment. "It is pretty cool, and so fucking surreal."

"I bet." She pauses for a second before she adds, "I think L.A. is going to be a real game changer, though."

"Oh, yeah? Why's that?"

"I just have a feeling," she says vaguely. "Anyway, tell me more about what it's like living on a bus."

We chat for an hour, the guys chiming in and insisting I tell her shit when they catch bits and pieces of our conversation. I don't mind, well aware that privacy isn't something we're rewarded much of anymore. In any case, most everything they want me to say makes Rosy laugh, and it does my heart good to hear it. She fills me in on what's been going on at home, promising that she'll send pictures of our nephews, Henley and Carter, and our niece, Sophia, in a couple of days, when she sees them on Thanksgiving. She then makes me swear to call mom and dad on the holiday, too.

"I'll come out there and kick your ass myself if you forget. You know they'll gripe about you *all day* if you don't—so make sure you call early."

"Rosy—I got it. Listen, I've got to go."

"Yeah, okay. It was good to hear your voice, Sage. I really do miss you."

"Miss you, too."

"I love you."

"You, too. Talk to you later."

"Wait—Sage?"

"Yeah?"

"Milk L.A. for all it's worth, okay?"

I furrow my brow, curious as to why she's so adamant about the significance of L.A. I don't bother to ask, and we hang up after I assure her that I'll do my best. If there's one thing I'm sure of, it's that I won't let my audience down. When I'm on that stage, none of the other shit matters—it's all about the music, and I'll never compromise that.

Millicent

I FEEL LIKE I'M going to throw up.

Violet and I touched down in Los Angeles almost three hours ago. As soon as we stepped foot into LAX, she had her phone out so she could call JJ. She informed him that *she* had just landed—keeping my presence a secret—and found out that they had not yet arrived. This news did not deter Violet at all, who was following signs and walking with determination to the airport's exit. Neither of us checked a bag, leaving us the freedom to go where we pleased without delay. Before I knew it, we were flagging down a taxi.

Violet had done her research. She knew where the bands and the entire tour crew would be staying for the next couple of days, and she had already called ahead to book a room. When it had been her and Rosemary who were coming out to L.A., they agreed to split the cost of lodging, knowing that Sage and JJ would have a room and they could just switch bed fellows when the time came. Feeling wildly optimistic, Violet was sure that everything would work out just as before. I'd room with Sage and she'd stay with JJ.

I won't lie and say that I don't hope it works out that way; that Sage will want to see me and that the privacy of a room would be a necessity. To deny that I miss all of him, including his cock, would be a lie unworthy of the effort. He owns my orgasms and we both know it.

Check-in at the motel was at four. By the time we arrived, we were able to head to our room and freshen up before we left to meet the boys at tonight's venue. JJ informed Violet that she could wait in the parking lot, outside of the barriers that closed off where the tour busses would settle, and he would come find her. After another taxi ride, we found ourselves at The Wiltern, along with dozens of other fans hoping to catch members of each band before the show.

My stomach was in knots at the sight of so many people—the numbers growing the longer we stood waiting. I'd never experienced anything like it, and I realized that I was standing in the midst of my biggest fear. I was standing in a crowd that was a representation of exactly where Sage is going. I was standing on the precipice of a dream come true—*his* dream come true. I felt so small.

Now, as I watch the tour busses roll into the lot, I feel even smaller. My hands are shaking, my palms are sweating, my mind is racing, *and I feel like I'm going to throw up.*

"JJ?" I look to Violet and see that her phone is pressed against her ear again. "I'm here, baby! I can't wait to see you," she exclaims, the grin on her face a pretty sight to behold. She laughs at something he says and then I watch as her eyes scan the line of busses. "Which one are you in? Oh—oh, shit, I see you!" I follow her gaze, my heart pounding as I see him burst out of the second tour bus. She grabs my wrist, tugging me toward the front as she says, "Babe, oh, my god! I'm to your right. Do you see me? Holy hell, you need a hair cut," she laughs. "Come get me!"

My eyes flick from him, watching as he tries to find his girlfriend, to the door of the bus. Knox comes out after him, followed by Maddox and then Alex. My eyes are back on JJ when he spots us. I can tell he's spotted *both* of us because he stops dead in his tracks.

"Surprise!" Violet giggles into her phone.

He looks back over his shoulder and I'm sure I'm about to have a panic attack.

"Violet—what if—shit. *Fuck*. What if—" I draw in a deep breath, closing my eyes as I try and get a hold of myself. For a second, I'm not here. I'm not in this moment. I'm not in this place. Rather, I'm at home, three weeks ago, pleading with Sage to let me go. Suddenly, I feel like the biggest idiot in the world.

I'm an idiot for thinking that I could actually let him go.

I'm an idiot for thinking that I could abandon my heart in his care without slowly withering away day by day.

I'm an idiot for questioning the depths of his feelings for me.

But most of all, I'm an idiot for showing up uninvited and unannounced, now fully aware that I'm not worthy of him. Not at all. Not after the way I've treated him.

"I shouldn't have come," I whisper.

"Millie, he loves you, remember?" she murmurs softly, giving my wrist a squeeze.

I nod, not because I agree, but because I wish it was enough to erase all that I've done. When I exhale, I open my eyes, knowing that I deserve whatever happens next. I spot JJ first, jogging toward us. Violet pulls me past the last couple of people that stand in our way, and then I see him, my eyes growing blurry in an instant.

I blink, not at all concerned when my tears trickle down my cheeks. I don't care what I look like—all I care about is *seeing* him. He looks exhausted, but even still, he's unbelievably sexy in a pair of faded, fitted blue jeans, a black graphic t-shirt, and his favorite pair of red Converse. I blink again, freeing more tears as I take in the tattoos that scale his left arm, my hands itching to touch them—to touch *him*.

I'm so busy staring at him, I don't notice when Violet steps away from me, or when she throws herself into JJ's arms. I don't hear them when they tell me to join them on the other side of the barricade fence. Not that it would matter if I did. The moment Sage's eyes lock with mine from behind those horn-rimmed glasses, I'm completely paralyzed.

He freezes for a second, as if he's unsure if it's really me. Then he starts walking toward me, his gait unyielding, confident, and sexy as hell. He doesn't stop until he's on the other side of the fence, standing right in front of me. Then, before I can even think, his hands are cupped around my face and his mouth is closed around mine.

I'm his.

His touch awakens every nerve ending in my body, and my fingers grip hold of his t-shirt right away, pulling us closer together. When his tongue grazes over the entrance of my mouth, I push myself up on my tiptoes, opening up for him as I seek to taste *my dreamer—my fucking rock star.* He hums, kissing me deeply, and the whimper that spills out of my mouth and into his cannot be silenced. The firm yet gentle touch of his hands, the wall of muscle that is his chest beneath the fabric I grip with all my might, his wet lips, and his greedy tongue all work together to stir the desire that's currently soaking my panties.

I don't know when the cat calls and whistles start. I don't know how long he consumes me with a single kiss in front of the crowd. I care about neither of those things, my focus saturated by all that is *Sage.*

"Fuck," he mutters against my lips, causing me to open my eyes. I find him gazing down at me, and my knees grow weak. I lean against him, in need of his support, but he's ready to move. He grabs one of my wrists, yanking my hand from his shirt before he marches his way back to the bus, pulling me after him.

He doesn't say a word to anyone, and neither do I. I'm not even aware of who we pass as I try my damnedest to keep up with him in the wedge-heeled sandals I picked out to go with my short, spaghetti strap, paisley print, cotton, summer dress. I know how much Sage likes my legs, and I figured the California sun was all the excuse I needed to pack the ensemble. So far, it appears as though I made a splendid choice.

He guides me onto the bus hurriedly, and I barely have a chance to look around before he's got me by the waist. He lifts me up onto the kitchen countertop, and then his lips are smashed against mine once more. I forget my surroundings as I circle my arms around him, content to follow his lead. My breath catches in my throat when he pulls away from me only to push up the skirt of my dress and tug at my panties. He tosses them over his shoulder before he reaches for the top button of his jeans, and my pussy pulses with need. We're both panting when he pulls his gorgeous cock out of his boxers, and I don't even have a second to question him before he thrusts his way inside of me.

He frees a long, deep, indulgent groan and my eyes grow wide as I bury my fingers in his hair, gripping him tightly. He feels *so* good—so *fucking* good that I can barely breathe. It isn't until he pulls out and rams back in that I realize I'm *not* breathing. I inhale so that I might free an uninhibited moan, my eyes locked with his. It isn't until his third stroke that I understand why he feels so good—why this feels different, *better*—god, so much fucking *better.*

He's not wearing a condom.

"Sage..." I force his name through my lips, but he shuts me up with a kiss. My eyes roll into the back of my head as his tongue sweeps through my mouth just as he grabs hold of my ass, pulling me close as he pounds into me harder.

"*Fuck,*" he growls before burying his face in my neck, his lips grazing the skin just behind my ear.

"Sage—"

"Doll face," he breathes, cutting me off again, his thumb finding its way to my clit.

I gasp, circling my legs behind his back as I feel my orgasm rushing to the surface.

"Sage, baby!" I cry as my insides clamp down around his dick, pleasure crashing through me like a freight train.

He growls, and I feel his cock swell and twitch inside of me as he fills me with his release. I'm trembling from head to toe, holding onto him with what little strength I have left—my head buzzing, and my heart so completely full. He's the first man who has ever spilled his seed inside of me, and I am unequivocally aware that this feels *right,* and I'm not sorry that he took what he wanted, what he *needed*—I'm not sorry at all. I belong to him. I love him, and I'm his to mark as often as he pleases.

"Fuck," he mutters, yet again, before he glides out of me with ease.

I look down between my legs as I feel his cum dripping out of my center and onto the floor. I bite my lip, a little unsure how we'll explain that, and then I look up at him. When I do, I see that he's already zipping up his pants.

"Sage—"

"Don't speak," he demands, gripping my jaw with one hand. I seal my lips closed, confused by his tone of voice. "*Fuck.*" He kisses me, *hard,* and then pulls away from me abruptly. "Goddammit. I'm so fucking pissed at you."

As soon as the words are out of his mouth, he lets me go and storms out of the bus, slamming the door behind him.

FIVE

Sage

I pause for just a second, reaching down to button my jeans closed before I head for the street. I have no idea where the fuck I'm going to go, but I know I sure as shit can't stay here. Unfortunately, I don't get very far before I hear the sound of familiar voices calling my name, their shouts accompanied by the noise of running feet.

"Sage—hey, where are you going?" calls Knox.

"Where's Millie? What's going on?" I hear Violet ask.

"The fuck, Sage—*stop!*"

I whirl around to face them only after Maddox grabs hold of my shoulder in an attempt to get my attention. When I see them all standing there, every single one of them, I want to yell at the top of my lungs for them to mind their own damn business. Derrick speaks before I get the chance.

"What gives?"

"I need to get out of here. Now," I grunt.

"What the hell, Sage? What about Millie?" Violet protests.

"I can't deal with that shit right now."

"What do you mean? Did you talk to her?"

I move to turn away from them, no longer wishing to engage in this conversation, but Maddox pushes against my shoulder with a scowl.

Violet eyes me up and down before she gasps, "Oh, my god—tell me you didn't just get your dick wet and then leave her in there." I clench my jaw closed tight and then watch as her face scrunches in anger. "You *asshole!*" she cries before she hurries back toward the bus. She stops when she's halfway there, turning back and pointing an accusatory finger at me before she yells, "Now I know why she was scared shitless to come see you even though she's missed you like crazy. I told her over and over that you'd be *happy*. Didn't know you had it in you, Sage."

I don't say a word as I watch her walk away, but her words hit me square in the gut. I *feel* them, and the regret that follows is like acid pumping through my veins. Even so, I know I can't go back there. Not now. Not yet. The numbness is gone and *everything* that it repelled before is now crashing down all around me. It's too much. I need to get out of here—away from the catalyst herself.

This time, when I start to head for the street, no one stops me. I don't think anything of it until I hear the footfalls of my company. I look over one shoulder and then the other, spotting a Bradley brother on my right and on my left.

"Go away," I grumble.

"Like hell," Maddox scoffs.

"*Maddy—*"

He grabs hold of my arm, spinning me around before he lays into me. "Don't *Maddy* me. I don't want to hear that bullshit. You're about to fly off the handle, and we've got your flank, whether you want it or not, so deal with it."

"I don't need your supervision," I mutter, furrowing my brow in frustration.

"You ever been to L.A.?" asks Knox. "Do you have any idea where you're going? No! You're pissed, you're hyped, and we are not about to let you loose three hours before a gig in a city where your pretty ass could get raped and beat to a bloody pulp in some gang related shit you stumbled into because you're being a jackass."

I stare at him like he's lost his mind before I say, "You're stupid."

"Ha, right. The girl you've been moping about for the last three weeks just flew out here to surprise you and you left her ass high and dry—and *I'm* stupid? What does that make you?"

Another jab to the gut. Another shock to the system. Another injection of acid through my veins.

I don't argue before I continue my journey to nowhere in particular, in a city I don't know, with my boys at my flank.

"Sage—you pain in the ass—stop walking like you know where you're going. We're hailing a cab," Maddox announces, grabbing a fistful of my shirt at my back.

"Like you know where you're going?" I bite back.

He smirks at me before looking down the street for a taxi. "I know enough to know we're about to hit an In-N-Out Burger. When in Rome, loser. When in Rome."

Millicent

The nausea I felt before I saw Sage is long gone, now replaced with a desire to cry—and cry *hard*. I don't. I *can't*—but I want to. Instead, my state of shock leaves me walking through the motions, completely numb.

I slide off of the counter and reach for my panties before searching the bus for a bathroom. I barely make note of the place the boys and Alex call their home on the road, too worried about cleaning myself up before someone makes an entrance. Once I've gotten myself straightened out and I've mopped up our mess in the kitchen the best that I can, I hear a knock on the bus's door. I don't move to answer it, feeling like it's not my place, but Violet only waits a second before she invites herself inside.

"Millie? Hey…"

One look into her dark blue eyes and I know Sage is gone. That's when the tears hit and I cry—*hard*. I sink down onto the couch, covering my face with my hands as my whole body shakes with my sobs. I know that I brought this onto myself. I know that I'm the reason he's pissed. I know that I can't blame him for the way he feels, not after the weeks of *silence* I forced onto him—but he's *never* treated me like that. Not *ever*. It hurts in a way I wasn't prepared for, and I can't even begin to figure out how to fix it. Now that I'm here, and after the way he fucked me, it all feels so much messier than before.

Violet sits down beside me, running her fingers through my hair as I allow myself to wallow in my tears. More than ever, I long for Sage. The taste I got just a minute ago was ripped away from me too soon, and the ache of his absence is exponentially worse than it was before I got here.

I hear someone clear his throat, and my head shoots up to see Derrick, JJ, and Alex standing in front of me. Alex's dark eyes look at me with a sadness I don't know how to interpret, JJ's eyes are trained on Violet, and Derrick looks angry; though, not in a way that scares me, especially when he speaks to me softly.

"Why don't we get you out of here. Have you eaten?"

I sniff, shaking my head at him as I reply, "I'm not hungry. I think—I think I just want to go back to the motel."

Derrick nods as Violet says, "Okay. We could let you get some rest and then pick you up before the show."

"I don't think I should go to the concert," I mutter, standing to my feet. "He won't want me there."

"You're almost all he thinks about," Alex chimes in hesitantly. "I think he *would* want you there."

I remember the look on his face just before he left, and I'm forced to swallow the knot in my throat as I reply, "No. I can't. He's not—I'm not—no. I'll just stay at the motel. When he's ready—*if* he's ready, he'll know where I am."

"He's being a dick," Derrick declares. "It was good of you to come."

I blink and a couple renegade tears escape from the corners of my eyes, falling down my cheeks. When I can't find my voice, I force the tiniest of smiles. It's a pathetic response, I know, but it's all I have to give.

He nods, as if he understands, and then assures me, "We'll take you wherever you want to go. Come on, darlin'."

Sage

My head feels like the size of Texas, and there's a pounding at my temples that makes me want to whine like a fucking pussy. I don't, but I sure as hell want to. I draw in a deep breath instead, suddenly aware that I'm stretched out, face down, in an unfamiliar bed that smells way too good. I open my eyes and see nothing but a wall. With a groan, and a great deal of effort, I twist my neck and rest my head on my opposite cheek. Now all I see is someone's jean-clad, little ass; or, rather, the side of it. I force my eyes to look up and I recognize the person sitting up next to me is Alex. I scrunch my brow in confusion, wondering where I am and why Alex is here.

"Morning, sunshine!" she yells.

"Holy shit, don't do that," I moan, sealing my eyes closed tight as the pounding in my head intensifies.

"Sorry," she laughs. "I couldn't help myself. You deserve far worse, but I'll be nice."

I grunt, not sure what she means by that, and then I try and think back over last night. I'm still not sure where I am or how I got here. When I attempt to retrace my steps, I realize that I don't remember anything after the show. Not a damn thing.

"Where am I?" I grumble, peeking open one eye to look up at her.

"On the bus. In my bed."

"That explains the smell."

"Pardon?"

"You smell good, Zip."

"Oh. Thanks."

I sigh, closing my eye again, feeling exhausted all of a sudden. "Why am I in your bed, Zip?"

"You refused to go to the motel and your bunk was too much of a challenge to conquer. And when I say that you refused, I mean Mad Lips is going to wake up with a shiner this morning because you were so damn adamant that you *were not* going to the motel."

"Shit," I mumble with a scowl.

"Yeah. You have quite a few people to apologize to today. You were kind of a douche."

I sigh, no longer sure that I want to know the details of last night.

"Why are *you* in your bed? Why aren't you at the motel?"

"Someone had to stay with you to make sure you didn't fall asleep and choke to death on your own vomit. You didn't puke, by the way. Thanks for that. I genuinely appreciate it."

"You volunteered for Sage watch?" I ask, opening my eyes to peer up at her.

"I'm the only one you *weren't* being a complete jerk to. Don't get me wrong, you were being a pain in the ass, but I didn't want to take a swing at you, so, yeah. Here I am."

"Shit," I sigh.

"You're welcome," she says with just a hint of sarcasm.

"Sorry, Zip."

"Ah, one down, six to go. You're doing good, Sage. Want some coffee?"

"Fuck, yes."

She laughs and then informs me, "I'll be right back."

While she's gone, I manage to roll over onto my back. My entire body protests as I push myself up to sitting, leaning back against the wall as I look around the room. I can't see far without my glasses, and I squint at Alex when she re-enters the room.

"Oh, glasses?" she asks, picking them up off of the table beside her bed before handing them to me. I slide them onto my face and she hands me a mug full of steaming, black coffee.

"Thanks," I mutter as she occupies the space next to me.

"All right, here's the deal," she begins to say as I take a swig of Joe. "We all put up with you when you got completely *smashed* after yesterday's show, I stayed up most of the night making sure you were still breathing, *and* I've made you coffee. Now, you listen."

I offer her a small nod, certain that I owe her more than a listening ear. "Okay."

"You told me once that praying isn't your thing, so I'm going to assume that God isn't really a big part of your life, either."

"Zip—"

"No, no, no—you've got your *listening* ears on now, Sage. Besides, I'm not here to preach at you. What you believe is your business, but I believe in God. It shapes my entire outlook on the world, and I want you to understand what I see when I look through that belief system into *your* world.

"You've been hurting. Since we started this tour, you've been hurting so much that you're barely you. I won't lie. I miss you. The only time I get *you* is when we're out on that stage and you let the music take over. Whatever's going on with you and Millie is so all consuming that no one can break through it, not that you would even let us try. You shut down every time we try and talk to you about it.

"I know how much you were looking forward to this tour. I know how much this band's success means to you—to all of you. I'm new. I'm here, I'm excited, and I hope that this is just the beginning, because it's so much better than I imagined it would be—but I've been dreaming about this for a couple of months. *You've* been dreaming about this for *years,* and you're letting it pass you by because you're off center. Your focus is scattered.

"When I look at you, I see a guy who loves *hard* and works *hard* and dreams *big*. It's quite admirable. I don't know many guys our age who are so driven and optimistic and determined. You're passionate. I see it when you're performing. I used to see it when you were sitting around with the other guys, just enjoying each other's company, because they mean so much to you. You appreciated every moment. I mean, I know I haven't known you for that long, but before the tour, you soaked up all that life had to offer. Then you hit a rough patch."

She pauses, reaching up to tuck her hair behind her ears before she shifts just slightly to look at me dead on. "I think you're barely holding on. I think your music is your center. I think that's what you've been clinging to as you're dealing with whatever it is that's going on between you and Millie. I think that's probably how you always cope. The problem with that is, your music is ever changing, which is good in terms of our sound, but not in regards to your well-being. It's as unreliable as your emotions. You've got to find a center that you can rely on—something you can lean on, no matter what; something that'll help ground you and give you perspective so that your world doesn't fall apart when the unexpected happens.

"God is my center. Obviously, I would suggest giving Him a try, but, again, that's just my personal preference. The thing about God is—He *never* changes. He will always be love; He will always be grace; He will always be mercy. He provides peace and rest and *purpose* and *meaning* to everything. He gave me the gift of music. So I know that no matter where it takes me, whether this works out and we hit it big, or even if we don't, I know that He gave me the ability to play and He'll always give me a way and a place to use my talent.

"And when my relationships are hard, when *life* is hard, I know that it'll all be okay. I know that I can lean on Him and He'll grant me perspective; He'll keep me grounded; and He'll give me hope. Every challenge I walk through, if I lean on Him, He'll teach me something, He'll make me stronger, and He'll shape me into the person that I'm supposed to be. All things work together for my good."

She sighs, reaching for my hand. For a minute, she doesn't say anything. My mind is muddled and I'm not sure what to make of everything she's just said. It must show on my face, because she gives my fingers a squeeze and offers me a small smile before she continues.

"I had a lot of time to think about this while I was on *Sage watch*. But, look, all I'm saying is, you've got to get it together, Sage. You've got to figure out what it is that brings you back to good. And it can't be Millie and it can't be your music or even the guys—because all of those things are imperfect and they can all let you down, and then you'll be right where you are now."

I shake my head carefully, looking down at her small hand wrapped around mine. "I don't know what that is," I say contemplatively. "I don't know if I've ever had that. Music has never failed me."

"Music drives you. But here you are, deep in your music, and you're still miserable. Life's a journey, Sage—your path has led you here, to this very moment where you question your stabilizer. Now, you look for it."

"That simple, huh?"

"I didn't say it was simple," she replies with a grin. "Anyway, your path to discovery isn't necessarily something you'll figure out while nursing a massive hangover. We'll start with something smaller today—like doling out *I'm sorrys*. I think you know who deserves the first one." She squeezes my hand again and then crawls out of bed. "Finish your coffee and then hop in the shower. We'll catch a cab to the motel when you're ready."

"Alex?" I call out as she makes her way to the door.

"Yeah?" she asks, turning back to look at me.

"Thanks. For...all of it."

"It was my turn for a pep-talk," she says, winking at me before she's gone.

SIX

Sage

As soon as we get to the motel, Alex points me in the direction of the room that was supposed to be mine, assuring me that's where I'll find Violet. She then abandons me to go catch some shut eye. I rap my knuckles against the door and then run my fingers through my hair, feeling both anxious and a little nauseous. JJ answers a few seconds later, wearing nothing but a pair of jeans, despite the fact that it's one in the afternoon.

Then again, if I were him, I'd be in my bed with my girl for as long as possible, too.

"Hey," he mutters.

"Hey," I reply. "Listen, I don't remember a whole lot, but I'm sure I owe you an apology, so—sorry, man."

He stares at me blankly before he speaks again. "Don't fuck this up. Fix you and Millie and then we'll deal with the rest—but this is your one chance, Sage. Don't. Fuck. This. Up."

I nod once. There's nothing to be said. He's right. I know he's right. Last night was apparently rock bottom, and if I don't get my act together, everyone is fucked.

Violet joins us, wearing little more than one of JJ's t-shirts, her hair still a mess from sleep—or lack there of. She curls into JJ's side, her gaze locked on me as he wraps his arm around her. If looks could kill, I'd be a pile of ashes. I've never seen Violet so pissed off before.

"Vi—"

"Fix it," she says, thrusting a key card at me. "That's the only apology I'll accept." I look down at the card and then back at her, not quite sure what she's offering me. "She's down the hall and around the corner. Room one-eleven."

I draw in a deep breath and then reach for the card, spinning it with my fingers as I stare down at it.

"Um, hello!" Violet snaps. "We've been here for almost twenty-four hours and she's seen you for all of fifteen minutes. Get your ass out of here."

Her words strike a chord, jogging a memory. Millie didn't come to the show last night—not at all. I had no right to be pissed, but I was. When I found out she'd stayed behind, *that's* when I decided copious amounts of whiskey was in order.

I shake my head a little, wishing to be rid of the memory. My head pounds in response, but I ignore it. I lift a hand to wave goodbye and then I make my way down the hallway, headed for my girl.

When I reach her door, I think about knocking and then decide against it. Violet gave me a key, and I see no point in letting it go to waste. I enter the room cautiously, noting right away that the curtains are still drawn closed, leaving the room shrouded in shadows. When I've made it past the bathroom door, standing in the mouth of the room, I see my girl sitting cross-legged in the middle of one of the double beds. The top cover is folded neatly at the bottom, but the sheets are made up. Millie is wearing a pair of jeans and a loose fitting, flowy, white tank top—her long, ashy brown hair draped over her shoulders and down her chest. Her pretty green eyes, red-rimmed from crying, grow wide at the sight of me. She sits up a little taller, but she doesn't say a word. At first, I don't either. Instead, I sit at the foot of the bed and rest my forearms atop my knees.

I don't know how long we sit, neither of us saying a word. All I know is that being in the same room with her, breathing the same air as her, it's like having a piece of home with me. I'm angry at her, *that* I can't deny. But I love her; and just like I knew I would, I love her *hard*. Whatever shit lies in our past, we have to deal with it—right here, right now, because no matter what, she's my gorgeous girl. Life sucks ass without her.

Millicent

He doesn't speak for so long, I wonder if he will. The longer we sit in silence, the more frightened I become. I have no idea what he's thinking and no clue what he's feeling. All I know is that he saw me, fucked me, and abandoned me last night. I can't say for certain what all of it means, but I don't have a good feeling. I don't have a good feeling at all.

"I've wanted this since I was sixteen years old," he begins, his rich, tenor voice smooth and soft. "When Knox, Maddox and I started Mountains & Men, this was always where we wanted it to go—touring the country, touring the *world*, sharing our music—*that* was the dream. It's what we've been fighting for—since I was *sixteen*. Now, it's happening. Or, at least, it's starting to happen; and instead of having the time of my life, instead of enjoying every single moment, I'm over here worrying about whether or not my girl is still going to be *my girl* when I get back home. I'm wondering how the fuck I'm supposed to convince her that I'm in love with her when she won't even answer her damn phone."

I suck in a quiet breath, my heart constricting as he turns his head to look at me.

"You fucked with my head, doll face, and that shit wasn't cool."

"I know," I whisper through the tears that congest my airway, not knowing what else to say. He's right. I got scared, tucked tail, and ran. He didn't ask for this. In fact, he demanded the opposite. "I'm sorry."

"What are you doing here, doll? Why did you come?"

I cried half the night. I cried so much, I'm surprised I have any tears left. I cried harder than I've ever cried before. I couldn't stop myself. I couldn't calm myself down. I couldn't explain or rationalize any of it. The tears just kept on coming. Now, looking at the man who holds my heart—*hearing* him ask me why I'm here and remembering the way he treated me yesterday—every ounce of hope that I've been building up and clinging to just evaporates. My eyes well up and I try my hardest not to let a single tear spill onto my cheeks as I scoot out of bed and onto my feet, sliding into my flip-flops as I begin to walk toward my bag.

"I'll just go."

"Baby, fuck!" he mutters exasperatedly, reaching for my hand before I step out of reach. "Just answer the question. Why did you come?"

"Because I love you," I cry, my eyes betraying me as they overflow with tears.

He stares at me, appearing surprised but not shocked at my declaration. Then he stands, gently cupping his hands around my face, wiping my cheeks dry with his thumbs.

"I love you, too, baby."

For a fraction of a second, I'm overwhelmed with relief. But that only lasts until I draw in a deep breath and reality wedges a gap between us. He leans in to kiss me but I shake my head at him, taking a step back as he drops his hands. "It's not supposed to be like this," I protest, reaching up to bury my fingers in my hair.

I was prepared to wait. I was willing to suffer for another eighteen days before I saw him again, when he'd tell me he loved me and *mean* it. Instead of being marred by *goodbye*, it was supposed to be drenched in the hope of *hello*, and I was supposed to get my chance to tell him I felt the same. Now, none of that has happened. Instead, our words are coated in the bitterness of *anger* and *hurt* and *regret*.

"Millie—"

"No," I cry, shaking my head at him. "Last night, you fucked me—*without a condom*—and then you *left* me."

His face falls before he murmurs, "Shit. Are you on the pill?"

"God, *yes*. I'm on the damn pill!" I groan, letting my hands fall to my sides. "That's *not* the point."

"Then what is?"

"No one has ever been inside of me bare. *No one*. You took that—I *let you* take that—and then you *left!* I hurt you. I know that, and I'm sorry. But then you hurt me right back and—shit, Sage…it's not supposed to be like this." By the time I'm done speaking, my voice is hardly more than a whisper, but I forge on. "I messed it up. I messed it all up. I was just *so scared*. I still am, and—"

"Baby—"

"No, Sage—"

He grips his hands around my waist and pulls me against him, silencing me as he rests his forehead against mine and mutters, "Millicent…"

I suck in a breath, reaching up to grip his t-shirt, loving the sound of my name falling from his lips.

"I'm sorry. I'm sorry I hurt you, baby—but you're here. I'm here. We're far from perfect, but we're nowhere near finished, doll face. It's like I told you, we're not breaking up, no matter how bad the shit storm. I love you and I'm not letting you go."

"Sage." I close my eyes, pushing myself up on my tiptoes as I circle my arms around his neck and whisper, "I love you so much."

"Fuck," he breathes before his lips brush against mine in a light kiss. "Feels good to hear you say it, doll."

He doesn't give me a chance to respond before he's kissing me again. Unlike yesterday, his lips caress mine softly, slowly, *seductively*. He teases my tongue with his and I melt against him, longing only to be as close to him as possible. My entire body tingles with excitement when his hands slip underneath my tank top, easing the fabric over my torso until we're forced to sever our kiss so that he can pull the garment over my head. When I'm free, I reach for the hem of his shirt, wishing to feel my skin pressed against his, and he helps me remove it. My eyes devour his sculpted chest, my fingers grazing along his tatted sides as I drag my lips across the art that covers his pecs. He grabs two handfuls of my ass, making me whimper as I press my chest against his.

I love how much he adores my ass. Always have. Always will.

He dips his head to kiss the space between my neck and shoulder as he guides me to the bed. He leans into me, encouraging me onto the mattress, and I kick off my sandals and scoot to the middle. Rather than join me, he reaches for the top of my jeans, unfastening the button and sliding down the zipper before tugging them off of me. My panties are discarded next, and then finally my bra, leaving me completely exposed.

He licks his lips, pulling his bottom lip between his teeth as he admires me. When he reaches down to give his cock a squeeze through his own jeans, I part my lips, suddenly in need of more air—my entire body ready and waiting for him. Thankfully, it's not long before he's divested himself of the rest of his clothing. He sets his glasses aside before crawling between my legs, resting his weight onto his forearms on either side of my head.

He rubs his cock over my clit, causing my arousal to drip out of my core as I gaze up into his eyes. I lift my hips, silently begging for more, and a small smirk tugs at the corner of his mouth.

"Who owns your orgasms, baby?"

"You, Sage," I whisper, reaching up to comb my fingers through his hair.

Without another word, he slides into me, and I can't help but arch my back, pressing my breasts against him. He feels so warm, so hard, so perfect—his cock filling me up like only it can, reminding me that he's all I'll ever need.

"You're my best girl, Millie," he whispers, his lips grazing mine. "Shit, you feel so good—my best girl."

I'm speechless. Completely and utterly speechless. But it doesn't matter.

He's here. I'm here. We're far from perfect, but we're nowhere near finished—just as he promised.

God, she feels sensational—her tight pussy so wet, so soft, and so warm. This is what I've wanted, my dick claiming ownership of what is mine; and her delicious cunt is exactly that. *Mine.*

I take my time, gliding in and out of her slowly, ignoring my headache as I make love to my girl. Her dark green eyes are locked with mine, and I dare not look away, wishing to take everything she's offering me. *Finally.* When she frees a moan, her lids drooping closed, I lean down and kiss her lips, needing another taste. As her tongue tangles with mine, she hitches up both of her legs around my hips, allowing me to sink my dick a little deeper. She hums a sigh into my mouth, and I wonder just how the fuck I've lasted so many days without this—without *her.*

Her fingers leave a trail across my shoulders, down my back and up again, tickling the nape of my neck before she buries them in my hair. When she grips onto me, pulling the strands in her fists as her swollen pussy swallows my dick, I know she's getting close. I pull my mouth from hers and the sound of her heavy breaths fill the room.

"Sage—oh, god—baby, I'm gonna come," she moans.

I free a grunt when her core flutters, squeezing my cock as she emits a soft cry. I keep my slow pace, drawing out her orgasm. She's still trembling beneath me when I hook one arm and then the other under her knees, pressing her thighs further up my sides as I roll my hips even slower, plunging as deep as I can go. She groans, the sound that pours from her mouth melodically deep and beautiful, and her fingers curl around the back of my neck as she holds on tight. Her pussy flutters and clenches again, and I roll my hips even slower, grazing my pelvis over her clit with each stroke.

"Fuck—*Sage!*" she whimpers, her core clamping down around me yet again, this time drawing out my release. I prop my forehead against hers as I groan through the duration of my climax, pumping in and out of her until I am spent.

I shift to free her legs and she wraps them around my waist as I surrender some of my weight on top of her. She reaches up to touch her lips to mine, and I don't deny her, taking her mouth in a deep, wet, sexy as fuck kiss.

"Baby, you just made me come three times in a row," she whispers against my lips.

I chuckle, pulling away to grin down at her. "I think my girl likes it slow." She nods, chewing her bottom lip, trying to hide her own smile. "Give me a few and maybe next time I'll try for four."

She giggles and my dick twitches inside of her.

Fuck—if I could bottle that sound.

I pull out and I can see it as the light in her eyes fades a little. I press a quick kiss against her lips and then ease her onto her side before positioning myself at her back, pulling the sheet up over us before I curl my body around hers.

"Rough night, baby doll. Could use a little more shut eye. You with me?"

She presses her body closer to mine before I feel her relax as she assures me, "I'm with you."

"Fuck you when we wake up," I whisper, pressing a kiss against her shoulder.

"Promise?"

"Hell, yeah."

SEVEN

Millicent

HE DOESN'T FUCK me after our nap. Instead, he's gentle and slow as he makes sweet love to me. He takes his time, showering my body with affection, singing to me and whispering to me about how much he's missed me and how much he loves me. I get so lost in him that nothing else in the whole entire world matters. It's just him, hovering over me, buried deep inside of me, staring down at me—his icy blue eyes so gorgeous, so full of longing, so all consuming that I can't help but fall in love with him all over again as I stare right back.

I once swore that his ability to move his hips the way that he does was nothing short of magical—now, as he rolls them over and over, so unbelievably slow, I come again, and I know that I was not wrong. I come so hard, I swear to god, I see stars. My whole body is a quivering mess beneath his, the walls of my center constricting around him so tight. I can barely take a breath, let alone utter a single sound, and I can tell that he's hanging on by a thread as he allows my body to enjoy my *fourth* consecutive orgasm.

"Jesus—fuck, Millie," he grunts when he can no longer hold himself back. As I begin to come down from my release, he speeds up his pace, pounding into me harder as he chases his own climax. When he finally comes, his whole body tenses, his muscles flexing under my hands as his cock swells and jerks inside of me. It's so incredibly hot, I almost come again just looking at him.

He collapses on top of me, and I wrap my arms and legs around him, wishing to keep him close. We're both slick with sweat, the room laden with the heady scent of our love making, and I know there's no where else in the world I'd rather be. Right here, right now, filled to capacity with my dreamer, I'm *home*.

When his phone rings, he starts to lift himself off of me to go searching for it. I whine in protest, tightening my limbs around him, not ready to let him pull away from me.

"Baby," he chuckles, pressing a kiss to my lips. "Haven't seen the guys all day. Fucked up last night. I don't remember it, but one of the highlights was punching one of my oldest friends in the face. I have to see who that is."

"Oh," I whisper, loosening my grip around him.

He smacks another quick kiss against my mouth before he slides out of me and sits on the edge of the bed, reaching for his jeans. He pulls the device out of his pocket and barely even looks at the screen before he slides his finger across the display and answers the call.

"Hey," he mutters apprehensively. I watch as he listens to whoever is on the other end of the line. "Yeah, we're good," he says, resting a possessive hand on my leg as he looks over at me. "Yeah, okay. Half hour? All right." He doesn't say goodbye before he ends the call, tossing his phone back onto our pile of clothes on the floor. "Band meeting. We're going to get a bite to eat. Hungry?"

I sit up, drawing my knees to my chest as I run my fingers through my hair. "Yes. But, Sage, maybe I should—"

He shakes his head, as if he knows already what I'm about to suggest, and interrupts me before I can finish. "You're with me, doll face. It means you're part of the fold, just like Violet."

I furrow my brow, my mind busy constructing a list of all the ways in which Violet and I are *not* the same. Her contribution to Mountains & Men is certainly far greater than mine. She's dubbed herself M&M's hottest roadie—and all of them know better than to argue. I, on the other hand—

"What'd I say, doll face?" he mutters, reaching over to cup his hand around the side of my face. "You're with me, Millicent. Band business is not a secret. Besides, I don't show up with you on my arm, I'm sure they'll all kick my ass. I'm going to hop in the shower, you with me?"

I let his words sink in, remembering the way Derrick, Alex, JJ, and Violet saw to me yesterday. It's not news to me that they're all really close. They consider each other family. I've seen it first hand, and I've felt what it's like to be welcomed by them—but I was never bold enough to consider myself *one* of them. Family is such a foreign concept to me; and yet, something tells me that I'm going to be part of theirs whether I want to be or not. In some ways, based on the definition of family, that strikes me as beautifully *normal*.

"Baby—you with me?" Sage repeats.

I lean into the palm of his hand and offer him a nod, accepting the fact that with Sage comes an entire family of friends, and I'm now *one of them*.

"I'm with you."

He wastes no time taking my hand and pulling me off of the bed and into the shower. We spend the next twenty minutes making out under the water before we wash each other clean. We're late by the time we get out. Sage is ready two minutes later, and I do my best to make myself presentable as quickly as possible. I hop back into my jeans before I dig through my bag for a fresh top. I throw on a strapless bra and then tug on a simple coral-colored, deep V-necked t-shirt. I then toss my hair up into a stylishly messy bun before applying a bit of eye liner and a touch of mascara.

"Millie—baby, you good?" Sage calls out from inside the room.

"Just need my shoes," I tell him before I tuck my feet into my wedge-heeled sandals.

I take a deep breath when I'm finished, reaching for my purse before I face him. He slides his phone into his pocket as he smirks at me and then circles an arm around my waist, pulling me against him tightly.

"You're so gorgeous."

"I'm a mess," I laugh, leaning into him. "But I'm showered and somewhat presentable."

He smacks a kiss against my lips and repeats, "You're so gorgeous."

I don't know what to say, so I don't say anything at all. He smiles at me before he taps my ass and then grabs my hand, leading me out of the room. We're the last to arrive in the parking lot, and everyone is standing around waiting for us next to a big, black SUV. They fall silent as we join the circle, and I cling tightly to Sage's arm, feeling a little unnerved under their collective stare.

"Fuck, Mad Lips," Sage hisses. My eyes search for him in the group. When I find him, I flinch at the sight of his black eye. "I'm so sorry, man. I—*shit...*"

"You back?" Maddox asks, folding his arms across his chest. I'm not sure what he means, and my stomach knots up when his eyes shift from Sage to me and then back again.

Sage squeezes my hand before he nods. "Yeah. I'm back."

"Next time, I'll pummel your drunk ass."

"Fair enough."

"Millie?" I jerk my head in the direction of his voice, surprised to find Derrick addressing *me*. "By the looks of things, I take it you're good?" he asks, lifting his chin in our direction.

Sage squeezes my hand once more, and I look up at him. He's got a small smirk on his lips as his eyes dance around my face, and I know he's thinking of the multiple orgasms he gave me to ensure that I was *good* after yesterday's fiasco. I fight a blush as I look back to Derrick. The expression on his face makes my heart swell. His attention is focused on me—not Sage, but *me* and *me* alone. Everyone waits for my response, as if to say that it's all well and good that Sage is back, but how I feel matters to them, too.

It hits me anew—*I'm one of them.*

"I'm great," I murmur honestly.

"Thank fuck that's over," pipes in Knox. "Meeting adjourned. Let's grub!"

"You sure you don't want me to drive?" Derrick asks Stefany as she heads for the front seat.

"Please, drummer boy," she scoffs. "Trust the professionals to handle the streets of L.A. Ride shot-gun and I'll show you how it's done."

The guys all burst into laughter as we make our way to the vehicle, squeezing into every available seat. I'm the last in, and Sage guides me down into his lap, the only spot left, before he tells me, "Hold on tight, doll face."

And I do.

Sage

I FEAST ON MY girl for Thanksgiving.

When Thursday morning rolled around, I was up before Millie, allowing me the chance to call my parents, as I promised Rosy I would. We didn't talk long before I called Pepper and then Rosy, who fessed up to her part in Millie's visit. She was irritated to learn that I didn't handle the surprise very well, but soon forgave me when I told her Millie and I were fine. *More* than fine.

Knowing that I had company, my sisters didn't keep me on the phone. As soon as I disconnect from my last call, I abandoned the device altogether and focused all my attention on Millie. We didn't leave the room for hours, snacking on shit from the vending machine down the hall when we got hungry. Millie griped about how unhealthy our food options were, but she didn't seem at all disappointed about spending her holiday in a motel with her boyfriend, no turkey in sight. I wondered about her usual Thanksgiving plans, but I didn't ask, knowing how much she hates talking about her family. I wanted the day to be about us—and it was.

We fucked, we talked about the tour and the cities I'd been to, then we fucked some more. She told me about how Violet came to see her, and how Rosy insisted she come out to L.A. in her place, and then I made love to my gorgeous girl. It was late in the day when we decided we should see about a legitimate meal. I called up my boys and we all headed out for dinner before we agreed to hit a bar or two. We found this local dive with live music and stuck around for a while. At the end of the night, I could honestly say that if I had to spend my Thanksgiving away from my family, this was certainly an acceptable alternative—on the road with the band and my girl.

Now, as I watch Millie pack up the last of her things, I wonder where the last two days have gone. She'll be flying out this afternoon as the tour takes us northeast. Our next stop is all the way in North Dakota. We've got a gig Sunday night.

"This sucks."

"What sucks?" she asks, looking at me from over her shoulder.

"Now that I know I can get you out on the road with me, I don't want you to go home."

"I have to go back to work on Monday, Sage," she murmurs, turning back to her bag.

I stand to my feet and close the distance between us, sliding my arms around her waist as I press my chest against her back. "Are you saying that if you *didn't* have to be to work on Monday, you'd stick around?"

She laughs softly, shaking her head at me. "Didn't you say that JJ sleeps on the couch? You don't need another body on that bus."

"Not a problem. You'd bunk with me, doll face."

"Sage, don't be ridiculous."

When I bury my face between her neck and her shoulder, kissing her soft skin—fragrant with the familiar scent of vanilla—I decide I don't think I'm being ridiculous at all. Selfish, maybe, but not ridiculous. Before I can say as much, she spins around in my arms and reaches for my face. The look in her eyes causes me to furrow my brow in confusion.

"Don't stop calling," she whispers anxiously. "I promise I'll answer whenever I can. I swear it."

"Baby," I start to say, burying my fingers in her hair. I grip the back of her neck with one hand, my other arm pulling her against me closer. "Don't you get it by now? I was never going to stop calling. I'm not going to start now."

She stares at me for a moment before lifting herself up to press her lips to mine. I hold her tighter, kissing her in return. For a second, we both get carried away; then I remember, as much as I don't want to, we've got to get out of here. Time is our enemy, and he's a punk-ass bastard. I sever our connection, sliding a hand down and around Millie's ass before I give her a squeeze.

Fucking love her sweet, little ass.

"We gotta jet. I need to feed my girl."

"Okay," she murmurs, turning away from me once more.

It's another couple of minutes before she deems herself ready, zipping up her carry-on roller bag. As she slides her purse over her shoulder, I reach for her luggage, and then we make our way out of the building. We grab a taxi and make a stop back at the bus, so we can drop off Millie's stuff, and then we hitch a ride to the nearest diner. We're seated in a booth. Rather than sliding in on the opposite side of the table, I sit my ass right next to Millie. When she smiles at me, I know I made the right choice.

Our waitress's name is Betty. She's got to be at least forty-five, and she looks like she walked right out of the eighties, with her big hair, her bright makeup, and a shirt that's at least a size too small. As she takes our order, she calls Millie *honey* and dubs me *good-lookin'*, and I make a mental note to leave her a nice tip just for being the perfect combination of amusing and sweet.

"So, North Dakota this weekend, and then where?" asks Millie as Betty heads for the kitchen with our order.

"Man," I sigh, resting a hand on her thigh. "Missouri, Illinois, Ohio, Tennessee, Georgia, Florida, Mississippi, and then home."

"Wow," she whispers. She shakes her head before she says, "Hearing you talk about it back home is so much different than being here with you, in California—just one of your many stops—and hearing you talk about the rest of your trip."

"Yeah," I reply with a smirk. "Halfway through and it still feels so unreal."

Her eyes drift away from me and then I watch as she sinks a little into the booth, as if she's trying to make herself smaller. I follow the direction of her gaze and spot a girl, probably still in high school, apprehensively approaching our table.

"Sorry. Um, I'm sorry—you just look like—" she hesitates, her cheeks heating in a blush before she blurts out, "Did you play at a concert the other night? At The Wiltern?"

"Yeah," I reply with a nod.

"You're the lead singer of Mountains & Men, aren't you?"

"That's me," I chuckle.

"Oh, my god!" she cries as her blush deepens. "My friends are going to *flip* when I tell them I met you. That's the first time we ever heard you—but you were so good. We all downloaded your EP! *Just Tonight* is, like, totally my new favorite song."

I grin at her, giving Millie's leg a squeeze—my girl. My *muse*.

"Thank you," I tell the young stranger.

"Could I get your autograph?"

Before I can even answer, she turns and stops the nearest waitress, asking to borrow her pen. She then plucks a napkin from out of the napkin holder at the table beside ours and hands me both.

"What's your name?" I ask, both humbled and flattered by her attention.

"Sonya—with a y," she tells me.

I write her a short note, thanking her for her support, and then sign my name before handing her the napkin. She thanks me a few times before she turns and heads back to her table, and I think back on the words I had spoken no longer than five minutes ago.

...it still feels so unreal.

When I turn my gaze back to Millie, I find her staring down into her lap, fidgeting with her fingers. I reach for her hand, and she peeks up at me from beneath her lashes.

"What's wrong?" I ask with a frown.

"Nothing," she says softly.

"Bullshit, baby—what's wrong?"

Her green eyes plead with me even before she says another word.

"You'll call, right? You promised." She squeezes my hand, leaning closer to me before she continues. "And we won't grow apart, right? Not this tour—or the next—or the next; not when you get busier, and not when you're so well known that you can't go anywhere without people knowing exactly who you are? Not when—"

"Millicent, hey, slow down," I insist, reaching up to press my hand against her cheek. "What are you so worried about?"

"I love you," she whispers. "You have all that I have to give—it's why I got scared; it's why I'm *still* scared. Sage, I don't want to lose you. I *can't* lose you. Dammit," she mutters, her eyes filling with tears. "Even just thinking about losing you to them..."

"Them?"

"*Everyone*," she blurts out. "The people you sing for." She closes her eyes and a single tear rushes down her cheek. "You don't see yourself the way I see you—the way *they* see you. They won't be able to get enough of you; I just know it. You're already on your way, and I'm not just saying that to blow smoke up your ass, Sage. You're brilliant, all of you. Soon, you'll be so much bigger than your hometown; bigger than The Brew Cycle; bigger than the second slot on someone else's headlining tour...bigger than me."

"Doll face, open your eyes." She does as I ask and I look at her for a moment, *really* look at her. I know that right now, she's offering me something she's never offered me before. Total transparency. She's not running, she's not pushing me away, she's being honest. She's being real. And *fuck me*—it makes me love her *more*. Hearing her admit just how much she wants this, how much she wants *us*, it suddenly makes the last three miserable weeks totally worth it. It brought us here.

I prop my forehead against hers before I tell her, "I know what I want. I want *you*. From day one, all I've wanted is *you*. You haven't been able to shake me yet—and I'm not going anywhere, doll."

"No matter what?"

"I won't lie to you. I want it *all,* baby doll—the record deals, the crazy fans, tours that take us all over the world—but I want you right there by my side when it happens. No matter what. You with me?"

She nods her head against mine, breathing out slowly before she murmurs, "I'm with you."

EIGHT

Millicent

Once Sage and I return to the bus, Violet and I have an hour before we have to leave. Everyone is on board, the band doing what they do any other day as they wait to take off again. Derrick is on the couch next to Alex, coaching her as she faces off with Maddox in some video game that's displayed on the television. Knox is right there with them, laughing and supplying commentary while he casually strums his acoustic guitar. Violet and JJ sit across from Sage and me at the little kitchen table, and it all feels vaguely familiar—like we're sitting around in the boys' garage in Colorado, rather than a bus in California.

When it's almost time for us to go, JJ calls Violet and me a cab to take us back to the airport. Too soon, we hear the driver honk his horn, announcing his arrival. My entire chest cavity fills with a sadness I'm not prepared for. I look at Sage, remembering our conversation back at the motel, and all of a sudden, staying on the road with my dreamer doesn't seem like such a ridiculous idea after all.

He offers me a small, encouraging smile, as if to silently assure me that everything is going to be all right, and then he leans into me, tightening his grip around my shoulders as he presses his lips against mine. I grip a fistful of his t-shirt, not the least bit shy to kiss him back fervently. He pulls away before I'm ready, but he doesn't let me go, his lips still grazing mine as he starts to sing to me.

"Hello was never meant to feel like this
Heavy with regret/I'm still hoping you'll forget
Hello was never meant to feel like this
Up against the sun/In the shadow of goodbye
Would rather you just hold me
Would rather you just stay here
Would rather, baby, anything but This."

I sigh into his mouth as he finishes, my skin covered in goosebumps and my heart racing.

"Holy shit," JJ mumbles.

It isn't until he speaks that I remember where we are, and I turn my head only to realize that we've got an audience. Everyone is staring, and Violet has a huge grin on her face.

"Not to sound like a total pussy, but that was pretty fucking epic," states Knox.

"What?" I mutter.

"He couldn't finish the song," Maddox tells me. "We started working on it a few days ago, got most of the way through it, but he couldn't write the second verse. He kisses you and—*bam!*"

"That's so romantic," Alex whispers.

"Well, *damn,* now I want to hear the rest of the song!" Violet insists. Sage chuckles, drawing my attention back to him, and then we hear the honk of our waiting taxi once more.

"You gotta go," JJ murmurs somberly. "We won't debut it without you in the audience. That good enough?"

"Yeah, babe, that's good enough," she tells him, standing to make her exit.

"I'll grab your bag. Meet you out there in a sec," Sage tells me, reaching up to tuck a few strands of hair behind my ear. I nod and then we both get up.

JJ tosses Violet's bag in the trunk of our ride just as another taxi pulls into the lot. While I wait for Sage, I watch as two guys climb out of the vehicle. I recognize them right away, though I don't remember their names. It's been a while since I've seen anyone from Lawful Sinners or Twisted Tuesday, but it's hard to forget someone who looks like *that*—his dark hair pulled back into a low bun, his face covered in a few day's worth of stubble, his broad chest covered in a black tank that could only be worn in a place like this, just days before December.

"Well, *fuck me,* look who it is," one of them calls out as they both make their way toward me. "That offer still stands, by the way," he continues with a cocky grin.

I quirk an eyebrow at him, ignoring his friend as I reply, "*Still* not interested."

"Clay, man, leave that one alone."

"Nate's idea is a pretty good one," says JJ from behind me.

I turn my head to see him standing with Violet tucked under his arm, his gaze trained on *Clay*—the asshole who invites me to bed every time he sees me. Looking at him now, I realize he's so far from what I want, it's laughable. I used to think that Sage was an arrogant little shit, but he is nothing like this guy. When we met, Sage was simply a man fully aware of what he wanted and he took it, knowing even before I could admit it that I wanted him just as much.

"I'm just sayin'," Clay chuckles, folding his arms across his chest. "Three weeks left—*anything could happen*," he whispers the last bit, as if to taunt me, but I refuse to let his words get to me. Not this time. Sage loves me. He would never betray me. Not like that. I know it.

"And *I'm just saying*, get over yourself—for the sake of all womankind."

"You'd be singin' a different tune if you—"

"You motherfucker," Sage growls as he prowls toward us. My eyes grow wide when I catch the look on his face just before he drops my bag and steps in front of me, filling the gap between Clay and me. "Back the fuck up off my girl."

A sneer spreads across Clays lips and Nate reaches up to grab his shoulder. "Clay," he says, his tone clearly meant to express a warning.

"Not this again," says Knox. I look beside me as the rest of Mountains & Men join the showdown, which, according to Knox, isn't the first one they've seen.

"What'd I say?" Sage speaks through a clenched jaw. I reach for his hand, hoping to calm him down. He squeezes my fingers tightly, and I start to get the impression that he won't relent until Clay does as he says.

"What's going on out here?" I look in the direction of the new voice and see another member of Lawful Sinners exiting their tour bus, the last of their group trailing behind.

"Clay's dumbass talking shit," Nate grumbles.

The lead man makes eye contact with me before a smirk curls at the corner of his mouth and he coughs out a laugh. "He can't help himself. He's got a soft spot for the rare beauties. Give it up, Clay. She's taken. We're rollin', fuckers. Break it up," he says, turning to head back to the bus.

Clay shrugs out of Nate's hold before he directs his eyes on me and offers me a wink. Sage starts to move, but I grip his hand with both of mine, and he relents as all four of Lawful Sinners' men head back to their bus.

"I'm pretty sure I hate that guy," Sage mutters.

"Hey," I say softly, moving to stand in front of him. "It's not a big deal."

"He knows you're mine. He did that shit on purpose."

"Let it go," I plead, wrapping my arms around his neck as I press my body against his. "I'm leaving, Sage. Don't rob me of a proper goodbye."

He sighs in resignation, locking his arms around my waist before he leans in to kiss me. And, oh, how he kisses me. It's hard, wet, unrelenting, possessive, and absolutely incredible. As his tongue sweeps through my mouth, his hand sliding down over my ass, I know he's making a point. He's staking his claim, sending a message, and soaking my thong. I love every moment, and I don't care who sees. I'm his, totally and completely, and I'm not the least bit ashamed.

When he finally pulls away, I'm panting, my fingers buried in his hair. I know my lips are swollen and red because his are too, and I can't help but wonder how in the fuck I'm going to last another fourteen days without him.

"I love you," he says, his voice husky and sexy as hell.

"I love you, too, baby," I whisper, the ache of goodbye overwhelming me.

"Call me when you get to the airport."

"I will."

"Get out of here, doll face—before I steal you away."

I giggle and he smacks one last quick kiss against my lips before he turns toward the taxi. Violet is already inside, speaking softly with JJ through the open window as they wait for me. Sage opens my door and I slide into my seat, already feeling too far away from him. He shuts me in and then deposits my bag in the trunk. As the cab driver begins to pull out of the lot, both Violet and I twist around to get one last look at our men. She blows JJ a kiss and I wave, staring at Sage until he's out of sight.

I draw in a deep breath and free a heavy sigh as I turn back around, settling in for the duration of our ride. After a moment, I take stock of my emotions and realize that while I'm sad to see him go, the weight of despair is no longer pulling me down. I'm buoyed by the knowledge that I'll see him again in just a couple of weeks—as soon as my semester is over. Furthermore, after I get to the airport, I'll hear the sound of his voice, reminding me that we're still *us*. We're in this—*together*.

"You all right over there?" asks Violet, breaking the silence between us.

I shift my gaze from the window and find her smiling at me kindly. I can tell that she misses JJ already, too, but she also remains light with the hope of the future.

"Thank you." The words fall from my mouth without a second thought. As soon as I hear them, I know they bear repeating. "Thank you for getting me here."

"Wasn't hard," she says with a grin. "It's where you belong."

I smile then, sure that she's absolutely right.

Sage and I sent a volley of texts back and forth Friday night, after I made it home safely. I didn't last long once I was settled, sleep coaxing me under until I woke late Saturday morning. When he called me in the early afternoon, we spent *hours* talking as the band continued to travel east. He made me laugh, keeping the conversation light and fun, telling me more tour stories and also filling me in on a few things Stefany has been trying to line up for them when they get back. We said goodbye when they stopped for dinner and he promised to call me later.

Later ended up being the next evening. We didn't talk long, as they were gearing up for their show, but I was just happy to hear from him—knowing full-well that's the kind of woman I am, the kind who needs to hear the rich, alluring, sexy tone of my man's voice. I went three weeks without it, and I'll never choose that ever again.

The rest of my night was spent preparing for work the next day. I then retired to bed, where I finished a book and then drifted to sleep, my head replaying my favorite memories from my time in L.A.

Now, as I stare blankly at the computer screen in front of me, I can't seem to reign in my thoughts. Instead of reading, replying, and deleting emails, I'm too busy remembering what it felt like to have Sage inside of me, bringing me to orgasm right on the heels of my third.

"Millie?"

My whole body jolts as I'm pulled from my thoughts, my gaze shifting toward Lindsey as she enters my office. She's wearing a burgundy sweater-dress that clings to her noteworthy curves, nude panty-hose, and a pair of Mary-Jane heels. Her loose, dark brunette curls dust her shoulders, and the pleasant *glow* that usually lights up her face is perfectly intact.

"You're *blushing*. What were you just thinking?" she asks, occupying the empty chair on the opposite side of my desk.

"Uh..." I reply dumbly, bringing my hair to one shoulder simply to busy my hands.

"Something happened. I'm missing something. What is it?" she asks, crossing one leg over the other before leaning her forearms atop her knee.

"What do you mean?" I inquire evasively, still trying to combat my inappropriate thoughts of Sage. Naked. Whispering my name...

"I *mean*, you've got color in your face again. You haven't looked this happy since—oh, my god," she gasps, sitting up straight. "Something went down with you and Sexy McHottington!"

I can't help the grin the spreads across my face at the mention of her nickname for Sage. It's certainly not one that can be denied.

"Millie Valentine, I want details—*now!* You were a ghost of your former self when we left for fall break. *What happened?*"

"I went to see him," I confess.

"Thank god!" she cries, clapping her hands against her chest in relief. "Seriously, I was worried about you. When you told me you two were putting the breaks on your relationship, I thought you were outside your mind. That guy is *hot!* Not to mention the way he makes your face go soft when you think about him—just like *that*."

She points at me, and I wonder what it is that she sees. I don't think on it long as she continues speaking.

"So, what's the story? Was it romantic? I bet it was romantic. Girl—I need romantic. We both know *my* life is lacking in that department."

I shake my head at her, a small smile playing at my lips as I tell her, "I don't know that *romantic* would be the term I'd use. We had a couple issues we had to iron out."

"But you're good now, right?"

"Yeah," I reply softly with a nod, the memory of our panty-melting kiss goodbye flashing through my mind. "We're good."

For the next twenty minutes, she peppers me with questions about my trip. Seeing as how Sage and I spent half of my stay in bed, there isn't too much for me to share with her, but I tell her as much as I can. I then inquire about her holiday, and she chats about her time with family and friends.

She stands to leave when she notes the time, her next class only fifteen minutes from now. When she gets to the doorway, she turns abruptly before she asks, "Hey, any chance you spent some time with the guys from Lawful Sinners while you were in L.A.? I'm still waiting on that autograph," she says teasingly, lifting an eyebrow at me.

I frown at her, vaguely remembering her request to get an autograph from the band's lead guitarist, back when I first saw them before the tour. "Which one is he again?"

"His name is Clay," she answers with a smirk.

I shake my head at her, knowing Lindsey's far too sweet to entertain any sort of attraction to that arrogant asshole.

"He's bad news, Lindsey."

"What? No," she pouts. "Let me guess—typical rock star? Mad talent with a god complex?"

"Something like that."

She wrinkles her nose in disappointment before she says, "Well, I suppose they can't all be like Sage. You got yourself a good one, Millie." She offers me a wink before she turns, slipping into her office across the hall. I replay her words in my head and smile as I think about my dreamer. Sage—my fucking rock star.

She doesn't know the half of it.

NINE

Sage

THE LIGHTS ARE brighter. The crowd is louder. The band is tighter. The music is better. I'm rockin' out harder than I ever have before, and I'm having the time of my life.

I thought my music kept me whole during a time when I needed something to hold onto—but here, now, I understand that Alex was right. I was barely holding on. My music drives me; it defines who I am—but it isn't everything.

The adrenaline that courses through my veins makes me soar. As the lyrics to our best songs pour out of me, I know I'm in the right place at the right time. I'm on top of the world. I'm on top of my fucking mountain. Every bead of sweat that trickles along the sides of my face and down my back reminds me how hard I've worked to get here—how hard I'll work to *stay* here. On the stage is where I belong, where we *all* belong.

"If I sneak you out the back, will you let me come?
Take a chance, just one glance, and we'll both be gone.
Let's run real fast, drive real slow where you wanna go.
We'll blow through perfect towns/ We'll leave a mess behind.

"Forget the girl you were/ I'm not the boy I was
You turn me upside down/ I'll make your world go 'round.

'Cause it's just you and me/I swear it's destiny
Forget the girl you were/Let's go, just you and me."

Under the lights, engulfed in the noise of wild screams, my band at my back, our music filling the atmosphere, it's where I realize just how much she means to me. She changed everything in just one night—the woman who makes my heart sing. I'm not the boy I was because of her. I love her deep, and I love her hard. My muse. My inspiration. My girl, worthy of more than an encore, lights up my world.

When we come to a stop, I open my eyes and take a deep breath, ready to get off the bus and breathe in a bit a fresh air. We hit Jacksonville tonight. I'd be lying if I said I wasn't looking forward to another show, but I sure as shit miss my own bed. I miss Millie's bed, too. Four more days and we'll be home. When we get there, I'll crash wherever she is—and I'll crash *for hours*. I feel like I haven't had a decent night's rest since L.A. I won't complain, though. Sleep and the comfort of home are small sacrifices I'm willing to make for the sake of a dream come true.

"All right, boys and girl—how much do you fucking *love* me?" asks Stefany as I hear her burst on board. I slide on my glasses and then peek my head out of my bunk, curious what all the excitement is about.

"Stef, we're on the last leg of our first national tour. Our Facebook page has literally thousands of likes we didn't have five weeks ago. People are starting to actually download our shit on iTunes—I think it's safe to say we love you a lot," Knox yells from behind the curtain of his bunk.

I chuckle as I watch her grin, pressing her fists against her hips as she looks in the direction of his voice.

"It's like I said, you do your part, I'll do mine. But this is just the beginning, guys, and you're about to love me a whole fuck-of-a-lot more."

"You always do this," Maddox mutters from where he sits, slouched on the far end of the couch. Derrick occupies the other end while Alex sits between them, her feet in Derrick's lap as she leans back against Maddy's shoulder. For a second, I can't help but be amused by the way the guys have adopted Alex into the fold. Especially Maddox. He was the most apprehensive about her; now, I swear, she's like the little sister he never had.

"I always do what?" asks Stefany innocently, pulling me from my thoughts.

"You dangle big news in front of our faces without coming out and telling us what it is. Spit it *out*, woman!"

"Do I?" she asks, playfully scrunching her nose.

"Totally," JJ laughs from where he sits, propped up on the kitchen counter, eating cereal right out of the box.

"Okay, well—if you're in hiding, get your asses out here, 'cause this news isn't big. It's *huge*."

I jump down from my bed just as Knox rolls out of his, and we both make our way toward the front of the bus. Once she has all of our attention, Stefany bounces on her toes, clapping her hands together in front of her before she speaks.

"I found a label that wants to take on Mountains & Men."

No one speaks. The only sound in the cabin is that of the bus's clicking engine as it sputters to rest. Stefany looks at each of us expectantly, and I shake my head, trying to conjure up a single word.

"*What?*" I manage.

She laughs before she repeats, "I found a label that wants to take on Mountains & Men."

"Are you shitting us?" asks Maddox.

"That would be cruel," she states, folding her arms across her chest. "I'm not cruel—I just kick ass at what I do. Lucky for me, you kick ass at what you do, too. I told you in the beginning, it's all about the *music*—and your music is fantastic. You might be the new kids on the block, but I've been screaming your name from every rooftop imaginable over the last few weeks, and I finally got a bite."

"Holy *shit*," Knox murmurs beside me.

"Who are they?" asks Derrick.

"All right, this is where I need you to hear me out," she says, holding her hands out as if to brace us for what's to come. "They're called Potential Records. They're pretty new themselves, located in Boulder, Colorado. They've got, like, five bands signed to them right now. But here's the deal, they're all about keeping the integrity of *your* sound. They've heard your stuff, they love *your* stuff, and they want you to do *you*. You define Mountains & Men and they won't change that or manipulate it into whatever the industry thinks you should be.

"They're an independent label that's willing to take on the risk of producing your record and getting it out there. The thing is, you have to earn your keep. They'll front the cost of *everything* that goes into creating your first album. I, of course, am going to keep doing my thing, and together we'll make it profitable. When your album makes money, as soon as production costs are covered, they get a cut, you get a cut, and we go from there."

Another moment of silence passes as we all let her words sink in. I tug my eyebrows together, trying to stay level headed. Truth be told, I don't give a shit *how* small they are. The fact that they're willing to take a chance on us is outrageous. I'm ready to go all in. I also know that I'm still so fucking green. I don't want to dive into the deal without asking questions.

Then again, Stefany hasn't steered us wrong yet.

"Should we take this deal because it's the right fit for us? Or is this about taking the only thing that's been offered to us?" asks Derrick.

I breathe a small sigh of relief, glad that *someone* knows what to say. Until Stefany came along, he was our business guy. I suppose I can't be surprised that he's thinking one step ahead.

"Honestly? This is your first offer, but I think it's a *great* offer. I could shop around some more. We could wait, sit on this deal—but if we do that, not only would we potentially lose this opportunity, but we'd lose the momentum we've been building the last five weeks. If I get you boys—and *girl*—home, and we spit out a single to your new record the first of the year, it'll keep this train moving, full speed ahead."

"Sounds to me like the worst thing that could happen is—we record an album and it goes flat. Potential Records are the ones taking the hit if we suck," says JJ.

"We won't suck," Alex pipes in, rolling her eyes.

"She's right. You won't," replies Stefany. "You're right, too, JJ. You lose nothing if we can't make your album a hit."

"That doesn't sound very business savvy of them," Knox mutters suspiciously.

"The owner—he's a kid who's got money to blow; but he's also got a good ear. I've talked to him, he's a smart guy, and he knows the industry."

"Stef's right," I jump in, too excited to listen to anymore. "Fuck, guys—a label wants to give us a chance. I think we can do the same. I say we do it."

"I'm with Sage," states Maddox, lifting his chin in my direction.

"Shit," says Derrick, a slow grin spreading across his face. "Are we really doing this?"

"Aye," I reply, casting my vote.

"Aye," Knox and Maddox add in unison, chuckling when they do.

"Aye," Alex and JJ chime in.

All eyes fall on Derrick, silence settling in the cabin once more. He laughs, shaking his head before he agrees, "Aye."

"Yes!" Stefany cheers, throwing her hands up in the air. "I've got a call to make. We're celebrating after the show!" she demands, pointing back at us as she steps out of the bus.

Maddox hoots before he cries, "Hell—*fuckin'*—yeah!"

Hours later, after we all freak out with excitement, we play one hell of a show and then we party our asses off. We don't get back to the bus until three in the morning, but I'm still buzzing from the adrenaline of being on stage and the alcohol that I guzzled down all night. I'm so hyped, I feel like I could howl at the moon—so I do.

"What are you doing?" Alex giggles as she clings to Adrian's arm. I smirk at them, wondering the same thing about their flirty shit.

"So, what's the deal with you two, anyway?" I blurt out, walking backwards across the lot.

"Now *that* is a fucking *fantastic* question," Maddox slurs, draping his arm around my shoulders as he leans against me. "We can't boink the church mouse—but Adrian can do as he pleases. So?"

"Maddy! Did you really just say that?" Alex gasps, trying and failing to deliver an intimidating frown. She's unbearably cute when intoxicated.

"Hey—don't call me that!" he grunts.

"I thought we agreed, no speaking of my *kitty cat!*"

We both burst out laughing, falling against each other as we do.

"Fuck, why doesn't that ever get old?" asks Maddox as he tries to control his laughter.

"I'm going to be her boyfriend," Adrian announces, silencing us both.

"You *are?*" she asks, halting her steps.

"Yeah, babe," he replies with a shrug, smiling down at her.

"You haven't even kissed me yet."

"We've been on the road for almost six weeks, and you haven't kissed our church mouse? You're doing it wrong," I tell him, shaking my head in reprimand.

"Trust me—I've wanted to. We've got a good thing going; I didn't want to be a dick."

"Well, right now you're being a pussy!" announces Maddox.

"You're gonna be my boyfriend?" Alex whispers, as if she didn't hear Mad Lips at all.

"Babe…" He chuckles, grabbing hold of each side of her face before he leans down and kisses her. I watch as she leans into him, another smirk tugging at my lips.

"'Bout fucking time!" hollers Gabe as he and the others catch up to us.

"Ow, ow!" Knox yells, making us all laugh. Adrian and Alex laugh too before they pull away from each other, Alex melting into his side.

"You know your girl plays circles around you, right?" says JJ with a grin.

"I do not!" Alex protests bashfully.

"It's okay, Ali. No need to lie about it. He's a man, he can take it. Right, Adrian?" asks Derrick, clapping him on the shoulder as he passes.

"Ain't no shame in my game."

"And then there were three," Knox declares, throwing his arm around his brother's shoulders. "Mountains & Men are coupling off, droppin' like flies. Gotta hold strong, lil' bro."

"Shit—ain't no shame in my game, either. There's plenty of Maddox to go around."

Listening to them talk makes me think about Millie. It's then that I realize I haven't spoken to her all day. After we got news about Potential Records, we were too excited to think about anything else. I have no fucking clue what time it is in Colorado, but I don't care—I need to hear the sound of my girl's voice.

I fumble for my phone and waste no time calling her up. When I don't reach her the first time, I hang up and dial again.

"Sage?" she finally answers, her voice raspy and sexy as fuck.

"Hey, doll face."

"Sage—it's almost midnight. I'm sleeping. I have to teach in the morning," she says shortly.

"Uh-oh. I'm in trouble," I mumble. She doesn't reply and I reach up to run my fingers through my hair. "Baby?"

"Are you drunk?"

"Fuck, Millie, just hearing your voice is making me hard, baby."

"You're drunk," she deadpans.

"Doesn't make it any less true," I reply, looking down at my crotch, my jeans barely hiding my semi.

"You didn't call me today…" she whispers.

"I'm calling you now, doll." Another moment of silence passes between us and I try again. "Got some pretty big news today, baby. Mountains & Men is putting out an album. We'll be signing with a label when we get back home."

"What?" she breathes. "Really?"

I smile, pleased as fuck to hear the excitement in her voice. "Yeah. I'll tell you all about it when I see you. Three more days, Millie—I'm comin' home, gorgeous."

"I miss you."

"Oh, yeah? What do you miss?"

"Sage…" she groans, the sound going straight to my dick.

"Shit," I sigh, dropping my chin to my chest as I reach for my hard-on through my jeans. I hardly pay attention as all the guys and Alex mingle just a few feet away, still rowdy and carrying on. My focus is elsewhere—in a bed, thousands of miles away. "Miss your pussy, baby. God—I need a taste."

"Sage," she whispers, her tone more inviting than it was before.

"Miss hearing the sounds you make when you come," I murmur. A crooked grin curls my lips at the sound of her breaths, increasing in speed. "Will you come for me right now, doll face? Hmm? I want to hear you."

"Sage, I should—"

"What are you wearing?"

"What?"

"What are you wearing? Tell me."

"Sweatpants and a t-shirt," she replies dryly, as if that's supposed to deter me.

It doesn't.

I know my girl.

"Are you wearing panties?"

She hesitates and I grin wickedly. "No," she finally answers.

"Take off your t-shirt."

"It's cold," she protests.

"Fuck, Millicent, take it off—you won't be cold in a minute, I swear."

"Christ…I can't believe I'm doing this." Her words are muffled, as if she's set her phone aside, and I listen to the rustling sound of her sheets. "Sage?"

"Put me on speaker."

"Okay."

"Take your pants off, baby, spread those legs wide for me." I hear more rustling before I ask, "Millie?"

"I should be sleeping."

"You'll sleep better when I'm through with you. Are you naked?"

"Yes," she replies quietly.

I bite my lip, *hard*, wishing I was there with her.

"Are your nipples hard?"

"Yes," she breathes.

"Play with them, baby."

"*Sage*," she sighs, my confirmation that she's done as I've asked.

"Are you wet for me?"

"God—I wish you were here."

"Pretend I am, doll face. Close your eyes and slide your fingers through your pussy. *Are you wet for me?*" I repeat, my voice husky as my mind fills with the image I'm sure she's creating right now.

"I am…"

"Touch yourself, Millie—make yourself come. I want to hear it," I grunt, my dick now completely hard. I give myself another squeeze as I hear her sigh. "Do your fingers feel good, baby?"

"Yes..."

"Mmmm," I hum, pulling my bottom lip between my teeth again as my eyes seal shut. "Bet you look so sexy right now—your fingers pumping in and out of that sweet pussy. Love the way you taste, baby doll. *You're my favorite fucking candy.*"

"Sage," she moans.

"Could eat you every day, doll—lick that pussy and bite that clit before I suck on you until you start to shake."

"Oh, baby—I'm so wet."

"You wet for me, gorgeous? Are you going to come for me?"

"Yes. Shit, *yes*," she says on a groan.

"Let me here you come. Fuck, my dick is so hard for you, Millie."

"Sage! Baby—I'm—" she sucks in a breath and then frees a whimper.

I open my eyes, a sly grin pulling at each corner of my mouth as I mutter, "That's my girl."

"Come home," she whispers.

"One more show. Three more days."

"One more show. Three more days," she repeats, as if she's chanting a mantra that's meant to keep her sane.

"Love you, doll face."

"I love you, too."

"Get some sleep, yeah?"

"M'Kay."

"Stay naked," I demand before she can hang up.

She giggles groggily before she agrees and we say goodnight. As I slide my phone into my pocket, I look up at the moon and chant—"One more show. Three more days."

TEN

Millicent

"Hey, it's late. What are you still doing here?"

I look away from my computer screen, where I'm submitting the last of my grades, and spot Lindsey in the doorway of my office. She's already in her coat and gloves, her purse and an extra bag slung over each of her shoulders. It's almost six o'clock on a Friday night, the last Friday of the semester. Most of the campus has been deserted already, students fleeing happily after the completion of their last finals.

"I was scheduled for a late exam slot. Three o'clock. I just finished grading and wanted to get these scores in the system before I left."

She smiles at me mischievously, leaning her shoulder against the doorjamb. "You mean, a certain *someone* is due back this weekend and you didn't want to have any last minute work to do."

"That, too," I admit, not even attempting to hide my smile. "He texted a little while ago. They were crossing the Colorado state line."

"I'm happy for you. You know what? No—it's more than that. I'm proud of you, too."

I scrunch my brow at her in confusion, shaking my head as I start to say, "Lindsey—"

"I'm serious. I won't claim to know you particularly well, but I know enough. I've been across the hall from you long enough to know that what you have with

Sage? It's outside of your comfort zone. Yet, even so, you've stuck with it. I've had my eye on you over the last couple of weeks, and the difference between now and when he first left is night and day. He makes you happy, and it's really good to see. So, Millie Valentine, I stand firm on what I said. I'm proud of you for letting yourself enjoy him."

I'm not sure why, but when she's done speaking, I have to take a breath to help ease the tightness in my chest. No one has ever said anything like that to me before, and it makes me both sad and incredibly encouraged. Once I know I'm not going to start crying, I open my mouth to speak, not even thinking about the words that fall from my lips before I say them.

"I love him. I love him more than I've ever loved anyone before. I'm not sure how it happened."

"In my experience, it's not so much the *how* that matters so much as the *why*. I'm sure that if he's earned your heart, he's deserving—which only makes me like him more," she says with a wink. "I'll leave you to it so you can get out of here. You have my number. Use it, especially if your hottie is playing a show during the winter break."

"Okay, I will," I promise. She waves at me and then I watch her leave, feeling surprisingly disappointed to see her go.

She had it right earlier, when she said that she didn't know me particularly well. I don't know her particularly well, either—my tendency to guard myself against any and all relationships keeping her at arm's length. Now, though, I feel as if something has shifted in our friendship. I like it, and I decide here and now that I fully intend to do as I promised and call her up a time or two over the course of the next month that we have off.

I'm at my desk for another hour as I tie up any and all loose ends. By the time I bundle up and head out to my car, the sun is long gone, and the chill of the night bites through my coat. I don't mind much. I'm too distracted by the excitement I feel knowing that my man is only a few hours away. I'm sure it'll be pretty late when he makes it back to town; I also know how much he's looking forward to being in his own bed. He made no promises that I'd see him tonight, but I won't lie. I hope that I do.

Driving through town on my way home, I sigh heavily as I pass countless displays of *Christmas* along my journey. Wreaths hang from city street lamps; lights scale the selected clusters of trees, illuminating the landscaping at neighborhood entryways; and at least one house on every street is decked out in decorations. I've never really been a big fan of Christmas, so I don't appreciate most of what I see. Honestly, for as long as I can remember, the holiday has hardly been more than any other ordinary day.

Since I was six years old, my world consisted of my mother and me. To this day, she'll deny it, but the abandonment of my father made her so bitter that it sucked all the life out of her, leaving barely anything left for me. I had to grow up pretty fast under her roof, taking care of myself in ways that she wouldn't. By the time I was seven, I was consumed by my desire to find some sort of order, to create a system of sorts in order to establish a routine. I was the organized one because I had to be. My mother spent too much time lost in her anger and resentment to do much more than clothe and feed me. I suppose I should be grateful she did that much. Even that was a sacrifice she made on my behalf, a fact that she's reminded me of constantly over the years.

Needless to say, we didn't celebrate anything. Not birthdays, not Christmas, not even my high school graduation. By then, I was too old to be disappointed by her lack of enthusiasm for any of my accomplishments. When I ran away from her, settling thousands of miles across the country in a picturesque college town, I did it with no regrets. Yet even now, I bear the scars of my childhood, and I feel it even more during seasons like this. For eight years, I've been free from under her thumb, and I still can't appreciate the beauty of a Christmas tree.

It's been two months since I've spoken to my mother. The dust has long since settled after our last fight, and yet neither of us has broken the silence. I'm not sure what to make of the fact that she kept her word, staying true to her oath that she was done with me. I didn't think she was capable of letting me go. I've always been the reason behind her misery, the reason behind every bad thing that's happened to her, and she was never shy about reminding me. She had to tell *someone*, and I was that someone—her social life even more isolated than mine. Now that we're not speaking, I wonder who she's latched onto? Who has been given the unfortunate task of listening to her countless woes?

As I pull into a parking space in front of my apartment building, I shake away all thoughts of Natalya Valentine, wishing to think of her no longer. Instead, I gather my things and head inside, allowing my thoughts to drift back to Sage. Knowing that he's so close, and yet still so far away, makes me anxious. Aware that I have a few hours to kill, I change into a pair of sweatpants and a long-sleeved shirt—*sans any and all underwear*. I then pour myself a glass of wine before curling up on the couch with a book: Ken Follett's *Pillars of the Earth*, a new *Violet approved* title.

A few days after we returned from L.A., she came over and noticed I was reading another piece of classic literature. She then proceeded to drag me to the bookstore, demanding I pick out something written in the last ten years. It had taken some convincing, as she was hoping I'd opt for a book that wasn't so *dense*, but I argued that the publication date fell within her parameters. I'm now halfway through and pleased to admit that I'm loving it. Even better, it'll occupy my mind for the next few hours.

Still, every few pages, I stop and cling to the giddy feeling that makes my stomach tingle when I remember—*Sage is almost home.*

Sage

I'M HOME LONG enough to look yearningly at my bed, where I've discarded my bags, and then I've got my keys in my hand and I'm out the door. I hop in my Audi and let it run for a few minutes. My brother-in-law, Harry, was kind enough to stop by once a week to take it for a spin around the block while I was away. Now, as it growls at me, I know it's just the cold that makes it angry and not neglect. I can't say I blame the thing. After having spent the last couple weeks in temperatures far warmer than what December in Colorado has to offer, I can honestly say that I didn't miss the twenty-degree chill that's welcomed me home tonight.

By the time I get to Rosy's apartment building, it's almost midnight. Even so, I don't hesitate to pound on her door excitedly, knowing she's up and waiting for me. I chuckle when I hear her squeal loudly seconds prior to her opening up, her small body crashing into mine before I can even get a look at her.

"You're *home!*"

"Feels good, too," I reply, earnestly returning her embrace.

We separate at the sound of Maestro's bark. He barks once more as he scurries toward me, pawing at my legs as he wags his whole behind.

"Hey, buddy," I say in greeting, lifting him up into my arms. He wiggles wildly as he licks at my neck, his tongue reaching for my face, and I pull away from him. "Missed you, too, Maestro—but you still lick your junk with that tongue. Lay off, bud."

Rosemary giggles and reaches for my elbow, tugging me inside.

"Baby girl, I can't stay," I inform her as I follow her pull.

"Hey, Sage. Welcome home," says Samantha, my sister's roommate. Her dirty blonde hair is in a messy knot on top of her head, and she's in a pair of tight, cotton shorts and a hoodie. She looks like she's ready to hit the sack, but not as if she was woken up by my arrival.

"Thanks, Sami. And thanks again for being cool with keeping Maestro."

"No trouble at all," she replies with a grin. "He's the sweetest."

I smile down at the little guy and he tries licking my face again. I chuckle before setting him back on the floor. "I'll be out of your hair in a minute. I just need to grab his stuff."

"I'm suddenly second guessing whether or not I like Millie right now," states Rosy, folding her arms across her chest.

"Don't lie," says Sami, playfully nudging Rosy with her elbow. "When she paid you back for that plane ticket, you said she was just right for Sage."

She rolls her eyes and blows out a sigh. "That's just because I told her *not* to worry about it, but she refused to leave until I took the money. Sage needs a woman who can hold her own. Doesn't mean I'm not totally jealous that he's about to leave me to go see her—even though they saw each other *three weeks* ago!"

"Rosy," I grin, palming the top of her head and twisting it so that she's got nowhere to look but at me. "I'll see you tomorrow night, remember?"

"Yeah, yeah," she concedes, turning to go gather the bag full of Maestro's things.

"No pouting," I insist, taking the small duffel and throwing it over my shoulder. "If you're good, I'll treat you to breakfast sometime next week."

"Just you and me?" she asks, quirking an eyebrow at me.

"Just you and me, little lady."

"Okay," she replies with a smile. "Tell Millie I say hi."

"I'll try to remember—but I make no promises," I tell her, picking up Maestro once more. "Haven't seen my girl in three weeks; my hello might not include any words."

"*Oh*-kay. You can go now," she says, shooing me out the door.

I laugh and then call over my shoulder, "Bye, ladies."

"Bye," says Sami.

"Love you," replies Rosy.

"Love you back."

As soon as I hear the door latch closed behind me, the deadbolt sliding into place, I hurry down the stairs and back out to my car. I load Maestro into the front seat and waste no time heading to Millie's place. She doesn't know I'm coming, or even that I've made it back to Fort Collins. The last time I made contact was when the bus brought us over the state line. I wanted to surprise her.

It's twelve-thirty when I put my car in park and grab Maestro. I wonder if Sarah is home or if Millie will be inside alone. I scan the parking lot for Sarah's car, but I don't look too hard, anxious to get inside and out of the cold—impatient to be buried inside of my girl. Thinking about it takes me back to a couple of nights ago, when she came for me over the phone. My dick jerks at the thought as I knock on her door.

I hear her footsteps and set Maestro at my feet. I see it as light suddenly appears beneath the door, and my pulse begins to race. When she opens the door, she takes my breath away. Her hair is pulled back into a low ponytail and her face has been washed clean, allowing her natural beauty to shine through—how I like her best. She's in a pair of gray sweatpants and a tight, white, thermal shirt. I can see the hardened buds of her tits through the fabric, and my dick stirs at the sight. Without a word, I take one, long step toward her, circling my arms around her waist as I pull her against me. I tear my eyes away from her gorgeous green ones just long enough to watch Maestro trot inside, and then she's got my undivided attention.

She grips the lapels of my coat, pulling me down while pushing herself up on her tiptoes. She brings her lips a hair's breath away from mine, and I can feel her shallow exhalations against my mouth.

"You came," she whispers.

A smile pulls at my lips as I murmur, "Not yet—but I think we can do something about that."

I swallow her laugh when I cover her mouth with my own. Her amusement is soon forgotten as I thrust my tongue between her lips, kissing her hungrily. She sighs dreamily, sliding her arms up and around my neck, and I back her further into her apartment so that I might close the door behind me. Blindly, I fumble for the lock, twisting the deadbolt before I sever our kiss. I flip off the lights and she gasps excitedly as I reach for the back of her thighs, hoisting her up off of her feet. As soon as she locks her ankles behind me, my lips capture hers once more.

"Sarah?" I mumble between kisses.

"In her room. With Brandon. Sleeping," she mumbles in return.

"Fuck," I hiss, grabbing a handful of her ass. Her legs squeeze my hips and my cock grows fully erect. "Don't have it in me to hold back, doll face."

"Then don't," she whispers, her fingers finding their way into my hair. "God, I've missed you. Every part of you, Sage."

A grunt crawls its way up my throat as I plunge my tongue back into her mouth, carrying her down the hallway, Maestro at my heels. When we cross the threshold of her room, I close the door behind us before whirling her around and pressing her up against it. She whimpers, pulling at my hair as she kisses me desperately, like she's thirsty and she can't get enough.

I shrug my way out of my coat, letting it drop to the floor. Maestro growls, probably having been in the drop zone, but I don't pay him any mind as I slide a hand underneath Millie's shirt to palm her breast. Another soft sound spills from her mouth into mine at my touch, and her kisses turn more frenzied. When I slide my other hand up her stomach and around her other tit, she pulls her mouth from mine and reaches for the bottom of her shirt, yanking it off without delay.

I press my lips against the hollow of her throat, sucking and licking my way to the soft spot behind her ear as she claws at the shirt on my back, working the fabric off of me. I move my hands off of her, reaching behind my head to grab at the shirt before pulling it over my head. As soon as I'm free of it, I latch on to one of her nipples, sucking her into my mouth without restraint.

"Baby," she sighs, her back bowing away from the door as she pushes her chest out.

I swirl my tongue around the hardened bud and she rocks her hips, seeking friction against her core. I let her go with a pop before grinning up at her, the lamp beside her bed illuminating the room just enough to clearly make out the unmasked lust on her face.

"Who owns your orgasm, Millie?"

"Hurry," she begs. "I want to feel you."

I lick my lips, wondering how long I can resist her. I decide to tease her a little bit more. I want her so worked up, she's dripping wet for me. I ignore her plea and dip my head down to take her other boob into my mouth.

"*Sage*," she moans, rocking her hips again.

I grab hold of her thighs, keeping her still, and she grunts in frustration. Chuckling, I free her nipple and then carry her to the bed, tossing her onto the mattress. She shrieks in surprise and then giggles as I hook my fingers into the cuffs of her pants and rip them down her legs, leaving her naked.

"Let your hair down," I instruct, toeing my way out of my shoes before I drop my boxers and my jeans in one fell swoop. I turn my back to her only long enough to set my glasses on top of her dresser, and then I'm at the foot of the bed. I kneel down, spreading her legs and pulling her closer. She sucks in a breath just before I flatten my tongue over her slick entrance, licking all the way up to her clit.

"*Fuuuuuck*," she cries.

I repeat the act, humming between her pussy lips, loving the way she tastes. There's a sweetness to her natural flavor, making her both savory and delicious. When I slip my tongue inside of her, lapping up all she has to give, she whimpers, her hands finding their way into my hair. I insert my tongue as far as I can reach, my dick growing painfully hard with every sharp breath she takes.

"Shit, baby, don't stop—just like—" She bucks her hips, her grip in my hair tightening to ensure that our connection is not lost.

As if I would ever let that happen. Fuck—she tastes like a dream.

"Sage!"

I reach down and give my dick a few rough strokes as her cunt flutters around my tongue. I've never made her come orally like that, usually paying more attention to her clit, and it's so fucking sexy. It's also proof that my girl really did miss me—her pussy desperate and waiting for my return.

Now she's in luck, 'cause I'm not done with her yet.

Millicent

Before I can catch my breath, Sage is on his feet, his hands wrapped around my hips before he flips me over and tugs me up to my knees. I prop myself up on my forearms and look back at him from over my shoulder, just in time to see his hand descend and smack against my ass.

My pussy pulses greedily, my mouth falling open in a silent O as I arch my back, lifting my ass higher. He smacks my opposite cheek, and my fingers curl around the covers beneath me.

"Fucking hell, I love this ass," he growls, grabbing onto me with both hands.

He smacks my right side again, then my left, rubbing the sting away affectionately, and I can no longer look at him. I want him too much—I want him so much I can hardly *breathe*. If he doesn't fuck me soon, I swear, I might die. I rest my forehead against the bed between my arms, whimpering in desperation before he *slams* his cock inside of me.

I gasp loudly, my head shooting up as I moan, "Sage, *baby!*"

"Shit," he hisses, pounding into me with abandon. "Jesus—you feel so good, baby doll. So goddamn sexy."

The sound of his voice spurs me on and all I want is more. Now that he's here, now that he's inside of me—stretching me open and filling me up—I realize just how much I missed him. It was more than I thought. *This*—our connection, our passion—it's undeniable. It always has been, and I hope with everything I have in me that it always will be. I hope that I always want him; always want this; always want *more*.

"Harder," I groan.

He frees another grunt and I feel it as the bed dips a little. I look back and see that he's planted one foot on the mattress as he rams back inside of me.

"Oh, *fuck*," I cry out—his dick plunging deeper, hitting me at a new angle that sends a rush of tingles throughout my entire core.

"You like that, baby?"

"Yes—*yes*," I pant as he continues to fuck me like only he can—his cock the most magnificent I've ever had.

"Need you to come, doll face. You close?"

"Almost," I answer, my orgasm brewing just below the surface, heating up my entire body.

"Get there, Millie," he demands, reaching around me to rub circles against my clit.

A deep groan spills from my lips, and I bury my face in the covers, attempting to muffle the sound as I get closer and closer to my release. He rubs faster, thrusting harder, and when I feel him start to expand inside of me, my pussy responds immediately. We come together, the sensation so warm, wet, and *perfect.*

He exhales, his foot slipping from the bed as he plants a fist on either side of me, lowering his lips to kiss my bare shoulder. He rocks his hips lazily as he starts to go soft inside of me, and I free a sated sigh.

"Fuck, it's good to be home," he mumbles against my skin.

I smile dreamily, my heart swelling at his words. I know what he means. I'm sure he doesn't think of it the same way I do, but *home* to me is this very moment—Sage and I connected as one body. *This* is home, and I'm so glad to have him back.

He kisses my shoulder again before he slips out of me, breaking our connection. "Don't move, doll face. I'll be right back."

I flop onto my side and watch as he steps into his boxers before heading to my dresser to don his glasses. He sneaks out of my room only to return a moment later, a wet washcloth in his hand.

"Let me clean you up, baby."

I roll onto my back without protest, opening my legs for him. Gently, he rubs the warm cloth over my center and the inside of my thighs, wiping away his release and mine. When he's finished, he crumples up the cloth and tosses it into my hamper before removing his boxers and returning to bed. He kisses my lips, then starts to turn down the sheets, and I move to slip between them as he crawls in beside me. He discards his glasses on my nightstand, turning off the light before he reaches for me. He pulls me close, and I let him, curling myself up against him tightly. When his lips touch mine again, I open up for him immediately. He kisses me slowly, deeply, *lovingly*, and I get lost in him completely.

We don't stay lip-locked for too long, his exhaustion catching up to him quickly. As soon as he pulls away, he silently encourages me to roll away from him, so I do, allowing him to spoon me. He slides a hand up and grabs hold of one of my breasts, tucking his nose in my neck as he begins to grow heavy with sleep.

"I love you," I whisper, my eyes drifting closed.

"Love you, too, gorgeous."

ELEVEN

Millicent

I WAKE TO THE FEEL of Sage's lips as they kiss along my shoulder and then down my arm, all the way to my elbow.

I missed that, too.

Sage's sweet morning kisses are the best. It's my favorite way to wake up. I breathe deeply, curling myself back against him as I slowly start to let sleep fall away from me. He leans into me, slipping a hand beneath my cheek before turning my head so that I'm looking up at him. His icy blue eyes dance around my face, and an amused smirk curls his lips before he presses them against mine.

He pulls away and smiles at me as he asks, "How is it possible that on my first night home, after being on the road and sleeping on a bus for six fucking weeks, you *still* manage to out-sleep me?"

I laugh, my voice thick and husky from slumber. "It's the first day of winter break." I'm interrupted by a yawn, which makes him grin before I finish speaking. "It's practically a requirement to sleep in as late as possible today."

"Well, it's eleven. Is that late enough?"

I flip around and press my body against him, coaxing one of my legs between his so that we're tangled tightly together. "Are you trying to get me out of bed?"

He shakes his head at me, reaching up to run his fingers through my hair. He tucks a few strands behind my ear before his fingers trace along my jaw; then he uses the pad of his thumb to caress my bottom lip. His touch is gentle and I relish every moment of it.

"What are you thinking?" I whisper.

"You're on winter break."

"Yeah."

"So I can have my girl any time I want for the next month."

I fight a smile as I offer him a shallow nod. "Yeah."

"I don't know when our next tour is coming. I hope sooner rather than later. It was one hell of a ride, and I can't wait to do it again. But, *fuck*—it's good to be home."

He rolls his body, taking me with him and pinning me to the bed. I can't suppress the soft moan that escapes through my lips at the feel of his warmth between my legs. He chuckles and then kisses the tip of my nose.

"I hear you, baby. I'll take care of you soon enough."

I nod again. I won't pretend that even after last night, I don't still hunger for him.

My thoughts shift when I hear the jingle of Maestro's dog tags. I turn my head in the direction the sound came from, but I can't see him from where I am.

"He's been out and fed."

I pull my eyebrows together as I focus my gaze back on Sage. "How long have you been awake?"

"'Bout an hour."

"Why didn't you wake me?"

He smiles slyly, and it's so sexy, I feel myself growing slick with arousal just *looking* at him.

"I thought you could use the rest. We're going to have a lot of sex today."

"Oh, really?" I ask, unable to hide my amusement.

"Mmmhmm," he hums before pressing a kiss against my lips.

"M'kay," I mutter into his mouth.

He then pulls away from me and says, "Got dinner tonight at Pep's. You're coming."

A slight frown pulls at my face as I think about the last time I was supposed to show up for dinner at his sister's house. When I open my mouth to express my concern, he shuts me down before I can utter a single syllable.

"I can have my girl any time I want for the next month—you just admitted it, Millie. I want you with me all fucking day, so that means dinner tonight at Pep's. You with me?"

I barely have time to even think about a response before he's kissing me. When I part my lips, his tongue snakes inside of my mouth, and I realize his question wasn't meant to be answered. No matter. As he eases his hardened dick inside of me, I can no longer think of a single reason why I should refuse him. And as he begins to make love to me, I spread my legs wide, signifying that *yes*, I am with him. To deny it would be a lie unworthy of the effort.

Sage

MILLIE AND I spend all day in bed, leaving only to piss and eat. It isn't until five o'clock that we hop in the shower and get cleaned up. I put on the clothes I had on yesterday while Millie gets dressed in a pair of jeans and a plain, V-neck, teal sweater. It sculpts her figure perfectly, reminding me of all that I enjoyed throughout the day. As I watch her pack an overnight bag, I'm already thinking about the ways in which I will have her later. I feel like such a horn-dog, but I could give a fuck. She didn't push me off once today, taking all I had to give and begging for a little bit more.

My gorgeous girl missed my dick as much as my dick missed her.

When she's ready, we stop by my place so I can change my clothes and she can drop off her things. It was her suggestion that we stay here tonight. I honestly don't give a fuck where I sleep, so long as she's with me, but she insisted that I deserved a night in my own space. I didn't argue.

I change into a fresh pair of boxers and jeans, donning a flannel button-up and my black boots. I throw on a beanie for good measure, and then grab my girl and my pup on my way out the door. On our drive to the Montgomery residence, I can practically *feel* Millie's nervous energy. This isn't the first time she'll be around my sisters and my brother-in-law. Why she's so anxious about it, I have no idea.

"Hey," I begin to say, sliding my palm over the top of her hand and lacing our fingers together. I then lift her hand so that it's resting on top of my gear shift and offer her a squeeze. "What's wrong?"

"What? Oh," she shakes her head, as if to clear her mind, and a false smile appears on her face. "I'm fine."

"You're a terrible liar, did you know that?" She doesn't say anything in reply, and I take her silence to mean that she's well aware. "Millicent?" I ask, giving her fingers another squeeze.

"I know you want to pretend that it doesn't matter, but the last time I was invited to your sister's house, I refused to go—and then *you* didn't go."

"Water under the bridge, doll face."

"Maybe Rosemary feels that way, but Pepper—"

"Baby, it'll be fine. I swear. Was Pepper pissed that she didn't get to send me off? Yes. Was she disappointed that she didn't get the chance to spend some quality time with you? Yeah. But that was six weeks ago, and we're on our way over right now. It's all good, Millie. Just relax."

"She wanted to spend quality time with me?" she asks, her tone full of surprise.

"Of course," I reply with a shrug. "Why wouldn't she?"

"I don't know," she murmurs.

"My sisters mean the world to me, you know that. We're really close. It's not one sided; they feel the same way about me."

"Yeah, I know. I've seen it."

I bark out a short laugh and shake my head at her. "You've gotten a small dose, doll. They'll both be all over your ass soon enough."

"Wait, what?" she squeaks.

"You're with me now, Millie—and I'm not fucking letting go. Once they see that—like, *really* see that—they won't just let you be my girlfriend. You'll belong to them, too. You'll be family, baby."

Suddenly, she tries pulling her hand out from beneath mine. I grip her fingers tighter, chancing a glance in her direction. I can see the look of fear on her face as she tries to pull away from me again.

"No," I declare. "Don't you fucking dare, doll face." I focus my eyes back on the road, but I can feel it when her eyes shift to look at me. "Don't pull away from me. We're done with that shit."

"What if—?"

"You're my girl. I'm your guy, remember? We go together. You don't need to worry about *what if*."

"Sage, I don't know how to do this," she whispers as I turn into their neighborhood.

"Do what?"

She pauses for a few seconds before she answers. "*Family*."

I think of all that I know about her and her family—or the lack there of. I know her mom's a bitch, and her dad's a fuck-face who left when she was just a kid; I know she's an only child, and I know that in order to find her happiness, she needed to move across the country from the woman who gave birth to her and then made her life a living hell. I know the facts, but I'm big enough to admit that I don't have a single clue what that life feels like.

Besides my two sisters, Harry, my nephews and my niece—my parents have siblings, and I've got dozens of cousins. They're scattered all over the country, but we all saw each other from time to time when I was growing up. All I know is family. Even though my parents and I don't see eye to eye on just about anything, I still love them. I still see them. Not as often as my sisters, but still.

"Listen to me, baby doll, it's going to be fine. Trust me. You don't have to *do* anything; just be yourself. That's the thing about family—the good ones accept you for who you are. My family's not perfect, but we're a pretty good one. Besides," I pause for a second, parking my car along the sidewalk in front of our destination. I kill the engine and then turn and direct my full attention onto my girl. "I love you," I remind her. "That automatically earns you brownie points with them."

She sighs, looking over her shoulder at the big house we're about to go into. When she doesn't say anything, I reach over and cup my hand around her cheek, turning her face back toward mine. I lean in to kiss her lips, and she instantly relaxes into me, kissing me in return. I tease her mouth open with my tongue, but I keep it sweet, not wishing to get too carried away in front of my sister's house.

Once I feel as though I've kissed away some of Millie's nerves, I pull away and remind her, "I love you."

"I love you, too, baby."

"All right then. Let's do this."

She inhales deeply, blows out her breath in a big sigh, and then offers me a slight nod. I smirk at her and then reach to swipe Maestro from out of the back seat. I set him down outside and he follows Millie and me up the driveway and to the front door. I'm just getting ready to knock when my older sister appears with a huge-ass grin on her face.

"You're *home!*" she cries before she barrels toward me. I catch her in an embrace, laughing as she squeezes me tight. "Shit," she whispers, pulling away from me just seconds later, backing up into the house. Maestro takes her lead, stepping inside and making himself at home— no doubt, searching for activity. "No shoes," says Pepper, pulling me from my thoughts. I look down at her socked feet and shake my head at her. "Well? Get in here where it's warm. Hi, Millie!"

I smile at my gorgeous girl, reaching for her hand. She laces her fingers with mine as our eyes lock, and I offer her a wink, as if to say, *I told you so.* She smiles back at me and I can tell she's still a little freaked, but not as much as she was a few minutes ago.

"Uncle Sage!" I hear Henley before I see him come flying around the corner in his grippy-socked feet.

"Hey, buddy," I reply as he comes crashing into my legs.

"Did you miss me?" he demands to know.

"You bet I did!"

When I hear the sound of a little gasp, I look up and spot Carter peeking his head into the entryway. He then hurries toward me, working his arms almost as fast as his legs. As he comes to a stop in front of me, he doesn't hug me, but holds up his palms and says, "Su-pwise!"

Pepper giggles, looking lovingly at her youngest son, and I can't help but laugh, too.

"Surprise?" I ask him.

"He's just a tad bit early. But we were practicing," Pepper says endearingly. "Good job, Carter!"

"Uncle Sage?" asks Henley, tugging at my coat.

"What's up?" I reach down and ruffle his hair, but he steps away from me, making quick work of smoothing his soft, blonde strands back to right with this little hands. When his eyes dart up to catch a glimpse of Millie before they dart back on me, I have to fight a laugh. "Oh, I see—you want to know who the pretty girl is, huh?"

He tugs at the bottom of his shirt, curling it over his arms and revealing his little belly.

"Keep your clothes on, kid," I chuckle, leaning down to help him out. "She's a taken woman."

"What does that mean?" he asks, looking between the two of us once more.

"Means you've got to get your own, squirt."

"Don't listen to Uncle Sage," Pepper jumps in, moving to stand behind him. She rests her hands on his shoulders as he twists his neck to gaze up at her, but she's too busy glaring at me. "He's *four*," she states, as if I need reminding. Before I can say another word, she kneels down between her boys and points to Millie. "This is Sage's friend, Millie. Can you say *hi?*"

"Hi, Millie," Henley murmurs bashfully.

"Hi, Miwwie." Carter is more brave with his hello, stepping toward her and waving wildly.

"Hi. It's nice to meet you," Millie replies.

Pepper grins and then asks, "Can you tell her your name?"

"Cartoor," Carter proclaims proudly.

Millie giggles, and I can tell Henley wants in on the action.

"I'm Henley," he announces.

"I like that name."

He blushes, and it's so fucking cute.

"Okay, boys, go keep Maestro company for a few minutes until dinner is ready. Go on, scoot." They obey, hunting for their favorite furry friend, and Pepper stands to her feet with a contented sigh. "Get those coats off, you two. You're staying a while."

Millicent

SAGE HELPS ME out of my coat, heading to the coat closet to my immediate right in order to hang it up. As he stows his away too, I can't help but notice how the rack is just about jam-packed, filled with coats of all different types and sizes. I also glance down along the bottom, spotting a wicker basket full of an array of snow gear; little boots, gloves, hats, scarves and snowsuits, ready and waiting for the next snowfall.

"Look who's home." I recognize the voice that steals my attention, and my gaze falls on Harry as he makes his way toward us. He's exactly as I remembered—well built with blonde hair, blue eyes, and a sexy-stubbled chin—only, now he has a baby all pretty in pink tucked into the crook of his arm.

"*There's* my sweet girl," says Sage, closing the closet door before meeting Harry halfway. He reaches for his niece without a single hint of hesitation, cuddling her in his arms as he leans down to kiss her forehead. "D-a-m-n, what are your parents feeding you, Soph? You're getting so big."

"She'll be five months, soon," says Harry before he looks around Sage and offers me a wave. "Hi, Millie."

"Hi, Harry."

"Come on in," Pepper insists with a wave. "Can I offer you a drink, Millie? Water? Milk? Hot cocoa?" As she lists my options, she leads us all further into the house. Unlike the last time I saw her, she's dressed down this evening. There's no makeup coloring her brown eyes, and her shoulder-length, dark auburn hair is pulled up into a ponytail. Regardless of her change in appearance, she's still really beautiful. Between her and Harry, it's no wonder their children are so incredibly adorable.

"If you couldn't tell, she's used to entertaining toddlers. We also have wine and beer," offers Harry.

"Water will be fine," I assure them both.

"Just opened a bottle of red, Millie!" Rosemary's voice floats from the kitchen. I spot her at the counter with two glasses of wine, her back to us as we approach. "Pep is breastfeeding, Harry is a beer guy, and Sage is a toss-up depending on the menu, so it's you and me. And since it's a rare occurrence that my siblings even *let* me drink, I'm taking full advantage; but I'm not doing it alone. I'm pouring you a glass."

"She can be a bit bossy," Sage stage-whispers. "You'll get used to it."

"Oh, shut it," she grumbles. Two seconds later, she turns and flashes her brother the most brilliant smile. "I think, since I only got to see you for two seconds last night, I have the right to another attack hug."

"You'll crush my Sophia," he warns, angling his body away from her as he gently places a hand around the back of Sophia's little head.

She rolls her eyes and then points at me. "Has Millie met Sophia? I'm sure she could hold her for a minute, right Millie?"

In an instant, my hands grow clammy in anxiety. I look to Sage and shake my head, silently insisting that he need not surrender the precious bundle into my care.

"You don't want to meet Soph?" he asks, as if the very idea of my refusal is terribly offensive.

I look to Pepper and then Harry, noting the way they eye me with curiosity before I shift my gaze back onto Sage. "I don't want to hurt her," I admit timidly.

"She's not as fragile as you might think," Pepper tells me. "You're welcome to hold her, if you'd like."

When Sage starts to step toward me, I take a step back, my stomach a mess of nerves.

"Millie?" he asks, scowling in confusion.

I feel like all eyes are on me. Probably because they are. In this very moment, I realize that I've been in the house all of five minutes, and the impression I'm making is taking a nose dive. Uncertain how else to get out of this awkward situation, I decide to tell the truth.

"I've never held a baby before," I blurt out.

"*Never?*" Rose gasps. I shake my head and her brilliant smile returns. "It's magical. I mean, no, it's not always rainbows and sunshine; sometimes it's spit-up and exploding diapers—but there's nothing like holding that warm, tiny body against yours. Right, Pep?"

Pepper smiles at me before she says, "Not everyone likes babies. To that I say, to each his own. I, on the other hand, still think holding her is one of the best feelings in the world—and she's my third."

"What do you say, doll face? Should we let Sophia pop that cherry?"

"Sage!" Rose mutters in disgust, smacking his arm.

Sage only chuckles before taking another step toward me. This time, I don't back away.

"What if I drop her?" I whisper, my hands trembling.

"You won't, baby. Hold out your arms."

I do as he says and he turns Sophia so that she's facing me. She looks at me curiously, which only makes me more apprehensive as Sage props her up against my chest. Instinctively, my body wraps around hers—one arm beneath her little booty, one hand pressed against her back. She turns and looks at Sage, as if to ask him why he passed her off, and then her head twists in my direction. Her body jerks as she looks at me, and I tighten my hold around her, afraid of losing my grip of her wiggling body.

She shifts her attention to my hair, her tiny fingers grabbing a fistful, as if it's the most fascinating sight she's ever seen. Then she sneezes. Her whole body jolts and she tugs at the strands. I don't mind. The little noise of her sneeze is too cute, and it makes me giggle. She shoots her eyes up at me at the sound, and then she smiles at me. Suddenly, I'm completely in love with her.

"See? You're a natural."

It isn't until I hear Pepper's voice that I realize the room has fallen completely silent. When I look up, I see that Sage has backed away from me, and he's now holding his sister against his side—both of her arms wrapped around his waist as she smiles at me. Harry offers me an encouraging smile when my eyes find his, and Pepper looks quite pleased.

Sophia tugs at my hair again, winning my full attention. I rub her back gently, and she continues to play with my hair until a loud round of little-boy laughter fills her ears. Her head pops up, knowing exactly who those voices belong to, and then she squeals in delight.

"Sage, why don't you show Millie to the table. She can hold Sophia while we serve dinner and get the boys ready to eat."

"You got it. It's through here, doll face." He takes two steps and then stops. "You guys," he says, turning to grin at his sisters. "You didn't have to do all this."

Very carefully, I close the distance between us in an attempt to see what he's talking about. On the other side of the counter is their kitchen table, set up to accommodate all of us. Above the bay windows hangs a handmade banner with words strung together that say, *Welcome Home Sage!* It's very colorful, and I can tell that some of the letters were filled in by a couple of young artists.

"Surprise!" Rose replies with a chuckle.

"This is why I love you. Star treatment, right here," he says, making his way around the counter. I follow him and he pulls out a chair for me on the opposite side of the table, below the banner. As soon as I sit, Rosemary appears with my glass of wine. She puts it down in front of me with a wink.

"Just because you're on baby duty doesn't mean you can't sip. Only, maybe don't share— 'cause, you know, backwash," she teases before she breezes back into the kitchen.

"See, what'd I tell you?" Sage murmurs into my ear. "You're doing great, baby."

He presses a kiss against my temple and I close my eyes for a second, relishing this very moment. When he pulls away, leaving me at the table to go round up his nephews, I let myself relax a little bit. The truth is, he *was* right. His family is pretty great. From the oldest down to the youngest, they've welcomed me as if I belong. I'm not certain that I do—I've never really belonged anywhere—but I have to admit, right now, I don't want to be anywhere else.

TWELVE

Sage

After dinner, we abandon the dishes and head into the living room so that the boys can play while we hang out. Conversation while we were at the table was all about the tour—what I had seen and experienced during my six weeks away. When we settled into the comfortable couches and overstuffed armchairs in the next room, Pepper shifted conversation in Millie's direction.

The first and only time Pepper was in the company of my girl, we were at The Brew Cycle for one of my shows. The environment was loud, the crowd and live music making it difficult for her to really get a chance to chat with Millie. I know how much she's been looking forward to a night like tonight. It's been a long time since I've claimed anyone as my girlfriend. The fact that Millie and I have been seeing each other for almost three months now says a whole lot. My sisters know it—and so do I.

Pepper starts off innocently enough, asking Millie about her job and what she likes best about teaching. Millie's answers are simple and straight forward. I watch her as she speaks, realizing that she doesn't talk about being a professor like I talk about Mountains & Men. She's an advocate for higher learning, though I know she doesn't judge me for being the college drop-out that I am. She's got a thing for numbers, and she's obviously good with them, but teaching them isn't her passion.

I wonder what her dreams are. I wonder what drives her, my gorgeous girl.

It's not the first time I've wondered about it. In fact, I remember asking her once, and she didn't know the answer herself. I know there must be something that lays dormant inside of her—something that gives her life purpose and brings her happiness. *Everyone* dreams of something.

"What about your family? What are they like? Do they live around here?" Pepper asks casually, pulling me from my thoughts.

Fuck.

I actually *see* it as Millie shrinks back into the sofa at the mention of her parents. *That* right there—*that's* what's buried the dreamer inside of her. Her spirit has been crushed by the people who were supposed to love and encourage her. My parent's aren't in favor of my life choices, but they fostered my passion for music all my life. In a way, it's their fault that I want the things that I want. It's their fault that I dream as big as I do. They might not know it, but it is. For Millie—it's the exact opposite.

I reach over and take hold of her hand. Her fingers grip mine tightly in return.

"Uh-oh," Pepper murmurs. "Sore subject?"

"I don't really know my father. He left when I was young," Millie confesses, her gaze locked on our hands resting in her lap. "My mom lives in New Jersey. That's where I'm from. We don't get along."

"Yikes," says Rosy. "I think that's *definitely* a sore subject."

"Hey, babe," Harry begins to say as he stands. "How about we save the rest of the inquisition for another time? I'll put the boys down while you see to Sophia, and then Sage can tell us more about this label deal."

"We'll take care of the kitchen while you're upstairs," pipes in Rosy as she gets up to deliver goodnight kisses to Henley and Carter.

Pepper agrees, and the boys offer a very reluctant farewell. I let Maestro out back, and by the time I join the ladies in the kitchen, Millie's already busy rinsing and loading the dishwasher while Rosy clears the table. I stand at the kitchen's entrance, listening as Rosy chats idly with my girl about the end of her semester and what classes she intends to take next spring. Millie asks a couple of questions in reply, and Rosy is more than happy to answer. I know she's loving this night just as much as Pepper is.

I won't lie. I fucking love all of it.

Feels good to know that Millicent fits in with the people I'm closest to. It's not that I doubted she would—but believing and *seeing* are two different things. I fall for her a little harder in this very moment, and I know without a doubt that what I told her earlier is *fact*. I'm not fucking letting her go.

Having withstood the distance between us for too long, I enter the kitchen, coming up behind her as I wrap my arms around her waist. I pull her back against me tightly and then reach up to move her hair away from her neck so I can kiss her there.

"Sage," she states, as if my affection in present company embarrasses her.

She twists enough to look up at me, and I smile as I inform her, "I need a taste."

"I don't think right now's—"

"Doll face," I murmur, bringing my lips closer to hers. "I *need* a taste."

I dart my tongue out, licking her bottom lip, and she sucks in a quiet breath, leaning back against me. "You're not playing fair," she whispers, her eyes traveling down to my lips and then back up to my eyes.

"I know," I chuckle, grazing my nose along hers.

"Go for it, Millie," says Rosy, totally interrupting us. "I've seen you two…well, I'm just saying, I can handle a little lip action."

Millie groans softly, turning away from me and busying herself with the dishes.

"The fuck, Rosy?" I ask with a glare. "I'm going to need you to stop finding excuses to bring that shit up."

"Geez. I just meant—" I scowl at her, and she breaks off her sentence with a huff before she furrows her brow at me. "Ugh. You're annoying," she says, stomping into the next room.

When we're alone, I give Millie a squeeze around her middle. She ignores me, closing the dishwasher before wiping her hands on a nearby towel.

"Hey, sorry about that. She's—"

"She was traumatized," Millie states, spinning around to face me. "I'm sure you would be, too, if you walked in on her fucking someone in the middle of the day."

"Whoa—don't put that shit in my head, baby doll. And Rosy better not be fucking *anyone*, let alone in the middle of the afternoon."

"All I'm saying is, it's probably, unfortunately, an image that's etched into her memory for the foreseeable future. Let's try not to give her more ammunition." She tries moving out of my grasp, but I hold her tighter, earning me a quirked eyebrow as her dark green eyes blaze with irritation.

Fuck, if it doesn't make my dick jump.

"Wasn't going to rip your clothes off in the middle of my sister's kitchen, baby—but I sure as fuck need a taste, *right now.*"

"Sage—"

I slide my hands down around her ass, giving her a squeeze while simultaneously pressing her against the semi hidden in my pants. The look in her eyes softens just a little—just enough. I lean in and kiss her hard before she can attempt to move away from me again. I force my tongue into her mouth, and she sighs into mine as her hands reach up to grip the fabric of my shirt at my sides. The longer we kiss, the harder my dick becomes, but I don't stop. She feels so damn good.

"Incoming," Pepper announces. I pull away from Millie as my sister enters the kitchen. She takes one look at us and laughs softly, shaking her head as she turns back toward the living room. "I would invite you to rejoin us when you're done making out, but from the looks of things, we might be waiting all night."

Millie yanks her hands away from me and runs her fingers through her hair, pulling the long strands to one shoulder before she starts to go after my sister.

"Baby," I say, stopping her with another squeeze of her ass.

"I don't know why I let you kiss me like that here."

"I do," I reply with a sly smile, dipping my head to kiss the soft spot behind her ear. "And there's more where that came from when I get you in my bed, doll face."

She shivers and I chuckle before kissing her once more. When I lift my head to look into her eyes, her expression is gentle. I slide my hands up, pulling her against my chest as I hold her tight.

"We can be exactly who we are here, baby. They wouldn't have it any other way. So I'll kiss you any time I want, any way I want. You taste good, Millie," I whisper, bringing my lips to hers. "Needed a quick fix."

"Sage," she breathes, reaching up to wrap her arms around my neck. She pushes herself up on her tiptoes and tightens her grip, burying her face beneath my chin.

"What is it, baby?"

She shakes her head but holds me tighter. I'm not sure what she's feeling, but I like the way she's wrapped around me, so I let her have her moment. When she finally pulls away from me, I see that her eyes are glassy. I frown in concern, but she shakes her head once more before kissing my cheek and stepping away from me. I let her go and she reaches for my hand, leading me back into the living room.

Millicent

As I DRAG SAGE after me into the next room, I envision the look on Pepper's face when she came into the kitchen a moment ago. Then, when Sage and I return to our seats on the unbelievably comfortable sofa in the Montgomery living room, I look over and see it again. It's as if her knowing smile hasn't left. Hasn't and probably *won't* until someone speaks, drawing her attention elsewhere.

I breathe a small sigh of relief when Rose says something. Though, I don't know what it is. My mind is still back in the kitchen; my thoughts are still swirling around what Sage said to me...

"We can be exactly who we are here, baby."

I force in a deep breath and lean into Sage's side, curling my legs up beside me. He smirks at me, unaware of the ache in my chest, and then he wraps his arm around my shoulders and holds me close.

I'm overwhelmed.

Rosemary has, inadvertently, seen me riding her brother's dick; Pepper has now seen me, a first time guest in her beautiful home, making out with him in her kitchen. While one is certainly less embarrassing than the other, neither of them has taken the opportunity to think *less* of me. To them, I'm not a whore or a stupid girl—I'm the woman in love with their brother.

"We can be exactly who we are here, baby."

I could never do this with my mother. I can never take Sage to Jersey and introduce him to the only blood relative I know. We wouldn't be able to sit cuddled together on my mother's couch, talking and laughing about everything—about *nothing*. She wouldn't be kind to him, and she definitely wouldn't be kind to me. And for reasons I cannot adequately explain, being here, now, in the company of Sage's siblings, I just want to cry.

"We can be exactly who we are here, baby."

Here—here is *home*. At Sage's side, in his arms, I'm *home*. And when I'm home, I can be exactly who I am; whether that be here, with his family by blood, or with the band, his family by choice. It doesn't matter how different we are. It doesn't matter what each of us has been through in our pasts. I'm accepted by these people—*all* of them—without judgment or condemnation.

I can love Sage as much as I want, as much as I do, *and that love will not be damned.*

I slip my arm around his stomach, holding onto his side, needing to feel close to my dreamer in order to keep myself together. He tilts his head and looks at me—*studies* me—trying to figure out what's wrong. Of course. That's Sage, capable of reading me and understanding me better than anyone I've ever met.

"You okay, doll?" He asks so softly that I'm sure only I can hear him.

"I will be," I whisper back.

"Tell me later?"

"Yeah," I barely manage.

He dips his head in a nod and then presses his lips against my forehead. I try immersing myself into the conversation in the room.

"I want to know more about Potential Records," says Harry, leaning forward as he rests his elbows against his knees. "How does this whole thing work?"

"I'm sure there's a bunch of logistical shit that needs to be ironed out, but I'll know more about that on Monday. We're heading down to Boulder to meet Greg, the owner, and we'll go from there. Stefany's done her research, though. Apparently this guy's dad is a big time producer in the music biz. He started Potential Records because he didn't like how the bigger labels were handling their bands—changing their sound and shit.

"Anyway, he seems to know what he's doing, and he likes our music. Stef says she hopes that we'll have a single off of our new album ready to release in January."

"Oh, my gosh, this is *so* cool," Pepper chirps with a wide grin.

"That, big sis, is a fucking *understatement*," laughs Sage.

"So, does this mean your days with Brandon at Little Bird Café are over?" asks Rose.

"Actually, I need to talk to him about that. I know December is a crazy month for him, because he does a lot more baking—doing special orders and shit. I was going to see if I could help out until the New Year; then, yeah—I've got a little money saved up, but hopefully Mountains & Men gets some regular gigs. Stefany is a badass, and we're her top priority right now, so I'm not worried."

"And you're going to fill mom and dad in about all of this…when?" Pepper asks, eyeing him warily.

"I'll tell them soon," he replies with a nonchalant shrug.

"Soon as in—*before* Christmas?" asks Rose.

"Sage, I swear to god, if you don't tell them your plans before Christmas—"

"You guys, I'm a grown-ass man. I don't need to answer to my parents."

Harry chuckles and all eyes fall on him. He shakes his head, lifting up his hands as if to ward off our questioning stares. "Not saying you're wrong, Sage—but even *I* get grilled by your old man."

"Exactly!" says Pepper, pointing at her husband.

"You guys," Sage starts with a groan.

"Just don't ruin Christmas, big bro. *Please?* Please talk to them before Christmas."

I peek up at Sage as he tilts his head back, resting it against the top of the couch. He frees a heavy sigh and then levels his gaze once more. "Fine," he mumbles.

"Great. You have fifteen days," announces Pepper. "Oh, and speaking of days until Christmas—we're putting our tree up tomorrow night. We've been waiting for you, and the boys are getting antsy. Millie," she says, her facial expression softening when her gaze meets mine. "You're more than welcome to join us."

"You *want* to join us," Rose insists, leaning forward to look around Sage at me. "Pepper makes peppermint hot chocolate, and Harry pops a boatload of popcorn. He makes *the best* popcorn. He seasons half of it for us to eat, and then we string up the rest and put it on the tree."

"Just a little tradition the four of us started after Harry and I got married," Pepper informs, smiling at her siblings before reaching over to kiss her husband's cheek.

"We welcome the strays, so Henley and Carter are in on the action. This will be Sophia's first year—so you wouldn't be the only newbie." Harry teases.

"What do you say, doll face? You with us?"

I pull my bottom lip between my teeth, biting down hard as I try my damnedest not to cry. I haven't cared about Christmas in over twenty years. As a kid, and even now, it simply serves as an excuse to get some time away from school. I'm well aware how *abnormal* that is. People go crazy over the holiday—or crazy *because* of the holiday. Nonetheless, I never was one who latched onto the festiveness of the season. Now, I'm being invited into a Christmas tradition. Something special. Suddenly, the magic of Christmas doesn't seem like such a foreign concept.

I look up at Sage, knowing that he'll help me keep it together. I can see his encouraging smile in his icy blue eyes, and it's as if he's caressing my heart, reminding me that it's in his care and he's not letting go.

"Yes," I murmur with a nod. "I would love to come."

THIRTEEN

Millicent

It's after eleven by the time we leave Harry and Pepper's house. The nerves that I felt upon entering their abode are so far gone, I barely remember them. In their place are a dozen other emotions. Love. Excitement. Anticipation. Curiosity. Apprehension. Fear. Doubt—to name just a few. As we exit the neighborhood, Maestro sitting poised in my lap as he stares into the night, curiosity fights its way to the top of the list.

"Earlier, when Pepper and Rose were talking about you telling your parents about your plans, were they exaggerating, or will your parents really freak out that much?"

He coughs out a humorless laugh before he answers. "On a scale of *We-don't-care* to *What-in-the-world-are-you-thinking?*, when they find out I intend to quit LB to pursue music full time, they will lose their shit—putting them at *What-the-fuck?*"

"At this point, it honestly can't be a surprise, can it?" I ask, not understanding how their reaction could be expected to be so intense. "You just got back from a nationwide tour. They must know you're serious."

"Millie, my parents are still holding onto the hope that this is just a phase."

"A phase," I deadpan. "A *five-year* phase? A five-year phase, during which you have made *major* life-altering decisions? A five-year phase that you've continuously expressed *isn't* a phase at all?"

"God, I love you," he laughs.

I look at him, unsure why he finds the state of his parents' denial amusing.

"So, what will they say? What kind of argument will you have? It's not as if they support you financially."

"You're right, they don't—a fact that I will remind them of when they lose their shit. They worry too much. They'll be all up my ass about losing my one steady source of income. They'll gripe at me about how reality is going to come *knocking on my door* and they won't be there to clean up my mess because I'm *grown*—which, I will then argue, is *exactly* my point. It's also bullshit. *Not* that I'm ever going to fail and need their help anyway, but even if by some chance I *did* need them, they wouldn't hesitate to help me. It's just a scare tactic—one they've been trying to use since I was nineteen."

I shake my head, knowing good and well that my opinion is bias, but also recognizing that Sage is a man worthy of my faith. I've seen him on that stage more than a few times, and I know that he's someone to believe in.

"They haven't even seen you perform. How can they argue so adamantly when they don't have all the facts?"

"They just do, doll face. Pepper says they're afraid."

"Of what?"

I hear the rustling of his coat as he lifts and drops his shoulders in a shrug. "The unknown. The unpredictable. I'm their wildcard—the course I've taken has never lined up with whatever plan they had for me in their minds. I guess it leaves them unsettled."

I grow silent, letting his words sink in. My mother didn't have a plan for my life. She barely had a plan for hers. I didn't disappoint her because she had no expectations for me at all—except for me to remember that men ruin everything, love is not worth a damn, and that life is *not* what you make it; rather, you are its victim. When I didn't live according to her views, I don't think it was *disappointment* she felt so much as *disgust.*

Deep down, if I allow myself to think about it, I believe that she's always been jealous of me—jealous of the life ahead of me when I was a child; jealous of my freedom when I left Jersey; jealous of my success or any potential relationships. She's a deeply unhappy woman, but I'm beyond the point of being able to feel sorry for her.

I may not understand why Sage's parents think the way they think, but even Sage admits that he loves them and they love him; that if anything were to happen and he needed their help, he could rely on them. They might be a pain in the ass to deal with, but they are probably a walk in the park compared to my mother.

"When will you talk to them?" I ask softly, breaking the silence between us.

"I don't know. Maybe next weekend sometime. It's best to come at them with as much info as possible, so I definitely want to wait until after our meeting with the label on Monday."

"That's smart."

"Enough about my parents," he grunts, reaching over to run his hand over my hair. He stops when his hand reaches the back of my neck and gives me a slight squeeze before he lets me go. "Did you have fun tonight?"

"Yeah," I answer honestly.

"Good. Get used to it. They'll want you around a lot."

"They will?" I ask, surprised by the hopeful note in my tone.

"Baby—you were invited to put up the Christmas tree with us. That means they think you're the shit and they want you around."

I shift my gaze out the window, feeling oddly bashful about the smile that pulls at my lips.

"I like them, too," I say quietly.

"Glad to hear it, gorgeous." He pulls into the vacant spot in his driveway and shuts off his car before looking over at me. "You head on in. I'll stay out while Maestro does his business and meet you upstairs."

"Okay." I get out of the car, setting Maestro down, and hurry in out of the cold.

The television is on in the sitting room. As I step away from the door, I peek over at the couch to see who's here. Violet is cuddled up against JJ, sleeping, and Derrick is stretched out on the adjacent sofa.

"Hey, Millie," greets JJ when he spots me.

"Hi," I reply with a wave.

Derrick jerks his chin up at me before he asks, "What's up? Want to chill?"

I offer them both a smile as I shake my head *no*, and I feel it as my ultra sensitive emotions trigger my tears. Obviously, I've had an exhausting night. I'm no longer capable of keeping myself in control. The joy I feel in this moment is too overwhelming, and I need to hurry upstairs before I embarrass myself.

"No, thanks," I murmur, backing my way to the stairs. "I think Sage and I are just going to head to bed."

"Cool," says Derrick.

"Night," JJ calls.

"Goodnight," I whisper, turning to rush up the stairs.

I make it all the way to Sage's room, closing the door softly behind me before I let the tears fall.

Sage

I come to a stop in front of my bedroom door, scrunching my brow as I lean in to see if I'm hearing correctly. When I hear her sniff, I swing open the door and there she is—my gorgeous girl, sitting on the edge of my bed, her face buried in her hands as she cries.

What the fuck?

I close the door behind me gently. When the door latches shut, her head shoots up. Before I can utter a single word, she's on her feet, running toward me. She wraps her arms around my waist, burying her face in my chest, and my heart pounds loudly in my ears.

"Millie? What happened?" I ask, closing my arms around her as I press my lips against her hair. She shakes her head at me as she continues to cry, and I'm taken back to a few hours before. She was acting strange at Pepper's, too. She told me she'd tell me what was up later.

Well, later is now, *and I need to know—what the fuck?*

"Baby, you're freaking me out."

At my confession, she lifts her head and presses herself up on her tiptoes so that she can reach for a kiss. She puckers her lips and I lean down the short distance to give her what she wants.

"I'm sorry," she mumbles as she continues to kiss me. "Don't be freaked out, baby."

"Millie…" I pull my mouth from hers, bringing my hands up to hold her face, brushing away her tears with my thumbs. "You're crying and I don't know why. Don't tell me not to be freaked."

"I'm fine. I promise. I'm *happy*," she stutters, tears still leaking from her eyes.

"*This* is you happy?"

"Sage," she cries, burying her face underneath my chin. "I don't know how to explain it. I've never had what you're giving me. Not ever. No sisters. No babies. No adorable nephews. No friends to come home to. I don't remember the last time I helped anyone decorate a Christmas tree." She sucks in a shuddered breath, her hands gripping two fistfuls of my jacket, as if she can't get close enough. "I was happy to just have *you*—but it's like tonight, tonight I realized that you aren't *you* without all of them. And loving you means I get everything that comes with you. It *terrifies me*, but not because I don't want it—it's because I *do*. And I didn't know how much I wanted it until tonight."

My chest grows tight as I listen to her cry. Her reaction shocks me, but the reason behind it doesn't. It makes me angry. It makes me angry that the simple things in life, the things and the people that often get taken for granted every day, she doesn't know the beauty of them.

At the same time, it makes me incredibly proud that *I* can be the one to give her these things. Now, more than ever, I want to give her *everything*.

"Millicent," I hum into her hair. "Millie, baby, look at me."

It takes her a second to calm down enough to pull away in order to meet my gaze. I wipe away her tears once more, staring down into her pretty green eyes, knowing that the woman in my arms is giving just as much to me as she thinks I'm giving her. I'm one lucky, motherfucking bastard.

"I forgot what *home* felt like," she speaks before I can, her voice husky and sexy as hell. "Or maybe—maybe I never knew. Not until you. You're my home, Sage—you're my home, and I love you so much."

Her words *wreck me*.

Whatever I might have said before, it can't compare to that. *Nothing* I say can match that. Abso-fucking-lutlely *nothing*. So I don't say anything at all. Instead, I close my eyes and press my forehead against hers. After a moment, I slip my hands into her coat and ease it off of her shoulders. She drops her arms, allowing the garment to fall to the floor. I discard mine, too, and then reach for the hem of her sweater. She helps me pull it off and then reaches for the bottom of my shirt as I toss my glasses onto my dresser. Slowly, we help each other undress until we're both completely bare. Then I reach for her face and lower my mouth to hers. I kiss her gently at first, and then her words replay in my head. I realize that tonight she's given me *all* of her. Somehow I know, there are no longer any barriers between us. No secrets. No fears. It's just her and me.

She's mine. Wholly. Completely. All fucking mine.

I kiss her deeper, groaning as I wrap my arms around her middle, bending down to crush her against my chest. She whimpers, snaking her arms around my neck as her tongue tangles with mine. My dick is stiff and anxious, and when I stand to my full height and lift her from her feet, she brings her legs up and circles them around me. Her pussy now fully exposed, I don't hesitate to reach down and guide my way in.

"*Sage*," she moans as I grab hold of her waist, easing her all the way over my dick.

"Millicent—*fuck*—I love you too, baby. You're all I want."

She squeezes her legs, trying to pull herself closer, and I know what she needs. I walk her to the bed, my dick easing out and in with every step. When I lay her down across my bed, I'm careful not to sever our connection. As I begin to pump in and out of her, she pulls me down to kiss me.

We devour each other fervently, both of us trying to say what words could never express. It's a hard, wet, deep, and wild kiss. When she sucks on my bottom lip, I thrust into her a little harder, unable to stop myself. She sighs, freeing my lip, and I pound into her harder still.

"Mmmm, yes—more, baby."

I increase my pace, ramming into her until I'm balls deep. Her legs squeeze my waist as she arches her back, her mouth falling open in silent pleasure.

"Millicent, fuck, you're so goddamn beautiful."

"Say it again—my name," she pleads, breathlessly.

"Millicent," I groan.

She whimpers, calling out, "Sage—*yes!*"

She feels so damn good, her pussy slick, tight, and swollen, hugging my dick just right. Her hands are everywhere, tracing over each and every one of my tattoos. Every sound she makes brings me closer and closer to orgasm, but I hold on, keeping my shit together, wanting this to last.

It's not long before we're both covered in sweat, the room heavy with the scent of her sweet arousal. She smells incredible, and it turns me on even more. I reach down and grab a palm full of her ass, squeezing the flesh as I continue to take all that I want—all that she gives me. There's something indescribable happening between us. It's not so gentle as love, but it's not as animalistic as just sex, either. Every thrust, every grunt and moan, every whimper and sigh, every touch—it's greedy, it's passionate, and it's fucking delicious. Whatever it is, it's something I've never had with anyone. I know with all my heart that I'll never find it with anyone else—and I sure as hell intend to hang the fuck onto *this*.

When I can't hold back any longer, I lower my lips so that they're pressed against her ear, and I fuck her good and sweet as I whisper, "You're my best girl, Millicent. My *only* girl, baby. Come for me, gorgeous." Then, as I flick her lobe with my tongue, I slide my hand away from her ass and in between us, reaching for her clit. I barely graze the surface and she cries out loudly, her swollen center clenching my dick. I come seconds later, driving in and out of her slowly as I fill her with my seed.

I release my weight on top of her, needing just a second to catch my breath, and she runs her fingers through my hair. When I start to move, her whole body locks around mine in protest.

"No. Not yet. Please? Don't go."

I tilt my head down to graze my lips against her shoulder before I assure her, "I won't fucking dare."

FOURTEEN

Millicent

THERE AREN'T MANY DAYS IN my past that I cling to. I don't have a lot of memories that I deem important enough to cherish. Even my most significant milestones have been tarnished, knowing that I didn't have anyone I loved or anyone that loved me there to celebrate with me. Some things I remember against my will—glimpses of my childhood, moments I wish I could forget. But yesterday I will hold dear, filled with memories I wish never to forget.

Sage and I were up for hours Saturday night, loving, fucking, and worshipping each other's bodies. Including the marathon we had had earlier in the day, I'm sure I've never had so much sex in a twenty-four hour period. Not that I had anything to complain about. As always, he took very good care of me, owning every single one of my orgasms.

Sunday morning was spent sleeping. I was woken by his sweet kisses in the early afternoon. He had made us breakfast in bed—a stack of grilled cheese sandwiches. We laid around, eating until we were full, and then lazed for a few hours, watching movies and dozing in each other's arms. When the sun went down, we shared a shower and then we each got ready to head back over to the Montgomery residence.

As soon as we got there, I could hear the Christmas music wafting from out of the house. Once inside, we found Rose was dancing with Sophia in her arms, and Harry was carrying up boxes from the basement—his boys trailing behind *helping*.

Pepper was in the kitchen, finishing up her preparation of heavy snacks for us to munch on while we got started.

Upon entering the sitting room, I was impressed to see so many boxes scattered about, ready to be unpacked. Sage helped Harry piece together their artificial tree—since, I learned, Harry is allergic to the real ones—and then Harry disappeared to start his first batch of popcorn. We ate while we decorated, and everyone was having such a marvelous time. Sage sang along to the music, his sister's joining in. Pepper can barely hold a tune, which made us all laugh, but she kept on, and everyone encouraged her. The comradery and love between the three siblings was palpable, and I could tell that Harry and the little ones were in on it, too. Their festive joy was contagious—especially Henley and Carter's—and as I took my turn holding Sophia, even she had a twinkle of amazement in her sweet, brown eyes.

When the tree was complete, and all the empty boxes were stowed away for the next couple of weeks, I stood back and admired it. For the first time ever, I saw the beauty in a Christmas tree. But it wasn't the tree itself that was exceptional; it was the the memories that hung on the tree, and the memories of putting it up that made it so special.

Since Sage had an early morning, we didn't stay late. Knowing that he'd be out the door before I was ready to get out of bed, he insisted we stay at my place. I didn't argue. He left while I was still half sleeping, kissing me goodbye and promising to call me later. Now, after having dressed in a pair of sweatpants, a racerback workout top, and a light hoodie, I wander down the hall to the kitchen, pulling my long hair back into a ponytail as I let my mind drift back to last night.

Rose was spot on about Harry's popcorn; and just now, I could go for a big mug of Pepper's hot cocoa. Instead, I settle for what I have in the fridge—a cup of yogurt and an apple.

My plans for the day are completely low key. I decided not to do any school prep until after Christmas, so while Sage is in Boulder, I'll finish reading my current book. Later, we're supposed to go out so he can tell me all about his meeting. I check the time, noting that it's nearly eleven o'clock. They were scheduled to meet at ten, which had them on the road a little after eight. Sage says they won't always have to go so far as Boulder and that most of their recording time will be spent in Denver; nevertheless, I see a lot of hours on the road in their future. Yet, I know that they all consider Fort Collins home, and they don't mind the drive.

I'm pulled from my thoughts at the sound of my phone. Finished with my breakfast, I hurry back to my room to see who it is. I notice right away that it's a New Jersey area code, but the number is not one saved to my phone. I furrow my brow in confusion, but slide my finger across the screen to take the call anyway.

"Hello?" I answer.

"Hello. I'm looking for a Tatiana Valentine."

My brow scrunches lower. That is my name, of course, but only the name by which my mother addresses me. "I'm Millicent Tatiana Valentine. With whom am I speaking?"

"My name is Detective Cody D'Ambrogio. I'm with the New Jersey police. There was a mugging two nights ago, ma'am. The victim was stabbed and killed."

In an instant, my blood runs cold.

Why is he telling me *this?*

"Her purse was stolen, along with everything inside, so that is why this call is delayed," he continues. "I'm sorry to inform you that we have reason to believe the victim we found is Natalya Valentine. You are listed as her only emergency contact on her employee records at her place of work."

"*What?*" I find myself saying, surprised my lips can form the word. "My mother is—my mother is…*dead?*"

"I'm sorry, ma'am. Evidence suggests that, yes, the deceased is Ms. Valentine. We'll need you to ID the body to be sure."

I shake my head, as if rattling my brain a little will somehow make this phone call make sense.

It doesn't.

"I notice that you are currently residing in Fort Collins, Colorado. Ideally, we'd like you to come to the morgue in person—"

My entire body flinches at the word *morgue*.

"—but if it's more convenient for you, we can send you photographs."

The thought of seeing a picture of my dead mother on my phone makes me shiver.

"*No*. No—no pictures. I…"

For a second, my thoughts hit a wall—a big, steel, mental wall. I can't see around it. I can't *think* around it. I feel cold. When I look down at my hand, I see that it's trembling, and I can't seem to manage a deep breath.

*My mother is—my mother is…*dead*?*

"Miss Valentine?" asks the detective, whose name I can no longer remember.

"What?"

"You were speaking. You said you didn't want us to send any photographs. Does that mean you'll be coming to New Jersey?"

"Yes." The word falls from my lips without a thought. I don't think about whether or not I actually *want* to go to my home state. I don't think about what it will be like to step off that plane only to head to the *morgue*. I don't think about any of it—I just answer *yes*.

"Okay. I'd appreciate a call, once you've got your travel plans in order, so we can arrange to meet. I'm truly sorry about all of this, Miss Valentine. I wish this wasn't the call I had to make."

"I understand," I reply, even though I'm sure that I don't. I don't understand a single thing that's happening right now.

*My mother is—my mother is…*dead?

"Well, you have my number. I'll be awaiting your call."

"Okay."

He starts to say something else, but I don't hear it. I drop the phone away from my ear as I end the call. I stand frozen for I don't know how long, trying to process what just happened.

There was a mugging.

It's cold in Jersey this time of year.

Is there snow?

I'm still cold. Still shivering.

There was a mugging.

The victim was stabbed.

*My mother is—my mother is…*dead?

Not breathing.

No pulse.

Cold.

Fuck, why am I so fucking cold?

There was a mugging.

Two nights ago.

Two nights ago, I was—

Sage!

I don't think. I don't want to think. I *can't* think; so instead, I *move.*

I hurry to my closet, grabbing a pair of fuzzy boots. I don't bother with socks before I shove my feet inside. I then hurry to the front, grabbing my coat from out of the closet. I shrug it over my shoulders and button it all the way to the top.

It's so cold.

I take a look around, seeing nothing, and then realize that I need my keys. I head to my room, snatch up my purse, and then go straight to my car. I barely give it a chance to warm up before I pull out of my spot and hit the road. I know that Sage won't be home, but it doesn't matter. I don't care. I just need—I need—

Fuck, my mother is dead?

Not breathing.

No pulse.

I shake the thoughts away and focus on the road. It looks like it snowed last night. The sun is out now, melting winter's efforts already. Yet, regardless of the affect the heat seems to have on the snow, I can't feel it. I can't feel it *at all.*

When I pull into the boys' driveway, I park just behind Sage's Audi. I get out and head for the front door. It's locked, though I can't say that I'm surprised. No one is home.

I'm halfway to my car, determined to wait it out, when I remember the back door. I turn on my heel, heading for the gated fence, and hurry toward my alternate entrance. I breathe a sigh of relief when I find it unlocked. I let myself in and shut and lock the door behind me. I then make my way to Sage's room, closing myself inside.

I'm still *so cold,* so I kick off my boots and crawl into his bed, pulling the covers all the way up to my chin. I smell his scent in the sheets that surround me, and I wish that he was here. I need him here. I'm just so cold.

It's cold in Jersey this time of year.

There was a mugging.

The victim was stabbed.

Two nights ago.

My mother is…dead?

Not breathing.

No pulse.

Sage

Gregory Black doesn't look much older than me. He's a short dude, standing no taller than five-seven, but you can tell it doesn't hurt his ego any. He's in jeans and a t-shirt, his curly, light brown hair cropped short—and if I had to guess, the sports jacket he threw on was a formality. He's got more energy than he seems to know what to do with, and at first glance, I think all of us were a bit apprehensive—but then he got to talking.

An hour later, all of us sitting around his conference room table, I get the feeling that Stefany's gut instinct was right. This guy knows his shit. He's got vision. He's got drive. But most of all, he's got passion. He's also got money and an eye for detail; the very room in which we sit showcasing the latter. The wall-to-wall windows face the foothills, giving us a great view, and I know he paid a pretty penny for this spot.

"Bottom line," he states, clapping his hand against the table. "I don't have a lot behind my name, but my name is not worthless, and *your* name has just the potential I'm looking for. Mountains & Men might be a fucking gold mine, and I'm willing to invest.

"Signing with Potential Records isn't just a deal. It's not about money. We're all going to have to work our asses off, but that's how the greats became legends. Don't be fooled by *instant* fame. YouTube superstars are quick to be forgotten, and what we're building here is going to be better than that."

"Brooks took a look at this—it all checks out," says Stefany, pushing our contract toward Knox, who sits directly to her right. Brooks is the lawyer who walked us through our deal with Stefany. He's on the up and up, and I'm content with his go ahead.

"Let's fuckin' do this," says Knox, reaching for a pen.

Greg stands, propping himself up against the table with one hand as he raps his knuckles against the wood with the other. "You made the right choice," he assures us. "I know you boys—and *girl*—just got back into town, and we're running out of shopping days before Christmas. We won't hit the ground running until after the New Year. Stefany and I will be in contact to set up your recording schedule. It's going to be busy, we want to get something out there as soon as we can, so be prepared. 'Round here, we go hard or we fucking go home."

"They'll be ready," Stefany states, grinning at all of us.

Greg nods and then steps away from the table, offering a blanket wave.

"Happy to be in business with you. I've got another meeting I've got to get to, but I'll see you later. Merry Christmas," he calls out as he leaves.

"That was painless," mutters Derrick as he stands.

"As it should be," says Stefany. "That's what you've got me for. Now, who's hungry? I'm thinking a pit stop in D-town for burgers and milkshakes."

"You and your celebratory milkshakes," JJ chuckles, shaking his head at her as we all make our exit.

"You're not turning me down, are you?" she gasps mockingly.

"Fuck no, babe," cries Maddox. "We are most definitely in."

As I follow the group to the parking lot, I pull out my phone and send my girl a text. It's almost eleven thirty, so it's a toss-up as to whether or not she'll be awake. When I don't hear back from her right away, a knowing smirk tugs at the corner of my mouth. I pocket my phone and hop into Derrick's SUV, suddenly craving a basket of fries.

It takes us about forty-five minutes to get to the burger joint, and we talk shop throughout our meal—reminiscing about our recent days on the road, talking about which songs the crowd responded to best, discussing which tracks we want to lay down for our first album, and working out a practice schedule for the next couple of weeks. By the time we're getting ready to head home, it's almost one-thirty and I still haven't heard from Millie.

I climb into the back row of Derrick's ride, intending to give her a call. When it rings through to voicemail, I'm quick to hang up and try her again. Still nothing.

After the weekend we just had, it doesn't sit right with me that she's not responding to my calls or texts. Something in my gut wonders if I should be worried, and I try to get her on the phone one more time. When I'm dropped into her voicemail again, I decide to leave a message.

"Doll face, why aren't you answering your phone? Call me."

As I disconnect, spinning my phone around in circles with my fingers, my worry starts to make me anxious.

"What's with you? Everything all right?" asks Alex, nudging me with her elbow.

"I don't know. Guess I'll find out when we get back to FoCo."

Traffic is light, and Derrick gets us back to town in an hour—but with every passing minute, my gut feeling weighs me down a little bit more, and then a little bit more. When we pull up to the house and I see Millie's Ford Focus parked behind my car, I don't know whether to feel better or worse.

"Did you give Millie a key?" calls out Knox from the front seat. "I swear I locked the door on our way out this morning."

"No," I state simply, too many questions buzzing in my own head to offer more than the one-word reply. The second I'm out of the vehicle, I jog up the driveway and through the opened garage door. "Millie?" I call out, looking around the living room as I pass it to get to the stairs. I take the steps two at a time and notice my bedroom door is closed. I don't hesitate to push it open, and what I find makes this moment feel a little bit like déjà vu.

She's not crying like the other night, but something is *definitely* wrong. Her face is pale, and I can tell from here that she's shivering beneath the covers.

"Shit, Millie, I've been trying to get a hold of you," I murmur, shutting the door behind me. "What's going on?"

"I can't get warm. I can't get warm, baby, I can't get warm."

I shrug out of my coat, moving to drape it over the back of the chair tucked in under my desk. "Are you sick? Did you catch the flu or something?" I ask, toeing my way out of my boots before making my way toward the bed. I lift the blanket to slide between the sheets, and I realize she's still got her coat on.

Shit—how can she still be cold?

"There was a mugging," she whispers.

I pause, the sheets still clenched and raised in one hand. "What?"

"The victim was stabbed," she continues, as if she didn't hear me speak. "Two nights ago."

"Millie—"

"My mother is…dead."

My stomach drops as I stare at her in shock. "*What?*"

"Not breathing. No pulse. I haven't spoken to her in two months. Our last conversation was a yelling match. She called me a bitch. Now she's…dead. Not breathing. No pulse…no pulse," she whimpers. "*No pulse*," she repeats, her voice cracking. "My mother—is *dead*."

She blows out a gust of air, as if what she's just told me has hit her square in the chest, knocking the wind out of her. Then she draws in a shaky breath, her watery eyes locking with mine as she sobs, "I'm so *fucking* cold!"

Immediately, I pull her into my arms, holding onto her as if it were life or death.

Fucking hell, I think to myself, *today—it really is life and death.*

"I'm all alone now," she cries into my chest. "She's all I ever had—I'm all alone now!"

"Shh, baby, you're not alone," I insist, pressing my lips against her hair, squeezing my arms and crushing her shivering body against me. "You've got me, remember? I'm not going anywhere, baby. Hold onto me, Millie. I'm not going anywhere."

FIFTEEN

Sage

SHE CRIES HERSELF TO sleep in my arms. I don't remember when she stopped shivering, but when her body grows heavy with slumber, I look down and see that her face is starting to break out in a sweat. I untangle myself from her grasp, careful not to wake her, and then gently work her out of her coat. Once I've freed her second arm, she whimpers and rolls away from me. I freeze for a second, waiting to be sure she's still sleeping, then I quietly make my way out into the hallway, shutting my door behind me.

I sure as fuck was not expecting to come home to *this*. Now that my girl isn't shivering and crying in my arms, I begin to process the reality of the situation. Her mother was *murdered*. I can barely wrap my head around the facts. I don't know much, as Millie was too distraught to tell me more, but the only family that Millie has was stabbed and killed for the contents of her purse.

Not the only family, I correct myself.

She's got me now.

My hands are shaking when I reach for my phone. I go to my saved favorite contacts and hit the third entry down. As I press my mobile to my ear, I reach up and run my fingers through my hair, willing myself to calm down.

"Hey, Sage? Can I call you back? Carter just—"

"Pepper, I need to talk to you."

She pauses, and I know she hears the twinge of desperation in my voice. "All right," she agrees softly. "Give me two seconds, okay?"

"Yeah," I mutter as I begin to pace up and down the length of the hallway.

Two seconds is more like *three minutes*, but I hold without complaint, my eyes looking at my door every time I pass it.

"Okay. Sorry about that. What's the matter?"

I stop pacing and take a deep breath. "Millie's mom was stabbed to death in a mugging."

Pepper gasps. "Oh, my *god!* Oh, my god, Sage! That's…*shit*," she whispers her curse. "That's horrible."

"I don't know what to do, Pep. What do I do?" I ask, knowing she'll know.

No one in our family has died since we've been alive. I have no idea how Millie is feeling. I have no idea what she needs from me; but Pepper has been through this before. Harry's dad passed away a few months before Henley was born. Pepper was there for him. Pepper will know what to do.

"Oh, Sage," she sighs sympathetically. "You just love her, babe."

"When I got home, she was in my bed. She got into the house somehow and she was in my bed, under the covers, with her *coat* on. She was shaking like a leaf, Pep. I don't know how long she had been here before I arrived, but she kept telling me she couldn't get warm."

"She's probably in shock, honey. That news…it shook her up. How is she now?"

"She's sleeping."

"Good, she could probably use the rest."

"Pepper—I don't know what to do."

"Yes, you do, Sage," she coos encouragingly. "You make sure she stays hydrated and that she tries to eat. She might not have an appetite for a couple of days, but she's got to get something in her system to keep her strength up. Don't hover excessively, she might need a little space—but check in on her and be there when she needs you. You've just got to let her grieve, babe. Everyone does that differently. But you love her, so just listen to your heart—listen to her. She'll be okay. She'll get through it, and you'll help her. We all will."

"*Sage?*" I hear Millie murmur my name, and I turn toward the door.

"Look, Pep, I've got to go."

"Yeah. Go. I'll talk to you later."

"Hey, Pepper?"

"Yeah, honey?"

"Thank you."

"Love you."

"You, too."

We say goodbye and I slide my phone back into my pocket as I make my way into my bedroom. Millie's propped up on her side, leaning against her forearm as she searches for me about the room. Her puffy, red-rimmed eyes find mine as I shut the door behind me, and I watch as a couple tears trickle down her cheeks.

"Hey, doll face," I murmur, closing the distance between us. I slide back in bed, leaning back against the pillows before lifting my arm, signaling her to come closer. She snuggles up against my side, gripping a handful of my shirt as she cries quietly.

"I have to go to Jersey," she sniffles. "I have to…I have to ID the body. I have to—pack up her place."

Her grip on my shirt tightens as she buries her face in my chest. In this moment, I know there's no way in hell I'm letting her go all the way out there to deal with this shit on her own.

"I'm coming with you."

"What?" she asks, pulling away from me so that she can look at my face. "No, Sage."

"Yeah, baby—I'm comin'."

She shakes her head as more tears gather in her eyes. "You've got the band and—"

"They'll be fine without me for a few days. It's not an issue," I interrupt.

"But your parents—"

"I'll deal with them when we get back."

"Sage—"

"*Millicent,*" I sigh, gripping the back of her neck as I lean in to press my forehead against hers. "You're not going alone. I'm coming with you, and it's not up for discussion."

"Tickets will be expensive. It's Christmas," she replies meekly.

I lift my head from hers, reaching up with my free hand to hold the side of her face. "Don't give a shit, baby doll. You're not going alone. Not so long as you're my girl. You still my girl?"

Her breath hitches in her throat and then she offers me a nod.

"Then it's settled," I say, ending the conversation with a quick kiss.

She surprises me when she leans in for more, but I follow her lead. When she flicks her tongue against my lips, I open up for her, letting her take what she wants. As she presses into me, circling her arms around my neck, my caution slips out of reach and I kiss her deeper—needing a taste. I don't know how much time passes as we lose ourselves in each other, only that when she finally pulls away, we're both breathless. She stares into my eyes, neither of us speaking, and then her tears return.

She buries her face against my neck and I slide an arm under her knees, bracing my other around her back as I lift her up and across my lap. "I've got you, gorgeous," I assure her.

"I love you," she whispers, squeezing me harder.

"I love you, too."

This time, when her tears taper off, she doesn't fall asleep. Rather, she relaxes against me and remains silent, probably lost in her head somewhere. I don't know what to say, so I don't say anything, and that seems to be okay with her.

"We should look at tickets," she whispers, her voice raspy.

"Okay. I think you should try and eat something, first. Have you eaten today?"

She inhales deeply and exhales slowly, shaking her head at me. "I don't remember. But…I'm not hungry."

"Some water then? You need *something*, baby."

She hesitates before offering me a nod. "Okay."

I let out a small sigh of relief and then start to lift her off of my lap so that I can head down to the kitchen. As soon as my feet hit the ground, she reaches for my hand and starts to crawl after me.

"Take me with you," she insists.

I don't question her. Instead, I wipe her cheeks dry and help her out of bed, wrapping my arm around her shoulders as we make our way out of my room and down the stairs. I hear their hushed whispers before I see them. When we reach the mouth of the kitchen, Millie and I both halt in unison.

Derrick looks up, noticing us first, and clears his throat. Knox and Maddox, who are standing at the fridge, loading it with beer, look over their shoulders at the sound. Rosy and Alex, who are busy setting something up on the kitchen island, both spin around, their gazes locking in on my girl and me. Both Violet and JJ look at us with caution, and I wonder what's going on.

"Hey," Rosy speaks, taking a step toward us. "Pepper made a couple batches of her famous chicken lasagna. I whipped up some cupcakes. We just thought…we wanted to do something."

"We got booze," Maddox announces.

"Millie, we're so sorry to hear about your mom," Alex murmurs.

I feel it as Millie starts to tremble beside me, and I'm not surprised when she bursts into tears. Violet rushes over and pries Millie away from me, wrapping her in a big hug. Millie sags against Vi, and Rosy and Alex are quick to surround her. Seeing them comfort her makes my chest swell.

She's not alone.

She's got me now.

She's got all *of us.*

I DIDN'T MEAN TO lose it in front of everyone, but I couldn't help it. Knowing that they were all gathered together for *me*, it broke the loose hold I had on my emotions to begin with. It took me a minute, but I pulled myself up, wiping away my tears as I offered them a shaky smile.

Not long after, we were all spread out in the living room—some on the couches, some on the floor. Everyone had helped themselves to Pepper's lasagna and the booze the Bradley brothers supplied. I opted for water, managing no more than a bite off of Sage's plate. Any other day, I might have understood why Rose had dubbed it Pepper's *famous* chicken lasagna; today, I could barely taste it.

A movie played softly in the background, but I'm not sure anyone was paying attention. Conversation was quiet, as if the news of my mother's death weighed heavily on everyone, and I tried to listen; tried to focus on anything but my own thoughts; tried to forget all that lay ahead of me—but even more so, all the horrible memories that were behind me.

I tried. I tried and failed miserably.

When Sage was finished eating and I had satisfied him by downing an entire glass of water, he grabbed his computer and found us two plane tickets that would have us at the Newark Airport by tomorrow night. The airport is two hours away from our final destination, Steelmantown, New Jersey, but it was the cheapest he could find.

There's nothing that I'm looking forward to in regards to this trip; adding one more hassle wasn't going to make it any worse.

I helped him book us a rental car and hotel, knowing there was no way in hell I'd be able to stay at my mother's place. Then, with our travel plans made, he suggested we get ready for bed. I agreed, wishing to be out from under the gaze of so many people—despite their genuine concern and companionship—and he helped me off the couch before we bid everyone goodnight. When we got to the stairs, he kissed my cheek and told me to head on up, that he was going to let Maestro out and then join me.

As I lay in his bed now, watching him take off his clothes and slip into a pair of sweatpants, I realize that I'm incredibly relieved to know that he's coming with me tomorrow. At first, I didn't want him to come. Jersey is my past, a place I had no intention of returning to. Especially not like this. The burden that waits for me is mine to carry—but his refusal to let me face it alone only proves that he *knows* me and *understands* me in ways I cannot even fathom.

I don't want to do this alone.

I don't have *to do this alone.*

So long as I'm his girl, he won't let *me do it alone.*

"Mind if I put on a movie?" he asks, pointing toward his collection of DVDs and BluRays.

I shake my head *no*. It's still early, and I imagine he won't find sleep for a while. I, on the other hand, am exhausted. By the time he crawls into bed, I can already feel sleep pulling me under.

"Need anything, baby?"

He stretches out beside me, lifting his arm in invitation. I curl myself around him, resting my cheek against his warm, bare, tatted chest.

"No," I whisper.

He presses a kiss against my forehead and begins fidgeting with my long ponytail, shifting his focus onto the screen hung up across the room. I close my eyes and just enjoy the feel of his solid body beneath mine; his heart beating beneath my ear, his deep breaths causing my head to rise and fall with his chest. Every few minutes, I feel it as he dips his chin to check on me, his lips grazing my hairline when he does. I fall asleep knowing that I am loved—knowing that, whatever tomorrow brings, I am already home.

Sage

I WAKE UP EARLY, like usual, and find Millie still asleep. I slept like shit—but my mom is still alive and well, so I don't complain. Instead, I get my ass out of bed and head to the kitchen to start a pot of coffee. As it brews, I feed my pup and feast on a leftover cupcake from last night. I don't think twice before grabbing another when I'm finished with the first. I'm halfway through my first bite when I see Millie walking into the kitchen. She looks to be still half asleep, her hair loose and draped around her face and down her chest.

"Hey," I say in greeting as she shuffles her way toward me.

"Hi."

I set aside my cupcake when she leans her hip against the counter in the space just beside me. She eyes my treat as she reaches up and sweeps her hair behind her ears, and a smirk pulls at my lips as I slide it in her direction.

"Have at it, doll face."

She looks up at me, then back down at the red velvet cupcake covered in cream cheese frosting. When she picks it up and takes a big bite, I chuckle softly before turning to grab two mugs.

"Want some coffee with that?"

"No, thanks," she mutters with her mouth full.

"I think JJ might have some tea in the pantry," I suggest.

She shakes her head as she swallows and then asks, "Do you have any milk?"

"Yeah, doll, we've got milk." I dip my head and kiss her lips. "I'll get you some." I kiss her once more before turning toward the fridge. I pour her milk and then my coffee, swiping another cupcake as I prop myself right next to her again. We consume our breakfast in silence, and when she's done, she rests her head against my shoulder while I finish my coffee. "Called Sarah last night after you knocked out," I start to say, reaching for her hand. "Told her our plans. She said she would stay at your place last night and pack a bag for you. She's supposed to stop by on her lunch break and drop it off."

"I really wish people would stop being so nice to me," she starts to say, her voice weak, but her grip around my fingers strong. "I'll never stop crying if they don't cut it out."

I hide my smile in her hair, shaking my head at her slightly. "Cry on me all you like, baby doll, but we aren't going to stop taking care of you. This is what friends and family do. We look out for each other. Right now, you need looking after—so get used to it." I punctuate my statement with a kiss on top of her head and she lets go of my hand so she can slide her arms around my waist. I set aside my empty mug and fold her in my arms, rocking her back and forth a little.

"My phone," she whispers. "I need my phone. I have to call the detective to let him know I'm coming. I…I left my phone—"

"I'll text Sarah. Don't worry about it, Millie."

"Okay." She draws in a shuddered breath and gives me a squeeze. "I have to ID the body. I don't…I don't want to go."

"*Fuck*," I whisper, sure that there's no way around that shit.

"I don't want to go," she repeats.

"You're not going alone," I remind her. She nods, but I can tell my words haven't penetrated through her fear. "Look at me." When she does as I ask, I stare into her eyes, holding her gaze for a moment before I say, "You've got this, baby. *We've* got this. Do you believe me?"

"Yeah," she whispers.

"It's you and me. We're in this together."

"Okay."

"You and me," I repeat.

"We're in this together."

I press my lips to hers in a soft kiss before I mumble, "That's my girl."

SIXTEEN

Millicent

It's after midnight by the time we arrive at the hotel in my small town, and Sage and I both fall right into bed as soon as we get settled in. When the alarm on Sage's phone sounds eight hours later, even just the thought of waking up makes me weak. I know what lies ahead of me today, and I don't want to do *any* of it. Be that as it may, Sage gets me out of bed and in the shower. An hour later, we're on our way to the police department to meet Detective D'Ambrogio.

As soon as we arrive at the station, we're escorted back to his desk. He stands when he sees us, greeting us with a sympathetic smile and a handshake. He's not a tall man, standing a little taller than me, but shorter than Sage. I can tell beneath the black pants, the collared shirt and loose tie is a well-maintained body that makes him confident; and I imagine there are women who find him easy on the eyes. Yet despite all of that, and the kindness he bestows upon us, I wish to be out of his presence as soon as possible, a fact I think he picks up on. We're back in our rental and following him to the morgue in no time.

When we arrive, Sage turns off the car, but I don't get out right away. I close my eyes and try to mentally prepare for what I'm about to see, but it's no use. I know that it's going to be the kind of awful that I can't even imagine.

"Millie?" Sage murmurs, reaching over to take my hand.

"Let's go," I whisper, giving his fingers a squeeze before I let go and step out of the car.

Detective D'Ambrogio signs in at the front desk, and then we're escorted to the back. I reach for Sage's hand as the attendant locates the right *drawer* that my mother has been stowed into for the last few days. When he locates the right one and pulls it out, I grip Sage's hand with all my might.

Then, there she is, *Natalya Valentine*, my cold, dead mother.

As if something has come over me, I step away from Sage and closer to her body. When I look down at her face, I notice that in death…she's actually quite beautiful. Her face is relaxed, void of the bitterness, the sadness, and the anger that marred her features for as long as I can remember. Staring down at her, I feel devastated—devastated that her life was taken from her the way that it was. *No one* should be taken from this world as an innocent victim to a meaningless crime. Yet, even amidst my grief, as I look upon her, I acknowledge the fact that I do not love this woman. I haven't for a long time. And I know, wherever she is, she doesn't miss me because she didn't love me, either. It's an incredibly sad reality—but here it is, sitting right in front of me.

Knowing that this moment is our only goodbye, I simply hope that she's somehow found peace in death.

"Miss Valentine?" the detective speaks, breaking the silence and pulling me from my thoughts.

I step away from the body, colliding into Sage. He wraps his arms around me, and in his strong hold, I realize that I'm trembling again.

"That's her," I tell him. "There won't be a funeral. No one would come. I'll arrange for cremation if you're ready to release the body." The words fall right out of my mouth, my desire for *order* suddenly kicking into high gear. "Can we go now?"

"Uh—yeah," he mumbles, clearly caught off guard by my response.

"If you need anything else, we're in town until Friday." When I finish speaking, I turn in Sage's arms and look up into his gorgeous blue eyes—full of life, clouded with concern, but screaming of love. "Get me out of here," I whisper.

He nods once and then escorts me out.

A LOT HAS CHANGED around my hometown in the eight years that I've been away, but my mother's small apartment is exactly as I remember it—only messier. Without me around, there was no one to organize her chaos.

After we left the morgue, Sage and I stopped at the store to pick up a bunch of packing supplies, and we spend most of the afternoon tossing out the garbage and boxing up anything worth donating. There's not a single thing in the place that I want to keep, so I tell Sage to use his own judgement. He tackles the kitchen and I get through the mess that was her office—my old room. By the time evening hits, there are three garbage bags lined up beside the door and four boxes stacked neatly against the wall in the living room. After Sage takes out the trash, he insists we stop for the night and grab something to eat. I don't argue.

Later that night, when we're back at the hotel, my exhaustion hits all at once. I've never been as tired as I have felt the last couple of days, and I wonder when I'll feel truly rested again. I don't imagine it'll happen so long as I'm here. Colorado is where my life is. If I never have to come back to Steelmantown again, it'll be too soon.

"Hey, can we talk?" asks Sage as I rummage through my bag for my night clothes.

I look at him, surprised by his request, and he stands beside me, running a hand across my lower back. "Is everything okay?"

"I was going to ask *you* that. You've been all business since we left the morgue."

"Yeah," I admit, directing my focus back to my bag. "I want to go home. I don't want to be here. There's a lot of shit that needs to get done, and we have to be finished by tomorrow."

"Doll face, I hate to state the obvious, but you saw your mom's dead body this morning. You've cried a lot the last couple days, but today—*nothing*."

I offer him a shrug, too tired to even truly process what his observation could even mean. "I don't know what you want me to say."

He sighs, sitting on the bed beside my bag. "I don't either, baby doll."

I look over at him as he pushes his glasses up his face to pinch the bridge of his nose. My shoulders sag in guilt when I realize how exhausted he looks too. He's been by my side, just as he promised he would be, looking after me and helping me. He's been amazing. He is so much *fucking* more than the arrogant little shit that I thought he was when we first met. He doesn't back down from life, but puffs out his chest when it throws a challenge his way, determined to face it head on. He's not afraid, my dream chaser, and his bravery has been my comfort. His support has kept me sane. I have no idea how I would have handled any of this without him.

I let go of my clothes and push my bag aside, sitting next to him, my shoulder grazing his. I can feel it when he turns his gaze on me, but I don't look at him. Instead, I try letting go of my to-do list in order to allow everything else that lies beneath it to come out.

"I hated her," I confess what I've told him before, drawing in a deep breath before I continue. "She was a horrible mother. I know there are far worse, that there are people out there who would give anything for a mother like mine—but I wouldn't wish her on anyone. And at the same time, I know she didn't deserve to die like this. I didn't love her; I didn't miss her—but I never wanted her *dead*.

"It's scary. It's scary to think that the only person in the whole world who has known you your whole life—the one family member tied to you by blood that you know—it's scary to realize that they're gone. That it's only you. And I know I'm not alone…but she was my mother. Then today, I don't know. Today was our goodbye. She didn't leave me anything to hang onto. She didn't leave me anything to *miss*. We let go of each other in so many ways so long ago. The woman I saw today…"

I shake my head, reaching up to run my fingers through my hair. "Today was our goodbye," I repeat. "It hurts in ways I don't understand, in ways that don't make sense; but she's gone and I have to move on. I don't know how else to explain it. I just—" I shrug, turning to meet his intent gaze. "I want to go home, baby."

He nods his head slowly and wraps his arm around my shoulders, pulling me into his side. When he presses a kiss against my temple, I relax against him with a sigh.

"Let's hit the sack, then. Tomorrow, we'll get shit done, and then I'm taking my girl home."

"Thank you," I murmur, burying my face in his chest.

"We got this. You and me, doll. You and me."

Sage

I SEAL UP THE last box in the apartment, amazed. Not amazed that we were able to pack it all up in less than forty-eight hours—although, that's pretty fucking impressive—no, I'm amazed that I spent two days going through a mother's things and found not one trace of Millie's childhood laying around. No pictures. No crazy art. Nothing. It was almost as if Millie didn't even exist. I don't understand it, and I sure as shit don't like it, but I don't mention it.

Millie's been through enough this week. I don't need to dredge up the past even more.

"Okay," she says as she pockets her phone, her tired voice breaking through my thoughts. "The pick-up crew will be here sometime tomorrow to get all the donations. The landlord has been informed. We just have to hit the bank first thing in the morning to settle her accounts, and then I'm done."

"So we've got the rest of the night off?" I ask, closing the distance between us.

"Yeah. I suppose we do."

I circle my arms around her waist and pull her against me before brushing my lips against hers in a soft kiss. "Might I suggest something?"

"Sage…" She slides her hands up my arms, across my shoulders, and along my neck, her fingers toying with the hair at the nape of my neck as she stares at me with those pretty eyes. "I couldn't have done this without you. I know I've been single-track minded since we walked into this place." She pauses, looking around at the living room now filled with boxes and discarded furniture. "But this would have been torture without you. You were home for all of three days before you hopped on a plane with me. You didn't have to do *any* of this, but you did. I just…I say all that to say, tonight—we can do whatever you want. I don't care what it is."

I smirk at her, amused that after all we've been through, she still thinks that I had a choice in the matter. Then my smile slips when I remember that no one has ever loved her unconditionally before. She doesn't understand that I didn't have a choice—that I couldn't let her do this alone. She doesn't get it, but she will. I'll make sure of it.

"I was actually thinking we could go grab a shower and then I could take you to that little Italian place you love."

Her mouth falls open as her expression softens in surprise. "You remembered?"

"Millie," I start with a chuckle. "How could I forget our first date and why I thought it was a good idea to take you to my parents' place? I totally fucked it all up. Of course, I remember."

She pushes herself up on her tiptoes, holding me securely around my neck. I return her embrace, appreciative of the way her body feels pressed flush against mine.

If only we were naked…

God, I miss her naked body.

"Does this mean yes?" I ask, rubbing my hands up and down her sides, trying to shake my lustful thoughts.

"Yes," she murmurs with a nod, her grip around me not loosening in the slightest.

"Okay," I chuckle. "Whenever you're ready, baby doll."

"I need a minute."

I nod before burying my face between her neck and her shoulder. "Take all the time you need, baby."

Millicent

DINNER WITH SAGE was lovely. We took a cab, since both of us needed the night off, and indulged in a couple glasses of wine during our delicious meal. The entire time that we were at the restaurant, Sage helped me to forget why we are here. It was a date, through and through, and I felt like I was sharing something special with him—the one thing I missed about Jersey, my absolute favorite restaurant.

Now that we're back at our room, the alcohol in my system leaving me with a nice buzz, I'm not ready for our date to end. He shrugs his coat off, tossing it onto an armchair, and I follow suit before making my intentions known. I step in front of him, wrapping my arms around his waist as I reach up for a kiss. As soon as his lips touch mine, I slide my tongue along the crease of his mouth and he opens up for me. I sigh longingly and he reaches up with both of his hands to hold the back of my neck, angling my head so he can get a proper taste.

"Millie," he mumbles.

"I want you," I admit, sneaking my hands under the hem of his shirt and up the smooth, hard surface of his back.

"We don't have to, doll, it's okay," he says, as if he's trying to hold himself back for my sake.

"Sage, baby." I take one hand from off of his back and move it down over the front of his pants, gripping the bulge trying the seam of his jeans. "*I want you.*"

He groans, taking my mouth in a bruising kiss, and I know he now understands *exactly* what I want. Judging by the way his tongue explores my mouth, as if it's on a journey of rediscovery, I'm certain he wants this just as much as I do.

Abruptly, he breaks away from our kiss, taking a step away from me. I'm disappointed only until I see the fire burning in his icy blue eyes. As he reaches for the hem of his t-shirt, he commands, "Clothes. Off."

I obey, stripping down to nothing as quickly as I can. I haven't had his cock in days. In this moment, I'm so hungry for his touch, I wonder how I ever lasted weeks without him.

When we're both naked, he reaches for me, capturing my lips once more. Feeling impatient, I press my hands against his chest and guide him backwards toward the end of the bed, never breaking our kiss. His legs hit the mattress and I give him another push. He gets the hint and sits his ass down, his long, glorious dick jutting out from between his legs.

I drop to my knees, my center growing slick with arousal just *thinking* about the noises he's sure to make when I suck on his balls before I lick my way up and down the length of his shaft.

"Ah, hell, yes," he grunts, one of his hands finding its way into my hair as I begin.

I suck and then I lick, just as I had planned, and then I wrap my lips around his head, swirling my tongue across his slit.

"*Fuck*—you feel so good, Millie."

I bob my head, pumping what I can't fit in my mouth with my fist, my pussy growing slick and swollen with every murmur of pleasure that spills from his lips. When I can no longer deny myself, I kiss the tip of his dick and then climb into his lap, the top of my feet resting at his knees. Our eyes lock as I hold onto his shoulder with one hand, reaching behind me for his dick with my other. I line us up and then ease down over him. I rest my other hand on his opposite shoulder, hanging on as I begin to ride his generous length.

He feels marvelous.

The sound of my arousal coating his cock makes me whimper with delight, and I throw my head back, concentrating on the feeling of him filling me up every time I crash down. When he dips his head and captures one of my nipples in his mouth, sucking greedily as his tongue grazes my hardened bud, I shift my legs around his hips, causing him to go deeper.

"Oh, shit, yes—*Sage*," I cry out, rocking my hips with greater force—needing *more*.

He frees one nipple in order to taste the other, his hands reaching back to grab hold of my ass. As he squeezes, sucks, and hums, I become even more aroused. I arch my back, needing him to go deeper, but it's not enough.

I grunt in frustration and then shove at his shoulders. He chuckles, lifting his head to look into my eyes. "Please," I beg.

He smacks a kiss against my lips and then stretches out on his back. I spread my legs wider, sinking down further, and my eyes roll into the back of my head. Reaching behind me with both hands, I grip his thighs and thrust my hips with as much force as I can manage. As I climb closer and closer to the pique of ecstasy, my breathing becomes ragged. Then, just when I think I'm about to get somewhere, I'm airborne.

My eyes open in surprise as I gasp, reaching out to grab his biceps, the sensation I felt just a second ago slipping out of reach.

"Sage!"

"You're a tease up there, doll face. It's my turn."

Before I can utter a word of protest, my ass is on the dresser, his hands cupped beneath my knees as he spreads my legs open wide.

"Sage, I—"

A low, indulgent groan fills the room as he thrusts deep inside of me—I swear to god, I don't know if he made the sound or I did. No matter. I'm instantly lost in him as he pounds into me, every plunge making the dresser bang against the wall. It's loud, it's disruptive, it's rhythmic, and it's *amazing*.

His glasses slip down his nose a little, but he ignores them, pulling his bottom lip between his teeth as he grunts in determination. I press my palms flat against the surface behind me, leaving my breasts fully exposed as they dance a little for my man.

Soon, he's got my feet propped up on the edge of the dresser, his hands underneath my ass as he lifts me up and holds me close while he fucks me hard. He leans down and sucks on my lips, making me moan, and then he silences me with his tongue. I reach up and grip the back of his neck, rocking my hips in tandem with his, unable to stop myself. He growls and the budding sensation of a forthcoming release returns.

"Sage—baby, I'm going to come," I whimper, holding myself against him as my body starts to lock up.

"Fuck yes, you are," he grinds out, reaching between us to play with my clit.

I cry out and my knees press into his sides, my body stiff as my orgasm detonates inside of me. Just as my muscles begin to relax, he buries his face in my neck, muttering a string of curse words as he thrusts into me one last time and spills his release.

We're both breathless from exertion, but he still holds me against him, his hand under my ass, his dick still deep inside of me, my arms wrapped about his neck. After a minute, he lifts his head, using his free hand to slide his glasses up his nose. He then smirks at me and asks, "Again?"

I giggle, feeling lighter than I've felt in days. I don't want to lose this feeling. Tonight, I don't want to think about anything else. I don't want to *be* anywhere else. Tonight—I just want Sage, so I nod and insist, "Again."

SEVENTEEN

Milicent

I WAKE IN A FAMILIAR BED, feeling comforted by the knowledge that I'm back where I belong. Yet, even as I pull the comforter about me tightly, breathing in the scent of the man I adore, I can't escape the questions and the burdens that have been crowding my mind for the last couple of days.

After identifying my mother's body, I had one mission—take care of her outstanding shit, and bail as quickly as possible. With Sage's help, dealing with her belongings had been pretty cut and dry. It wasn't until our last day, when we went to the bank so I could deal with her finances, that my plans to leave all of my past in Jersey were suddenly thwarted.

I'm pulled from my thoughts at the feel of his warm, wet lips against my neck. I draw in a deep breath, freeing a sigh as his hand slips beneath the covers and down my side. Sage kisses me again, and I feel the bed dip behind me, surrendering to his weight. My lips part open and I gasp quietly just as his fingers find their way under the t-shirt I wore to bed. He flattens his palm against my stomach and then feels his way up to one of my breasts, which he fondles gently. I arch my back, unconsciously encouraging him as a soft whimper escapes from my throat.

"Morning, doll face," Sage mumbles into my ear.

I turn my head, not even bothering to open my eyes, knowing what I seek would have them closed again in an instant, anyway. As if he can read my mind, Sage presses a kiss against my lips, his tongue sweeping through my mouth without delay. I feel myself growing wet already, and I want nothing more than to see this through to completion—to forget what my mind was so adamant that I remember upon waking.

When he pulls away from me, tweaking my nipple before his hand disappears too, I whine in protest. I can't help it. I wasn't ready for him to stop, a truth I try to convey when I open my eyes, seeking his.

"Sorry, baby doll, I can't stay. I've got practice in five. Just wanted to tell you to come down and chill with us when you're ready. Dress warm—the garage is a little cool. We just turned the space heaters on."

I frown, looking up at the clock he's got hanging on the wall, and see that it's almost ten-thirty. It strikes me as an odd time to be up and dressed, getting ready to practice on a Sunday morning. I open my mouth to say just that, but then I remember that with us being out of town until last night, the band hasn't been together in almost a week.

"Hey," he murmurs, burying his fingers in my hair as he holds the back of my head. "You good?"

As much as I want to tell him that he needs to finish what he started a second ago, I don't. After the past week, he owes me absolutely nothing.

"I'm fine," I assure him with a small nod.

He studies me, unbelieving. "I know we didn't leave things the way you wanted, but we're home now—let it go for a while. It's your winter break, it's almost Christmas, don't worry about any of it. We'll deal with it later."

I pull my bottom lip between my teeth, my stomach tingling at his mention of *we*. He's been by my side since the moment I told him about my mother's death. Now, when he says *we*, I know that he means it, and it makes me want to do exactly as he's suggested. I offer him a nod and he kisses my forehead before he lets go of me and stands to his feet.

"See you in a few?"

"Yeah. I'll be down in a little bit."

I watch him leave, shutting his bedroom door closed behind him, and then I stare up at the ceiling.

For just a moment, I think about the unknown funds being deposited into my mother's account on a monthly basis—the funds that prevented me from being able to leave the bank completely free of her. Instead, I'm left with only the knowledge that she's collecting some sort of garnishment payment. The banker I was speaking to couldn't give me any further information; she only confirmed that I couldn't close the account as long as the funds were still being deposited.

With no time to dig further, Sage suggested that we leave it be until after the holidays. Just now, he reminded me again to let it go. Knowing that something far more pleasant than my own obsessive compulsive thoughts awaits me downstairs, I get out of bed, gathering what I need for a shower.

I don't linger under the water for long, deciding to skip my daily shampoo routine. As soon as we got back from the airport late yesterday afternoon, I washed away the stench of travel, so I don't think my hair will mind. Besides, hanging out in a chilly garage with wet hair is a recipe for a cold. Getting sick is the *last* thing I want to worry about right now.

Before I step out of the bathroom, I don my panties and my bra, tugging on my blue skinny jeans and a plain, olive green t-shirt. As I open the door to make my exit, I'm coaxing the hair tie from out of my messy mane. I'm startled at the sight of Violet, causing me to yank at the small band, my hair cascading past my shoulders as she clutches her chest and then giggles.

"*Shit*, Millie, I didn't know you were in there."

"Sorry," I murmur, offering her a tired, half smile.

"Totally my bad. I heard the band and just figured—" She cuts herself off, shaking her head as she waves her hand, dismissing her excuse. "Are you sticking around today?"

"Yes," I reply, combing my fingers through my hair, sure that it needs a brush. "You?"

"I have to step out for a bit—staff meeting at work—but I'll be back."

"Okay." I start to walk around her, assuming she still needs the bathroom, but she stops me.

"Hey, how are you doing? You and Sage looked pretty wiped last night."

"Long travel day," I reply with a small shrug.

She nods, and something in her striking, dark blue eyes tells me she wants to say something more. I'm not sure what she could be thinking, so I endure the awkward pause before she says, "Look, I'll be the first to admit, I have no idea what it is you're going through; but if you want to talk..."

I force a smile, my heart conflicted. I feel grateful for her offer, all the while knowing that opening up to Violet about my mother will likely never be something I'll feel comfortable doing. I'm not sure that I could explain what it is that I'm going through; I can hardly understand it myself. My relationship with Natalya—or, rather, the harsh feelings we harbored toward one another—it makes this whole situation so twisted and confusing, painful and yet liberating.

"Thanks," I finally manage to say.

She smiles at me and I take that as my opportunity to slip back into Sage's room. I get halfway across the hall before she stops me again.

"Do you have any plans tonight?"

I turn to her once more as I reply, "I don't think so. Why?"

"JJ and I are going to Sunset Canyon tonight. You and Sage should come with us, if you're up for it. I haven't been on a double date in ages."

I raise my brow in surprise, wondering if I've heard her correctly. "You and *JJ* are going to *Sunset Canyon?*"

She laughs, the look on her face expressing her understanding of my bewilderment. I've been to the club she's referring to only once, back when I was in college. It's a cowboy bar. Somehow, I have a hard time picturing either of them stepping foot in there—Violet with her pixie haircut and her urban-chic style, JJ with his mop of spiral, curly hair and his *obvious* rocker vibe.

"Don't let my handsome mutt fool you. He can two-step like nobody's business." With a grin she adds, "It's not exactly something he brags about, and most of the band really hates country music, so they never come, but I have a blast every time we go. You should come."

I think about it for a second, my curiosity getting the better of me before I realize, "I don't think Sage—"

"You're kidding, right? He'd do anything for you—including a night at Sunset Canyon. All you have to do is say the word."

A smile, a *real* smile, pulls at the corners of my mouth as I picture Sage, my sexy rocker, *line* dancing. The thought of spending the evening with friends—laughing, dancing, and drinking—makes me feel a little lighter than I did a minute ago. If nothing else, it'll provide just the distraction I need.

I dip my chin in agreement and Violet beams at me.

"We're going to have so much fun. I promise!"

"What time should we be ready?"

"They have a mini lesson at seven-thirty, and then the real fun starts at eight. Hell—let's go at six. We'll grab some dinner first and make a night of it." She looks down at her phone and then swears under her breath. "I've got to pee and then get out of here, but I'll be back in about an hour. We'll tell the guys our plans then."

"Okay," I agree with a nod.

She grins at me and then disappears into the bathroom. I shake my head as I make my way back to Sage's room, heading to his closet for something warm to wear. After I pull one of his sweatshirts over my body, I spot his red, flannel button-up, and I can't help but smile. I pluck it from the hanger and toss it on the bed before I slip my feet into my fuzzy boots. That shirt will be perfect for later.

Sage

IT WAS THE TWINKLE I saw in her eye when I looked at her that made me agree. Violet didn't so much *ask* if I wanted to go, more like demanded that I be ready on time—but one glance at my girl and I was in. Then, when we stopped by Millie's place so she could change for the evening, we almost didn't make it out the door.

It's the dead of winter, so she's not in anything skimpy, but she still dressed to kill. Her jeans are tight, showing off those long-ass legs I love, the cuffs tucked into a pair of black boots that come up to her ankles. She's got on a long-sleeved, white shirt that's cut so low I can almost make out the top of her bra, and the fabric clings to her tits, making me want to take them out and devour them. The sweater she put on is long and black, the entire back cut out into some sort of lacy pattern. She left most of her hair down, pulling half of it back and away from her face, and she looks gorgeous—especially now, as she throws me a playfully irritated expression.

We're standing, facing each other, listening to the guy at the front giving us instructions. I can hardly hear him. My girl is fine as all hell; and after the couple beers I had with dinner, I could give a fuck about the two-step, I just want my baby doll pressed up against me.

"Sage, are you even *listening?*"

I offer her a smirk and she smacks my arm.

"Baby, please?"

"Okay," I agree begrudgingly. I lean toward her and smack a kiss against her lips before looking at the instructor, trying to memorize what he's saying so that I might mimic his steps. The two-step isn't exactly rocket science, and I've got enough rhythm to conquer the basic idea. When Millie and I finally try it, we look like a couple of novices, but the smile on her face is all I care about.

After our lesson, we seek out Violet and JJ. They sat at a table and ordered a round of drinks during the tutorial. When we join them, I see a bottle of beer waiting for me, and a gin and tonic for my girl.

"You guys looked good out there," says Violet as we take our seats.

"Yeah. Not too shabby for a couple newbies," teases JJ.

I chuckle, lifting my bottle to take a swig. It's been a long fucking time since I've seen him let loose to a country jam. The last time I was here, I was still in college, still walking around clubs with those stupid X marks on my hands. The only reason I stepped foot in this place was because there was no way I was taking Violet on her word that JJ could *cut a rug* to some country twang. I thought for sure I'd come and laugh my ass off; turns out, Violet wasn't lying. His two-steppin' skills are definitely a hidden talent, buried underneath the true rocker that he is.

"Fuck, yes! I love this song. Come on guys, let's go," Violet insists as she stands to her feet, tugging JJ out onto the dance floor.

When I look to Millie, she offers me an apprehensive smile. I wink at her and then offer her my arm before leading her out with the others. We're barely two counts in before Millie's stopped in her tracks, her eyes glued to JJ as he twirls Violet this way and then that way. A smirk pulls at my lips as I draw my girl close, pressing my lips against her temple.

"Wow," she breathes.

"Right?" I reply with a laugh. When she doesn't stop staring, I smack her ass. She frees a yelp before looking up at me with her pretty, dark green eyes. "You're stuck with me *darlin'*," I drawl teasingly.

She laughs softly and then we get lost in the music, shuffling around the floor. The song that comes on after is accompanied with a line dance of some sort, and Violet is quick to jump between us, teaching us the steps. Millie picks it up with ease, and I stumble my way through—too distracted at the sight of her to give two shits about my feet. She's laughing, the combination of good food, good company, and good booze causing her to relax. After everything she's been through over the last week, this is exactly what she needs.

We line dance for a couple more tracks, and when the song changes again, people start to couple up. Before I can reach Millie, JJ takes her in his arms. I quirk a warning eyebrow at him and he laughs as he says, "It's time I show her how it's done. Watch and learn, Sage."

With a giggle, Violet links her arm through mine and nods toward our table. "I could go for another drink. You?"

"Yeah, sure."

We order a round for everyone before heading back to our seats. My eyes drift back to Millie immediately, watching as JJ spins her around effortlessly.

"How's she doing?" asks Violet.

I don't pull my gaze away from my girl as I answer, "Better than I'd be if I were in her shoes." I take a pull from my beer before I say, "She's strong. I mean, I always figured she was tough, you know? She's got that brain and that smart-ass mouth. She's stubborn as hell, too. But underneath all of that? She's more resilient than I think even she knows."

Violet reaches over and squeezes my arm, causing me to turn and look into her bright, blue eyes. "Don't count yourself out, Sage. She's got you, too. I see how she leans on you."

I don't say anything in reply, shifting my focus back out onto the dance floor. Truth be told, there's nothing to be said. I love her. I sure as fuck hope she knows I'm here for her, no matter what—and I'm not going anywhere.

As soon as the song ends, JJ and Millie make their way back to us. Millie sits, but JJ only takes a gulp of his drink before extending his hand to Violet. She's up in an instant, and they're back out there, showing off. I look to Millie, asking her with a single glance if she wants to be out there, too, but she shakes her head *no*. She then moves her chair closer to mine so she can lean against me as she sips at her drink.

"Sage?"

"Yeah, baby?"

She rests her head against my shoulder as she says, "Thanks for bringing me here."

I reach for her hand and bring it into my lap, lacing our fingers together as I twist to press a kiss against her forehead. "Any time, baby doll," I assure her. "For you, any time."

EIGHTEEN

Sage

I WAKE UP IN A quiet house.

It's been a week since Millie and I got back from New Jersey. I've kept her close, wanting to make sure she's okay. She's been pretty emotional since I got back into town, even before she found out about her mom. I know Christmas can take it out of people, but this is more than that. She's got a lot going on in that head of hers; and to be honest, I don't want to leave her alone with her feelings for too long. She does some fucked up shit when she lets her thoughts fester—*like try to break up with me.*

I'm not afraid she'll do something that stupid, but for now, I don't want to take any chances. Besides, she shouldn't spend the entirety of her winter break alone, anyway. Not while she's feeling sad and overwhelmed.

My plans to put in some hours at Little Bird were scrapped, the days before Christmas dwindling down to zero faster than I could keep track. Today, on the morning of Christmas Eve, it's only Millie and me in the house, my mates all gone to celebrate the holiday with their families. Derrick was the last of the bunch to pack up and go, leaving for Kansas to hang out with his cousins yesterday afternoon. Usually, I'd hit the mall and then head to Pepper's house to hang out, but not this year. This year, Christmas Eve is going to be for me and my girl.

I don't know what time it is, only that the sun is up and I'm hungry as a motherfucker. I think about all the food I *don't* have in the kitchen and all the warm foods that sound good that I *don't* know how to make. My stomach growls, and I decide it's time to wake Millie and coax her out of bed—bribing her with the idea of a nice, hot breakfast. It's been a minute since I've eaten at Morning Glory. They serve the best damn pancakes. My mouth waters at the thought, and I've made up my mind.

Looking at Millie, totally knocked out beside me—her hands tucked beneath her cheek, her bare shoulder peeking out from underneath the covers—I don't hesitate to just stare at her for a moment. *My best girl.* In every way, she's all that I've ever wanted in a woman. Gorgeous. Intelligent. Sweet, but with a smart-ass mouth I can't get enough of. She's tender on the inside, but tough on the outside. And most of all, she believes in me. She *sees* me for who I am.

I love her, and I love her *hard;* not because she makes my heart sing; not because she's—hands down, dick up—the *best* lay I've ever had in my entire life; not even because I fought so hard to get her. I'm in love with her because beneath that hard shell, behind that sassy mouth, underneath her stubborn nature lies a woman whose vulnerability is nothing short of sheer, fucking beauty. Every glimpse I see of *Millie*—my *Millicent*—it makes me want her more. And with every passing day, she invites me in a little deeper, proving herself to be a rare treasure worthy of the fight.

Suddenly, I'm craving something more than pancakes. I smile to myself and then sneak beneath the covers toward the foot of the bed. My feet stick out from under the warmth of our blanket, but I don't mind—my dick already twitching with excitement. I roll her onto her back, and she frees a sleepy sigh as I position myself between her legs, my mouth hovering over her pussy.

I flatten and then drag my tongue up her slit, repeating the act over and over until she begins to stir. I stifle a chuckle but don't fight my grin when her sweet cunt grows more delicious as she becomes aroused. Though, I laugh when I hear her sharp inhalation of surprise followed by her abrupt movement. She lifts the sheets and peers down at me, as if to confirm that it's me who's about to devour the hell out of her pussy—

Like it would be anyone else…

"Morning, baby doll," I mutter, my lips grazing her wet skin, my voice still hoarse from sleep.

She groans in reply, lifting her knees and spreading her legs as she drops the sheet and starts to relax. I wrap my lips around her clit, sucking her into my mouth before I flick the sensitive flesh with the tip of my tongue.

"Oh, *god,*" she moans airily.

I graze over her clit with my teeth as I pull away, and then I plunge my tongue into her entrance, lapping her up like the hungry man that I am. I free a grunt, voicing just how much I'm enjoying this. When she rolls her hips against my mouth greedily, I reach my hands up and flatten my palms against the inside of her thighs, pressing her down, making my desires known.

I own her orgasm.

Me.

My tongue does a figure-eight, teasing her entrance and her clit as I work her up even more. From down here, buried underneath the covers, I can still hear her ragged breathing, and my dick aches to take a dip. I resist and suck on her clit, determined to taste her orgasm.

"*Baby!*" she cries with a jerk. I can tell she wants to move her hips, but I won't let her.

I suck harder.

The deep, guttural sound she makes in response shatters my restraint. I run my tongue along the length of her slit once more, sampling her cum, and then I crawl up her body. I sink my dick into her swollen center just as my head breaks out from beneath the covers. "Mmmm, Sage," she sighs, her hooded eyes peering up at me.

"You're so goddamn sexy," I mutter before I lean down and capture her mouth with mine. She hums, her fingers sliding up the back of my neck and into my hair as I roll my hips. She's fucking tight, and her soaked pussy feels so good—warm and slick and inviting. "Fuck, baby, I love your pussy," I mumble against her mouth.

"Love your dick," she whispers in reply.

My lips curl into a grin and she giggles—the sound raspy and sexy as all hell.

"You gonna come again for me, baby?"

Her hands slide out of my hair and over my back as her eyes lock with mine. "You are the master of my orgasms—you own me, Sage. Every part of me, baby. So, you tell me—*am I* going to come again?"

"*Shit,*" I hiss, loving every single word of her goddamn challenge. I prop my hands on either side of her head, lifting myself up a little, offering myself more mobility. I roll my hips slower, careful to graze my pelvis against her clit with every thrust. Looking down between us, I have to bite my lip—*hard*—in order to keep myself from blowing my load. Fucking love the sight of my dick disappearing into her perfect cunt.

"Yes—*yes*, don't stop," she gasps, her fingers digging into my shoulders.

I don't stop. I go slower, exaggerating my every move. She sucks in a breath, arching her back as her pussy begins to flutter around me.

"Sage!" she moans loudly.

"Come for me, baby," I demand, seconds away from losing control.

"*Yes,*" she whimpers as her walls tighten, pulling forth my release.

I pump in and out of her lazily until she milks me dry, and then I settle my weight on top of her. She breathes a sated sigh as she clings to me. I brush my lips across hers softly before I say, "Merry Christmas Eve, baby."

Millicent

I'M SHORT OF BREATH, unable to inhale deeply with his weight resting atop my chest,but I don't give a damn. I've been awake for all of thirty minutes and it's already the best Christmas Eve I've had in my entire life. I don't want him to move. I don't want to breathe if it means the loss of him from chest to toe.

"Kiss me," I command in a whisper.

He smirks at me before he does as I say, kissing me thoroughly. I enjoy every second. With his tongue in my mouth, tasting of *Sage* and my arousal, I don't think of anything but the man I love. It's during moments like this that I'm reminded that happiness isn't something that I can escape; it's not something that can be stolen from me, despite what the past and the present may argue. No, happiness is languorous morning kisses, or driving through the snow-covered streets in the dead of night, admiring Christmas lights; it's the reality that while we might not be promised tomorrow, we were blessed with today, and *today* can be filled with love making, whispered sweet-nothings, and the memory of surviving yesterday.

Happiness is stopping to question mortality and eternity; stopping to question whether or not there is a God out there—someone who has watched me and allowed me to grow up in an environment void of love only because His plan the whole time was to bring me *here*—to *this* man, in *this* moment—to be on the receiving end of *this* love, a love I'm so unworthy to call mine. Happiness is wondering and believing that perhaps timing is everything and our experiences are not coincidence, but a series of choices that are laid before us so that we might chose our own adventure.

Happiness is knowing that I am loved because I chose *this* man—*this* man who kisses me like I'm the only woman in the entire world that he wishes to taste. And in this moment, death, abandonment, sorrow, and regret—they're not strong enough to rob me of my *choice*; my choice to choose him, to choose *Sage* and our future.

"I love you," I whisper into his mouth. "I love you so much, Sage."

"I know," he utters. "I know, doll." He groans before he starts to pull out of me. I whimper when he drives his cock back inside of my core, realizing that he's grown hard again. "I love you, too, Millicent."

He makes love to me all over again. Then, when he brings me to orgasm not just once more, but *twice* more, I decide that there must be a God out there somewhere.

Sage convinces me to get out of bed and into the shower so that we can go out for breakfast. I'm glad he does. He takes me to Morning Glory, where the wait is insane—especially considering the holiday. Or, I suppose, perhaps *because* of the holiday. Nevertheless, he insists that we wait it out. The cinnamon apple pancake with cinnamon brown sugar butter and a boat load of maple syrup with a touch of caramel glaze is outrageously delicious, and indulgent, and totally worth the wait.

When we're finished, he tells me that he's going to take me to the mall. The mall, on the eve of Christmas, seems like a horrible idea—but when he describes the sad look I'll see on Henley and Carter's faces if he doesn't show up with gifts for them tomorrow, I seal my lips shut and allow him to escort me wherever he desires. Besides, a bit of walking after our late breakfast would probably do me good.

An hour later, we're leaving store number three. Sage's latest purchase was a pack of pencils for Rosemary. Just…*pencils*. Earlier, he had gotten her a really pretty infinity scarf and a pair of monkey print socks. The pencils, however, totally throw me for a loop.

"I don't have much experience with Christmas presents. And not to question your gifting skills, but what nineteen-year-old wants pencils for Christmas, Sage?"

He laughs, dropping the small bag into one of the bigger ones before he grabs my hand and leads me through the crowd.

"In the McCoy family, we have Christmas present rules. Since Pepper, Rosy, and I were old enough to pick out gifts for one another, we were given a designated dollar amount. Our age."

"Wait, what?"

"Yeah. Our parents are exempt from the rule because they always got us things from our list, or clothes. My mom always got us a shit ton of clothes, wrapping them and shoving them under the tree. Padding the amount of gifts was more like it. Obviously, since we're all older, she doesn't do that anymore. Anyway—

"Before we were old enough to get jobs, our parents were stuck buying our gifts to one another. So, we were limited to our age. When we started working, the rule just stuck. We make it a point to spend as close to our age as possible. The scarf and the socks for Rosy were nineteen and change. The pencils were a dollar—so, almost twenty-one."

I knit my eyebrows together, turning my head to peer up at him as I ask, "So you spend as close to twenty-one dollars as you can on your sisters?"

"Plus Harry, the boys, and Sophia."

"So Rose spends nineteen and Pepper spends twenty-five?"

"Yup," he says with a nod.

A small smile pulls at the corner of my mouth. There's something really endearing about that tradition. I try not to think about the fact that I was raised as an only child, and the last Christmas gift I ever received was a plastic doll at the age of five. That was before my father left. My mother made certain I understood that it was the last gift my father would ever give me. It took a while to sink in, and I carried that doll with me almost everywhere. I loved it. I loved it until I realized that my mother was right; then it was just a reminder that she was telling the truth. He wasn't coming back.

"Millie?"

Sage's voice snaps me out of my thoughts. I look through his glasses and into his eyes, and then I shake my head in an attempt to clear it. "I'm sorry, what?"

"You okay? You zoned out for a minute."

"Oh," I mutter with a feeble shrug. I don't really wish to discuss the past, so I change the subject before he can press. "Are you sure it's not rude if I come empty handed? I know that I don't know your family very well, but you could help me."

"Nah," he insists, dropping my hand and wrapping his arm around my shoulders. He pulls me into his side as he assures me, "It's your first holiday with us, baby doll. Besides, you're going to have to put up with my mom and dad all day. That, in and of itself, is a gift to us all."

"Every time you say shit like that, it makes me nervous. You know that, right?" I tell him, circling my arms around his waist.

It struck me, like *really* struck me a couple of days ago, that I'm finally going to meet Mr. and Mrs. McCoy. *Finally* being an incredibly ambiguous term in this case. I won't lie and say that I'm not curious about them. I am. Their reputation proceeds them, and I don't just mean in the sense that their children speak of them often, painting them as both strict and successful. It's more than that. It's who their children are. Kind, considerate, beautiful people, all of them—which doesn't come from nowhere. They were raised that way.

Yet, it's not my curiosity that makes me nervous. It's the reality of knowing that tomorrow, I'm going to be the twenty-six-year-old college professor who is dating their twenty-one-year-old son. I know of the discord in their relationship; I know they are opinionated, and not at all shy about expressing what they think or how they feel about what's going on in their son's life. I just—I don't know what to expect, and it turns my stomach into a bunch of knots even now.

"Hey," he says, stopping abruptly. Someone bumps into my shoulder and I turn my neck to catch a glimpse of some frantic shopper who doesn't even realize that she just ran into a bystander. "Doll face?" I draw in a deep breath, shifting my focus onto Sage. "How many orgasms did you have this morning?"

My eyes grow wide and my mouth falls open as I stare at him, not at all prepared for that question—*here*, in the middle of a crazy mob of last minute shoppers.

"What?" I manage.

"Orgasms, baby. How many?"

"Sage—"

"How. *Many?*"

I scowl at him before I hiss, "*Four.*"

A sly grin pulls at his lips and the hand that rests on my shoulder slides down my back and over the top of my ass. He then pulls me into him closer, and my breath catches in my throat.

"Sounds like your man took care of you this morning. I'll sure as fuck take care of you tomorrow, too. I'm not going to toss you to the wolves, baby doll. What have I been telling you, huh?"

I tighten my grip around his waist, ignoring the people walking around us as I say, "We're in this together."

"Hell, yeah, we are. So you have nothing to worry about, got me?"

I nod and he leans down and smacks a quick kiss against my lips. He then taps my ass and winks at me. It makes me smile. I love my arrogant little shit—my dreamer—my badass rock star.

"Come on, doll face. There's more shopping to be done."

For the next couple of hours, we wander in and out of stores. Sage doesn't waste time, already fairly certain about what it is that he wants to get each member of his family, but the lines at each register are exhaustingly long. Over and over I think to myself: *Christmas is not a surprise. These people have had all year to shop—why are there so many crowding the mall today, just hours before the big day?*

Despite my confusion, and my desire to get away from the masses, having Sage at my side makes it all bearable. He promises that as soon as we're done, he'll take me back to his place and we'll lay low for the rest of the day. After he's made his last purchase, an *adorable* little, lavender dress that I helped him pick out for Sophia, I couldn't be more relieved.

"Next year, I'm making you shop earlier," I warn him as we begin to trek our way to the exit. "Like, September, I think."

He laughs, but I'm not even kidding.

I'm so busy thinking about how practical my idea is, I don't notice when he starts to steer me in a direction *other* than *out*. It isn't until I see the grand piano in the middle of the foyer, just beside the food court, that I start to question where he's taking me. He looks around and I follow his gaze, not sure exactly what he might be looking for.

"Sage? What are you doing?"

"Hey, excuse me," he ignores me as he calls out to a stranger, sitting at a table a few feet away. The man looks up and Sage nods over his shoulder as he asks, "Is someone playing that thing?"

The stranger points behind us, and we both turn to see a sign that says *Back in Thirty Minutes.*

Sage turns back to the man, calling out a thanks that I'm not sure he even hears above the chatter of people. Then Sage starts pulling me toward the piano.

"Sage? Baby, what are you doing?"

"Come 'ere," he insists, ignoring my question once more.

When we've reached the piano, he sets his shopping bags down and slides onto the stool.

"Sage!" I whisper shout in warning, looking around to see if anyone is watching.

He rifles through the music propped up in front of him, humming his approval and grunting his distaste when he comes across a piece he likes or dislikes. "Ah. Yeah. This one," he mutters, spreading out the pages.

"Sage!"

"Come 'ere," he repeats, offering me his hand.

"I don't think this is a good idea."

"I know how much you like it when I play. Haven't played for you since that first time. Come 'ere. I owe you for braving this place with me today."

I stare at him for a second, still unsure as to whether or not this is a good idea.

Those blue eyes behind those annoyingly sexy horn-rimmed glasses win.

I take his hand and he tugs me down beside him. He smiles at me, pressing a quick kiss against my lips, and then shifts his focus to the music in front of him.

"On my cue, turn the page for me, okay?"

"Okay," I murmur.

He places his fingers over the ebony and ivory keys, draws in a deep breath, and then starts the opening bars of Tchaikovsky's *The Nutcracker: Waltz of the Flowers.* My heart races as I watch his fingers move effortlessly and so gracefully. Within seconds, his performance takes me someplace else. I don't hear the the sound of people conversing; I'm no longer worried about whose seat we've taken; I barely remember where we are. As he plays, signaling with a chin lift when he'd like me to turn the pages of sheet music, it's just him and me and the grand piano. It's him and me and the *music.*

He takes my breath away.

In this very moment, in this particular space, Sage is offering me a little bit of magic. Just like the evening spent with his siblings and his niece and nephews as we all worked together to put up the Montgomery tree, I'm given another dose of what makes Christmas special. As I turn the last page for Sage, it hits me anew that the man I love is the greatest gift I've ever been given. I know that there's so much more of him that I've yet to discover, but I want to. I want all of him—I want *everything* with him.

When he lifts his hands and drops them into his lap, I'm pulled from my daze at the roar of applause that erupts from behind us. We both turn to look over our shoulders, and my stomach drops at the sight of a large crowd standing around and cheering Sage on. He offers them a sexy smile and a wave. Then, chuckling softly, he shifts his gaze back to me.

"I think they liked it. But I was playing for my girl."

Without thinking, I grab hold of each side of his face before I lean into him and kiss him. Immediately, his arms snake around my waist and he holds me close, the cheers around us growing louder.

I try pulling away, embarrassment suddenly making me less bold, but he grips the back of my neck and opens his mouth around mine. I whimper, my body and my brain in disagreement about what it is that I want.

"Sage," I manage, pushing away from him just slightly. "One performance was enough. Your encore is for me. Take me home."

"You got it, doll," he says with a smirk. "Let's jet."

NINETEEN

Sage

IT SNOWED ALL NIGHT. Now, as I stand looking out of my bedroom window, waiting for Millie to finish up in the bathroom, I let the beauty of the undisturbed blanket of white calm my nerves. I hope today is a good one. I hope that my parents don't scare Millie. They're good people, my parents. We don't always get along, and we certainly don't see eye to eye on a lot of things, but that doesn't mean that I don't respect them. I keep my distance because it's just easier. I get on Millie for being stubborn, but the truth is, I can be, too. That stubbornness against my parents' unyielding standards and expectations can be explosive. I'm hoping that today will be low on drama.

I promised my sisters that I would fill my parents in on the future of Mountains & Men before today. I haven't. In fact, I haven't seen them at all since I've been back from the tour. I called mom a few days ago to let her know I was bringing Millie, but we didn't talk for too long. She was busy with last minute restaurant business. Mom and dad always take the week between Christmas and New Years off. It's about the *only* time they take off, and the days leading up to their time away are always a bit hectic.

"I think I'm ready," says Millie, pulling me from my thoughts.

I look away from the window and find her standing in the middle of the room, looking absolutely amazing. She has on a pair of brown boots that come up to her knees, her wool, cream-colored socks peeking out over the top. Her legs are adorned in a pair of tight, dark red leggings, and the long-sleeved, cream sweater dress she's got on clings to her breasts and then hangs loose until the middle of her thighs. She's got a plaid scarf draped around her neck, and her hair is loose, falling over her chest and all the way down her back.

My dick jerks as I take her in from head to toe. *Twice*. When I cross the room, closing the distance between us, I get a whiff of the vanilla fragrance she wears. I'm sporting a semi I don't even try to hide as I slide my hands against the small of her back and pull her body to mine.

"Fuck—you look gorgeous, baby."

She looks down at herself, hiding her face from me as she says, "Thank you."

"Hey," I mutter, wanting to see those dark green eyes.

She peeks at me from beneath her lashes and I can't help myself. I need a taste. I dip my head, angling my mouth against hers, and her arms immediately find their way around my neck. I tease open her lips with my tongue before I dive in, seeking the warmth of her mouth. She sighs on a moan, and I'm suddenly fully erect. With a grunt, I pull her even closer, knowing already that I'm not going to be able to keep my hands off of her today.

By the time we manage to pull away from each other, we're both panting. Her lips are red and swollen and I have to look away before I decide to do something stupid—like reach my hand into her panties to see how wet she is right now. I pull my bottom lip between my teeth, biting down hard as I drop my forehead against her shoulder. The scent of vanilla is even stronger from down here, and I groan in frustration before I turn my face, tracing my tongue up the side of her neck to that soft spot just behind her ear.

"*Sage*," she whispers, a shiver running through her as she slides her hands over my back.

"Shit, doll face. You taste so good."

"Baby, we have to go." She's still whispering, her voice airy and sounding as desperate as I feel.

"Yeah," I reply, sliding my hands down over her ass. I give her a squeeze and she gasps.

"Sage, baby, if you don't stop touching me like that, it won't just be my thong that's soaked. I didn't pack another pair of leggings, and I really like this outfit."

"Jesus, *fuck*." I take a step away from her, reaching up to smooth my hand over my hair as I try and calm my dick down. She giggles and my eyes lock with hers before a crooked smile crosses my face. I shake my head at her. "That shit isn't funny, doll face."

"I wasn't the one to provoke you."

"You walked in here in those leggings."

She smiles at me, and the happiness I see in her eyes does me good.

"Fuck you later."

"Promise?" she hums.

"You bet your sweet, little ass."

We both grab our coats, shrugging them on before gathering the rest of our things. Millie throws her purse over her shoulder and then reaches down to pick up Maestro while I take the two bags of gifts I wrapped and packed last night. I run out ahead of my girl and my pup, tossing the presents in the trunk before I start the car. When they're both inside, I scrape off all the excess snow, and then we hit the road.

The neighborhood has yet to be touched, but all the main streets have been plowed, making our drive across town pretty painless. We pull into my parents' driveway at eleven o'clock on the dot. We're right on time, but we're the last to arrive. Rosy probably stayed the night, and Pepper has a habit of being early everywhere—even with three kids in tow.

I hear it as Millie draws in a deep breath and lets it out slowly. I look over at her and see her staring at the big, stone faced, two-story house in front of us. The McCoys have inhabited the place for the last seventeen years. A lot of great memories are inside that house. Yeah, there are some not-so-great ones, too—but that's life. That's family.

"Don't be nervous, doll face."

"We're in this together," she replies softly, turning to look into my eyes.

"You got it. Besides, there's only two people you don't know in there."

She coughs out a little laugh. "Right. Just two people. Just the two people who *made* you."

"Hey," I murmur, reaching over to bury my fingers in her hair. "We don't always get along, but that doesn't mean there's not love between us. I love you. You're with me. That makes you family, remember? Once they know you, they'll love you, too."

She nods, but I can tell by the look in her eyes that she's not so certain. I can't blame her—not with her history—but that's all about to change.

"Come on. Let's get inside where it's warm."

Millicent

He doesn't knock before he opens the front door and escorts me inside. I set Maestro down as soon as we cross the threshold, closing out the cold when my hands are free.

"*Maestro!*" Henley cries, running toward the dog.

"I come in with my hands full of presents and today it's *Maestro* you want? I see how it is," Sage teases, setting his bags aside as he slides out of his coat.

"Presents?!" Henley squeaks, shooting up onto his tiptoes.

"Yup."

"What did you get me?"

"You'll have to wait and find out, buddy," Sage replies with a laugh. "Why don't you take Maestro in to say hello to Carter?"

Henley obeys, as does Maestro when Henley's little voice beckons him down the hall.

"Let me take that for you, doll," says Sage as I begin to shrug my way out of my coat. "And leave your boots at the door. Mom hates shoes in her house."

I do as I'm instructed, anxiously tugging on my wool boot socks after I've stowed my boots with all the other shoes lined up neatly along the wall. Sage kicks his off and then grabs his gifts in one hand, taking mine with the other. I lace our fingers together and hold on tight, Sage giving me an encouraging squeeze in reply.

Carter's laughter can be heard from the entryway, and as we make our way further into the house, I make note of all the other noises I hear. Somewhere in the distance, there's Christmas music playing, battling against what sounds like a sporting event on the television. This, of course, is buried under all the activity that's happening, everyone talking jovially to each other.

When we first walked in, I noticed a large sitting room decorated elegantly. It seemed like one of those rooms where no one actually *sits* on anything, making its title a bit of an oxymoron. But as we bypass the flight of stairs that leads to the second level, the hallway opens up into a huge open floorplan, the kitchen and dining room to my left, and the living room to my right—and that's exactly what it looks like: a room in which this family has lived.

In a way, it reminds me of Pepper's home, only *older*; but not in an unattractive way, in an extremely *cozy* way. Their suede, leather furniture gives the room a comfy-cabin feel, with blankets draped over the back of every armchair and couch. Family photos are everywhere—across the mantle above the fireplace and hung up in large frames along the walls. The Christmas tree in the corner is gigantic, the vaulted ceilings accommodating its height just fine. On every end table, and in the center of the coffee table, there are dishes filled with candy.

The kitchen looks as I suppose it should, given the nature of Sage's parents' work. There are three ovens, all of which look to be in use, and an island where Mrs. McCoy's stove top resides, next to a beautiful, deep sink on a dark granite counter. Pots and pans hang above the island, but much like the sitting room, they don't look like they serve as much more than decoration. Then again, with all the cabinet space, I'm sure there's plenty of room to store what gets used from day to day.

When Sage suggested that we come inside where it was warm, I'm sure he was referring to the temperature. Now that I'm in here, I feel like it's so much more than that. Taking a second look around, I see Harry in the living room with his sons; a man I presume is Sage's father sits across from him, Sophia nestled in his arms. Pepper, Rose, and their mother are all in the kitchen, tidying up from what looks like a morning cooking marathon. Seeing them all together is proof that the atmosphere is inviting in and of itself. I understand Sage a little bit more just having stepped foot into his childhood home. I understand why—in spite of the rocky relationship he has with his parents—he still feels welcome here. This place wouldn't be complete without him. Somehow, I just *know* that.

Family. This house is a home because they're a *family*.

"Hey! Sage and Millie are here," cries Rose, turning away from the stove to rush over to us. She reaches up and presses down on Sage's shoulder, and he leans over so she can reach his cheek, greeting him with a kiss. "Merry Christmas," she tells us before wrapping me in a side hug.

"Here, let me take those," says Pepper, reaching for Sage's bags. "Merry Christmas!" She reaches up to kiss Sage's cheek, too. Then, to my surprise, she presses her cheek to mine in a friendly hello. "It's really great to see you, Millie," she says sincerely, offering me a sad smile before turning to head toward the tree to deposit gifts.

I watch her go, combating the memories of Christmas past; ignoring the unexplainable sadness of knowing that I can neither re-write my history with Natalya Valentine, nor change our future. To think on such things is a fantasy based on the the improbable thoughts derived from *what if*. In reality, deep down I know that if my mother were still alive, today would be no different than any other day. There would be no visit. No phone call. No card. Nothing.

Sage's lips press against my temple, pulling me from my thoughts. I close my eyes, relishing in the feel of his warm, wet lips against my skin, and then free a soft sigh.

"You okay, baby doll?"

I look up at him and offer him a small smile, his amazing blue eyes bringing me back to the present—back to reality—back *home*. "Yeah," I reply with a nod. "I'm good."

"Good. I've got some people I want you to meet."

My stomach knots up, but I dip my head in a nod anyway. He then leads me into the kitchen just as his mother turns away from one of the ovens. She's taller than both of her daughters. Taller than me, too. She can't be any shorter than five-nine. She's got a curvy figure and dark features—her eyes the same color as Pepper's, her hair the same color as Sage and Rosemary's. Her thick mane is pulled up into a bun on the top of her head, a couple gray strands hanging loose around her face. Not surprisingly, she's *beautiful*. I imagine that in her day, she turned more than a few heads.

I watch as her eyes glance at me before they settle on her son. She smiles at him, as if just the sight of him in her kitchen warms her heart. Closing the distance between them, she lifts her hands up to hold his cheeks and says, "How I've missed this handsome face."

"Hi, mom," Sage replies, a smile in his voice.

"I don't see you enough."

"I've been busy, mom."

"Gallivanting around the country, I know," she says with an eye roll. "Doesn't change the fact that *I don't see you enough*."

"I'm here now," he reminds her, reaching up to cover one of her hands with his free one.

"Yes, my sweet boy, I suppose you are right."

"Mom," he starts to say, pulling her hands away from his face. "I want you to meet Millie, my girlfriend."

"Ah, yes—the older woman I only know about because my daughters are gossips. Thank the heavens for that," she says, lifting an accusatory eyebrow at Sage before her big, brown eyes settle on me. She studies my face as if she's sure she'll be able to find something there. In spite of the small smile that plays at her lips, her perusal is very intimidating.

"Millie, this is my mom, Abrielle," Sage continues, ignoring his mother's comment.

"It's nice to meet you," I say, offering her my hand. "Thank you for allowing me to spend the holiday with your family. Your house is beautiful, and it smells delicious in here."

She presses her lips together and hums a laugh. I'm not sure what's funny, and suddenly I feel a blush creeping up into my cheeks.

"Flattery is not necessary, Millie," she tells me, reaching for my hand. She doesn't shake it, but instead curls her fingers under mine. She looks back at Sage, causing me to do the same. He must feel my gaze, because his eyes meet mine before he winks at me.

"He loves you," Abrielle says softly, earning my attention once more.

Her eyes linger on her son for a moment longer before she shifts her stare back onto me. I'm not sure what to say in response, so I say nothing.

"You wouldn't be here if he didn't. He's not brought a girl into my home in years—let alone a *woman*."

I hold my breath, still uncertain what to make of all that she's saying.

"What I mean is, if he loves you, you don't need to thank me for allowing you to be here today. If he brought you, there is a certain amount of significance to your presence, one that my husband and I will respect. Not to mention, if you are as important as my girls claim that you are, it's about damn time that I met you."

"You can stop saying *if*, mom," Sage insists, dropping my hand in order to wrap his arm around my waist.

She purses her lips together, like she's fighting a grin, but the twinkle in her eye as she looks upon her son cannot be hidden. I wonder what it means—all the things she says with her eyes; all that goes unspoken but not misunderstood by the ones who know her.

"Very well," she says, letting go of my hand. I'm startled when she reaches for my chin, gripping me gently as she takes a step closer. "I heard about your mother, Millie," she practically whispers. "Simply *dreadful*. I can't even imagine, especially on days like today. I lost my mother when she was far too young, before I was a mother myself. It is a loss you will carry with you; a loss that will define you in ways you might not ever notice. I am so sorry. So long as you are here, if you need *anything*, don't hesitate to ask."

My mouth falls open, my words fleeing my brain. I have no idea what I was expecting her to say upon our introduction, but certainly not any of that. Furthermore, I'm not so sure that our losses can be compared. I don't know that the death of my mother will define me. I lost her a long time ago—when I was six years old. Nevertheless, Abrielle's kind words are not ones that I wish to take for granted.

"Um—thank you," I stutter.

She offers me a nod before she turns back to the kitchen. "Introduce her to your father, Sage. We'll do presents in a few minutes."

"Yes, please, introduce me to the illustrious woman who has been a topic of conversation at my dinner table more than once over the past few months," a voice booms from directly behind us.

I jump in surprise, and Sage chuckles before turning me to face his father.

Unlike his wife, who seems tall by a woman's standards, Mr. McCoy seems short by a man's. Or, I suppose, short*er* than I expected. He's probably a tad bit taller than Abrielle, but Sage has him beat by at least an inch or two. Yet, despite his stature, he's a very well-built man with broad shoulders and what looks like plenty of lean muscle. His irises are as blue as the sky, and I now see where Sage and Rose get their eyes from. His hair, cut much like Sage's—parted down the side and slicked back—is a light brown with just a kiss of red in its hue, explaining where Pepper got her auburn hair.

"Dad, this is Millie," says Sage, interrupting my thoughts. "Millie, this is my dad, Ewan."

Sophia, who is still in Ewan's arms, frees a squeal of delight at the sight of me. She then launches her body in my direction. Ewan laughs, taking a step toward me, and I gasp, holding my hands up to catch her.

"Well, if my granddaughter likes you, you've already earned the best character reference around," he says, relinquishing the baby into my arms.

Sophia squeals again, her fingers grabbing two fistfuls of my hair. I smile at her before I look at Ewan and explain, "I think it's my hair she likes."

"I'd say that's a fine start. It's good to see you, son," he says, clapping a hand on Sage's shoulder.

"You too, dad."

"Well, don't just stand there. Offer the lady a seat. The fun's about to start."

"Time fo pesents?" Carter calls out, his little head popping up from over the couch.

"Yeah, little man," Sage replies with a laugh, escorting me to the next room. "Time for presents."

TWENTY

Sage

PRESENTS TAKE FOREVER, as usual. Mom only ever allows one person to open a gift at a time, not wanting to miss a thing. It was torture when we were younger, now it's mostly fun to watch the boys wait anxiously for their turn. I like to mess with them, taking my sweet-ass time when I'm up. Yet, as fun as it is, I'm starving by the time we're finished.

Harry and I help dad pick up all the wrapping paper trash while my mom starts ordering Rosy and Pepper around the kitchen. They set the table and finish prepping the food while Millie holds Sophia, who dozed off about fifteen minutes ago. When we're finished in the living room, Harry spreads out a blanket on the floor so that Soph can continue sleeping while we eat. Maestro lays down on the far corner of the blanket, as if keeping watch, and Pepper snaps a picture before we all head to the table.

Mom went all out, as she always does, and the food is fucking amazing. Rosy takes credit where credit is due, and we all sing their praises as we devour our meal.

"So, Millie, Rosemary tells us you're a college professor," says dad as he wipes at his mouth with his napkin.

"That's right," my girl responds with a nod, setting down her fork. "I teach calculus."

"No kidding?" he asks, his eyebrows shooting up in surprise.

"Yeah." Millie smiles at me, as if expressing her amusement of my old man's reaction. "I just finished my fifth semester on staff."

"Well, I'll be. Pretty *and* smart—how'd you end up with my boy, here?"

"What are you trying to say, dad?" I ask jokingly.

"I'm just curious to know how you two met. I know you didn't bump into each other on a college campus."

I clear my throat, his not-so-subtle dig extinguishing my amusement. I don't say anything in return, biting my tongue as I look to Millie to answer his initial question.

Her eyes meet mine and I'm gifted another smile as she says, "I actually met him at one of his shows. My roommate invited me out, and Sage—he was incredible."

Reaching over underneath the table, I rest my hand on her thigh, giving her a gentle squeeze.

"It's refreshing to see a woman of your age with your caliber in such a noble profession," says mom. "Perhaps you can convince our son of the finer parts of obtaining a proper education." I fight a groan, suddenly feeling nauseous at the sight of the dead horse she just threw in the middle of the table. They've been beating the shit out of the thing for years. "He can hardly consider it a possibility to make a sustainable living working at a coffee shop for the rest of his youth," she goes on to say.

"Actually…" Millie starts and then she stops. She turns to catch my eye as her hand covers the one I have resting on her leg; then she clears her throat as she looks back at my mom. "As much as I believe in the power of knowledge and the advantage of an education, I can also understand why it isn't for everyone. Sage has a brilliant mind. He's very creative and talented. His keys to success aren't lying in wait in a classroom. At least, I don't think so."

"She's a goner, Abbi," dad says with a knowing grin. "We've lost her to the other side."

"I suppose we never stood a chance, as she's been kept in captivity all these months," mom teases in return.

"You guys are ridiculous," Rosy says with an eye roll. "Millie's right, though. Besides, Sage is doing great! And his days at Little Bird are over, so he won't be living the coffee shop life anymore, anyway."

"What do you mean, *his days at Little Bird are over?*" mom asks, no longer amused.

Rosy sits bolt upright, her wide eyes seeking mine from across the table.

"*Sage,*" Pepper mutters with a glare. "*Tell* me this is not news to our dear mother."

I clear my throat as I lean back in my chair, smoothing my hand over my hair as I avoid eye contact with either of my sisters.

"Oh, for crying out loud, would *somebody* tell me what's going on?" asks mom.

"I'm not going back to LB," I confess.

"What will you do for work?" asks dad.

"The band is taking off," I tell them, looking from one end of the table to the other. "Stefany, our manager, found us a label. We'll be recording our first album starting next month."

"Son—we've been over this. Your little band is not a job. Neither is it a reliable source of income. You can't escape the real world. You can't shirk on your responsibilities chasing after some fanciful dream."

I scowl, my grip around Millie's leg growing tighter as I try and keep my irritation under control. "My *little band* just got back from a six-week tour around the country. We're selling our music, dad—people want to hear us. This record deal isn't some small accomplishment. It's fucking *huge*."

"*Language!*" mom, Pepper, and Rosy all cry at once.

I look to Henley and Carter, neither of whom seem the least bit interested in our conversation. I'm about to continue my argument, but my mom jumps in before I can.

"Sage, *Sage*—your more ignorant than I thought if you think that some small town rock band will sustain you. The odds are against you; don't you know that? Your classical training, on the other hand—"

"You want to talk about me using my *classical* training as a means to a profession? You're joking, right? As if my chances would be any higher at reaching success."

"With the proper education and training, it *would* be!"

"*God!*" I groan, looking up at the ceiling. "Would you just stop? Would you just *stop?* Please—I'm begging you. I'm not going back to school. I'm sure as hell not going back to school to be trained as a pianist. I know how to play—I use my skill often. I compose music all the time."

"Fame and fortune are a pipe dream, son," says dad, earning my attention. "Using your gift as a pianist could take you much farther. You could teach *and* play, providing you with some sort of stability."

"I'm twenty-one years old!" I spit out, slamming my palm against the table. "I'm not settling down and starting a family. Stability is *not* on my radar. Stability will come when I've *earned* it. How is it even possible that I learned that from *you*, and yet you don't understand it when I tell you I'm building something that I actually believe in?"

"How is it possible that you guys can have the *same* argument over and over for *three* years?" Rosy mumbles under her breath.

"Good question," I grumble.

"When you stop acting so irresponsibly, we'll stop having this argument," says dad.

"Your father is right. It's not our fault that your actions require us to broach this topic over and over. Quitting your *job?* That doesn't even make any sense! We understand your passion lies with music—we've never discouraged you from perusing that avenue, but—"

"You're discouraging it *right now!*" I erupt, throwing my hands up in frustration. "Just because I'm not doing it the way *you* want me to. I mean, for fuck's sake—"

"Sage!" Pepper hisses.

"I'm sorry," I mutter, tossing my napkin on the table. "Don't worry, I'm done. I'm not talking about this anymore. Excuse me." I get up from the table and make my way back into the front room. I need a minute to calm down.

I shouldn't get so worked up. Like Rosy said, it's nothing new. We've been having the same *fucking* argument over and over. It's frustrating as all hell. I don't know why I even bother telling them anything at all. If we just avoided it altogether, maybe we could get through a visit without the drama. Then again, I know that could never really happen. Mountains & Men is my life. To keep them out of the loop, no matter how much they hate it, would mean kicking them out of my life. I can't do that. *I* know it. *They* know it—we're just both too stubborn to come to some sort of consensus.

But I won't back down. I'm going to prove them wrong.

"Hey."

Millie's soft voice pulls me from my thoughts. I don't realize that I'm pacing until I stop. She approaches me slowly, her hands sliding around my waist hesitantly as she looks up at me.

"Fuck," I grunt, leaning down to touch my forehead to hers. I reach up and grip the back of her neck with my hands, squeezing her affectionately. "I'm sorry, doll face."

She doesn't say anything for a moment, but runs her hands up and down my sides as she continues to stare into my eyes. I wonder if we've freaked her out—if she won't accept my apology. It worries me. What she just saw was child's play when it comes to my parents and me.

"Pepper was right," she finally speaks. "They worry about you." She hums a laugh, but I can tell it's void of any humor. "It's kind of beautiful."

"What?" I ask, lifting my head just slightly, not understanding what she could mean.

"My mother and I used to fight a lot. It was never about me. I might have been the subject of the argument, but it was never about *me*. What I just witnessed…it was about *you*."

"Baby—" I start to disagree, but she interrupts me.

"Trust me, they don't want to see you fail. I get where you're coming from. I'm on your side. I support you and you know that," she insists, gripping my shirt in her fists. "But they are fighting *for* you. I know that it doesn't feel like it, and in a lot of ways, I think they're wrong. But they can't see around the reality of how few people make it the way that you want to. Their ability to see around that reality is hindered by their lack of control. But you—my dreamer..." A small smile plays at her lips before she pushes herself up on her tiptoes and brushes her mouth against mine in a soft kiss. "You've never let statistics stand in your way. You're not a quitter. Not to mention, you know what you're capable of—and *I* know that what lies within you is only going to grow brighter. You just have to show them that.

"You guys will fight until you have nothing to fight about. Or until you find something else to fight about. They'll argue with you until you show them that you are more than capable of doing this. They're just worried. They don't want the world to swallow you up. I can see it in their eyes—their love for you. It's...beautiful."

By the time she's done speaking, her eyes have grown glassy with tears. As I admire her, letting her words take root, I feel my frustration from before evaporating into nothing. In this moment, I realize that that argument—every argument we've ever had, every argument we will have—it's a byproduct of the love they have for me and the love I have for music. They clash—but it's with a passion that I hope we never lose.

Just now, Millie has made me appreciate it more than I ever have before.

"Millicent," I whisper, running my thumbs across her cheeks. She blinks, fighting her tears as she draws in a deep breath. At a loss for words, I decide to kiss her instead. "I love you," I murmur against her lips.

"I love you, too."

I kiss her once more and then pull her against my chest, holding her close. She feels good in my arms, and I allow myself to breathe her in for a moment. After a few minutes of silence, I press my lips against her hair as I mumble, "We should probably get back in there."

"Yeah. I think you're right."

With a sigh, I pull away from her and reach for her hand. She laces her fingers with mine and I shake my head, a smirk tugging at the corner of my mouth.

"What's that look for?" she asks me.

"You're my best girl, baby doll. I'm never going to let you go."

"Promise?"

"You bet your sweet, little ass."

Millicent

Magic. That's what Christmas is—pure *magic.*

When Sage and I returned to the table, he sat down and asked, "So, how about dessert?" It was hours before we actually dug into the cakes and pies that Rose helped Abrielle make last night, but his comment seemed to sweep the tension right out of the room, just like magic.

I help with the dishes after our meal, against Abrielle's wishes; there was just no way that I was going to come into her house and celebrate with her family all day whilst contributing absolutely nothing. I was stubborn and, with Rose and Pepper's help, I won. She gave me her apron, telling me that she wanted no part in any potential stains to my sweater, and then she supervised while the three of us ladies cleaned and stowed away leftovers.

Sage made himself comfortable in front of the television in the living room with Ewan, Harry, and Sophia, who managed to sleep through most of dinner. Pepper had fed her at the table, handing her off to Harry shortly there after so she could put the boys down for a nap upstairs.

While at the sink, my hands elbow deep in bubbles, Pepper and Rose chatting easily with their mother, I'd feel Sage's eyes on me every few minutes. When I looked up and caught his gaze from across the room, he'd offer me his signature smirk. Like always, it made the back of my neck heat up—the thrill of simply knowing that he's mine sending a rush of tingles down my spine.

After our kitchen duties were complete, we joined the men in the living room. Sage pulled me down next to him on the couch, wrapping his arm across my shoulders before tucking me into his side. As Pepper and Rose argued with their father about what we should all watch—basketball or a movie from their collection—I nestled against my man, taking in everything each moment had to offer.

In the end, a compromise was made. We watched basketball *and* a movie. And despite my lack of interest in either choice, I loved every minute of it.

Hours later, as I lay naked in Sage's bed, wrapped up in blankets, I replay the day from start to finish. Odd as it may sound, I feel as though some of the missing pieces of my heart have suddenly been restored. There's a part of me that's terrified by that notion—afraid of what might happen should those little pieces be torn from me later; but there's another part of me—a *bigger* part of me, that cannot help but to embrace the gift of the present. And when Sage walks back into the room in just his boxers, Maestro trailing behind him, I realize that the part of me that isn't afraid is that part of me where *Sage* resides.

"You still awake?" he asks, setting his glasses on the nightstand before dropping his underwear.

"Yeah," I whisper.

"Does that mean I didn't wear you out enough?" he asks, slipping between the sheets as he slides into bed behind me.

I chuckle as he pulls me back against him, his hand cupping my breast as he buries his nose in my neck. "No. You did a marvelous job, I assure you." I scoot back a little more and he tightens his hold around me. "I just didn't want to fall asleep without you."

He kisses my shoulder, my skin still sticky from our tumble in the sheets a few minutes ago. "Well, I'm here now," he mumbles, kissing me a second time.

I close my eyes, and the day flashes before me once more.

"Sage?" I murmur, breaking the silence between us.

"Hmm?" he hums sleepily.

"Thank you for today," I whisper. "It was wonderful."

He gives my boob a squeeze, making me smile as he says, "Get used to it, baby doll."

TWENTY-ONE

Sage

"DAMN—FEELS FUCKING good to be back up here."

I grin like a fool as the room fills with the cheers of the crowd. The dance floor is *packed*, the whole bar buzzing with excitement, booze, and the promise of a new day—a new dawn—a *new year*.

Even filled to capacity, The Brew Cycle is nothing compared to most of the venues we played at during our trek across the country. As always, the dream of bigger and better is still alive and well. We want to pack *stadiums* all over the world. Nevertheless, tonight holds just as much significance as our last show. There's nothing like playing for our home fans—the people who sang along with us when no one else would. For Mountains & Men, *this* is home, and there's no place else I'd rather ring in the New Year.

"Is anyone having fun out there?" I ask, ignoring the sweat that drips down the side of my face. The cheers turn into screams and I chuckle, looking back at my mates. "Yeah," I drawl into the mic. "I might be a little biased—but I think we picked the right place to party tonight."

Maddox sidles up next to me, propping his elbow against my shoulder. I look over at him with a sly grin and he reaches for the mic. I surrender it without question.

"Sounds kind of like you missed us." His comment is met with a roar, and we grin at each other, eating this shit up. "Think we should give them something new?"

I frown, shrugging playfully, and they all cheer us on.

"Nothin' like ending the year with a new jam, right?"

He smiles at me, handing back the mic before he readjusts his guitar and starts strumming the opening lick to our latest song on a loop.

"This is a little something we wrote while we were on the road," I tell the room just as Knox adds another layer of guitar—the Bradley brothers showing off the best way they know how. "If you like what you hear, you can find it on our first album, coming out early next year. This one's called, *Anything but This.*"

I nod back at Derrick and he looks over at Alex, both of them joining the groove at the same time. As JJ starts in on the keys, I scan the crowd for my girl. She's exactly where she was the last time I locked eyes with her. I smile knowingly, watching as she pulls her bottom lip between her teeth.

"Doll face—love you, baby," I say, pointing right at her.

All the ladies in the room seem to sigh collectively. I grin, running my fingers through my hair before I begin.

"Goodbye was never meant to feel like this
The dissonance so loud/ The distance too far
Goodbye was never meant to feel like this
Moving in the dark/ Hiding in the light
Would rather you just hold on
Would rather you just give in
Would rather, baby, anything but this

"Would rather hear you scream
Would rather see you fight
Would rather taste your tears
Would rather/ Would rather
Would rather, baby, anything but This

"Hello was never meant to feel like this
Heavy with regret/ I'm still hoping you'll forget
Hello was never meant to feel like this
Up against the sun/ In the shadow of goodbye
Would rather you just hold me
Would rather you just stay here
Would rather, baby, anything but This.

"Would rather hear you scream
Would rather see you fight

Would rather taste your tears
Would rather/Would rather
Would rather, baby, anything but This

"The silence of This
Not ignorance, not bliss
Would rather/Would rather
Baby, anything but This."

Millicent

IT AMAZES ME that he's able to turn the darkest part of our relationship into a song that's so hauntingly beautiful, it makes my heart race as my skin breaks out into goosebumps. I stand perfectly still, engulfed in the mob of revelers who fill the dance floor, but totally consumed by all that is Sage. I feel desperate to catch every word, hear every phrase, and understand everything that he went through while we were apart. To say that I'm relieved that we're so far away from *This* is an understatement.

"Holy *fuck*," cries Violet into my ear as the song comes to an end. "That song was *amazing*—I'm really glad you two didn't break up, like, *really* glad—but, wow!"

I can't help but laugh as I turn to look into her eyes. She grins at me, hooking her arm through mine before she nods up at the stage.

"We get to call those men *ours*. How lucky are we?"

I sigh wistfully, directing my gaze back up to the stage. Sage looks *so* incredible up there—his shirt damp with sweat, clinging to his chest and back, reminding me of all the tatted gloriousness that resides underneath. As he throws his left arm in the air, his colorful sleeve of ink glistening in the stage light, all I can think about is what it feels like to be wrapped up in him.

He swivels his hips suggestively, and feeling a bit tipsy and turned on, I imagine the strong legs and the long, thick cock those fitted jeans cover up. Then he smiles mischievously, pushing his glasses up his nose, and my pussy pulses with need. I swear to God, no one could rock those horn-rimmed frames and look as drop dead sexy as the one and only *Sage Lawrence McCoy*.

My dreamer.

My sexy as hell rocker.

My *love*.

They play for another twenty minutes, all of us in the crowd dancing, singing, and enjoying every fucking moment. It's beyond hot out on the dance floor, and

I'm glad I decided to ring in the New Year in a dress more befitting of the occasion than the weather. The spaghetti strap, rose gold, sequin slip dress I've got on has just enough fabric to cover me from my boobs to my ass. Tonight, I wanted to look pretty. I also wanted to drive Sage crazy, exposing as much of my long legs as possible. I even bought a pair of red, platform stiletto heels to make them look even longer. I braided the front of my hair, adding a little character to my ponytail, leaving my neck and shoulders on display as well. I did it all for Sage—but in the middle of this throng of people, I'm grateful I'm not covered up in a sweater dress.

The band is more in sync than I've ever heard them—which is saying a whole hell of a lot—and it hits me that this is the first time I've heard them play since the last time they played in Fort Collins. I shove aside the memories of why I didn't see them perform when I was in L.A., and instead, I stand in awe of what six weeks together on a bus, focusing on their music, has done to them.

By the time their set is finished, it's almost midnight, and their fans are screaming, begging for an encore. They're off stage just long enough to tease us, and then they hurry back to their instruments, Sage clutching the microphone from where it rests in its stand.

"Really? You really want one more?" Sage quips.

"Encore! Encore! Encore!"

He laughs, the sound making my belly warm.

"Okay—*one* condition. It's just about midnight." The patrons cheer at the news. Speaking through his smile Sage says, "I'm gonna need my girl up here for this one."

My stomach drops, the warmth I felt a moment ago turning into a pang of nerves.

"What do you say, JJ? Think we need a little back up?"

I don't notice as JJ responds, distracted by the giddy squeal of Violet from beside me as she grabs my hand and starts pulling me toward the stage.

Shit!

I try to get my feet to stop, but once the audience catches on that *we're* the backup that Sage is referring to, they usher us encouragingly to our final destination.

"Oh, shit—I almost forgot. Adrian, you out there, man? Guys, give it up for Adrian—our brother from Lawful Sinners!"

The crowd applauds, parting like the Red Sea as they allow him to pass through them to the front. He winks at me once he's reached us, and then he says, "Need a lift?" Before I can register what it is that he's doing, his hands are around my waist.

"Come 'ere, gorgeous," says Sage so that only I can hear, reaching for my hands.

Together, they help me concur the lifted platform of the stage, both of them helping Violet up next. Adrian manages on his own, an advantage he earned by dressing in jeans and boots tonight. He makes his way to the far side of the stage, headed straight for Alex. Apparently, they're now a couple—a recent development. In this moment, I wish I could join him, out of the center stage spotlight. However, Sage has me by the hand, and he's not letting go.

"Who's ready to ring in the New Year Mountains & Men style?" he calls out.

I look down at our conjoined hands, certain that there's an electric current flowing through him—almost as if his very *presence* sparks all around him.

"This is a favorite of mine. Sing along if you know it."

When the music starts, I recognize the song right away. As Sage begins to sing, their fans start to sing with him. Only, while Sage leads them through the lyrics, he sings them to *me*. He sings me *my* song. Then, when he starts to dance with me, everything else grows a little dimmer, all my attention focused in on my man. His hand still wrapped around mine, he spins me so that I'm facing away from him, hooking my arm around my waist as he pulls me back against his front. He moves his hips, guiding mine as he sings:

"Can't stop the beat, can't stop my feet, just want to dance
I'll set you free, but will you let me go?
You cage me in and now I can't let go.
All night/One song
This room/My home
Set me free but, baby, don't let go
Tonight/ Just give me tonight."

At some point in the middle of the song, the clock strikes midnight, but the band plays on. I don't mind a single bit, for I cannot imagine a better way to start the year—in my lover's arms, lost in his icy blue gaze as he sings to me with his rich, alluring, sexy tenor voice.

As soon as the song is over, he abandons the microphone, spinning me around before he crushes my body against his. He then takes my lips in a hard, deep, long, wet kiss that makes me weak at the knees. I cling to him, no longer feeling self-conscious standing center stage. All I feel is his tongue tangled with mine, his hands squeezing me tight, his hard cock pressed against my stomach through his jeans.

All I feel is *Sage*.

All I feel is *love*.

Sage

SHE TASTES LIKE GIN, *and she feels like a sin for which I do not wish to be forgiven.*

As the band and I come back inside from out of the cold, the trailer loaded up with all of our gear, memories of my midnight kiss still make my dick twitch. I shiver, having left my coat out in the car; but as we emerge from backstage, the warmth of the crowded room washes over me. I head directly for the bar, ready for a drink, thirsty for my girl.

Once we've waded through the masses, the guys and I are all served right away—our drinks on the house. I order a beer for myself and a gin and tonic for Millie before I go hunting. I find her a few minutes later, at a table with Rosy, her roommate, Sami, and Violet. Her back is to me, so I walk up right behind her, molding my body around hers as I set her drink down.

She arches her back, pressing her ass into my crotch as she turns her neck in order to meet my gaze. "Hi," she murmurs, her voice so low I can barely hear it over the house music.

"It's about damn time! You guys took forever to pack up," says Violet just as JJ arrives.

"It was twenty minutes, babe—quit your whining and kiss me," he insists in reply.

"'Kay," she says with a smile before their lips are locked.

"Are you ready for this?" Rosy asks Sami. "This is the price we pay for volunteering as designated drivers—we're forced to sit front row center while they get drunk and make-out all night," she says with a teasing half smile.

Sami laughs, shaking her head as she replies, "We're also with the band—making us the only two bitches under twenty-one who got into this party. I can deal with a little tongue action."

I smirk at my sister who has no smart-ass comeback. Sami is right. While most nights the bar is eighteen and up, tonight was for the older crowd. They really are the only two in here with giant X's marked on the back of their hands.

"Is this for me?" asks Millie, abandoning her empty glass for the full one I just brought her.

"Drink up, baby," I instruct, speaking softly into her ear. "It's time to party. New year, big dreams, and great plans, doll—it's going to be *insane*. I can feel it." I slide my arm around her, resting my hand against her lower belly. She rests her hand over mine, tilting her head back to prop it against my shoulder.

"Maybe I'll learn to dream again, too."

"You will," I tell her. "I mean it, Millie—you will."

She raises her glass before she says, "Happy New Year, baby."

I clink my bottle against her drink and then we both down a healthy swig.

Knox and Maddox show up at the table a few minutes later with a bucket full of ice and beer, and a bartender behind them with a tray full of shots. *Tequila*. We wait for Alex, Derrick, and Adrian to join us, and then we all take one before Knox insists on another round, then we all take another. By the time Millie's finished with her gin and tonic, she's as drunk as I've ever seen her.

I won't lie—it's pretty fucking hot.

Her back is to the table, her chest pressed against mine, and her hands shoved down into the back pockets of my jeans. She massages my ass as I throw back the rest of my beer, my free hand giving her backside a squeeze in return.

"I love how much you love my ass," she starts to say. "I think I don't praise yours enough. Perhaps I owe you an apology for that."

I laugh, which makes her smile as I set aside my empty bottle.

"No apologies necessary, doll face," I assure her, now palming her ass with both of my hands. "I know you appreciate *other* parts of me a whole lot more, and I sure as shit can't complain about that."

"Mmmm," she hums, pressing into me as she tries pulling me closer—the hard-on in my jeans far from a secret. "You're right. You've got the biggest cock I've ever seen. It's perfection. I'm sure of it."

"Yeah?" I chuckle, lowering my lips to hers.

"Mmhmm," she murmurs with a slight nod, kissing me in return.

I flick my tongue out flirtatiously and she frees a soft moan, her hands coming out of my pockets as she reaches up to claw at my shirt greedily. My dick grows harder as she plunges her tongue into my mouth, as if she could give a fuck that we're still in the middle of a packed bar. When one of her hands slides to my side, then over my stomach, only to descend until she's got a firm grip around my cock, I know she's trashed.

"Want you inside of me," she whimpers against my lips. "Need you to fuck me—over and over, Sage. Over and over."

"*Jesus*," I mutter, crushing her against me as I look behind her at our table of friends. Everyone is drinking, laughing, and having a good time. We're here to party, and I'm sure our night has barely just begun. There's no way we're getting out of here any time soon.

There's no way I can keep my dick in my pants with Millie's hands all over me, either.

Her lips press against my neck as she rubs my erection shamelessly. I stifle a groan and make up my mind all at once. I'm going to fuck my girl—*right now*.

I take her hand away from my dick, wrapping my fingers around hers tightly.

She frowns at me and I smirk at her in return before I begin dragging her through the bar. I have every intention of taking her to the bathroom and locking us into a stall until she's screaming my name. I've never been so brazen before, but at the moment, I really don't give a shit.

Yet, as soon as we find our way to the back, I notice immediately that there's a line for both the men and the women's bathrooms. I don't stop to question why the hell so many guys are lined up to take a piss, my mind too busy trying to think up an alternative plan. I'm stumped for only a second; then I make a bee-line for the backstage entrance.

"Sage? Where are we going?"

I look around the dimly lit space, noticing for the first time that there's not a single covert place to be found back here. It's too fucking cold to take Millie outside—a fact that I remind myself of when I look beside me and give her a once over.

Then all I see is *her*.

Her long legs, bare and fully on display in her gold dress.

Her narrow hips, begging to be held between my hands.

Her perfect tits, smaller than average, but perfect for biting.

Her straight hair, pulled up and away from her face.

Her sweetheart lips, just plump enough to suck on.

Her eyes, green and gorgeous.

Her eyes, haunted but no longer so mysterious.

She's my gorgeous girl—and I can't wait a second longer.

I take her to the back door and position her so that I'm blocking her from the entrance before I lift her dress up. She gasps, but I grip her hips tightly, pressing a kiss to her bare shoulder before I whisper, "No one will see you, baby. This is gonna be fast and hard. You with me?"

"Fuck," she groans, running her hands down my chest before she reaches for the top of my jeans. She unbuttons and unzips, shoving my boxers down as she takes out my cock. I grin wickedly as she says, "I'm with you. I'm *always* with you."

I reach down and slide her thong to the side before grabbing the back of her thighs. She sucks in a sharp breath as I lift her up and press her against the cold door, her hands fisting my shirt at my shoulders. Then, as I thrust my throbbing dick into her tight, wet pussy, she locks her legs around me and frees an uninhibited groan.

"Perfect," she sighs.

A growl rumbles from my throat, everything about her in this moment turning me on. I take hold of the outside of her left thigh with one hand, pressing the palm of my hand against the door above her head with my other. Then I do *exactly* as she's requested. Exactly what I promised.

I fuck her—*fast and hard.*

The door rattles against its hinges as I pound into her. Every time I ram back inside of her, she sighs, whimpers, or moans—calling my name over and over. Her fingers let go of my shirt, and she feels her way up my neck before grabbing hold of my hair. She pulls me toward her, her mouth open and wanting, and I kiss her hungrily, my groan traveling down the back of her throat.

"Oh, fuck, *Sage!*" she cries out as she breaks our kiss, gasping for air. "Yes-yes-yes—god, you feel *so good.*"

I watch as her eyes fall closed, her head tilting back as she climbs closer and closer to her release. She's so fucking hot. So fucking gorgeous—all fucking *mine.*

"Need a tit, doll. Take one out," I demand, panting greedily.

She doesn't hesitate before she tugs down the fabric from over one of her breasts, arching her back as she pushes her chest out. Her drunken desperation makes me wild and I thrust harder as I lean down and suck her nipple into my mouth.

"Shit! *Oh, shit!*" she whines, her legs squeezing me tighter.

I buck my hips faster, ready to lose my load. Just when I think about reaching for her clit, she screams, her walls clamping down around me, bringing me to orgasm right on her heels. She slumps against me as she descends from her euphoric high, and I pump in and out of her lazily until my dick goes soft.

"I love you," she mutters breathlessly into my shoulder. "You make everything better. Everything is better with you, Sage."

I pull her away from the door and wrap my arms around her, holding her trembling body close. My buzz fades a little, but I don't mind. I want her words—her confession—her *truth.* I want more of her. I want all of her. I always have.

Something tells me I always will.

"I love you, too, baby doll."

Carefully, I slide the sequined fabric of her top back up over her exposed boob before pulling out of her and setting her on her feet. She giggles and then groans as I set her down, and I'm both amused and confused as I help her straighten out her short dress.

"What's up?"

"What's *down,*" she corrects me. "Your jizz is running down my leg."

I fight the urge to smile like some fucking Neanderthal, proud to have just marked the hot as shit woman in front of me—backstage—in the middle of a bangin' New Years Eve party.

"Sorry, doll. I don't have a napkin on me," I tell her, tucking away my dick and adjusting my clothes.

"Please tell me you can do better than that. I am *not* going back out there covered in semen."

Now I can't help it. I laugh, earning me a frown. I grab the back of her neck before smacking a kiss against her lips. "I'll be right back," I say, delivering another kiss.

"Hurry," she whispers against my lips.

I kiss her once more, tapping her ass before I hurry to the bar.

Five minutes later, sated and straightened out, we're welcomed back to the table with knowing smiles. Rosy crinkles her nose at me and I toss her a wink and a smirk before she laughs, whispering something in Sami's ear. Knox, with some groupie on his arm, declares it's time for another round of shots—and the revelry continues.

TWENTY-TWO

Millicent

It takes two days for me to recover from the party that brought me into the New Year. After a lot of gin and tonic, sex with Sage against a freezing cold door, more gin and tonic, a few shots, a three a.m. breakfast at an all-night diner I'd never been to, and then more sex—this time in my warm and exceedingly more comfortable bed—I finally went to sleep around six in the morning.

Never—*in my life*—had I been as reckless as I was that night. It was as if I'd had an out of body experience, spending the night in some twenty-one-year-old's body—and certainly not *my* twenty-one-year-old body. I would have never behaved that way at that age; neither did I have the friends to encourage me to do as I damn well pleased, regardless of the consequences. I'd never let loose that much before.

And never had I ever had so much fun.

I slept through most of the following day, wrapped up in Sage's arms. For once, he didn't give me a hard time for indulging in my slumber. He needed it just as much as I did. We woke sometime in the late afternoon, and we stayed awake long enough to eat, hydrate, and then fall back asleep. The following day, I spent most of my time with Violet, curled up with Maestro under a blanket on the couch in the garage as the guys and Alex practiced all day, preparing for their first recording session of their upcoming album.

Today, I've made the trip down to Denver with all of them so that I might spend another day hanging out with Violet while the band works. We're in the same recording studio that they used to record their EP, and Tank is playing the part of sound engineer again. I know that when school starts next week, my trips to Denver will be a lot fewer, and I want to spend as much time with everyone as I can. I'm well aware that everything about their schedule is up in the air right now. They don't have another tour on the books yet, but Sage tells me that Stefany is working on it. They want to be able to promote their album not long after they release it.

I don't want to even *think* about being apart from him again—not after the last few weeks that we've had.

"Hey," says Violet, nudging my knee with her sock-covered toe. I'm sitting on one side of the couch with my legs folded beneath me, Violet on the other side, her legs stretched out between us. "What are you working on? Can you take a break?"

I look down at the class syllabi in my lap. I was trying to go over it and tweak it as part of my semester prep; but honestly, my mind is elsewhere. I shrug at Violet before I reply, "Yeah, a break would be nice."

"Just got a text from Stefany," she says, holding up her phone. "Her meeting is running late. She was going to bring lunch for everyone, but she doesn't know how much longer she'll be. She asked if we wouldn't mind going out to grab something. I've got JJ's keys—will you come with?"

"Yeah, sure."

She grins as me and then hops into action as only Violet can. While she slides her feet into her boots, she takes Tank's lunch order. Then, when the band is done with their current take, she memorizes their orders as well. In no time, we're out the door, headed to the nearest burrito shop.

"Are you sure you don't need to write any of that stuff down?" I ask, impressed by all that she's now holding in her brain.

"I'm good," she says with a laugh. "You forget—I do this almost every day."

"Right," I reply, shaking my head at myself. "Do you like it? Working at Jo-Jo's, I mean."

"If you're asking if I'm living the dream, then *no*," she chuckles, peeking over at me before focusing back on the road. "I studied fashion design. Some days I have to remind myself that choosing to major in something I cared about instead of something more practical was *not* a mistake. Some days, though..." She pauses, shaking her head. "I worked at Jo-Jo's through my undergrad and couldn't find anything in my field—not even an internship—in the entire *state*. I know Fort Collins isn't exactly the fashion district, but I was willing to move down here, to Denver, if the right opportunity presented itself. It didn't. New York was my best bet, but I was too afraid to go."

"The city isn't that bad," I say encouragingly. "I didn't grow up there, of course, but I've been. It's expensive and competitive—but I'd imagine if you wanted it enough, you'd thrive there."

"I wasn't afraid of the *place*; I wasn't afraid of *failing*. I—" She pauses again, giving me a sidelong glance before offering me a shrug. "I was afraid of losing JJ."

"Oh," I say on an exhale.

"Yeah. Sounds silly, right?"

I open my mouth to protest, but she goes on before I can get in a word.

"My parents thought I was being ridiculous at the time. Even now, I know they want better for my professional life, but they can't deny that JJ was a smart choice. I'm sure we would have given long distance a good try, but it would have been so hard. I didn't want to take that risk. JJ is the love of my life—I'm sure of it.

"I'm not one of those people who believes you can only find one. I'd like to think that if I ever lost JJ, or if he ever lost me, we'd be able to find someone who could help us heal and enjoy companionship for the rest of our days. But so long as JJ roams this earth, I know that he's the only one I want. No one could make me as happy as he makes me. The thought of being without him—" She shudders. "Anyway, to go back to your question, Jo-Jo's somehow manages to pay my bills. I still have a passion for fashion. I've got so many design ideas that I've sketched out and saved, just in case one day I can start my own line. For now, though, I'm content."

I process all that she's shared with me for a moment. I'm not at all surprised to learn that she has an interest in fashion. She has her own style, which I've always considered *rocker-chic*. I love it, and I can imagine that she's got some great design ideas. I'll have to remember to ask her to bring some of her sketches over to the house sometime.

What intrigues me the most about what she confided in me is how important it was for her to stay with JJ. It's no secret that they are completely in love with each other. Their loyalty runs deep, and I've come to appreciate that they work as a team. She supports him in everything that he does; and even though she's not exactly chasing after her fashion career like he's chasing after his dream, I'm without a doubt that he supports whatever decisions she decides to make for herself. And yet, I can't help but ask—

"What about JJ's career? I mean, they've already been on one tour; the next one is bound to come around sooner than later. He'll be away from you all the time."

"It's his turn," she states without hesitation. "I can't figure out how to explain this without me sounding like some anti-feminist. What I want professionally is no less important than what he wants. If I decided to pack my bags and head for New York tomorrow, he'd help me pack, he'd drive me to the airport, and he would call me every single day that we were apart. But two years ago, it broke my heart just thinking about the hours and miles that would separate us.

"Now, we're in a different place—it's his time. I might have an eye for fashion and an education to back up my vision, but it's different with JJ. He was *made* to play. I believe that with everything I am. More than anything, I want to see him accomplish all that he's ever dreamed of. It's starting to happen, and I couldn't be more excited. Yeah—long distance will suck. But you better believe that when they make it big, I will not be in Fort Collins working at Jo-Jo's pizza," she says with a laugh. "I'm just bidding my time, is all."

Again, I fall silent, contemplating what she's just said. In a way, I envy her. Her life might not be perfect, and it might not be all that she wants it to be, but it's a life full of hopes and dreams, with a *love* that carries her through. She believes in *one* day; and even though the road seems long, she has faith that it'll all work out. She knows who she is and what she wants; she knows her heart's deepest desires, and she clings to them completely unapologetically.

I love Sage more than I ever thought possible, and it still scares the shit out of me. I want to see him succeed, just like Violet wants to see JJ succeed; but while I know that Sage is destined for greatness, I'm still so afraid that I am not.

"What about you?" Violet asks, interrupting my thoughts. "Do you like teaching?"

I take a moment to think about her question, really think about it—and yet I know before I speak a word that I already have the answer. That I've *always* known the answer.

"I enjoy it," I begin hesitantly.

"*But…?*"

"I don't love it like Sage loves music. It's just comfortable. I'm good at math, *really* good. Teaching seemed like a logical and smart career move."

"So, what would you rather do? If you could do anything?"

"That's the problem." I speak so softly, I'm not even sure she can hear me. "I don't know."

Suddenly, I'm overwhelmed by the realization that until Sage, I wasn't *living*. I was only *existing*. Now all of that is changing. I'm surrounded by people who are full of passion and drive and *love*. The very atmosphere that they create is different than any I've ever been fully immersed in. It feels amazing. And since I've been invited into a life abundant with friends and family who encourage and support one another, it's now glaringly obvious that my life is still *lacking*. I don't know what it is that I want to do with my life; I don't know what I'm passionate about. It's that very truth that fuels my fear that Sage will outgrow me.

"Hey," says Violet, reaching over to pat my knee.

It's not until I feel her touch that I realize we've stopped moving. I look out the windshield and see that we've arrived at our destination. When she continues speaking, I turn to look at her.

"Not everybody's journey is the same, you know? You'll figure out what it is in life that you want. I met JJ when I was nineteen, you met Sage at twenty-six. It happened for both of us when it was supposed to happen. Life is all about timing, you know? So what if you don't have it all figured out now? You'll find your way."

I nod, not because I believe her, but because I *want* to.

"Thanks for saying that."

"I say it because I mean it," she insists with a smile. "Now, come on—we've got a hungry band we need to get fed."

Sage

THE TEN HOURS WE spent in the studio today wore me the fuck out—but it was totally worth it. We managed to nail four songs, and I can't wait to see this project continue to unfold. We're scheduled to meet up with Tank again next week, and as tired as I am, I'm already itching to be back in the booth. Knowing that this is how the next few weeks are going to go, the first few weeks of the new year, I can sense a change in the atmosphere. This is our year, and I'm prepared to work my ass off to insure that I'm right.

The ride back to Fort Collins is a quiet one. Violet drives while JJ rides shot gun. He passes out before we even hit the interstate. My mind is too busy to sleep, my thoughts wandering aimlessly as I stare out the window and fidget with Millie's hand, which is resting in my lap. Every once and a while, I look over at her and find her doing the same as me—looking out into the night, lost in her head. I wonder what she's thinking, but I don't ask, not with Violet in the car.

She seems to be doing okay as the days go by, the shock of her mom's passing settling into reality, and the holidays now behind us. I know that it had been a while since she last talked to her mom, and that their last conversation was far from pleasant, but she still had to mourn. In some ways, I think she still is. But she's still Millie—*my Millicent*—strong as she's ever been, facing the world one day at a time. Nevertheless, her far off look doesn't go unnoticed.

Alex met up with Adrian after we wrapped up with Tank, and he said he'd get her home. When Violet pulls up to the house, I see that we're the last to arrive. We couldn't have been but ten minutes behind them, yet Derrick and the Bradley brothers are already sprawled out in the living room, parked in front of the TV with a brew in their hands.

"I'm heading up," says JJ with a wave, not even stopping before he climbs the stairs. Violet follows behind him, saying goodnight to Millie as she goes.

"Maestro was pretty excited when we got back. I let him out to drop a shit. He should be good," Maddox tells me, lifting his chin at my dog, who lays stretched out by his feet.

"Thanks."

"Sage?" Millie speaks, earning my attention. "I think I want to go home," she says softly.

I cough out a humorless laugh as I reach for her hand.

I knew it. Her mind has been busy.

"Think again," I tell her as I head for the stairs. She follows me without protest but then lets go of my hand as soon as I shut my bedroom door behind us. "What's going on, doll face?"

"Nothing," she says with a sigh, dropping her oversized purse on the floor. "I just—I have a lot on my mind. School's coming up, and I can't find my focus here."

"It's almost eleven, doll. What, are you going to go home and *work?*"

She opens her mouth to speak, but no words come out. Instead, she shakes her head, her dark green eyes staring helplessly into mine.

"Millicent," I murmur, reaching out to pull her against me. "We're both beat to shit. It's been a long day, so just spit it out."

Her fingers grip the lapels of my jacket, her eyes following her hands before she says, "You're not so average. You never have been. Everything I ever expected from someone your age—*you're not average.*" She grips at my coat tighter, and I furrow my brow, confused by what she's trying to say.

"You're a fighter," she continues. "You don't just take life as it comes, you chase after it. My chaser—*my dream chaser.*" A small smile plays at the corner of her mouth, but it only lasts a second. "You're so strong and resilient, and I admire you so much. It's like your music—it calls you to tap into something, tap into the deepest parts of who you are; it demands for you to see the world differently. You're wise beyond your years and it's..."

She hums a humorless laugh, abandoning her sentence. I wish I could see into her eyes, see what she's feeling so that I might understand what she's trying to say. I reach up and run my fingers through her hair, gently tilting her head back so that she'll look at me.

"You want to sing with the world," she whispers, her voice shaky with some emotion I still can't identify. "You want it so badly that you've turned into this *man* who will give it his all until he gets exactly what he wants. I don't feel that way about *anything*. What if I never do? What if I don't discover my dream? What if I become undesirable to you because I'm—"

"Don't. Don't you fucking dare think like that."

"But, Sage—"

"I mean it, Millie," I insist, frowning at her. I don't know how she gets this shit in her head. It's like she has *no* idea how much she means to me; like her eyes are closed to the way she impacts my entire fucking world. "How do I get it through your head? How do I make you understand? I *love* you—"

"I know, but—"

"But nothing!" I cry out. She jumps, startled by my volume, and I'm quick to give the back of her neck a squeeze. I lean down, inching my face closer to hers before I repeat softly, "But *nothing*. What we have? This love? You know what we're like without each other. I'm a sack of shit without you."

"Don't be ridiculous, Sage—"

"Maybe I wasn't before. Before I met you, I was all I could be. But then I met *you*. I fell in love with *you*. Now I'm not me without you. And you aren't you without me. So stop it—stop thinking of reasons, no, *excuses* for why we aren't going to work out. We are. I'm not fucking letting you go. I'm not leaving. *You're* not leaving. Got it?"

She draws in a shuddered breath, nodding her head as she leans into me. "Yeah," she whimpers.

"Good."

I press my lips against hers, completely closing the door to this stupid conversation. When I slide my tongue along the seam of her lips, seeking entrance into her mouth, she opens up for me, and I kiss her deeper. She pushes herself up on her tiptoes, circling her arms around my neck, and our exchange turns wet and greedy. My hands slip from out of her hair before I wrap my arms around her middle, splaying my hands against her back, pressing her against me tighter. We don't do anything but kiss, and it's as if we both know that *this* is exactly what we need right now.

I kiss her long and hard, and she kisses me back harder and longer. In this moment, we're both fighting for us—fighting for each other—and I know I'll never stop fighting. My girl is worthy of the dissonance, and our song will play on.

TWENTY-THREE

Millicent

Getting out of bed on the first day of the semester is always a challenge. Getting out of bed on the first day of the semester is nearly impossible when I wake up naked, tangled in the sheets with Sage. Lucky for me, he knows a trick or two that have always proven quite useful in rousing me from my sweet slumber. This morning he played me with his fingers before encouraging me into the shower. In spite of the cold, my cheeks grow warm as I replay the memory while making the trip from my car to the building that houses my office.

I have five classes this spring; my first three happen to be back to back on Mondays, Wednesdays, and Fridays. I spent most of the weekend preparing for today, knowing that it would be one hell of a morning.

I make it to my office without turning into a popsicle, and I'm just shrugging my way out of my coat when I sense someone's presence in my doorway. I direct my gaze over my shoulder and find a very impatient looking Lindsey.

"Oh, shit," I mutter under my breath. It isn't until this very second that I remember I had promised to call her and get together with her over the break. I did no such thing. In fact, the thought never even crossed my mind.

Clearly, I'm still working on the friend *thing.*

"Oh, shit—yeah, that about sums it up. You're lucky I'm as nice as I am. I think I can manage to forgive you for standing me up the last month if you agree to grab some lunch with me later."

"Um, yeah, okay," I mumble, draping my coat over the back of my chair before sweeping my hair behind my ears. "I should be free around one."

"Great. I'm free then, too. It's settled," she says, flashing me her brilliant smile. "I'll want details during lunch, but how were your holidays?"

Without warning, my chest begins to ache. I look away from her, my mind flipping through a reel of memories that make up the last four weeks of my life. Truth be told, there is no simple answer to her question.

"I guess—" I start and then I stop, lifting my shoulders in a shrug as I look at her from where I stand. "Honestly, I don't know how to answer that. There were highs and lows."

She folds her arms across her chest, her brow dipping in curious concern, and I decide now's as good a time as any to tell her the news. There really is no *good* time to speak of your mother's murder. Even just thinking about it makes me short of breath. It's such horrific news to share.

"Millie?" she asks, her arms falling to her sides as she takes a step further into the room. "Something happened—what? What is it? Are you and Sage—?"

"Oh, no, Sage is good. *We're* good. It's just—"

I'm interrupted when a tall, slender yet sturdy looking man fills my doorway. He's in a pair of navy dress slacks and a pale blue, button-up shirt, the collar left open. He's got a long, gray, heavy wool coat on, and the scarf draped around his neck hangs down his chest. In his hands are a pair of leather gloves with which he fidgets, as if he's anxious. He looks slightly familiar, though I can't recall where I might have seen him before. When he doesn't speak, but instead looks at me with rapt fascination, I straighten my back and take him in again, now apprehensive about the handsome stranger.

My eyes roam over his ashy brown hair, cut short at the sides but a bit longer on the top, his temples highlighted with gray. His face is covered in a couple day's worth of stubble, and I notice it's also speckled with gray. But it isn't until I look into his eyes that I realize who he is. It isn't until I see the reflection of my own dark green irises that my hands begin to tremble and my lungs seem to shrink.

"*Hello*," Lindsey speaks, breaking the tension filled silence. Without actually looking away from the man, I can tell that her gaze is bouncing back and forth between us. "Can we help you?" she asks him.

If I could manage a proper breath, I might sigh in relief at hearing her question. I'm suddenly desperate to know the answer to that, myself.

"I'm here to speak to Millicent."

"And you are…?"

"Christopher Valentine," he replies, his eyes still locked with mine. "Millicent's father."

Lindsey

I flinch at his declaration, surprised as all get out to hear his response. Then I study him openly—not that he would notice, his gaze trained intently on Millie, admiring her as if he's seeing her for the first time. It takes me a second, but when I squint, I see it. Millie's hair. Her eyes. Her nose. I call them *hers* because to me, that's who they belong to—not the man who has made Millie fall mute.

I whip my head back in her direction. I've never heard Millie talk about her father. By the pallor of her gorgeous face, I can tell that there's a reason *why* I've never heard his name pass through her lips. I can't say for certain what that reason is, but the appearance of one Mr. Christopher Valentine doesn't exactly look to be one that brings her an abundant amount of joy.

When Millie sways on her feet, I hurry to her side, securing my arm around the back of her waist. She leans against my side, and I can feel her whole body trembling. I have no idea what's going through her head right now, but I don't feel comfortable leaving her alone with him—not unless I hear her tell me that's what she wants.

"Millie?" I ask softly, giving her a gentle squeeze.

She sucks in a shallow breath, blowing it out quickly before sucking in another. It's as if she's trying to breathe deeply, but she can't.

"Hon, I think you should sit down. Can you sit down for me?"

She nods, allowing me to guide her the short distance to her chair. After she plops down, I shift my attention back to *Christopher Valentine.*

"Look, I understand that you'd like to speak to Millie, but she seems rather incapable of managing that right now. Also, we've got a busy morning."

Truth be told, I have no idea what her schedule looks like today, only that we had planned to have lunch at one—but I'm not above making up some crap story to get him to give her some breathing room.

"Is it possible for you to come back? Perhaps this afternoon?" I shift my gaze back and forth between the two of them, hoping to get some sort of *okay* from Millie at my suggestion.

"What time would be convenient for you?" he asks his daughter.

She stares at him, still stunned, and I continue to act as her mouthpiece.

"One o'clock. She's free today at one o'clock."

"Millicent?" he murmurs, his voice deep and his tone unsure.

Millie jerks back at the sound of her name on his lips.

"Please don't call me that." Her request is spoken so softly that I'm surprised he even hears her from where he stands—still just outside of her door.

"Millie, then. Does it suit you for me to come back at one?"

She seals her eyes shut tight and offers him a nod. When she shows no sign of opening her eyes and addressing him any further, *Christopher Valentine* gives a curt nod before uttering, "Right. I'll see you at one o'clock." Without another word, he turns and makes his exit.

I kneel down beside Millie, giving her shaking hands a squeeze as I assure her, "He's gone. You can open your eyes now."

She does just that, sucking in a deep breath sharply.

"I take it you don't see your father often?"

With a slight shake of her head, she whispers, "Not since I was six."

Goodness gracious! No wonder she looks like she's seen a ghost.

"Do you want to talk about it?"

Abruptly, she pulls her hands out from underneath mine. "No," she answers shortly. She then meets my gaze, her eyes softening a touch. "No, thank you. I—I have to get ready for my classes. I—I have three classes this morning."

"Okay," I say, returning to my full height. I eye her warily, trying to assess whether or not she's even capable of standing in front of a classroom just now. The look in her eyes tells me that there are a lot of things going on in her head at the moment. But as I stare at her, it's as if I can see her shoving them all into some dark corner in the deep recesses of her mind. "Okay," I repeat. "You know where to find me if you need."

She nods and then reaches for her bag, pulling out what is necessary to get started with her day. I decide it's best not to push her and then begin making my exit. I'm halfway across the room when she calls out.

"Lindsey?"

"Yes?" I turn back to find her on her feet, her hands speaking of the anxiety she's trying desperately to hide.

"Thank you."

I smile encouragingly before I declare, "That's what friends are for."

Millicent

I WATCH LINDSEY as she disappears into her office across the hall, then I take my seat once more—my legs still feeling a bit unreliable. I try my damnedest not to think of the reason *why*. I don't think about the man who just darkened my door. I don't think about the ways in which we look alike. I don't think about how different he appears in comparison to the fragmented memory I have of him. I don't think about the way my name sounded falling from his lips. I don't question why in the hell he's here or how he found me.

I don't think about *any* of it.

Instead, I shove it all aside, abandoning it to be dealt with later. *Later* being one o'clock this afternoon. For now, it's only eight-thirty, and I have a class to prepare for.

Yet, try as I might, I cannot *un-hear* his voice wrapping around my name.

Millicent, he called me.

There's only one person—one man—who's allowed to call me that. Only one voice that makes it sound beautiful. I could care less who gave me the name, it's *mine,* and it is to only to be spoken in love. There's a reason my mother could never speak the name—why she *refused.* And I don't know the man who just left, but I'm certain he doesn't love me. There is, however, one man who does—one man whose voice makes my name sound like a song.

*Sage stole my heart by simply speaking my name, and it belongs to him—*I *belong to him forevermore.*

Sage

When I pull into the driveway, I run my tongue along my lip. I still taste like Millie—the remnants of her arousal sucked from my fingers tormenting me. My dick jerks and I free a heavy sigh. I'm such a pussy for that pussy.

Shaking my head at myself, I step out of my car. I'm surprised when I see Alex sitting inside of hers, parked on the side of the street in front of the house. It's still pretty early, a little after eight a.m., and I'm sure some of the guys are still sleeping—but surely she could have snagged someone's attention to get inside and out of the cold. Not to mention, we've still got a couple of hours before we're supposed to meet for practice, so I'm not sure why she's here so early.

When she doesn't even look up to notice me staring at her, I make my way toward her. That's when I notice her car is packed full of her shit, and she's not just sitting in the front seat of her car—she's sitting in the front seat of her car *crying.*

Shit.

I walk around to her door and open it without prompting. She gasps, looking up at me with her dark, red-rimmed eyes, her cheeks soaked with tears. I don't say a word as I hold out my hand, silently beckoning her to come with me. She comes without question, placing her hand in mine and following me inside of the house. I lead her to the couch and then hold up a finger, signaling for her to wait. I don't know what's going on, but it isn't good—and since whatever is wrong has brought her *here,* I decide she needs all of us.

I head upstairs first, pounding on JJ's door before I call out, "You decent?"

"Yeah," he grumbles. I open the door and find him in bed with Violet, both of them propped up on their elbows, their sleepy gazes now trained on me.

"We've got tears downstairs. Something's up with Alex. Band meeting. Wake Knox, will you?"

They both offer me a nod before they start to get out of bed, and I hurry for the basement to rouse Derrick and Maddox. Five minutes later, we're all in the living room—most of us half dressed, all of us with bed head. That is, everyone except for Alex.

Derrick sits beside her, and she immediately rests her head on his shoulder. Maddox takes the spot on her other side, resting his forearms against his knees as he looks back and her and says, "Lay it on us, church mouse. What's going on?"

"Is this about Adrian?" Derrick asks.

"No," she sniffs, shaking her head.

"Whatever it is, you can tell us," Violet says encouragingly. She sits directly in front of Alex on the coffee table. Knox sits down on the corner, running his fingers through his hair before he speaks.

"Like a Band-Aid, Alex—let her rip."

"When we got back from tour, I moved out of my apartment. It was campus housing and—even though I still managed to pass most of my classes last semester in spite of being on the road, I knew I was going to have to take this next semester off. I told my parents. It wasn't a secret. I was going to stay with them. Longmont isn't that far from here, and I didn't mind making the drive most days. Then last night—my parents told me I couldn't stay."

"Wait—*what?* Why?" Maddox asks, scrunching his brow.

"They said that if I was adult enough to make life altering decisions—like dropping out of college with only one semester left—then I was adult enough to figure out a place to stay that wasn't under their roof. They said that they didn't care if I wasn't in school, that it was my life and I could do with it as I pleased, but that they weren't going to hold my hand while I tried to figure it out."

"So they just *kicked* you out?" I ask, still trying to process all that I'm hearing.

"They gave me a week, but we got in a big fight about it, which only made it worse." She sits up straight, her face growing angry as she says, "I just don't get them! They told me that they were proud of me before the tour—that they were happy to see me going after what I wanted. Then the second this band became my life, the *moment* they realized that I love being here more than going through the motions of my old, ordinary life, they freaked. All of a sudden, they thought I wasn't thinking things through and I was acting impulsively."

I cough out a humorless laugh and she looks at me in surprise.

"I get it, Zip. I've been there. Trust me, what your parents said to you, I've heard it all."

"He's not shitting you," says Knox with a nod. "I've witnessed it. Not all of us have parents who are brave enough to support our choices—brave enough to trust what it is that we're doing."

"For some of us, our parents aren't a factor at all," Derrick murmurs. We all fall silent and he shakes his head before he continues. "What I mean to say is, we all get push back. It doesn't look the same in all of our lives, but it's there. It doesn't matter, though. We don't succumb to the bullshit. We're in this together; we know what we're about, we know what it takes to succeed, and we're willing to stick it out no matter what. We make it or we don't, but we aren't going down without a fight. So shake it off, Ali. You've got us. We're out to prove them all wrong."

"And don't worry about someplace to stay," pipes in JJ. "We've got two couches right here. It's not glamourous, but you're welcome to stay."

"Really?" she asks, sounding relieved.

"The fuck? What'd you think we'd say?" asks Maddox, patting her on the back.

She laughs, wiping away her tears with a shrug.

"If you can handle us for six weeks on a tour bus, I think you can survive around here," I tell her with a grin.

"Thanks, guys."

"And thank fuck that's over," says Knox with a big sigh. "Meeting adjourned. Now I'm hungry. Let's grub."

TWENTY-FOUR

Millicent

I DON'T REMEMBER A second of my morning classes. All I know is that I somehow managed to get through them. Now that they're behind me, I hope that I won't have too much damage control to handle on Wednesday when I see my students again.

My stomach growls, but I'm not sure why. I have absolutely no appetite, my nerves and apprehension serving as my fodder. As I continue to pace back and forth behind my desk, I check the time. *Again.* It's probably only been thirty seconds since the last time that I looked. It's three minutes after the top of the hour, which makes him three minutes late. I make up my mind that he gets seven more before I bolt.

Just then, a knock sounds at my door. I halt all movement, my eyes connecting with *his* as he fills my doorway. I'm not sure what it is about him—maybe just the fact that he's *alive* and well and *here,* after twenty years of simply *not* existing in my life—whatever the case may be, I find myself falling speechless at the sight of him all over again.

"May I come in?"

I nod and he steps inside. As soon as he crosses the threshold, I see movement behind him. My eyes flicker into the hallway and I spot Lindsey. She doesn't say a word, but merely nods at me, as if trying to communicate that she's here for me should I need her. Before I can offer her so much as a blink in response, Christopher closes the door behind him.

He fidgets with his leather gloves, just like before, and I wonder what the act means. When he sees that I've noticed, he shoves his hands into his coat pockets before he says, "I understand that my being here is probably somewhat of a shock—"

"Do you?" I ask, finding my voice, suddenly bothered that he thinks he knows *anything* about what I may or may not be feeling. "Do you understand what it's like to come to work, as if it were an ordinary day, only to have not one but *two* encounters with your father, whom you haven't seen or heard from in over twenty years? *Do* you understand that?"

"It was never my original intention to stay away from you this long, Millie."

I open my mouth to speak and find that I have no idea what to say. I'm nowhere near mentally prepared for this conversation. I was never under the impression that this day would come—the day when I could stand in front of the man who left me as a child, abandoning me in the hands of a woman who refused to love me because of *his* decision to leave. For so long, I dreamed of the day when he would come back to me. For so long, I held onto the idea of him—the *hope* of a future with him, until *time* shattered my hope and crushed my dream into nothing.

It hurt too much to even *resent* him. Instead, I thought nothing of him. I let him go completely. I didn't wonder about what I would say if I was ever given the chance, because I didn't think that a day like today would come. I certainly wasn't going to go *searching* for such an opportunity, either. Life with one difficult parent had been hard enough to endure. I saw no point in looking to add to my troubles.

"Perhaps this would be easier if we both sat?" he suggests, motioning to the two chairs placed in front of my desk. I ignore his invitation but take his advice, occupying my own chair. He nods, as if he *understands* something, and then shrugs out of his coat before taking a seat himself.

"I don't understand why you're here—*how* you're here," I murmur in an attempt to start solving the mystery of his presence.

"I read about Natalya's death in the paper. I'm sorry for your loss, Millie, I truly am."

I knit my eyebrows together, confused by his words—bewildered by his condolences.

"I decided to take a chance and searched for you on the internet. It didn't take me long to find you."

"It—it didn't take you long to find me?" I stumble over my words. "Oh, my god, you're joking, right?" I ask, my lungs shrinking again. I try my best to draw in a deep breath, but my chest aches and I can't manage more than my shallow inhalations. "My mother dies and you decide to search for me? After twenty years? Why? Did you think I needed looking after? Because I *don't*."

"Millicent—"

"Don't call me—"

"I apologize," he mutters, his feathers obviously ruffled. "But you need to know this isn't the first time I've tried to make contact with you."

"It isn't?" I whisper, my fight instantly evaporating at his confession.

He takes a deep breath, relaxing the features of his face before he begins speaking. "Four years after your mother and I split, I remarried. Her name is Gretchen. She didn't know about you at first. It's not something I'm proud of, but it's the truth."

I try to school the features of my face to express a state of indifference, but I'm not sure how successful I am. The more he speaks, the more grateful I am that I *didn't* spend years painting a picture of him. If I had, I would have been more disappointed than I already am at hearing that he didn't just *leave* me, he acted as if I didn't even *exist!*

"What happened? You grew a conscious?"

"Your mother happened," he answers. "After I left, she spent years trying her best to keep tabs on me. Just when I thought I was rid of her, there she was. She stopped tracking me after she found out about Gretchen, but not until *after* Gretchen learned about the two of you. It wasn't easy news for her to swallow, but Gretchen is a forgiving woman. It was she who insisted I try rekindling a relationship with you. However, your mother wouldn't hear of it."

I stand abruptly, suddenly unable to sit still. This is all so much so fast—I can hardly wrap my head around it.

"You—you *wanted* me?"

"Millie, my leaving was never about *you*."

At his words, my anger flares. "You left me to get away from *her?*"

"You knew the woman," he says, scowling in frustration, as if his reasons should be self-explanatory. "How could you possibly blame me?"

My eyes burn with tears I wish not to cry as I argue, "*You* knew the woman and you *left* me with her!"

He draws in another deep breath, relaxing his shoulders and softening his face. When he speaks, his voice is calm and steady. "Millie, I'm trying to tell you, I saw the error in my ways and I sought to correct them, but it was too late. Your mother would hear nothing of it. It was both of you or neither of you. I knew, even if I got the courts involved, even if I got what I wanted, she would win. She'd be in my life forever."

"That thought never crossed your mind when you were fucking her without a condom?"

"Millie—"

"And what about when I was older? I'm *twenty-six years old!* If my mother was the real reason you stayed away, what's your excuse for when I was no longer under her thumb? Why didn't you come for me then? I've been on my own for eight years—and you choose *now* to *drop by?*"

"I have an entire life! I've had children and a wife to look after, I—"

"*Children?*"

"Two girls and a boy. Your half siblings. I—"

I don't hear the rest of his sentence, the pain in my chest so unbearable, I wonder if I've actually been stabbed. I press my hands over my sternum, pressing down hard in an attempt to relieve the pressure, but it does nothing. Then I realize, as long as I'm breathing the same air as he is, I *won't* be able to take in enough oxygen. His every word is *suffocating* me.

"Get out," I demand, pointing to the door.

"Millie," he starts to protest, standing to his feet.

"I can't. I can't do this right now. It's—*get out!*"

"Millie, please—"

"I'm sure that you can *understand* that your reasons for choosing to live a life without me in it are *nothing* short of *pathetic*. And if you think for one second that you can come in here and speak to me of your *family*, as if I should give a single shit about the other *obligations* in your life that kept you from considering me and *my* life, then *you* are the sorry bastard here—*not* me. Now *get out!*"

He stares at me, obviously stunned, and clearly at a loss for words. My eyes are so full of tears, I can barely see through them, but I refuse to let him see me cry.

I refuse.

It takes him a few seconds, but then he finally resigns himself to the fact that I'm not the little girl he left. I have no intention of welcoming him with the love of a daughter who longs for her father. That girl is long gone—crushed by his cowardice.

"I never imagined that this would be easy," he starts to say, sliding his coat over his arms before shrugging it onto his shoulders. "Twenty years is a long time. But I didn't come all the way out here to be dismissed." He reaches into his pocket and pulls out his wallet. I then watch as he slides out a business card and tosses it in front of me onto my desk. "I'm here for the remainder of the week. If you don't call me, I *will* be back, Millie."

I stare down at the card, a single tear trickling down my cheek as he makes his exit.

Sage

We spend most of the day practicing, addressing our weak spots so our time in the studio tomorrow won't be wasted. It's after five before we decide to call it quits, and the kitchen is everyone's first stop. I'm just peeking into the refrigerator when Alex tells us that she wants to make us all dinner as a way of saying thank you for letting her crash at our place. We all agree that she's doled out enough thank yous already, but none of us are about to turn down a free meal. After announcing that she needs to make a quick run to the grocery store, she's out the door. Not two minutes later, I hear my girl.

"Sage?" she calls out.

I head out of the kitchen, stepping into the front hallway, and smile at the sight of her. "Hey, doll face," I say in greeting. I kiss her once I've closed the distance between us, but she's distracted and barely kisses me back.

"What's going on? What's all this?" she asks, pointing into the living room.

Alex's things are stacked in a neat pile just beside the TV. We helped her unpack her car after breakfast this morning.

"Alex moved in. She needed a place to stay, so she's crashing on the couch for a while."

"*What?*" Millie mutters, a deep scowl pulling at her brow.

"Yeah. Her parents kicked her out. It's all good, though. We got her covered," I say with a shrug.

"So—you're telling me you now live with another woman?"

I frown at her, wondering why she seems so bothered by this. "Yeah, I guess."

She looks me square in the eye and states, "No."

"Uh, what?"

"No. No—I don't like this."

Before I can utter another word, she turns on her heel and hurries up the stairs. Confused and annoyed that she seems upset over something so minor, I follow after her. By the time I make it to my room, she's already in my closet.

"Millie, what are you doing?"

She emerges with my duffle bag, which she deposits on the bed before she goes back into my closet. This time, she comes out with an armful of clothes. I watch as she dumps them carelessly into the bag, hangers and all, before turning to make yet another trip to the closet. I stop her before she can get there, gently grabbing her shoulders.

"What the fuck?" I demand to know.

"You can't have a girl roommate. That makes me uncomfortable. You have to stay with me."

She tries shaking me off, but my grip tightens as I say, "It's just Alex. What's your deal?"

"My *deal* is, I don't want you *living* with a pretty, little someone sleeping on the couch night after night!"

Again, she tries to maneuver out of my grasp. Again, I hold her still.

"You do realize you're being ridiculous, right? Violet's here all the time."

"*Violet* shares a bed with *JJ*," she spits out, pointing a finger in the direction of his room.

I shake my head, totally confused how that makes any difference. "Baby, I don't know what the big deal is. It's Alex. She's one of us."

"I don't care," she mutters, pushing my hands off of her. "If *she's* here, *you're* staying with me. You're *mine*."

"Whoa, *what?*" I ask, catching her around the waist before she gets two steps away from me. "What the fuck is that about? Alex is with Adrian, remember? She's not going to make a play for anyone in the house. Not to mention, nobody messes with the church mouse. Band rule."

"I don't care about your stupid rules!" she erupts, shoving at my chest. She catches me by surprise, and I take a step back as she yells, "I said I don't like it!"

"Millie—"

I hardly get her name out before she bursts into tears. I stand stunned, watching as she crumbles right before my eyes. She covers her face with her hands as her tears fall, her shoulders shaking with her sob. This morning, when Alex was crying on our couch, feeling desperate and frustrated, I never imagined that agreeing to let her move in would lead to *this*—my girl, crying in front of me, feeling desperate and frustrated. I don't understand it, but I know I have to fix it.

"Hey," I say softly, running a hand over her hair before taking hold of the back of her neck. "Millicent..."

"Sage," she cries, dropping her hands only to wrap her arms around me. She buries her face in my neck as she sobs, "My father—my father is in town. He came to my office today. He—he's *here*."

Every muscle in my body locks up as I crush her against me. I have to replay her words in my head a couple times before it *really* sinks in. Her dad—her dad who left her when she was just a kid—he's *here*. In an instant, it clicks that the fit she just threw over Alex, it didn't have shit to do with Alex. My girl has seen a fucking ghost.

"Jesus, doll face—you *lead* with that shit, baby," I mutter, pulling her even closer. "What happened? What's he doing here?"

She shakes her head, signaling that she's not ready to talk about it. Instead, she whimpers, "Will you just come home with me? Please?"

"Yeah, doll," I reply without a hint of hesitation. She draws in a calming breath, pulling away from me with a nod. When she heads toward the bed, straightening out the clothes in my duffel, I stop her, reaching for her hand. She looks at me with her pretty, haunted eyes—*there are demons in those eyes*—and I tug her toward me. "Forget the bag. I'll come back for it later. Let's get out of here."

She nods once more and I reach up to dry her cheeks, kissing her lips softly before I tuck her underneath my arm. I grab my coat, and we're out the door.

TWENTY-FIVE

Millicent

Sage and I have grilled cheese for dinner. He makes it for me while I change out of my work clothes, ridding myself of my undergarments before slipping into a pair of sweatpants and a long-sleeved t-shirt. By the time I've washed my face and run a brush through my hair, I feel a little less frazzled. Nevertheless, Sage doesn't push me to talk while we eat. Instead, he gives me the space and the time to gather myself.

The meltdown I had in his bedroom earlier couldn't be stopped. I had been gripping my emotions in a tight fist all day. When I walked into that house, I didn't have the strength to hold on anymore. I needed to cry; but something tells me that I'm not done yet. I know that when I confide in Sage, my guard will be down again. He does that to me—he makes me feel safe, allowing me to be exactly who I am without my defenses up. He has my heart. He *provokes* my vulnerability.

When we're finished eating, he takes our plates to the kitchen without a word. He returns a moment later, reaching for my hand. I slide my fingers between his and he leads me to my room, shutting out lights as we go, Maestro on our heels. After he closes the door, he turns on my bedside lamps and then flicks off the overhead light.

"In the bed, baby," he tells me as he toes his way out of his boots.

I don't question him. I turn down the covers and slip between the sheets, watching as he strips down to his boxers. His naked torso isn't new by any stretch of the imagination, but I admire him anyway—my eyes devouring the defined muscles of his chest and his sculpted arms. My gaze roams over the artwork that spans across his pectorals—the cassette tape with uncoiled ribbon that turns into the jack for the headphones inked in the middle of his sternum; the sound of music is depicted by two EKG lines that span the space between each headphone, continuing on the other side until just over his heart, where the lines turn into script. Each of his sisters' names are inked over his heart.

On his right side, he's got lyrics across his ribs underneath his arm. Down the length of his left side, he's got an image of sheet music that appears to be under his skin. The same technique was used on the inside of his forearm where he's got the keys of a piano—his very first tattoo. Then, on the front of his arm is a guitar propped up against an amp, the strings of the guitar turning into a music staff that wraps around his arm and coils around an old school microphone that stands out stunningly against his upper arm, just below his shoulder.

I've tasted every inch of artwork on him, including the mountain-scape that spans across the length of his shoulders on his back. While I can't see myself ever getting a tattoo, I love his. I love the way they tell his story—how they speak of who he is.

"What are you thinking?" he asks, climbing into the bed with me. He sits on my right side, tucking me against him, wrapping his inked arm around me. I reach my hand out and trail my fingers down his right arm, void of any markings.

"Why don't you have any tattoos on your right arm?" I ask softly.

"I guess you could say I'm saving it."

I tilt my head back so that I can see into his eyes as I ask, "For what?"

"I don't know," he replies with a little shrug. "Life. I've got a lot left to live. Needed to live a little to find the inspiration for more ink. I'll know what to get next when it hits me. Just have to be patient. Can't erase that shit."

"True," I whisper, resting my cheek on his chest.

"Doll face?" he mutters, pressing his lips against my hair.

I know what he wants. I know it's time to tell him what happened today. I've stalled for as long as I can. Now, I have to face the truth—the truth that my father is a coward who didn't fight for me; didn't care for me; didn't *love* me. I thought about it all afternoon, about what he said. I thought about the lies he must have told his wife before my mother unveiled the truth. I thought about his reasons for staying away and how incredibly selfish he was—then and now. As the day wore on, my thoughts consumed by him, my indifference morphed into distaste. He wasn't anyone to me before, just the man who left once upon a time. Now, he's the father that I don't like.

I tell Sage everything, leaving out not a single detail. When my tears come back in full force, he holds me lovingly, saying nothing as he lets me get it all out. I feel better after a few minutes, his arms reminding me that I'm not alone. I'm comforted knowing that I'm *home*, wrapped in the embrace of my dreamer. What I have with him is something that I've never had before, and I cling to it—I cling to *us*.

"He sounds like a prick," Sage mutters after I've calmed down. "What do you want to do? Are you going to call him?"

"He didn't really give me much of a choice. He won't leave without seeing me again."

"Okay. Then call him. We'll do it on our terms."

"What?" I murmur in surprise, pulling away from him as I sit up to look into his face.

"He cornered you today, he's not cornering you again. You held your own; my girl's strong, but you've been through enough hell. I'm sick of this shit—I want you back to happy, and that starts with dealing with him and getting him out of here. So we do it on our terms. Dinner. Wednesday night. I'm coming with."

"You are?" I breathe.

"Yeah, baby, I am."

I draw in a deep breath, relief freeing me of the ache I've carried in my chest all day. I don't know what tomorrow will bring. I don't know what might come out of another conversation with my father—I don't even know if I *want* to have another conversation with him. There's so much that I'm completely unsure of, this whole day filled with more than I can process in one sitting. But Sage...

"You make everything better," I say, reaching out to touch his cheek. "I don't know how I would have handled any of this without you. My mother—my father—I just—"

"Don't even worry about it," he tells me, leaning in to kiss my lips. "Doesn't matter," he says, kissing me once more. "I'm here now. You don't have to go it alone."

I seal my eyes closed tight, buoyed by his compassion and generosity. I kiss him hard, circling my arms around his neck. He amazes me every day. I don't know how life brought us together. I feel so unworthy of all that he has to give—but worthy or not, I'm not letting go.

"I love you so much," I mumble into his mouth.

"Feels good to hear you say it, baby," he replies before thrusting his tongue between my lips.

Wishing to be closer, I shift positions, straddling his lap. He grunts, his hands gripping my hips in earnest. I kiss him deeper, sighing when I feel him grow hard beneath me. Now, I don't want to think about my day any longer. I don't want to think about *anything*. I want to get lost in this moment—lost in *Sage*.

I grind down against him, letting my body do the talking. He hears me loud and clear, and the next thing I know, his hand is in my pants, his fingers tracing over my slick entrance.

"Fuck, I love how fast you get wet for me," he mutters before pushing a two fingers inside of me.

"My body is yours," I say on a moan, riding his hand.

He grins at me, then dips his head, kissing my neck as he continues to work me up. The feel of his tongue against my throat spurs me on, and I want more. I grind down over him harder and he chuckles, sucking on my earlobe before his whispers, "Does my girl need my dick?"

"Yes—*please*, yes."

He pulls his hand out of my pants and immediately tugs my shirt over my head. He then holds my waist, flipping me over so that I'm on my back. I don't resist him in the slightest. I am his ragdoll to do with as he pleases.

He tosses his glasses onto my nightstand as I start to wiggle out of my pants. I get them to my knees before he takes over, freeing my legs and tossing the sweats on the floor. His boxers are next—then he's on his knees, hooking his arms beneath mine. He pulls me closer, my hips lifted off the bed as he sinks his long, hard dick inside of me. I moan at his intrusion, savoring every bit of him.

As he thrusts in and out of me, his grin returns. The sight of his smile fills me with an abundant amount of contentment, and I can't help but smile back.

"God, this pussy—I can't get enough."

"I'm yours when you want me, Sage," I promise, repeating the words he promised *me* months ago.

"Fuck, yes," he grunts.

He wraps my legs around him and I lock my ankles behind his back as he leans over me, propping himself up with one hand against the bed, his other grabbing a palm full of my ass. He fucks me faster, the friction wet, warm, and *marvelous*. Our breathing grows heavy as we surrender to our desire, our bodies helping us escape the world that's just outside the door. He claps his hand against the side of my ass, sending a ripple of pleasure up my spine. I arch my back, reaching for my aching breasts.

"Hell, yeah, baby doll—play with those nipples."

I do as he says, staring into his eyes as I obey. He looks so hungry for me that I can barely contain myself. He's *so* fucking sexy. I pinch my nipples hard, seeking to remind myself that this is real—*he is mine*. The more I touch myself, the closer I get to finding my release.

"Harder, baby," I plead.

"Shit—you're so tight, doll. You gonna come for me?" he asks, driving into me harder, just the way that I need.

"*Yes*," I answer, tweaking my nipples some more. "Don't stop. Fuck, don't stop, Sage!"

He doesn't.

I cry out as my orgasm crashes through me. I reach down to rub my swollen clit, wishing to make the sensation last as he continues to pump in and out of me. When I start to come down from the high of my release, I unlock my legs from behind his back and push on his chest a little. He leans away from me, sitting on his haunches, and I sit up to kiss his lips.

"Lay down, baby. I want a taste," I insist, my voice low and sultry.

I don't have to tell him twice. He stretches out across the bed, his dick standing to attention just for me. I position myself between his legs, swallowing him up without a hint of hesitation. I suck away the taste of my arousal, leaving nothing but the tangy, manly taste that is *Sage*. I hum around his cock, my head bobbing, my fist pumping, my pussy throbbing with the memory of him filling my core.

He fists his hands in my hair, groaning with pleasure as I continue my ministrations.

God, how I love the sounds he makes when I suck him off.

"Jesus, Millie—I'm gonna come."

I suck harder and he bucks his hips, the head of his dick hitting the back of my throat. He grunts, pulling at my hair, and then he swells and ejaculates inside of my mouth. I swallow every last drop of his climax, licking him clean before I crawl up his body, propping myself against his chest.

"Hands down, dick up, *the best fucking lay*, baby doll—every goddamn time."

I chuckle, pressing my lips against his, and he locks me in his arms, prying my mouth open with his tongue. I can tell, with just this kiss, that he's not done with me yet. Not even close.

"That was good, guys," says Tank, his voice coming through our headphones. "You got one more in you?" he asks us.

We've been working this song for almost an hour, playing it over and over. Some takes sound exactly the same to my ears, but we all trust Tank. If he's asking us to do it again, we'll fucking do it again.

I look over my shoulder at the rest of the band, all of which offer Tank some sort of signal indicating that we could do this all day. I toss him a chin lift myself, reaching for a bottle of water to coat my throat before we hit the song again. Just before we get ready to start, I watch as Stefany rushes into the room with Tank, talking fast. He nods at her and then she's gone, only to appear in the room with us.

"I've got news, boys and girl—sorry to interrupt. Although, not really, because you're going to fucking *love* what I have to tell you."

I slide my headphones down around my neck, folding my arms across my chest as I wait for her announcement. She bounces on her toes, and a small smile tugs at my lips. That's her *tell*. She's got something big in the works.

"What's cookin', babe?" asks Maddox.

"I just got off the phone with Greg. He's listened to the tracks you laid down last week and decided that he wants to release *You and Me* as your single."

"We still have eight more songs he hasn't heard," says JJ.

"That's okay. Trust me. Trust *him*. Trust his ear—the song is great; it's the perfect length, it's catchy, it's upbeat, and it showcases your sound just enough to offer an enticing tease."

Her reply must satisfy JJ, for he simply nods in response.

"But that's not all. He wants to put this single out there with everything we've got. We're talking radio, Apple music, iTunes, Spotify, Amazon and—" She pauses for dramatic effect. "We're shooting a video."

"For real?" asks Knox, sounding about as astonished as I feel.

"I shit you not," Stefany replies with a grin. "It won't be anything crazy fancy. What we want to do is get a camera in here—in the studio. We want to do this candid. We'll keep it simple. It'll be a way to introduce your faces to the world along side the single. We'll slap that thing on YouTube and watch it spread. Videos are easy to share all over social media. Hopefully, you guys will catch like wildfire."

"Hell, yeah. That's what's up," says Maddox.

We all pipe in our agreement, earning us a laugh from Stefany.

"Told you you'd love my news. Now, get back to work," she says with a wink, backing her way toward the door. "I'll have more details for you later."

Excitement now filling the room with a new energy, we do exactly as she commands and get back to work. After we've played through our current song, we get two thumbs up from Tank before we dive into our next track. We work for another hour and then he says we've earned ourselves a little break.

As I make my way to the lobby, I pull out my phone, thinking about Millie. By the time we went to bed last night, I'm certain her dad wasn't at the forefront of her mind; but when we got up this morning, I could tell that she was in her head. I let her be, knowing that calling her dad to set up a meeting wasn't going to be easy. Now, as I hit the call button, I hope she's doing all right.

"Hello?" she answers on the second ring.

"Hey, doll. What's up?"

"I actually just got back to my desk. My office hours start in a few minutes. Are you guys done?"

"Not yet," I reply, leaning against the wall. "We're just taking a breather. Got some exciting news, though. I'll fill you in tonight."

"Okay."

"Did you call your dad?"

She inhales deeply and blows out a sigh before she says, "Yeah. I did."

"You okay?"

"Yeah. I'm okay. Um—I told him I wanted to have dinner a Giuseppe's."

I lift my eyebrows in surprise. "Are you sure about that?"

"I know that you don't like to go there, but your family will probably be there and…"

Her voice trails off, as if she's apprehensive about giving voice to her reasons. But I don't need to hear more. "It's perfect," I tell her, suddenly bursting with pride. "You're one of us, baby."

She doesn't respond right away, and I can imagine the look on her face right now. I wish I was there, or that she was *here*, and that I could pull her against me and chase away those demons in her eyes.

"I—I should go," she says, a slight tremble in her voice.

"Yeah. Me too. Love you."

"I love you, too."

"See you tonight."

"Bye."

As soon as I disconnect, I shoot my sister a text, asking if she'll be working a shift at our parent's restaurant tomorrow night. I'm making my way back to the sound booth when my phone alerts me to a new message.

Rosy: No. Why?

Me: Want to pick up an extra shift?

Rosy: Not really. Why?

Me: What if I promise to tip really well?

Rosy: For real?!?!

Rosy: Okay, maybe.

Rosy: But WHY???

Me: Call you later. Thanks, little lady.

Rosy: I only said MAYBE.

Me: Trust me. You'll be there.

TWENTY-SIX

Millicent

I'VE CHANGED THREE TIMES, my discarded choices now strewn across the bed. I'm not exactly sure why it matters what I'm wearing. I'm not trying to impress the man. Not to mention the fact that I hadn't gone to great lengths to pick an outfit for the first time he saw me. Then again, I had no warning. This time, I suppose I could argue that I simply wish to feel comfortable in my own skin, so the perfect outfit is necessary.

I decide on a pair of skinny blue jeans, a plain white, long-sleeved shirt, and my tan, cowl neck, poncho sweater. It's both warm and flattering, a combination I appreciate, and it gives me an excuse to wear my brown, suede ankle boots with the double buckle on the side. I touch up my makeup—darkening my eyeliner and adding another coat of mascara—before I see to my hair. I'm just finishing up my loose top bun when I hear Sage let himself into the apartment.

While my request for him to stay at my place was a bit hysterical, I told him yesterday that I really did mean it. Our civilized and honest conversation sent him back to the house to pack a bag, and my spare key was added to his keyring without further argument. Now, hearing him waltz right in fills me with a sense of security that I cling to. It's a relief knowing that he's here because he loves me, because he cares about what matters to me, and because he wants me back to happy.

With him by my side, I know I'll get there.

"Doll face?"

"In the bathroom," I call out.

No sooner are the words out of my mouth, and he's filling the doorway, his icy blue eyes behind those horn-rimmed glasses giving me a proper once over.

"Damn," he mutters.

"What?" I look down at myself and then turn to face him directly. "Should I have picked something else? Is this too casual? It's probably too—"

He interrupts me with is body, his hands reaching out to grab my hips before he pulls me flush against him.

"Need a taste," he says before capturing my mouth in a kiss.

For a second, I'm absorbed in him. Then, before I'm ready, he pulls away from me.

"You look good to me, doll."

"Thanks."

He taps my ass before he lets me go, and I get a look at him, too. He's got a worn, gray sweatshirt on, with a faded Mountains & Men logo across the chest, his white undershirt peeking out around the collar. He's in his black leather jacket, a pair of dark washed, fitted blue jeans, and his black, high-top Converse sneakers. As usual, he makes the simplest attire appear mouthwateringly sexy. I would be jealous—but I'm smart enough to realize how ridiculous that is. I'm the girl on his arm. I don't need to be jealous.

"You about ready to jet?" he asks, pulling his phone out of his pocket to check the time. "If we don't leave soon, we'll be late."

"Let me grab my coat and my purse."

While I'm in my bedroom gathering my things, I hear the front door open and close again.

"Hey, Sage," greets Sarah.

"Hey, what's up? Haven't seen you in a few days."

"Yeah, I guess we keep missing each other," she says as I join them in the hallway. "We miss having you at Little Bird. Though, news on the street is you're a busy guy these days."

"Tryin'," he says with a chuckle.

"Hey, Millie." Sarah greets me with a smile and a wave. "You guys headed out for dinner?"

"Yes. We'll be back a little later."

"Don't let me keep you," she insists, heading toward her room. "I'll probably be at Brandon's tonight, so if I don't see you, have a good night."

"You, too," Sage and I reply in unison. He then takes my hand and leads me to the door.

For the duration of our drive, he talks to me about what's going on with the band. They spent the afternoon practicing, as they so often do, gearing up for the end of the week. They'll be back in the studio on Friday, and they're hoping to finish up the album by then. It surprises me that they were able to get so many songs out so quickly; then again, they've been preparing for this for a while—for some of them, it's been years. They're certainly not messing around.

They've got a gig in town this weekend, and another lined up in Boulder for early next week. Before the month is out, their single will be released, and what comes after that could be anything. There's been no talk of another tour yet, but I know it's coming. Right now, I'm just happy to have Sage with me. I'll soak up our time together as best as I can so that I'm ready to let him go when the time comes. I know, no matter when it happens, I'll survive it a hell of a lot better than I did the first time. I have to.

"You ready for this?" he asks me as he parks the car across the street from the restaurant.

"As ready as I'll ever be, I suppose."

Truth be told, I'm not really sure what to expect. I don't know what my father wants from me. The more I think about it, I'm not sure that I want anything from him. No matter what he says, he left me with Natalya and made one half-assed attempt to contact me after his next wife suggested he do so. He may have said that his leaving had nothing to do with me, but I was a casualty of his escape, and he can't undo that. Definitely not after twenty years.

"Rosemary's inside. She sent a text when she arrived informing me that both my parents are in tonight. I told her not to tell them we were coming. They'd make a big deal of it. But if you need me to, I'll go get them. If you want me to have him kicked out, you just say the word, doll face."

"I don't think it'll come to that," I say, shaking my head at him.

"The offer still stands," he says, leaning over to press a soft kiss against my lips. "Let's get inside, yeah?"

"Yeah," I reply before we both climb out of the car.

The closer we get to the front door, the more nervous I feel. The overwhelming sensation of shock that I felt the other day seems to be making a comeback. Only this time, it's accompanied by a whole slew of emotions that I now associate with the man who is my father. There are so many things that were never dealt with between him and me, so much baggage that has gone ignored for most of my life. I hate that we're now doing this on *his* terms. Sure, Sage and I set the time and place for tonight's meeting, but Christopher just *showed up* in Colorado—without my permission; without so much as a phone call in *twenty fucking years!*

I stop before Sage can reach for the door handle, suddenly in need of another minute.

"Millie?" Sage speaks, reaching up to rest a hand on the small of my back.

I turn to face him, gripping onto his jacket as I peer into his eyes—his face lit by the street lamp and the Giuseppe's sign above our heads. I don't know what to say, so I say nothing. I feel like a child, unequipped and unprepared for what lies on the other side of the door.

"Baby," Sage murmurs, wrapping his arms around me. "Listen to me. You got dealt some shitty parents—but you turned out just fine anyway. *Better* than fine. You don't need him. You don't. When we go in there, you've got all the power, not him. Hear me?"

I suck in a deep, cold breath and offer him a nod. I do. I do hear him, and he's right.

I've got all the power. Not him.

"Let's go."

Sage

When we walk in out of the cold, I see Rosy shootin' the shit at the hostess stand. I don't recognize the girl she's laughing with, but the longer I stay away from this place, the less familiar the staff becomes. As we approach them, Rosy spots us and offers us both a grin.

"Hey, guys!"

"Hey," I mutter, wondering why she's so chipper.

"Your dinner companion has already arrived," she says with a smirk. "I'll take them, Jill. Be back in a minute."

I frown at my sister. I didn't tell her all Millie's business, but she knows enough to understand that this isn't some joyful reunion. Why she's acting so weird about it, I have no idea. Then, as we walk into the main room, it all makes sense. Rosy looks back at me from over her shoulder, as if to make sure that I've spotted them, and then giggles. I nudge Millie, who looks up at me distractedly, and point to a corner booth on the far side of the room. Harry and Pepper are here with the boys and Sophia. Pepper looks away from Henley just in time to see us staring. She winks and then shifts her attention back onto her son.

"Did you tell them to come?" Millie whispers.

"No," I reply with a knowing smile. "Remember what I said a few weeks ago? Told you my sisters would be all over your ass."

A small smile tugs at the corner of her mouth as we continue to follow Rosy. That smile disappears when we reach our table. My eyes roam over the prick Millie told me about the other day, and I'm immediately unimpressed. He's a slim dude, his face covered in a few day's worth of scruff, a look that clashes with his collard shirt underneath his sweater. I can barely see how he and Millie resemble one another, but I can't deny the dark green eyes that stare me down look familiar.

I like those eyes a lot better on my girl, I think to myself as I stare right back.

"Hi," Millie speaks, drawing his attention in her direction.

"Hello," he replies as he stands to his feet. "I was under the impression that you'd be coming alone."

"I'm Sage," I tell him, holding out my hand. I might not like him, but I was raised with manners. He shakes my hand, still looking at me with a perturbed expression on his face.

"Sage is my boyfriend," says Millie. "Sage, this is my father—Christopher."

He nods at me, as if he *gets* something I don't, and then takes his seat. Millie and I take our coats off, hanging them on the back of our chairs, and then sit across from him.

"Sage, Millie, can I get you something to drink?" asks Rosy.

"I'll just have water," answers Millie.

"Me too."

"Coming right up."

"I take it you come here often?" asks Christopher.

"Not really," Millie replies, opening up her menu.

"The waitress knew your name."

"She better," I say with a smirk. "She's my sister."

"I see," he mutters, shifting his focus onto his menu.

I don't bother looking. I always order the same thing. Even if I didn't, the menu hasn't changed much since I stopped working here three years ago. I could probably still recite the whole thing.

The silence that settles between us is awkward, but I keep my mouth shut. The way I see it, Christopher wanted Millie here. She's here—the ball's now in his court. I push the sleeves of my sweatshirt up my forearms before resting them on the table, looking around the room as I wait for father and daughter to decide what they want to order.

Christopher clears his throat, earning my attention. I catch him studying the bottom of my inked sleeve as he asks, "What is it you do, Sage?"

"I'm in a band. I sing lead."

Fuck, it feels good to say that.

"You're in a band?" he asks skeptically.

I ignore his tone and reply, "Yup."

"And how old are you?"

"Twenty-one."

He coughs out a laugh and Millie sets down her menu before she says, "Don't. Don't do that—don't start interrogating my boyfriend as if you have the right to know *anything* about him. You don't know anything about *me*."

His lips press into a hard line, his minor amusement replaced with what appears to be impatience. He then looks to me and asks, "Is it lucrative? This *band* of yours?"

"We're getting there."

He grunts in response.

Just then, Rosy returns to the table with our waters. Impervious to the tension at our table, she asks if we're ready to order dinner. We each take our turns telling her what we'd like, and then she collects the menus before disappearing again. This time, before silence overtakes the conversation, Millie jumps in.

"I still don't understand why you're here. I don't know what you want. I'm not sure what we're doing—*here*."

I watch as he takes a breath, lacing his fingers together as he leans against his forearms on top of the table. "It was time, Millie."

"Time?" she asks, confused.

"Look, I'm sorry I didn't come sooner; it just didn't work out that way. But I'm here now, and I'm willing to put forth the effort if you are."

"Put forth the effort into what, exactly?"

"Our relationship," he replies with a scowl.

"*What* relationship? We don't have a relationship. You made sure of that."

"I told you—"

"Yeah," says Millie with a laugh void of any humor. "You told me you couldn't deal with my mother so our *relationship* had to be sacrificed. Now she's dead and you're here."

"It's not as simple as you think," he mutters, shaking his head.

"Right. Because you had another family to take care of."

"Look, I'm not a bad guy," he insists, planting a finger on the table as if marking his point. "I did the best that I could under the circumstances."

"The best that you could?" Millie scoffs. "It took you twenty years to get here. I grew up without a father because of you. I barely had a mother. I did the best that *I* could—I—I don't know that it's fair for you to say the same."

"I can't change the past." He shrugs. "We could sit here all night talking about what *was*. But what's the point in that? I can't go back in time."

I force in a deep breath, leaning back in my chair as I stare down this douchebag. He's treating Millie as if she should just sweep the majority of her life underneath the rug; like his excuses are worth a damn and he deserves a second chance. His apology is flat out *shit*, and it's pissing me off.

Millie falls silent, and I reach over to rest my hand on her thigh. She places both of her hands on top of mine as I give her leg a squeeze.

"I still don't understand," she murmurs, her gaze in her lap. "I *can't* understand what you want from me."

"You never will if you don't forgive and move on. I can't make myself anymore clear. I traveled across the country to have this conversation with you. I'm *here*. I can't make up for twenty years. You can't hold onto my mistakes forever—you can't hold it against me."

Millie's fingers curl around mine, her nails digging into my skin as she shakes her head from side to side. "Do you hear yourself?" She looks up then, her eyes glassy with tears. "You left me—you left me with full knowledge of who Natalya was, of what kind of *monster* she was capable of being. She made me miserable, and you weren't there. Not for any of it. And now you want me to forgive you? You want me to *move on?*

"Christopher—I think what you fail to realize is that there's nothing to forgive. You're my father, but you aren't my family. You haven't been my family in decades. And I *have* moved on—*without* you. I had no choice. You gave me no choice. And here you are again, trying to rob me of my choice. I didn't ask you to come here. I didn't ask for any of this."

He taps his fingers against the table, like he's losing what little patience he has left, a snide smile crossing his face.

"So, let me get this straight—I've come offering you an olive branch and you're tossing it back in my face?"

"What the fuck, dude?" I scowl, unable to keep my mouth shut any longer. "What did you expect? Red carpet treatment?"

"You stay out of this," he mutters, pointing a finger at my face. "This doesn't concern you."

"*Bull-fucking-shit*," I state, enunciating every syllable. "You couldn't be more wrong. See, unlike you, I love this woman. I want her to be happy. Right now, you're not making her very happy. That makes you *my* problem."

"Cute. How about you let the grown-ups talk?"

"Don't speak to him like that," Millie hisses, leaning against the table to shorten the distance between him.

"I will not be treated with disrespect."

"I'll show you respect when you've earned it, Mr. Valentine," I mutter.

"For Christ's sake, what am I doing here?" he mumbles.

"What?" asks Millie.

"I knew I should have just gotten straight to the point. Reconciliation is bullshit."

"Wh-why did you come?" she asks, her voice breaking. "You told me—you told me in my office that you knew this wasn't going to be easy, but you're not even trying. You're not listening to me. You don't even seem sorry."

He twists in his chair, pulling an envelop from out of his coat pocket before throwing it down on the table. "It wasn't *me* who found out about your mother. It was Gretchen. *She's* the one who insisted I come out here, though it didn't take much convincing. I want this garnishment to stop just as much as she does. It was a ridiculous move on your mother's part in the first place."

My eyes shoot to Millie when I hear her gasp. She sits up taller, staring at her father in some sort of enlightened shock. Suddenly, she's got answers to questions that have been sitting stagnant in the back of her mind for the past few weeks.

The money being deposited into Natalya's account each month—it's his.

"What garnishment?" she manages to ask.

"Back child support," he states, his face contorted in an expression filled with contempt. "That bitch didn't ask me for a single *dime* in all the years that you were under her roof. Not a *penny*. Then, out of nowhere three months ago, she comes at me with this nonsense. She claimed I was in arrears for twelve year's worth of child support. *Twelve years*."

Millie shakes her head, and I watch as she gets that look on her face that she has when she's working on grading homework assignments. I wonder what she's thinking until she says, "After our fight." She coughs out a sad laugh and shakes her head again. "She needed a target. She didn't have me anymore, so she went after you."

"Are you saying I have *you* to thank for this?" he asks, lifting an eyebrow at her.

"You've *got* to be fucking joking," I spit out, scrunching my brow at him. "This isn't Millie's fault, and you know it. What the fuck is wrong with you?"

"Sage—" Millie murmurs.

"No, Millicent, I won't let him talk to you like that," I insist, relaxing my face as my eyes lock with hers.

"I named you. I named you and I'm not allowed to call you by that name, but *he* is?"

I want to reach across the table and punch this dickhead in the nose. I haven't wanted to hit someone this badly since Clay and I got into it on tour. I don't realize I'm squeezing Millie's hand too tight until she pinches at my skin, gaining my attention. When I look back at her apologetically, her eyes tell me to back down. With a deep breath, I concede, surrendering the floor to my girl.

"If you're here about the garnishment, fine. She's dead; can't you just tell the courts and make them stop it?" she asks with a shrug.

"No. It doesn't work that way. You, as the owner of her estate, will have to forgive the debt. It's all in here," he says, pushing the envelop across the table. "Technically, you're supposed to appear in court. However, it can be arranged for you to call in, if that's more convenient."

"Fine. Whatever," she mumbles, taking the envelop and shoving it into her purse.

He studies her for a moment as silence invades the space between us and him. Then, without any preamble, he stands and begins sliding on his coat.

"Wh—that's it? You're leaving?" she breathes.

"You're right. I don't know you. I look at you and I see who you are, but I see her, too. My blood might run through your veins, but you don't belong to me. Now we can both move on, assured that we're doing just fine without the other. At least I'll leave with the peace of knowing you didn't turn out like her."

Millie's mouth falls open as she watches him retrieve his wallet, throwing a couple bills on the table. Without another word, he turns and makes his exit.

"Oh, my god," she whispers. "Did that just happen?"

I debate whether or not I should go after him and kick his ass for about two seconds. Then I'm on my feet, hurrying after him. He hasn't gotten very far, and when I call his name, he stops and looks over his shoulder. I jog toward him and he turns to face me. I come within inches of his chest, looking him straight in the eye.

"You're such a fuck-up."

"Get out of my face, kid."

I scrunch my face in disgust, ignoring his request. "What is *wrong* with you? You keep walking out on her like she's garbage. She deserves better than that."

"Who the hell do you think you are? I'm not going to explain myself to some punk-ass loser who doesn't know *shit*. And if you know what's good for you, you'll make sure she follows through with forgiving this debt. Don't think for one second that I'm going to fund your lifestyle while your *band* is *getting there*."

I take a step closer, eradicating the space between us as my chest bumps his. My blood is *boiling*, and I have to ball my hands into tight fists to keep from knocking the shit out of him. Then I look straight into his eyes—eyes the same shade as Millicent's—and I realize that he's no more than a cold-hearted bastard. He's not even worth it. Hitting him wouldn't change the last twenty years; it wouldn't get Millie her father back. Even more, it wouldn't mend the heart of the woman I've left at the table inside. She's all that matters. Not this prick who has no fucking idea who he's throwing away.

"I don't want to ever see your face again. Not that I think you will, but don't come back. Don't even call. Just stay away. For good."

A snide smile crosses his face, and my gut tells me I need to back down before I do something supid.

"How noble of you."

"Fuck off," I spit out before I turn and walk away.

It isn't until I'm back inside the warmth of the restaurant that I realize I left my jacket on the back of my chair. I shake off the chill as I walk past the hostess station, stopping dead in my tracks when I spot our table. Pepper's in my seat, smiling at Carter with Sophia resting against her chest. Carter's sitting across Millie's lap, showing off his activity page on the reverse side of his kid's menu. The anger that coursed through my veins just a moment ago begins to dissipate as I make my way toward them. I don't stop until I'm just beside Millie. She looks up at me when I reach up and give the back of her neck a squeeze. She forces a smile, but I can see the pain in her eyes.

"Please take me home," she whispers.

"Whatever you want, doll."

"Hey," Rosy speaks softly, approaching hesitantly. She's got a to-go bag in her hand, which she hands to me as she says, "I saw the dramatic exit. Thought you two might be next. Try and eat anyway, okay? On the house, of course."

"Thanks, sis."

She nods before scooping Carter out of Millie's lap. She whispers something in his ear and then tickles his side, making him laugh and squirm as they head back toward Harry and Henley.

"Dinner at my house on Sunday," Pepper says as she stands, giving Millie's shoulder a squeeze. "I won't take no for an answer."

"We'll be there," I say, my gaze still trained on Millie. She offers no more than a slight nod, but Pepper doesn't mind. She comes toward me and kisses my cheek before offering me a wink as she heads back to her table.

Millie stands without a word, and we both slip into our coats before making our way to the exit. She clings to my arm as we walk out into the cold. I press a kiss against her forehead, wishing I knew what to say.

"Sage?"

"Yeah, baby?"

"Why do you love me?"

I jolt to a stop, my stomach dropping at her question. Suddenly, I wish I hadn't held back against that son of a bitch. I should have broken his nose.

I slip my arm from out of her grasp, wrapping it around her shoulders and pulling her against my side as I look into her green eyes. "You make my heart sing, doll." I shake my head, sure that there's no other way to describe it. "It sounds cheesy as fuck, I know. I could stand here and list off all the reasons why one night with you was never going to be enough; I could tell you why the thought of losing you after I fought so hard to win you turned me into a pathetic sack of shit; I could explain the way you make me feel just by entering a room—but it all comes down to one simple truth. You make my heart sing. You're my best girl, baby. I love you because I can't help it."

She circles her arms about my waist as a single tear races down her cheek. I lean down and wipe it away with my lips. Before I pull away, Millie turns her head until her lips meet mine. She kisses me tenderly, holding me close.

"You're all I want," she whispers into my mouth. "We're in this together. You and me. Right? It's you and me."

"Hell, yeah, doll face," I grunt before I slide my tongue between her lips, this time taking her mouth in a hard, possessive kiss. I ignore the cold, crushing her body against mine, reminding her with this kiss that there's no doubt about it—she's *mine*.

TWENTY-SEVEN

Millicent

"You guys, guess what?" Violet shouts the second she steps foot into the house.

Sage, JJ, Maddox, Rosemary and I are all in the living room. Night has just fallen and there's barely any Sunday left, making Monday an unwelcome reality that's lurking over my shoulder.

Rose and I are sitting side by side on the couch; she's got a textbook in her lap, her notebook sitting in between us. She's a diligent note taker, I've noticed, and has no trouble focusing in a room full of people. I, too, am trying to get work done. My tasks have picked up over the last couple of weeks, homework assignments pouring in almost as fast as I can assign them. Yet, unlike Rose, my focus comes and goes. Sage, who sits on the opposite side of me, is a frequent distraction. It can't be helped—not when it's his voice that pulls my attention in his direction.

He's working on a composition with JJ, Maddox offering his opinion as the song continues to evolve. I like hearing the way the sound changes, taking on a definite shape as they progress. Besides, I could listen to Sage sing the same three lines over and over and not tire of his sexy voice.

When Violet bursts into the room, a couple boxes of pizza in her hand, everyone stops what they're doing to look at her. She sets the pizza in the middle of the coffee table and immediately shrugs out of her coat as she announces, "I heard your single on the radio at work today *three times!*"

"How many times did you call to request it?" asks JJ with a grin.

Violet returns his grin with one of her own before she confesses, "Twice. But I *swear* it was only twice."

"Baby McCoy?" Maddox coaxes, a sly grin on his lips as he looks beside me at Rose.

She fights a smile and offers him a shrug. "I don't know what you're talking about."

All three of the guys laugh, the three of us girls joining in a second later. *You and Me* was released last week. Even though they said otherwise, I know Alex and the guys were nervous about how it would be received on such a large scale. For the first time ever, Mountains & Men is being promoted on a global level. It's only been a few days, but it's obvious that they had nothing to worry about.

Violet and Rose call the radio station at least once a day—*each*—requesting to hear the song. But even if they didn't, the single is getting some pretty impressive play. The music video that they released has been viewed over ten thousand times already, and their social media fan pages are growing daily. Stefany says their number of downloads is climbing, and they're right on track with where they want to be.

I'm pulled from the conversation when my phone alerts me to a new message. I reach down to dig it out of my purse, and then sink back into the couch cushions as I unlock my screen and open it up. I find a text from Sarah, my stomach filling with butterflies as I read over what she says.

Sarah: We just got word. We can move into our new place at the end of the week! I'll be out by Saturday. Have you found someone to sublease my room?

A couple weeks ago, on the night my father walked out of Giuseppe's, Sage took me home and rocked my world. While we were eating our dinner, he suggested that he move in with me—permanently. At first, I was speechless; but as he began to process his own idea out loud, I became more and more attached to the possibility. He reasoned that Sarah was hardly ever around anyway, and he proposed that I give her an *out* just to see if she would take it. He said he wouldn't move in unless she wanted to find a place with Brandon, but if she did, it would work out perfectly for the band, too. Alex could take Sage's room, freeing up the couch, and he wouldn't have to worry about packing a bag to stay with me all the time.

I talked to Sarah about it the next day, and she immediately agreed. I never imagined that they would find someplace so fast, but she and Brandon were diligent in their hunt—and this text proves it. Now that she has a move-out date, I'm both excited and nervous. I'm excited because I believe, with all that I am, that if Sage moves in with me, my apartment will be *our* apartment. For the first time in my life, I'll inhabit a place that feels like home because Sage *is* my home. Yet, I can't ignore the reality that I've never been so deep in a relationship before. I've never lived with a boyfriend, and it's a big step—just as daunting as it is exciting.

I stretch out my hand, resting it on his back to catch his attention. He looks at me from over his shoulder, his smile from a moment ago still on his lips. It slips a little when I hand him my phone, but then spreads even wider once he's read the text. He drops the device on top of the homework assignments in my lap before he reaches for my face and smacks a kiss against my lips.

"Does this mean what I think it means?" he asks, running his nose along mine.

"Yeah. I think so," I whisper, reaching up to grab hold of his wrists.

He kisses me again before he mutters, "Fuck, yes. I'm movin' in with my girl."

"Wait, what did you just say?" Rose gasps.

Sage and I both turn our heads to find her gaping at us with wide eyes.

"I'm moving out," Sage announces. "Giving Alex my room."

"You're moving in with Millie?" Violet gushes, pressing her hands over her heart. "That's awesome!"

I blush as all eyes fall on me. Sage kisses me once more before Maddox teases, "There's a no return policy, babe—you're stuck with his ass, now."

Sage flips him off as I free a giggle, and Rose grabs her phone before she says, "Oh, my god, Pepper is so going to freak out!" She presses her mobile to her ear and then looks at me as she asks, "Is your apartment child-proof?"

"Oh, no, no, no," Sage protests. "We're not going to have some sort of open door policy where you can just drop by any time you two damn well please."

She grins at her brother, ignoring him as she slides her textbook out of her lap and heads for the kitchen. "Pep, guess what?" I hear her say before her voice trails off.

Sage groans, resting his head on my shoulder. "Sorry, baby," he mumbles. "You're fucked. No return policy and, apparently, an open door policy."

I reach up and bury my fingers in his hair, resting my cheek against his as I whisper in his ear, "As long as I'm fucked by you, I think I'll be just fine."

He chuckles, turning his head until his lips brush against my chin. "Mmmm, speaking of fucking—I might have to fuck you in this house at least one more time."

"Sage," I murmur in warning, my body heating up in spite of our company.

"I say we grub and then you help me start packing. We'll start with my dick," he whispers huskily in my ear. "I know the perfect place for it."

My fingers tighten in his hair, the feel of his breath against my skin making the back of my neck warm. "I'm not hungry," I reply.

"Fuck," he grunts.

In the blink of an eye, my lap is empty and I'm on me feet. Sage drags me toward the stairs calling out, "Save us some pizza. We're gonna start packing."

An hour later, as I come around his cock for the second time, my body covered in sweat as I writhe beneath him, we've long since forgotten about pizza and packing—and I don't even care.

"KNOCK, KNOCK," SAYS Alex, tapping her knuckles against the open door.

I look up from where I'm sitting at my desk, a box full of random shit at my feet. "You know, it's amazing the stuff you accumulate but don't realize. It's like I don't even know who this desk belongs to."

She hums a laugh, running her fingers through her hair as she sits at the foot of the bed. Recently, her died purple ends were exchanged for a sapphire looking blue. I totally dig the change. It's also quite fitting. Her hair's not the only thing that's different around here.

"Tell me again that you're not doing this for me," she says, looking around the room.

All week, if we weren't playing, I was packing or tossing shit out. Millie made it pretty clear that she doesn't do *clutter*, so I've been trying to downsize a little. Now, the room is just about cleared out. Tomorrow, the band is headed down to Boulder to meet up with the label to discuss our album release, and then the day after is moving day.

"I'm *not* doing this for you, Zip—you just get to reap the benefits of my departure."

"You're not going to miss it around here?"

"You're kidding, right? First of all, we practice here. I'll be back just about everyday. Besides, it'll be nice to get away from all of you when we get back home from being on the road," I say with a chuckle.

"True," she replies with comfortable smile. "Plus…Millie."

"Yeah," I murmur with a reverent nod. "Millie."

"You guys seem really good." She sweeps her hair behind her ears before she continues. "I mean, I know a lot has happened in the last few months—with the tour and then her mom and everything; but things seem really good right now."

"Yeah." I inhale deeply, leaning back in my chair as I think about how far we've come. How far *she's* come. "We're in a good place. Finally. Hopefully it stays that way."

"I bet it will. You love each other enough to fight for one another."

I nod and then lift my chin in her direction. "What about you? How are things going with you and Adrian?"

"We're good. It still kind of surprises me," she responds with a laugh and a small headshake.

"Why does it surprise you?"

"I don't know," she shrugs. "He's the bass player for one of Denver's hottest bands. They've got a place to play just about every night. He's busy, I'm busy, we live an hour apart and—I'm just surprised."

"That's a good thing though, right? You mean enough for him to stick around."

"No—*yeah*—it's a great thing. I like him a lot."

I nod, turning to reach inside of the desk drawer in front of me. I grab an old notebook filled with scribbled lyrics and toss it into my box. "Well, for the record, if you need us, you've got a band of brothers ready and willing to kick ass in the event that he does something stupid."

"I know," she says with a laugh. "Thanks."

"It's how we roll, Zip."

"Well, I'm free for a while. Want some help?"

"Sure. I've still got some clothes in the dresser. Grab a box."

"You got it."

Millicent

MOVING IN THE MIDDLE of a Colorado winter is a bitch. It's been snowing off and on all day. I'm going to have to shampoo the carpet after all the wet foot traffic that was in and out of the apartment today. Yet, surprisingly, I'm not the least bit bothered by that knowledge. Not with the view I've got in front of me right now.

The spare room is now full of Sage's things. At the moment, it's just a bunch of scattered boxes, his mattresses propped up against the wall, and his desk pushed up underneath the window. I already know that getting him to unpack is going to be a nightmare, and making this room presentable will be interesting, but I don't care. Not today, anyway. Today I'm too busy basking in the reality that at any moment, Sage will walk through the door and he'll be *home*.

He left about an hour ago, riding back to the house with Derrick and the Bradley brothers, who helped load all of Sage's things in the back of the trailer that usually transports their equipment. He said he'd be back as soon as he picked up his car. I'm surprised he hasn't arrived, yet. Though, if the snow has picked up, that could be the reason for his delay.

I'm still standing in the doorway of the spare room when I hear the front door finally open. As Sage makes his entrance, I see that he's got two bags in his hands. One, a to-go sack from Giuseppe's, and the other, a brown paper bag which clearly holds a bottle of wine. I tilt my head to the side, squinting my eyes at him suspiciously as I begin to close the distance between us.

"Honey, I'm home," he greets with a cheesy smile.

I can't silence the giggle that bubbles out of me as I come to a stop just in front of him. "You were gone a while. What are you up to?"

"Well," he says before he smacks a kiss against my lips. "This is probably one of the only Saturday nights I'll have off for a while. We got lucky—so tonight, I thought I'd treat my girl to dinner. Then—" He kisses me again, lingering a little longer this time. "Then I thought we could get lucky *again*."

"Oh, yeah?"

"Yup. You hungry?"

I offer him a nod, and he kisses me one more time before he heads to the kitchen. I follow him, getting out plates and glasses while he unpacks the bags. I set the little dining room table while he goes to hang his coat, and then we both sit down and enjoy our meal together. It's delicious, and I love him a little more for going out of his way in order to make tonight even more special.

When we're done eating, we clean up together. I wonder how many nights we'll get to share like this. I know that we'll soon fall into a routine and it'll all seem mundane and normal, but as I've said before—everything is better with Sage. I mean that, and I look forward to every single ordinary night at home with him.

After the dishes are loaded into the dishwasher, leftovers stored in the fridge, and the empty containers thrown in the trash, Sage hands me a full glass of wine and then escorts me down the hall to our bedroom.

"I'll be back," he tells me, setting his glass down on my dresser. "I'm going to take Maestro out really quick."

"M'Kay," I say softly, watching as he taps his leg to signal his pup to follow. He goes obediently, leaving me all to myself for a couple of minutes. Feeling happy and a tiny bit tipsy, I take a large swig of my wine before I strip out of all my clothes. I then head to his duffle bag, laying on the floor at the foot of the bed, and dig out one of his t-shirts. I've just slipped it over my head when I hear the front door open and close.

Quickly, I crawl on top of the bed, stretching out on my stomach before he enters. I can feel the cold from outside wafting off of his clothes as he crawls over me the second he reaches the bed.

"If I didn't love you, my cold hands would be all over your ass right now, gorgeous," he mutters into my ear.

"Get warm fast, baby—I want you to touch me," I insist, peeking at him from over my shoulder. He kisses me, lowering his hips to rub the bulge in his pants over my ass. I arch my back, lifting my hips in response, and he grunts before pushing away from me and onto his feet.

I watch him strip down naked, my pussy growing wet just looking at him. I find myself short of breath when he reaches for his cock, stroking himself as he looks down at me.

"Need you naked, doll."

I roll onto my back without another word, reaching for the hem of his shirt before tugging the garment over my head and tossing it onto the floor. He then signals with his free hand for me to roll back onto my stomach, so I do, spreading my legs open invitingly.

He crawls on top of me again, this time running his dick along my seam and then between my ass cheeks. Even though he's just teasing me, it still feels amazing, and I prop myself up on my forearms, spreading my legs even wider. Over and over again, he coats the head of his dick in my arousal, which only makes me wetter. When he grabs hold of my ass with both of his hands, still teasing me with his dick, I whimper in frustration.

"Please," I beg.

"Please *what*, baby doll?"

"I need you inside of me—stop teasing me, please!" I barely get the words out before he slowly sinks his cock into my core, burying himself until he's balls deep. For a second, he doesn't move—a new form of torture—but props himself up on his forearms. I can feel the heat of his chest against my back, his breath making my hair tickle my ear.

"Fast or slow?" he whispers.

"Slow," I reply on a moan.

"Hard or soft?"

"Mmmm, *hard*."

"That's my girl," he says, sliding out of me slowly. Once he's almost all the way out, he slams back inside of me. I cry out in pleasure, in love with the way he fills me completely.

He sets a steady rhythm, fucking me nice and slow, the room filled with the sound of my desire coating his dick. He sweeps my hair to one shoulder, exposing my neck and back, giving him the opportunity to kiss, nibble, and lick as he continues to thrust in and out of me. When I turn my head, hungry for the taste of his mouth, he doesn't hesitate to give me what I want. He kisses me slowly at first, teasing my tongue with his. But I want more. I kiss him deeper and he growls into my mouth, his hips picking up speed.

"Shit, Sage," I pant. "I want to touch you."

Immediately, he pulls out of me, flipping me onto my back. He spreads my legs wide and eases his way inside of me before propping himself over me once more. I run my hands down his chest, up his sides, across his shoulders, over his arms, along his neck, and into his hair. I can't get enough of him. He stares down at me all the while, his icy blue eyes smoldering and filled with lust. It's so sexy, it only makes me want him more.

"I'm so glad you're here," I whisper, wrapping my legs around his back.

"Me too, baby," he breathes, resting his forehead against mine.

He exaggerates the roll of his hips, his pelvis grazing my clit with every thrust, and I suck in a breath, pushing out my chest. He leans against one arm, using his free hand to palm my breast and tweak my nipple. I groan, my legs squeezing his sides tighter.

"In the dark of night is where I want to be
Baby, in your arms, where no one else can see
No longer bound by light, we can both be free
'Cause you're my ecstasy, my only ecstasy."

I suck in a sharp breath, my body locking around his as he hums the tune once more. My pussy clenches down on his cock and he slows his pace to an excruciatingly pleasurable tempo, no longer taking me hard, but loving me gentle, singing the words over again.

"*Sage*," I moan, my second orgasm overtaking my first.

I've barely caught my breath when he pushes himself up onto his hands, his thrusts picking up in speed and force as he chases his own release.

"Fuck, Millie," he mutters, taking all that he needs. It's not long before he groans, his body growing stiff as he twitches inside of me. When his muscles begin to loosen up, he lowers himself on top of me, giving me all of his weight. I cling to him, knowing there's no place else I'd rather be but here—*in his arms, where no one else can see.*

TWENTY-EIGHT

Sage

"Encore! Encore! Encore!" our fans chant in unison.

Knox drapes his arm across my shoulders and I reach around and pat his back. "This is no fucking joke," he says in awe.

The band is standing just off stage, another local gig in the archives. Tonight, we took over The Wash Bar, hoping we'd need a bigger bar than The Brew. And what do you know? As luck would have it, the place is *packed.* Only this time, the milestone we celebrate makes tonight unlike any other.

"Just when I think shit couldn't get more surreal," says Maddox, speaking over the cry of the crowd. He throws his arm over his brother's and I'm suddenly flanked by the Bradley's. I give Mad Lips a pat on the back, too. I know exactly what they're feeling—know exactly what this night means to them. To us. To all of Mountains & Men, really; but it was the three of us who started this dream—messing around when we were just kids, shootin' the shit, talking about putting together a band. Now, almost six years later, here we are.

"I think it's time we give them what they want, eh, guys?" calls out Derrick, joining our ranks.

"Not so fast." We all turn at the sound of Stefany's voice. She's got a wicked grin on her face as she makes her way up the short flight of stairs to join us in the wings. "I have a little something for your fans."

Without further explanation, she walks right past us and onto the stage. The mic stand is too high for her, so she grabs the mic and sets the stand behind her before she addresses the crowd.

"Give it up for Mountains & Men! They played one hell of a show, don't you think?" Everyone in the bar cheers and the six of us look at each other, wondering what Stefany's up to. "When I first heard them play, about four months ago, I knew I had to get my hands on them." Someone cat whistles and laughter fills the bar. Stefany joins in on their laughter before she continues. "Turns out, I'm not the only one who believed in their potential, which is why we're here tonight—celebrating the release of their first album—*Of Mountains & Men.*"

I couldn't keep the wild grin off my face even if I tried, so I don't. Instead, I bask in the moment, hoping to commit to memory every detail of tonight.

"Now's the part where I insert my little, shameless plug—if you haven't heard it, what the hell are you waiting for? You can download it right now! *But* that's not the only reason I'm up here. I've got a little surprise for our boys and girl."

"Here we go," says JJ with a chuckle. "Classic Stef. What's she got up her sleeve now?"

She looks our way with a wink before she turns back to the crowd and asks, "How many Kings & Crowns fans do we have in here?"

"What did she just say?" Alex yells over the noise of the excited audience. She ducks her way between Knox and me so she can stand in front of us and see. "Did she just say *Kings & Crowns?* That band is *amazing!*"

I fold my arms across my chest, my stomach in knots as I study Stefany with intrigue. I don't know where the fuck she's going with this, but Alex is right—Kings & Crowns *is* amazing. They've been on the music scene for the last couple of years, after they blew up with their first hit single. They got their start in Cali, but if you don't know who they are in even the smallest Podunk town, you've been living under a rock.

"Well, as some of you might know, they're heading out on tour next month," Stefany continues. "They'll be on the road until July; and when they heard M&M's single, they wanted to hear more—so we might have slipped them an advanced copy of *Of Mountains & Men*, and they *loved* it."

"Holy. Shit," Maddox mutters.

"Now, if you've ever met the guys from Kings & Crowns, you'd know that they're a bunch of bad-asses with big hearts—and they enjoyed this album so much, they decided they wanted to help promote it. So," she pauses and turns to face us. "Guess who's going to be opening up for Kings & Crowns for four months?"

In an instant, we all go insane. We were already on top of the world, but Stefany just catapulted us even higher. Maddox is the first to attack, running out on stage. He grips Stefany around the waist and lifts her up in the air. I follow after him, and soon, Stefany is propped up on both of our shoulders, everyone in the band yelling and cheering with the crowd at the news.

"Okay, okay—*Christ*, put me down," Stefany says into the mic. "You've got an encore to perform!"

It takes us a minute to calm down enough to get our shit together, but when we do—we give our fans exactly what they want. I sing my heart out, more excited than I've ever been in my life. We've worked so hard to get here, and doors are starting to open—our dreams are coming true. I know that this is still just the beginning, because we won't stop fighting until we make it to the top.

We were born for this.

This is who we are.

Playin' from the heart.

Rockin' from the soul.

Millicent

I've never been so proud of anyone in all of my life. Standing in the middle this mob of fans, crowded in a bar that seems big on any other night, but so small tonight, I'm beside myself. Watching him up there—my dreamer, my rock star—I'm sure that he's exactly where he belongs. He shines so bright, and I admire him so much. The look on his face after Stefany announced the news of their next tour broke my heart and mended it together all at once. This opportunity is bigger than big. I know this because even *I* know who Kings & Crowns are. I really am excited for him—for *all* of them—and I'm *so proud*.

But I won't lie to myself. Four months is *not* six weeks—it's *four months*. Just thinking about being away from Sage for that long makes me miss him even while he's still in reach, still right in front of me, still singing to me as only he can. Stefany said that they'll be leaving next month. March will be the middle of my semester; even if I wanted to meet him somewhere for a short visit, it wouldn't be until *May*.

"Come on, Millie," Violet yells over the music, grabbing hold of my forearm. "Let's head back now! I can't wait any longer."

The smile on her face makes her blue eyes more vibrant, and I know she's over the moon with the news we just heard. As I follow her tug, I'm reminded of the conversation we had a few weeks ago about her relationship with JJ. She believes that it's *his* time. I don't have to ask her if she'll miss him, or if she's not even the slightest bit sad that they'll be apart for weeks and weeks. She loves him. Of course she'll miss him—but she's strong enough to let him go. They're strong enough to let each other go. Right now, they want the same thing. Right now, they share the same dream—the success of Mountains & Men.

I still don't know if I'm capable of dreaming.

Am I strong enough to let Sage go? Can I latch onto his dream? Will goodbye be any easier if I do?

I don't know the answer to any of my questions; but as Violet and I find our way backstage and the band's song comes to an end, I know one thing for sure. I wish to be brave. I love Sage more than I've loved anyone, and for *him,* I wish to be brave.

"Thank you!" Sage says as the rest of the band starts to exit the stage. "You guys are awesome—we wouldn't be here if not for your support, so *thank you!* Now, let's party!"

My eyes are glued to him as I watch him run off stage after the others. I see it as his eyes spot Violet, wrapped in JJ's arms, before he starts his search for me. When our gazes align, the sight of his grin makes my knees weak. He runs toward me, not even slowing down before he collides into me, locking his arms around my legs before he picks me up off of my feet. Laughter pours out of me as I grip hold of his shoulders to keep myself upright.

"*Fuck!* We're going on tour, doll face! Did you hear that? We're touring with fucking *Kings & Crowns!*"

"I heard, baby," I tell him, unable to keep the grin off my face. His excitement is contagious. "I'm so proud of you, Sage," I say, reaching up to run my fingers through his hair, damp with sweat from his performance.

"Get down here, gorgeous. I need a taste."

I hold each side of his face as I lean over to kiss him, my hair falling around us like a curtain. The second my lips touch his, he darts his tongue out, telling me what he wants. I open up for him and lean into the kiss a little bit more. One of his hands slides up, gripping my waist as he holds me more securely. He groans, kissing me deeper—his mouth devouring mine with his greedy lips and delicious tongue. He takes. I give. And as I surrender to him in this moment, I vow here and now that I *will* be brave.

I will be brave because he makes me brave.

We're in this together. He promised.

Sage

GODDAMN, MY GIRL can kiss. I don't want to let her go—but I know the night has just started, and we've got some serious celebrating to do.

I clap my hand against her ass, the impact making her shriek. I chuckle and she smiles down at me, reaching up to sweep her hair behind her ears.

"Fuck you later," I say, giving her a squeeze.

"Promise?"

"You bet your sweet, little ass."

"You guys, I have *one* last surprise to throw your way before you get your drink on," Stefany calls out. We all turn our heads in her direction, and I set Millie on her feet as she continues. "Actually, Greg wanted to get you something. It's out back—follow me."

We all exchange curious looks, no doubt wondering the same thing. Instead of asking questions, we do as we're told and follow. I take Millie's hand and she laces her fingers with mine, clinging to my arm as we make our way to the back exit. None of us have coats on, but fear of winter's bite is definitely not going to hold us back.

Alex is the first to walk through the door, right on Stefany's heels. When she gasps loudly, everyone starts running. We crowd behind our little bass player, our mouths falling open as the *something* that Greg wanted to get us is revealed.

"Holy fucking shit—he got us a bus?" I exclaim.

"Yup," Stefany replies with a knowing grin. "The second Kings & Crowns extended the invitation, he started making calls. He knows more than a few people—as you're well aware—and he was able to score this black beauty for his newest up-and-comers. A small time band by the name of Pinstripes was in the market for a new ride, so Greg took this one off their hands." she says with a shrug.

"Pinstripes?" Knox utters in surprise.

Stefany is so full of shit, and she knows it. Pinstripes is no *small time band*. They're a fucking award winning group, bigger than Kings & Crowns.

"Our new bus used to belong to Pinstripes?" Knox asks once more.

"Yup," Stefany repeats. "Don't worry—it's been properly cleaned and sterilized," she adds with a laugh.

"Can we look inside?" asks Alex.

"Absolutely!" She tosses the keys to Derrick and he catches them against his chest, looking at her in question. "We'll let Big Shot, here, open her up. Though I doubt even *you* could handle these wheels."

He chuckles, shaking his head at her before jogging toward the driver's side door. We all head to the opposite side and wait anxiously for him to let us in.

"All aboard!" he yells as the door hisses open.

We climb inside, each of us silent as we take in our new digs. The front of the bus has two black, leather sofas—one on either side of the walkway. There's a flat-screen TV mounted on the wall that sections off the driver's seat. Just beyond the sofas is the breakfast nook and the kitchen—everything decked out in chrome. Then, after the door I assume closes off the bathroom, there are six bunks. Finally, at the very back, there's an open space—big enough for us to have a place to jam. JJ's keys would fit in there perfectly.

"Oh, my gosh," Alex sputters. "This is…this is…"

"Fucking *perfect* is what it is," pipes in Maddox.

"This is nicer than Lawful Sinners' bus. Adrian is going to be so jealous," she teases, reaching for her phone as she hurries off the bus.

"Looks like JJ get's a bed this time," says Derrick, sliding back the curtain to one of the empty bunks.

"Thank fuck," he replies, plopping down onto the couch. He pulls Violet into his lap and she snuggles up against him, her eyes still roaming around the bus.

"Black Beauty—that's her name," says Knox, running his fingers across the black kitchen countertop.

"Hell, yeah," Maddox agrees. "I think Black Beauty deserves a toast. Who's coming?" He doesn't wait for anyone to answer before he makes his way off of the bus. Derrick and Knox follow after him, Violet and JJ trailing behind.

"Hey, wait," I murmur, gently pulling on Millie's hand as she turns to leave. I'm not ready to go. Not yet. I peek into one of the bunks and then climb inside, stretching out across the bed.

"What are you doing?" she asks, sounding amused.

"Get in here."

"What? It's too small."

"No it's not. Come on, get in here."

"Sage—"

"*Millicent*."

She purses her lips at me and then rolls her eyes before she climbs into the small space with me. It's just big enough for her to lay on her side, half of her body draped over mine.

"This is ridiculous," she mumbles.

"Relax, baby—just lay with me a minute."

She looks up at my face for a second and then gives in. Her body melds further into mine, her cheek resting on my chest as she frees a sigh.

"I almost can't believe this is happening," I admit, tracing my fingers up and down her arm.

"Which part?"

"All of it. The tour. The bus. I mean—*fuck*—we never could have gotten here on our own. Big things are happening, really big shit. I just…it's almost too good to be true."

"It's pretty remarkable." She pauses for a beat before she murmurs, "You might not have been able to accomplish this on your own, but you're here because you earned it. Mountains & Men—who you are, the music you put out—*that's* what got you here, in the hands of the right people at the right time."

"Yeah," I whisper, allowing her words to sink in.

"I'm going to miss you so much."

I wrap my arms all the way around her, holding her tight. For a second, flashbacks of the last time I set out on tour are at the forefront of my mind. I push those thoughts aside, sure that this time will be different; confident that we're in a far better place—*she's* in a far better place.

"We're going to be okay. You know that, right?"

She nods against my chest, her fingers clutching around the fabric of my shirt. Her actions contradict themselves, and I can tell she *wants* to know that I'm right, but a part of her is scared. I get it. If I've learned anything about my girl over the past couple of months, it's that she's still learning that people are capable of loving her and not abandoning her.

She might be older than me, she might be smarter than me—but her book smarts don't compare to what I know; and what I know can't be learned any other way than by experience. I just have to prove to her that my leaving is not goodbye. It doesn't have to be like that. No matter how incredible life on the road might be, I found a girl worth keeping—a *woman* worth fighting for. She's the dream, too. I want it all, and I want her by my side.

"Come with me." The words fall out of my mouth without thought. Even still, when she jerks her head up to look at me, one glimpse into those pretty eyes and I know that's what I want. "I mean it, doll. Come with me."

"What? Sage—I can't come with you."

"Why not? Spring break is next month, right? Wherever we are, wherever we're going—just take the week and come with us."

"Sage," she starts to protest, shaking her head at me.

I shake my head right back, a smirk tugging at my lips as I argue, "It's perfect. The bus is plenty big—"

"It's not," she laughs. "There are six beds and six of you."

"You'll sleep here with me."

"Baby, we barely fit in here."

"I don't mind sleeping with my girl wrapped around me."

"Sage, you're—"

I cut her off with a kiss. When she opens her mouth to speak, I thrust my tongue between her lips. She hums as I reach up and bury my fingers in her hair, keeping her close. After a moment, without breaking our kiss, she maneuvers her way on top of me. With our legs locked together, her thigh brushes against my dick, and I slide a hand down to grab her ass. She whimpers, and the sound makes me smile. I drag my lips along her jaw and down her neck, fisting her hair in my hand and turning her head where I want it to go.

"Come with me," I whisper against her neck before licking her skin. "We'll make it work, baby doll." I kiss the spot at the back of her jaw and then press my lips against her ear as I say, "You make everything better, Millicent. Everything's better with you. I love you, baby—I want you with me. Say you'll come."

"Okay," she breathes, nodding her head in agreement. "I'll do it. I'll come."

"That's my girl."

"Yo, Dweeb!" Derrick calls from the front of the bus. "Get your asses inside—we're partying!"

"Aye!" I shout back. I then look up at Millie, smiling before I smack a kiss against her lips and clap my hand on her ass. "Come on, doll. Let's get drunk."

TWENTY-NINE

Millicent

"HEY," HE MURMURS BEFORE kissing my hair. "Wake up, baby. Time for grub." I draw in a deep breath, trying desperately to shake off sleep, and turn my face to look into his eyes. He smiles at me, kissing my lips before drawing back the curtain to our bunk.

"Up, sleepy head!" calls out Maddox as he passes behind Sage, heading for the front of the bus.

Sage chuckles, turning to watch him go, and I fight to keep my eyes open. I'm exhausted, though I can't say for sure why. It seems that so long as the bus is moving, I'm overwhelmed with the desire to sleep. Not wanting to miss my time with Sage while we're away, I try my best to keep myself alert—but this afternoon I just couldn't do it. My stomach was bothering me so much that I didn't have it in me.

Turns out, riding on a bus for hours at a time makes me slightly nauseous. Couple my motion sickness with the fact that I'll be flying back home tomorrow, and my stomach has enough reason to pit itself against me.

As luck would have it, Kings & Crowns' tour was slated to start at the same time as my spring break. Almost one week into the tour, and Sage and I haven't said goodbye yet. We packed our bags together, loading up with the rest of the band at some ungodly hour last Saturday. It wasn't until after I agreed to come that I wondered how the guys and Alex would feel about me tagging along with them. Fortunately, none of them minded. In fact, they were disappointed that Violet couldn't join us, too; she'll be meeting up with them in a few weeks, when she can get the time off work.

"Up you go, baby doll. You need to eat—you'll need the sustenance for later." He wiggles his eyebrows at me before kissing me once more and heading toward the front.

Tonight, Sage promised me we'd check into a motel. They'll all be in Minnesota for a few days before they head to their next stop. Kings & Crowns are scheduled to do a couple radio shows while they're in town, which is why we're here today instead of tomorrow. They'll be performing in St. Paul tomorrow night. I wish I could stay to see it, but my flight leaves in the afternoon.

I don't know where time has gone. It's more than just this week and the six days that have disappeared right before my eyes. It's the last *month*. It flew by before I had a chance to grasp hold of it. One day, Sage was moving into my apartment; the next, I was putting the final nail in the coffin that is my connection to my father, dealing with the court and the bank to put an end to my mother's last act of retaliation against my father; and then the next, I was boarding Black Beauty, headed for Nebraska with Mountains & Men. Now I'm sick at the thought of leaving Sage in the morning.

"Doll face—come on."

"Yeah. Sorry. I'm coming."

I roll gently out of bed, running my fingers through my hair as I make my way to the front of the bus. I slip my feet into my warm, fuzzy boots and slide into my coat before grabbing my purse and hooking it over my arm.

"Hey, you okay?" asks Sage, running the back of his fingers down the side of my face.

"I'm fine. Probably just need some fresh air."

"Let's get out of here, then."

The brisk cold air that greets us feels good against my skin. Like a jolt of caffeine, it wakes me up, which is just what I need. Sage and I join the others in the cab of the suburban that takes us to the nearest restaurant, which ends up being a bar and grille with something on the menu for all of us.

We take our time eating, talking, and laughing. It's during moments like these that I understand why Sage loves this so much. I'm not one for the spotlight, certainly not like he is, but sitting around the table at a restaurant, miles away from home, it almost feels as if we never left. The comradery between them is contagious; and it's just about impossible to avoid growing closer to one another while on the road.

When they got back from their first tour, I remember thinking that they'd never sounded so in sync before. Now I understand why. This is part of their journey—

perhaps one of the most important parts—and it means so much that Sage wanted to share it with me. A month ago, I asked myself if I'd be able to latch onto his dream; I wondered if I could somehow make it *my* dream so that it would be easier to let him go. After the week I've had with all of them, I realize that Sage's dreams are not mine—but I love him, and part of what it means to love him is to want what he wants for himself, and I do. With all my heart, I want him to shine as bright as I always imagined he would. I want him to share his music as much and as often as possible. I want the whole world to sing with him.

I'll admit, that's not going to make goodbye any easier. Seeing him this past week, watching him burn blue—like the hottest part of a flame up there on that stage—it makes me love him deeper. Seeing him in his element, experiencing his journey right along side of him as he grows into the man that he's destined to be—it just makes me admire and adore him even more. Goodbye is going to suck ass. But I will hold true to my vow. I will be strong. For him, I'll hold fast to who we are, to the promises that we've made to each other, and to the hope of our future. For him, I'll be brave.

Sage

"Don't go to sleep, yet," I insist, looking down at my gorgeous girl.

We've been fooling around for hours. She's come four times. Before the break of dawn, I intend to make her come at least four more.

"Stop touching my face like that and maybe I'll have a fighting chance," she murmurs, her eyes fluttering as she tries to keep them open.

I slide my fingers down her cheek and along her neck, flattening my palm against her chest as I drag my hand over her stomach and around to her side. I pinch her and she giggles, turning her naked body toward mine. I smirk down at her, loving the sound of her sexy, groggy laugh.

"Fuck. I'm not ready for you to go," I tell her.

I lean down to brush a kiss against her lips, and she rests her hand against my cheek, staring up at me without a word. For a moment, neither of us moves or speaks, as if our silence might slow down time.

"I know now," she whispers before reaching up for another kiss.

"You know what, baby doll?"

"I know that this is our best chance." She runs her fingers through my hair, the sensation of her touch making my dick jerk. "Before, I was afraid. I was afraid that if

I let you go while we were still together, I'd lose you—that you would get swallowed up by the attention and the success that's right at your fingertips. I was afraid that you'd outgrow me. Honestly, I'm sure you will. Outgrow me, that is." I start to shake my head at her, but she continues before I can get a word in. "You will. It's how this works—it's the *only* way this works. You can't have the dream and *not* outgrow me. You'll see too much, experience too much, *live* too much. It's destiny. I'm sure of it. But I'm no longer afraid of it.

"You have to go. I have to let you go. It's our best chance at survival. You won't love me if I hold you back; and it's not love at all for me to want to. I've never wanted you to sacrifice your hopes and aspirations for me. Not ever. I see you," she says, holding my face between her hands. "And I love the man I see. I won't run from you. I couldn't even if I tried. I *did* try, but you have my heart. All of it. So while I'm not ready to say goodbye, I will—I will, knowing that it's the only way we make it."

"Baby," I sigh, leaning down to rest my forehead against hers.

For a second, I don't know what to say. She blows my mind. Just when I think I love her as much as I ever will, I fall for her a little bit more. She's unlike any other girl I've ever met. Sexy, smart, stubborn, soft, sweet—and she can be a smart-ass, but it's hot as hell. Then, when she opens up, when she allows herself to be vulnerable with me, I wonder how the fuck I got to be so lucky. Getting here sure as shit wasn't easy, but it was worth the struggle. I wouldn't trade her for anyone.

"No one—*no one* has ever believed in me the way you do."

"I don't believe that," she says softly.

I furrow my brow, lifting my head so that I can look her in the eye as I reply, "Swear to god, doll face—no one. Not like you. It means everything to me." She smiles and I tighten my hold around her hip. "I'm not going to outgrow you, baby. We're going to grow together."

"Sage, I—"

"What'd I say?"

She seals her lips shut, saying nothing as she stares up at me, her hands falling away from my face. I fight a smirk. That's my girl. So fucking stubborn.

"I'm *not* going to outgrow you. You'll figure it out. The dream—*Millicent's* dream—you'll figure it out. And when you do, we'll fight for it together." I dip my head down and kiss her lips, barely pulling away before I whisper, "I believe in you too, doll face. And I love the hell out of you."

"Dammit," she mutters, her voice trembling as she wraps her arms around my neck. "If you don't shut up, I'm going to cry—and I sure as hell will not be able to get on that plane tomorrow."

I seal my lips around hers, chuckling into her mouth.

"How about I fuck you instead?"

"No," she whispers, tightening her hold around me. "Make love to me, Sage. Take me slow. Make it last."

I respond with a kiss, more than willing to give her exactly what she wants. She parts her lips, and I don't hesitate to sweep my tongue through her mouth. As she hums a sigh, my dick starts to get hard. I kiss her deeper, rolling on top of her, the warmth of her body beneath me—her peaked nipples grazing my chest—her smooth legs rubbing against mine—it all excites me even more, stirring my desire for her. Only for her. Always for her.

I kiss her harder as her hands begin to roam—and, fuck me, her light touch makes my skin tingle and my dick grows fully erect. I rock my hips, causing my length to glide over her clit. She whimpers, making me harder still. I kiss her even deeper, desperate to taste her, and she hooks her legs around the back of mine before lifting her hips.

I pull my mouth from hers with a grunt. "Who owns your orgasm, baby?"

"Sage—I need you. I'm so wet—*please*. Don't make me wait anymore."

"Who owns your orgasm, Millicent?" I ask again, rubbing my hard-on over her clit once more.

She digs her fingers into my arms as she moans, "*You!* God, Sage—you own all of me. My heart, my body, my soul—it's yours, baby. I belong to you."

My chest swells at her words and I don't waste another second before I ease my cock into her tight, warm, soft pussy. I can't stop my eyes from rolling back as my lids close. She feels perfect wrapped around me. She wasn't lying—*she's drenched*.

I push all the way in, until I'm buried as deep as I can go, and then I pull out slowly. I take my time, wanting to give her exactly what she asked for—wanting to make this moment last. I don't think about the fact that this will be our last night together for who knows how long. I don't think about how much I'll miss her body cuddled against mine in my bunk on the bus. I don't think about how awesome it's been having her on the road with my closest mates and me. I don't think about anything but right now. And as I make love to my woman, time ceases to exist. We get lost in each other and the pleasure that we can only find together.

"Kiss me," she pleads.

I do. I kiss her until neither of us can breathe. When I pull away, she arches her back, crushing her chest against mine.

"Oh, *Sage*, baby—I'm going to come!"

Her words spur me on, and it takes everything in me to keep my slow pace. When her pussy clamps down around my dick, I thrust into her hard, pausing for a beat before I pull all the way out. Her body still trembling from her climax, I roll her onto her side and curl myself around her from behind. I slide my hand between her thighs, lifting her leg before I sink back into her core. She moans and I bury my face in her neck, breathing her in as I begin to pump in and out of her.

"Fuck—I love your pussy, doll face."

"Mmm, I love your dick, baby."

Her back bows as she reaches behind her to grab a fistful of my hair. I thrust in and out of her faster, harder, sure that I won't last much longer.

"You're going to come again for me, Millie."

"M'Kay," she mutters, breathless.

I reach down between her legs, my fingers finding her clit, and she sucks in a breath. She's still swollen and sensitive from her last release, and I know I can get her where I want her with just a little coaxing.

I nibble on her ear, massaging her clit as I bury my dick inside of her over and over. When I start to sing to her, she presses her ass into me even more, her grip tightening in my hair, and I'm sure she's close.

"Come for me, baby," I murmur once I've finished the phrase. "Strangle my dick, Millie." I pinch her swollen nub and she cries out, her pussy squeezing me tighter than before, pulling forth my own release. I hold her tight against me as I pound into her until I'm spent, and then we both sink further into the mattress, panting.

"Shit," she sighs. "I love you."

"I love you, too, gorgeous," I say, cupping one of my hands around her breast as I hold her close.

"I'm so tired," she whispers.

I can hear it in her voice, hear her succumbing to her exhaustion, and I don't try and stop her. I listen as her breathing grows deeper, her body becoming heavy as she drifts off to sleep, my dick still tucked inside of her. I don't move. Not yet. I want to feel at home for just a little while longer.

Goodbye is a bitch I wouldn't fuck if she was the last cunt on earth. Watching Millie board that plane, seeing her as she looked at me from over her shoulder one last time—her long hair pulled up into a ponytail, leaving her face fully on display so that I could see the tears in her eyes as she waved at me with the tiniest of smiles—yeah. It was a bitch.

But as I stand in the middle of this stage, wading in the spotlight, drowning in the music, the sea of *thousands* within arm's reach as we rock our way through *Anything but This*—I'm reminded that we've had worse *goodbyes*. We'll survive this one, just like she said. It's all part of the chase, part of the journey, part of the *climb*. The distance between us is a mountain we both have to face—but it sure as fuck won't stop us. It won't stop *me*. Right here, right now, in this place, with these people, it's where I belong.

This is the life I want.

This is what I've been waiting for.

This is what I've been *fighting* for.

This is the dream.

EPILOGUE

Millicent

"Uh, Millie?"

I suck down a deep breath, opening my eyes as I right myself in my chair. When I look over at the entrance to my office, I see Lindsey with her knuckles still touching the door. It isn't until I register her stance that I realize she must have knocked, rousing me from sleep.

She never actually *knocks.*

Then again, I never fall asleep at my desk.

"Oh, my god." I reach up and run my fingers through my hair, gathering the long strands to drape down my chest. "I meant to rest my eyes for just a second—literally a second—but I must have fallen asleep. What time is it?"

"It's just after five. I was stopping in to see if you wanted to grab a bite for dinner, tell me about your spring break—but we could always go another time. You seem pretty tuckered out."

"Yeah," I start to say as I stand to my feet. "I think maybe I'm coming down with something. I've been really drowsy and a little nauseous for the last week, but I figured that was just my body responding to the tour bus. I thought it would go away as soon as I got home." I shake my head, reaching for my tote bag so that I can pack the work I need to take home with me this evening. "I'm sure I just need a couple nights of really decent rest. Maybe we could do dinner Friday night?"

"Sure, okay," she mutters distractedly. I look over at her and see that she's staring at me, her arms folded across her chest. "Did you say that you've been tired and nauseous?"

"Yes. But I—"

"Millie," she interrupts, taking a couple steps further into the room. "By any chance do your—" she pauses, looking over her shoulder before she leans toward me conspiratorially. "Do your *girls* feel especially tender?" she asks, pointing at my breasts.

I look down at my chest, and then scowl at her in confusion. The truth is, they *have* been a little sensitive to the touch—but it's nothing I thought I should worry about. Now, I'm not so sure.

"Why are you asking me that?"

"Uh, Millie," she continues to say, ignoring my question. "When's the last time you had your period?"

"*What?*" I mutter, my head still fuzzy from sleep. I mean, it must be. She's not making any sense.

"My sister, whenever she's growing a human, she sleeps, like, *all* the time. She could fall asleep anywhere. *You* do not fall asleep at your desk. Ever. And you don't look ill, but you say you're nauseous. If your boobs feel sore and you can't remember the last time Aunt Flow came to town, you *might* want to head to the drug store and pick up a pregnancy test. Just an idea."

My stomach drops and my pulse begins to race as I replay her words in my head. For a second, I'm absolutely certain that she's wrong—but then I remember that my period is late. It's two weeks late. I didn't think anything of it because I thought it was stress. It's happened before! I figured the reality of Sage's leaving was taking a toll on me, nothing more.

"I'm on the pill. I *never* forget to take my pill," I blurt out, my voice airy and not as confident as I wish it was.

"Please don't tell me we have to have the sex talk," Lindsey says, arching an eyebrow at me. "The amount of action I'm sure you see with Sexy McHottington as your personal boy toy is probably enough to make me want to disown you as a friend because I'd keel over from envy if I really knew. You can't possibly need me to tell you that the pill is not super-sperm proof."

"Shit," I sigh as my hands start to tremble. "You think he has super sperm and I'm pregnant?"

She laughs as she closes the distance between us. She gives my elbow a squeeze and says, "You won't know unless you take a test and find out. I'll come with you, if you want?"

"No. No—thank you, I'm okay," I insist, willing myself to calm down.

"All right. Well, you know how to get a hold of me should you need a friend."

I offer her a smile and she pats my shoulder before she starts to make her exit. "I'll see you tomorrow, Millie."

"Yeah. Tomorrow."

Once I'm alone, it takes me a few minutes to gather my wits about me. I stand over my desk simply concentrating on breathing in and out, combating my unsettled stomach. Then I finish gathering my things and hurry to my car. I decide not to panic until I know for sure what my body is telling me. Though, I can't stop my thoughts from crowding around the concept of a *baby* as I head to the nearest drug store and purchase the most expensive at-home pregnancy test I can find.

When I get home, Maestro greets me at the door. I know that I need to take him out for a quick walk and then feed him, but my nerves have readied my bladder, and I decide to take the test first. I slip out of my jacket, discarding my things on the couch before I grab the small box and make my way to the bathroom. I don't look at myself in the mirror as I close myself in. I don't need to see the evidence of my anxiety on my face.

After I've done my business, I set the stick on a piece of toilet paper on the counter and wash my hands. In an attempt not to stare at it while I wait for the results, I let my eyes wander around the sink. Sage isn't here, but the evidence of his presence still remains. He left behind a bottle of cologne and forgot his aftershave, both of which sit next to my small collection of body spray and perfume. Suddenly, I wish he was here.

Then again—I have no idea how he'll react if this test is positive.

Feeling like I might throw up, I leave the bathroom and head for the door. I grab Maestro's leash, calling him to me, and then hurry outside. The cool breeze alerts me to the fact that I left my jacket inside, but it doesn't matter. The chill does me good, and I breathe deeply while I watch Maestro trot a little ways ahead of me. Now, no longer confined within the four walls of my bathroom, I try again to imagine the possibilities that just might be in my future.

The truth is, Sage and I haven't been together for that long. Six months is nothing to scoff at, and we *are* living together—when he's in town—but we've never discussed *children*. He's twenty-one, almost twenty-two, and while I'm flirting with twenty-seven, I've never really been afraid of my biological clock running out of time. In fact, I've never really thought about my biological clock at all.

I have no idea what kind of mother I would make. I didn't have a very good example. Not to mention the fact that after I'd had my heart broken one too many times, I hadn't planned on falling in love or settling down with someone. Then Sage happened. I know that neither of us are promised tomorrow—nobody is—but he is the man I want to be with forever. Violet said it best: as long as she and JJ are still on this earth, she doesn't want to be with anyone else. I feel the same way about

Sage. I know what it's like to be without him, and I don't want that—I don't *choose* that. So, if we did make a baby, if a human being is going to tie us together forever…

My thoughts instantly shift to my own parents. *I* was supposed to tie them together, but I didn't. We were never really a family. Sure, my father stuck around until I was six, but you don't *abandon* your family, no matter what.

My feet slow to a stop as I realize that I'm aware of this truth for no other reason than that I'm in love with a man who has welcomed me into his family. And when I think about that family—when I remember my time with them, and the way they make me feel—I realize that I want that. I want something beautiful like that. I want to be a mother who loves like Abriella and Pepper do; and I want a man by my side, a man who *won't* leave, but who will stay and be a father like Ewan and Harry. A man like Sage.

I turn back toward my apartment, the anxiety that makes my stomach knot up in fear now laced with a hint of excitement. I can't explain the hope that I feel. Logically speaking, Sage and I aren't ready to have a baby. Not even close. But in my heart, I somehow know and understand that *no one* is ever *ready* to have a baby.

It's entirely possible that I'll walk into my bathroom and find a negative result. In a way, it would be a relief. Regardless, this false alarm might just be the catalyst to an epiphany I've been waiting for. It's as if my eyes have been opened and there's a small seed of hope that may take root and grow into a *dream*.

I scoop Maestro into my arms as I hurry up the steps that lead to my door. Once inside, I set him down and let him off his leash. Sucking in a deep, calming breath, I make my way back to the bathroom. I remind myself that one stripe means *not* pregnant and two stripes means I am. As I reach for the stick, I notice that the tremble in my hands is back and my nausea has returned. I seal my eyes closed tight, in this very moment no longer sure *what* I want it to say. Then, when I can't handle the suspense any longer, I open my eyes.

"Holy shit," I breathe.

I'm pregnant.

Worthy of the MELODY

MOUNTAIN AND MEN BOOK FOUR

Author's Note

If you're reading this, you should know that I appreciate you. From the very bottom of my heart, I do. If you're reading this, you've stuck with me for two and a half novels, and you're probably anxious to dive into the last of this saga. If you're reading this, some sort of attachment has blossomed between you, my nerdy rocker, and his sassy heroine, and that—*that* is incredible to me.

Thank you for investing in this journey—this story—this couple. I've never held on to characters like I've held on to these two; and knowing that you've enjoyed them enough to pick up this book—it's special to me. I just wanted you to know that.

As you turn this page, you should also know that the novel that follows is a happily ever after only a true Sage and Millie fan could appreciate.

You're welcome...

Sincerely,

R.C.

Every great dream begins with a dreamer.
Always remember,
you have within you the strength, the patience,
and the passion to reach for the stars to change the world.

Harriet Tubman

PROLOGUE

Sage

"If you're just tuning in, this is Harley with *The Record Times*, streaming live for this Tuesday's podcast. I'm here with a couple of my favorite badasses—Lewis and Kent from Kings & Crowns. They're currently halfway through their stateside *Royalty Unleashed Tour*, and if you haven't gotten tickets for a venue near you—you're shit out of luck."

We all laugh, but my heart isn't in it. The truth is, Harley's right. Word has it, we're rockin' at sold out venues for the rest of the tour. It's more than I could have possibly dreamed of for our second trek across the nation. Like everything that's happened over the last eight months, it's fucking *surreal*. I'm so pumped, I swear I feel high half of the time. But right here, right now, I'm just plain, fucking nervous.

"You could always come jam with us in Europe," says Lewis with a grin, pulling me from my thoughts.

He's the drummer for Kings & Crowns—if you want to call him that. Derrick calls him *The Beast*. When he gets behind that kit and lets loose, the music changes him; it unleashes him. It's fucking epic. Now, sitting with him at this table, he's nothing but chill. He's down to earth, mellow, and so easy to get along with. It's almost as if he's not the same person.

"Hell, yeah. Dates for the global leg of *Royalty Unleashed* will be announced in a couple of weeks. Tickets will be on sale next month," pipes in Kent.

Kent sings lead. Unlike me, he also plays guitar. On stage, it's almost like, with his electric in his hands, the sound his guitar creates fuels his vocal strength, making him the power-house that he is. I've learned so much from him over the last few weeks just by watching him. He's also thrown a few tips my way after a couple of our shows, proving that Stefany was right about these guys. They're a bunch of bad-asses with big hearts. They've not only taken Mountains & Men along for the ride, but they've brought us under their wing.

That's how we ended up here. In Philadelphia—home of The Record Times, *which just so happens to be one of the biggest music magazines around. They've earned their relevance, ranking up there with titles that got their start in New York and L.A., and today—they're bestowing the same opportunity to us; the opportunity for Mountains & Men to earn our relevance.*

"All right, all right—be sure to keep a look out, all you Kings & Crowns fans; but for those of you who will be seeing these guys in the next couple of months, they've brought with them a rather talented opening act."

Harley nods at JJ and me from where he sits across the small conference room table, leaning against his folded forearms as he speaks into his mic.

"Kent—K&C has been known to bring along a lot of up-n-comers over the years, but none quite like this one. What made you pick Mountains & Men?"

"We actually had a band picked out for the tour," he begins to say, running his fingers through his shaggy, blond hair. "Shit went down, and we had to scramble. At the time, Mountains & Men was starting to get a bit of a buzz going. They had released an EP in the fall of last year, they had just gotten back from their first tour around the U.S., and we heard one of their songs and wanted to hear more."

"It was actually Brock who heard the track," Lewis jumps in. "He brought it to us, we brought it to our manager, one thing led to another, and we got a sneak peak of their latest album."

"They didn't sound nearly as green as I thought they might on their first record," says Kent. "They sure as hell know how to put on a show, too. Probably the best pick we've ever made."

"Careful, guys, you'll make Sage blush," teases JJ into his mic.

The room fills with laughter again. This time, as I look over at JJ, I fight to let my amusement sink in and calm me the fuck down.

"In all seriousness, they're legit," Lewis adds, scrubbing his hand over the dark stubble that covers his jaw. "We've all said it before: if we could take them with us everywhere, we would. But they're not some bitch band. They're putting in their time now, and all I can say is—we all got lucky."

"Well, if that's not one hell of an introduction, I don't know what is. Here with me now are Sage McCoy and JJ Reston from Mountains & Men. You're a six-man crew—Sage, you sing lead; JJ, here, is on the keys. Are you two the brains behind the sound, or what?"

I draw in a deep breath, shaking my head as I look at JJ. He grins at me and then tips his chin, telling me it's my cue. Mountains & Men is far from a solo act, but I'm here because I'm, quite literally, the mouthpiece of our sound. Now *is* my time to speak up. Now is my time to speak out on the airwaves that will, no doubt, thrust us into a whole new spotlight.

Now is my time to fucking shine.

Millicent

I HEAR IT AS they shuffle down the hallway, and I hurry to the door, peeking my head out.

"You're late!" I hiss, waving them in my direction.

"Shit—I *know*. Did we miss any of it?" asks Violet, tossing her blonde bangs out of her face as her dark blue eyes meet mine.

"Kings & Crowns just finished. Come on."

"It's totally my fault. Sorry! My class got out late and—"

"Everyone take a breath," Lindsey says with a chuckle, cutting Rosemary off as she and Violet enter my office. I shut the door as Lindsey continues to explain, "They haven't even been introduced yet. Sounds like Harley is transitioning now. You're just in time."

Rose nods, dropping her backpack before reaching up to readjust her long, dark brown ponytail. When JJ cracks a joke about Sage, the most beautiful grin breaks out across her face. The sight of her beaming blue eyes—lighter than Violet's and a tad bit darker than her brother's—make my chest ache. She looks so much like Sage. Every time I see her, I miss him a little bit more.

"Can you turn it up a tad?" asks Violet, taking the seat on the opposite side of my desk next to Lindsey.

I sit down in my chair, reaching out to turn the nob on my monitor to increase the sound. Rose hops up and sits on the edge of my desk—reminding me of her brother again. It's been so long since he's been in here.

"Well, if that's not one hell of an introduction, I don't know what is. Here with me now are Sage McCoy and JJ Reston from Mountains & Men. You're a six-man crew—Sage, you sing lead; JJ, here, is on the keys. Are you two the brains behind the sound, or what?"

"Oh, my god! This is really happening!" Violet squeals.

"Shhh," Rose hushes with a giggle.

"Yes—but—but, no," answers Sage.

My stomach clenches at the sound of his voice. I hear it every day, and yet hearing it now feels different. It's as if his tone is even more alluring and sexy streaming through the airwaves of this live podcast than when I speak to him on the phone.

Yet, there's also something different about it today. There's a slight hesitancy I've never heard before. He's *nervous*. If I didn't already have a good idea about how *huge* this interview is for them, I certainly know now.

"I write the lyrics," he goes on to say, "and sometimes I compose the melody. Sometimes JJ does—but it takes all of us to put it together. It takes all of us to create the sound that we call *ours*, you know?"

"Team work makes the dream work?" asks Harley, sounding amused.

"Exactly," JJ replies. I can hear the smile in his voice just as clear as I can see the smile on Violet's face.

For just a second, I think back to yesterday, when I got the text from Sage that said this interview would be happening. Violet called me not five minutes later, practically screaming at the top of her lungs with excitement. Apparently, the decision to pick Sage and JJ had been unanimous. For obvious reasons, Sage was a no-brainer. As for JJ, they felt he had the temperament and the knowledge to talk about their sound in a way the others couldn't quite articulate. They certainly all wanted the chance to be there, but they also recognized that this stepping stone would soon put all of them into the spotlight.

"And the *team* is made up of six Coloradans," says Harley, earning my attention. "Tell me, how did Mountains & *Men* end up with five guys and a girl? She didn't object to the name?"

"Alex was actually our last addition. She came way after the name," says JJ. "She's the first girl we'd ever auditioned—but, I mean, listen to her play..."

"That little thing packs a punch—right to your fucking balls, if you aren't careful," Lewis teases, making us all laugh.

"We aren't M&M without her," says Sage, getting them back on track. "The thing about our name, though—at the root of its meaning, it's not sexist. It's universal," he continues, the confidence in his voice growing with every word he speaks. "We all have our mountains to climb; we all have our struggles to overcome; but that's what makes the dream—any dream—worth fighting for. The view at the summit, in that single moment when you look around you and realize how far you've come, how much you've sacrificed, and how hard you've worked—it's everything. For that one period of time—however brief it may be before you go barreling after your next peak—that view, man...it's *everything*."

ONE

Millicent

I NEED A DRINK.

Preferably a Snapple peach iced tea. I can't get enough of them. I drink at least four a day. I'm not sure why, seeing as how I've never gone out of my way to buy them before. Or *ever*.

That's a lie. I *do* know why. I know *exactly* why.

I draw in a slow, deep breath, peering down my chest at my belly. If I were anyone other than me, I'd have no idea that there's a child in there. Or, rather, a little below there. It might look like I've been putting back one too many iced teas, but my body hasn't yet begun to change very much—unless you count my boobs. Those seem to be growing a little more each day. Soon, I'll have to invest in a couple of new bras.

Every morning, when I stand in my underwear, admiring my figure in the mirror above my dresser, I can't help but wonder if Sage would appreciate the way my breasts barely fit into the cups I've got now.

He's always been more of an ass guy.

That man adores *my ass.*

Thinking about Sage in this moment sends a pang of longing through my chest. That longing is accompanied by a twinge of guilt that I try to ignore as I slip my hands away from my keyboard and press them lightly against my lower abdomen. He still doesn't know. I haven't told him. Every time I think that it's the right moment, I panic and don't say a word.

At first, I thought maybe I should wait until I had more than *one* at-home pregnancy test off of which I had based my theory. After two more positive sticks, I convinced myself that a doctor's confirmation would be even better. Never mind the symptoms that served as their own confirmation that I'm no longer in this body all by myself. Regardless of all of the above, I set an appointment with my doctor for a few weeks out, as I was instructed. The wait about killed me, as I hate keeping this news from him; but then after my doctor told me that I was, indeed, approximately eight weeks pregnant, I grew even *more* scared of sharing the truth.

Now, it's not *just* the truth that I'm worried how he'll take. I'm ten weeks pregnant, and I've known for thirty-two days. Thirty-two days I've been keeping this from him. We're not supposed to have secrets between us. There aren't supposed to be *lies* that separate us. We've got enough geography doing that on our behalf.

My list of excuses seems pathetic even to my own ears. Sage is…*my dreamer*. I can tell him anything. In my heart, I know that we're in this together, no matter what. It's a promise we've made to each other over and over again. Yet, there's always one more excuse as to why I continue to hold back, the most legitimate one I've come up with being the one I don't know how to alter.

It just doesn't feel right to tell him he's going to be a father over the phone—me here, him there—wherever there *is on any given day.*

"Knock, knock," murmurs Lindsey as she takes a step into my office.

My head shoots up, and I drop my hands into my lap immediately. I can tell by the knowing smile on her face that it wasn't quick enough.

"Just checking on our resident mama," she whispers, inviting herself further into the room.

I reach up with one hand and sweep my hair behind my ear as I assure her, "I haven't fallen asleep at my desk all week. I'm doing fine, I promise."

"And does daddy know that you like to take naps in odd places with his little peanut?"

I roll my lips between my teeth, avoiding her gaze while simultaneously avoiding her question.

"*Millie—*"

I interrupt her, sighing loudly before I moan, "I know. I know. Believe me. It's killing me." For reasons I can't quite explain, I use my eyes to plead with her, needing someone to understand. "We've just never talked about this. We've not made plans. He's in the middle of a tour. I just—I don't know how he'll feel about it." I bite my lip, looking back down at my belly. "I mean, *him* or *her*. I don't know how he'll feel about *him* or *her*."

"Honey, you *won't* know until *he* knows. And he *can't* know unless *you* tell him." She pauses, and I lift my gaze back up to meet hers. Arching her brow, she says, "If ever there was a time to discuss your future and make plans for what's to come, it's *now*."

I nod, knowing she's right, but not knowing what else there is to say.

With a small sigh, she flips her wrist and checks the time on her delicate time piece before tucking her hands into the pockets of her dress. "I'm getting ready to head home. You about out of here?"

"Yeah," I reply, suddenly feeling both defeated and exhausted. My focus has been shit lately, and it seems like I'm working double time to stay on top of my tasks, making each day feel a little bit longer than the last.

"You know to call me if you need anything, right?"

I smile, feeling a bit more at ease as she reminds me—like she so often does as of late—that no matter how alone I feel right now, I'm not.

"I know," I tell her, standing to gather my things. "Thank you."

"Any time. I'll see you tomorrow, Millie."

"See you tomorrow," I echo.

Fifteen minutes later, I'm in my car, heading for the closest supermarket. I'm hungry; and despite the food I know I have in my fridge at home, I'm sure nothing will satisfy me if I don't have my peach iced tea to wash it down.

"My sweet baby has a sweet tooth," I whisper to myself.

Speaking the words out loud makes my skin break out in goosebumps while my stomach knots up with a nervous excitement, and my chest tightens with fear and guilt. This baby makes me feel an overwhelming amount of emotions. And while I'd like to blame my hormones, I know it's not as simple as all of that.

It's the secret.

I can't hold onto it much longer.

I *won't*.

I'll find a way to tell him.

Soon.

I WATCH AS KENT pulls the groupie's hair back as she holds the rolled up bill to her nose and inhales the line of coke straight from the kitchenette counter. She lifts her head, sniffs, and wipes her nose before Kent grips her hair tighter and draws her in for a kiss. That's when I look away, taking a pull from my beer as I look around Kings & Crowns' tour bus.

It's filled with a surprisingly large crowd. Their band, our band, a few roadies, and a handful of fans—of the female persuasion—that got picked up after the show tonight. Brock disappeared into the back room with a couple of girls a while ago, and I can only imagine what he's gotten himself into—in Kent's room, no less. Though, Kent's so high at this point, I'm sure he could give a fuck.

Needless to say, as I take another pull from my beer, I'll admit that there are a few lessons I've chosen *not* to learn from Kent. Mainly, how to handle blow. To be honest, drugs freak me the fuck out, especially knowing how careers and lives have been destroyed after taking just one hit. I know what it's like to get high. I feel it every time I walk out onto that stage. That shit's addicting, and the bigger the crowd, the more I want it. Feeling that yearning over a substance is just dangerous. I can get drunk off my ass, maybe suffer a little alcohol poisoning and one hell of a hangover—but you do enough drugs, you'll end up dead.

I'm sure as shit not going to be digging my own grave. I've got too much life left to live.

That's just me, though. To each his own. I don't really give a shit what these guys are into, so long as they're still around to rock. Luckily, I'm not the only one in my band who feels this way. None of us are really into the hard stuff, but that doesn't mean we don't often find ourselves here—partying our fucking asses off after another killer night on the road.

I look across the aisle from where I sit, slumped into the couch, and see Lewis pass Derrick a joint. I can't hear what he's saying, as the music is blaringly loud, but it makes Derrick laugh before he takes a hit and passes the green back to his fellow drummer. When two tall, leggy girls walk up to them, they look at each other, then up at the girls before they share a smirk. Then they've each got a groupie in their lap, and their *puff, puff pass* becomes a party of four.

I cringe when I see Derrick thrust his tongue into the brunette's mouth, averting my eyes immediately. Unfortunately for me, the next thing I see is Knox with his hand down the front of some girl's pants as she sits on the dining area table, her legs spread, and her tits practically falling out of her tank top.

Fuck. This is going to get nasty. I need to get the hell off of this bus.

I down the rest of my beer, setting the empty bottle beside me before I make my exit. I have no idea where Maddox is, no doubt baggin' himself a groupie. He's been whining about needing a good fuck. For all of our sakes, I hope he's getting some. He can be a real bitch baby when it's been a while since he's had his dick wet; but he's picky as fuck. Won't bag anyone that reminds him of his ex, Andrea. And when he's drunk—they *all* remind him of Andrea.

The night is a perfect one, the slight breeze reminding me that spring is well on its way, and summer will be here before we know it. We've got another few weeks along the east coast, and then we'll be traveling south before we end the tour hitting venues scattered all over the west—every last one of them *sold out.*

That shit still blows my mind.

When our manager, Stefany, told us what a tour with about a hundred stops full of packed houses meant for our bank accounts, I about shit myself. Mountains & Men's cut—after we pay the label and cover the cost of travel and shit—is enough for each of us to go home with forty grand in our pockets. I know to some people that's nothing to write home about. But I've never made that kind of money in a year, let alone in four fucking months. And that doesn't include our record sales—which have already started to skyrocket after our interview with *The Record Times* just a couple of days ago; plus, we've got the shows we'll have on our schedule for the rest of the year.

We're on our way.

We're on our fucking *way.*

It's surprisingly quiet under New Jersey's stars, the sounds of the party muffled as I walk further away from the bus. I look up into the sky, disappointed when I don't see much. Being here, just a couple of hours away from where Millie grew up, makes me miss my girl. The moon shining through the scattered clouds makes me miss home—miss the field on Derrick's land that I'd drive to when I needed to clear my head and let go of all the bullshit. I'm in a good place right now—no bullshit to shed—but that doesn't mean I wouldn't mind being out there, lounging in the back seat of my Audi, Millicent in my lap.

As I make my way to Black Beauty, I reach into my pocket and pull out my phone. I note that it's just past one in the morning, making it a little after eleven back home. I know it's too late to call my girl, but I want to anyway. She'll complain about having to teach in the morning, but at least I'll get to hear the sound of her voice.

When I climb aboard our bus, I hear JJ's laughter before I see him. He's stretched out on the black couch to my right, a remote control in his hand and his focus on the television mounted on the wall just behind the driver's seat. Taking another step up into the cabin, I start to understand why his game is so amusing. On the couch to my left, Alex is sitting up with the other remote. She's laughing, too. It's only Maddox, who is laying with his head propped up against Alex's thigh, who doesn't seem amused as he scowls at the TV.

"The fuck, Zip? Have I taught you nothing? Give me the fucking control."

He reaches for it lazily, his inebriated state making it easy for Alex to twist her body away from him, pulling the remote out of reach as she giggles some more, her attention still glued to the screen.

"Give me a break, Mad Lips. This is a new track. And stop reaching! You're messing me up."

"Oh, for fuck's sake. This is painful."

"Stop your bitchin'. Finish your beer," JJ demands good naturedly.

Clearly—Maddox had Andrea on the brain tonight.

For the life of me, I can't understand it. She was a total bitch. She treated him like shit, and he needed to cut her loose long before he did. I'll have to make it a point to play the part of his wingman the next time we go out. His ass needs to get laid.

"'Sup, Sage?" asks JJ, his focus still on the game. "Got sick of beating off the girls over there?"

"Nah," I reply, chuckling as I run my fingers through my hair. That's not to say that I didn't have to tell a few to scoot. I always do. It doesn't bother me much. It's easy to push 'em away when I've got a gorgeous girl waiting for me at home. "Just needed a breather. It was getting hot as fuck in there."

Literally.

"You're gonna drunk dial her, aren't you?" Maddox mumbles, nodding toward the phone in my hand. I offer him no more than a smirk before I start to head back to my bunk. "Pussy!" he calls after me.

"I've got a woman," I call back over my shoulder. "What's your excuse?" When he doesn't answer, I shake my head with a grin before I yell, "Pussy!"

He mutters something under his breath, but I pay him no mind, kicking off my shoes before climbing into my bunk. I pull the curtain and flick on the light before I tap on the screen of my phone. I open up my favorite contacts, hitting her name at the top of my list. The phone rings through to her voicemail. I hang up and try again. For the second time, I get her voicemail. I know this means she's sleeping, but I'm drunk enough to keep this up for a while.

It's been a month since I've seen her. Having her around for the first week of the tour was such a tease. Now, with every day and every mile that stretches on between us, she seems farther and farther away from me. It's not a body thing, either; it's a heart thing. I talk to her every damn day, but it's not the same as being in the same room with her. It's not the same as touching her—kissing her—*fucking* her. I know my girl needs that. Fuck, I need it, too. But she's been acting strange, which makes me sure that she's been in that pretty head of hers.

It's scary as shit up there, sometimes.

So today—right here, right now—I'm going to remind her that I love her. She needs to hear it. When I get her voicemail for the third time, I don't even hesitate before I hit redial.

I want to hear my girl's voice, and I want to hear it now.

Millicent

By the time I reach for my phone, it has stopped ringing. Peering through bleary eyes as I struggle to pull myself out of sleep, I notice that I've got five missed calls. Before I can register what that could mean, the device starts ringing again in my hand. I slide my finger across the screen and bring it to my ear.

"Hello?"

"Baby—*fuck*—hi."

"Sage? Baby, are you okay?" I ask, shaking my head to ward off sleep as I prop myself up on my elbow.

"I miss you, doll face," he murmurs.

I free a sigh, falling back against my pillows. In this moment, I'm not sure if I'm relieved or irritated. I was cocooned in the arms of sleep—sleep that I *really* needed.

Then again, he doesn't know that. He has no idea how much *more* precious my sleep has become to me. If he thought I was bad before…

"Millicent?"

The sound of his voice speaking my name coaxes me out of my thoughts, my heart assuring me that I don't have to pick whether I'm relieved or irritated. I can be both. And I am. I'm irritated that he woke me up, but I'm relieved that his incessant calling isn't cause for any sort of alarm; furthermore, I'm relieved to simply *hear* him.

"I'm here."

"*I miss you*," he repeats pointedly.

"I miss you too, Sage."

God—what a fucking understatement.

"What are you doing?" I ask softly.

"Laying here. Fully clothed. Drunk. Wishin' my girl was here—preferably *naked*."

Suddenly, I'm no longer sleepy. Neither am I entertaining wild thoughts of being *naked* with my boyfriend. Rather, I'm assaulted by the reality that my *boyfriend* is the twenty-one-year-old lead singer for a band that's on tour. My boyfriend is drunk, calling me from somewhere out east in the middle of the night.

Somewhere out east. I can't even fucking remember *where*, because where he is today isn't where he was yesterday. *This* is his life. *This* is his dream. *This* is what he's been fighting for; what he's been sacrificing for. *This* is one of many reasons why I haven't told him that I'm pregnant. I'm overwhelmed with the fear of how it'll all play out. It's not right, keeping this secret. It's not *fair*, and I know that; but I also know that a baby will change everything. Our baby will alter the entire trajectory of his future—of *our* future—and the outcome is completely unknown.

I've thought this out a million ways. There are two scenarios that frighten me the most.

Either he learns that he's going to be a father, he freaks out, then he feels somehow obligated to make all of these sacrifices for us—giving up nights just like this one so that he can be with us—and then years from now, he resents me for robbing him of the chance to be all that he was *supposed* to be during this time in his life.

Or he continues on his path to stardom so that he can provide for me and the child; only he's never around—because he's too busy fighting to ensure that he's got us covered. And while that's both noble and totally something Sage would do, I hate the idea of being away from him. It pains me to think of my child growing up hardly ever seeing his or her father. I know it wouldn't be the same as my childhood, but I want our baby to have *both* of us as often as possible.

In no scenario does he not love me. We're in this together—*always*. I believe that. I *have* to believe that. Also, in no scenario does he not adore his child. I've seen how he is with his nephews, with his *niece*. I know that he loves his family more than anything and that he would do anything for them. Yet, that doesn't change the fact that this could all turn out so wrong.

We have no plan.

I always have a plan—and now—

"That's it. I'm buying you a fucking plane ticket."

His declaration yanks me from my thoughts, my mind suddenly racing in an attempt to catch up.

"What?"

"Right now, Millicent. I'm getting out of my bunk, I'm headed to the back to power up my damn computer, I'm taking out my fucking wallet, and I'm buying you a motherfucking ticket. You're calling out for work tomorrow, you're getting on a plane, and you're coming to New York. We'll be there mid-afternoon, and we're there until Monday. I'll meet you at the airport."

"Sage," I begin to protest, pushing myself up into a seated position. "I can't just—"

"You can and you will, baby. I'll call Rosy or Pepper, or whoever the fuck, as soon as I hang up with you, and I'll tell them you need a ride to the airport."

My head feels like it's spinning, and suddenly I'm craving peach iced tea like nobody's business. I try and ignore my thirst as I rake my fingers through my hair, closing my eyes tight as I explain, "Next week is the week before finals, Sage. I don't have time to travel. We've talked about this. I can't come out until—"

"Bullshit, baby doll. Need to see my girl. Need to see her *pronto*. Besides—it's your birthday Sunday. My dick is so much better than the bouquet of flowers I was gonna send you."

I cough out a laugh, caught off guard by his declaration. While I can't argue that he's wrong, that's not what has me speechless. The truth is, I totally forgot it was my birthday this weekend. I've had so much on my mind; I hadn't given it a single thought. Not to mention the fact that I can't even remember the last time I celebrated my birthday.

"Do you hear that?" he asks, his voice soft and low.

"Hmm? Hear what?"

"The sound of those wheels turning in that pretty head of yours. It's so loud, it's drowning out every word you're saying."

Suddenly, my chest aches, my guilt so heavy I fear that I'll crumble beneath the weight of it. He's right. I've barely said a word to him since I answered the phone, and it's not because I'm half sleeping. I'm wide awake, lost in my thoughts, unable to focus on anything longer than a few seconds without getting distracted. I know that I won't get past this until I've confessed the truth.

In a few minutes, thirty-*two* days will turn into thirty-*three* days. *Thirty-three* days I've been harboring this secret, carrying his child with not a clue as to how or when to tell him. I still don't know the *how*, but it appears as though the *when* has been decided for me. I bite down on my lower lip, willing myself not to cry. He knows something is going on; he knows I'm holding back, and instead of picking a fight about it over the phone, he's buying me a plane ticket.

He's not fighting *with* me.

He's fighting *for* me.

"I love you so much," I whisper past the knot in my throat.

"Feels good to hear you say it, baby. Check your email. Your flight leaves at ten."

I don't argue. There's no point. I need this. *We* need this, and there's no sense in denying it. So instead, I simply reply, "Okay, baby."

"I'll see you tomorrow. And doll face?"

"Yeah?"

"I fucking love you, too."

TWO

Sage

KNOX VOLUNTEERED TO come with me to the airport. Now, as we sit waiting for Millie's plane to arrive, he's going through the shit-ton of notifications we've accumulated on our Facebook page over the last couple of days. The amount of social media attention we're getting now is *wild*. It takes all six of us to keep track of each different platform, our fan base growing by what feels like the hour. It's humbling, and exhilarating, and overwhelming all at once. It has taken us *years* to get to where we are, and now, everything seems to be happening in the blink of an eye.

The weekend we have ahead of us is going to be fucking *insane*. We've got a show later on tonight; then tomorrow, Kings & Crowns will be performing on *The Late Show* with Johnny Bash. *Johnny*-fucking-*Bash*. While Mountains & Men won't be playing, we'll be in the audience. To say that we're stoked would be putting it mildly. I'm sure we'll hit a party or two after the recording, and then we've got a day to chill on Sunday before we hit the road again Monday.

When my phone rings from inside of my jacket pocket, I'm quick to pull it out. It's not Millie, like I was hoping, but I shouldn't be surprised. Her flight hasn't even landed yet. I nudge Knox with my elbow, showing him it's his brother calling, and then I slide my finger across the screen and bring the device to my ear.

"Yo," I answer.

"Are you sitting down?"

I furrow my brow, my eyes locking with Knox's as I reply, "Uh, yeah. Why?"

"Remember when Stefany first told us about Potential Records, and Derrick was wondering if signing with Greg was our *best* offer or our *first* offer?"

"Yeah," I mutter, wondering where he's going with this.

"Best. Fucking. Offer. This guy has got *crazy* pull in this industry."

I shake my head, wondering why he's telling me something we already know. Before he started his own label, he was kind of a big deal at a label that was more than a big deal. His dad has been working in the music business his whole life, so Greg knows his shit. He also knows his people—it's how we got Black Beauty, his gift to us after we released *Of Mountains & Men*.

"Mad Lips, you've been spending way too much time with Stefany. Just tell me what's up."

He chuckles before he says, "Tomorrow afternoon, we've got a date with VH1."

My spine goes rigid as I sit up straight, my eyes wide in disbelief. "Stop the fuck lying."

"I shit you not."

"What? What's going on?" asks Knox. I can tell by the way that he's smacking the side of my knee that he's more than anxious to hear the news that's got me wound up. "Put him on speaker," he demands.

"Maddox," I begin to say, holding the phone out between Knox and me. "You're on speaker. Say that again."

"Tomorrow afternoon, we've got a date with VH1."

"Are you *shitting* me?" Knox exclaims.

"I don't know how the fuck he did it, but we're all going to the studio for an interview. They're doing a *Behind the Music* that's geared toward up-and-coming bands. Apparently, they only do this theme, like, once or twice a *year*. I cannot believe our fucking timing. We're seriously the luckiest motherfucking bastards on the planet. It airs in a couple months, and Greg got us a spot. Stef said it won't be very long, but they want us all there for the interview; and when it airs, they'll play the video of *You and Me* right after."

"Holy. *Shit*," Knox mutters.

My heart is pounding in my chest, my head spinning so fast that I can't think of a single word to say. Mountains & Men is going to be on *national* television. This is *huge*.

When we were talking about signing with Potential Records and recording our first full-length album, we agreed that the momentum we had gained from our first tour with Lawful Sinners was one we couldn't let slip from our fingers. Now—I swear to god—it's like we're rolling downhill so fast, we can't be stopped.

Eight months. Eight fucking months ago, we got hooked up with Stefany after playing a gig in Greeley, Colorado. Fucking *cow-town* Colorado. Now, we're in New York City talking about *air time* on *VH1*. I seriously have no words.

I don't even realize that my phone is ringing until Knox snatches it out of my hand and starts talking.

"Bro—his girl's calling. We gotta go. We'll meet you at the hotel in a few."

"Word," Maddox replies before Knox switches the call over and presses my phone to my ear.

"Sage?"

The sound of her voice is like a shock to my system, bringing me back to the here and now. I reach my hand up to hold the phone, my heart now pounding for different reasons.

My girl's here.

"Hey, doll face. Where are you?"

"We just landed a moment ago. We're almost to the gate. I should be out in a few minutes."

"I'll meet you there. God, I can't wait to see you."

"Me neither," she murmurs.

We disconnect a second later, and I stand to make my way to her gate. I look back at Knox to see if he's coming, but he just smirks at me as he shakes his head.

"I'm no *voyeur*. I'll wait here."

I laugh, flipping him off as I walk away, knowing good and well that he's smart to stay put. It's been too long since I've seen my Millie—our *hello* will consist of a lot of tongue.

Millicent

A KIND, OLDER gentleman helps me pull my roller bag from the overhead bin. I whisper my thanks, not capable of much more as my nerves and excitement start to overwhelm me. Walking off of the plane, I rest a hand over my lower abdomen. There certainly isn't much to see down there, especially with the loose knit top that I'm wearing over my jeans, but I'm *beyond* nervous just the same.

Fortunately, morning sickness—or *anytime* sickness—isn't one of my pregnancy symptoms. However, I do have a tendency to grow nauseous off and on throughout the day. Normally nothing comes of it, other than an upset stomach. Right now, I'm not certain whether or not that will hold true. Furthermore, I'm so anxious, I can't even tell if it's the baby or knowing that I'll be seeing Sage in a few seconds that has me overexcited.

When I step out of the corridor that opens into the airport and my eyes sweep the area surrounding our gate, I spot Sage and immediately get my answer. It's *him* that has my whole body abuzz. The baby just multiplies every emotion I feel by a thousand. I almost cry when those icy blue eyes meet mine from behind those horn-rimmed glasses. A huge smile lights up his face, and my stomach clenches. He really is marvelously beautiful. My dreamer. My rock star. My *love*.

He hurries toward me, and I hurry toward him—my heart instructing my feet that the distance that separates us must be eradicated. I let go of the handle of my bag the moment Sage's arms wrap around me, pulling me into his hard chest just as his lips crash down onto mine. I grip onto the lapels of his jacket, holding on tight as my knees grow weak and my body melts against his. When his tongue seeks entrance into my mouth, I part my lips willingly, allowing him to taste me.

As he devours me like a man whose thirst cannot be quenched, I slide my hands over his shoulders, circling my arms around his neck. I kiss him back hungrily, pushing up onto my tiptoes, and he holds me tighter against him. In this moment, there is no fear. There is no worry. There is only *love*. There is only *hope*. There is only *Sage*; and for the life of me, I can't remember why I ever doubted him—doubted *us*. This kiss, this *one* kiss isn't just our hello. It's a declaration. It's a promise. What we have is forever. I am his and he is mine, no matter what.

I whimper when he severs our connection, both of us breathless as he props his forehead against mine. I wasn't ready to lose the feel of his lips so soon, but I know that I've only just arrived. Knowing Sage, there's certainly more where that came from.

I *feel* his scowl before he pulls away, and then I see his scrunched brow. I don't understand his expression until he reaches up and runs the back of his hand over my cheek as he asks, "Doll face? Baby—why are you crying?"

I shake my head, surprised when I feel more tears spilling from my eyes. "I didn't know that I was," I whisper, suddenly feeling the knot in my throat.

He holds both sides of my face, sweeping away my tears with his thumbs as his gorgeous blue eyes search my green ones. "I thought after that kiss I had nothing to worry about—but fuck, Millie. Are we okay?"

For a second, I get lost in his gaze—full of concern, yet warm with yearning and overflowing with love. In his stare, I see that I am *exactly* where I belong, and I can't silence the sob that spills from my mouth as I bury my face in his chest and mumble, "I'm *home*. I've missed you so much, Sage—I needed this. I needed to come home."

I feel it as he breathes out a sigh of relief, his arms engulfing me against him once more. He holds me so tight, I can barely breathe, and it feels perfect.

He presses his lips against my hair as he murmurs, "Fuck, I love you."

"I love you, too," I manage, trying my best to silence my tears.

I genuinely feel on the verge of a complete breakdown.

That's how happy I am.

That's how pregnant I am.

Nevertheless, I try my best to pull myself together. I'm here, in New York City, and I have just two and a half days with the man that I love—the father of my child—and I can't waste any time being unexplainably emotional.

His whole body jolts, as if something has startled him, and then he exclaims, "Shit, doll face, you will not believe the news we just got." Before I can move to look up at him, he does it for me. Gripping my shoulders, he separates us and then gently slides his hands up the back of my neck and into my hair. "M&M is going to be on VH1."

His announcement stuns me into a stupor. I wasn't at all prepared to hear what he just said, and my mind feels ill equipped to even begin to process his news. It takes every brain cell I've got to conjure a single word in response. "*What?*"

"Yeah," he laughs, giving my neck an affectionate squeeze. "I guess Greg pulled some strings or some shit. I don't know—Maddox just called before you landed. We'll find out more when we get back to the hotel." He pulls away from me and reaches for the handle of my bag as he asks, "This all you got?"

I nod, wiping away the remnants of my tears before adjusting the purse on my shoulder. "Yeah, that's all."

He smacks a kiss against my temple and then snakes his arm around my waist, tucking me against his side. He then lifts his chin toward the exit. "Let's jet, baby doll. We'll grab a bite to eat with Alex and the guys, and then we've got sound check at six."

I follow his lead without a word, all the while wondering how long it'll be before our next minute alone. I have only about a week's worth of experience being on the road with the band, but that's long enough for me to have learned that privacy is a rare commodity while on tour.

"There she is!" yells Knox as he stands to his feet. We're still several yards away from each other, but I can still recognize his tall, built frame and his handsome smile from here. His welcome makes me smile right back. Then, once the distance between us has been closed, he tugs on my arm, pulling me away from Sage before he wraps me in a friendly embrace. "Good to see you, Millie."

"You too, Knox."

"Also," he continues in a mock whisper, keeping me close. "Thanks for answering his calls. Morale is *way* up this time around," he teases as he lets me go.

I blush, remembering their first tour. While I never intended for all of Mountains & Men to be a part of my relationship with Sage—or the lack there of—I learned the hard way that their bond runs *way* deep. If one of them has a broken heart, they all feel it. It's just how they function. They're more than friends; their more than band mates. They're *family*.

..ight, all right, enough of that shit," mutters Sage with an eye roll.

Knox laughs before he nods to the doors leading out to the curb, lined with people waiting to hail a cab. "Ready to bounce?"

"Yeah. Let's get the fuck out of here," says Sage, grabbing my hand and lacing his fingers through mine. "The birthday girl has arrived. Our weekend has *officially* begun."

THREE

Millicent

The Beacon is probably the prettiest venue Mountains & Men has ever played in. Upon our initial entrance a couple of hours ago, I was taken aback by the grandiose classical feel of the place. As the guys and Alex went about their sound check, I wondered how two rock-n-roll groups would manage to make such a historical space fit their modern sound.

Now, standing in the shadows of the wings, watching as Sage struts his way across the stage singing his heart out, I wonder what it is about my silly brain that dares to question what he's capable of—what they're *all* capable of. I can't see the back of the crowd very well, or make out all of the people seated in the balcony, but I'd be willing to bet that there's not a single ass in a seat right now. This band is every bit as good as everyone is saying—and the energy in the room is electric, practically *demanding* that you stand up and dance like no one is watching while you sing along, even if you don't know the words.

I think back to the looks of awe on all of their faces when they first walked out on stage and caught a glimpse of the empty space, soon to be packed with a sold out crowd. Their excitement and wonder was a familiar sight, reminding me that this is just their beginning. They're still getting used to all of this. I got to witness their amazement during their first week on the road, and it is still just as apparent all this time later. It astonishes me how the very setting that humbled them hours before seems to be under their command now.

"I've never seen anyone like him, you know?"

I jump, startled to find someone standing beside me. When I look over and see Lewis, the drummer from Kings & Crowns, I breathe a sigh of relief before I replay the words he just shouted into my ear.

"Like Sage?" I yell back, pointing a finger at my boyfriend.

He nods, his eyes still drawn to that blue flame. I follow his lead, immediately mesmerized by the bright light that he is. I swear, Sage burns hotter and hotter as time goes on.

"It's all in his name," he continues, speaking just loud enough for me to be able to hear him over the roar of the crowd and the sound of loud music. "He is a sage. Fuck of a lot smarter than I was at twenty-one. He knows when to paddle and when to ride the wave."

To be honest, I'm not sure what the hell Lewis is talking about. I seriously wonder if he's high right now, but I try and make sense of his words anyway. It is true that Sage is wise beyond his years. He's still young in all the best ways; it's the dreamer in him that preserves that little boy optimism he clings to so fiercely. Yet, at the same time, it's the *man* in him that defines his strength and determination; his stubbornness and his resilience.

"Hold onto that one, lassy." I look at him once more, his tone taking me by surprise. "He's solid, Millie. He's unwavering. He's loyal. He's fucking *good,* is what he is. And I don't just mean his talent. That will take him far—all of them. Their talent will take them anywhere they want to go. But it's the integrity of a man that keeps him alive in this business. People don't realize that. They don't want to believe that. They don't want to *see* it." He pauses, shifting his gaze to peer down into my eyes. "He sees *beyond* it. He's all about the music. He's *pure.* Just take my advice, eh? Hold onto that one."

I smile, still not sure whether or not Lewis is under the influence, but certain that his words come from someplace honest. I know it because I *feel* it in my heart. I've said it before, and I'll never stop believing that Sage is not average. He's undeniably rare. And while I consider myself unworthy of him, he holds every single piece of my heart. I'm his, totally and completely.

"I'm not going anywhere, Lewis."

He chuckles, offering me a conniving smirk that confuses me. Then, before I know what's going on, his hands are on my shoulders, pushing me out onto the stage.

I start to protest, planting my feet in an effort to stop him, but he's stronger than I am. Panic washes over me, and then I see Sage looking right at me—a huge grin lighting up his face.

Shit. What did I miss?

"She's a little shy," he speaks into the mic, walking toward me with an outstretched hand. "Can you guys give her a little encouragement?"

The crowd erupts, snatching my attention. Suddenly, the room feels a lot bigger than three thousand strong.

"Come on, doll face," says Sage, grabbing hold of my hand. I snap my focus back on him, realizing that Lewis is no longer at my back. I turn to glare at him, now catching onto the fact that he was distracting me for a reason. He winks at me before he starts clapping, whooping and hollering with the rest of them. I twist my neck to catch the eyes of anyone in the band, stupidly believing that one of them might help me. Their knowing smiles are proof that I'm fucked—they're in on this, too.

Under the spotlight, I have nowhere to run.

"My old lady has a birthday this weekend," Sage announces, tucking me under his arm.

Still in shock that he's pulled me out here, I don't have the wherewithal to reprimand him for calling me his *old lady*. Instead, I shrink into his side in a feeble attempt to hide.

"The guys back here can't sing for shit," he teases, making the audience laugh. "But I thought maybe you all could help drown them out in a chorus of *Happy Birthday*. What do you say, you with me?"

I choke out a laugh at his question, not at all surprised by their riotous agreement. Mountains & Men has been on the stage for twenty minutes. They only need *three* to prove their worth and captivate their listeners. Sage only needs *one* to wrap them all around his finger. *Of course* they're with him, which is how I find myself standing center stage while three thousand people sing to me for my birthday.

I'm *mortified*.

Yet, in the same breath, I will not deny that I've never felt so special.

These New Yorkers don't know me from Adam, but in this single moment in time, they're celebrating my birth with more gusto than anyone ever has before. I force myself to let my eyes scan the crowd once more, truly taking in the scene before me. Then I peer up at Sage, who is staring at me as he sings, looking as happy as can be—and it hits me like an explosion.

Right here. Right next to him, wherever he is, this *is where I want to be.* This *is where I need to be—where* we *need to be—soaking up every ounce of his love.* This *is the Sage I want my child to experience. Every single day.* This *is the love I want wrapped around our baby. I'll do anything to make sure that happens. Anything.*

"Happy birthday, Millicent," he says so that only I can hear.

Without thinking twice about it, I reach for his face with my hands, pulling my sweaty man down for a kiss. I ignore the cheers of his fans, pressing my body against his as I shower him with affection. His arm tightens around me before his hand glides down over my ass, and I giggle against his lips as he gives me a squeeze. I don't even care how many people just saw that.

My man adores my ass, and I love it.

Sage

I CAN'T HEAR HER giggle over the sound of the crowd, but I feel it—her chest pressed up against mine, her lips still grazing my mouth as I squeeze her ass. She offers me one more kiss, and then shoves her way out of my arms before hurrying off stage and back into the wings. I watch her go, my thoughts temporarily honed in on the semi I'm sporting in my jeans.

Fuck—having her out here with me felt awesome. She was glowing under the lights, looking more beautiful than ever. My girl is hot as hell, and I won't deny that I'm counting down the hours until she's underneath me, soaking my dick as she screams my name.

I shake the thought away as I look back out into the auditorium, bringing the mic to my lips before I say, "Thanks, guys." Their response sends another rush of adrenaline through my veins, and I chuckle before I reply, "Now, how 'bout I teach you a new song?"

Derrick clicks the beat without further ado, and Alex kicks us off—playing the *shit* out of that bass. I grin over at her, nodding my head to the beat. Then I turn back to the crowd as I tell them, "We wrote this a couple weeks ago. You don't mind if we debut it now, do you?" They cheer wildly, pumping me up even more, and I start to jump up and down just as the Bradley brothers join Alex, adding another layer to the sound. JJ comes in on the keys for a few bars while I continue to ramp up the crowd, and then I suck in a huge breath, throwing my fist in the air as I belt out my first note.

This is the dream. This is the life. This is who we are. This is what we were born to do.

My band at my back, our new fans before us, my girl at my flank—yeah, I'm high as fuck right now.

After one hell of a show, I stand with my girl wrapped in my arms as we watch Kings & Crowns rock the shit out of their set. It feels good having Millie with me. I've missed it. I've missed *her*. It might make me sound like a pussy, but I could give a fuck. I'm not some punk-ass wanna be kid chasing a pipe dream; I'm a man chasing my destiny, and I know what I want. I want it *all*, and that includes Millicent right by my side.

I know that the future scares her—that *my* future scares her. She believes in me, and she knows this is just the beginning. So far, my career has been one hell of a wild ride, and all the unknown leaves her feeling unsettled. Nevertheless, she wants this—she wants *us*. We're in this together, a promise we've made to each other more than once; but I can tell that as the future of Mountains & Men becomes more real, she's getting more and more overwhelmed. The distance was one thing, but even now that she's here, I can feel something is different.

I decide that flying her to the city this weekend is even more perfect than I realized. I'm determined to show her that she's meant to be a part of this life with me. I want her to see that what's ahead of us isn't something to worry about, but something to look forward to—an adventure to *experience* as it continues to unfold.

"We're hittin' some clubs," Brock shouts as he walks off stage after their encore. "Let's get fucked up and then get fuckin' *laid!*"

I chuckle, thinking that's exactly what I want to do. I haven't been inside of Millie for far too long. My dick twitches just thinking about it.

"Hey—*D*," I call out, catching Derrick's attention as we all make our way backstage.

"What's up, Dweeb?" he asks, offering Millie a chin lift and a wink.

"Do me a favor, will you? Make sure Maddy get's some pussy tonight. I was going to play wingman but…" I nod down at my girl and Derrick laughs before smacking me on the shoulder.

"I'll see what I can do."

"No blondes!" I insist as he walks away.

"Dude—I know. I got this."

Millie twists her neck and frowns up at me. "Maddox is still messed up over Andrea? It's been months."

"Yeah," I reply with a smirk. "Nobody gets it. Nobody has *ever* gotten it. Since day one, they were the definition of dysfunctional. He's fine—he just needs to stay away from the diva type; and the blondes—he's such a fucking sucker for the blondes."

She hums but shakes her head, letting me know she's on the same wave length as the rest of us. We don't get it; we just roll with it.

"You ready to have some fun?" I murmur in her ear, no longer wishing to discuss Maddox.

"Actually, I was hoping maybe we could just, um, maybe head back to the hotel?"

As much as I like the idea of taking her back to our room, stripping her completely naked, and fucking her until the sun comes up—that won't exactly work with my plan to immerse her in M&M's world for the weekend.

"Ahh, come on," I croon, freeing her from my arms before I take her hand and give her a tug. "We're in NYC, doll. Not to mention, we're hitting the streets with Kings & Crowns. You *don't* want to skip this."

I don't miss the apprehension that flashes in her eyes as she opens her mouth to speak, but she surrenders without argument, sealing her lips closed. When she shrugs and offers me a slight nod, I dip my head and smack a kiss against her lips.

"We'll have fun, I swear," I whisper before brushing my lips against hers once more. "Then later, I'll take care of that greedy pussy. I'll make you come so many times, you'll be begging me to stop."

She runs her teeth over her bottom lip before she murmurs, "Promise?"

"You bet your sweet, little ass," I reply, reaching around to clap my hand against her backside.

"Let's roll, Sage. You can back that ass up at the club," Kent shouts down the hallway leading to the rear exit. He's got a girl under each of his arms—their VIP passes still wrapped around their necks.

"We got a spot. Brock knows a guy," announces Rex, Kings & Crowns' fourth man. As he passes us, he slips on a pair of shades. It's almost midnight and the guy pulls those fuckers off so well, it makes me question why I'm not wearing sunglasses under the pale moon, too.

I give Millie's hand a squeeze and then we follow after them, out into the cool, calm night of late April. Still riding the adrenaline high from performing, we're loud and obnoxious as we walk the few blocks to the club of Brock's choosing. We end up at a place called Vibe, and the line to get in is outrageous. Brock doesn't even blink, leading us to the front of the pack. I don't hear what he says to the bouncer at the door, but I watch as he nods and then points back at all of us. The bouncer says not a word in response; he simply nods, unhooking the velvet rope, allowing each of us to pass.

"That's what I'm fuckin' talkin' 'bout!" cries Maddox as he makes his entrance.

I laugh at him, slinging my arm around my girl's shoulders as we make our way to the bar. The club is pretty badass, the room decked out in black with neon green accents, making it look respectfully retro-chic. There are four bars that span the length of the four walls in the room shaped like a box. The back-lit shelves make the stock of booze a focal point, and each stretch of wall is lit with a different bright color. Pink. Purple. Yellow. Blue. There are high tables scattered around the perimeter, packed with groups of people forming clumps around them as they drink and socialize.

Glancing up, I see what looks like some sort of exclusive lounge a level above us—the partitions made up of frosted panes of glass, giving the illusion of some sort of privacy. I watch as a couple comes out from behind the glass, the entire panel of wall swinging open like a door. Then, down a level in the center of the room, there's a dance floor packed full of people—the DJ set up in the center of all the madness; the dance floor lined with green LEDs.

"Birthday shot for the birthday girl?" asks Knox, speaking loudly over the music as he looks back and points at Millie.

She shakes her head before she replies, "No, thanks!"

"What?" I scoff. "Think again, doll face—we're celebrating."

"Sage, *really*, I don't want anything," she insists, surprising me with her resolute stare.

"A gin and tonic, then."

I start to motion to the bartender, but Millie grabs my wrist, lowering my hand as she says, "I'm not kidding, Sage. I'm not drinking. Order for yourself if you want. I'll just have some water. It's hot in here."

I furrow my brow, wondering what her deal is, but she ignores me and looks about the room. I've never known her to turn down a drink, and I don't understand why she's suddenly feeling *responsible*—unless maybe she's worried about us getting trashed in an unfamiliar city as big as this one.

"Doll, I got you—you know that, right? We'll make it back to the hotel just fine. Have a few drinks."

She reaches up and kisses my cheek before she shakes her head at me and says, "Thanks, baby. I just don't feel like it."

Before I can open my mouth to respond, she's turned her gaze away from me again. There's something about her that's making me anxious. I don't like it. It's like she's not telling me something, like all those times on the phone when she'd get quiet, lost in her head—except we're not on the phone. We're standing right next to each other.

"Hey," I start to say, gently taking hold of her chin before directing her focus back on me. "What's going on? What aren't you telling me?"

I wait what feels like a full sixty seconds for her to respond. She doesn't. She just *stares* at me, her eyes holding some sort of truth she's not fessing up to. All of a sudden, I'm frustrated—my good mood evaporating into thin air. Now, the club is too loud, too hot, too crowded, and I don't feel like celebrating shit.

"Let's go," I mutter, shaking my head as I begin to make my way to the door.

"Sage? What—? Where are we going?"

"You wanted to go to the hotel? We're going to the fucking hotel," I announce, suddenly getting the impression that sex was *not* what she had in mind earlier.

Fuck—what the fuck is going on?

"Sage, wait!"

I stop just on the other side of the door, looking down at her as she reaches up to run her fingers through her hair. For a second, I think she's about to tell me that she's changed her mind and that we should go back inside. Instead, she softly asks, "Shouldn't we tell someone we're going?"

"I'll send Alex a text from the cab," I mumble, heading for the curb to hitch a ride.

I do exactly as I said I would, letting Alex know that we've left as our driver weaves us through traffic. For a while, neither of us speaks. The longer we sit in silence, the more pissed off I get.

"Don't be mad," she whispers, reaching over to take my hand.

I cough out a humorless laugh, annoyed by her request, but I don't shake away her touch. It's been so long since I've had it, and in a couple of days, it'll be gone again. I'm upset, but I'm not an idiot.

"Sage?"

"What the fuck, Millie? For real—I'm asking—*what the fuck?*"

She doesn't get a chance to respond before we pull up in front of our destination. She's quick to make her exit while I pay the driver, and then I climb out after her without delay. When I find her waiting for me on the curb, I stand as close to her as I can without touching her. I can feel her anxious breaths against my lips as she looks up at me, and it makes my dick jerk.

Fuck.

"Millicent," I start on a growl. "If you even *think* about breaking up with me, I will lock you in Black Beauty until Monday morning, and then drag your ass to the courthouse and marry you."

I watch as her eyes grow wide in shock before she loses her balance and falls against my chest. I catch her with ease, clamping my hands around her biceps to right her and keep her steady.

"Sage…" She gulps and then shakes her head at me. "I'm not breaking up with you."

"Then what the hell is going on?"

Sliding her hands around my waist, she gives me a light squeeze before she begs, "Please—can we please just go upstairs?"

"Yeah. Okay. Fine. And then you're telling me *everything*."

FOUR

Millicent

SHIT. I'VE MADE SUCH A *mess of this.*

Sage is pissed. He's pissed and he doesn't even know why. When I tell him—when the truth comes out that I'm not only pregnant, but that I've known almost the entire time we've been apart and haven't said a *word*—I can only imagine this bad situation will get even worse.

I wish that all of this could have happened differently. I wish that I wasn't so scared, that I could just trust my heart, trust my gut, trust *Sage* and know that everything is going to be all right. I never wanted him to find out quite like this. I don't want him to be *angry* with me. Knowing that it's entirely my fault that he is only makes me feel worse.

The second we walk into the room, he strips out of his jacket and tosses it onto the foot of the bed before he turns and looks right at me. He lifts his eyebrows expectantly, and I know it's time for me to come clean. Only, I can't find my words. I've rehearsed this a hundred times in my head, but not once did I imagine that I'd be telling him with *that* look on his face.

"*Goddammit,* Millicent."

My tears hit me instantaneously, and I can't stop them. I try everything—biting the inside of my cheek, holding my breath, keeping my eyes from blinking—but it's no use. As soon as the tears start to fall, Sage's hands are holding my face.

"Doll face," he says, his voice so soft I can hardly hear it. "You're freaking me out."

"I'm pregnant," I blurt.

He goes stock-still, his eyes wide and unreadable; but just like my tears, now that I've started to tell the truth, I can't stop.

"I found out almost as soon as I left the tour. I had my first doctor's appointment two weeks ago. In a couple weeks, I'll be three months along. I'm sorry I didn't tell you. I didn't know how! And I..."

My words trail off as I watch his facial expression slowly begin to change, and my heart skips a beat as a boyish grin pulls at his lips. His eyes dance around my face as if he's somehow *seeing* me for the first time since I got off of the plane. My pulse spikes and my tears pick up speed when I realize that I've never, *ever* seen him look so...*happy*.

He startles me when he crushes his lips against mine, his grip around my face tightening. I then feel it as his smile returns and he chuckles into my mouth.

"Holy shit," he breathes.

He kisses me again, his hands leaving my face as he pushes my jacket from off of my shoulders, letting it drop to the floor. He then reaches for the hem of my shirt, carefully pulling it over my head before he takes a step away from me—his eyes studying the entire length of my torso.

"Holy shit," he whispers. He trails the tips of his fingers over the swell of my breasts before dragging them down the length of my abdomen.

"My doctor says it'll be a few more weeks before I really start to show," I murmur, because I feel like I need to say *something*. He still hasn't really said anything, and I'm beginning to wonder if he's just in shock.

"Oh, you're showing, baby," he grunts, his hands molding around my front. "*Fuck* me." He grips my sides, pulling me flush against him as he rests his forehead against mine.

"Sage?" I question hesitantly. "Are you...*happy*?"

I need to hear him say it. I need to hear him say that he's in this with me.

His hold around me tightens before he asks, "We're keeping it, right?"

My chest *aches* with an abundant amount of joy at his use of the word *we*. "Yes," I reply assuredly, reaching up to grip the back of his neck. "*Yes*, of course."

"Then, yeah, gorgeous," he replies softly, running his nose down the length of mine. "I'm happy. *Fuck*," he smashes a kiss against my lips, crushing my body against his. "I'm beyond happy." As he mutters the words, he drags his lips across my cheek and down my neck, causing my stomach to flutter with excitement. "Need to be inside you, doll."

The next thing I know, my bra is on the floor and his mouth is sucking one of my nipples. It hurts, but I don't care. As his tongue swirls around my hardened bud, I concentrate on the heat between my legs as I grow slick and swollen with arousal.

It feels like it's been forever since I've had his lips on my body, and I endeavor to make the most of this moment.

Once he's shown a fair amount of attention to each of my nipples, he kisses his way back up to my lips, thrusting his tongue deep into my mouth. I moan, feeling abnormally turned on all of a sudden, and he reaches to unbutton my jeans. When they're unfastened, he severs our kiss and drops into a squatting position to help me out of them—along with my shoes. As soon as my panties are dealt with, he stands to full height, and I watch as his eyes rake over me.

"I know this is going to sound stupid," he begins to say, shaking his head as if even *he* can't believe what he's thinking. "But I've never wanted to beat my chest as much as I do *right* now."

I burst into a fit of laughter, awash in the blissful relief that accompanies the revelation of my secret. I've been waiting for this moment for a *long* thirty-three days, and I never came close to imagining Sage making me feel the way he's making me feel *right now*. When I look at him and find him still staring at me possessively, I quell my laughter, biting my lip as I rest my hands over my lower belly.

He is ours. Sage Lawrence McCoy belongs to us, and forever and ever, we belong to him. To know that he's not just happy, but proud*—it makes my heart unbearably full.*

"Do it," I tell him.

His eyes are staring straight into mine, and I see them dilate as he draws in a deep breath. My stomach clenches when he reaches behind his head and yanks off his shirt—revealing his spectacularly chiseled, tatted torso. I suck in a quiet gasp when he lifts his fists and pounds them against his chest, freeing a sexy as hell growl.

Fuck. That's hot.

He smirks at me, as if he's read my mind, and then immediately toes his way out of his shoes before he drops his pants and kicks off his boxers. My gaze falls down to his long, thick cock, now fully erect, and my mouth waters.

"You want a taste, baby?" he asks, his voice husky and heavy with lust.

"Yes," I whisper, my pussy pulsing and my heart racing.

"On your knees, gorgeous."

He doesn't have to tell me twice. I'm knelt in front of him instantly, my hands skimming up the back of his toned, bare thighs as I stare at the tip of his dick, watching as his pre-cum leaks from the head. I dart my tongue out, wanting to taste it, and the slight contact makes him hiss. I then tilt my head, allowing me to lick his entire length. I repeat the act twice before he grows impatient, fisting my hair with a grunt. I smile, peering up at him from beneath my lashes, and then I take him into my mouth as far as he'll go. I relax my throat and breathe through my nose, wanting to take him a little deeper—deeper than I've ever taken him before.

"Oh, *shit*," he groans as he hits the back of my throat. "Fuck, yes, baby—you feel so good."

I pull away from him until my mouth is empty. Then I take a deep breath and engulf him between my lips once more—slowly easing him all the way to the back of my throat.

"*Jesus,* you're gonna make me lose my load."

I back away again, looking up at him as I say, "Fuck my mouth, baby—but don't come down my throat. I don't want to swallow. I'm eating for two, now."

He grunts, biting down on his lip as he gently tugs on my hair. Without a word, I open my mouth and he shoves his cock inside, pumping in and out of me as I suck and hum around him. I close my eyes, lost in the pleasure of pleasing my man. My desire is so much, I can feel my arousal dripping between my thighs, and it makes me want to touch myself.

I don't—knowing full well that Sage is the master of my orgasms. I come by my own hand only when he demands it.

Without warning, he pulls out of me, reaching down to grab hold of me from underneath my arms. He lifts me off of the floor, and I'm quick to circle my legs around his middle. When I grab onto his shoulders, he slides his hands down my back, reaching for my ass as he carries me to the bed. I whimper at his contact, squeezing him with my legs.

"Holy fuck—" He looks down between us and then back into my eyes. I'm sure he can feel it—my drenched pussy smearing my arousal onto his stomach. "You're *soaked*," he exclaims with wide eyes.

I simply nod before pressing a kiss to his lips, holding him tight around his neck. He reciprocates hungrily, his grip around my ass making me wonder if he'll leave bruises. Not that I would mind. He feels *so* good.

He severs our kiss and reaches for the itchy coverlet that rests on top of the bed, ripping it back and tossing it onto the floor. He then turns and sits on the edge of the mattress before laying down on his back. Pulling his glasses off, he tosses them onto the pillows as he mumbles, "You smell good enough to eat, baby doll. Need a taste, Millie. Get up here."

Slowly, I lean over him and crawl up his body until I'm straddling his head. I suck in a breath of air as he curves his arms over my backside, flattening his palms on my spine before he pushes down. My legs spread a little wider, opening me up for his kiss. I'm trembling after one luxuriously lazy swipe of his tongue. He groans as he savors me, and then—

"You're my favorite fucking candy
I'll always lick, lick, lick
'til the center of your tootsie pop
And if I bite/just know I might

You'll taste just right, all night
'Cause you're my favorite fucking candy."

I smile, because I can't help myself, because I love the sound of his rich, tenor voice when he croons to me, and because as he sings, his lips graze over my sensitive flesh—but deep down, underneath my longing for him, I want to smack him for singing about my *vagina*. When I open my mouth to tell him as much, he distracts me as he thrusts his tongue into my core. He feels so warm, wet, and *amazing* that I forget to speak, already climbing closer and closer to my release.

"*Sage*," I call out airily.

I rock my hips, my body acting of its own accord, seeking the *more* that it needs, and he smacks my ass in response. At first, I think he's silently reprimanding me for moving; but then he smacks my opposite cheek before he commands, "Ride my face, doll. Take what you want. Come all over my tongue, baby."

He doesn't say another word as he inserts his tongue between my slick lips, and I circle my hips, grinding down on his mouth like the greedy woman that I am. The closer I get to my orgasm, the louder I moan, my desperation stronger than it's ever been before. Then, right before I lose my mind, he wraps his lips around my clit, sucking *hard* as he flicks his tongue across the nub. I scream, my whole body trembling as my hips buck out of my control. His mouth devours me, his tongue lapping up the evidence of my orgasm.

I'm concentrating so hard on keeping my arms from buckling, I don't even realize that Sage has moved until I'm flipped onto my back, my hair a mess covering my eyes. With shaky fingers, I reach up and brush the strands out of my face, looking down just in time to see Sage press a delicate kiss to my stomach, right above my hips. My breath hitches in my throat, and I'm overwhelmed—yet again—by the man that I love and all that he's giving me in this moment.

"Fuck," he whispers before brushing his lips against my skin once more.

He rests one of his hands where his lips just touched, saying nothing as he stares at my baby bloat. I wish I could tell what he was thinking; I wish I could crawl into his head and know all that he's feeling, but I know that I can't. Neither do I ask after his thoughts. Instead, I reach down and lovingly run my fingers through his hair, understanding that he needs to process this news in his own way.

After a few quiet seconds, he crawls over my body, making room for his hips between my thighs as he presses his forehead against mine.

"I love you. I love you so damn much."

"I love—" My words dissolve into a deep, indulgent groan as he sinks his cock inside of me, stretching me open and filling me up like only he ever has. It's because of *him* that I know how a man is supposed to fit inside of a woman. And as he gazes into my eyes, his body locked with mine, I know with all of my heart that I was made for him. "I love you too, baby," I choke out. "I love you, too."

We don't say anything else as he begins to make love to me, easing almost all the way out of my center before burying his dick until the hilt. Each time he returns, I have to remind myself to breathe. He feels so much better than I remember. I hate the weeks that we spend apart, but I won't deny that absence makes our reunion *that* much sweeter. I cling to him, needing him as close as he can possibly be.

Wrapped in each others arms, his hips rocking steadily against mine, we pant together—swallowing each others moans as we surrender to the pleasure we find only in one another. Our skin grows slick with sweat, the room heady with the scent of our love making, and the slow burn of my climax grows hotter and hotter as time passes. When I bend my knees, pressing them into his sides, he thrusts a little harder, sinking his cock deeper. For a moment, his eyes roll into the back of his head as his mouth falls open with a grunt. I reach up to sweep my tongue over his, and he reciprocates my kiss immediately, driving into me even harder.

"*Millicent,*" he breathes.

Something about the way he utters my name causes me to arch my back as I hold on to him tighter. I know he's on the brink of losing control when he rolls his hips faster, chasing his own release.

"Oh, Millicent—*baby—fuck,*" he groans, pounding into me with more force.

"Yes, *harder!* Sage, *shit*—just like that!"

My arms and legs lock up around him as my core clenches down on his cock, my whole body on fire as wave after wave of glorious ecstasy rolls over me. He pumps into me a few more times before his muscles tense beneath my grasp and he groans, spilling his seed inside of me. When he is spent, he settles his weight on top of me for only a second. Then, too soon, he rolls to my side, taking me with him but breaking our connection.

I stare into his eyes as he tucks a bit of hair behind my ear. He then traces his fingertips along my hairline, both of us still working to catch our breath. His gentle touch makes me suddenly sleepy, and I curl into him a little bit more. While we haven't really discussed the reality of this new life inside of me or where we go from here, right now—I don't give a single shit. He *knows*. The burden of my secret is no longer something I must carry, and the truth has made Sage...*happy*. Right now, being here with him, resting in the knowledge that our love was strong enough to conceive a child—our child, our *family*—it's all that I want.

"We made a baby," he whispers, cradling the back of my head.

"Yeah," I barely manage, a new knot clogging my throat. The awe and wonder in his eyes fills me with both regret and hope. I regret that it took me so long to get here; that it took me so long to find the courage to tell him. Yet, I'm also comforted by my renewed hope in the future, knowing that my dreamer is capable of being the man of *my* dreams. He will not leave me; he will not run from *us*. I always knew it, always *assumed* his faithfulness—but to *feel* his affectionate acceptance? He is so much more than the arrogant little shit I thought he was when we first met. He is the reason why I even *dare* to dream. For so long, I pushed such silly notions aside, merely existing in the mundane of reality. But Sage—Sage has breathed life into me. He's put back together the pieces of my heart, filling in the holes I thought would always remain, and this—*this* is the father of my child. I love him deeply; and I know, without a shadow of a doubt, that every moment we share like this one will only make me love him *more*.

My eyes drift closed as he presses a soft kiss against my forehead, his lips grazing my skin as he repeats, "We made a baby."

FIVE

Sage

SHE FALLS ASLEEP ON top of the sheets, and I continue to stroke her face long after her breathing grows deep and even. I know I should cover her up, but I can't bring myself to do it. I want to look at her; I want to admire every inch of her naked beauty. She thinks the evidence of our baby is still too subtle to make out, but I know her body well. I've played it, explored it, memorized it, loved it, dreamed of it—her body is *mine,* and I can see how it's begun to change already. Her tits are bigger, and there's a roundness to her stomach that was once perfectly flat.

There's a *roundness.*

Fuck me.

There's a *baby* in there.

I knew something was up. It's why she's here. She was being fucking *weird,* and I wanted to get to the bottom of it. But never—*never* in my wildest dreams did I think that *this* would be the reason she's been so distant. Even after the way she refused to drink any alcohol earlier, I still didn't expect for her to tell me she's *pregnant.*

Fuck me.

I rest my hand in the shallow curve of her waist, gently sweeping my thumb back and forth across the front of her stomach. I think about the way her body will continue to change, and the corner of my mouth twitches with a small smile. There's a shit ton I don't know about pregnancy, but my sister has had three kids. I know enough to understand that a woman's body is a fucking temple, capable of the most amazing things. I've watched Pepper grow three babies, and it's nothing short of a miracle. Now, it's Millie's turn. *My* Millicent. I get to watch her body change as she grows a baby. Our baby.

Fuck me.

I press a soft kiss against the top of my girl's head, wishing she was awake so that I could fuck her all over again. No one has ever made me feel like more of a man than Millie. To know that I put a baby inside of her—I swear, I feel like some caveman, proud as hell that she's carrying the fruit of my seed.

Since the first time I met Henley, just minutes after he was born, I was sure that I wanted kids. By the time Sophia came around, I knew I wanted a house full of them. My niece and my nephews are some of my favorite people. I spend as much time with them as I can. They're constantly changing and growing into themselves, and it's incredible. I definitely want that. Sure as shit didn't think it was going to happen this fast; thought I had a long while before I made a kid of my own, but I know one thing for damn sure…

There's no one else in the world I'd rather have kids with than Millicent. No one. I love her deep and I love her hard. We've been through hell and back to get to where we are now, but I'd do it all again. For her, I'd do it all again. She's worthy. She always has been.

Despite the late hour and the exhaustion that's settled over me after the adrenaline crash that hit me a while ago, I can't sleep. I look at the bedside clock, squinting to make out the time, and see that it's two in the morning. I know I should try and get some shut-eye, but I feel restless with this news. I want to tell someone.

I reach for my glasses, sliding them on my face before I gently crawl out of bed. Millie's out like a fucking light, and she doesn't even stir when I pull the sheets from underneath her in order to cover her up. For a second, I just stand and stare down at her, remembering how she said she's known for the last month that she's knocked up. Running my fingers through my hair, I scrunch my brow, wondering how much longer she would have gone without telling me if I hadn't insisted that she come out this weekend. I get it that it's not exactly the easiest thing to tell a guy, especially because we weren't *trying* to make a baby, but still. Why was she so afraid?

The thought doesn't sit well with me, but I shake it off for now and search the floor for my pants. I don't bother with a shirt before I tuck my feet into my shoes and grab my phone and the room key. Once I'm out in the hallway, I don't even think twice before I dial my sister. She's always been my best friend, and if there's anyone I want to hear the news first, it's her and Pepper. Not to mention, if they found out that they *weren't* the first to know, they'd bust my balls.

"Are you butt-dialing me, drunk-dialing me, or all of the above?" she answers without a hello.

"Fuck, Rosy—what kind of greeting is that?"

"It's late. At least it is *there*, and you usually only call me this late if you need a DD—which I wouldn't be able to help you with; though, you wouldn't be cognizant of that if you're shitfaced—or you've butt-dialed me. Though, you don't sound drunk, and clearly this isn't a butt-dial. What's up?"

I cough out a tired laugh, shaking my head at her as I ask, "What are you doing right now?"

"Hanging out with my main man, binge watching *Friday Night Lights*."

I furrow my brow, sure that I'm too tired and distracted to understand her answers. "You've seen that show, like, a million times. And who's over there at this time of night?"

"Sage, it's the weekend before dead week. Need I say more? And no one is here. It's just Maestro and me."

I hum my approval, smiling as I ask, "How's my little guy?"

"Loving every minute of cuddle time. What are *you* doing? Where's Millie?"

I start to answer and then I stop, a *zing* of excitement shooting through my chest. Something about saying it out loud, saying it out loud to someone else, it makes me anxious and nervous.

"I want to tell you something—let's try and call Pepper," I suggest. For the first time since I left Colorado, I suddenly wish I was home.

"Sage, I take it back. Maybe you *are* drunk. You want to call Pep after midnight?"

"Yeah. I do. Hold on."

I pull the phone away from my ear, tapping the screen so that I can add Pepper to the call. When the line starts ringing, I bring it back to my ear.

"She's going to kill you if you wake her up. You know that, right?"

"She's not going to kill me."

"Hello? Sage? Are you okay?" Pepper answers, her voice raspy from sleep.

"Dead man," mumbles Rosy.

"Rosemary?"

"Hey, Pepper—we're both here."

Pepper moans before she mutters, "It's a quarter after midnight, Sage. Soph will be up in no less than an hour. I might kill you."

"Hold that thought until after I tell you why I'm calling. You can't kill me. I need to stick around for a while."

"Is this about VH1? Rose already told me. Can I go back to sleep now?"

"Millie's pregnant," I announce without preamble.

A grin spreads across my face when they both gasp.

"Oh, my god! *Oh*, my god! Oh, *my god!*" cries Rosemary.

"She's—she's *pregnant?* As in—*with child?*" asks Pepper.

"You're going to be a daddy!" Rosemary exclaims.

"Oh, my god," Pepper chokes out, her voice now laden with tears. "You're going to be a daddy?"

My skin breaks out into goose pimples as I reach up and tug on my hair, needing some sort of reminder that this is real. This is my *life*.

"Yeah. Yeah, I guess I am."

"This is exciting, right? I mean—this is good, yeah?" Rosemary sputters enthusiastically.

"Yeah," I chuckle, imagining her bouncing up and down in her seat. "It's a surprise, but, yeah, it's a good surprise."

"I hate you for being so far away from me right now," Pepper sniffles. "I'm going to be an aunt! Come home so that I can hug you."

I laugh and then remind them both, "The tour will bring us through town mid-June."

"That's so far away," grumbles Pepper.

"Just in time for his birthday, though."

"I'm too tired to appreciate the silver lining. And how I'll ever get back to sleep now is beyond me." She yawns and then asks, "Babe—when will you tell mom and dad?"

"I don't know. But don't spoil the mood, okay? They'll flip out, and not in a good way."

Pepper hums before she says, "They might surprise you. They're quite fond of their grandchildren. Yours won't be an exception."

I know she's right. I know they'll love any addition to our family. But I'm not stupid. Just because they love my kid doesn't mean they'll stop fighting with me. It's what we do. It's how we love, my parents and I.

"Tell them when you're ready," says Rosemary, her tone still bright and excited. "When you're *both* ready. *Man!*" she exclaims. "I took her to the airport and I had no idea. She must not be very far along."

"Ten weeks," I tell them.

"She'll start showing soon. With Henley, I didn't start showing until almost four months. Sage—tell Millie that when she gets home, I'm here if she needs anything. Anything at all."

"I will."

Hearing her talk of Millie being back in Colorado brings me out of the excitement of the moment. I don't like the thought of being away from her for the next two and a half months. If I thought missing her before was bad, this—this is going to suck some serious ass.

"I should go," I tell them, suddenly wanting to be with my girl.

"All right," Pepper murmurs.

"Thanks for calling!" Rosy practically sings.

"I love you guys."

"We love you, too," they reply in unison.

We say our goodbyes and then I slip back into the room. I plug in my phone and take off my glasses before stripping out of my clothes once more. I'm headed to turn out the light when I hear the sheets begin to rustle.

"Sage?" Millie calls out softly, pushing herself up onto one elbow.

"Go back to sleep, baby. I'm right behind you."

She lays down as I hit the lights, and I climb into the bed, wrapping her in my arms. She curves her back, pushing against my chest in an attempt to get closer, and I give her a gentle squeeze.

"Are you okay?" she asks sleepily.

"Yeah." I kiss her hair and then tell her, "Just got off the phone with my sisters."

"You told them?"

"Yeah." I give her another squeeze and she hums a tired sigh.

Then, her voice so soft I almost don't hear it, she says, "You're happy."

"Yeah, doll face." I close my eyes, pushing aside the reality that I'll only have this—her, here, in my arms—for another two days. Instead, I rest in the here and now, sliding my hand over her belly. "I'm happy."

I SLEEP LIKE SHIT, waking up with the sun. I don't even really understand why, but I don't fight it. Instead, I sit up, tug the sheets around my lap, and watch Millie sleep. Moments like these are the kind people take for granted. I don't want to do that shit. Especially not now.

The band is on the rise, and every new city, every new venue—every show, every interview—it's all paving the way to the road of success that Mountains & Men is on. We're not even halfway through the tour, and the publicity we're getting is fucking insane. We're writing new songs along the way, and this year is turning out to be as epic as I thought it would be. Then there's Millie…

Everything is happening all at once. If I blink, I'll miss it. Maybe that's why I can't sleep. *Dreamers don't sleep, they* do—and I'm nothing if not a dreamer.

My phone alerts me to a text, pulling me from my thoughts, and I reach over Millie to grab it, along with my glasses. Once I can see, I read that I've got a message from Stefany. It's been sent to everyone in the band, reminding us that we're to meet in the lobby at eleven to head over to the studio for our interview.

With two hours to spare, I wonder if I should wake Millie. Then my mind starts buzzing with questions—questions I don't know the answers to. Like, does she get morning sickness? Will she want breakfast? Pepper was sick with Henley and again with Sophia. With Carter, she wasn't sick, but she'd only drink these gross veggie, peanut butter smoothie things in the morning. It was weird, but Pepper always said that each pregnancy brought with it a new baby that treated her body differently. I've known about Millie's pregnancy for less than twelve hours. I know *nothing* about it, which brings me back to the question I asked myself last night.

Why did she keep this from me?

Sliding back down between the sheets, I set about waking her up like I usually do—with my lips. I start at the curve of her elbow, trailing kisses up her arm until her shoulder.

"Millie," I mumble, my lips brushing against her neck.

She turns her head, her gorgeous, dark green eyes opening to look at me. She blinks slowly and then flips over so that she's facing me. I rest my arm around her, my dick twitching when she coaxes her leg between mine before she reaches for a kiss. When she opens her mouth and slides her tongue over mine, I rule out morning sickness and kiss her deeper. She hugs me closer and my dick starts to get hard. As I swallow her airy moan, I almost forget why I was waking her up.

With a grunt, I roll us over until I'm resting between her legs, my weight supported on my arms as I smirk down at her.

"Not so fast, baby doll."

"I don't know what you mean," she replies flirtatiously.

The way she's looking at me right now, coupled with her sexy as fuck morning voice, turns me on even more. It takes every bit of self restraint I can manage *not* to rub my hard on over her center to see how wet she is.

I love how fast she gets wet for me. Every time.

I ignore my dick and tell her, "We need to talk."

In an instant, the playful glint in her eyes vanishes. "Okay," she whispers, her body now completely still beneath mine.

"Why didn't you tell me? We've been apart for five weeks, baby—you said you found out right after you left the tour. When were you going to tell me?"

"I…" She starts and then she stops. When she doesn't continue, I lower my hips and rub my cock over he clit. She arches her back with a sigh, but I shake my head at her.

"Tell me."

"Sage, I—I was going to tell you. I was going to tell you soon, I just—"

"You just *what*, doll?"

"I don't know how this is going to work."

My heart sinks and I pull my eyebrows together, wondering what the hell *that's* supposed to mean. Before I can ask, she rests her hands on my chest and continues to explain.

"We've never talked about having kids. Until a few weeks ago, I'd never even really thought about it. Then I found out I was pregnant and—I got scared. We don't have a plan. I don't know where we go from here. I don't know how to make this work."

I sigh, propping my forehead against hers. "Baby, how many times do I have to tell you—we're in this together. It's you and me."

"But, Sage, look at you. Look at where you are. Look at where you're going."

I jerk back, wondering if I'm hearing her correctly. "Do you mean to imply that you thought I'd bail on you? It's my kid down there. Not to mention, I love the fuck out of you. What—? I mean—that's bullshit, Millie."

"No. No, you don't understand. That's not what I [illegible]"

"Okay, then what?"

A few seconds pass without her speaking a word. She just stares at me, her hands gliding up my chest and around the back of my neck. She buries her fingers in my hair and then closes her fists, pulling the ends.

"I found it," she whispers. I watch as her eyes fill with tears, studying her as she seems to grow frustrated with herself.

"You found what?"

"My *dream*."

Her words hit me like a punch in the chest. Before I can ask any questions, words start tumbling from her mouth as tears stream down the sides of her face, disappearing into her hair.

"I want you. I want this baby. I want *our family*. I want it more than anything. More than *anything*, Sage. But I—I don't want to do it without you. I don't want you to miss it. When you're gone, I miss you so much; but since I found out about the baby, it's like I miss you a thousand times more."

"Baby—"

"No, listen! Please," she insists, wrapping her legs around me. "I don't ever want our baby to forget the sound of your voice or forget the warmth of your embrace or the touch of your kiss. I don't want our baby to know what it's like to say goodbye to you for weeks or months at a time. I want you with us. I want us to be together. It means *everything* to me—*everything*. I don't know what it's like to have a father, and I know you'd never leave us, but I just—*need* you with us.

"And I know—I know that I can't ask you to give this up," she goes on to say, looking around the room. "This is who you are. This is *your* dream, and this is what I want for you. I want you to be the man that I love, and the man that I love is the lead singer for a kickass band. I want our child to know my dream chaser. I want him or her to know *you*. But…I don't know how we make it work. I don't know how to make both of our dreams come true. That's why I didn't tell you. I'm afraid. I'm afraid of letting go of my dream. I just—"

I interrupt her with a kiss. I kiss her hard and long, twisting my tongue with hers in a furious exchange. It's the only way I can think to respond to everything she's just said to me. And when my dick grows fully erect again, I don't hesitate to bury myself in her heat. It's where I belong. With Millie is where I was meant to be. I know this as certainly as I know that I was meant to be on stage, singing with the world.

"We're going to make it work, do you hear me?" I grind out, my lips still grazing hers as I drive my dick inside of her over and over again.

"*Sage*," she groans.

"I mean it, baby. We'll figure it out. You're not letting go of *shit*. You want me around all the time, I'll fucking be around. I don't want to miss a thing either, doll. It's like I told you before—I want it all, and I want you by my side. So that's where you'll be, Millicent. Right by my side."

"Sage—*baby!*"

She squeezes her legs around me tighter, arching her back as her hands move frantically all over my body. I reach down and hook one arm and then the other under her knees, pulling her legs apart and spreading her open as I prop myself up and pound into her harder.

"Fuck, yes—yes," she whimpers.

I look down between us, watching as she takes all of me, and the sight makes me even harder.

"So beautiful," I breathe before leaning over and kissing her lips. The act causes her to bend even more, and she gasps, reaching out to grip hold of my biceps.

"Oh, baby, I'm gonna come! Don't stop—don't—"

She throws her head back, freeing a deep, melodic sound as her pussy strangles my dick. I don't bother holding back, surrendering right on the heels of her release, allowing her to milk me dry with a grunt. When we're both spent, I free her legs and then fold her in my arms as I roll onto my back, careful not to break our connection. She rests on top of me, her face buried in my neck as we work to catch our breath.

"Meant what I said, Millie."

"Okay," she whispers with a nod.

"I promise you, baby."

"We're in this together."

"You bet your sweet, little ass," I assure her, reaching down to give that ass a squeeze. "You and me."

SIX

Millicent

I'M *STARVING* BY THE TIME SAGE and I are showered and dressed. With a half an hour before we're to meet the rest of the band in the lobby, we find our way to a bagel shop on the corner of our block. I order mine toasted with extra cream cheese, and I don't waste any time eating it as we head back to the hotel. When I see a 7-Eleven across the street, I gasp, almost choking on my bite. Sage reaches up, pressing my damp hair around my neck as he holds me there, stopping us both to make sure I'm okay. I only nod before I insist we head over to see if they have any peach iced tea. They do—which makes me way happier than it probably should—and he smirks at me, amused when I shove four into his arms.

After we've purchased my stock of beverages, I stow three of them in my purse before I practically chug my first one. By the time we make it back to the hotel lobby, I realize the error of my ways. My stomach, now full of tea and half of my breakfast, sends a message to my brain that I've over indulged too quickly. I feel nauseous, something that's become quite familiar, and I quietly tuck away my almost empty tea bottle and the remainder of my bagel. I slide a hand over my belly, willing myself to keep down the contents of my stomach, and Sage pulls me under his arm and against his side.

"You okay, doll?" he murmurs, pressing a kiss against my temple.

"I'll be fine," I whisper in assurance. "I ate too fast."

He studies me carefully, reading me in that way that he does, before he kisses my lips softly. "If you need anything, you tell me," he instructs before gracing me with another kiss. I nod and he kisses me yet again before we're interrupted.

"Hey," greets Alex as she and JJ approach. She offers us a kind smile that warms her dark brown eyes, but JJ only lifts his chin before eyeing us suspiciously.

"You two good?" he asks.

"Yeah. Why?" Sage answers.

"Knox just made it seem like—never mind."

I look up at Sage just as he looks down at me. A small smile plays at the corner of his mouth before he shakes his head and directs his attention back to JJ. "We're good." I wait for him to say more, but he doesn't. At first, I wonder if he's being tight lipped about the baby until the rest of the band arrives, but when Knox and Derrick show up, he still says nothing.

"Morning boys and girl," chimes Stefany as she joins us. She looks around before inquiring, "Where's Maddox?"

No sooner are the words out of her mouth, and Maddox comes strutting through the front doors. *Strutting* being the operative word. When he sees all of us, he grins—his tired eyes glistening as he claps his hands together before rubbing them against one another.

"Are we rollin', or what? Let's do this!" he says excitedly.

Sage coughs out a laugh before looking over his shoulder at Derrick. I look back too, just in time to see his wink. I take that to mean that Derrick pulled through as wingman last night, and Maddox got laid. With everyone in good spirits, Stefany doles out instructions, and then we're all hopping into cabs on our way to VH1 Studios.

Sage and I share a ride with Alex and Knox, which doesn't allow for me to ask him why he hasn't told his friends our news. I know he told his sisters last night before he went to sleep, so I expected he wouldn't be able to keep it secret from the band, either. I try not to read into it, sure that he—along with the rest of them—are preoccupied with their forthcoming appointment.

It isn't until we pull up to the high-rise building that I can *feel* their collective nerves. Sage grips my hand with a sweaty palm, and my nauseous stomach knots up with sympathy anxiety. In my heart, I'm absolutely certain that he has no reason to be nervous. He's fabulous, something the world is about to find out, and each member of the family that makes up Mountains & Men is special in their own right. Yet, at the same time, I feel ill equipped to offer him any sort of adequate encouragement. Sage has always been braver than me. They *all* are. I was not meant for the spotlight like them.

Once everyone has arrived, Stefany turns to them, looking each and every one of them in the eye before she says, "You belong here. You've earned the right. Now, let's go." She winks and then turns on her heel, leading us inside.

She stops at the front desk, and after a short exchange with the person manning the entrance, we're directed to a bay of elevators. We wait for only a moment, and then the chime of an awaiting car sounds. The doors open and Sage squeezes my hand so tightly, I look up at him in surprise. He doesn't pay me any mind, though, his attention focused on the guy coming out. When I shift my gaze, I take in the tall man built like a super hero. He's got broad shoulders and huge arms, but a trim waist. And his thighs—*good god*. He's clean shaven, and his deep, dark brown hair is cut shorter on the sides and longer on the top, swept back and out of his warm eyes. He offers us a nod and a small smile before making his way through us, and I notice I'm not the only one who watches him leave.

"Holy. Fucking. *Shit*," Maddox mutters once we're all inside the elevator, breaking the silence as we make our accent. "That was—"

"Ashley. Fucking. Hicks," his brother finishes for him.

"Um, who's Ashley Hicks?" I ask, now certain that while I was mesmerized by the guy's size, everyone else was in awe of his musical position, whatever that might be.

"Shit, Millie—he's only the greatest guitar player of our time," Maddox announces, sounding as if I've offended him in some way.

"He's played for some of the biggest names in the industry," Knox informs me. "He's so underappreciated, it's not even funny."

Suddenly, I don't feel so bad for not knowing who Ashley Hicks is. As the guitarists of the band, it seems only appropriate that the Bradley brothers know his name.

"Rumor has it that he's just signed with a label to release his first solo album," says Stefany with a knowing smirk.

The Bradley brothers almost lose their shit. I find it quite amusing, their excitement contagious. In fact, by the time we exit the elevator, it feels as though the nervous energy has shifted into something else entirely. Then, almost as soon as we step out of the car, Sage is swept away from me. It happens so fast as all the guys and Alex are introduced to one of the produces before they're hustled away to hair and make-up.

Hair and make-up!

Thankfully, Stefany makes sure that I stay close, and I hang out with her as she talks business with someone from the network. I don't really pay attention, distracted by my surroundings. There's a bunch of activity going on—considering that it's Saturday—but I suppose in the city that never sleeps, Saturdays are just as lively as any other day. Not to mention, there's always something on television.

I wish Violet was here with me. I know she'd get a kick out of all of this. She might not be a part of the band exactly, but she was made for this fast paced life, just like the others. And while she might not crave the spotlight like our men do, I believe that she, too, is meant for much greater things. Thinking back on a few of the conversations we've had, I'm sure she feels the same way. She's got dreams she's holding onto; dreams she's confident will come true in the right time. Right now, she's adamant that it's *JJ's* time.

Time. It always seems to be working against me. Even now, when it seems like everything is going exactly as it should, it feels as though the timing is all wrong. Sage promised me that we would make this work—the baby and us, together—but as I cling to his promises, as I cling to the hope that's wrapped up in my love for him, I'm afraid *something* has to give. Now, as I stand in this studio, reality feels so heavy and so *real.*

Violet was right. This is JJ's time. It's Sage's time, too. It's *their* time. Mountains & Men are going to make it, and it's moments like these—stolen opportunities not taken for granted—that are going to propel them onto center stage. The *world's* center stage. I'm proud beyond measure, and yet I can't shake the feeling that compromises have to be made, *something* has to give, and no matter how deep his well of optimism goes—perhaps Sage won't be able to deliver on all of his promises. He's moving full speed ahead, and he can't be stopped. But neither can this baby. In six months, our baby will be here, and it hurts to admit that I have no idea where either of us will be.

Sage

It's in the middle of the interview that I realize—*I can do this.* All of it.

I once told Millie that everyone has dreams, and that until she found hers that she needed to hang onto me. Now that she has, now that my girl has a dream she's fighting for, I realize that destiny or fate or whatever the fuck—it has knotted us together with one dream. We have the *same* dream. Now, it's two against the world, and we're going to conquer that shit.

It's after one by the time we leave the studio, and we have just enough time to go grab a bite to eat before we head over to *The Late Show* to meet up with Kings & Crowns before they go on. My head is all over the place, thinking about *Behind the Music,* thinking about getting to meet Johnny Bash—one of late night's best—and, of course, thinking about Millie, the baby, the tour, and the idea I got. I'm pretty sure she's going to think I'm crazy. Maybe I am—but I can do this. *We* can do this. All of it.

I'm so caught up in the moment, it isn't until we're backstage on the set of Johnny's show that I realize Millie has been really quiet. She ate at lunch, which

I thought was a good sign, but something's off. *Again*. This time, I blame myself. Before I can do something about it, we're escorted into the dressing room for Kings & Crowns. We shoot the shit for a while, and then Johnny comes in. Turns out, he's even funnier in person than he is on TV. While I'll admit I'm incredibly star-struck, he really is just a cool guy. When he starts asking us about our music and the tour, I almost forget who I'm talking to.

He only stays for a few minutes before he leaves us to finish preparing for the filming of tonight's show, and then we're escorted out of the dressing room to our seats. Not sure when I'll have another chance to speak with Millie alone, I squeeze her hand and hold her back, leading her down a semi-deserted hallway we just came from. She looks up at me curiously, and I wrap my arms around her, pulling her closer.

"Hey."

"Hey," she murmurs in reply, curiosity evident in her dark green eyes.

"How're you feeling?"

"I'm fine. Tired, but otherwise fine. I get sleepy easily," she admits bashfully.

"Tomorrow won't be so busy. We'll do whatever you want, I promise."

"Okay." She sweeps her hair behind her ears as she speaks, looking away from me. That's when I know she's been in her head.

Fuck.

"Baby?"

"We should join the others, don't you think? We don't have much time."

I tighten my grip around her, watching as her lips part when she sucks in a silent breath.

"I've been thinking. Looks like you've been thinking, too; but I'm sure my thoughts are a fuck of a lot better than yours." She curls her fingers around my shirt, holding onto me, but doesn't offer anything else in response, so I continue. "I want you to come with me."

"What?" she whispers, tugging her eyebrows together.

"I want you to come with me. I've got to run it by the band, but I know they won't care—especially not after I tell them why."

"You mean the tour?"

"I mean all of it, baby. I mean *Mountains & Men*. I want you to come with me."

She shakes her head, and I can tell by the look in her eyes that she's not hearing me.

"I don't understand."

"You've got two weeks of school left, right? After finals, quit," I state with a shrug. "Pack your shit, spend the summer with me, and then whatever happens next—we'll do it together."

"Quit my job? That's your solution? Quit my job?"

There it is. I can tell by the tone of her voice that she thinks I'm nuts. Nevertheless, I have to convince her that my idea is not as crazy as it seems. It's actually kind of perfect.

"Doll face, this is it. This is our best chance," I insist.

My heart is racing, knowing that right here, right now, *this* decision—it will define our future. It'll define who we are. I rest my forehead against hers, sealing my eyes closed tight, absolutely certain that Millie and I are at the bottom of a mountain—a mountain we must face *together*.

"Millicent, we can do this. Don't you see?" I open my eyes to stare into hers as I explain, "I want it all. I want this life. It's *right* within my reach, and I won't stop until I'm on top. I *won't*."

"I know, but—"

"Listen to me, baby. None of it means shit without you. I know it. You know it. We've been there, and we're not going back."

"But, Sage—"

"We're *not* going back." She nods, her grip tightening around my shirt, tugging me toward her. I touch my nose to hers as I continue. "I can take care of you. I *want* to take care of you. *Both* of you. We can both have everything we want, because everything we want is the same damn thing."

"How?" Her voice is strained, and the look in her eyes tells me I've got to fight harder.

"I am Mountains & Men. We all are. And you love me—you *believe* in me more than anyone, which means you want what I want. My dream matters to you, and it damn well should, because it includes you, too. I want to be on top of the world, and I want my girl by my side. And you want me. You want me at your side, so it's simple, really. *Be at my side*. Come with me."

"Come with you?" she asks, her voice trembling. "Just like that?"

"Just like that. I mean, think about it. What are you leaving behind? A job that's just a job? It doesn't even excite you. Think of the adventures we'll have together!"

"Sage—we're about to have a baby. We need a plan. That's not a plan."

"It's enough. We'll figure it out as we go along. The important thing is that we'll be together. You'll have me. The baby will have me—and I'll have you. I'll have everything, and I'll share it all with you."

She pulls me even closer, and I can feel the rise and fall of her chest as she pants for breath. With a whimper, she pushes herself up on her tiptoes, bringing her lips to my ear before she whispers, "I'm scared."

I wrap my arms around her back, hugging her close, and her arms circle around my neck as I reply, "Fear is sometimes good. It makes us fight harder."

"I don't want to mess up. I don't want to make the wrong decision. We have another *life* to consider."

"Do you trust me?"

Until just now, I never doubted the answer to that question. I know she trusts me to be faithful. She trusts me to call when I say I will, and to make her come as often as I can. I know she loves me, almost as much as I love her—but the trust I'm asking about goes deeper than any of that. I feel it, and I know she does too. 'Cause this isn't about just us. Like she said—we have another life to consider. So the question is, does she trust me with that life?

When she doesn't respond right away, I squeeze her harder before I repeat, "Do you trust me?"

She pauses for another moment before she nods, burying her face in my neck as she says, "Yes. With my whole heart, yes."

"Then *come with me*."

She sighs and another beat of silence passes between us.

"Did you mean what you said last night? About marrying me?"

I stifle a laugh but don't bother fighting the grin that spreads across my face. As if she can sense this shift in my thoughts, she pulls her head back so that she can see me, and her eyes narrow on me when she sees my smile. Before she can say a word, I smack a kiss against her lips.

"You're mine, whether you like it or not. I'm not fucking letting go. But doll face, you want me to put a ring on it, I will."

Her eyes stare into mine, almost as if they're looking for something. Patiently, I wait. Staring right back, I silently promise that I won't back down. I won't stop fighting. Not for us. Not ever.

Then, all of a sudden, her eyes soften before she says, "Okay."

"Okay?" I ask. I quirk an eyebrow, not sure what she's agreeing to, exactly.

She giggles, presses a kiss to my lips, and then whispers, "Okay—I'll come with you. I'll give my notice when I get home."

"For real?" I mutter, still managing to be surprised after all of that. "You're with me?"

She nods. My eyes then drop, watching as she brings her lips as close as she can get them to mine without touching me before she breathes, "Don't let me go."

"I won't fucking dare."

Seven

Sage

I MAKE THE DECISION TO find some sort of take-out and spend the rest of the night in my room with my girl when she almost falls asleep during *The Late Show* three different times. She wasn't kidding when she said she gets sleepy easily. I know how much she enjoys her slumber, but this is something else entirely. That's why, as soon as the recording is finished, I call an impromptu band meeting, asking the guys and Alex to meet us outside before we part ways until Monday morning. Millie's decision to quit her job and attach herself to me is a big deal, and I want her to know she doesn't have to be afraid; that she's not in this alone. In order to do that, I have to assure her that the band will have her.

And the band sure as fuck will have her. Selfish or not, I won't have it any other way.

Now, all eyes are on me as I look around the circle of my mates. JJ stands with his hands in his jacket pockets; Derrick and Knox both have their arms folded across their chests; Maddox has his elbow propped against Alex's shoulder, and Alex stands, seemingly unperturbed, with her fingers tucked into the back pockets of her jeans.

"What gives, Dweeb?" asks Derrick, tipping his chin up at me.

I look down at Millie, who looks anxious and exhausted, and give her hand a squeeze before I shift my focus to the band and ask, "Millie's coming on the road with us in a couple of weeks, you cool with that?"

They all look at me with blank stares before Knox grunts, "Yeah. Okay. What's the big deal? She's been out with us before."

"I'm not talking about a week. I mean for the rest of the tour," I clarify.

"Yeah. Okay," Knox repeats.

Millie's grip around my hand loosens as she asks, "That's it? You don't mind?"

"Babe, why would we mind? You bunk with your boy, you're not a buzz kill, and Black Beauty is a fuck of a lot cleaner when you're around. I mean, it might cramp our style if we all started bringing our girls around—but seeing as how JJ's the only one with a girl and Alex, here, has a dude who has his own shit to worry about, having you along for the ride is not an issue."

"You say that now," she says softly, so softly that no one else hears her but me.

Before I can figure out what she means, JJ asks, "Not that being on the road isn't the shit, because it is, but I'm kind of curious to know *why* you want to come? Even Violet will admit that she misses her space after a while."

"She's coming because I want her to. I don't want to miss it," I confess, looking down at my girl. Her grip tightens around my hand once more as she smiles up at me. Her green eyes are soft, and the hope I see there fills me with courage and makes me want to kiss her. I don't get the chance as Alex interrupts me.

"You don't want to miss what?" she asks.

A smirk tugs at the corner of my mouth as I look to the band and reply, "Watchin' my baby grow."

Alex gasps and I chuckle at the sight of each and every one of them in shock.

"Are you fuckin' around?" asks JJ, his wide eyes pinned on Millie.

"No. I'm pregnant. Really," my girl replies.

"That's why you wouldn't let me buy you a birthday shot last night," says Knox with a grin. "Shit, Sage—your girl is knocked up!"

I laugh, shaking my head at him before Alex steals my attention as she tells us, "Congratulations, guys! Seriously. That baby is so lucky to have both of you." She wraps her arms around Maddox's waist, as if she's too excited to contain herself, and Maddox smirks at her before slinging his arm around her shoulders.

"She's right. That baby is lucky to have you," he says. Then he winks and adds, "But even *luckier* to have all of us."

"Sage McCoy, M&M's baby—a dad. *This* I gotta see," says Derrick, shaking his head at me with an amused look on his face. I flip him the finger for pointing out that I'm the youngest member of the band, but I do it with a smile.

"He's going to be the best dad I've ever known. I'm sure of it," Millie declares, leaning into me.

"I don't doubt it, darlin'," he replies, offering her a wink.

My chest swells, pride filling me up as everyone congratulates us in their own way. It feels good knowing that they have my back at every turn, including the unexpected ones. They're my closest friends—my brothers—and this family, tied together by music, it's one that I'm proud to be a part of; one that I hope to be a part of for years and years to come.

"So what are we going to do to celebrate?" asks Knox.

"Go out—have a drink for me. I'm taking Millie back to the room for a nap."

"Oh, my god, yes. Please," she sighs, resting her head against my shoulder.

I chuckle before Maddox shrugs and announces, "You heard the man. I'm ready to grub."

"Meeting adjourned?" asks Knox.

"Aye," Millie and I agree together.

Millicent

WAKING UP FROM my nap, pressed against Sage's side, his whole body making me feel warm and cozy, I breathe deeply. I slept really hard, and now I feel well rested and full of energy. I'm sure it'll only last a few hours, but that's long enough for Sage and I to go out and explore a little bit. I look over my shoulder and see that it's only eight o'clock. Then I look up at Sage, and all thoughts of going out are immediately silenced.

He's sleeping.

It's so incredibly rare that I ever get to see him sleep. Now, I can't stop myself from nestling back into his side, tilting my head back so that I can watch him for a while. As I admire him, I think back over this afternoon—about the conversation we had in regards to our future—about my decision to leave everything and follow him.

Even just *thinking* it sounds crazy, and stupid, and reckless. The list of reasons why I would never have come up with this idea on my own is so long, it's laughable in comparison to the list of reasons why I decided that I was actually going to do it. But as hard as it is to ignore reason, and logic, and common sense—as hard as it is to ignore the *fear* that's clawing at my back even in this very moment—I do my best to focus on what my heart wants.

Just last night, I told myself I'd do *anything* in order to have the life I wanted, a life spent at Sage's side. I didn't know what that meant until now. *Anything* is a risk unlike any I've ever taken, but I think that's what fuels my bravery. I've never wanted anything this badly. Not anything—not *ever*. I understand, now, why Sage fights the way that he does for what he wants; why he is the man that he is on the

the path that he is on. I understand his passion and his drive and determination. I understand because I feel the tug that's pulling me toward him and away from everything I've ever believed. Sage and his very *unplanned* out plan is calling me away from the limitations I have always placed around love, relationships, and *life*. I don't want to live within the confines of those limitations anymore. I want to be bold, I want to love with everything I have in me, and I want to do it without regret.

I hated my mother, and I thought nothing of my father until he gave me a reason to dislike him, too. I wasn't raised to believe in fairy tales. Hell, I wasn't raised to believe in *anything* except the notion that men always leave. It was a lie my mother lived and *died* by; a lie that almost cost me the love of my life. It's by some power greater than me that I learned at a young age to believe in myself. That belief got me as far as I could go, living within the walls I had built up around myself to survive the toxic relationship that I endured with my mother. Then I met Sage. Since the moment I met him, nothing has been the same.

I am not the same.

So I'm going to do it. As scary as it may be, I'm going to be the mother that I never had, and I'm going to give my child the best chance of knowing a life bursting with love—and I'm going to do it with Sage. It's what I want, and I'm clinging to the bravery it takes to admit that.

I have enough money saved up to last me six months without a job. It's not much, certainly not with a baby on the way, but I trust Sage. I trust his ambitions and his talent. I trust his music and his heart. I trust my dream chaser. My rock star. My lover. My man—and that is precisely what he is. A man who knows exactly what he wants.

I press deeper into his side as I reach up to place a kiss underneath his jaw. He jerks, suddenly awake, and draws in a deep breath as he looks down at me. He makes a noise, something that sounds like a mix between a hum and a grunt, and then dips his head so that he can kiss my lips.

"Nap felt good," he mumbles before kissing me again.

"Mmmhmm," I agree with a smile, giggling as his lips start an exploration of my neck. "Sage, baby, I thought maybe we could go out for a while."

"Oh, yeah?" he asks, gently fondling my breast over my shirt. "Is that what you want?"

I sigh, arching my back, my nipples growing hard at his touch. "Yes," I reply.

"Had a dream about you." As he speaks, he rolls on top of me, settling himself between my legs. My core heats up and my breathing grows heavy as I try and focus on his words.

"What kind of dream?"

"Let's just say..." He thrusts his hips, making me well aware of the bulge that's trapped in his pants, and I can't silence the whimper that escapes my lips. With a smirk, he goes on to say, "It had a happy ending."

"Oh," I sigh, the heat at my center rising to my stomach, where a warm pool of longing now simmers.

"How about you come—*then* we go out for a while?"

"I like that I idea," I reply airily.

"I thought you might."

Sage

It's easy to lose track of the day when you're on the road. Mondays don't usually feel like Mondays when work doesn't feel like *work*. Today, however, I'm reminded why the day after Sunday has such a bad reputation. In just a couple of hours, I'll be headed back to the airport to send Millie home before we board Black Beauty, headed further north. We've got a show in Boston tonight. The show—I'm looking forward to. Saying goodbye to my girl—not so much.

We slept in for her birthday and then went out for brunch, just the two of us. New Yorkers don't fuck around with brunch, either. After we ate way too much, we roamed around the city with no particular destination in mind. The weather was perfect, and it was nice to just chill with my girl for a while.

For dinner, we met up with the rest of the band, who wanted in on the celebratory day, and then we all ended the night at this hole in the wall dive bar with some kick ass live music. By the time we got back to the room, Millie was so tired, I swear she almost fell asleep while she was brushing her teeth.

Looking at her now, I push the sheets down over her hip before gently pulling up the cotton of my t-shirt, uncovering her stomach. I gaze down at the subtle curve of her growth—or her *baby bloat*, as she calls it—and I wonder how big she'll be when I see her next. Turns out, I'll have to wait a little longer than I want to before I get her back.

After looking at the calendar, Millie convinced me that it would be too much of a hassle for her to try and join us before her sixteen-week check-up. Apparently, she's got doctor visits every four weeks, and she wasn't down with the idea of making two trips home just for a check up—so we'll be going another six fucking weeks without seeing each other. It's not exactly what I planned when I told her to come with me, but I don't argue. After these six weeks, it'll be a long while—if *ever*—before we have to be apart for so long again.

In a way, I guess it's a good thing. Even though I won't be around, she'll have my sisters. They're sure to be all over her ass, making sure she and the baby are okay. And Pepper, being Pepper, I bet she'll have all kinds of advice. That's certainly not something any of us around here can offer. Then, of course, there's my mom—though, I still haven't figured out how we're going to tell my parents they're going to be grandparents again.

I shake the thought away, deciding to cross that bridge when we get to it, and slide my palm over Millie's belly. She wakes a few minutes later, with my hand on her bare skin, my mind thinking nothing while I take advantage of the few moments I have left to hold her like this before she leaves.

"I miss you already," she whispers, her raspy voice going straight to my dick as she slides her hand over mine.

Fuck, I love the sound of her voice in the morning.

"Still right here, doll face," I assure her before pressing a kiss into her hair.

She turns over so that she's facing me, and then she pushes me onto my back and rolls on top of me. The weight and warmth of her body stretching down the length of mine makes my dick hard. I know she feels it when her eyes dilate as she stares down at me. She doesn't act on it, though. Instead, she reaches up and buries her fingers in my hair, pausing for a second before she presses a feather-soft kiss to my lips.

"I'm so proud of you. I hope you know that. I hope you feel that." I don't say anything in response, somehow knowing that I don't have to, and she continues. "I know you're right where you belong, and not one sliver of my being wishes for you to be anywhere else. But..."

She sighs, touches the tip of her nose to the tip of mine, and then closes her eyes.

"It doesn't make it any easier," I mutter, finishing her sentence for her.

"Not even a little."

"I know."

She presses another kiss to my lips, this one a little harder than the first. Then she opens her eyes and stares into mine before she says, "Thank you for my birthday weekend. Best birthday ever."

I smirk at her, sliding one of my hands under the shirt and over her back, the other down her panties and around her ass. "Get used to it, doll." Holding her tight, I tease, "Told you my dick was better than flowers."

She laughs and I grow even harder, my desire to be inside of her now pretty damn undeniable. I tell her as much, lifting my head to touch my lips to hers. I open her mouth with my tongue and she hums her approval, kissing me deeper. When I reach the hand in her panties down even further, rounding her ass until my fingers find the wet entrance of her pussy, she sighs my name into my mouth.

"I want these panties off. Want you on my dick, doll face."

"M'kay," she says, kissing me once more before rolling off of me and onto her back. I make quick work of my boxers while she shimmies out of her panties, and then she's straddling me—my cock in her fist. She strokes me slowly, torturously, and then she watches me as she lifts up onto her knees and rubs my head along the slick seam of her pussy, all the way to her clit. My jaw clenches when she does it again, whimpering as she makes a figure eight around her sensitive nub before sliding me back down.

I reach out, sneaking my hands underneath the shirt that covers her body, skimming my fingers up her sides. I hold her around her ribs as she continues to play with my cock. Just when I think I can't take her teasing another second longer, she lines us up and takes me in.

"Fuck," she whispers when she's completely full of me. For a second, she doesn't move. Her head rolls back as her breathing turns ragged, and then she reaches for the hem of my t-shirt and yanks it off. Her hair falls down her chest and back as her eyes lock with mine, and I move my hands to grip her breasts. She hisses, and I start to pull away, but she grabs my wrists and shakes her head. Then, without letting me go, she begins to rock her hips.

She moves slowly at first, making little noises that threaten to unravel me before I'm ready. She looks hot as hell on top of me, her dark green eyes darkened further by the lust I see there. When she starts to move faster, my hands are everywhere, seeking to spur her on. She props herself on my chest, using me as leverage as she rides me harder, and I groan at the feel of my girl taking what she wants.

"I can't get enough of you," she pants. "Shit—I love your dick. You feel so good."

"It's all yours, baby doll—just like your pussy is all mine," I grumble, gripping her thighs.

"Forever and ever," she insists, her hooded eyes staring straight into mine.

"Always, baby."

She throws her head back and moans, grinding down on me even harder. Her desperation is hot as fuck, and I reach around to palm her ass. I give her a squeeze before I smack her cheek, and she shrieks as her pussy begins to flutter around me. A grin spreads across my face and I squeeze and smack her other side.

"Mmm, Sage, I'm gonna come, baby."

I smack her ass again, and she sucks in a sharp breath, her mouth falling open in a wide O as she grabs hold of my sides. With a long, deep moan, her cunt strangling the life out of me, she comes. Her hips slow to a stop, so I take over, tightening my hold around her ass as I buck my own hips, seeking the friction I need to push me over the edge. As I pump in and out of her wildly, owning her wet cunt with each thrust, she wraps her hands around my shoulders, digging her nails into me as she tries to hang on. It feels good, and a growl rumbles from my throat as I get closer to finding my own release.

My spine starts to tingle as my dick expands, and I'm just about to explode when Millie comes again.

"Oh, *shit*," she gasps, trembling around me.

At the same time, I roar, "*Fuck*—yes!" as her pussy demands my climax and I come inside of her.

She collapses on top of me, and I can feel her hard nipples pressing into my chest as her warm, heavy breaths blow across the skin of my neck. I wrap my arms around her back, holding her close. We're both hot and sweaty, but I could give a fuck. I want her right where she is.

"I love you," she whispers, still breathless.

"Love you too, doll."

For a few minutes, neither of us says a word. We don't move, either, and it feels so damn good. I try not to remember the fact that I won't get to feel this again for six fucking weeks. Instead, I just breathe her in, tightening my grip around her.

"Sage?" she murmurs.

"Yeah?"

"I need some peach iced tea now."

I chuckle, making a mental note to stock up on the stuff before she gets back, and then kiss the top of her head as I reply, "You got it, doll. What my babies want, my babies get."

"Mmmm," she hums, lifting her head as she offers me a lazy, sated smile. "That's why we love you."

With a wink I grunt, "You fucking better."

EIGHT

Millicent

It's the Monday before finals week. I should be doing study prep with my students, going over questions they may have in regards to the abundant amount of material I've managed to dole out over the semester, and updating grades. Instead, I'm in Denver, getting off of a plane that brought me from New York, where I spent my weekend in my lover's arms *not* thinking about finals week.

Sage was right. The job I'm about to leave is just that. A job. I won't deny that I've enjoyed it over the last couple of years. I certainly could have done worse for myself, but school has always been my safe place. Inside the walls of the institution that brings about knowledge, I found myself. From grade school until now, academia has been a constant friend; numbers and equations the stimulating challenge that kept me intrigued while simultaneously keeping me protected from falling into the pits of despair that surrounded me when I was immersed in a toxic environment I couldn't escape. Then when I *did* escape, I knew nothing else.

Now—I want *more*. Now, I understand that there *is* more, and I don't have to be afraid to step out of my comfort zone in order to enjoy it. If I've learned anything over the course of the last eight months, it's that outside of my boundaries, there is a whole new world worth exploring. And the best part is, I have someone to explore with me.

I might not know what the future holds, but I know that I'm ready to step into it, with Sage and the new life that's growing inside of me.

First, I have to endure the next six weeks without him. That is what has me in a foul mood as I walk through the terminal, tugging my bag behind me on my way to the arrivals pick-up area. My mind wanders as I ride the shuttle-train that carries me to the other side of the airport, and I start formulating a checklist of things I need to catch up on over the next week. As I follow the crowd getting off the train and heading for the escalators, I start mentally constructing my letter of resignation, which I will prepare tonight in order to deliver tomorrow.

My stomach knots up with nerves at the thought.

I'm really doing this…

I'm so lost in my head, I almost don't see them when I walk off of the escalator, turning toward the direction of baggage claim. Though, I'm sure I'm the *only* one who could possibly miss them, as they went out of their way to make their presence known.

Standing amongst a small crowd of people waiting for other travelers are Pepper and Rosemary. Henley and Carter both flank Rose, each of them with two strings attached to two balloons tied around one of their little wrists. The pink and blue helium-filled bulbs are jerked to and fro as the little boys wave wildly at me. Rose has a huge grin on her face and she's practically bouncing, holding a small sign with my name scrolled out in pink. Standing next to them, with Sophia tucked into one of those cloth-sling-things that hangs across her chest, Pepper is holding another small sign, this one written in blue. It reads, *Baby McCoy*.

Like someone flicked a switch, all at once my belly warms, my chest tightens, and tears are streaming down my face so fast, I don't even try to stop them. I feel both incredibly overjoyed and genuinely annoyed. Overjoyed that I'm met with such kindness, acceptance, and excitement; and annoyed that I can't stop myself from sobbing like a loon.

Pepper hurries toward me, her smile still intact as she wraps her arm around my shoulders and pulls me in for a gentle hug. I rest my forehead against her shoulder, careful not to squish Sophia, and try my damnedest to shut myself up.

"I'm guessing now is a bad time to mention that we're taking you out to lunch before we drop you at home; and Rose already promised the boys cupcakes—so we're celebrating with those, too."

Managing a deep breath, I pull away from her, reaching up to dry my cheeks with the back of my hand before I shake my head. "You don't have to do all of that. It was really nice of you to all be here to pick me up."

"Honey, let me fill you in on something," she starts to say, resting a hand on my shoulder as she pierces me through with her warm, brown eyes. "As long as you're home, the Montgomerys and the McCoys are banding together to do everything we can to stand in for Sage while he's away. We're not being *nice*; we're just being *family*.

We're filling the gap. I know we're not your man, but collectively, we're here to keep an eye on you and to make sure you have whatever you need whenever you need it.

"Now, I would tell you not to cry about it, but I've had three babies. I won't ask you to do the impossible. So—are you hungry?"

I stare at her for a second before I nod, the knot in my throat preventing me from offering much more. She smiles at me in response and tilts her head, signaling toward the rest of my welcoming committee. I follow after her, managing to laugh when Rose throws her arms around me.

"Congratulations, Millie. I'm so happy for you guys."

"Thanks," I whisper.

When she pulls away from me, I feel a little hand slip into mine. I look down and find Henley gripping onto my fingers. Before I can say anything he tells me, "When mommy had Sophia in her tummy, she cried sometimes, too. Daddy said if he wasn't around, that I should just hold mommy's hand." He reaches up and haphazardly brushes his slightly overgrown blonde bangs out of his face before he continues. "Mommy said you have a baby in your tummy. Uncle Sage isn't here to hold your hand, so I will. Okay?"

Fuck, I think to myself as I gently squeeze his fingers. My throat is so tight I feel like the sob that's trying to work its way up just might strangle me. By some miracle, I manage not to dissolve into a blubbering idiot, and I squeeze his fingers again before Pepper announces that it's time for us to go, for which I am grateful.

Now—if I could only get my hands on a bottle of iced tea.

"Oh, my god, you're here! *Yes!* Stand up—let me see, let me see!"

I look up from my desk, my eyes wide as I remain seated, startled by Violet's very *loud* entrance. Her eyes are bright and she appears breathless as she tosses her purse into the empty chair across from me, clapping her hands as soon as they are free.

My head is still stuck in calculus mode, so I don't move. *This,* apparently, is the wrong thing to do. I realize my mistake when Violet presses her hands to her hips and cocks an eyebrow at me.

"Do you know how many hours it's been since I found out? Like a gazillion! I wanted to come with Pepper and Rose to the airport, but I had work. Then I was going to just drop by last night when I got off, but rumor has it, *preggers* gets tired pretty easy these days—and since you were traveling yesterday, I thought I should cut you some slack. But I literally cannot wait another second. So—Millie Valentine, if you don't get your ass out of that chair—"

"Hey, ladies."

I sigh in relief at the sight of Lindsey darkening my doorway. My respite only lasts but a moment, and then I realize that a couple hours ago, I tendered my resignation—news that I'll have to tell Lindsey. It took me a while to realize it, but I have a true friend in her. In this moment, I'm fully aware of the fact that I'll miss seeing her just about every day.

"What's all the excitement about?" she asks, lowering her bag from off of her shoulder.

I look to Violet just as she looks to me. The alertness in her eyes lets me know that she doesn't want to make an announcement without my permission; but since Lindsey was the first to know, I simply nod, answering Violet's silent question.

"I'm trying to get Millie to show me her baby bump!" she gushes.

"Ahhh," Lindsey murmurs with a knowing smile. "Daddy knows?"

I nod once more before I reply, "Yeah. Daddy knows."

"You knew?" Violet gasps, narrowing her eyes at Lindsey.

With a smirk and a wink, she replies, "I knew," before she looks at me and prompts, "Well?"

The memory of Sage beating his chest flashes before my eyes and I feel my cheeks heat in a blush as I stifle a giggle. Sweeping my hair behind my ears I tell her, "He's whisking me away."

"What do you mean?"

I look to Violet, sure that she must already know. She's got an informant on the inside. Then, after I take a deep breath and stand to my feet, I announce, "Next week will be my last. I won't be back next year. I've decided that the best thing for the baby and me is to be wherever Sage is. Soon, he'll be all over the map—" I pause, flattening my hands over the slight curve of my lower belly, turning to give Violet the view she's been waiting for before I continue. "And we'll be with him."

Violet grins so big, I'm afraid she'll hurt herself if she doesn't relent soon. But when I look at Lindsey, the calm expression I find on her face as she studies me makes me feel ill at ease. I stare at her, wondering what she could possibly be thinking—a little worried that she's judging me for my decision—but then she speaks.

"This is what I love about you two. You don't make any sense at all; and for all the reasons you don't, you *do*. If you were anyone else, I'd call you crazy. You, a first time mother, traipsing around with Sexy McHottington as he barrels his way into stardom? It sounds reckless."

"It is," I whisper, my heart beating wildly as my mind reminds me of the truth.

She chuckles softly, dipping her head in a subtle nod. "But it's *you*. You'll take care of each other, of this I have no doubt. You'll do the best you can, following your heart every step of the way, and *that* is what will make you outstanding parents." She shrugs and frees a sigh before she admits, "I sure will miss you, though."

"I'll miss you, too," I insist, the words falling from my lips without the slightest bit of hesitation.

"That kid is going to have an amazing life," pipes in Violet. "Raised by a pack of wolves and the women that love them."

We all laugh, the mood in the room shifting into a lighter one. When Violet inquires about my birthday, Lindsey reprimands me for not telling her of my twenty-seventh anniversary, and then promptly insists that we round up all my girls in order to celebrate. I'm beside myself at the thought that I *have* a group of girls to *round up*, and agree for a low-key night after finals are behind us.

Violet sticks around to chat for a little while longer after Lindsey slips into her office to get back to work and prepare for her next class. By the time Violet leaves, Pepper and Rosemary have been brought to speed on my belated birthday gathering, and Pepper has volunteered to host. All the excitement of the last hour makes me tired, but I push through the rest of my day. As soon as I'm able, I pack up my things and head home, anxious for the chance to relax.

Sage calls me just before nine, as I'm getting ready for bed. We don't talk for long, but it comforts me to hear his voice, and he promises me he'll call again when they hit the road tomorrow afternoon. After we say goodbye, I realize that while I miss him, it feels different than the last time I left him on tour. This time, the six weeks that lie ahead of me aren't so ordinary. I have preparations to make and things to wrap up as I say goodbye to my old life and step into my new one.

When I crawl into bed alone, thinking of Sage, I do so *not* thinking about the weeks we'll spend apart, but of all the ones after that we'll get to spend *together*.

As I STAND IN the doorway of my office, now completely empty, I wouldn't say it is *sadness* that I feel. Nevertheless, my eyes are still glossy with tears that I refuse to cry as I blink them away. The last week and a half went by so much faster than I thought it would, but the fear and anxiety I felt before is not with me just now. Instead, I feel at peace. Looking around, it seems as though the empty space in front of me was never really *mine*, but rather a borrowed opportunity; someplace for me to be until I found my way. Now, a door has opened for someone else to take this vacated space—a space where they belong.

When my phone alerts me to a text message, I take that as my cue to leave. Pulling my phone from my purse, I start to make my way to my car. The message is from Sarah, asking for Pepper's address. She'll be joining us tonight, and I have to admit that I'm actually really excited about my evening plans. I respond with the information she's after, and with an hour before we're all supposed to meet up, I head home to change.

After my *third* attempt to put together an outfit, my excitement starts to wane. In the last two weeks, I've managed to outgrow at least half of my wardrobe. The only pants that fit me without hurting me are my sweatpants or yoga pants. I wore dresses to work all week, but even those felt uncomfortably snug. I feel as though I'm being blown up like a balloon. I know I shouldn't complain. So far, the only parts of me that seem to be inflating are my boobs and my belly, but I can't help my frustration. Now, rifling through my closet, I curse myself for owning so many damn *fitted* clothes.

With not enough time to run to the store, I suck it up and decide to embrace the bump and aim for comfort. I pull out a pair of olive green leggings and shimmy into them. Then I don a white, cotton camisole, stretching it out a bit as I adjust it low around my hips. I grab my long, light-weight, pale pink cardigan and slide that on, too, then remember I have a little, tan belt that I can tie around my waist; it matches a pair of sandal wedges I can wear.

For a moment, before I leave to search for the accessory, I abandon *my* side of the closet and begin looking through Sage's clothes. I find a thin, long-sleeved blue button-up—one I've never seen him wear; one I'm sure would make those icy blue eyes pop; one I'll take with me on tour so that I can see how it looks on him—and I bring the sleeve to my nose, inhaling deeply. His scent is beginning to disappear entirely, given that I'm the only one who comes in here these days; but if I think hard enough, I can appreciate the slight whiff of my man.

Knowing that if I think too much about his absence, I'll start to miss him too much, I make my exit, headed for that belt. Once I've found it, I strap it around my waist before standing in front of my vanity mirror to assess my appearance.

I look completely understated, but in that cute way that implies that I did it on purpose. Honestly, though, I just feel like I'm in the middle of a fight between my brain and my body as I struggle to keep my confidence in my appearance. I don't feel like myself, and it's weird. My baby bloat has definitely turned into a prominent bump that would make someone look twice in passing. With the belt holding my cardigan close around me, you can tell that I'm just a couple weeks away from *really* starting to show. I'm certainly not ashamed of my growing belly, knowing the reason behind it, and I actually look forward to stretching out a few of my t-shirts in the coming weeks—but at the moment, *pants* are my problem, all of them making me feel bloated and gross. I can't live in leggings and sweatpants all summer, which means I'll definitely have to do some shopping in the next four weeks.

With a sigh, I head to the bathroom to freshen my make-up and run a brush through my hair. When I'm finished, I tuck my feet into my sandals and then grab my purse and a bottle of iced tea before I put Maestro on a leash. We make our exit together. Looking down at Sage's French bulldog, I wonder if we can arrange for him to come with me when I meet up with the band. Perhaps with me around, it'll be easier to keep track of him. I know they miss each other. Though, tonight, at least Maestro will get to hang out with two little boys who happen to love him almost as much as Sage does.

Twenty minutes later, pulling up behind Rose's old, red, VW Bug along the curb, I notice I'm one of the first to arrive. I waste no time getting out of my car and escorting Maestro to the front door. I'm about to ring the bell when suddenly a little face appears in one of the narrow windows that flanks either side of the door.

"Aunt Miwwie!" Carter smacks the glass, making Maestro bark. *That,* of course, makes Carter squeal in delight before he cries, "Maestro! Mommy, open," he demands, looking back over his shoulder.

Two seconds later, his wish is granted and Pepper stands before me. Maestro tries to run inside, but I stop him so that I can unhook his leash. Once free, he and Carter disappear.

"Hey—come in, come in," Pepper insists, opening the door wider.

As I step inside, I don't miss the way her eyes scan over my body from head to toe. Neither do I miss that *look.* I've seen it before. In fact, I'm growing quite used to it. Usually, she gets the look when Sage is around and he does or says something to me that she wholeheartedly approves of. Apparently, she sees something she approves of now.

As flattering as that might be, it doesn't stop me from blurting out, "None of my pants will fit."

She fights a laugh, but looses the battle against her smile before she replies, "You're expanding, huh?"

"My inability to fasten the top button of any of my jeans without extreme discomfort would imply that, yes, I'm *expanding,*" I mutter.

With a grin, she shuts the door and then signals me to follow her further into the house. "You need a belly band."

"A what?"

"It's a band of fabric that you wear around the top of your jeans to cover up the fact that you can't close them. We'll pick a couple out this weekend. We'll also make sure you're stocked up with a few items for your trip. Are you free Sunday afternoon? Harry will be home. We can go while he watches the boys."

"Oh, go where? I want to come," chimes in Rose, who is in the kitchen mixing together some sort of pink drink in a gigantic bowl.

"Are you making…punch?"

"Yup!" she answers with a nod, her long, dark ponytail dancing across her back. "Just because we're keeping our beverages virgin tonight doesn't mean they have to lack some spunk. Now—back to this *outing* that involves Harry staying home with my nephews. When and where?"

"Just a little maternity clothes shopping," Pepper answers, heading to check on something she's got in the oven. "Not that I think you'll really need a bunch of maternity stuff. It can get pricey. But we can get you a couple pairs of shorts and some jeans. I bet we could find some cute non-maternity shirts that would work for you. We just have to buy bigger than normal. That's what I did when I was pregnant. Oh, and we'll invest in some maxi dresses. One of the perks to being pregnant during the summer."

"Oh, shopping. Yay! When?" Rose asks again.

"Sunday?" Pepper looks at me from over her shoulder, and I offer her a shrug and a nod. She then looks to Rose and confirms, "Sunday."

"Awesome! I work Saturday, so my Sunday is free. Oh, and, um—*speaking* of work, have you and Sage talked about telling mom and dad? Keeping baby McCoy on the DL is starting to get *really* hard. I almost accidently said something just about every time I saw them this week."

I look everywhere but into Rosemary's blue eyes, making sure to avoid Pepper's brown ones, too. The truth is, Sage and I haven't really figured out how to handle that. I know we need to tell them soon. *No—they should have already known—* but he's not exactly clear about how they'll take the news. And, like me, he's not convinced over the phone is the best idea. In my head, I've worked out the only other possible option. *Me, alone,* showing up on their doorstep. But I won't lie—just the *idea* scares the shit out of me.

"Millie?" Pepper calls softly. "Look at me, honey."

She's a year younger than I am, but there's something about her—something about the *mother* inside of her that makes my heart warm at the sound of her term of endearment. It's also what makes me obey her in this very moment. Once my gaze is locked with hers, she offers me an encouraging smile before she speaks.

"Our parents are strict, but that's only because they care. You've met them. You've seen how gentle they can be."

"She's also seen how unyielding they can be," mumbles Rose.

Pepper glares at her as she grumbles, "*Not* helping." She shakes her head and then shifts her focus back to me. "I'll just say this much—that baby is coming. Whether they think you and Sage are ready or not, their grandchild is coming. At the end of the day, all they want is what's best for all of you. What's best for that child is to have two grandparents who love the hell out of them. I promise you, *that's* who they are. Besides, mom won't want to miss all of this. So don't keep it from them much longer, okay?"

"Okay," I assure her, suddenly feeling a little braver than I did a moment ago. She's absolutely right. This baby is coming, and whatever qualms they may have about it, they should at least have the option to be involved in every moment of this baby's life that they wish. "We'll tell them. Soon. I promise."

"Good."

Before another word can be said about it, the doorbell rings.

"I'll get it," I insist, happy for an excuse to change the subject. "Keep doing—whatever it is you're doing. Let me make myself useful."

To my surprise and relief, neither of them protest, and I make haste to the front door. When I open it, I find Sarah on the porch, a *Brandon's Bakery* bag dangling from her wrist.

"Hey," she greets with her signature bright smile. "I know you said I didn't have to bring anything, but I couldn't help myself. Brandon and I came up with this amazing recipe for red velvet scones," she shakes her head, her smile growing wider. "You just have to try them to understand."

Noting that I don't feel sick at the moment, I agree to her suggestion and step aside before inviting her to come in. I barely get the door closed behind her before she's calling my name—her tone no longer giddy with the excitement of a new recipe, but rather hesitant and confused. When I turn to face her, I watch as her gaze travels up the length of my torso before her eyes settle on mine.

"Um—did you have a really big lunch, or..." She blushes, almost as if she's afraid to finish her sentence from fear of offending me in some way.

Resting my hand on my belly, I think back on the lunch I was too nauseous to finish and then announce, "I'm pregnant, Sarah."

Her eyes grow wide as her jaw falls open, and I can't help but smile.

"Come on," I murmur with a giggle. "I'll catch you up in the kitchen."

"Please," she says, motioning for me to proceed. "I'm all ears."

NINE

Sage

NEVER THOUGHT MY FIRST trek around our nation's capitol would be in the dead of night after playing for a packed venue in downtown DC—but after we close out the show, that's exactly what we do. We wander around the National Mall, our feet treading over historical ground. Swear to god, I've never felt so glad to be free.

By the time we've walked off our post-performance high, we've made it to the White House. Sick of being on his feet, Brock insists we find a place to drink before the morning sneaks up on us and we miss last call. That's how, twenty minutes later, I find myself walking into a strip club. Something tells me my girl wouldn't approve, but we've got Alex with us, and I sure as fuck am not leaving her to fend for herself in this place with these clowns.

"Come 'ere, Ali," calls out Derrick as we all make our way onto the main floor. He holds out his hand and she takes it as he nods to the bar. "I'll be your wingman tonight, Zip. Unless, of course, you want a front row seat to the show?"

"Nope. The bar sounds fantastic," she replies, tugging him that way.

Derrick chuckles, winking back at me as he follows. I contemplate joining them, but Kent throws his arm over my shoulders as he follows the others to one of the tables near the platform. I look over and see a woman in nothing but a bra, a thong, and ridiculously high heels. My eyebrows shoot up in surprise when she throws herself at the pole, latching on before skillfully twirling around it a few times.

"Fuck, she knows what the hell she's doing," Kent hollers over the music. "See—*this* is the shit you're going to miss out on with your girl on the road with you. I still think that decision is unwise, my friend."

We sit and I shrug, knowing there's no use in arguing. He'll never get it. He likes the easy pussy that comes backstage night after night. I'm not interested in that shit. Millie's better than all of that. Not only does she know how to ride my dick, she'll do it often and beg for more. Besides the fact that she's not into me for any other reason than because she wants *me*. She gets it—knows who I am. She knows that my music isn't just about scoring chicks and fame. Yeah, those things come with the territory, but at the root of my passion, I just want to share my music with as many people as possible.

She fits—like the harmony to my melody—and that makes her better than some random piece of ass who wants to wet my dick just to say that she did.

"Look, McCoy, I get it," he says, waving his hand to signal a waitress. "You're a good guy. Loyal and shit. But come on, man. You're about to hit the big leagues. The places you'll want to go? The people you'll want to see—the people who will want to see *you*? I'm not fuckin' around, man. You don't want to miss any of that shit. It can get wild as hell, and it sure as fuck isn't meant to be experienced with your girl. Especially if she's knocked the fuck up!"

"Say what you want, he's not one of us," says Knox. He doesn't bother looking in our direction when he speaks, his attention glued to the bare tits on stage. "Not anymore, at least."

I smirk at one of my oldest friends, and, as if he can feel my gaze, he looks back at me with a smirk of his own.

"He's a wolf, Kent. Fucked around for a while, but he's found his mate. He's done. A lifer. Trust me—Millie's pussy is the only pussy his dick will even get up for."

"Okay, so you got a woman. Good for you. I mean it, mate—good for fuckin' you," says Rex, smacking his palm down on the table. "But that doesn't mean she's got to be a part of the joy ride. Kent has a point; you just don't know it yet."

The waitress arrives and we all order a drink before I return to the conversation, explaining, "She's not a ball and chain. She doesn't hold me back. She never will."

"Never say never," mutters Kent. "As soon as that baby comes, you're fucked. She'll have expectations, they always do. But you've got work to do, man!"

"In this industry, business deals, collaborations, fucking entire albums are *birthed* over a shot of tequila, a line of coke, a joint—whatever the fuck. Pick your poison. If you aren't in the room, if you aren't in the *life* rubbing elbows with the right people at the right time, you might as well just quit while you're ahead," Rex argues, looking at me from over his sunglasses. He shrugs and then finishes with, "Just think twice about that woman."

"You can always bail now and come around when you're ready. The kid will always be yours. But your induction into this world—it waits for *no* man," says Kent.

I stare at Kent, processing his advice. It takes me a second to realize that he means I should abandon my family for the sake of my dream. In his eyes, I can't have both at the same time. In a way, I realize that he's right. Wild parties, nights spent drinking until the sun comes up, bar hopping after a kick-ass show, I might be able to do that with Millie on my arm—but not after she has the baby.

I look at Knox and find him looking at me. He quirks an eyebrow, silently asking me what I think. I return the expression, wanting to know what's on *his* mind. When he shrugs, I wonder if he thinks they're right—if he thinks that having Millie and our baby at my side will be a death wish for Mountains & Men. The very idea that one would hinder the other makes me sick.

When my beer arrives, I wrap my hand around the bottle, but I don't bring it to my lips. I shift my focus to the stage, looking but not seeing the entertainment. I want to go outside, get some fresh air; but I don't want to look like a fucking pussy, storming off after hearing opinions that I don't like. Opinions that make me question *everything*.

I throw back my beer, downing half of it in one pull. When a woman comes over, dressed in almost nothing, her fake-ass tits barely covered, she says that she's been sent our way by a table of fans across the room. Playing coy, she asks who we are, and Knox is quick to introduce us. Her eyes grow wide before a wicked smile pulls at her lips and she offers our entire table a lap dance. Knox is the first to agree, and I roll my eyes before abandoning my beer and heading for the club's exit. I don't realize I'm being followed until I hear D call my name.

"Where's Zip?" I ask, looking back at him from over my shoulder.

"Left her with JJ. He knows his dick is toast if word gets out he let some naked ass in his lap."

I pull in a deep breath, reaching up to run my fingers through my hair as I tilt my head back and look into the clouded sky. "*Fuck*," I moan.

"Yo, what gives?"

I drop my hands and turn so that we're facing each other before I point back to the club and declare, "We're not like them. Not really." I shake my head, dropping my arms to my sides. "We can hold our own. We've been doing it for two months now, but *we aren't like them*."

"Dweeb, what the fuck are you talking about?" Derrick asks with a scowl.

"We've got a church mouse who, I'd wager a guess, doesn't know shit about the sex we sometimes sing about. I've seen her drunk, but I've never seen her smashed. Then we've got JJ—fucking twenty-five-year-old dude who refuses a lap dance *just in case* one of us gets stupid and slips up and tells Violet, which we *wouldn't* do, and he knows it but denies himself anyway. We've got the Bradley brothers who are down for anything—groupie pussy, open bar, wild nights—but hold the illegal substances, 'cause that shit's just crazy. We've got you, and I don't know what the hell you've got going on—but you'll walk into a strip club and offer to sit with our church mouse so she's not all alone. And then me. Fucking *me*. I'm about to be a dad, and I'm stupid enough to believe that I can do this—*all of it*—and bring my kid along for the ride? I mean, what the fuck?

"Sex, drugs, and rock-n-roll. That's what Kings & Crowns are about, that's what this *life* is about. We want their success, we want more than their success, but what the fuck does it cost? We don't know what the hell we're getting into. We're a bunch of green motherfuckers walking in *blind* into an industry we've only ever gotten to taste. And we want it all?" I scrunch my face, realizing how fucking crazy we are. "We're going to get eaten *alive*. And the worst part? I thought it was just about the music. To me, it's *always* been about the fucking music."

I watch as Derrick opens his mouth to speak only to seal his lips closed. He sighs, tries again, and still nothing. Then he folds his arms cross his chest and stares at me for a second before he finally speaks.

"Scared?"

I frown at him, wondering how that's the only thing he could possibly say. "What?" I ask incredulously.

"Are you scared? I mean, you just lost your shit for no good reason, so I'm asking—*are you scared?*"

"This isn't fear. This is a reality check."

"Check this," he states, taking a step closer to me so that we're standing toe-to-toe. "*We* are Mountains & Men. We've said it before, we'll say it again—fuck, we'll shout it from the fucking summit—*we* are Mountains & Men. We're a garage band with a church mouse, the banger brothers, a classical pianist who sings lead, a techy, and me. I just want to play. I want to beat the shit out of my kit night after night. That's what I want. To *play*. That's what we *all* want. To fucking *play*. It *is* about the music. To us, it's *always* been about the music. It's why we are who we are—it's why we sound the way we sound—it's how we made it *here*.

"Look around, Dweeb. We're almost there. We didn't come this far because we weaseled our way in. We *played* our way in. And when we get to the top, we're staking our claim and owning that spot until *we* decide we're done." He coughs out a humorless laugh, taking a step back as he shakes his head and nods toward the club. "Whatever bullshit they threw at you, don't buy into it. They're good, yeah. They've got my respect, for sure. They've earned their place and they did it their way. We'll earn ours, too—and we'll do it *our* way.

"We are Mountains & Men. We will keep our integrity. If we lose it, we lose everything. If you stop being you, we lose our sound. *You are* Sage *fucking* McCoy. Dweeb, you're the weirdest son-of-a-bitch I've ever met. Grounded, focused, determined like you wouldn't believe—and you dream so fucking big. There's a reason the baby of the band is also the leader of the band. So you want your kid along for the ride? Bring your kid along for the ride. Who the fuck says you can't? Certainly not any of us. We know who you are. You're one of us. And we don't quit. *Mountains & Men*—we face our shit head on.

"Now—are you fuckin' scared?"

I stare at him blankly for a minute, wondering where the fuck that came from. Then I think about his question—*really* think about it. I set aside the bullshit that Kent tried to feed me and I realize that Derrick is right. We're going to do this our way. I might be the new kid on the block, but I can't forget that the people who have come before me—the artists that I've admired—the legends that will always be great. It was their hard work and integrity that got them there. There's not one way to the top. There are a million ways. You just have to have the endurance to keep on climbing.

"No," I declare with a shake of my head. "I'm not scared."

"Good. Come on, then," he mutters, heading for the door. "I got next round."

"You saw what, where?"

I hear JJ and groan, rolling over in my bunk to check the time on my phone. It's ten a.m. on a Sunday morning, and the pounding in my head is demanding that I close my eyes and continue to sleep off the alcohol I poured down my throat last night. Then I realize that we're moving, Black Beauty headed south, and I know *for sure* I need to make my ass go back to sleep.

"For real? Shit!" he mutters, his voice now louder.

"Shut the fuck up," Maddox moans from the bunk on the opposite side of my head.

"You guys—we were spotted," JJ announces before he tells the person on the phone, "Babe, I just want to state for the record—" Violet cuts him off and says something to make him laugh.

"JJ, *seriously?*" grumbles Derrick.

"No, babe. Vi, they're mad. We had a late night."

Suddenly, Violet's voice fills the cabin as JJ puts her on speaker and she yells,

"Get your lazy asses *out* of bed and get on the *fucking* internet *right now! US* magazine spotted you guys last night. I mean—you're like a byline to a byline—but there's a picture!"

"Wait, what?" Alex mumbles from above me before I hear a bedside curtain slide open. I do the same, squinting out at JJ who appears to be smiling.

Violet grunts her frustrations before she explains, "I couldn't sleep. When I can't sleep, I celebrity stalk. Much more fun than Facebook scrolling. Anyway! I saw something about Kings & Crowns so, duh, I clicked on it—and there you were! Leaving the club with them. I mean, that wouldn't be my first pick for the location of your first tabloid spotting," she mumbles. I can practically see her eyes rolling from here. "But that's not the point. The point is—"

"We're fucking *famous!*" Knox rumbles from behind his closed bed curtain. "I'm looking at it right now. Ha! Holy shit."

I reach behind me and feel for my glasses, sliding them on my face as I hop out of bed. When I reach Knox's bunk, I stick my hand through the curtains and he responds a second later, pressing his phone into my waiting fingers. I yank it in front of my face, and there we are. Well, some of us. The picture is mostly of Kent and Brock, but Derrick, Alex, and I are in the shot too—and all the band members not photographed are mentioned in the two sentences attached to the photo.

We stayed at the club until after two. When D and I headed back inside after our talk, I proceeded to drink my face off. He was right. I had lost my shit, and I needed to get it the fuck together. Obviously, that meant forgetting that I had lost my shit by consuming a hell of a lot of whiskey. To be honest, most of the morning is hazy—but I vaguely remember the table of fans joining us. Then, by the time we were headed out, there were a few people calling out for pictures just beyond the door. I really didn't think anything of it.

"I *cannot* believe my *face* is on the internet on a *gossip* magazine website!" Alex mutters. It isn't until I look back at her, hanging out of the side of her bunk with her gaze trained on her phone, that I realize she's *smiling*. "Adrian is going to be *so* jealous!" She giggles and then rolls back into her bunk, presumably to call her boyfriend to give him the news.

I think about calling Millie, but then stop myself. The strip club part I think she'd get over. Me waking her up at eight o'clock in the morning? Not so much. Instead, I toss Knox's phone back at him and then snatch mine up before heading to the front of the bus. I sprawl out on one of the couches, still in nothing but my boxers, and proceed to call Rosy. She can wake her ass up. *This* she's gotta see.

"A STRIP CLUB?" she says, seemingly unimpressed.

I chuckle, looking down at the remnants of milk from my cereal still left in my bowl. After I woke Rosy up, I went back to sleep for a couple of hours. I didn't even bother to get up from the couch until Knox turned on the TV. I hopped in the shower for a quick wash and then realized I was hungry as a motherfucker. I'd just finished my last bite when my phone started ringing. I grin at her greeting, sure that Rosy or Violet, or *both*, spilled the beans.

"We try and keep it classy, doll face."

"Mmmhmmm," she hums.

"It's pretty sick, though, right?"

"Yeah, baby," she says on a sigh.

I push away my bowl and lean back in my seat at the table, now fully aware that something's wrong. I didn't really think she'd be *this* upset about our whereabouts last night, but her tone says otherwise.

"What's going on, doll face?" I ask gently. "Are you mad?"

"What? No—no, I'm not mad. I mean, I'm over here getting fat and my boyfriend is looking at naked women on poles, but right now, I just don't have it in me to be mad."

I pause a beat, at a loss for what to say. I can't tell if she's being a smart-ass or if something else really is bothering her. Thankfully, she doesn't make me guess as she goes on to say, "I feel like shit today. I just really wish you were here to hold me right now."

My shoulders deflate at her confession, and I stare out the window, suddenly wishing it was four weeks from now. "It won't be long before you'll be wishing you could have a break from me," I tease, trying to make her laugh.

She doesn't.

"I'm sorry, baby doll. I wish there was something I could do. Really."

"Let's talk about something else."

"Okay."

"I have my shopping trip with Pepper this afternoon. It'll be nice to have some bottoms that fit. Though, if I outgrow any of my new things, your wardrobe might become *our* wardrobe."

A sly smile pulls at the corner of my mouth as I think about every time she's ever worn a piece of my clothing. Usually, it doesn't stay on her body long—the sight making me want her naked as soon as possible.

"I think I can live with that," I assure her.

"Sage?"

"Yeah?"

"We need to tell your parents. Before I get any bigger. I'm thirteen weeks along, and this secret is literally getting heavier and heavier every day."

I pull in a deep breath, holding it in my lungs for a second before blowing it out in a huff. I know she's right, but I can't deny that there's a big part of me that just wants to wait until I'm home. Though, something tells me my parents would be furious if I showed up at their house with my girlfriend five months pregnant and them none the wiser. Then again, the lecture I'm sure I'd get if they found out *now* isn't exactly something I want repeated over and over for the next couple of months. They'd call every time they had a mind to lay into me about the whole situation. I'd bet on it.

"Sage?"

"Yeah. I hear you."

"I'll do it," she states, making my whole body jolt in surprise. "I'll go see them this week. I'll tell them."

"No. Fuck," I mutter, pushing my glasses up my nose. "I can't let you do that."

"But—"

"I'll call them. Today. Okay?"

"But you said—"

"When I tell you I have no idea how they'll respond, I mean it, baby. I'm not throwing you to the wolves like that. If they lose their temper, I don't want them taking it out on you. So just—don't do anything. I'll handle it."

"Okay," she whispers.

Silence passes between us again as I think about the rest of my day. We should be in Virginia Beach within the hour, and we've got the night off. I'll text them and let them know we need to talk as soon as they're free.

"Baby?"

"Hmm?" I hum, readjusting my glasses before shaking my head clear.

"I'm sorry, I need to go. I just—can I call you later?"

I frown, feeling too far away and completely useless. "Okay, doll. Call me when you feel up to it."

"I will. I love you."

"I love you too, Millie."

We say our goodbyes, and when I pull my phone away from my ear, I stare at it for a moment. Then I realize I'm not completely useless after all. I open up the text app and send a message to my dad.

TEN

Millicent

I RUN MY FINGERS THROUGH my hair, bringing it over my shoulder before I smooth the long strands down my chest. I pull in a slow, deep breath and close my eyes, willing my upset stomach to go away. I'm almost certain that the nausea I feel is not baby McCoy's doing as, fifteen minutes ago, I was feeling just fine. In fact, better than I have been all week. It wasn't until I got into my car that I regretted eating lunch. Now, as I stand beside my vehicle, looking at my reflection in my driver's side window, I remind myself that what I'm about to do is not only necessary but *crucial*. What happens in the next few minutes will impact not just my relationship with the McCoys, but it will also shape the way I mother this child.

Sage told his parents about the baby on Sunday, as he promised he would. Unfortunately, it went exactly as he feared. The way he described it, it's not that they're *angry* with him, or even me for creating this new life; rather, they are *furious* with Sage for not taking responsibility—as they understand the term. They're under the impression that he should come home to find a *respectable, stable* job that will enable him to support his child. Furthermore, they seem to be questioning *my* sanity, as I not only support Sage in his endeavor to continue pursuing his dream, but I also intend to chase after it with him.

Currently, Sage is ignoring all of his parents' calls. And, as I found out yesterday afternoon, he's no longer answering for his sisters, either, as they have somehow gotten thrust into the middle and are trying to get Sage to try and fix things with his parents. To be quite honest, I understand his reluctance.

While his parents feel as though he's merely "road-tripping" around the country with a bunch of his friends, in reality, he's working his ass off promoting *Of Mountains & Men*. They're playing shows four or five nights a week, traveling almost non-stop. When they *do* get the chance to stay in the same city for a couple of days, Stefany has them making as many publicity appearances as she can possibly manage. They're doing radio show and podcast interviews; they're meeting with bloggers or journalists; and in any down time they have, they're working on their music. Essentially, they're laying the groundwork for what happens *after* they get home from tour. And from what I can tell, they're doing one hell of a job.

I'm not exactly one for social media, but I've been stalking them since they started this tour. Their fan base is growing faster than I think any of us saw coming. In the last couple of months, their numbers have catapulted from a few thousand to just shy of one hundred thousand—*and counting*—with half of the country left on this tour. Kings & Crown has a massive following, which is doing wonders for Mountains & Men. The fact that M&M can captivate an audience the way that they can just makes it even easier for them to get their fan base to stick.

This is all stuff that Abrielle and Ewan McCoy don't really know or understand, mostly because they don't take the time to know or understand. However, it's important to all of us—Sage, the baby, and myself—that they open their eyes and see that the son they raised is more remarkable than they know; and the future he's building is exactly the one I want for our child. In confronting them this afternoon, I'm positive I'm doing what's best for all of us.

I didn't tell Sage I was coming, sure that he would try and talk me out of it, but his parents are the only grandparents our baby will ever know. They're unaware of it, but Abriella and Ewan are a part of the dream I'm fighting for, too. I grew up in an environment completely void of love. My support system was shit, and I didn't have any extended family to run to or lean on when I needed it. Sage grew up in a family that's the exact opposite of mine—and I want to give that to my child. It means everything to me.

So, as I pull in another deep breath and tug my shirt down over one of my new belly bands, I remind myself that just like the man that I love—I have to fight with everything I've got for what I want most in the world. If he can stand up to his parents, so can I. Today, I intend to do so in a shirt that *doesn't* show my growth, in hopes that if they can't see the evidence of the baby, perhaps they'll feel less worried.

When I walk into Giuseppe's, I'm relieved to find that the Thursday afternoon crowd isn't heavy. The young woman at the hostess stand is busy rolling silverware when I approach and ask if I can speak with the owners of the establishment. At first, she gives me a strange look, but when I assure her that I'm a family friend, she relaxes and disappears into the back. When she returns, Ewan is right on her heels.

"Millie—this is a surprise," he says in greeting, his light blue eyes mirroring his words.

I offer him a small smile, clasping my hands together as I take a step in his direction. "Hi, Mr. McCoy. I'm sorry to drop in unannounced, but it's important."

He studies me for a moment before he nods once and replies, "My grandchild grows inside of you—you must call me Ewan. Follow me. I'm sure Abbi would appreciate being a part of this conversation as well."

Without another word, I do as he says, following him through the heart of the restaurant and into the back. He leads me in and out of the kitchen, still buzzing with activity—no doubt preparing for the dinner hour—and then down a narrow hallway. At the end, there's an office with the door partially opened. He pushes it all the way ajar, signaling for me to precede him inside. I do, and upon my entrance, Abrielle—who sits behind one of two desks in the surprisingly spacious place—looks up at me immediately. I can tell by the look on her face that she's surprised to see me, too. Though, by the time Ewan steps into the room and shuts the door behind him, she's appraising me suspiciously.

As frightening as it may be, I don't let her intimidate me.

"Millie, how are you?" she asks, her eyes flickering over my body.

"I'm well, and you, Mrs. McCoy?"

She smiles, but it doesn't reach her eyes. "*Concerned*," she answers honestly. "And please—if the child in your womb is to call me *nana*, you must call me Abrielle."

"Okay."

"I was wondering when we'd be seeing you. After speaking with our son, I'll admit, I didn't suspect it would be this soon."

I nod, absentmindedly smoothing my hands over my middle. "Pepper told me that you wouldn't want to miss this part. I don't want you to, either," I admit. Feeling bold, I add, "I'm not under any illusion that Sage and I won't need your help and guidance. Neither do I wish to pretend that we know what the hell we're doing. Furthermore, since the moment that I realized that this baby existed, I've wanted nothing more than to ensure *this* family is the one that he or she is brought up in."

"Sweet sentiments from a smart girl," says Ewan as he goes to stand behind his wife. "But how do you expect us to help you if neither of you will listen to reason?"

Before I can speak, Abrielle adds, "Sage's problem has *always* been that he listens but doesn't *hear* what we have to say. He throws up shields, deflecting our advice as if it is his sole purpose in life to go against our wishes."

"You raised him to be independent, did you not?"

"Of course," says Ewan.

"Then how can you be surprised that he's so incredibly independent?"

Abrielle shakes her head, freeing a sigh. "He's not just independent, his *defiant*.

I get it, I do. He's young and idealistic—but your lives are about to change in ways that you can't possibly imagine." She lifts her hand to her chest as she continues. "Millie, every child is a blessing. I feel extraordinarily fortunate that I've been given the opportunity to be a grandmother four times over. There's a certain joy that only a grandchild can bring—but I harbor serious doubts as to the decisions you're *both* making in regards to this baby. I might still be healthy and energetic, but I do not wish to raise a child in this season of my life."

A scowl pulls at my brow as I insist, "We're not asking you to."

"And what will you do when you run out of money? Where will you go when neither of you has a job and you have a tiny mouth to feed and to clothe?"

"That won't happen," I state with certainty.

"Sage tells us you've quit your job," says Ewan. "Months ago, he admitted that he wasn't seeking stability, thus the reason why he felt he could chase after this dream of *rock-n-roll*. But now, stability is exactly what you need, and yet he refuses to change his course."

"A choice I fully support."

"Then perhaps you aren't as smart as we assumed," says Abrielle, shaking her head once more.

I cough out a humorless laugh, wondering why I'm surprised our conversation has come to this place so quickly. Since the first time Sage spoke of his parents, he's made it clear that they don't support his music career; and every time that I've been around them, they've reiterated that truth. I have no idea how I'm going to get them to see where I'm coming from, but I came here to try and do just that.

I pause for a second, not really sure where to begin. Then I decide all I can do is explain how I feel—explain how safe and secure their son makes me feel.

"Your son loves me." I pause again, a knot suddenly forming in my throat. I try my best to ignore it before I continue. "He loves me more than anyone ever has, and I'm not saying that to be dramatic. It's true. No one has ever fought for me the way he has—the way he *does*. No matter where he is, no matter what he's going through, he's made it a point to *fight* for me because to him, I'm important. And I know that if he will fight that hard for me, he'll fight a hundred times harder for his child. He won't give up, not on us. Not ever.

"I wish that you could see that he gets that from you. I wish that you could see that so many of his most admirable qualities are ones that you have instilled in him. He's not *defiant* and he's not actively going against what you want for him—he's chasing after everything *you* told him he could accomplish. Mountains & Men might not look like your business, but it is *his* business. Just like you have invested your time and efforts into building this place, just as you have worked tirelessly to be able to provide for your family, *he* is also doing the same for himself—for me and our baby.

"I know you don't see it that way. I know that it's hard for you to understand, but that's because you're so uncomfortable with the way his lifestyle and his choices *look* that you haven't taken the time to really explore what it is he's all about. You haven't taken the time to *see* him. You haven't seen him light up that stage. It's incredible—and please," I insist, holding out my hands to protest their apparent desire to cut in. "Don't diminish my words to nothing more than those of a woman in love, as if I'm just some fan who hopes that her boyfriend will make it big so that I can enjoy the ride. That's not at all who I am. In time, I hope you'll come to see that.

"The truth is, just like you think he *listens* to you but doesn't *hear* you—you do the same to him. Until you've seen him perform, you haven't *heard* him. He's good. *Amazing*, actually. And while I'm sure his pride would prevent him from telling you, the tour he's on right now is bringing in more of an income than he's ever made in a span of four months.

"I know you're scared. I understand your fear, but you've got to have faith in him. I would also appreciate it if you put a little trust in me. I know that might be asking a lot, as we hardly know each other, but I already love this baby *so* much. I want nothing but the best for my child, and my decision to be at Sage's side as he pursues his career is not one that I've made lightly. I'll admit that the road ahead of us is uncertain, but *you* raised one hell of a son. No matter what happens, he'll make sure we're taken care of. He promised—and in my experience, as long as he can help it, Sage Lawrence McCoy does not break his promises."

I don't realize I'm crying until Abrielle gets up from her seat and comes to stand in front of me. She reaches out to cup her hands around my face, gently brushing away my tears as she gazes down at me. Her tenderness doesn't surprise me, as I've experienced it before; but instead, it makes my heart swell. She has the gentle touch of a mother, the likes of which I've never known, reminding me that *this* is part of the reason I'm here.

"Let him shine, Abrielle. Let him show you—let him prove to you that he's so much more than you've given him credit for. Come see him perform. The tour comes to Colorado in June. I know a guy," I say with a little laugh. "I can get you tickets. Just—stop fighting him and let him show you who he really is. When you see, you'll know that he's not being selfish or irresponsible. He's being the man you raised him to be, building a life that he wants to share with us."

I don't know how long we all stand in silence. Ewan still behind Abrielle's desk; Abrielle studying me with her rich brown eyes. What I *do* know is that in this moment, I cannot back down, so I don't. I return her intent stare, willing her to see that I believe every word that I just said. Furthermore, *she* should believe them, too.

"Oh, Millie," she sighs, finally dropping her hands from my face. "Your passion for him is remarkable. You being here, pleading his case, it is an admirable sort of love. It is the sort of love that I always hoped my children would get to experience. My husband loves me thus. He fought for me with a passion that can be matched with yours. I appreciate it. I really do.

"You might not think that I understand my son, but in a lot of ways, I do. He is a brilliant soul. I've known this about him since he was nothing but a child. For him to have found someone like you during this season of his life—I guess you could say I'm just *grateful*."

She doesn't say anything else before she turns to make her way back to her desk. I watch her go, my eyes flicking back and forth between her and Ewan, wondering where this leaves us. It isn't lost on me that neither of them has agreed to my proposition.

"I know you have a history that I've not felt," I start to say, still refusing to give up. "You love each other, you're devoted to each other—you're family; but I know that it hasn't always been easy and that fighting with one another has left bruises that are re-inflicted just as soon as they start to heal. But all is not lost. Trust me when I tell you that I know what it's like to lose that emotional tie with a parent. He hasn't let you go. Don't let this be the time that he does.

"He might act like he doesn't care what you say or what you think, but I know that your support would mean the world to him. To know that you believe in him and stand behind him—not just as a performer, but as a *man* who is about to be a father... Please. If not for him, then for his child. Please, just give him one chance to show you the part of him that you've never seen."

I watch, almost breathless, as Ewan rests his hand on top of Abrielle's shoulder, giving her a slight squeeze. She looks up at him and he nods once before he looks back at me and says, "Send us the information, and we'll put it on our calendar."

I puff out a sigh of relief, a small smile curling my lips. "I will."

"And take down my number," Abrielle insists. "I'd like to be kept abreast about the progress of my grandchild, if you don't mind."

"No. I don't mind. I don't mind at all."

ELEVEN

Sage

As I climb in the back of the cab, I realize that it's been two and a half months since I've driven myself anywhere. It's weird; and yet, I've adapted to this way of life without a hitch. As much as I miss home and my family, as much as I miss Millie—I love being on the road. It's exhausting, but even more so, it's exhilarating. The rush that comes from being on stage in a different city every night, each crowd welcoming us with frenzied excitement—yeah, it's a high I doubt will ever get old.

Now, as I head to the airport to pick up my girl, I'll have one less thing to miss. Or, rather, *two*. It's hard to believe that it's been six weeks already. On the one hand, it feels like time has gone by so slow. Every time we speak to each other and I can tell she's not feeling well, I know I'm too far away and the countdown to when we'll be together again seems endless. But then when I think of all the places I've been in the past month, I wonder where the time and miles have gone? We've got five weeks left on this tour, and we're finally inching our way back west. I intend to milk it for all it's worth—and when we're back home, we'll be back to a whole new grind.

Stefany says that she's heard from Greg, and a couple clubs opening up in our home state this summer requested that we be there for their grand openings. One of them is in Denver, three weeks after we get home. The other in Boulder, home of our label, Potential Records, a couple weeks later. It blows my mind that we've reached a place in our career where people are requesting *us* months in advance, knowing we'll draw a crowd.

Then again, it's nothing I didn't expect. This is the future of Mountains & Men. No doubt in my mind.

The drive to the airport feels long. When we finally arrive, I ask the driver to park while I head inside to get Millie. She texted ten minutes before our arrival, informing me that they'd just landed, and that she was on her way to baggage claim. I hurry inside without delay, anxious to see her. *Finally.* It takes me a few minutes to figure out where she is, but as soon as I spot her, my feet slow as my eyes take her in.

She's standing with her back to me. From this angle, I'd never guess that she was pregnant, making me wonder if she's grown as much as she says she has. She's wearing one of those dresses that looks like a really long, collard shirt, the fabric draped over her ass just right and hanging to mid-thigh on her long, gorgeous legs. The peach color stands out against her skin, and the belt she's got wrapped around her waist makes me want to put my hands there.

It isn't until my eyes land on her sandaled feet that I notice the small kennel that sits just beside her.

"*No. Fucking. Way,*" I whisper as a lazy grin tugs at my lips.

She brought Maestro.

Just when I thought this day couldn't get any better.

I walk right into her, my chest pressed against her back, my arms circling her waist beneath her new, full tits, and I pull her against me closer. She gasps in surprise, but quickly relaxes into me, reaching up to rest her hands around the back of my neck.

"*Baby,*" she whispers, as if that's all she can manage.

I squeeze her tighter before I reply, "You brought my dog."

With a nod she says, "He missed you. I thought I could help keep an eye on him while I was here. I read somewhere that French bulldogs don't mind small spaces, so the bus shouldn't be too uncomfortable for him. Plus, I thought the band would—"

"Millicent," I grumble, my longing to taste her suddenly undeniable. Hearing that she researched whether or not Maestro would be comfortable on the bus because she wanted to do something kind for me, but also my favorite pup, makes me weak. "I'm going to turn you around and I'm going to kiss you so hard, you won't be able to think straight. You good with that?"

She sucks in a breath, but she doesn't get the chance to answer me before I turn her around. Then, as she grabs hold of my biceps, just before I lean in to kiss her, I see her belly and freeze.

"Holy shit, doll face." My hands slide around until they're resting over her protruding middle. She's still got a ways to go, but there's no denying she's pregnant now. Seeing it makes my chest swell, and as I lower my head to kiss her lips, I murmur, "You're fucking gorgeous, baby."

She parts her lips to respond, but I beat her to it—thrusting my tongue inside of her mouth. With a moan, she leans into me, and the feel of her body pressed against mine after all this time makes my dick start to harden. I don't even try to fight it as I savor the taste of her mouth, enjoying the feel of her tongue tangled with mine.

I don't know how long we kiss before she pulls away from me, planting her hands on my chest before she says, "I need a breath."

With a chuckle, I press my lips against her forehead, looking over her to see that the bags have started to come out. Remembering we've got a ride waiting, I reach down and tap her ass before I nod and tell her, "Point out your stuff. I'll grab it."

Five minutes later, I've got one bag full of Maestro's shit slung over one shoulder, Millie's suitcase in one hand, and Maestro in his kennel in the other. Millie keeps insisting that I should let her help, but I remind her that she's got her own precious cargo to worry about and that I'm fine. Once we're all piled into the cab, Maestro—whining and impatient to be let out of his cage—sitting between Millie and me, I tell our driver that we're ready to head back to the bus.

We don't talk much along the way. After I find out that her flight was fine and she's not hungry, she grows quiet as she stares out the window, taking in the little bit of San Antonio that she'll get to see while she's here. We'll be leaving for Albuquerque around midnight, so she won't get to see much. I'm not exactly sure why she's being so silent, but when I reach for her hand, she laces her fingers with mine. I take that as a good sign and decide to let her be. Something tells me traveling with Maestro today wasn't exactly easy.

By the time we make it to the bus, she's asleep. I lean over and kiss her temple before I speak softly into her ear. "We're here, baby doll."

She draws in a deep breath, opening her eyes and looking right at me before offering me a small smile and a nod. As soon as she climbs out of the car, Knox and Derrick step off of the bus.

"Whoa! Look at you," calls out Knox as I step out of the cab, Maestro in hand. "Lookin' good, mama."

Millie laughs and he pulls her in for a hug as the rest of the band comes out to greet my girl. I watch as Millie says hello to all of them, resting her hands around her middle when someone says something about the bump. The look on her face does me good. Even after just waking up from a short nap, she looks more alive than I've ever seen her. *This* is who my girl is—who she was meant to be—*where* she was meant to be.

I no longer have to wonder what her dreams are; I no longer have to ask what drives her. The baby that she carries, the life that we're starting to build here and now, *that's* it. This is what her dream is—*this* is what drives her. My strong, stubborn, sexy as fuck girl dreams of having the family she never got, and I'm the lucky bastard that gets to help make that happen.

"Hell, yeah!" cries Maddox, pulling me from my thoughts as he walks toward me. "M&M's mascot. It's about time you joined us, Maestro."

I can feel it as Maestro grows excited at the sound of so many familiar voices. I chuckle, setting the kennel down before opening the door and letting him out. He wastes no time racing out before he's trembling with excitement at my feet. I pick him up and he immediately tries to lick me as he wiggles around in my arms.

"Some things never change, huh, buddy?" I ask, yanking my face out of reach. "Missed you too, little guy, but I'd like my girl to kiss on me later—so that means you can't."

"Need help with your bags?" asks JJ.

"Oh, shit. Yeah." I hand Maestro to Maddox, who takes him willingly, walking him over to a patch of grass so that he can do his business as I pay the cab driver and grab Millie's things.

Once we've got everything on board, I feel Millie's touch at my back. When I turn to face her, I see an apprehensive smile on her face. Before I can question her, she asks, "Can we go for a walk? I think Maestro and I could both use it."

"Yeah. Okay, sure. Let's go."

Millicent

KNOWING THAT THEY keep bottled water in the fridge, I grab one before stepping back off of the bus. The Texas humidity is certainly not something I'm used to, but I'm not ready to be closed into the bus after traveling all day. Besides that, I need another moment alone with Sage.

It's been a couple weeks since I went to talk to his parents. While he's aware that we conversed and his sisters have phone privileges with him again—as they aren't calling to talk about their parents but to check in on him—everything isn't exactly out in the open yet. I still haven't told anyone that I got Ewan and Abrielle to come see Mountains & Men when they perform in Colorado in two weeks. Sage might have appreciated me standing up to them, but he still hates that I felt that I had been put in the position to do so.

To say that he's still not exactly *pleased* with his parents would be completely accurate. Months ago, maybe even weeks ago, I never imagined that I would be stuck in the middle of their unique and turbulent relationship. It's amazing how the reality of parenthood makes you do things and see things and understand things in a whole new way. I've been a mom for all of sixteen weeks, and already the world looks different.

"Hey." Sage pulls me from my thoughts, pressing a kiss against my temple as he takes my hand. I look down and see that Maestro has been leashed, and Sage nods to a sidewalk behind the bus. "Ready?"

"Yeah."

We walk a few paces, neither of us speaking before Sage asks, "So, are you going to tell me what's on your mind?"

"I have to ask you something," I admit, giving his hand a squeeze. I look down at my feet, the view of the parking lot we're circling not exactly a view to miss.

"You're being weird, doll. Just spit it out."

I stop walking and he stops too as I look up at him and blurt out, "I need you to arrange for two backstage passes for your show at Red Rocks. Or, well, maybe five, if Pepper can get a sitter."

He knits his eyebrows together before he asks, "*Five?* For who?"

"Your family."

He shrugs, as if this is no big deal—and then he does the math and lifts an eyebrow at me. "*Five?*" he repeats.

"I invited your parents, and they've agreed to come."

I hold my breath waiting for his response. Though, it isn't long before I have to draw in a fresh intake of air. The silence continues to linger between us while he stares at me blankly.

"Sage? Baby, say something," I plead, letting go of his hand to reach up and brush my fingers along his cheek.

As if my touch has pulled him out of a different place entirely, his icy blue eyes focus on me before he wraps his arm around my waist and pulls me against him. I expect for him to say something, but when he *still* doesn't, I try and find the words to coax out a response.

"I told them that there's no way they could know who you are until they saw you perform. They don't understand how good you are or where you're going, and if they could just—"

I squeak my surprise when his lips crash against mine, taking me in a kiss so hard it almost hurts. Nevertheless, I don't pull away. Instead, I circle my arms around his neck, already damp with sweat from being out in the Texas heat, and I kiss him back. The longer we kiss, the softer he becomes, and I hum into his mouth.

He growls when he pulls away just slightly, just enough to tell me, "I love you so fucking much. If I could, I'd take you back to the bus and fuck you right now to remind you that you're my girl—*mine*—and you belong exactly where you are."

My breaths come in short spurts, still trying to recover from that kiss, but I realize that his words don't have their usual affect on me. As much as I love it when he talks dirty to me, I'm not the slightest bit turned on right now. In this moment, I realize that, in spite of the fact that I feel fine, I have *zero* sexual appetite. Without Sage with me, I never noticed before—but it appears as though I've misplaced my sex drive; or maybe it's more accurate to say that baby McCoy has hidden it.

"Millicent," he breathes, pulling me back into our conversation. I blink my eyes closed tight, willing my thoughts to shut up as I focus on Sage. "In six years, not *once* have my parents come to see us play. They've never seen me behind a mic. Ever."

"I…" I start and then I stop, not really sure what to say.

"I don't know how you got through to them; hell, I don't even know if it'll matter. But—*thank* you."

I sigh in relief, holding him tighter as I press myself up on my tiptoes. "I did it for all of us. I did it because I believe in you."

"My best girl," he whispers, propping his forehead against mine. "You're my best girl."

We stand together until the heat forces us to pull apart, and then he takes my hand once more and we continue our leisurely stroll, giving my legs just what they want. By the time we make it back to the bus, I'm hungry, so Sage asks the band if they're ready to head downtown for their last dinner in San Antonio before we get ready to leave. Everyone agrees that they could eat, and then we're off—just Mountains & Men—my family of friends.

Sage

When we got into town yesterday, we didn't really get a chance to explore before the show. Now that we're downtown, I'm glad that we won't be leaving until later. This place is awesome. We eat dinner at this Mexican restaurant where I have the best smothered burrito I've ever had in my life. Then, we wander down to the Riverwalk where we stop and listen to a couple musicians along the way.

"Hey, let's go on one of those river boats," suggests Alex, pointing to a couple boats filled with people as they pass us on the water.

"What are we, tourists?" scoffs Maddox teasingly.

"As a matter of fact," Alex retorts with a smug smile. "Come on, it'll be fun. We can all go."

"I'd like to go," says Millie, her hand tightening around my arm in order to grab my attention. I look down at her and she gives me a smile before her pretty, dark green eyes shift to look out onto the river.

For just a second, I'm struck with the truth that we *are* tourists, which is part of the reason being on the road is so adventurous. There's so much of the world I want to see, so much of the world I've always believed I *would* see while taking my music as far as I could. Now, I'm not just taking my music, I'm taking my girl, too. She used to be afraid that I'd outgrow her—that who I was, where I was going, and what I dreamed would somehow make me *more* than her. I told her I didn't think this would happen. Now, I'm sure that it won't.

I'm going to show her the world, starting with this damn river.

"Come on. Let's go," I tell the band, wrapping my arm around Millie's shoulders before I start heading up stream. "I think I saw a place to purchase tickets back this way."

"*Yes!*" cries Alex, skipping ahead of us. Maddox grumbles something but follows, and we all laugh when Alex turns around and sticks her tongue out at him.

We wait in line to purchase our tickets, and then we move to another line to wait for our turn on a boat. When a group comes up to stand behind us, I catch a word or two of their conversation, and my ears focus in on what they're saying when I hear them mention our name. Knox must hear it too, because he turns to casually look over his shoulder. He nods when he makes eye contact with one of them, and when I hear her gasp, I can't help but chuckle.

"Oh, my gosh—that *is* them, y'all!" one of the girls whisper-shouts, her Texas accent heavy.

"I *told* all y'all I recognized the guy with the glasses."

Millie's grip around my hand loosens and I feel her take a step away from me at the same time that one of the guys in the group calls out, "Y'all opened up for Kings & Crowns last night! That was an awesome show!"

"Oh, my god, what're all y'all doin' down here?"

"Alex, here, wanted to ride the boat," Maddox says with a lazy grin, propping his elbow against her shoulder as he winks at one of the Texans.

"Holy shit. You're a lot smaller than ya look up on that stage," says one of the guys, his eyes roaming up and down Alex's short length. "You sure can play."

"Thanks," Alex murmurs, her cheeks tinted a soft pink.

"I can't believe we ran into y'all!" gushes the girl who mentioned my glasses earlier. "Is this y'alls first time to San Antonio?"

"Yup," Derrick answers for all of us.

"While we're waitin', mind if we get a picture? I've never met a rock star in person before."

JJ catches my eye and we share a knowing smile, both of us realizing that *this* is fucking awesome. Then, for the next five minutes, we take pictures with our fans, chatting about last night's show and how much they're sure we'll enjoy our ride on the river. Apparently, they're playing host to a couple of friends who came from a small town to see Kings & Crowns perform. We move closer to the front of the line as another group fills a boat, and I notice that Millie is farther away from me than I thought. I step away from the guys and Alex, who are all still lost in small talk, and close the distance between my girl and me—our gazes locked the entire time.

When I've reached her, I slide my arms around her waist, pulling her against me. A smile pulls at my lips when her belly presses against the top button of my jeans before her hands slide up my arms and around my shoulders.

"What are you doing all the way over here, doll?" I ask, running my hands up and down her back.

Her eyes look behind me before they settle on my face again. She squeezes my shoulders and then shakes her head, but I'm smart enough not to fall for that bullshit.

"Talk to me, doll face."

She sighs before she tells me, "You were meant to grace the spotlight, not me. You know that."

"What, them?" I ask, nodding back at the group behind me. "It was just a few pictures, Millie. They aren't the paparazzi."

"Yeah. Okay," she mutters, pushing me away.

I don't let her go, holding her tighter against me. "Don't you fucking dare. You're not going anywhere. Not until you tell me what's going on in that head."

"I just told you. You weren't listening."

The slight frown on her face forces me to take a beat and replay the last few minutes. I think back to the moment she let my hand go, as soon as one of the girls recognized me. Pulling my eyebrows together, I ask her, "It really makes you uncomfortable? The band getting noticed in public? That's going to happen, baby—you know that."

"Of course it's going to happen. I *want* it to happen—for *you*. But not for me."

My stomach drops, immediately aware that what she's saying will soon be impossible. She must know that. She must know that the bigger my name gets, the more people will know about hers. She's my girl. My muse. My inspiration—it's inevitable.

"Baby..." I pause, reaching up to grip the back of her neck. She stares at me intently. I stare right back, silenced by the stubbornness I see in her gorgeous eyes. It makes me chuckle, and I sigh, lowering my head until my forehead is pressed against hers. "Right here, right now, I promise you just one thing, baby—are you listening?"

"Yes," she whispers.

"I'll never ask you to be anyone other than who you are. You don't want to be the center of attention? I'll do my damnedest to make sure that you aren't. You're my girl, the mother of my kid—not my eye candy. No matter where we go from here, anyone who cares to know will know *that*. I promise."

"Okay."

"But you have to promise me something, too."

"Hmm?" she hums, her fingers grabbing two fistfuls of my shirt.

"Trust me. Promise you'll trust me."

"I *do* trust you."

"No, Millicent, I don't mean trust me with your heart—I mean, trust me with your name. Trust me with your image. Trust me to protect you as my girl." She pulls back a little, scowling up at me in confusion, and I continue to explain, "I won't lie to you. I have no idea how this is going to unfold. All this attention is going to be new to both of us, but we'll figure it out along the way—and as we do, hold my hand when I hold yours, step back when I let you go, and trust that either way, it's because I'm keeping my promise. Okay?"

She pulls her lower lip between her teeth, her eyes searching mine as she processes all that I just said. When she nods her agreement, I dip my head and press a soft kiss against her lips. She tilts her neck, tipping up her chin to kiss me back a little harder, and I can't help but to sneak my tongue out, taking a small taste before I pull away.

"What am I always telling your stubborn ass?" I ask, running my nose along hers.

She smiles knowingly and laughs quietly before she murmurs, "We're in this together."

"And don't you forget it."

"Come on, you two—stop being all gross. Our boat is here," calls out Maddox, making Millie giggle.

God, I love that sound.

I tell her as much with one more quick kiss and then take her hand, holding on tight as we join the others.

TWELVE

Millicent

THERE ARE PEOPLE EVERYWHERE *as we exit the building. The show ended more than an hour ago, and yet the crowds don't seem to have diminished in the slightest. I watch as Knox and JJ push their way through the people, girls screaming and reaching out to touch them. Derrick looks at Sage, who looks at me, before he tucks Alex under his big, huge arm and leads her into the madness. Alex clings to his side, but as large as he is, he's no match against their wild fans. I lose sight of them just as they are* ripped *apart and swallowed by the masses.*

My heart is beating so fast, I'm afraid that it's going to fly away. Sage's hold around my hand is so tight that I'm not sure there's any blood circulating through my fingers.

"I won't let you go, doll face. You hear me? I won't fucking let you go."

"Maybe we should wait?" I plead over the noise of screaming people.

"Let's go, guys. We can't wait any longer," Maddox insists as he walks by us. "Ladies, ladies!" he yells at the crowd. "There's enough Maddox to go around, no need to fight."

"Come on, Millie. It's fine. I won't let go. I promise."

I draw in a deep breath and offer him a nod before he winks at me, turning to finally make his exit. The second he steps foot into the miniscule aisle meant to be our pathway to the car, the shouting and screaming grows even louder and the aisle begins to close in around us.

Suddenly, I can't take a deep breath. There are so *many people, all of them calling*

Sage's name—all of them desperate for his attention. Hands grab at him from every which way, and while his grip around my hand gets tighter, I still feel it as my fingers begin to slip out of his grasp.

"Sage! Baby—don't let me go!" I cry.

He can't hear me. He doesn't even look back at me. Then, before I can do anything to prevent it, my hand is no longer locked in his. I scream as we're separated, the fans unstoppable as they surround him, swallowing him up. Still, he cannot hear me.

He doesn't even look back at me.

Frantic with panic, confused by what has happened, I plant my feet. For a moment, I imagine that he'll turn back—that any second now he'll be right in front of me, folding me in his arms. But as time passes, the crowd begins to thin around me. The noise starts to die down, and the people move away from me. Too soon, I'm standing in the middle of a littered parking lot—alone.

I'm all alone.

He let me go.

With a gasp, I open my eyes and try to sit up. I don't get very far, my body weighed down by Sage's arm slung over my middle, his hand resting protectively over my growing belly. As I realize that everything I've just experienced was nothing more than an incredibly vivid dream, I'm pulled further into reality by the feel of an intense burning in my chest. Now positive that I cannot stay in our bunk, I lift Sage's arm from around me and gently climb out.

The bus is moving. I'm not entirely sure what time it is, but something tells me it's still the middle of the night. The sun isn't out yet, and everyone is sleeping. Well—everyone except for Derrick. I see the light on behind the curtain of his bunk. I think about going to check on him, but then decide that I'm not exactly in the right frame of mind to be any sort of good company. So instead, I make my way to the kitchen in search of the bottle of Tums I've been consuming since just before we left San Antonio. I thought maybe my indigestion could be blamed on the spicy salsa I had with dinner Saturday night—but more than a week later, it plagues me just about every night, no matter what I eat.

I turn on the small light above the kitchen sink and find the bottle on the counter. I pop a couple in my mouth and chew them up as I open the fridge and pull out a bottle of peach iced tea. Then, leaving the light on, I head to the front of the bus, sitting on one of the couches beside the window. Curling my legs beneath me, I stare out into the night, thinking back on my dream.

I read somewhere that pregnant women have very intense dreams—but that one has left me troubled. It was a nightmare that hit way too close to home. The truth is, the scenario that played out in my head isn't as impossible as one might imagine. I can't ignore that; furthermore, I cannot run from the fear that I now feel. I made Sage a promise.

Then again, he made me a promise first. In that dream—it was a promise he broke.

"Millie?"

My head snaps up at the sound of his soft, husky voice, and I watch as my man comes toward me, rubbing his tired eyes. He's in nothing but his boxers, and his hair is wild, reminding me that I probably don't look much better in a pair of short cotton shorts and one of his t-shirts.

"Yeah, I'm here."

"Fuck, baby," he sighs plopping down on the couch behind me. "It's three in the morning. What are you doing up?"

Before I can even open my mouth to answer, he has his arms wrapped around me, pulling me back against his chest. He rests one hand over my belly, using his other to cup my breast. I sigh, suddenly reminded that while I have absolutely *no* desire to have sex, Sage's desire grows hungrier and hungrier with every passing day. I wonder if my dream had something to do with that—if maybe I'm losing him and there's absolutely nothing I can do about it. I'm not at all in control of my body, and the body he loves is now bigger and *dryer* than ever.

"Sage," I start to say, trying to wiggle out of his grasp.

"No fuckin' way," he mumbles. He then shifts us both so that I'm resting between his outstretched legs, his hold around me a little tighter than it was before.

Something about his adamancy makes me pause; then I relax, resting my head against his shoulder, reminding myself that I can't dream into existence something that hasn't happened. Right now, in Sage's arms, I'm exactly where I want to be. I'm exactly where I belong.

"I had a bad dream. It woke me up," I confess. "Or maybe it was my indigestion. Whatever it was, I can't go back to sleep. Not yet, anyway."

"What happened in your dream?"

At first, I think about not telling him. But before I open my mouth to refuse him an answer, my heart begs me to tell him the truth, knowing that he'll reassure me that it was nothing but a dream.

Reaching up to grab a fistful of his hair, I murmur, "You let me go..."

I feel it as his muscles lock up, his body immediately tense. He doesn't speak right away, and I wait patiently for him to respond. He doesn't disappoint me. His body melts around mine, his arms holding me even closer as he buries his nose in my neck and mutters, "It was just a dream, baby doll. I'm right here, and I'm not going anywhere."

"I know," I whisper, turning my face to press a kiss against the top of his head.

He returns my affection, pressing a few wet, lazy kisses against my neck. I feel his dick start to harden at my back, but he lifts his mouth away from my skin before resting his chin on my shoulder. While he doesn't complain much, I still feel guilty every time he gets hard for me. Now, feeling tired and anxious after that dream, I wonder if I could rally and make him come while the bus is quiet. Maybe if I made him feel good, I'd trick my subconscious into straying away from such horrible dreams.

Willing myself not to second guess my decision, I reach behind me, arching my back as I feel for his cock. When I grip him through his boxers, he grunts before he warns, "Millie—don't start something you can't finish."

"Who says I can't—"

"God, baby, don't play with me," he practically begs, pressing his forehead against my shoulder. "Been sleeping with your sweet, little ass pressed against me for a week now, and I can't do a damn thing about it. *Don't* play with me."

"I might not be in the mood to ride you right now, baby, but if you promise to be quiet, I'll take care of you."

"*Fuck*—are you messing with me right now?"

"Do you promise?" I ask in reply.

"Hell, yes," he hisses.

He lets me go as I sit up, setting my tea on the floor before I kneel just beside it. He moves with me, shifting so that his back is to the couch and he's got a leg on either side of me. Still working to not second guess myself, I slide my hands up his thighs all the way to the waistband of his boxers. I gently lift the fabric up and over his hard cock, a little saddened by the fact that the mere sight of it doesn't cause the throbbing between my legs that it should.

I shake the thought away and then waste no time before I take him into my mouth. A sound that resembles a whimper spills from his lips, and I know he's trying to hold back the moan I'm sure is lodged in his throat. I know my man. I know the sounds he makes when I blow him. I know how long he's gone without the pleasure of my body. And I know my demand for his silence is killing him—but he wants this, so he's doing his best to remain silent.

"Fuck, fuck, fuck, fuck, fuck," he whispers, his hands finding their way into my hair as I glide up and down his long, thick length, pumping his base with my fist.

I suck him hard, trying to keep my slurping noises to a minimum, and I find myself getting into it more than I anticipated. I'm certainly not wet, as baby McCoy seems to be completely against that, but I can't help but feel a bit of pride—pride in knowing that while I may dream of crazy fan girls stealing my man away, in real life, my mouth is the only one he'll let swallow his dick.

"Uuhh, *Millicent*," he groans as he fists my hair, bucking his hips a little. "Shit, baby, you feel amazing. Fucking hell."

With every word he speaks, he gets a little louder, but I know I can't stop. Not now. He's too far gone. While I'd be completely humiliated to wake up anyone on this bus and have them find me like this—on the floor, in my pjs, round with child, with Sage's dick shoved down my throat—I also know that to stop now would just be cruel. He said it himself—I shouldn't start something I have no intention of finishing.

So instead of stopping, I suck *harder*, wishing to bring him to orgasm as quickly as possible. When he starts to thrust his hips more aggressively, I surrender to him, moving my hands and letting him have his way with my mouth. I gag a little, but he doesn't hurt me as he takes what he wants—what he needs. Then, just before he comes, he pushes me away and jerks himself off, groaning softly as he comes all over his own stomach.

Before he's finished, I'm on my feet, headed to the bathroom for some toilet paper to clean him up. When I return, he's slumped lazily on the couch, his dick going soft in his hand as he peers at me through the darkness. I don't say a word as I clean him up, tucking him back inside his boxers before going to dispose of the tissue. When I return for the second time, he sits up and reaches for my belly. He lifts his shirt and presses his lips against my bare skin before he murmurs, "Hey, baby, it's daddy. Just wanted to say, whatever the hell you did to mommy tonight, *thank you*. I owe you one."

Sage

SHE GIGGLES, BURYING her fingers in my hair as she murmurs, "I don't think the baby can understand you. It'll be a few more weeks before your voice will be recognizable as *daddy*. He or she does have ears now, though. I'm at seventeen weeks, so I think he or she can hear music."

My head snaps up, and I look at her in the darkness as I ask, "For real? My kid can hear music?"

"Mmmhmmm," she replies with a nod.

A tired smile curls my lips, and I refocus my attention on Millie's belly. I press a couple kisses around her belly button before I whisper, "It all started with this, baby..." I kiss Millie's stomach once more and then sing softly.

"I see the demons in your eyes and I want to dance
Can't stop the beat I hear from one haunted glance
Take my hand, baby, don't let go
I'll set you free, baby, won't let go

All night/One song
This room/My home
I'll set you free, baby, don't let go
Tonight/Just give me tonight."

I stop singing when I hear Millie sniff. When I look up, her fingers slide all the way through my hair then over my ears until she's holding my face. I can't see her tears, the small light from the kitchen too dim to illuminate her face, but I can hear them in her voice as she speaks.

"I love you so much. Please don't ever leave us. Don't ever let me go."

I frown, seriously concerned about this dream that has her so shaken up. "Come 'ere," I insist, pulling the shirt down over her belly before guiding her down onto the sofa next to me. She leans into my side, still crying quietly, and I lift her legs so that both of them are hooked over one of mine. I then wrap her in my arms and hold her close.

"Shhh, doll face," I whisper, pressing my lips against her forehead. "It was just a dream, Millie."

"They *all* wanted you," she whimpers. "They took you from me, and you let me go. There were so many people screaming your name."

"I'm right here, Millicent. I'm *right* here." I hold her tighter, not sure what else to say; not sure what else I can do.

"It felt so real."

"This is real," I declare, giving her a small shake. "You and me and our baby that can hear music. If you think for one second that I'd let anything happen to you, or that I'd leave either of you, you're crazy, doll. Are you crazy?" I ask teasingly. "You just gave me head on Black Beauty, I sure as hell hope that's not because you're going insane."

She snuggles against me even closer, sniffing as she says, "I'm not crazy."

"That's a relief." I reach up and bury my fingers in her hair at the back of her head, keeping her close as I let the quiet that only comes in the middle of the night on the open road settle around us. I close my eyes, feeling slightly sated and content with my girl in my arms. I try to stay awake, wanting to make sure she falls asleep before I do, but it's a fucking struggle.

"At my last appointment," Millie starts to say a few minutes later, "the doctor tried to find out the sex of the baby, but she couldn't see. She told me at my next check in, she might have more luck. Do you want to know the sex of our baby?"

My eyes snap open and I tell her through a smile, "Hell, yeah." My excitement wanes for a moment and I confess, "It sucks that I can't go with you to any of your appointments."

"I'm not even halfway through my pregnancy, baby. You'll be home for plenty of appointments. Besides, as long as you're there when the baby comes, that's all I care about."

This. This is why I love my girl. My time away has never been something she's held against me. It scared the shit out of her at first, but she's never wanted anything less for me. She knows me. She *sees* me.

Fuck, I love this girl.

"I'm glad you want to know the sex," she says softly. She tilts her head back and I look down at her as she tells me, "As appropriate as it may be to call the baby *baby McCoy*, I'd like to start calling the baby by a first name."

My chest tightens with excitement and I dip my head to kiss her lips before I ask, "Have you thought of any names?"

"Not exactly. But I was thinking that I wanted it to be a little like your name. Just one syllable."

"Really?" I ask, not sure why I'm surprised that she would think of such a detail. "I kind of like how long your name is."

"How about a compromise? Short first name, long middle name? That's how your name is."

I smirk, admittedly quite proud that she'd like my kid's name to resemble mine in some way. "Okay."

"Okay," she repeats, circling her hand around the back of my neck as she reaches for a kiss. "When you think of something, tell me. I'll do the same."

"Okay."

She kisses me again before she whispers, "I think I'm ready to try and sleep again. Can we go back to bed?"

"Fuck, yes."

She hums a quiet laugh and I brush a kiss against her lips before I scoop my arm under her legs and stand to my feet, cradling her against my chest. I carry her to the kitchen and nod toward the light. She turns it out and I then carry her toward our bunk. I stop when I see the light on behind Derrick's curtain.

Shit, I think as I cough out a laugh.

With Millie still in my arms, I walk past our bunk until we're right in front of his. "D?" I call out, keeping my voice low.

"Yup," he mutters.

Millie gasps and then buries her face in my neck. Speaking through a grin I ask, "How long have you been awake?"

"Long enough."

"Fuck. I'm sorry, Derrick," Millie mumbles into my neck.

"Don't mention it."

"I hope you get some sleep."

"Thanks, darlin'. You too."

Without another word, I carry her back to our bunk, setting her on her feet before I climb in first. She follows shortly after, and I tuck my leg between both of hers, draping my arm around her as I rest my hand over her middle.

"Next time, we check bunks before you get head," Millie whispers.

I chuckle, burying my nose between her neck and her shoulder, pleased as fuck that she's promised me a *next time*. "Deal."

THIRTEEN

Sage

As luck would have it, the week of my birthday is one of our lightest performance weeks of the tour. We've got three stops, Colorado, Wyoming, and Utah, with a day of rest in Colorado after we arrive this morning. We play Red Rocks tomorrow and roll out for our show in Cheyenne Thursday night. Even though my birthday isn't until Saturday, I'm happy to be in town to see my family a few days before.

Kings & Crowns will be spending the night at a hotel in Denver; but since Mountains & Men is finally home, we've all arranged to stay where we want for the night before we meet tomorrow for our sound check. Pepper offered to drive down and pick Millie and me up. Adrian is supposed to grab Zip, and Violet will play chauffer for the rest of the band, taking them back to the house.

When we pull into the parking lot of the hotel and Black Beauty comes to a stop, we're all anxious to unload. Alex and JJ are the first to make their exits. I hear Violet's shriek of excitement, and I'm not at all surprised to find her small frame wrapped completely around JJ when Millie, Maestro and I step off of the bus. Alex and Adrian's reunion is a bit tamer, but not by much. I smirk, looking over as she smothers his face in kisses. Watching both couples, I'm reminded that I'm one lucky bastard. They've gone almost three months without seeing each other, something Millie and I aren't familiar with.

Something Millie and I will *never* be familiar with, if I can help it.

"Uncle Sage!"

I turn in the direction of Henley's voice, beaming at the sight of him running toward me, Carter right on his heels. I crouch down just in time for him to come crashing into my chest, and I hold him tight before Carter makes room for himself in my grasp.

"Unka Sage, unka Sage!"

I chuckle, squeezing them tight as I stand to my feet with a playful growl. "Holy cow! What has your mom been feeding you? You're so big!" I gasp.

"Gween beans make me stwong!" declares Carter.

"God," I mutter, propping my forehead against his little one. "I missed you, buddy."

"We missed you too, uncle Sage," says Henley.

"Not nearly as much as mommy, though," announces Pepper.

I shift, watching her approach. She's smaller than she was the last time I saw her, having dropped a little bit more of Sophia's baby weight, and she looks awesome. Though I think my sister is beautiful at any size, I can tell she feels more confident now. It's all in her smile.

"Hey, big sis," I say in greeting, leaning down to kiss her cheek.

"Hey, baby bro." She cups her hand around my cheek, her eyes dancing around my face as she says, "D-a-m-n, it is so good to see you."

"You, too, Pep."

She winks at me and then nods down at Sophia, whose gaze is jumping everywhere. I set the boys down and hand Henley Maestro's leash before scooping my niece into my arms. "Hey, beautiful," I coo. When I shower her neck with kisses, she frees the cutest fucking giggle I've ever heard in my life, and I can't stop myself from attacking her again.

When I've had my fill, I grin at her, an expression she returns, showing off a few new baby teeth. I then press a kiss to her chubby cheek, muttering, "Stop growing up so fast, Soph."

"Oooh," Pepper says through a laugh, earning my attention. I look over to find her standing with her arms wrapped around a crying Millie as she says, "I know. That's going to be your kid in his arms before you know it."

"Come 'ere, gorgeous," I insist, holding out my arm. She pulls away from Pepper and buries her face in my chest as I hold her against me, trying not to laugh. It really amazes me how just about anything can make her cry these days—my tough girl.

Looking over at Pepper, I watch as she bites her lower lip trying to stifle her own amusement. She draws in a deep breath and winks at me again before she says, "We've got a few hours before dinner at mom and dad's. We can do whatever you want. Rose will be off at four."

"Honestly, I'd be cool with going back to your place and just hanging out."

"Sure. I can whip something up for lunch."

"Grilled cheese?" Millie mumbles into my shirt.

"Yeah," says Pepper with a grin, reaching out to rub Millie's back. "I can make you a grilled cheese, hon."

I chuckle, press a kiss against Millie's head, and then tell Pepper, "I'm just going to check in with Stefany really quick, then we can go."

"You got it. I'll load up the clan."

DINNER WITH MY parents was *interesting*, to say the least.

Knowing that a lot has happened over the course of the last few weeks, I was curious to see how an evening in their company would be. Of course I was welcomed with open arms, as I usually am, and conversation was casual for a while as we dug into the dinner dad had grilled up for us. When conversation shifted to the topic of baby McCoy, I could feel the tension in the room, but it wasn't nearly as heavy as I thought it might be, given the last conversation I had with my parents on the subject. It was quite apparent that whatever happened when Millie went and spoke with them a few weeks ago, it had a lasting effect.

Then, when dad started asking questions about the tour and what plans I had after we returned, my jaw almost hit the fucking table. Granted, the skepticism in his as well as my mother's expressions was glaringly obvious, but they listened to what I had to say. They also weren't shy about expressing their doubts, but they were careful not to turn it into an out-and-out argument. When conversation shifted to a different topic entirely, I sat in complete shock for a while, replaying what happened over and over.

Now, as I lay in our apartment, Millie asleep on my chest as we lay in our bed, I replay the whole evening all over again. I told Millie that I wasn't sure that seeing me perform would change my parents' minds about the decisions I'm making; honestly, I'm still not sure—but my hope is greater than it's ever been. If tonight proved anything, it's that they're at least *trying* to be more opened minded.

Tomorrow night's show was already going to be something special—Mountains & Men playing at home. Now, it holds an entirely different significance, one that wouldn't be happening if not for Millie. It's the best birthday gift my girl could've ever given me.

I'm pulled from my thoughts at the sound of her gasp. I dip my chin, looking down at her as she claws her fingers into my bare chest. Frowning, I realize that she's still asleep. When she calls my name, I tighten my grip around her shoulders.

"No, no, no," she whines.

"Millie—doll face, wake up," I insist, giving her a gentle shake.

"Sage! No—don't let go."

Fuck—"Millicent," I call out, louder this time. "Open your eyes, baby. It' s just a dream."

She sucks in a breath, sitting up immediately as she pulls at the fabric of my shirt at her chest. I sit up with her and she looks beside her, taking me in through the darkness before she wraps her arms around my neck, pressing her cheek against mine.

"Promise me, baby. Promise me you'll—"

Rubbing her back, I interrupt her before she can finish. "Not going anywhere, doll face. I promise you."

"Okay," she breathes with a nod.

"You know what I find interesting?" I ask after her breathing returns to a normal pace.

"Hmmm?" she hums.

"Just that you only started having nightmares *after* we stopped having sex."

She laughs, which soon turns into a groan. Then she kisses my cheek before she lets me go, laying down once more. "Sorry for waking you."

"You didn't, doll."

"Oh. You should get some sleep. You've got that photo shoot tomorrow."

I grunt in remembrance. After our sound check tomorrow, Stefany arranged for some official band photos. Thinking Red Rocks would be the perfect space, that's how we'll be spending the second half of our afternoon before we grub and then take the stage.

"Sage, baby," Millie murmurs, reaching her hand behind her to find mine. When she does, she pulls it around her before she pleads, "Hold me."

"All right, gorgeous," I reply, curving my body around the back of hers.

"Get some sleep, baby. I love you."

"Love you, too."

I close my eyes, listening to her breathing as it grows deep and even. Then, before I realize it, I fall asleep right along with her.

Millicent

"Oh, my god," Rosemary sighs in reverent wonder as she, her parents, Harry and Pepper are escorted into the green room where the band, Adrian, Violet and myself are sitting around, just hanging out before the show. Her eyes grow wide as she looks around. I must admit, I appreciate her admiration of the space. It feels almost as if we're in a cave, one of the walls made of the red rocks that this outdoor amphitheater is famous for.

"This is pretty cool," Pepper murmurs quietly.

"That, sis, is a fucking understatement," says Sage as he stands to properly greet his family. I keep a close eye on Ewan and Abrielle, who look completely out of their element. This, of course, is no surprise. Yet, seeing them has me filled with anticipation and a little bit of anxiety—add to that a bit of indigestion—excited for them to see Sage take the stage in less than an hour. Knox and Maddox, the only other two members of the band who have any sort of history with Mr. and Mrs. McCoy, stand to say hello as well. Then, Sage introduces the rest of the crew.

"I'm not even going to lie," Harry starts to say as he stands, his arm resting around his wife's shoulders, "but as many times as I've seen you guys perform, I might be a little star struck right now." The band laughs and he smiles as he continues, "Do you have any idea how many amazing musicians have graced this very room?"

JJ grins as he says, "Trust me, the significance of this night is not lost on us. We've just had half the day to lose our shit over it," he laughs.

"The walls are covered in signatures of those who have come before us," Alex tells them.

My heart swells with pride as I remember all of us crowded into the hallway, the cement walls and steps covered in names of various artists and bands. They let Sage have the honor of etching their own band name amongst the others in black Sharpie while Kent did the same for Kings & Crowns.

"I still can't believe you made it here before me," says Adrian, pulling me from my memory. I look over at him, surprised by the tone of his voice. Then I catch a glimpse of his face, which seems soft, and I frown in confusion before I shake it off and let it go.

"Ah, don't be jealous, Adrian," teases Maddox.

"Yeah, you know your girl plays circles around you," adds Derrick.

Alex rolls her eyes but doesn't argue, and then Stefany comes into the room, stealing everyone's attention.

"Look who I found wandering around, looking for a great band he could watch perform. I told him he picked the perfect night for an epic show," she says just before Greg enters the room.

I've only ever met him once before, but it's kind of hard to forget him. He's not particularly tall—probably standing only an inch taller than me—but what he lacks in height, he makes up for in energy.

"Hey! What's up, man?" calls out Knox as he makes his way across the room to shake Greg's hand. The rest of the band follows suit, and then Sage turns and introduces him to his family, saving his parents for last.

"You've got one hell of a kid," says Greg, clapping a hand on Sage's shoulder. "With his talent and brains, I bet you couldn't be more proud."

Abrielle and Ewan both smile and nod politely but offer up nothing else. I catch Rose's eye and she rolls hers at me before a grin spreads across her face, lighting up her pretty blue irises. I smile back, but my anxiety rises a little, desperately hoping that the pride Greg speaks of is exactly how they'll feel before the night is through.

As time passes and we get closer and closer to show time, I feel it as the band's excitement begins to build and shift into an energy that I've only ever felt just moments before they perform. I watch as each and every one of them goes through their pre-show routine, focusing their minds on the forty minutes of music that lies ahead of them. When it's time for them to hit the stage, Sage grabs my hand and leads me out of the room, nodding at his family as we pass.

I don't get a chance to see how Ewan and Abrielle respond.

When we reach the wings of the stage, I lose my breath as I look out into the night. The sun is starting to set, and I know that we'll be under the moon soon, surrounded by the beautiful red rocks that rise above us. The stadium seating of the amphitheater is completely packed—as we knew it would be—but my heart skips a beat anyway.

"Tell me something good."

I look around Sage and see Alex on his other side, her hand squeezing his fingers as she looks out at the thousands of people waiting for them to take the stage.

"This is home, Zip. Our fans are out there—people who knew who we were long before we started touring with K&C. There are people out there who came to hear *us* play—and we're going to give them one hell of a good show."

She smiles up at him and then nods before she lets go of his hand. That's when I see Adrian shaking his head at her. She doesn't notice, but it bothers me anyway. He knows their ritual as well as I do, so I'm not exactly certain why he's so bothered by it. Before I can think too hard about it, Derrick claps his hands on her shoulders and I watch as she arches her neck, looking up at him with an upside-down smile.

"You got this, Ali."

"You too, D."

He growls, sticking out his tongue as he shakes his head, and she laughs as he lets her go and starts jumping around. Maddox joins in, then Knox—then they're all circled together, jumping around, pushing and slapping each other's backs, shaking off their nervous energy.

"All right, boys and girl—get your asses out there and play your hearts out," cries Stefany as the stage lights go up. The crowd starts to cheer, and one by one they make their way out on the stage.

Derrick goes first; after giving Adrian a quick hug, Alex goes next, followed by the Bradley brothers, who each make their way out after clapping Sage on the back. JJ kisses Violet then comes over and holds up a fist for Sage, who knocks his knuckles against the ones offered.

"Kill it," JJ yells over the sound of the screaming crowd before he goes to take his place behind his keys.

Derrick clicks out the beat just as Sage goes and hugs both of his sisters, and the band starts to play the intro to their first song on a loop. I know the song even before Sage starts singing the words. It's the first single they released off of their first album. But more than that, it's the song he started writing what seems like ages ago—the morning that Rose walked in on us while we were having sex. Just as I was getting ready to leave, he sang the words to me after he kissed me, amused that I had every intention of sneaking out the front door.

Sage brings me back to the here and now when he rests his hands around my stomach, bending down to kiss my bump before he brings his lips to mine.

"Love you."

I don't get a chance to respond before he runs out on stage. The crowd gets even *louder* as he yanks the mic out of the stand and immediately starts singing. I bite my lip, fighting the tears that threaten to fall as I watch him out there, doing what he does best. I resent my stupid hormones for making me so emotional; but then I remember that the music that is blaring right now is music that our sweet baby can hear, and I smile as a couple tears trickle down my cheeks.

Rose steals my attention as she reaches up and dries my face before taking one of my hands. Violet takes the other, winking at me before she directs her attention back out on stage and starts singing with Sage at the top of her lungs. Rose joins in, and soon all three of us are singing with my man.

Sage

After the best forty minutes I've ever spent under the lights, I stalk off stage, headed straight for my girl. I'm so fucking high, and all I want is a taste of her sweet mouth. I watch as her eyes grow wide in surprise. Then, as my hands grip hold of her hips and I pull her close, my dick twitches at the sight of the smile that curves her sweetheart lips.

I smash my lips against hers and then pry her mouth open with my tongue. She responds immediately, wrapping her arms around me as her hands skim up my neck until her fingers are buried in my hair. I don't hear anything but the residual sounds of the crowd, bidding us goodnight, and the soft hum of my girl's moan as she twists her tongue with mine. I kiss her deeper, my adrenaline rushing through me making me want to push her against the wall and fuck her. Knowing this isn't a possibility, I force myself to find satisfaction in all that she's giving me right now—but I don't stop myself from reaching down and grabbing a handful of her ass.

"Sage—I don't think mom and dad need a visual presentation of how their fourth grandchild was created!" Rosy yells, her words somehow breaking through the glorious noise of the audience.

I pull my lips away from Millicent, but I don't let her go, both of us short of breath as we stare into each other's eyes. I don't know how long we stand in one another's arms, trying to breathe deep as the road crew tears down our stage to put together Kings & Crowns' set, and I don't care. Right here, in this moment with my girl—it's exactly where I want to be.

"I love you, too," she tells me, pushing herself up on her tiptoes so that she can touch her nose to mine. "You were amazing, baby!"

"Thanks, doll face," I reply, brushing my lips against hers softly.

A hand grips my shoulder and I know before I even look beside me that it belongs to my dad. I don't let Millie go as I turn to face him. I tuck her under my arm and she holds me around my waist. I can see it in his eyes that he understands what I'm doing. I'm making a fucking statement. *This* is my family, and *this* is how I intend to take care of them—whatever he says right now, my mind is made up. It's *been* made up, because this is who I am.

My chest tightens when he moves his hand from my shoulder, gripping his fingers around the back of my neck. He gives me a squeeze, shaking his head as he says, "I had no idea, son. I had no idea." He stares at me a second longer before he wraps his arm around my shoulders, pulling me against his chest before he kisses my forehead. "You've got yourself a good woman. She knows a good man when she sees one, and she's not afraid to fight for him. Hold on to her, and you keep fighting, too—your efforts," he shakes his head again, looking back out at the crowd. "They aren't in vein."

He pulls away and I offer him a nod, my throat suddenly clogged with an emotion I can't quite identify. Then I see my mom and I feel like I can't breathe. She walks right up to me, cupping her hands around my cheeks before she whispers, "*Wow.*"

That's all she says. That's all she needs to say.

FOURTEEN

Millicent

"YOU AND THE OLD LADY COMIN'?" calls out Brock as he walks backwards along the sidewalk, all of us headed to the hotel.

I'm still undecided as to how I feel about being referred to as Sage's *old lady*. Lewis explained to me that it's not supposed to cause offense; that in some circles—like motorcycle clubs—it's some sort of badge of honor to wear the title. Except, we're not in a motorcycle club, and I'm five years older than Sage, not to mention twenty weeks *pregnant*—all of which has me leaning toward *not* in favor of the name.

Nevertheless, at Brock's question, I look up at Sage, his face illuminated by the lights of the hotel entrance we pass under as we make our way down Freemont street in downtown Las Vegas. They wrapped up their show over an hour ago, and now there's talk of a party in Kings & Crowns' hotel suite. I'm exhausted and want nothing more than to be off of my feet in a quiet room, but I know how Sage gets after a show—and tonight, I assume his high is even stronger than usual.

Kent called him out on stage in the middle of their set. Kings & Crowns was playing a cover song, and he wanted Sage to sing back up. I hadn't heard the song before, but Sage knew all the words and jumped in like the pro that he is. It was awesome, and the crowd loved it. I could tell that he had a blast doing it too.

That said, I wouldn't be surprised if he wanted to join them for a few drinks in order to unwind and expend any excess energy that might be coursing through him. When he looks down at me, those gorgeous icy blue eyes framed by those horn-rimmed glasses make my knees weak, and I can tell that my assumptions are correct; but as he studies my face, I watch as he makes up his mind.

"Nah," he answers, his eyes still looking down at me. "Not tonight."

"What?! Come on, man! It's our last night in Vegas!" hollers Rex.

"Sage, if you want to go, go," I tell him, giving his hand a squeeze.

"You look beat," he replies, squeezing my hand in return.

"It's late and my feet hurt and I really just want to go back to the room—but that doesn't mean you have to," I say, meaning every word.

The last thing I want is to hold him back. It's something I've thought about since before I told him I was pregnant. I understand who he is and where we are. I understand that he'll never be twenty-two and at the forefront of his amazing career ever again. The *last* thing I want is for this time in his life to be remembered as the beginning of him being *tied down* by his *old lady*.

He responds by letting go of my hand only to wrap his arm around my shoulders, pulling me into his side. He then tells the guys, "I'm taking my girl to bed."

"Good call, my friend," says Lewis with a wink.

I roll my eyes and I hear Knox and Maddox snicker behind me. I'm sure they know Sage is *not* getting laid, but it appears as though the men of Kings & Crowns are ignorant of Sage's present plight. Nevertheless, not another word is said about it as we arrive at our destination. Most of M&M follows after Kent and his crew, while Alex decides to retire to her own room. Sage and I say goodnight as we pass, and then we're finally alone.

"Baby, if you want to go, you should—"

He turns me around, and I have to reach up to grab hold of his arms to catch my balance. With my growing belly beginning to protrude more and more, I find my equilibrium is frequently off. I don't really get the chance to think about it too much before Sage's lips are on mine, his tongue seeking entrance into my mouth. Holding on tight, I return his kiss, enjoying the taste of him until he pulls away abruptly.

"I have to put you on a plane tomorrow, doll face. Not looking forward to it. Sure as hell am not going to go get wasted on your last night of the tour and leave you in here all by yourself."

I stare up at him for a second before I circle my arms around his neck and pull him down to my lips once more. "I love you," I confess, whispering the words into his mouth.

"You fucking better," he teases, smacking a hand against my ass. "Let's get you off your feet, yeah?"

"Yeah."

Ten minutes later, after we're both ready for bed, we slip under the sheets. Sage sits up with his back propped against the pillows, and I recline against his chest between his legs. As is becoming routine, he lifts up the hem of my shirt, exposing my bump before splaying his hands around it. On his birthday, the baby started moving. It's an incredible feeling, one that still makes me stop and gasp, but Sage hasn't been able to experience it yet. So whenever we're alone, just sitting around, he uncovers me and waits.

"Have you thought of anymore names?" I ask, my eyes growing heavy as my fingers trace up and down his tatted arm.

"Mmmm," he hums, resting his chin on top of my head. "I did think of one. Actually, I saw it online the other day and I really like it."

I wait for him to tell me, and when he doesn't, I giggle and ask, "Well?"

"It's for a boy," he hints.

I move my head so that I can tilt it back and look at him as I say, "Baby, the suspense is killing me."

When he looks at me, I realize that he wasn't kidding. He *really* likes whatever name is being held captive in his brain. We've discussed at least fifty names—mostly girl names, but quite a few boy ones, too—and while a couple of them are ones we agree are good, we haven't loved any.

"Okay, what do you think about Jace?"

"Jace," I whisper, wanting to see how it feels falling from my lips. "Jace McCoy." A smile pulls at my lips as I look down at my belly, Sage's hands still spread around me, and I say it again. "Jace…I love that," I admit, looking back up at him.

"Really?" he asks, his eyes alight with excitement.

"It's kind of badass."

He grins as he chuckles and says, "I thought so, too."

"Middle name?"

"Not for a boy—but for a girl, maybe."

Now *my* eyes light up as I demand, "Spill it."

"I was kind of playing around with my mom's name and stumbled across Ariella."

I close my eyes, pressing my forehead against his neck as I couple the beautiful name he thought up with the name I decided I liked earlier today. "I think we have a name for a baby girl."

"Spill it," he insists, stealing my words.

I tilt my head up until my lips are grazing the the underside of his chin as I whisper, "Eve Ariella McCoy."

Before he gets a chance to respond, I gasp and he mutters, "Holy shit!" as the baby moves inside of me. "Our baby moved! Did you feel that?"

His question makes me giggle and I reach up to touch his cheek as I assure him, "Yeah, Sage—I felt it."

Dipping his head, he buries his face in my neck, kissing me before he mumbles, "I think the baby likes the name, too. Eve Ariella. That's it."

"You hear that baby?" I ask, resting my hands over Sage's. "You've got a name. Jace or Eve—I can't wait to find out which one."

"Just a couple more days," Sage reminds me.

"One more week until you're home, baby," I say, turning to speak into Sage's hair. "I can't wait for that, either."

"I'm ready too, doll face."

Saying goodbye to Sage is never easy, especially not with my hormones all out of whack, but I made it through the weekend with a surprisingly low amount of tears and a pleasant amount of anticipation. Five days from now, Mountains & Men will *finally* be home from tour. Something tells me that four months will soon feel like nothing when they're discussing dates for future tours that will likely take them all over the world; and while I can't imagine being away from home for longer, I'm not afraid of the possibilities. I rest in the security of knowing that once Jace or Eve is born, Sage will take us wherever we want to follow, and I won't have to worry about months and months spent without him.

As for now, talk of *tours* are not in the works. In fact, Sage is fairly certain that any traveling that the band does for the rest of the year will be minimal. He's not exactly sure what to expect when they get back, but he's sure they'll be in the studio at the beginning of August to start work on their second album. I'm still wildly impressed that they were able to write an entire album's worth of music while touring. I've been fortunate enough to hear some of their newest songs, and I'm certain that their sophomore release will be even more of a hit than their debut. Sage says that if everything goes the way they want, they'll be able to release their first new single in October and then put out their entire record before Christmas.

Two full albums released in one year.

They truly are remarkable; and to say they've got momentum is an understatement. They've been working so hard, and I'm so proud of each and every one of them. It's hard to believe that less than a year ago, I had no idea who any of them were. Now, I consider them part of my family, and hundreds of thousands of people follow their music. And after tonight, I'm guessing that number will increase by leaps and bounds.

A knock sounds at my front door and Maestro's head pops up from my lap before he looks at me with a question in his eyes. I pat his head before I stand, all the while assuring him, "We've got company, Maestro. You'll like them, I promise."

He jumps down off of the couch and follows me to the door, seemingly acting as my protector. Though, when I open up and he sees Rosemary and Violet standing on the other side, he stops thinking about me, entirely too excited to see Rose.

"Hi, puppy!" she gushes excitedly, squatting down to shower him with attention. "Hey, Millie," she says, smiling up at me.

"Hey, preggers," Violet greets before coming to wrap me in a hug. "My god, this baby is *growing!*" she says when she pulls away from me. It's the first time she's seen me since I was here with the band two and a half weeks ago.

"I know," I laugh, running my hands over my belly.

"You still look hot, though," Rose comments as she stands and enters the apartment, closing the door behind her. "Are you eating enough?"

"Trust me, I'm eating plenty. I have the indigestion to prove it."

"Well, I hope the baby likes cupcakes and sparkling cider," says Violet, holding up a brown paper bag with *Sprinkles* written on the front. I recognize the logo as that of one of our local cupcake shops known for outrageously decadent treats. "We thought the occasion called for something special."

"You're right. It does. I'll go grab some glasses."

"No, no," insists Rose, gently pushing me toward the couch. "I'll get them, you relax and find VH1. The show will be on any minute."

I don't argue, knowing that it's useless, and follow Violet around the couch. I sit while she unpacks the bag. She pauses when she spots the envelop I left on top of the coffee table a few hours ago; the one I've been staring at off and on all evening.

Picking it up, she turns around and raises her eyebrows at me. "*Valentine/McCoy Baby?*" she asks, reading the writing on the front.

"I'll take that, thanks." I grab the envelop before she can protest, shoving it behind my back.

"Well, now I *really* want to know," she states, folding her arms across her chest.

"Know what?" asks Rose, entering the room with three stemless wine glasses.

"I went to the doctor today. She wrote down the sex of our baby and put it in an envelope. I'm going to open it tonight when Sage calls so we can find out together."

"*God,*" Rose groans, dragging out the word. "You guys are disgustingly adorable. Like, I can't take it. Also, screw my brother, give me that envelop!"

I giggle, shaking my head at her before I reply, "I did screw your brother, which is how the reason behind the envelop came about. And I'm not giving it up. Sorry. I'm sure he'll text you tonight, though."

"Have you guys picked out names? Valentine/McCoy—are you hyphenating the last name?" asks Violet, lowering herself onto the floor.

I swear, she never sits on the furniture when she's here.

"No. No hyphen," I state, shaking my head for emphasis. "I don't want my father's name anywhere near my child."

"'Nough said," she replies with a nod.

"What about the first name?" asks Rose.

"We have a full name picked out for a girl and a partial name picked out for a boy; but we aren't revealing either until we know the sex, and then we'll just share the one."

"*God*," Rose groans, dragging out the word again. "The suspense! I can't even. You know he's my best friend, right? You know he tells me everything first? Or, I guess, he *used* to until *you* came along," she mutters, lifting an accusatory eyebrow at me. She doesn't hold the expression for long, her grin breaking her sassy frown before she laughs and whines, "I'm so jealous right now! That's it—I get the chocolate cupcake."

We all share a laugh as Violet starts pouring the cider and I turn on the television, searching for the appropriate channel. By the time we've each picked out a cupcake—Rosemary surrendered the black forest chocolate cake with peanut butter buttercreme filling, chocolate icing, and a peanut butter cup on top to the baby, who insisted I have it, regardless of the burning in my chest I'm sure will follow—the opening credits of the show start to play. A quick preview shot of Mountains & Men flashes across the screen and Violet squeals with glee as Rosemary reaches over and grips hold of my thigh. My heart is still racing by the time the first commercial break starts.

"I bet my phone will be *blowing up* with notifications after this show. How much do you want to bet?" Violet gushes with a grin.

"What do you mean?" I ask.

"Oh, my god—Vi is *brilliant!* She set up a google alert for the band. Anytime google finds something new about them on the web, she gets an email. She hooked me up too."

I run my finger across the frosting of my cupcake before dipping it into my mouth. I savor it for a second and then ask, "Do you get a lot of alerts?"

"At first, not really. Maybe two or three a day. But that was when the *Royalty Unleashed Tour* first started. Now? I average about one hundred per week."

"*What?*" I gasp, my eyes growing round in shock.

Violet smiles at me wickedly and then holds out her hand, palm up. "Come on, preggers—hand it over. You know you want to."

Rose giggles as she adds, "You totally do."

I think about this new information, still in awe of how much they're being mentioned in the media. It's my curiosity that has me reaching for my phone. I unlock it and hand it to Violet who has me all set up in no time.

Fifteen minutes later, when Sage's voice fills the room, him and all of his band mates suddenly displayed on the TV screen, I get my first alert.

When my phone rings, I'm startled out of my sleep. I sit up and spot the book I was reading still open on the pillow beside me. All the lights are on in the bedroom, and I'm stretched out on top of the covers. I turn and look at the clock, noting that it's just after ten-thirty, realizing that I must have fallen asleep not long after the girls left.

Before the call goes to voicemail, I reach for my phone and hurriedly slide my finger across the screen. "Hello?" I answer, my voice huskier than I was anticipating.

"Hey, doll face, did I wake you?" asks Sage. I can hear a bunch of background noise, and then a door opens and shuts and it fades away.

"I didn't mean to fall asleep."

"It's late. I'm sorry, doll, I should have called earlier, but—"

"No, no. It's okay. How was the show?"

"It's good to be back in front of a California crowd. We may have stolen ourselves some Kings & Crowns fans tonight," he chuckles. I smile, knowing without a doubt that Kings & Crowns may be playing in front of their home crowd this week, but Mountains & Men will *definitely* earn some respect out on stage. "Anyway, we just finished up and K&C just started their set. I was going to call you after, but I couldn't wait."

"You guys were great on VH1, Sage. Really. They put you in the top three bands to watch for."

"Baby doll, that's awesome—but I'm not talking about VH1."

I gasp, my stomach tingling with excitement as my heart melts and my brain finally wakes up, remembering why he's calling. "Oh, my god—the baby!"

"Yeah," he laughs. "What are we having, gorgeous?"

"One second." I twist around, reaching for the envelop on the night stand. I tuck the phone between my shoulder and my face and then take a deep breath as I rip the envelop open and peek inside.

My heart swells as I think back to a couple nights ago, and the look Sage got in his eyes when he was talking about naming his son. I don't even try and fight my tears as I whisper through the phone, "Jace."

FIFTEEN

Sage

BEHIND THE *MUSIC* AIRED Monday night. By Tuesday morning, we had two radio show interviews scheduled with the top rated stations in San Francisco, and an invitation to perform on *The Late Late Show* with Kristin Prince in Los Angeles on our last day of the tour, just hours before our final *Royalty Unleashed* gig. There really were no words to describe how any of us felt. And when we finished recording our performance of *You and Me* and Kristen Prince came up to thank us, congratulate us, and give a shout out to our debut album, *Of Mountains & Men*, I'd never felt so high.

Not high on adrenaline, though that was there. This was a different kind of high—like I had reached a new height. It was like, if I looked over my shoulder, I'd be staring down the biggest mountain I've ever tried to climb. Mountains & Men have fought our way this far, this *high*. We aren't at the top yet, but we sure as fuck can see the summit a lot better than we could four months ago.

"Okay, I'm pretty good at keeping my shit together, but I need you guys to spare me a moment," says Stefany as she enters the dressing room.

My mates and I exchange dubious looks with one another before Maddox mutters, "All right, babe, lay it on us."

She takes a deep breath, runs her fingers through her wavy, blonde locks, and then puffs out a sigh before she squares her shoulders. "In five minutes, you're closing out your stint on this tour." She stops, shakes her head, and offers us a shaky grin before she continues. "When I first saw you guys and girl on stage, I knew I wanted to work with you. I had this gut feeling that with the right connections, the proper exposure, and hard work, your music could take you just about anywhere. Yet, no matter how awesome I thought you were, I didn't imagine we'd be here in less than a year. And believe me when I say, *here* is a fucking *fantastic* place to be.

"Guys, my phone will not stop ringing. When we get home, be prepared to take it to a whole new level. This really is just the beginning. The things Greg and I have in the works already would make your head spin. It makes *my* head spin. I'm so proud of you, I can't even think straight. It is my honor and my privilege to represent you and your music. Mountains & Men is a class act, and you're headed straight for the top. There's not a doubt in my mind.

"So, *thank you*—from the bottom of my heart; thank you for trusting me and allowing me to be a part of your incredible journey." As soon as she's finished, a single tear leaks out of the side of her eye, rolling slowly down her cheek. She sighs in annoyance, reaching up to swipe it away as she murmurs, "Damn."

"We owe you thanks, too," says Derrick. "No way in hell we'd be here if I was still handling all the business shit."

"You took a chance on us. We needed you, and you delivered just like you said you would," Knox adds.

"*Shit*," she grumbles as a couple more tears leak from her eyes.

"Fuck it. Bring it in," Maddox demands, standing to his feet. He wraps his arms around Stefany, who laughs when Mad Lips looks back at us and then waves us over. "Bring it the fuck in!"

"Group hug!" cries Alex, extending one arm around Maddox and the other around Stefany.

We all jump up and get in there, huddling around Stefany. This is how the stage manager finds us when he opens the door and announces our two-minute warning.

"All right guys—last show before we go home," I begin to say, ready as ever to get out on that stage. "Make it count."

"You're coming with us tonight—we *won't* take no for a fucking answer!" cries Kent, hooking his arm around my neck as he heads for the back exit. He's a little shorter than I am, so I have to bend at his will, but I do it with a laugh and no argument. "We're home, and we're going to show you how we *really* party on our turf."

Rex lets out a hoot of excitement from behind us, and the Bradley brothers join in. Then, as soon as we step foot outside, we're *swarmed* by the paparazzi. Cameras are everywhere, and I have to hold up my arm to get one guy out of my face.

Kent shouts in my ear, "Welcome to the big leagues, my man," before he lets me go.

I look back over my shoulder and catch JJ's eyes. He winks at me before he yells, "Smile!"

I chuckle, shaking my head at him, and then search for Alex. There's so many people—fans, security, photographers—I just want to make sure she doesn't get lost in the crowd. Derrick catches my attention and holds up his hand, his fingers wrapped around hers, and I nod, satisfied to know that our little church mouse hasn't been swallowed up by the masses.

"Sage! Sage! Can we get your autograph?"

My senses are being flooded by everything that's going on around me, but when my ears tune in and I hear our fans calling for us, I don't hesitate to stop and return the favor of their attention. I sign shit and pose for selfies until I hear Brock bellow my name. When I look in the direction of his voice, I find him with three girls draped all over him. He jerks his head, signaling for me to follow, and I wave to the group beside me before I start to join the others.

"Aww, Sage is all alone! That doesn't seem fair. He's *hot!*" The sound of her high pitched voice seems close, so I turn to see who's talking. By the time I spot her, she's got her hand wrapped around the back of Knox's neck as she coos, "Not nearly as hot as you, baby—watching you play got me so turned on. I can't believe I'm touching you right now."

I roll my eyes, looking away just as Knox leans in to kiss her.

"Come on, guys!" cries Alex, tugging Derrick past me. "This is crazy!" she adds with a laugh.

JJ sidles up beside me, clapping a hand on my back before pointing a little ways ahead of us, where I see Maddox macking on some blonde.

"Oh, shit," I laugh, headed his way. "Mad Lips—not that one. Not today!"

"Wha—"

I cut him off as I pull him away from a very disappointed looking girl. "You're sober now. Give it an hour. You want to get laid tonight, you'll thank me for that later."

"Sage! Sage *Lawrence* McCoy!"

I stop dead in my tracks, as do JJ and Maddox, and we all exchange a glance. My middle name isn't exactly public knowledge, so as I look through the crowd, I wonder who the hell just called out to me.

"Over here, McCoy!" she calls out again.

"*Holy fucking fuck*," Maddox bites.

I jerk my head in his direction, startled by his reaction. He shakes his own head before jerking his chin, and I follow his gaze until I see her.

"What. The. Fuck?"

She doesn't look much different than the last time I saw her. Her hair is shorter, her golden blonde strands hanging straight until just above her shoulders. And she's got bangs. She didn't have bangs before. She's wearing a strapless top that stops just below her belly button, showing off her defined waist; and the jean shorts she's got on are cut so high, you can see the tips of the pockets peeking out from underneath. It also doesn't go unnoticed that *she* hasn't gone unnoticed, the people that stand closest to her looking at her and snapping pictures of her with their phones.

I don't know what that shit's about, but I also don't fucking care.

"Ah, come on, babe—are you going to leave me hanging?"

"Is that who I think that is?" I hear JJ ask. I don't know if he's talking to me or Maddox, and I don't bother to find out.

In any case, Maddox doesn't miss a beat before he mutters, "Yup. Nora *fucking* Hampton. Fucking bitch."

Nora Hampton.

The girl who cheated on me after I refused to follow her to New York.

The girl who threw me out like I was trash for choosing M&M over Julliard.

Maddox has it right. She's a bitch.

"Sage," she says, coughing out an exasperated sigh as she tilts her head to the side. "It's been forever! Get me over this thing." She motions down to the metal barricade fence that stands between us. "Don't pretend like you don't know me."

I lift my eyebrows, folding my arms across my chest as I ask, "Who's pretending?"

"You know this guy?" asks Rex, appearing out of nowhere.

"Sure do," she answers, turning on her charm.

Rex holds out his hand and she doesn't hesitate to take it as he announces, "You're fine as hell, and you're coming with us."

Before I can utter a word of protest, she's over the fence, clinging to Rex's arm. As he begins to lead her toward our waiting vehicles, she looks back over her shoulder and smirks at me. Fucking *smirks*.

Shit.

We all pile into the two SUVs owned by Kings & Crowns, headed I don't even know where. Luckily, the one I end up in doesn't include Rex and Nora, which is why I feel free to ask, "What the fucking hell is she doing in Los Angeles?!"

"Who are you talking about?" asks Alex.

"His ex, Nora. We don't discuss the bitch," grumbles Maddox.

"Holy shit—Nora is here? What is she doing in L.A.?" asks Knox, temporarily distracted from the chick in his lap.

"Did you see the way people were looking at her?" JJ mutters, his focus zeroed in on his phone. "Oh, shit."

He turns the device, holding it up so that I can see the screen. On it is a picture of Nora. She's in a cut-off t-shirt and a pair of sweatpants that sit low around her hips; her hair pulled up into a high ponytail, but her face done up like she's about to go out. She's smiling wide, her arms folded and propped on the shoulders of some guy who's leaning to accommodate their height difference as he, too, smiles at the screen. They're surrounded by at least four other people, dressed in workout clothes, in a room that's unmistakably used for dance—the walls behind them made up of mirrors.

"What is this? What are you showing me?" I mutter, too annoyed by the sight of her to comprehend.

"According to this, she's a choreographer for one of those dance competition shows. She's about to shoot her third season. Apparently, she's pretty good."

I scoff, looking away from the screen and fixing my gaze straight ahead of me. "So she's a reality TV star. Fucking figures."

"You know why she's here, right?" Derrick asks, his voice calm and even, but dark and certain.

"Yeah," Knox jumps in, not missing a beat. "She's probably been hearing our shit everywhere, can't escape the truth that she was wrong about you, and now she wants back into your good graces."

"I'm thinking she wants *more* than his good grace, bro."

"Fat chance," I mumble, repulsed by the very idea.

"Wow," Alex murmurs. "Now I really wish someone would fill me in on this girl."

Maddox barks out a laugh before he tells her, "Let's just say, she created an animal that only Millie could tame."

It takes us almost an hour to arrive at our destination. When we climb out of the vehicle, we're standing in the middle of a huge wrap-around driveway in front of house that's got to be at least three times the size of the one the band stays in back home.

"Where *are* we?" Alex breathes, her head craned back to take in the structure before us.

"Hollywood Hills, little bit," says Lewis. He offers her his elbow in dramatic fashion, which she accepts, and then he nods at the rest of us as he explains, "Natalie

Woods is a friend of a friend. Try not to act too impressed, her ego doesn't need a feeding," he says coolly.

"Natalie Woods? As in *the* Natalie Woods? The actress?" gushes Alex as we begin to make our way to the front door.

"Did you get that out of your system?" Lewis chuckles.

"I make no promises."

When we enter the house, we find it filled with people and loud music. I swear, it looks like something straight out of a movie—mainly because half the people here *are* in movies. I try not to stare, like some nobody who took a wrong turn and ended up at the cool kid's table, but it's pretty fucking badass.

The main room has long, plush, black couches with zebra print throw pillows, and there's a gigantic leopard print rug under a big, round coffee table littered with various bottles of beer, glasses of wine, handles of liquor, and a few recreational drugs that appear to be up for grabs. Everyone seems to be pretty chill, lounging, talking—a couple people making out, but nothing out of control.

There are more people in the kitchen, their conversations louder and filled with more laughter—the kind that broadcasts exactly how intoxicated everyone is already. When we make our entrance, some offer no more than a glance or a chin lift; others—friends of Kings & Crowns—come and greet us, introducing themselves and striking up conversation while offering us a drink. I work the room, casually hopping from one conversation to another, actively working to keep as much distance between Nora and myself as possible.

An hour later, I've got a couple beers in my system and I'm starting to relax. I'm on the couch in another room—this one decorated in brown with cheetah and giraffe print accents—shooting the shit with Kent and some well known DJ I just met a few minutes ago. I'm so caught up in our conversation, I don't notice when Nora enters the room. When she plops her drunk ass in my lap, I go stock-still, sure that she's lost her fucking mind.

I can't help but notice her perfume as it wafts around me. It's exactly the same as it's always been. Not sweet and simple like the vanilla Millie always wears, but decadent and floral.

"You didn't think you'd be able to avoid me all night, did you? We've got some serious catching up to do, handsome."

"Get up," I mutter through clenched teeth.

She doesn't listen, but instead props her forehead against mine, speaking softly when she says, "Sage, don't be like this. It hurts my feelings. I haven't seen you in so long. The least you could do is *talk* to me. Then maybe later you could show me your tats. They're totally hot, by the way—I remember how you used to talk about how you wanted a bunch."

"'Sup, Nora? You know Sage?" asks Bones, the DJ who apparently knows the woman I want out of my goddamn lap.

"Hey, Bones!" She turns her gaze on him, flashing a grin before she drapes her arms around my neck and proclaims, "We go way back. We were high school sweethearts. Isn't it crazy how we've both ended up here? Oh, my god, Sage—you totally have to hear Bones do his thing. I swear, he makes me want to dance all night!"

"Nora—get the hell up," I grind out, two seconds away from standing and dropping her on her ass.

"This is what I'm talking about, man," Kent calls out, speaking around Bones. "While the cat's away, the mice will play."

I shake my head, trying to express that he's got it all wrong, and I'm about to say as much, but then Nora's got her phone out. With her arm still wrapped around my neck, she holds it up as she demands, "Come on—a selfie, for old time's sake."

Just as she's getting ready to take the picture, I grab hold of her waist and squeeze her—*hard*. I turn my head so that my lips graze her ear before I growl, "You need to get the *fuck* out of my lap. I've got a girl, and you are not worthy to eat from the ground she walks on. You don't know me—never did—and I sure as fuck don't need the shit you're feeding me right now. So get the fuck up before I drop you on your ass."

When I've finished, I remove my hands and wait for her next move. She turns her head slowly, her smile from before now *conniving*. "Okay, handsome," she practically purrs. "I get it. I left a bad taste in your mouth the last time we saw each other. But know this—I'm sweet as sugar, babe, and now that we're both here—exactly where we hoped we'd someday be—*destiny* has brought us back together. You'll see."

She stands from my lap, *fucking finally*, and saunters out of the room. I don't watch her go. I'm not the least bit interested in whatever game she's playing. She's clearly delusional.

"Shit," says Bones with a laugh. "She looks like trouble."

"No shit."

"And *you* look like you need a drink. Shots?"

The thought of drowning out the feeling of her anywhere on my body is enough to have me on my feet. "Fuck, yes. I'm down. Let's go."

SIXTEEN

Millicent

I TOSS AND TURN FOR half the night, feeling uncomfortable and lonely in the bed. It isn't until well past two in the morning that I fall into a deep sleep. It's eleven when I finally decide to get up and act like a functioning human being. I take Maestro out to do his business before I feed him. Then I eat before I shower, taking my time as I blow dry my hair, since I am in no particular hurry. When I'm finished, I lather my body in lotion and then pick out something casual to wear for the day. I slip into a pair of shorts—a new pair with the belly band already sewn in—and layer a couple tank tops over my chest, stretching them over my now spectacularly round middle. Admiring myself in the mirror, I'm proud to say I've finally reached that stage in my pregnancy where I look *pregnant* and not just questionably so and bloated.

"We're over halfway there, Jace," I say out loud, holding my bump. "Mommy can't wait to meet you."

Just like every time I say it out loud, or *anyone* for that matter, I get goosebumps when I refer to myself as *mommy*. It's who I am, it's who I long to be, but I can't help but think about how I don't even remember my own *mommy*. I remember my *mother*—but not mommy. I was quite young when she became *mom*. Then, soon after my father left, she was always my mother. Cold. Bitter. Resentful. With all my heart, I hope those are traits that I never adopt.

I want Jace to know how much I love him every day. I don't want him to question it; I don't want him to doubt it; I want him to be wholly aware of it. I want him to *exist* in it, his entire reality consisting of absolute truths, the most important of which is that he is loved beyond measure by his mother *and* his father. His mommy and his daddy.

"Speaking of daddy, he'll be home tomorrow," I tell my belly as I walk to the nightstand and grab my phone and current read. "I bet he'll be so excited to talk to you."

I make my way out into the living room and arrange myself until I'm comfortable on the couch, sitting with my legs crossed underneath me. I check my phone for messages, and when I go to my inbox, I find fifteen google alerts. It makes me smile, and I think about how excited Violet and Rose must have felt when they woke up and found these.

Just like Violet predicted, after seeing them on VH1 Monday night, the number of alerts for M&M have increased. They were on *The Late Late Show* with Kristin Prince last night, which has contributed to today's alerts as well. I missed the performance, having dozed off for a few minutes while waiting for it, but one of my alerts takes me to a YouTube video where I can watch. I set the volume extra loud, wanting Jace to be able to hear it, and I couldn't hide my grin even if I tried—which I don't.

After watching the clip twice, I peruse the other alerts.

Then I spot one that makes my heart skip a beat.

The gossip site, TMZ, has posted a short report about a tweet that's apparently getting a lot of buzz. That, in and of itself, isn't what makes my chest start to ache. It's the headline, which reads: *Nora Hampton and new sensation Sage McCoy? Give us more!* Below that, I skim the text that explains why the hell anyone gives a shit about *Nora Hampton*. Apparently, she's a TV personality people love. She's a choreographer known for her lyrical pieces that *"always touch on matters of the heart."* Now, TMZ is wondering if her heart has been *"stolen,"* or perhaps, *"according to the tweet, recaptured."*

I skip the rest of the text, scrolling down to see the tweet posted by @ twirlingnora95. In an instant, my lungs are *burning*, my nose is tingling, my eyes are stinging, and it feels as though the ground has fallen from beneath me. In the picture, captioned: *Reunited and it feels so GOOD!*, it looks like Nora is sitting in Sage's lap, her arm wrapped affectionately around his shoulders. She's smiling at the camera, but he isn't. His lips are pressed against her ear, as if he's whispering something intimate.

Something *intimate!*

I don't know a damn thing about *Nora Hampton*—TV personality/choreographer—but what I *do* know is that Sage was once in love with a girl named

Nora. It doesn't take a rocket scientist to figure out that this must be her. And considering I *am* a mathematician, I know the chances of this being anyone other than the girl he told me about out in the barren field, where bullshit is shed, are slim to none.

I don't realize I'm panting until my rapid breaths are the only sound that I hear. My heart is pounding, my mind is racing, and I'm *overwhelmed* with just how much I hurt. It's more than the ache in my chest. It's more than my heart. It's as if my whole body is in pain; as if Sage's betrayal has ravaged me heart, body, and *soul.*

I wail, unable to keep silent as my pain begins to multiply. I don't know how long I cry, weeping for myself—but even more so, sobbing for my son. My Jace. My sweet baby boy. I'm blinded by my emotions, unable to even *think* about any other explanation than the one I've just read. I can't imagine how Sage could explain away that picture. I can't figure out how this could be anything other than exactly what it appears to be.

I lose track of time as I wring myself dry. Just when I feel like perhaps I can take a breath, my phone starts ringing. I look down at the device, still clenched tightly in my hand, and see *Sage* lit up on the screen. I think about answering. My whole body trembles with rage as I imagine the things that I would scream at him. Then I start crying again, and I know that I'm in no state to tear into him. The truth is, I know I'd crumble if I heard his voice.

His voice. It's what drew me to him when we first met. It captivates me still. His rich, alluring, smooth tenor voice has brought me to my knees more times than I can count—and at my knees is *not* where I desire to be. So I ignore his call. And the next one. And the next one.

Then it dawns on me—*he'll be home tomorrow.* He won't have to call. He'll be here. Which means only one thing.

I can't be here when he gets back.

I don't even bother wiping my face when I get up, ignoring the *thud* of my book hitting the floor as I hurry to our room. I grab my suitcase, so recently stowed away at the bottom of the closet, and throw it onto the bed. I open it and start throwing clothes inside. I keep it simple, grabbing mostly sweatpants and t-shirts, a couple pairs of jeans, and shorts. I then race into the bathroom, grab my essentials, and hurry back to my bag before I toss them inside. Deeming myself ready as I need to be, I zip my suitcase closed and grab Maestro's leash. I don't bother packing any of his things, sure that I can send Violet or Rose back for it, if necessary.

When I have everything I need, I'm out the door—lugging my bag and Maestro with me. I'm out of breath by the time I sit down behind the wheel of my car. I look out at my apartment building, my lip trembling when I realize I have no idea when I'll be back. Of course it's not the building itself that I'll miss, but the hope that Sage would be walking up those stairs tomorrow. That hope is now gone—shattered into a million little pieces, just like my heart.

I take a deep breath, willing my tears not to fall, realizing that I can't worry about me. I can't worry about *my* heart or how Sage has broken the piece of me that he himself put back together. I can't afford to fall into despair. I have a child to worry about. I'm a mommy, and I aim to be a damn good one.

It takes me twenty minutes to reach my destination. It takes me another five to pull myself together enough to brave approaching the front door. When I ring the doorbell, I'm surprised when Rosemary answers. She takes one look at me and then her shoulders fall as she steps out onto the porch and wraps her arms around me.

"You saw," she whispers—a statement, not a question.

"I saw."

"Hey, Millie." Rose let's me go and I look behind her to see both Harry and Pepper filling the doorway, Sophia resting against Pepper's chest. Harry steps onto the porch as well, signaling to my bag before he takes it from my hand. "I'll get this. Come on in."

Sage

I CHECK THE TIME, confused why Millie isn't answering her phone. It's the middle of the afternoon. I know, since the baby, she's been known to nap here and there on her busy days, but she told me she didn't have anything going on today. She told me I could call any time. When I get her voicemail for the dozenth time, I start to worry.

What if something happened to her?

What if she fell?

What if something's wrong with the baby?

With my mind slowly filling with *what ifs*, I decide to call one of my sisters. I need someone to check on my girl to make sure she's all right. I dial Pepper first, thinking she's got the most experience, and stand to my feet as I listen to the phone ring. By the third ring, I'm pacing back and forth along the length of the bus, getting nervous glances from Derrick, JJ, and Alex, who are all camped out in front of the television playing a video game.

"Hello?"

"Pepper!" I exclaim, stopping dead in my tracks at the sound of her voice. "Hey, I need you to check on Millie for me. I've been trying her phone for hours, and I can't get an answer."

She hesitates—the silence before her reply loud as fuck—and then she says, "Millie and Jace are okay."

"What? How do you know that?"

"Millie's here. She's at the house, Sage."

"Oh-*kay*, well, she's not answering her phone. Put her on, I want to talk to her."

"Um…honey, I'm sorry, she doesn't want to speak to you."

I scowl out the window, seeing nothing as the highway scenery passes us by, too concerned about why the fuck my sister sounds so guarded and my girl doesn't want to speak to me.

"Pepper—what the hell? Put Millie on the phone."

She draws in a deep intake of air and lets it out in a slow sigh before she tells me, "You screwed up, babe." She lowers her voice as she continues. "I don't want to believe what we've seen. In fact, I *don't* believe it. I know you. I've seen you with Millie. I know how excited you are about Jace, and there's no way that you would throw all of that away for no reason. There is just *no way*. But Millie…Millie is twenty-one weeks pregnant. *Rational* is not exactly how I'd describe her, and you screwed up."

My stomach drops and my mind races as I try and figure out what she's talking about. When I come up short, I ask, "Pep—you're going to have to be more specific. I don't know what the fuck—"

"Nora. She knows you saw Nora last night."

All the air in my lungs just disappears, my jaw falling open as I replay her words in my mind.

"How—"

"I've got to go, Sage. Google your name with Nora's and you'll understand why your girlfriend is bursting into tears every ten minutes."

"What? Pepper! Wait—"

"Get your shit together, baby brother," she whispers through the phone. "You have *got* to fix this."

She hangs up before I can get in another word. Immediately, I open the google app and type in my name with Nora's, like Pepper said I should. What I find makes me sick to my stomach—hyperlink after hyperlink that lead to gossip about the two of us. Then, when I open the image she posted on Twitter, my rage is all consuming.

"*FUCK!*" I roar, chucking my phone blindly.

"Whoa, what the hell?" asks Maddox, his voice groggy from sleep as he pokes his head out of his bunk. I look at him, and all I want is to bash his face in. I want to hit someone. I want to break something.

I don't—a small voice reminding me that it won't solve my problems. My problems being that my girl, my Millicent, thinks I've betrayed her. Instead, I clench my fists and turn my back to Maddox, pacing across the length of the bus. With every step I take, I realize that Pepper is right. I didn't do *shit* with Nora last night—

but that's not what it looks like. That's not what it looks like at all. It's true that Millie should trust me, that she should know I would *never* walk out on her, but that picture—that goddamned picture.

"Ah! That fucking cunt!"

"Shit, Sage—calm down. Tell us what's wrong," says JJ as he stands to face me. He's holding his arms out as if I'm some sort of crazed animal he has to approach with care. Truth be told, I feel a little unhinged. He's not wrong to practice caution.

I don't answer him, though. I nod down at my phone, which landed at the front of the bus, just behind him, and then I continue pacing. I know when he's seen it because I hear him whisper a curse under his breath.

"Has Millie—?"

"Yes! Fucking *yes*—Millie has seen it. It's why she's not answering my calls. God!" I reach up and bury my fingers in my hair, my blood still boiling. "I thought Nora was a bitch before—I was wrong. Fucking hell, she did that shit on purpose. I told her—*shit*."

"Sage, take a breath. For real."

I hear Knox speak just as I turn around to pace back toward the bunks. I almost collide into his chest, but he doesn't move. I glare up at him and he shakes his head at me before he goes on to say, "Take a breath. I'm not fucking joking. We're on our way home. We'll be there tomorrow. You'll sort it out. This is you and Millie we're talking about. But you going on a rampage in Black Beauty? That's not going to fix shit. So, take a breath. You'll get your girl back tomorrow."

I stare up at him for a minute and then do as he says. I take a breath. Then I take another. As I start to calm down, I realize that while JJ is still standing behind me, everyone else is at Knox's back. I'm caged in, and they're not going to let me lose my shit—not here—so I take another breath.

"Tomorrow."

"Tomorrow," Knox repeats with a nod.

"I'll get my girl back tomorrow."

I TURN OFF THE SINK and dry my hands before looking over at the kitchen table. Millie is still sitting with a half eaten plate in front of her. It's been more than twenty-four hours since she showed up on our doorstep with Maestro and her suitcase, and she still hasn't found her appetite. She's stubborn, though. Like last night, I'm sure she won't let me take her plate until she's eaten every last bite—even if she ends up sitting there until after I put the boys down.

I admire her tenacity. She's eating for Jace's sake, not her own; and if I wasn't confident about it already, I'm certainly without a doubt now—she's going to be a fantastic mother, always putting that baby's needs before her own.

Turning my back to her, I reach for my phone and pull up the image that has her so upset. I stare at it, studying it, trying to pick it apart piece by piece. I see the same details I noticed last night as I obsessed over the image until Harold insisted I lay down and go to sleep. I spot the glint of mischief in Nora's eyes, past experience—hazy as it may be—reminding me that her brown eyes sparkle when she's happy, and what I see isn't happy. I also notice the way Sage's jaw is clenched, like he's angry, and whatever he's saying into her ear is in no way *romantic*. Knowing their history, I bet it wasn't even *kind*.

Nevertheless, I keep these details to myself, knowing that they will provide little to no reassurance to Millie. All she can see is Nora wrapped around her man and his lips on her ear. I love my brother. I believe him innocent, and I have faith that he can put things back to right—but I cannot deny that *this* looks bad. *Really* bad. Nora's caption makes it worse, and the media even more so.

Goodness—the media. My baby brother's name carries enough weight to be written about in the media. Right now, I find it both exciting and terrifying. Is this what his future looks like? Lies and misconceptions intruding upon his personal life?

"Babe," Harold murmurs softly just before his lips touch my temple. "What'd I tell you about that? Stop staring at that thing. It'll only make you crazy."

He puts his hand over my screen, covering up the image. I lower my phone and turn my head to look up at my handsome husband, offering him a small smile.

"You're right," I whisper. "I know. I just—I want to help."

"You're doing what you can. There's only so much you *can* do."

"Yeah." I sigh, wishing I could do more, and then peek around my husband to catch another glimpse of Millie. I find her looking right at us, tears rolling down her cheeks, and my heart breaks. "You have to go, honey. We're making her upset."

"How are—?"

"Just trust me on this one." I reach up and press a light kiss against his cheek before I say, "I love you. You're a wonderful, wonderful man—but scram."

He nods once, calling out as he leaves the kitchen, "Let me know if you need anything."

I look back at Millie just in time to see her sweep her fingers across her cheeks. She really is a beautiful woman. Everything about her is delicate, graceful, and elegant. Pregnancy looks great on her, and if I were a lesser woman, I'd be jealous of how well she's managed to keep her figure so far. Fortunately for me, I'm well aware that comparison is for the small at heart, and I harbor no jealousy. She's my sister, and I've come to care for her so much. All I want is for her to understand that Nora is not a threat.

She won't say much, so it's hard for me to combat any of her destructive thoughts, and she's still not taking Sage's calls. I'm certain only he can get through to her. She just needs to listen.

I'm pulled from my thoughts at the sound of a pounding fist against my front door. Millie gasps, sitting up straighter, instantly shaking her head at me. Silently, I try pleading with her, but she only shakes her head harder. I wait a second longer, hoping she'll change her mind as the pounding at the door grows even louder. When she doesn't, I turn to make my way to the front door. I arrive just as Harold opens it.

"Hey, Sage."

Sage looks right past Harold and straight at me.

"I'm taking my girl home. Where is she?"

"She's not ready. She doesn't want to speak to you right now."

"Bullshit!" he cries, moving to take a step inside. Harold blocks his entrance, causing Sage to lift his eyebrows in surprise. "Uh, Harry, I'm going to need you to get the fuck out of my way."

"I understand you're upset, I get it that you'd like to speak with Millie, but until she's ready, I can't let you do that."

"You've got to be kidding me," he grunts.

"She came here seeking shelter, and that's what we're giving her."

Sage's brow shifts, dipping into a deep scowl as he mutters, "I'm not some fucking wife-beater. Let me in." When Harold doesn't move, Sage looks over his shoulder at me. "Pepper?"

It kills me to say it, but I force the words out anyway. "Honey, she needs a little more time."

"Time? No! *No*, she does not need *time*—she needs the truth!" He growls before he yells, "Millicent! Millicent, baby, come on. Talk to me! Let me explain—it was nothing, doll face. Nothing happened! Nora is a liar and bitch, and that picture shouldn't have even been taken. I love you, baby—I wouldn't lie to you. Just—come on, Millie—come talk to me." When he gets no response, he smacks his hand against the doorframe before he moans, "Millie, baby, come on..."

We all stand in silence for a minute. Seeing the look of defeat on Sage's face almost makes me want to push Harold aside and drag Sage back to the kitchen, but I don't. Millie heard every word of his speech, I know she did, and she still hasn't shown herself. That's all the proof I need that she really, truly is not ready to discuss this with him.

"Sage," I whisper, stepping closer to the door.

"Don't," he mutters, taking a step back. "I don't want to hear it."

"Sage—"

"The next time I show up, I'm coming into the damn house and I'm taking my girl *home*. Just try and stop me."

Without another word, he turns on his heel and leaves.

SEVENTEEN

Sage

I DRIVE AROUND TOWN FOR AN hour. I don't want to go home. It's not home without Millie. She's the whole reason I'm in the building in the first place. I don't know where I'll sleep tonight, but it sure as fuck won't be in our bed. Not by myself.

I need to clear my head. I need to figure out how to make this better—how to make her hear me. This whole thing is so unfair, and it pisses me off. When Harry stood in front of the door, refusing to let me in, I thought I was going to lose it. The last twenty-four hours have been a nightmare. This was not supposed to be my homecoming. Nora came out of fucking *nowhere*. I was in her presence for *one night* and she managed to fuck shit up in two seconds.

As if my sub-conscious has taken the wheel, I find myself driving to Derrick's land. When I arrive, I put the top of my convertible down and I stretch out in the backseat, propping my feet up against the rim of the car. Looking up into the clear blue sky, the sun getting ready to set behind the mountains, my mind battles against itself. I keep going back and forth, being angry at Millie, being angry at myself—all the while being furious with Nora.

One second, I'm sure Millie is overreacting. She hasn't even given me a chance to explain. Hell, I shouldn't even have to explain. Millie's it for me—she knows that. We're in this together, no matter what. Especially with Jace on the way. I can't figure out how she could push me away like this.

Then the next second, I blame myself. Nora wouldn't have had a chance to snap the picture had I pushed her out of my lap the second she sat down. My attempt at avoiding a scene has caused more damage than a drunk girl on her ass at a party would have. And that picture—fuck—that picture looks shady as shit.

That line of thinking lasts just as long as the previous one, and then I'm back at being frustrated with Millie. It's a never ending cycle, one that's bound to drive me insane, so I do my best to let it go. Right here, right now, in the place where bullshit is shed, I let it go. All I can do is move forward. All I can do is remind my girl that she's just that—*mine*. Always.

I let my mind go blank, staring at the horizon as the sun paints the sky in shades of orange and red. When I reach up to shield my eyes from the bright light, I catch a glimpse of my right arm, my skin bare of any markings. I pull my hand away from my face and study my forearm as an idea comes to mind. I've barely thought it through before I'm pulling my phone from out of my pocket. I find the number to Generation Ink, dial, and wait impatiently for an answer.

"Generation Ink, this is Coder," he answers.

"Hey, Coder, is Trevor there?"

"Yeah. Can I tell him who's calling?"

"Tell him it's Sage McCoy."

"Sage! Shit, man, how the hell are ya? Don't answer that," he says with a chuckle. "I saw you on TV the other night—performing for Kristen Prince?"

"Yeah," I mumble, not in the mood to reminisce.

"You back in town? You should swing by the shop."

"Yeah, man, that's why I'm calling—was hoping Trevor could squeeze me in ASAP."

"For you, I think that can be arranged, my man. Here he is."

"Sage—the man who's going to make my art famous—what's up?" greets Trevor.

I chuckle in spite of myself, shaking my head. Trevor sure as shit doesn't need me making his art famous. He does that on his own—which is exactly why I refuse to get ink from anyone else. "I need some work done."

"It's what I'm here for. What do you want and when?"

"It's actually just a rough idea at the moment, but I trust you can make it work. And how about tonight?"

"Shit, I've got two appointments tonight. Hold on." I do as he says, listening as he shuffles around some papers. "You know what? If you don't mind me squeezing you in between the couple pieces I've got on my calendar, I'll fit you in. I've got someone coming in ten minutes—that shouldn't take me more than twenty—then I've got another at eight-thirty, also a small piece. We can do a quick consultation before my eight-thirty and I'll stay after close and get you inked. We talking something big, or—"

"Just my forearm. Maybe an hour, hour and a half."

"Come on down, man."

"You sure?"

"For Sage McCoy—fuck, yes."

Millicent

I MISS HIM. It's confusing. The pain is all mixed together now. It's indecipherable. With every beat of my heart, I feel his absence. I feel the distance between us, and it's cavernous. He's minutes away from me, and yet it is as if he's on a different continent. With every breath I take, my chest aches. It's as if there's a heavy weight pressing down on me, and that weight is the reality of the fact that three nights ago, *Nora Hampton* was all over Sage. She might be a liar and a bitch, as Sage proclaimed last night, but it doesn't change the fact that she was in his lap with her arm wrapped around him; it doesn't change the fact that as he spoke into her ear, she was able to smile for the camera; it doesn't change the fact that *something* happened.

This is my worst nightmare.

For that one moment in time, however long it was, Sage let me go.

And yet, I cannot help the way I feel drawn to him even now. Hearing him call out to me last night was almost unbearable. I wanted to go to him, to hear him out, but the thought of seeing his face and sifting through his excuses was too much. I don't know what I believe. I don't know what I feel. It's all so—*indecipherable.*

"Millie?" I look beside me at Pepper.

She's got Sophia strapped across her chest as we make another circle around the block. Our pace is slow, as we let Carter and Henley set our speed, the both of them holding onto Maestro's leash, but I don't mind. It feels nice to be in the sun, using my legs.

"Hmmm?" I hum in response.

"I know you're feeling a lot right now. I know that you're hesitant about speaking to my brother—and I get that. I really do. But you know Sage. He won't give up."

"Yeah," I murmur, looking away from her and down at the boys.

"I wish I could explain why I believe him innocent. I wish I could tell you all the reasons why I think that photo is b-u-l-l-s-h-i-t, but I know that it wouldn't mean a thing coming from me. He's my brother and I love him to death. I was also around after Nora. I know how he feels about her, and it's venomous. But I know this is his battle to fight. I know it's your trust in him that needs to be repaired. It's asking a lot, I know. I *know.*"

"It *is* a lot," I murmur. "I want to believe him, though. At least…I think I do."

"At this stage in your relationship, with Jace coming and the band taking off in a huge way, trust is *everything*. But Millie," she pauses, reaching over to grab my hand. I look over at her once more, her brown eyes waiting for me to meet her gaze. "He's going to mess up. *You're* going to mess up. That's life. Nobody is perfect. Trust me when I say, sticking it out for the long haul is often times painful. But it's also beautiful and full of love and totally worth it.

"I have learned so much putting up with Harry; and all the ways in which we have been forced to practice patience and forgiveness, it has made me a better mother, and definitely a better person. At the end of the day, I love him more than words can express, and I'd never choose to live life without him by my side.

"You and Sage, in the short time that you've known each other, have been through so much—you've built a foundation for a home. I think, deep down, you know that you're not even close to being over. It's why you're here, with us. And I'm happy to have you, but you can't keep hiding. You have to face him. You have to listen to him."

I give her fingers a squeeze but look away from her. She's right and I cannot deny it. I'm avoiding Sage. I'm angry and hurt. I'm sad and confused. My mind doesn't know what to believe, but my heart—the broken pieces are still in his hands. I can't ever get them back. I surrendered to him months ago, giving him all of me, and I can't take that back.

I don't want to, either.

I want the dream. I want it all. I'm not ready to give that up. I'm not ready to give *him* up.

I miss him.

"I miss him," I whisper, my voice shaky.

She lifts our hands and points a finger in front of us as she says, "He's right there."

I jerk my head in the direction she's pointing. In the Montgomery driveway, standing with his arms folded as he leans against his car, is Sage. The sight of him steals my breath. It's not just him, here, showing up without warning—it's him with his dark brown hair combed to the side and slicked back; it's his horn rimmed glasses framing his gorgeous icy blue eyes; it's the faded green, graphic t-shirt that hugs his chest, and the tattoos that scale from wrist to shoulder on his left arm; it's the way his blue jeans hang low on his hips and sculpt his legs; and it's those red Converse sneakers—his favorite pair.

It's *all* of him—every handsome and sexy inch of him.

I think of Jace and I wonder what color his eyes will be. I wonder what color his hair will be. I wonder if he'll look like his father. I hope he does.

The thought makes me stop, and I drop Pepper's hand, wrapping my arms around my belly as I try and keep myself together. I concentrate on my breathing, willing myself not to cry. I don't notice when Pepper and the kids leave my side, making their way back to the house. I don't notice as Sage leaves his car to close the distance between us. I don't notice that it's just the two of us until he pulls me into his arms and holds me tight.

With his lips pressed against my ear he mutters, "It's just you, doll. It's only you, baby. No one else. She took me by surprise, she sat in my lap, and I insisted she get up. When she didn't, I told her I was a taken man, that I wasn't interested in the shit she had to offer. That's when she took the picture. Everything about it is a lie."

I shake my head, ball my fists, and press against his abs. "She was all over you!" As I speak the words, its as if a dam has broken, and the sob that erupts from my throat is unstoppable. It makes me even more irritated, and I press against him again, but his hold is too strong, and he doesn't budge.

"I know. I know, doll face, and I'm sorry. I'm *so* sorry. Ask anyone—I was pissed she was even *there!* The last thing I wanted was for her to touch me. I swear to you, Millie."

"We're not having sex, and I'm only getting bigger, and she—"

"Whoa, *what?!*" he exclaims, pulling away from me. He brings one hand to the side of my neck, lifting my chin with the other until I'm looking right at him. "No. *No.* Fuck no! I do *not* want her. Baby," he groans the last word, moving to hold each side of my face.

It's then that I notice something is different about him. My eyes flicker to the dark spot on the inside of his right forearm, and I jerk away, grabbing hold of his elbow and his wrist so that I can see his new ink. It's a tree—a big, thick, *old* tree. Just above his hand, the roots of the tree look as though they're imbedded in his skin, as if the life source of the tree runs through his veins. The trunk takes up almost half of the length of his forearm, and then there are six thick branches that span across the rest of his forearm, smaller twigs growing off of them. There are no leaves, as if the tree is going through a winter season. The ink is so dark brown that it could easily be mistaken for black. It looks masculine and haunted and beautiful—but it also looks unfinished. Only one of the six branches is filled in. When I take a closer look, I suck in a quiet gasp as I notice a name hidden in the bark of the branch.

Hesitantly, I let go of his wrist and trace my finger over Jace's name. Now that I know it's there, I can see it as clear as day. Then Sage takes hold of my hand, gently moving my fingers down to the trunk. I follow our movements, all the air rushing out of me when I see *Millicent* in the grooves of the base of the tree. On my next inhale, it's as if, instantly, my heart has been made whole again.

"It's our family tree, Millie. We're just getting started, doll face."

I peek up at him from beneath my lashes, at a loss for words, and then my eyes drift back to the unfinished piece. It's a little intimidating, my name permanently etched onto his skin—but his name is written on my soul, so I suppose it's no different.

I graze my fingers over the five unfinished branches and a small laugh bubbles out of me. "Six? We're going to have six kids? That's…a lot."

He laughs softly, reaching up to hold my face once more as he says, "We'll have as many as you want, Millicent."

I smile at him, the hope I thought was gone now blossoming bigger than ever before. "Maybe three."

"At least four," he counters.

My heart swells as I reply, "Okay."

When he lowers his face so that his lips are a breath away from mine, my stomach starts to tingle and the back of my neck grows warm. He does this to me—only Sage. Always Sage.

"Don't let me go," I whisper, reaching up to grab hold of his wrists. I squeeze him tight as I repeat, "Don't let me go again."

"I never let you go, doll face—and I never will."

He kisses me, his lips gentle but his intentions sure, and I kiss him right back.

I need a taste.

Pressing myself up on my tiptoes, I circle my arms around his neck, parting my lips in invitation. He drops a hand down onto my back, burying his fingers in my hair with the other as his tongue makes contact with mine. The sensation goes straight through me, causing a surge of longing that rushes down between my legs. It's a feeling I haven't had in what feels like *ages*. Wanting to feel it again, I open my mouth wider, moaning when Sage responds in kind. His grunt makes my toes curl, and I'm suddenly breathless, desperate, and wet.

I'm wet!

"Baby, I'm wet," I murmur into his mouth, gripping a fistful of the shirt at his back.

"What?" he asks, trying to pull away.

I yank him closer, thrusting my tongue deep into his mouth as my pussy pulses with an urgent sense of desire. "Oh, my god—I need you to fuck me."

"Now?"

"Yes! I want you." I look into his eyes and grin, because I can't help myself, and then explain, "I haven't felt this way since New York. Do you know how long it's been since—"

"You're kidding, right?" he chuckles, a smirk pulling at his lips. "Come on."

He grabs my hand and walks me straight to the car. As he guides me down into the seat, I remember that Maestro and all of my things are still inside. I start to tell him as much, but he closes the door, leans over the side, and kisses me hard.

"I'm going to fuck you until you're exhausted and then I'll come back for your shit. Deal?"

I squeeze my legs together, biting my lips as I offer him a nod. I can't deny his impatience. I feel it, too. And when he hops over the driver's side door and slides down into his seat, I giggle, feeling way happier than I thought possible after the last two days. Then he rips his Audi out of the driveway and speeds down the street, the wind blowing my hair back, and my giggle is gone. I watch him drive, and I'm transported back in time to the first night we met. I remember wanting him this badly then, riding through the night with the top down. I was drunk, but I knew only he would satisfy my needs. Now, I'm feeling a different kind of high—the depths of my pain from yesterday now flipped on their head.

I replay Pepper's words of wisdom from just a few minutes ago. In this moment, I know that in the act of forgiveness is the gift of peace. Sage and I need to talk about how we're going to handle situations like this in the future. I'm not naïve. Celebrities and scandal seem to walk hand in hand, and my sexy rocker and I have to be smart. But right now, I choose to bask in the beauty of forgiveness—and the return of my libido.

Sage is mine. I was silly to think otherwise; and if I ever have any doubt, all I have to do is look on his arm. He's been branded. He's mine forevermore.

Sage

I DRIVE LIKE A bat out of hell for all of about two minutes, and then I realize *who* I'm driving and reluctantly slow down. At least a little. Needless to say, the thought of being inside of my girl after *weeks* of nothing but the occasional blow job has me a little excited. I'm hard the entire way home just thinking about seeing Millie naked.

When I finally pull into the parking lot, I can hear Millie's breath quicken. Turning off the car, I don't even bother putting the top on before I jump out and hurry around to the passenger side to help her out. As soon as she's on her feet, she reaches up and curls a hand around the back of my neck, pulling me down for a kiss. She moves her lips urgently, and my dick twitches, fully aware of what we're about to enjoy.

"I'd run up those stairs if I could," she whispers. "I swear, every time you moved that gear shift, I got turned on even more."

"You still wet for me, gorgeous?"

"Get me upstairs and find out for yourself," she challenges.

Without any hesitation, I bend down and scoop her into my arms. She's heavier than normal, but nothing I can't handle, and I'm spurred on knowing I don't have the patience to walk any slower than I have to. I set her on her feet only after we've made it to the front door. She stands behind me, her hands rubbing up and down my back as I unlock the the barrier before us. As soon as we're inside, I lock us in, caging my girl against the wall as I lower my lips to hers.

I kiss her greedily, and she returns my fervor with her own. We use our tongues liberally, making our exchange wet and sloppy. When she moans, gripping my shirt into her fists, I thrust my hips, rubbing my erection against her hip.

"*Sage*," she sighs, tugging on my shirt as if to beckon me closer.

I trail kisses along her cheek and down her neck, licking my way back up as I lift her shirt in search of the top of her shorts. When I slip my fingers under the high waistband, descending down into her panties, she spreads her legs in invitation.

"Jesus—*fuck*," I growl, my fingers soaked after one swipe through the seam of her pussy. She whimpers and my patience vanishes. "I need you *now*."

She looks up at me, her gorgeous dark green eyes hooded in lust, her voice airy as she asks, "What are you waiting for?"

She barely gets her words out before I begin stripping her clothes off. Her shirt and her bra are the first to go. Then I take her by the hips and position her behind the couch. When I yank her shorts and panties around her ankles, she cries out in surprise, reaching out to hold onto the back of the couch. I drop my jeans and my boxers, not even bothering to speak a word of warning before I line us up and ram myself all the way inside of her.

"Sage!" she screams, arching her back as she pushes her ass against me.

I pause for just a second, needing to regain full control. She feels so good wrapped around me, so tight, I can barely breathe. She's so wet and warm, and I know I'm not going to last long before I lose myself.

I pull almost all the way out before I slam back inside of her, and she gasps. On my third stroke, I grab a fistful of hair and tug lightly. She arches her back a little more, freeing a deep, guttural groan as I thrust in and out of her at this new angle.

"You feel so good. God, Sage—you fit just right, baby. I need more—faster! Harder!"

I don't stop rocking my hips steadily as I ask, "Are you sure?"

"Please! Fuck me, baby—*harder*."

I tighten my grip in her hair, increasing my speed as I pound into her with more force. I grip her hip, holding her steady, clenching my jaw as I try and keep my shit together. She feels incredible—*too* incredible—and I've missed this. *Fuck*, I've *craved* this.

When I tug on her hair again, causing her to bend a little more, she sucks in a sharp breath before she starts to tremble. Suddenly, the noises coming from her mouth are incomprehensible. Then, without warning, her pussy clamps down *hard* around my dick. I manage one more thrust, groaning loudly as I shove myself so far up her cunt, my balls are begging for entrance as I spill my release inside of her.

"Sage, baby," she whispers seconds before her legs give out.

I catch her, wrapping one arm around the front of her hips, the other secured beneath her tits. We lose our connection as my dick slips out of her, and I miss her warmth immediately.

"That was…that was…"

"Fucking *awesome*," I insist.

She giggles softly, nodding as she grabs hold of my arms and leans back against me, resting her head on my shoulder. "Yeah. Fucking awesome." We stand like this for a couple minutes, neither of us speaking as we both work to catch our breath. Then, twisting her head to look up at me, Millie asks, "Again?"

I smack a kiss against her lips before I answer, "You bet your sweet, little ass."

EIGHTEEN

Sage

After I fuck Millie on her feet, I make love to her in bed before she passes out. I don't bother with a shower, content with the smell of her coating my body as I leave the apartment to head back to the Montgomery house. I'm only there long enough to grab Millie's bag and assure Pepper that we're good. With some major plans in the works for the next couple of days, I ask if she'd be all right with keeping Maestro for a little bit, and she agrees. Shortly after, I'm back in my car and headed for home.

Millie's still asleep when I arrive, which is fine with me. As I enter the bedroom and spot her naked body resting on her side, the sheets resting low around her hips, her hands resting under her chin, her bent arms hiding her breasts, her round belly on full display, I stop and stare for a moment. She's fucking perfect, her body changing as my son grows inside of her. Shaking my head, I wonder how she could have ever thought I would ever want someone other than her.

I abandon her bag and start to rifle through mine. I toss a bunch of it into the laundry, but after a smell test, I set a couple things aside, one of which is the lightweight blue button-up Millie brought me when she joined us on tour. She told me she wanted to see how it made my eyes pop when I wore it; needless to say, she was pleased with the combination, which is why it makes its way back into my smallest bag.

Assuming I've packed plenty for our short trip, I head to the closet and start sifting through Millie's things. Knowing my girl, she had laundry done the day after she got back, all her clothes put away neatly shortly there after. When I find a couple things I recognize from her time on tour, I smile and count myself lucky. These days, I don't really know what she'll feel comfortable in and what she won't, but there are a couple things she wore repeatedly while on the road that I'm sure to pack now. One is a short, pink dress that hugs her all over, making her tits look *fantastic*; the other is another short dress, this one loose, light blue, and covered in some sort of floral design. Spotting the sandals I see her wearing all the time, I toss those in the bag too. Then I go through what she grabbed when she went to Pepper's, stuffing a couple items and all of her personal hygiene things into the one bag before zipping it closed.

When we're all packed, I print out our boarding passes and check the time. It's almost five, and I know we're going to have to leave soon, so I make my way to the bed and sit beside her. I prop myself up over her, placing a hand on either side of her head as I kiss my way across her cheek to her lips. When I stick my tongue out and run it across her bottom lip, she inhales deeply and turns toward me. I smile as she immediately wraps her hands around the back of my neck, keeping me close as she opens her mouth and invites me to kiss her deeper.

Fuck, yes. My girl is back, all right.

"Sorry, doll, you're going to have to hold that thought until later," I tell her, propping my forehead against hers.

"Why?"

"We've got a plane to catch."

She tilts her head, pressing it further into the pillow as she looks up at me in confusion. "What?"

"A plane. We're getting out of here for a couple days, just you and me."

"We are?" she asks, raising her eyebrows in surprise.

"Yup."

Her eyes narrow into slits as she asks, "Where are we going?"

I grin, smacking a kiss against her lips before I reply, "Vegas."

"Sage—we were just in Vegas; why would we—?"

My smile fades and I push myself up on my arms so that I'm propped above her higher. I gaze down at her for a moment, sure that the idea I got when I was under Trevor's needle was a good one. Even more so, a *necessary* one. I want Millie tied to me in every way.

"Sage?" she whispers cautiously as I reach up and tuck some of her hair behind her ear.

"Wasn't quite sure what shit was going through your head the last couple of days, baby doll. You wouldn't talk to me. The last time you wouldn't talk to me..."

I shake my head, wishing not to remember what that hell felt like, our most recent nightmare more than enough to bear. "Told you in New York that if you tried to break up with me, I'd marry you. Well, now I'm going to marry you just in case."

"Wh—what?"

"Our plane leaves in three hours. You've got time to hop in the shower if you want."

"Sage—"

"If you're hungry, we'll grab something on the way to the airport."

"Wait, Sage—"

"What, doll?"

"Just..." She takes a deep breath before she insists, "*Wait.*"

"Don't want to wait, doll face. Everything's happening so fucking fast these days, I feel like every time I blink, something else pops up. Mostly good, sometimes bad—but it won't stop, doll. We're moving full speed ahead, and we can't get off this ride. This is our chance, Millie. Marry me."

I count the seconds that tick by as she stares at me without a word. I make it to fifteen before she whispers, "Okay."

"Yeah?" I ask, my grin returning.

"Yeah, baby—let's get married."

Millicent

I SHOWER QUICKLY, deciding not to rewash my hair, and then have just enough time to shove some food into my mouth before Sage is hurrying us out the door. I frown in concern when I realize he's only got one bag over his shoulder, wondering what, exactly, he's packed. Looking down at my outfit of jeans and one of Sage's old, worn Mountains & Men t-shirts, I fear *this* is how I'll be marrying Sage.

At least my hair won't be wet.

We board the plane an hour after we arrive at the airport, and as I fasten my seatbelt across my lap, I question if what we're doing is slightly insane. Sage and I have talked about being married almost as much as we had talked about having kids, which basically means we've never seriously discussed it. In New York, on the set of *The Late Show*, I asked him if he'd meant what he said about marrying me, and all he'd told me in reply was that if I wanted to get married, we would. That's the last we talked about it.

He's right. Everything is happening so fast lately. The only time things seem to be moving along *slowly* is when we're miles and miles apart from each other. Even then, things were still going on with the band. We're halfway through the year and they've accomplished so much already; not to mention the fact that I'm over halfway through this pregnancy. Just as he told me a couple hours ago in bed, there's no getting off this ride. Not now.

I look over at Sage when he wraps his hand around mine, giving my fingers a squeeze. When our gazes align, he winks at me, and I can't help but smile. Suddenly, I understand that we're not insane, we're spontaneous. Millicent Tatiana Valentine is *not* spontaneous. I like to have a plan. I feel most comfortable when there's some sort of structure or order around me—but Sage has a way of making me step outside of my boundaries. Since the very beginning, he's challenged me to follow my heart.

Since the very beginning, my heart has wanted *him*.

I tricked myself into believing it was all just about *phenomenal* sex. I was lying to myself. The first time he entered my body, I knew my life had changed. Now, almost a year later, the man at my side, the child in my womb, and the wholeness of my heart are proof that I was wrong to believe that we could ever have been summed up to just great, earth-shatteringly amazing sex.

In a matter of *hours*, I'll be Millicent Tatiana McCoy, and as I gaze at my rock star—the man who burns blue—I feel no fear, no doubt, and no regret. I want to do this. I want to do this *now*. I don't want to wait, either. I belong to Sage. *His* is the name that I should bear, for I've never belonged to Christopher Valentine. Not really. But Sage…

"I love you so much," I whisper, leaning toward him and resting my chin on his shoulder.

"I love you, too, gorgeous," he mutters, running his nose down the length of mine.

I kiss his lips softly and then turn my head to rest it against him as I let my eyes fall closed. I'm asleep before we're in the air.

Our flight is just under two hours and, fortunately, I sleep the entire way. By the time we arrive at the hotel, it's after ten thirty. While I'd like to think that the excitement of the occasion and our location would have been enough to keep me awake, I don't think Jace would have given two shits. But after two naps, I'm currently not lacking in energy. However, I am starting to rethink whether or not Sage might be insane.

"The MGM?" I ask, gaping at him as we pull in front of the entrance.

"Your groom got paid, baby," he says, leaning over to kiss me. "I can spoil my bride for a couple nights." He doesn't say another word before he's climbing out of the cab, reaching his hand in to help me step out. I scoot toward the open door and place my hand in his before I join him, still incredibly surprised that *this* is where we'll be staying.

I adjust my purse on my shoulder and then rest my hand over my belly as Sage leads me inside. My eyes are everywhere, taking in the grandiose lobby. I barely pay attention as he checks us in, and then we're headed for the elevators.

"I say, we change really quick and then find ourselves a chapel."

His suggestion grabs my attention and I can't help but chuckle. He makes it sound so casual, so simple. In a way, it is. For me, with no father to walk me down the aisle, and no mother to plan such an event like this, I never dreamed of a wedding. Now that I'm about to have one—potentially in jeans and a t-shirt, depending on what I find in Sage's bag—I decide that this is just right.

Well, almost.

"Baby, who knows that we're here?" I ask as we enter the elevator.

He hits the button for the twenty-second floor before sliding his arm around my waist and pulling me into his side.

"Nobody."

I tilt my head back and stare at him with wide eyes. "*Nobody?* You didn't tell one person?"

"I just decided last night that we were coming. I had to get shit planned and then I had to make up with my girl. Didn't really have a whole lot of time to tell everyone."

"Oh, my god—your family is going to freak."

He grins at me before he admits, "Yeah. Probably."

"Not *probably*, Sage. Rosemary might have a coronary. Pepper will—oh, shit—what will your mom say?"

"I'm the wildcard, remember? Pepper had a big wedding, there's no doubt in my mind Rosy will, too. Two weddings is enough. They'll get over it."

"But—"

He cuts me off with a kiss, his lips crashing against mine hard before he forces his tongue into my mouth. The second it grazes over mine, a flicker of desire sparks between my legs. I swear, it's as if my body is making up for lost time. One kiss, and my pussy starts to get ideas.

"You changing your mind, doll face?" he asks when he pulls away, his lips still close enough to graze mine.

"No," I barely manage.

"Good."

He kisses me once more and then the elevator chimes, announcing our arrival to our floor. With his arm still around my waist, he guides me out of the car and then we find our way to our room. Once inside, I'm *positive* that Sage is insane. It's not a particularly large room, just big enough to house a bathroom, a king size bed, a desk, and a sofa—but the *view!* The floor to ceiling windows that make up the wall behind the couch looks out over the strip. The bright lights of the city look beautiful from here, and I can't stop my feet from taking me across the room so that I can get a better look.

"Sage," I murmur, my gaze still fixed out the window. "This is too much."

"Doll face?" He comes up behind me, resting his chin on my shoulder as he rests his hands around my belly. "This will soon be nothing. Just wait and see. Now, come on. Let's get dressed."

I draw in a deep breath, offering him a nod before I turn to face the room. He's got the bag on the bed, and I go to stand beside him as he opens it. When I spot two of my favorite new dresses inside, relief washes over me. I pull out the blueish teal one with three-quarter length sleeves; it cinches below my breasts, and the fabric is covered in simple, pretty floral accents. I start to take out the other one, but then I notice Sage has got a blue shirt in his hands. Instantly, my mind is made up, and I decide to wear the outfit that matches my groom.

After I dress, I head to the bathroom to try and do something with my face. I don't have much, but a little eyeliner and a bit of lip-gloss makes me feel like I tried. I then move onto my hair. All I have is the hair tie around my wrist, but I make do. I part my hair, braid two Dutch-braids, and twist the ends together to form a sort of knot that I hold together with the hair tie. I comb my fingers through the bottom half of my hair, which I've left loose, and then take one last look at myself in the mirror.

"You look perfect, baby."

I jump and then turn to see Sage in the doorway. He's in a pair of fitted, black jeans. His blue button-up is loose at the collar, and his sleeves are rolled and pushed over his elbows, leaving his tatted arms on display. He's got on his black Converse sneakers, and I love the contrast of his dark bottoms against his light top.

"You, too," I reply with a smile.

"You ready?"

"Yes."

"Let's get hitched."

NINETEEN

Sage

WHILE MILLIE WAS GETTING ready, I googled twenty-four-hour chapels. I found one just a fifteen-minute drive from where we are. As we ride down the elevator, I squeeze Millie's hand each time it hits me that she'll be my *wife* before the stroke of midnight. When the elevator chimes, announcing our arrival at the lobby, *she* squeezes *my* hand. I smile over at her and she wraps her free hand around my bicep, leaning into me as we step out of the car. I'm not looking ahead of me, so I don't notice that someone is about to board the elevator, and I accidently bump my shoulder against his.

"Sorry, I—" I start to apologize, and then lose all my words when I realize who I've just bumped shoulders with.

"Don't worry about it," he says in a heavy southern accent, dipping his chin as he looks at me. I'm still staring at him, shocked that this is the second time we've run into each other at an elevator, when he furrows his brow and asks, "Hey, have we met?"

"Uh, no. No, we haven't. Um—a few weeks ago, we were both at the VH1 studio."

He squints at me, turning his back to the elevator as the doors close. "You're in a band." A smile breaks out across his face as if he's suddenly remembered something. "Mountains-n-Men, right?"

"Holy shit," I say as I cough out a laugh. "You've heard of my band?" I turn my gaze to Millie and whisper, "Fucking Ashley Hicks has heard of my band."

"Music is my business. Kinda hard to ignore the buzz y'all are creatin'," he says, earning back my attention.

I shake my head—my mind *blown*.

"Ashley," he says, holding out his hand. I start to let go of Millie in order to return his gesture, but he notices and immediately extends his opposite hand. "See you're holdin' on to some precious cargo," he explains, offering Millie a wink.

"I'm Sage. This is my girlfriend, Millie."

"Nice to meet, y'all."

"I—I can't believe I'm officially meeting you. Here. Now. Knox and Maddox are going to lose their shit when they hear about this."

He chuckles, reaching up to scratch the back of his neck as he asks, "Friends of yours?"

"Guitarists in the band. They've been following you for a while. We heard you're working on a solo project?"

"That's right."

"Congratulations, that's really awesome."

"We'll see how it turns out," he says with a nonchalant shrug. "Anyway, I'm sorry, y'all. I don't mean to keep you from your plans."

"We're just going to get married, is all," Millie replies teasingly.

Ashley's eyebrows shoot up as he asks, "No joke?"

"No joke," I answer.

"Now *that's* awesome. Congratulations! Where you headed?"

I look down at Millie with a smirk before I tell him, "The Little White Chapel. It's a few minutes from here."

"Do you guys have a car?"

"I was just going to get a cab," I reply with a shrug.

He reaches up and runs his fingers through his hair, studying us for a second before he says, "I know we just met and all, but I'm guessin', since you're about to get married in Vegas, you probably wouldn't mind my asking if you wanted a ride? I've got a car with the hotel. I could save y'all the trouble of a cab if you don't mind me taggin' along."

I have to concentrate to keep my jaw from falling open at his suggestion.

"Actually, that could be nice. I mean—having a witness who knows more than *nothing* about us," Millie says hesitantly, looking up at me.

"You don't, um—you don't have any other plans?" I ask.

"You'd actually be savin' me from the plans I'm tryin' to escape at the moment."

"Well…*shit*. Okay. Sure!"

"All right. Let me just make a quick call; the car will meet us out front."

As he takes out his phone, he starts heading through the lobby to the valet drop-off. Millie and I follow behind him, and it's then that I notice Ashley isn't alone. By the looks of the big dude walking with us, I'd guess he's some sort of security for Ashley.

"Oh, sorry," says Ashley, turning to speak over his shoulder. As if he's read my mind he says, "Y'all, this is my guard, Leo. He doesn't talk much," he adds with a teasing grin.

I don't know what the smile is about, as Leo doesn't offer us anything but a nod, proving Ashley's point, but I don't mention it. Who the fuck cares? Ashley Hicks is about to be a witness at my wedding! Fucking *un*real.

Five minutes after Ashley hangs up the phone, a Bentley pulls up right in front of us. A *Bentley*, with four seats in the back. Leo takes the passenger seat up front, and when the valet opens the back door for us, Ashely insists that Millie climb in first. When we're all in, Ashley gives instructions to the driver who nods before we're on our way.

"So, you know why we're here. Why are you? Are you playing somewhere?" I ask, breaking the silence.

"Actually, a friend o'mine, it's his birthday. A few of us came out for the fight last night."

"Nice."

"Yeah, it was a good time. They're out gamblin' now, but that's never really been my thing."

For a second, no one speaks, and then Millie sucks in a breath and reaches for my hand, pressing it against the side of her belly. Jace moves again, and I grin at my girl. It's the first time I've gotten to feel him in a while, but I'm sure it'll never get old.

"If you don't mind my askin', boy or girl?"

Millie and I both look over at Ashley and I can hear the smile in Millie's voice when she responds, "Boy. His name is Jace."

"When are you due?"

"November." He nods and Millie asks, "Do you have any kids?"

"Not yet. Haven't found me a lady I like that much to make one with. But one day, hopefully. Not in any rush."

He answers casually, but I can't help but read into his last comment. His name, all on its own, is the evidence of a life dedicated to his craft. Like he said before, music is his business. He's been around for a few years. Even though he's just now branching out on his own, he's talented enough to have made a name for himself playing in the background for people who don't trust anyone else to deliver the sound they want. That said, he's basically at a level I hope to be at one day, and yet he's *in no rush* to start a family. I can't help but wonder why.

Kent's warning about leaving Millie behind was bullshit. I know that. I'm not going anywhere without her; but it makes me question if my *family* will force me to change my tactics. Somehow I know, I'd be a fool to let this once in a lifetime opportunity pass me by. I'd be a fool to not ask for a little advice from a guy who is obviously kind, generous, and completely down to earth. So I buck up the courage to speak.

"We just finished touring with Kings & Crowns on their stateside *Royalty Unleashed Tour*."

"Right, I heard that. I've never met them, but I hear they're pretty cool."

"Yeah, they are. Actually—Kent—" I start and then I stop, looking over at Millie. I never told her this before, and the last thing I want is for her to feel like I'm getting cold feet minutes away from the alter. I take her hand and lace my fingers with hers before I go on to say, "Kent offered me some advice. Told me to leave my family on the sidelines while I pursued my career. He told me that they'd hold me back if I kept them too close. Is that why you're in no rush?"

"Absolutely not," he answers without hesitation, shaking his head at me. He opens his mouth to speak and then shakes his head again, sucking in a breath before he says, "You know, I believe the company you keep decides where you're goin'. Now I don't know much about you, but I reckon the pretty lady at your side is far from a hindrance."

"Not at all," I confirm.

"There are no rules, Sage. Don't let anyone trick you into believin' they've got a formula to success. Hard work—everyone who has ever made it has put in the work. Everythin' else? Just depends on who you are, I suppose."

"Yeah. I agree. Thanks."

"Don't mention it." As soon as the words are out of his mouth, the car stops. We all look out the window and he chuckles before he says, "Y'all ready for this?"

I look back at Millie before I reply, "Fuck, yes."

Millicent

Sage and I order our wedding ceremony *a la carte*, which is so ridiculous, I can't help but laugh. Nevertheless, the little chapel that we choose, as there were five for us to pick from, is surprisingly appropriate. Admittedly, it's a bit gaudy for my tastes, but it *is* Vegas—though, I adamantly refused to be married by Elvis, which might have disappointed Sage a little bit. However, while I haven't ever really dreamed of this day, I *do* have *some* standards.

Ashley surprises me when he announces that he would like to purchase my bouquet. At first I politely refuse, but when he insists, I choose a bundle of pink roses. Then, he surprises me again when he offers to walk me down the aisle; this time, when I thank him and then decline, he doesn't press. For some reason, it just doesn't seem right to let a stranger walk me down the aisle. As kind and generous and *handsome* as he is, Ashley's been a part of mine and Sage's journey for all of a half an hour. The steps I take toward my groom have always been mine to take, and mine alone.

When the music begins to play and I start to make my way toward Sage, my belly flutters with nervous excitement. It all feels so surreal, so fast, and yet so *right*. Standing in front of him now, I realize that he's a dream I never really knew that I had. Yes, I want him and I want our family and I want *everything* with him—but in this moment, listening to him recite his vows, it dawns on me that even if all I ever got was him, he'd make me happier than I ever thought I could be. All my life, I have been taught that men always leave; but here and now, *my man* is promising me, in front God and Ashley Hicks, that in good times and in bad, and even until death, he will never leave me. That, all on its own, is a dream come true.

Considering the way this day has turned out, I shouldn't be surprised that when the officiant of our ceremony asks for the rings, Sage winks at me before reaching into his pocket. He places them on the book the elderly man is holding, and I see a plain, thin, rose gold band for me, and a thick, black ring with beveled edges for him. I barely hear the officiant as I look back at Sage, my eyes filling with tears. When it's his turn to slide the ring on my finger, my heart skips a beat.

"I know it's not much. Actually, it's less than that," he starts to say as he twists it around my finger. "But I'll get you something better when—"

"No, it's perfect," I tell him, squeezing his fingers. "I love it." And I do. It's understated and simple, but I swear it makes my whole hand look elegant and pretty.

I take my turn repeating the phrases spoken to me as I slide Sage's ring on his finger, and then, before I know it, it's over. Sage smiles at me and then takes hold of my face, bringing his mouth to mine. Before he kisses me, he whispers, "I love you, Millicent McCoy."

The sound that spills from my lips and through his as he kisses me is a mix between a giggle and a whimper. Hearing my name for the first time makes me overwhelmingly happy, and as I kiss my husband for the first time, I make sure he knows it. When his hands move from my face, sliding back around the nape of my neck and into my hair, I circle my arms around his waist. His kiss is slow and deep and *languorous*, and I melt against him, sure that I could stay in this moment forever and never tire of it.

I don't know how long my lips are locked with Sage's, only that his spread into a grin when Ashley hollers, "Hot damn!" A part of me wonders if I should be embarrassed, but I'm not. As Sage finally pulls away, I have to stop myself from leaning in for more.

Our officiant clears his throat, smirking at us when we turn to face him, and then he leads us to a nearby table. He waves Ashley over and the four of us sign the marriage license declaring by law that I really am Mrs. McCoy.

"Holy shit," I breathe, setting aside the pen. Biting my lip, I look up at Sage and then I murmur, "We're married."

"Here, let me get a picture for y'all," says Ashley, pulling out his phone.

Sage wraps his arm around my waist, tucking me into his side, and I press my left hand against his chest as we smile for the picture. The nice elderly man who married us offers to take a picture of all three of us, and Ashley—who is twice the size of Sage in bulk, and a couple inches taller, rests his arm around my husband, as if we've all been friends forever. The smile on Sage's face turns a little goofy, and it makes me grin just as the picture is taken.

We thank the officiant and then, just after midnight, we make our way back out to the car. By the time we arrive at the hotel, Ashley and Sage have exchanged numbers and Sage is in possession of our wedding photos.

"Are you sure I can't buy y'all a drink?" asks Ashley as we enter the lobby.

"Ashley, you've already done so much."

"Rain check?" Sage asks, giving my hand a squeeze.

"For when the lady can have a real drink," he says with a nod and a wink.

"Thank you, again, for everything," I murmur, truly hoping that we'll meet again.

"It was my pleasure, darlin'."

He gets a call as we approach the elevators and waves at us when we board the next available car. We both wave at Leo, and he simply dips his chin in return. Sage and I are not alone as we ride up to our floor, but the sweet way he rubs his hand around my lower back makes me anxious for the moment that we *are*. When we've reached the twenty-second floor, he takes my hand and hurries me into the hallway toward our door. Once we've arrived, he pulls the keycard out of his back pocket and hands it to me. I'm just about to insert it into the door when he bends down and scoops me up into his arms.

"Sage!" I laugh, holding him around his shoulders.

"Mrs. McCoy," he mutters before smacking a kiss against my lips. "I'm pretty sure this is how it's done. Get the door, doll face."

I nod and then reach down to insert the key. As soon as the light flickers green, I push down on the handle and Sage nudges the door open with his foot, carrying me over the threshold. He then takes me straight to bed, gently laying me across the mattress with my head and shoulders resting on the pillows.

"You tired?"

A sly smile pulls at the corner of my mouth as I reach out and carefully remove his glasses from his face. "Yes. But for my new husband, I think I can fight sleep for an hour."

"I can work with that."

He takes his glasses from my hands and sets them on the nightstand. Just as he's leaning in to kiss me, his phone starts to ring. He sits up, pulls it from his pocket, taps his screen to ignore the call, puts his ringer on silent, and then sets it on the nightstand with his glasses. Then, without a word, he leans in for that kiss.

I've got his attention for two seconds before his phone starts vibrating. He groans in irritation before he picks it up and ignores yet another call. Then he turns the device off and tosses it aside.

"Is everything okay?" I ask as he stands.

"Yeah, doll, it's just Rosy," he replies, toeing his way out of his shoes. "Whatever she needs can wait. Besides, I'm not there—I'm *here*," he says, unbuttoning a couple buttons on his shirt before he reaches over his head to yank the garment off of his body. "With my *wife*."

I giggle, holding out my hand to admire my ring. "That you are, my husband."

With my eyes still focused on my newest and most beloved possession, Sage kneels at the foot of the bed, ridding my feet of my wedge sandals one by one. When he starts to lift my dress up, I lock eyes with him, lifting my hips before sitting up and raising my arms for him. I can read the desire in his eyes already, and the lust that heats his gaze as he takes me in stokes my own longing. I don't hesitate to free my breasts, which are suddenly heavy, and I toss my bra onto the floor before leaning back against the pillows.

"Fuck, baby doll," he grunts as he rests himself between my legs, supporting his weight with a forearm on either side of me. I feel the bulge of his erection through his jeans as his mouth descends around one of my hardened nipples, and the combination of sensations causes me to arch my back, spurring him on. He sucks, which sends a surge of wetness to my core, and then his tongue swirls, and tingles rush up my spine. When he sucks again, he grinds his groin against mine, and a heatwave of pleasure washes over me.

"Sage—oh, Sage, yes," I say on a sigh, reaching up to bury my fingers in his hair.

When he pulls away, he lets me go with a pop before immediately seeking out my other breast. His ministrations make me impatient, and I know my panties are soaked through when I roll my hips up, seeking more friction. This causes Sage to pull away from me abruptly before he peeks up at me, his mouth still hovering over my nipple. His eyes are hooded, and he looks so sexy, with his body planted firmly between my legs, I can't help but roll my hips again.

He presses himself up on his hands, lifting himself off of me completely, and an unexpected whine claws its way out of my throat.

"Who owns your orgasm, baby?"

"Sage, baby, please—I need to feel you!"

"Who owns your orgasm, Millie?"

"Sage—"

"Who?" he asks, leaning back on his knees as he unfastens the top button of his jeans. My eyes drop to his fingers in an instant, my mouth watering at the thought of what lies hidden beneath, and he slowly unzips the fabric before he stops and repeats, "Who, Millicent?"

"You. Only you. *Always* you."

"And who am I, Millicent?" His voice has grown soft, his hands leaving his own clothing and moving to the last piece that I'm wearing. His eyes don't leave mine as he slips my panties down my legs leisurely. *Torturously.* "Who am I, doll?" he semi-repeats.

"My husband." As I say the words, my stomach clenches. Then, in the next second, my panties are yanked from around my ankles, and Sage's hands are spreading my thighs wide before his mouth is on me. I groan, my pussy fluttering instantly as his tongue glides through the length of my center. "Oh, shit—*baby,*" I cry out, completely unabashed, beyond grateful for the slightest bit of relief.

He hums, sucking on my clit, and my eyes roll back into my head as my fists close around the fabric of the blanket beneath me. When he thrusts a finger inside of me, I gasp, bucking my hips, feeling incredibly responsive and aroused. He pumps a couple times before he slips in a second finger, and my heavy breaths mingled with my loud moans fill the room.

"Come for me, Millicent—come for me, wife."

My body obeys not even a second later. I come *hard,* and as he sucks my clit, flicking it with his tongue, I put both hands on top of his head, silently demanding that he stays close as I ride out my pleasure. He strokes and sucks until I go limp, and then he lifts his head, inserting his fingers into his mouth.

"My favorite fucking candy," he drawls when he shoves himself out of the bed. I watch as he drops his pants and then his boxers, his long, thick cock jutting out all the while. My pussy pulses at the same time that my mouth waters, and I push myself away from the pillows before crawling to the edge of the bed. At this height, on my hands and knees, we're lined up perfectly—a fact he seems to notice as well. Neither of us speaks as he steps closer to me, his icy blue eyes starting down at me as he pumps his hand along his shaft a couple times. That only makes me want him more, and I open my mouth wide in invitation.

"Fuck—you're fucking beautiful. Just like this." He pauses, slowly sinking inside of me. I don't tear my eyes away from his as he gently cups the back of my head. "So fucking sexy on your hands and knees with my cock in your mouth," he praises. He holds my head still as he begins to fuck me gently. I swirl my tongue around the head of his dick when he's almost all the way out, and he groans before easing his way back in. I suck, the taste of him beckoning even more of my arousal. When his hands start to caress my back, the longing between my legs returns in full force.

I suck harder, causing him to pump faster, and I moan, eliciting a soft curse from his lips. Then, before I'm ready, he pulls all the way out of me. I bend my neck to look up at him, and he mutters, "First chance I get, I'm coming down your throat, doll face." I bite my lip and nod my head, wanting the same thing. "Between the sheets," he commands, lifting his chin at me. "I think I'll make love to my wife now, if that's all right with you."

"Yes." I breathe my assent before climbing to the head of the bed to strip back the sheets. I yelp when he slaps my ass, pausing my movements as I look back him.

"Love that sweet, little ass," he says, rubbing the place he just hit.

"You better," I tease, wiggling my hips. "It's yours forever, Mr. McCoy."

He grins, smacking the opposite cheek before he rubs the stinging area. Leaning over me, his cock pressed against my ass, he brushes his lips against mine as he whispers, "Damn straight, Mrs. McCoy."

He darts his tongue out and I stick mine out to meet his. Soon, we're both lost in our kiss. It's a lazy, loving, delicious kiss that makes my heart swell. Then, when he rubs his cock through my ass cheeks, I arch my back, pressing against him. With a moan, he reaches around and cups one of my breasts in his hand, tweaking my nipple. His other hand slides around my belly before he hooks his arm below it at my hips, and then I inhale his exhale as his cock finds its way home. His hold around me tightens and I twist my neck even more, reaching up to hold the back of his head as I kiss him passionately.

He makes love to me in a way he never has before, and I adore every second of it. He curves his body so that I feel his chest along my back as he thrusts in and out of me steadily. With my memory aware that this position is usually one in which he fucks me, a part of me wishes he would go faster—but the achingly slow build of my budding orgasm is glorious, so I let him lead. The master of my orgasms. My *husband*.

"Sage," I sigh, my lips still touching his. "I love you, baby—I love you so much. Forever and ever, baby. You're my everything."

He grunts, driving into me harder, but still keeping his leisurely speed. He squeezes my breast with one hand; his other hand descending down between my legs. I mewl as his fingers graze over my clit, curling my own fingers in his hair.

"Together. Always," he grinds out.

"Yes—*yes*," I reply on a moan, my orgasm building. "Sage, baby, I'm gonna come."

"We'll come together."

"*Together*," I breathe as I nod.

He rams into me harder still, the sound of his skin slapping against mine filling the room, his hips still moving at the same speed as before. His fingers on my clit circle faster and harder, and my breathing grows louder.

"Sage—"

"Wait." I seal my eyes closed tight and he squeezes my breast. "Open your eyes, gorgeous," he commands. "I want to see you when you come. My wife. Fuck—my *wife*."

"Oh, Sage," I groan, not sure how much longer I'll be able to hold on, *especially* not with him talking like *that*.

"Wait. Just wait, baby doll."

I bite down on my lip, hard, my gaze locked with his—his icy blue eyes so beautiful, so full of fire, so full of love. He possesses me completely, now more than ever before. In this stare, he's staking his claim—he's making promises—he's sealing his vow. And when I see his brow furrow in concentration, I understand that tonight really is the beginning of our forever. We're one, tied together in every way possible.

"Now, baby," he mutters, touching his lips to mine. "*Now*."

I let go, and my orgasm crashes over me with such intensity that I'm trembling from head to toe. My moan is lost in the sound of his roar as he spills his seed inside of me, and I savor every lazy thrust that follows. He hugs my body close to his for a few breaths before he lays me down on my side, my body feeling boneless and blissfully satisfied. I close my eyes as my head hits the pillow, and Sage presses a wet kiss against my temple. He doesn't climb in the bed right away, and I listen, fighting to stay awake as he goes to turn out the overhead light. A few seconds later, he's at my back, resting a protective hand around my middle as he tangles his legs with mine and buries his face in my neck.

"Best night of my life, doll face."

I smile, pressing back against him tighter as I whisper, "Mine too, baby. I love you."

"You fucking better." I giggle, my exhaustion making it sound funny, and he kisses my shoulder before he tells me, "You're my everything, too, Millicent. Always."

I fall asleep sure that I've never been happier.

TWENTY

Sage

Millie and I sleep through the morning. When we wake up, she insists that before we do anything, she needs to be fed; so we shower before we leave the room and I see about feeding my girl. *My wife.* After a buffet lunch, I drag her back to the room and strip her naked, reminding her that we're on our honeymoon and that means we need to fuck as much as possible. She doesn't argue, and after eight orgasms—six for her, two for me—and a long nap, we shower again and head out for another bite to eat. When we're finished with dinner, we wander the strip until Millie complains of her tired feet, and then we head back to the room. We make love before we fall asleep, and I do so with a smile on my face.

Being a husband feels pretty damn good.

It isn't until we're about to check out of the hotel that I remember I turned my phone off when we got back to the room after the wedding. When I power it on, I toss it onto the bed and finish packing our bag while Millie does her thing in the bathroom. I'm distracted from my task when my phone starts vibrating like crazy, alerting me to a shit ton of notifications received over the last day. I pick up the device and scroll, seeing missed calls from both of my sisters, my parents, everyone in the band, and Stefany. I've also got text messages from everyone, including the guys from Kings & Crowns. My Twitter account has me tagged in posts by Johnny Bash from *The Late Show*, and Kristen Price from *The Late Late Show*, along with Bones, the DJ I met in L.A., and a bunch of other people I've met over the last few months.

"Millie!" I call out, finally unlocking my screen. "Doll face, come 'ere."

"Hmm?" she hums as she comes from the bathroom. I look up at her and stare for a second. She looks cute as fuck in a pair of tight jeans and a V-neck t-shirt that dips low, the fabric stretched over her rounded middle. Her hair is still damp and she wears it lose, letting it hang down her chest and back. I shake my head, remembering why I called her in the room, and ask, "Where's your phone, baby?"

"Um…" She tucks her hair behind her ears as she looks about the room. When she spots her purse on the couch behind me, she walks to it and digs out her device. Turning back to me she holds it up and says, "I forgot to charge it. It's dead."

I nod in acknowledgement before focusing my attention back to my phone. I decide to check voicemails first, to rule out any sort of dire emergency. I've got five from Rosy, four from Pepper, one from my parents, a couple from Violet, and one from each of the Bradley brothers. I click on Rosy's first, putting it on speaker.

"I am going to KILL YOU!" she shouts. Millie gasps and my head shoots up to watch her close the distance between us as Rosy continues. "Married?! MARRIED?! And I wasn't even invited? Hell, I didn't even know you were *thinking* about it. I hate you. I love you. CALL ME BACK!"

I chuckle and Millie asks, "How did she find out?"

"I'm not sure," I reply before hitting her next voicemail. "Seriously, you need to call me back. Also, how did you manage to get that fine ass man to act as your witness? You know what, I don't even care. I should have been your witness. Ugh! I hate you. Mom is going to KILL YOU, by the way. Love you. CALL ME BACK!"

"Wait—how many messages do you have?"

"A lot," I reply with a grin. "And even more texts."

I skip a few of Rosy's messages and click on one from Pepper. "Explain to me how twelve hours ago, Millie was sulking on my couch, and now I've been woken up to find out that you're married. MARRIED! Mom is going to kill you—that is, if Rose doesn't do it first."

I click on her next one to hear, "I love you, by the way. And I'm happy for you both—ecstatic, even. Congratulations. Now call me back. But maybe wait until tomorrow. I've got to go back to sleep."

Next, I jump down to the message from my parents, and my mom's voice fills the room. "When my only son decides to get married, the least I deserve is an invitation. I expect to see you as soon as you get home."

Millie leans into my side and wraps her arms around my waist as she whispers, "She doesn't sound even a little bit happy."

"She'll be all right," I assure her, holding her tight against me with my free arm.

"I still don't understand how everyone found out."

"I wonder if Ashley posted something," I murmur distractedly as I navigate my way to my Twitter app. My eyes grow wide when I find I have over a thousand notifications. Fans and musicians alike congratulating me on my marriage. I also notice more than a few unkind posts, wondering who Millie is, and bashing her for being a homewrecker. These I scroll by quickly, thinking they must be from Nora's loyal fans or some shit. In any case, I don't want Millie seeing them.

"There," she gasps, pointing at a retweet of our wedding photo with Ashley.

I click on it, finding the original post from @ashleyhicksstrums which reads: *Congrats to @thesagemccoy and his beautiful bride! It was an honor. #newfriends #loveisgold #wheninvegas.*

"Holy shit," I laugh, in awe of his words and overwhelmed by the response that followed.

"Rose," Millie whispers.

"What?"

"Or Violet," she goes on to say, looking up at me. "He posted this and they got an alert. I probably have one on my phone, too—but it died before we could hear it. Sage," she buries her face in my chest before she mumbles, "Does the whole world know we're married?"

I laugh and then press my lips on top of her head in her fragrant hair. "Maybe not the *whole* world. Just a few hundred thousand people."

"They're *all* going to kill us—your sisters, your parents, the band—*all of them,*" she groans.

"They'll get over it," I say on a laugh. Then what she said a moment ago triggers and it suddenly hits me—"You got an alert."

"Hmm?" she asks, peeking up at me from beneath her lashes.

"About Nora. You got an alert when she posted that shit." When she nods, my stomach drops and I shake my head at her, "Baby doll, you've got to turn those things off."

She scrunches her brow at me before she asks, "Why? Do you plan on something like that happening again?"

She starts to push away from me, but I fold her in my arms, shaking my head as I declare, "Fuck no. But you don't need to see any of that shit."

"Sage—"

"No, listen to me, I'm serious. I get that it's new and insane and totally sick—but that bullshit Nora posted? It got to you before I could and had you believing a lie. Look, not all the things that are said about me on social media are going to be good," I explain, thinking about the posts I scrolled by bashing my bride. "I don't want you following the news about the band or me. I'm right here. I'm going to be *right here.* Anything you want to know, I'll tell you. Deal?"

"But Rose—"

"I'll deal with her. Just promise me, baby. Turn them off."

She hesitates for a few seconds and then concedes with a nod. "Okay. I'll turn them off."

We're interrupted when my phone starts ringing, and both Millie and I look down at my screen to see that Ashley is calling. Millie looks back at me, a question in her eyes, and I bring the phone to my ear as I answer.

"Hey, Sage—y'all still around?"

"Uh, yeah. We'll be checking out in a few and headed for the airport. Why?"

"I'm fixin' to head there myself. I'm out front, and there are paparazzi everywhere. They must have been tipped off that we were leavin' today. Look, my ride is full, but if y'all are plannin' on leavin' in the next few minutes, I'd like to send Leo up to escort you down. I'll have a taxi waitin' on you."

"An escort? You really think that's necessary?"

"These kinds of folks aren't exactly gentle, Sage—and with Millie—"

"We'll be down in ten minutes."

"All right. What's your room number? I'll send Leo now."

I tell him where we can be found and then thank him before we end the call. I kiss Millie, who is still looking at me curiously, and then let her go and head for our bag. "We've got to get out of here. Apparently, Ashley's drawn a little bit of a crowd and he's worried about us getting out of here with the paparazzi hanging about. Leo's coming up to walk us down."

"What? Are there really that many out there?" she asks timidly.

I turn to look at her, note the apprehension in her face, and move to stand in front of her. I know how she feels about the spotlight. *Any* spotlight. But I also know that this is our future and she's going to have to get used to it. We *both* are.

"Millie," I start to say, reaching for her hand. "I won't let go."

She draws in a deep breath and then lets it out slowly, offering me a nod before she hurries back into the bathroom to finish getting ready. By the time she comes back out, there's a knock on the door. She grabs her purse, I shrug our bag over my shoulder, and then we make our exit.

Leo nods at us in greeting before he instructs, "When we get down there, just stay close."

Millie reaches for my hand and I lace my fingers with hers, giving her a reassuring squeeze. Something about this feels different. Bigger. It's not that I've never been around the paparazzi before, I've just never been around them while I was doing something as simple as leaving a hotel for the airport, especially not by myself. Most of my encounters have been after we've performed at a show, or gone out with Kings & Crowns. I assume this won't be like anything I haven't experienced before, it's just unexpected. In any case, it won't hurt to have Leo to help me keep people away from my expecting wife.

The second we step off the elevator, I can hear them outside of the hotel entrance. They're murmuring and shouting, their cameras aimed and ready. My feet stutter for a second, appalled at what I see.

"I thought Ashley was already in the car," I mutter under my breath, confused why there's still so much commotion.

"He is," says Leo. "They're waiting for you."

"*Me?*" I reply, shocked and a little disbelieving. "We went out yesterday—nobody bothered us."

"Yesterday, they didn't know where you were staying. Today, they do," he states matter-of-factly.

Fuck me.

"Sage," Millie whispers, drawing closer to my side.

I shake my hand out of hers and wrap my arm around her shoulders. She slides both of her arms around my waist just as Leo pushes open the front door. The second we step outside, I'm bombarded with questions, cameras flashing in my face.

"How long have you been friends with Ashley Hicks?"

"What's your relationship with Nora Hampton?

"Does your bride have a name? Was this a shotgun wedding?"

"Sage, are you the father?"

"Are you and Ashley traveling together?"

"Are you collaborating on his new record?"

"Where's the rest of Mountains & Men?"

The questions come so fast, I don't even understand half of them. I speak not a word, holding Millie close as Leo makes a way for us through the crowd to the taxi Ashley promised would be waiting. When we're both inside, he closes the door behind us and nods before jogging to the Bentley I recognize from the other night. Then, just as the taxi driver begins to pull away from the hotel, my phone sounds with the alert of an incoming text. I open it right away, a smirk tugging at my lips when I read the message.

Ashley: Welcome to show biz.

Millicent

WHEN WE LAND in Denver a few hours later, my head is still reeling from everything that happened this morning. I was just starting to wrap my head around Mountains & Men being a band of note. Big music magazine interviews, radio shows, even live television I was starting to get used to. The fans were to be expected; and while my pregnancy brought about terrifying dreams of what those fans could do when they became a wild mob of people, I knew that the band was good enough to warrant such attention—not to mention they are all attractive enough to explain the fangirls and groupies that seemed to be multiplying each day. Even meeting other famous people was slowly becoming *normal*—though, I can't imagine it losing its shock value for me or the band anytime soon. But that was all *Mountains & Men*—five guys and a girl who made music people wanted to hear.

This morning—it was all Sage.

It's still hard for me to explain exactly how I felt when I saw the paparazzi waiting for us. Waiting for *Sage*. Yet, he handled himself with the maturity and ease of a seasoned veteran. I could feel his hands shaking as they held me, but his step didn't falter, he didn't speak a word, he followed Leo's instructions, and he didn't let me go. It was all as if he'd done it a million times; like he was in his element, even though this is all so new.

Sure, the first time he was mentioned in a gossip column, he was leaving a strip club. The second time, he was supposedly "rekindling" a lost love. And, now, days later, hundreds of thousands of people are talking about his wedding in Vegas. Not exactly the situations a *seasoned* professional would be caught doing; then again, he is—it seems—officially a rock star. Their rules are that they have no rules. Plus, I suppose I have to admit, he makes for good gossip.

Nevertheless, it's *our* wedding people are gossiping about. It's *my* husband that people suddenly find interesting enough to stalk outside of his hotel. It's a lot to take in. Not to mention what he told me about the media. I know he's right to insist that I stop the alerts, but I can't help but be curious. He thinks I didn't see any of those nasty posts this morning on his Twitter account, but I did. I only caught a glimpse of one of them, but it was as if my eyes couldn't miss the caption: *Who is that fat cow? He can do so much better!*

Needless to say, with my thoughts whirling around in my head, I didn't sleep a wink on our flight. Neither did I bother to think whether or not we'd run into more attention when we landed at home. So when we exit the plane and see Stefany waiting for us at the gate, my stomach drops immediately.

"Uh-oh," Sage mumbles, reaching for my hand. I take it and he leads me to where Stefany stands with an expression I can't exactly interpret.

"First of all, congratulations! I'm really happy for you guys. I'm sure you're going to hear that a lot, but if I had to bet on whether or not you two would make it, I'd put up cash that—hell yes—you're definitely going to make it."

Sage laughs softly, looking at me before we both shift our attention back to Stefany.

"Thanks—but why do I feel like there's a *but* in there somewhere?"

She grins, her smile lighting up her whole face before she forces a laugh. "*But*—your little trip to Vegas after that picture of you and what's her name, it's creating a different kind of buzz than we want for you right now. We're supposed to be focusing on the music, remember?"

"What, so, I'm not allowed to get married?" Sage asks, his tone instantly defensive; and if she didn't hear it in his voice, the shrug definitely gave it away.

"No, that's not what I'm saying at all," she says gently, holding her hands out as if to signal him to calm down. "All I'm saying is that we're now in a place where we have to *shift* all this talk in the direction we want it to go. They say no publicity is bad publicity, and in some ways that can be true, but we need to get a handle on this. So, Greg has called an emergency band meeting. I'm here to take you—unless you have your car here and you want to follow."

"Wait, what? An emergency meeting? For what? Not to mention, how did you even know we'd be here now?"

She smirks at him, resting her hands on her hips as she says, "I have my ways. And, yes, emergency meeting. You boys and your girl need a PR rep—*stat*. I'm drowning at this point, and some of this shit is way outside of my jurisdiction. Besides, I came back to a hell of a lot of free stuff from people wanting to talk endorsements so—"

"Wait, what?" Sage repeats, this time not sounding so irritated.

"It'll all get covered in the meeting. Let's go, or we'll be late."

She turns to leave without another word. Sage looks down at me, giving my hand a squeeze before we start to follow after her. In a voice low enough for only me to hear, he mumbles, "Welcome home, Mrs. McCoy."

Suddenly, just for a moment, I'm not worried about what we're about to walk into.

All I can do is smile.

TWENTY-ONE

Sage

MILLIE SHIFTS CLOSER to me, hooking her leg over mine until her thigh grazes my dick. As she presses further into my side, the warmth of her body and the feel of her tits—which she let loose almost as soon as we walked in the door—makes me hard. I don't even try to fight my erection. I swear, it's like she's trying to hump me in her sleep. It's hot as fuck, and I have to ignore the urge to wake her up and take her right now.

Instead, I pull at my jeans in a failed attempt to create more room, and with the arm draped around her back, I continue to stroke her side. I pick up and spin my newest pair of glasses with my fingers. They're a gift from *Ray-Ban*. It's actually one of five pairs of various horn-rimmed frames that they sent me. Stefany wasn't exaggerating when she said she came home to a bunch of shit. Each and everyone of us got a gift from someone, mostly just stuff we could use or wear—preferably when we're out, so we can get photographed with it. It's a small price to pay, so none of us are complaining. It's also pretty fucking awesome and totally surreal.

It's all surreal. I keep thinking I'm getting used to this lifestyle, and then I get hit with something new, something I never really thought about before, or something I didn't even know was possible. As the days go by, I'm realizing that my dream come true is a whole lot more than I ever imagined. I'm excited and scared as fuck at the same time.

Then again, that's always been my mountain. Fear. I've had plenty of opportunities to doubt myself; to doubt my talent, my sound, my voice. I've had enough people tell me that what I want is too much to ask for or that it's nearly impossible. I've heard these things from people who love me or care about me, people with good hearts but small faith. I won't lie and say that I've never let their words penetrate. I have. I have been afraid. I've never let it best me, though. Rather, it's something I use to propel me forward. I know that if my dreams don't scare me, they're not worth fighting for. And what's a dream if it's not worth fighting for? An idea. A hope. Nothing more.

I'm literally walking into the product of *years* of not giving up. A year ago today, Mountains & Men wasn't on anyone's radar. We were a band with a cursed bass slot, playing gigs at our local bars. Nobody gave a single shit who I was fucking or what brand of jeans I was wearing. Now? Now, I get married and suddenly that's news to people—fans—*strangers*. Fucking *surreal*.

Coming home only to be rushed to a band meeting wasn't exactly the homecoming I wanted for Millie. Even still, the reaction we got when we walked in the room was priceless. The guys and Alex all cheered before getting up to congratulate us. There were plenty of hugs, a bit of laughter, and a couple threats—mostly from the Bradley brothers—that if we ever hang out with Ashely again without them, they'd kick my ass. After that, we got down to business.

Greg talked about the benefits of a publicist, then insisted we hire one as soon as possible. Of course, Greg being Greg, he said he knew a few people who might be interested and that he'd put us in touch. We're supposed to start interviewing for the position next week. He wants us to have someone locked in by the end of the month, before we start working on our next album.

Outside of finding some decent PR, we've got two club opening gigs in a couple weeks. Greg and Stefany both suggested that we all lay low in the mean time and catch up on rest. None of us argued. After four months on tour, preceded by the recording and the release of our debut album, preceded by our first six-week tour—we've been on the grind for a while now. Three weeks with just a couple gigs sounds good. Especially knowing we've got money in the bank, so we can afford to chill.

When my phone starts ringing from inside of my pocket, I'm quick to pull it out, not wanting to wake Millie. Noticing that it's my sister calling, I smile and shake my head before sliding my finger across the screen and bringing the device to my ear.

"Hello?" I speak softly. Millie moves again, her fingers gripping my t-shirt.

"Family dinner. Tonight. At the restaurant. Seven-thirty," Rosy clips.

Obviously, she's still pissed.

I look at the nightstand and then furrow my brow. "That's in an hour."

"Yup. Better not be late. You know how dad gets when we're late. See you then."

She hangs up before I can say another word, and I groan, tossing my phone to the foot of the bed. Dinner with my family is one thing. Dinner with my entire family pissed off is another thing entirely. And when *Rosy* is upset, it makes it all ten times worse.

Millie sighs, flattening her palm against my stomach, and my dick jerks as I look down at her. Her lips are parted open, a sight that makes me want to kiss her; and when my eyes drop down to take a peek at her chest, I can see one of her hard nipples underneath the shirt that covers her. Thinking she'll probably want some time to get ready before we have to go face my family, I justify my actions with the intent to wake her up.

The low, V-neck she's got on makes it easy for me to slip my hand below the collar. I cup the breast that isn't smashed up against me, and start playing with her nipple. Almost instantly, she moans, her leg hitching even higher over mine. As I continue to work my fingers, I listen as her breathing starts to pick up, and I wonder just how turned on she is. When she moans again, I decide that if she's not as turned on as me, I'll fucking get her there. Now, there's no way in hell I can deny myself any longer.

I take my hand from out of her shirt, using my fingers to gently tilt her head back. With her mouth parted open, I don't hesitate to lean down and sweep my tongue through her lips. I kiss her slowly, waiting for her to wake up. I know I've got her attention when she opens her mouth wider and plunges her tongue into mine. I groan, my dick even harder as she proves to be not the least bit bothered by her wake up call.

Then she moves away from my side, straddling my lap, and I get my answer as to how turned on she is. She doesn't speak. She grabs hold of my face as she continues to kiss me, all the while grinding down on my erection.

"I thought it was a dream," she whispers, tilting her head back as she draws in a ragged breath. I watch her, speechless as she continues to rock her hips over me. She reaches up with one hand and runs her fingers through her hair, holding onto my shoulder with the other. "Oh, baby, I'm going to come just like this. Fuck—touch me!" she whimpers, her voice airy, and her tone desperate.

Holy shit—my wife is hot. I slip my hands under the hem of her t-shirt to palm each of her breasts.

"Oh, god, yes—*yes!*" Her hips start moving faster, pressing down harder, and as much as I wish she was riding me while I was inside of her, I can't deny that this is sexy as fuck. Just before she comes, she presses one of her hands over mine, applying more pressure to my touch as she grips a fistful of my shirt with her other. She sucks in a breath, her neck still arched back, and then her whole body trembles as she whispers, "I'm coming—I'm coming—oh, god, baby—I'm coming!"

I almost fucking come watching *her* come.

She sighs as her body starts to relax. When she rights her neck, her dark green eyes finding mine, I watch as her cheeks pink. She then pulls her bottom lip between her teeth before leaning forward, pressing her forehead against mine. "In my dream, you were touching me. It felt so real. And then it *was* real. I'm sorry I attacked you like that—I thought I might die if I didn't come."

I laugh, *really* laugh, and she sits up straight, her sweetheart lips turned down in a frown.

"Are you laughing at me right now?"

"Doll face," I chuckle, reaching behind her to wrap my hands around her ass. "Are you seriously apologizing for dry humping me?"

"You *are* laughing at me," she mutters, pressing her hands against my chest in an attempt to get away from me.

"I'm not!" I declare, gripping her tighter to prevent her from moving. I see it as her eyes dilate in response to my touch, and a grin spreads across my face. "Okay, maybe I am just a little," I admit. "But you're ridiculous if you think *that* was something you need to apologize for. Attack anytime you want, baby."

She fights a smile and I give her ass another squeeze before leaning toward her for a kiss. She kisses me back without hesitation and I grunt, forcing myself to pull away.

"How about we try that again—*naked*, and preferably not so dry. Though, if I had to guess—" I pause, bringing my lips a breath away from hers. I can feel her shallow exhalations as her arms circle around my neck. "Something tells me you're probably dripping for me already."

"Let me go," she whispers.

I scowl, pulling away from her slightly before I ask, "Uh, what?"

"Let me go, husband—I need to get naked."

WE'RE TEN MINUTES late to dinner, but I'm not sorry. In fact, I'm pretty proud of us for getting out of the apartment at all. A flip has *definitely* been switched on in my girl. For weeks, she had no interest in my dick. Now, all of a sudden, she's *dreaming* of it before she wakes up and rides it.

It's fucking *awesome*.

Now, as we walk into the restaurant—Millie in that tight pink dress that shows off her new curves, making me want to turn us around and take her straight back home—I barely notice how quiet it seems when we pass through the front doors. At almost eight o'clock on a Tuesday night, the dinner rush should still be in full swing. I'm so caught up in figuring out what my chances are that I'll get laid again tonight, it's not until we walk past the empty hostess station and onto the main dining room floor that I realize something is different. It's Millie's gasp that pulls me completely out of my thoughts. She then bursts into tears, burying her face in my shoulder at the same time that I bust out laughing.

"Surprise!" they all cry together.

The restaurant is obviously closed, but everyone is here. The band, my sisters, my parents, Stefany, Millie's friend Lindsey, Violet, even Brandon and Sarah. Wren, who used to play bass for Mountains & Men back in the day, and his wife and their kid. Knox and Maddox's mom and dad are here. *Everyone* is here.

The room has been rearranged, and there are two long lines of tables. One stretch of tables is surrounded by chairs, draped in white cloth, with vases full of bright, summer flowers placed sporadically down the center from one end to the other. From where we stand, I see two chairs at one end with little signs tied to the back that read *Mr.* and *Mrs.*

There's also a buffet table set up, filled with a spread of classic Italian favorites, and a tower of cupcakes at the far end. I'd bet money that mom made the food and Rosy the cupcakes—the little brat; pretending she was still pissed, all the while holding this secret up her sleeve.

As if she can read my mind, she shouts across the room, "You're late! And yeah, I'm still pissed." She folds her arms across her chest defiantly, but then Millie turns her head to look over at her, and she breaks. With a squeal, she steps out from the group and comes running toward us with a huge smile on her face. She stops abruptly once the distance between us is closed, and then gently—and barely, with her short arms—pulls the both of us in for a hug.

"Now you're *officially* my sister," she proclaims, stepping away from us.

"I apologize in advance," I mutter teasingly.

Rosy just rolls her eyes and then Pepper playfully pushes her out of the way as she insists, "We're not that bad. And even if we were, you're stuck with us anyway. Welcome to the family—officially, that is!" She pulls Millie away from me and wraps her in a hug, whispering something in her ear that I can't hear. Millie murmurs something back and then they both laugh, making my chest swell with pride.

I'm proud to be able to call Pepper my sister. She really is amazing. The way she stepped in and stood up for Millie a few days ago meant a lot to me. It pissed me off at the time, but now that we're all good, I'm glad Millie had someone to turn to. It's nice to know she'll always have that with both of my sisters.

More than that, I'm proud to call the woman at my side my *wife*. She belongs here, with me—with my family. It feels good to know that the people who have loved me my whole life, the people who know me so well, trust that I made a good choice with Millie. I made the *best* choice. She's the mother of my son, and the love of my life. She's more than the harmony to my melody. She *is* my melody. She's my everything. Always.

When my mom and dad approach us next, Millie reaches for my hand blindly, and I grab it and weave my fingers with hers. We both take a deep breath at the same time, which makes me chuckle as I look over at her. She catches my eye and I wink at her before she squeezes my hand and we shift our attention back to my parents.

"I know I don't even have to ask whose idea it was to get married in *Vegas*," my mom says, looking straight at me. "I swear, I don't know what I'm going to do with you. *You're* the reason I have gray hairs. And as much as I don't want to admit it, I know this won't be the last time you do something to drive your mother crazy." She sighs and shakes her head at me before reaching up with one hand to hold my cheek. She does the same with her other hand, wrapping it around Millie's cheek before she says, "Never give up on each other. Never stop getting to know one another. Remember that love doesn't always wear the same face, but your commitment to each other *does*. Challenge each other. Learn from each other. Encourage one another and *save* each other."

"And when you think you're at the end of your rope, you have us," says dad, resting a hand on mom's shoulder. "We'll help you through the best we can. We might not be experts, but we've got a few years' experience."

"Thank you," Millie whispers in a shaky voice.

"You're one of ours," he says to my girl. "We take care of our own."

"Oh, all right," mom mutters, dropping her hands and turning her back to us. "I'm not about to start crying in front of all these people. Let's eat!"

Dad barks out a laugh before hugging Millie and me, and then he goes to help mom start uncovering the food while our friends come up to say hello.

"Okay—let me see the goods!" cries Violet instead of hello. She holds out her hand expectantly and Millie chuckles before placing her fingers in Violet's waiting palm.

Lindsey steps up behind her, peeking over her shoulder before she says, "That's…a pretty color. It looks great against your skin."

Violet scoffs before she states, "It's tiny! It's like half the size of a regular wedding band, and there's no sparkle. Sage—how could you get her a ring with no sparkle?"

"It's just a placeholder," I defend, sliding my arm around Millie's waist as I tuck her into my side. "I'm—"

"I love it," Millie interrupts, resting her head against my shoulder. "To me, it symbolizes how urgent his need to marry me. *That* is worth more than diamonds."

Fuck. I press my lips against the top of her head, hiding my victorious smile. *There's absolutely no doubt in my mind—I'm the luckiest bastard around.*

"You two are disgustingly adorable," states Lindsey, a slow smile pulling at her lips. "And *you*, my dear, are *glowing*. That baby looks heavenly on you."

"Thanks, Lindsey," Millie murmurs, resting her hand on top of her belly.

"Speaking of—how about we feed my boy, yeah?"

"Mmmm. Yes, please!"

Millicent

SAGE AND I HANG out at our surprise wedding reception for a couple of hours. I'm just as surprised, overwhelmed, and deeply moved when we leave as I was when we walked in. I was prepared to face the firing squad of the McCoy clan, not a party in celebration of Sage and my impromptu nuptials. Though, when I think about it, I shouldn't really be as shocked as I am. The McCoys are the most loving family that I've ever met. They aren't perfect, but they care for each other above all else. Now, I'm one of them.

I sigh wistfully, running my fingers through Sage's hair. My body feels sated and happy. I'm exhausted, my day far more exciting than I expected, but I force my eyes to stay open for a few more minutes. I'm propped up against the pillows, laying naked across our sheets. Sage is stretched out naked beside me, his feet dangling off the bed as his head is level with my belly. I watch and listen as he sings to Jace, falling in love with him a little more in this moment.

When he's finished, he kisses my stomach before gently resting his cheek against it, gazing up at me. I continue to stroke his hair, and we say nothing as we just stare at each other. I think about the advice Abrielle spoke to us tonight, and I know I'll never give up on us. I'll never give up on Sage. Not ever.

My dream chaser.

My rock star.

My husband.

My love.

TWENTY-TWO

Millicent

As I walk through the halls, I feel strange and under dressed. I'm in a pair of mint green Converse sneakers—a recent gift from Sage—plain black skinny jeans—with a black belly band, of course—and a white t-shirt that stretches over my Jace-bump—which now feels a lot bigger than a bump; it's more like a basketball has been shoved underneath my shirt. My sweet boy is growing more and more, and at twenty-eight weeks, heels are no longer a preference, and my dress collection is small. I know I'm only here to meet Lindsey for lunch, but I feel out of place. It's odd, given how much time I've spent on this campus over the last couple of years.

Summer has all but disappeared, and I've been busy. For most of July, I was spending as much time with Sage as possible. He had a couple weeks off, and we took advantage of them. We had family dinners at the Montgomery residence, Sage attended one of my check-up appointments—which was so special for me—and during the week, we hung out at the band's house. Violet would sit with me and Maestro as the band rehearsed their newest songs, and it reminded me of days gone by.

Then, the rest of the time, we just stayed home. It was nice, being home. It had been so long since we had the chance to live *normally*—and the time we did have had been short before Sage left on tour. While at home, we made it a point to clear out the spare room to prepare for Jace's arrival. Sage got rid of the stuff he felt he could live without, and then the rest we stored in Harry and Pepper's basement. We also ordered a couple pieces of furniture that Sage promises to put together before his schedule gets really busy again. As the weeks continue to go by, I find myself more and more anxious to get a nursery put together. Our place is just an apartment, so I can't do much, but I'm determined to make the best of it.

Though, once August hit, nursery planning slowed a bit. Mountains & Men has been back in the studio, which incidentally means that *I* have been back in the studio, too. I go most days, because Sage wants me to, but also because I can. I've managed to find ways to be helpful—taking care of feeding the guys and Alex, mostly. I read when I want to, or chat with Stefany or Greg when they pop in. I've also taken on the task of managing Sage's schedule. If there's one thing above all others that makes me feel like a wife, it's managing my husband's schedule. And, being the woman that I am, I love it.

Since the band hired Todd, their publicist, Mountains & Men has a calendar full of events to keep track of. Lately, it's just been a few local gigs, but after they're finished recording, Todd has them going various places around the country to promote their single. They're mostly short trips, one or two every couple of weeks. I won't be able to go, since they'll be flying the majority of the time, but I'm not worried about it. I'm happy to be able to watch my man do his thing before he comes home to me. There's talk of a tour next year, but I'm beyond relieved to know that they don't plan on going anywhere until January or February, at the earliest. Sage has his mind set on taking Jace and me with him wherever he goes. I'm still not entirely sure how we're going to make that work, but at least Jace will be a couple months old. Not that that's saying much.

In any case, I know my dream chaser. He's just as stubborn as I am, sometimes a little bit more, and together, we'll formulate a plan. During the *Royalty Unleashed Tour*, it was hard for me to be away from Sage because *I* missed him. In the coming months, when Jace is here, I intend to cling to Sage's promises and trust him, as I said I would. I intend to stay by his side, not just for me, but for Jace. I don't want Sage to miss out on months and *months* of Jace's life, and I know he doesn't want that either. So, when the time comes, we'll figure it out.

Now that August is almost over, the band is starting to wrap things up in the studio. They plan on releasing their latest single, *In the Dark*, next month. Then, in November, they'll release their second album, which they've decided to call *Mountain Roads*. Being a part of their recording journey has definitely gotten me excited for them to share their new music. It's fantastic, and I know it'll be an even bigger success than their debut record.

With so much going on in my personal life and Sage's band business, I haven't really had a chance to think about how different this next season will be. Autumn means the first semester of a new year, and for the first time in my whole life, I'm not starting school with everyone else. Being on campus, seeing the students as they go to and from classes, I feel *weird* being here but not *being* here. Yet, knowing that this is my reality, and that I don't carry an official job title, I don't regret the choices that have brought me to this place in my life. When I left campus in May, I felt like I was doing the right thing. Now, almost three months later, I'm happy to note that I still feel the same way.

When I walk into the building that houses Lindsey's office, my sneakers silent against the tiled floors, I'm anxious and excited to meet up with my friend. I haven't seen her since that night at Giuseppe's, and I currently feel very proud of myself for taking the time and making the effort to ensure that we meet up. I'm usually so bad about that.

Rounding the corner down the hallway that I know all too well, I spot Lindsey right away. She's standing just outside her door, her purse hooked over her arm as she chats with another woman. The other woman looks to be a little younger than me, and she's dressed in a pencil skirt with a pretty, ruffle blouse. She must sense my presence as I slowly approach, not wishing to interrupt. Turns out, I don't have to. She gasps at the sight of me, halting her current conversation.

Lindsey turns to see me and a smile breaks out across her face as she says, "Hey, Millie."

"Hi," I reply hesitantly, my eyes darting back and forth between the stranger—who is staring at me—and Lindsey. "Are you ready for lunch?"

"Oh, my god, Lindsey—you *did not* tell me you were going to lunch with a freaking *celebrity!*"

My eyes grow wide as my mouth falls open, completely caught off guard. "Uh… I'm *not* a celebrity," I stammer.

"You're married to Sage McCoy. Oh, my god!" she gasps again, looking back at Lindsey. "Do you know Sage?"

Lindsey giggles, nodding her head as she says, "Yes, I know him. I met him, what, about a year ago now?" she asks, looking to me for confirmation.

I smile as realization strikes. "Yeah, actually. Wow."

"A year?" asks the woman whose name I still don't know. Her eyebrows shoot up in surprise as she presses her hands to her hips. "I didn't know you'd been together that long. Which means, speculation about your shotgun wedding might not be true, making Nora Hampton the skank in all of this. Oh, my god! This is amazing. I'm totally getting the inside scoop right now."

I open my mouth to speak, but then clamp my lips shut before I speak a word. The truth is, I haven't said anything. Not to this stranger, not to *anyone*. It was agreed upon, between Sage and myself, that our relationship wasn't going to be public knowledge. Sure, they know that we're married, but they don't need to know anything else. I am not the star in our partnership—*he* is. Furthermore, all attention revolving around him should also be attention that helps promote the band and their music. Not to mention the fact that I'd really like to avoid conversations like this in the future.

"So...you're a fan," I state, purposely avoiding everything she just said.

"Totally," she gushes. "I saw them perform at Red Rocks this summer. A friend of mine is a huge Kings & Crowns fan, so she bought two tickets and I tagged along. I expected I'd have a good time, but Mountains & Men? They were *electric!* I've been following them ever since. I mean, how could I not? They're from *Fort Collins!* Nobody famous comes from Fort Collins."

"Right," I say, offering her a small smile before I readjust my purse over my shoulder. "Well, I'm sure they appreciate your support. Maybe at their next release party, I could get you and Lindsey on a guest list or something."

"Oh, my god! Really?"

Her excitement is overwhelming, and I suddenly wish Sage was here to be on the receiving end of all of this attention instead of me. Lindsey must catch on to my state of discomfort because she closes the distance between us and hooks her arm through mine before she says, "She's his wife, remember? And I'll make sure to remind her. Anyway, Eden—we've got to get going. I've got class in a couple hours as *Mrs. McCoy* has lots to fill me in on."

"Oh, yeah. Your lunch date! Sorry. Please, don't mind me," she rambles, flailing her hands around.

"It was nice, uh, meeting you—um, Eden," I say just as Lindsey starts to turn us toward the exit.

"You, too!"

"Well, look at *you,*" Lindsey giggles as soon as we're out of ear shot. "A *celebrity.*"

I roll my eyes and sigh. "*She's* my replacement?"

"Eden is brilliant, really," she assures me with a grin. "Maybe not as quick with numbers as you, but she's got a fine brain. She's young, like you when you first started, and very spunky. I think she'll have a great first semester. We've gotten to know each other a little bit over the last couple of weeks. I like her. I bet you would, too."

"Maybe," I mumble dubiously. I think of how Eden talked about me, referencing Nora as if she's played a part in any aspect of my life with Sage. She hasn't. Not really. Then again, Eden *did* call her a skank. Maybe we could get along.

"Anyway, enough about Eden, where should we go for lunch?"

"You know, I could really go for a burger right now."

"Oh—I know *just* the place."

After lunch with Lindsey, I head home. I spend a little time picking up random things left about the apartment since the last time I cleaned, and then I decide to take a nap. I drift off in no time and sleep soundly for a couple of hours. When I wake up, I hear activity in the next room. I look to the clock to see that it's a little after five in the evening.

"Sage?" I call out, still a little groggy as I climb out of bed. "Baby, is that you?"

"Yeah, doll face," he mutters distractedly.

I run my fingers through my hair, pulling it back into a ponytail as I follow the direction of his voice. When I get to the doorway of the nursery, I find Sage in the middle of the floor, surrounded by a number of parts that are meant to make a crib. He's holding the instructions in one hand, separating the parts in various piles.

He looks up at me and I smile, feeling suddenly giddy at his choice of project for the evening. "I didn't know you were going to do this today."

"Neither did I," he says with a shrug. "Then Todd sent out an email with a few more interviews and events he's scheduled in a couple weeks. Did you see it?"

"Not yet. I haven't checked messages this afternoon."

"Yeah, well, I don't want to run out of time or get caught up in work shit before Jace gets here. Time flies, you know? I mean, look at you."

I do as he says, my eyes dropping down to my belly as I graze my hands over it. I then nod in understanding and offer him another smile. "Do you want some help?"

He chuckles, thrusting the directions at me. "You're the smart one. You read, I'll assemble."

"I am not the only smart one," I scoff, making my way further into the room.

As I approach him, he takes hold of my wrist and lifts up onto his knees before he says, "You're the good looking one, too. Get down here, gorgeous—need a taste."

Placing a hand on his shoulder, I lean down and press my lips against his in a soft kiss. When I pull away without giving him more, he grunts his disapproval, making me laugh.

"So, what did Todd add to the calendar?" I ask as I go to sit in our new, padded rocking chair. The frame is made of light wood, and the padding on the seat and along the back is covered in navy blue and white chevron fabric. I saw it and loved it for its simplicity, and Sage didn't deny me when I told him I wanted it.

"Actually, he found someplace for us to play *In the Dark* on the day we release it."

"Really? Where?"

"*The Dylan Show*," he says nonchalantly. It isn't until I gasp that he looks over his shoulder at me, a big grin plastered across his face. "Can you believe that shit?! I'm going to get to meet fucking Dylan!"

"Baby—that is huge! You've never been on daytime television before. And Dylan is, like, the queen of talk show hosts in the middle of the afternoon."

"*Someone's* been paying attention," he chuckles.

I fight my own grin now. He's right. Over the last several weeks, I *have* been paying attention to anything and everything that has to do with the promotion of Mountains & Men. I've never really spent a lot of time watching television or browsing social media. I spent most of my time working; and when I wasn't working, I was reading. I didn't have a bunch of friends I followed on any social media platform, and I didn't have friends who encouraged a TV habit, either. Of course, I didn't live under a rock. I do *own* a TV, and I go out enough to know what kind of music I like and what I don't; but my knowledge of the music industry and how it ticks is very limited. Now, I'm working to change that.

"So that means California in a couple weeks?"

"Yeah. L.A."

My mood plummets instantly. I dip my chin in acknowledgement, taking in a deep breath before shifting my attention to the crib assembly directions in my hand. I'd rather *not* think about L.A. That place has both great memories and horrible ones attached to it. Most recently, the bad has out-weighted the good.

"Doll face?"

"Hmm?"

"Millicent, look at me," he insists in a tone that makes me reluctant to ignore him. He doesn't speak again until I'm looking into his gorgeous, icy blue eyes. "I'm yours, baby doll. Got the ring to prove it. Nothing's going to happen. I probably won't even see her. It's been weeks, now, and we haven't heard her spout anymore bullshit. Don't even think about it."

He's right. Again. It *has* been weeks. I need to let it go. But even though it was a lie—the pain that shot through me when I saw the picture that Nora took of the two of them—I still haven't forgotten it.

"I can see it in your eyes that I'm going to have to fuck you later to remind you where my dick belongs—the only place my dick belongs—*in my wife*."

A shiver races down my spine, and I can't tell if it's from hearing him declare his dick belongs in *his wife*—or if it's the promise that his dick will later be *in his wife* that causes the reaction. Either way, I don't say a word of protest. Instead, I read step one of the directions aloud.

Sage

When Millie rolls away from me, resting on her opposite side, I inch the sheet up over her bare shoulder before I quietly slip out of bed. I pick up the first piece of clothing my feet touch, tugging on my jeans over my naked body. I don't bother zipping them as I make my way to the dresser for my glasses. Once I've slid them on my face, I step out of the room, cracking the door behind me before I go to the next room. I flick on the light, a small, proud smirk tugging at my lips at the sight of Jace's crib.

Putting that thing together was a bitch, but we figured it out. It looks fucking good, too. Propping my head against the door jam, I blow out a breath as I think about the next couple of months. I thought being home and not on tour would mean more time at *home*. While I won't be sleeping on a bus any time soon, between Todd and Stefany, starting next month, the band is traveling at least once a week until after we release *Mountain Roads* in November. I sure as hell won't complain about the opportunities that we've been given to promote our stuff, I just worry about Millie.

I made her a promise. I told her I wouldn't let her go. I told her I wanted her by my side—her and Jace. I told her we'd figure it out along the way. I meant every goddamn word. I just don't want to let her down.

I let my mind go blank for a while as I stand staring into the nursery. It's nowhere near finished, but I know my girl will do it up right. I don't know how long I stay unplugged, not paying attention to anything. I fold my arms across my chest, and my newest tattoo grabs my attention. Then, as if the silence was all I needed, I feel the surge of a second wind. I shake my head, reminding myself that any doubt that stands in my way is merely a hindrance that will become my bitch. I've come this far; I sure as fuck won't stop fighting now. I want it all, and I want my little family right there with me when I get to the top.

Taking one last look at Jace's crib, I flick the light out, thinking only one thing as I head back to bed.

That thing better stay in one piece.

TWENTY-THREE

Millicent

*H*IS TONGUE IS WARM AND WET, *and it feels good against my sensitive flesh as he drags it over my entrance all the way up to my clit. With his fingers, he spreads me wide open, blowing on my pussy, and I shudder in pleasure. He licks and blows again, and my center flutters as my arousal skyrockets. When he closes his lips around my clit, sucking me into his mouth, he hums, and I buck my hips, unable to stop myself. With a grunt, he holds me down while simultaneously thrusting his tongue inside of me.*

"Oh, Sage—yes—yes, baby, that feels so good!"

He hums again, pushing his face into me further, causing his tongue to go deeper. I can feel my budding orgasm as it grows bigger and bigger, and I'm short of breath, desperate for my release. He's relentless with his affection, and I'm right on the edge, but I don't come. I can't come.

I roll my hips, needing more, needing my body to reach its climax, but nothing happens. I cry out, feeling trapped in between unimaginable pleasure and the pain of the built up pressure at my core. I'm so wet, and he feels so good, but something isn't right.

Then, suddenly, he stops.

My eyes shoot open and I gasp, pushing myself up until I'm propped on my hands. I'm breathless, and my breasts feel swollen and achy. I look down at my chest, covered in one of Sage's old t-shirts, and my skin breaks out in goosebumps as I realize that my nipples are hard, the soft fabric rubbing against them as I pant softly, sending tingles between my legs.

With one hand, I grab hold of one of my breasts, squeezing it mercilessly, and my pussy pulses as my head falls back.

Fuck—that feels good.

I sit up fully, using my other hand to grab my other breast, and I can feel my arousal pooling at my center. I squeeze my legs together, my desire leaking out of me and onto the sheets. I'm not wearing any panties, and as I continue to massage my breasts, I decide that I don't want to be wearing anything at all.

The feel of the t-shirt scraping against my skin as I pull it off makes me hyper aware that my body is sensitive to *any* touch. I'm so turned on I can hardly stand it. I close my eyes, tracing my fingers down my neck, between my breasts and over my belly. I run my hands along the inside of my thighs, and then I remember my dream.

My pussy pulses at the thought of Sage's tongue inside of me, and I moan as I spread my legs. I need him. I want him. I want to taste him. I want to feel him. I need him to fill me up.

I look beside me and see that he's sound asleep, turned towards me on his side. I don't even hesitate to throw the sheets off of him before I lean close and slip my hand into his boxers. My fingers wrap around him as I begin to stroke, and I whimper, loving the feel of him in my hand; loving the way touching him makes my stomach clench.

I squeeze him tighter and he grunts, shifting until he's on his back. He's starting to get hard, which only excites me more. My heart is racing when I let him go only to pull his underwear out of my way. As soon as his cock is free, I position myself on my hands and knees, leaning down to take him into my mouth. I moan as I suck, and he's fully erect in seconds, a groan spilling from his own throat. I take him as deep as I can before I pull my mouth away. Then I twirl my tongue around his head, licking along his slit.

"*Fuck,*" he whispers.

I take him in my mouth again, and I can feel my arousal smearing between my thighs as I squeeze my legs together. I suck him hard, and then I hear him grunt before his hand is in my hair, gripping the strands in a tight fist.

"Shit—Millie," he hisses. "Fuck, yes."

I can tell by the way he guides my head that he's awake now, so I lower my head until he's grazing the back of my throat, and then I pull away, gasping for air.

"Baby, what are you doing?" he asks, still sounding half sleep.

I don't answer him right away. Instead, I move until I'm kneeling between his legs, and then I lean over him, kissing and licking my way up his chest. I spread my legs, my knees pressing into the bed on either side of his hips as I suck on his nipples, and I can feel it as his dick twitches underneath my belly. When I reach the base of his neck, I suck at his skin and his hands graze up and down my sides. Every time he skims the outer swell of my breasts, my pussy clenches. Then, when I finally reach is mouth, I immediately plunge my tongue inside, a deep moan pouring into him as I kiss him hard and wet.

He returns my affection greedily, lifting his head off of his pillow as his tongue twists with mine. His hands mold my ass and he squeezes me hard, kneading my flesh. My breasts ache to be pressed firmly against his chest, but my belly is in the way. Before I can think to complain, he rolls his hips, his hard cock grazing through my wetness.

"*Fuck*, doll face. Were you dreaming of my dick, baby? Hmm? You're *soaked*. You need my cock, Millicent? Is that what you want?"

I whimper before I nod as I admit, "Yes—shit, Sage, I need to fuck you."

He runs his nose down the length of mine before he smacks a kiss against my lips. His mouth still grazing mine, he murmurs, "Have at it, doll face."

Without further ado, I plant my hands on his chest before I push myself up until I'm straddling him. I reach behind me for his hard length, and then I line us up before I ease my way over him. I'm so swollen, and he feels so good, I can hardly think straight as I take him all the way in.

"*Jesus*," he grunts, his hands reaching for my hips before his fingers tighten around me. "So fucking good!"

I'm speechless as I begin to ride him, rocking my hips as I grind down over his length. I'm so worked up, I feel my orgasm starting to build almost immediately. I find a steady rhythm, rising and pounding down on his cock over and over again. My breaths grow shorter and shorter as the pleasure in my core builds higher and higher.

"Baby," I mewl, reaching for my breasts once more. "Sage! Fuck!" I pinch my nipples hard, and then he slaps my ass. The moment his hand makes contact, my orgasm explodes. I drop my hands to his chest, needing him to lean against as my body trembles and shakes above his. He groans, bucking his hips up a couple times until I've ridden the wave of my release, and then he taps the side of my leg.

"Off, doll face. My turn."

I nod, unable to find my words as I climb off obediently. I lay down next to him, my back to his front, and he grips a hand underneath my knee, lifting my leg. He lets me go just long enough to guide his cock inside of me, and then he supports my limb as he begins to fuck me from behind. I close my eyes, in love with everything about this moment, and I just *feel* him as he fills me up like only he can.

"You fit just right, Sage," I moan. "Oh, god—I love your dick."

He doesn't respond with words. Instead, he buries his face in my neck, licking and nibbling along my jaw before he brings his lips to my ear. I listen as he pants and grunts, working to find his release while coaxing out another one of mine.

"You're gonna come again for me, doll face," he grumbles.

It's not a question, it's a command, and I nod in acknowledgment. He then lets go of my leg, reaching around to play with my nipples. I arch my back, lowering my leg and pressing my ass against him, and he rams into me harder and faster.

"So tight. Fuck—I love this pussy. It's mine. All mine."

He lets go of my breast and skims his palm over my belly until he forces his fingers between my legs, finding my clit. I groan as they make contact, reaching back to grab a fistful of his hair. He rubs fast and hard, causing my orgasm to come rushing to the surface. It hits me without warning, and I cry out as my core squeezes his cock.

"Yeah, baby! Strangle my dick, doll—*fuck!*"

He pumps into me a couple more times and then I feel it as he swells and then erupts inside of me, freeing a long groan as he stills—buried as deep inside of me as he can go.

When we're finished, both of us trying to catch our breath, neither of us moves. My muscles feel useless, but I feel amazing, and now all I want is sleep. I press back against him a little more, freeing a sated sigh, content to have him still inside of me. He presses a kiss against the back of my head, and as sleep starts to pull me under, I don't fight it.

Just before I fade away entirely, I hear Sage whisper, "Best wife ever."

Sage

She doesn't stir when the alarm clock sounds in the morning. Then, an hour later, as I shrug the strap of my duffle bag over my shoulder, she's still completely knocked out. I guess I can't be surprised, not after our fuck-fest at three in the morning; and while I feel a little guilty for leaving without saying goodbye, I don't want to wake her.

I watch her as she sleeps, still naked and fucking gorgeous. Her hair is wild, fanned across the pillow and over her chest. She's got the sheets pulled up over her body, but I can still make out the slight swell of her tits and the roundness of her belly.

My wife. Six months pregnant and still sexy as hell.

I lean over her and tilt my head before I press a soft kiss against her lips. When she doesn't stir, I kiss her again before I begin to make my exit. I'm supposed to meet up with the rest of the band at the house. Stefany has arranged for us to be picked up and shuttled to the airport. Today, we're headed back to L.A. We just finished wrapping up the recording of our next album a couple weeks ago, and this morning we drop our single, *In the Dark*. For the next month and a half, we'll be promoting our album with this track; and this afternoon, we'll be performing it on *Dylan*.

I can't fucking wait.

It takes me fifteen minutes to get to the house, and when I arrive, I don't bother knocking before I stroll through the front door. I barely get two steps inside before I hear it. I know right away that it's Alex. I drop my bag by the stairs, abandoning it as I make my way into the living room. She's on the couch, crying into Derrick's shoulder. Maddox is on her other side, looking helpless as shit. They both look up at me, and I shake my head and shrug, silently asking what's up.

Maddox glowers before he nods at Alex and mutters, "Fucking fucker broke up with her. The jealous piece of shit."

My eyes grow wide as I look to Derrick for confirmation. He nods, but doesn't offer me anything else. Not that it matters, Maddox isn't finished.

"She stayed with Adrian last night, and then he brought her home like this," he continues, jerking his thumb in her direction.

"He said it was obvious my career was more important to me than him; that he wouldn't wait on the sidelines for me," she cries, turning her head just enough to look at me. "Like *his* career isn't important to him! I mean, what am I supposed to do? *Not* travel with the band? He should know better than anyone—this is important! It means something to me! I've worked hard for this." She sniffles, drawing in a broken breath, and Derrick gives her shoulders an encouraging squeeze.

"Like I said," mutters Maddox. "Jealous piece of shit. He just said that because our band is more relevant than his. We've outgrown Lawful Sinners, and he's come to the conclusion that your dick is longer than his."

"What?" she grumbles, lifting her head to look at him. "*Ew!* I don't have a—"

"We know you don't have a dick, Ali," says Derrick with a chuckle. "But you've always been a better bass player than him. We tried to tell him, but he wouldn't listen."

She sighs, shaking her head as she whispers, "I'm not—"

"Don't even fucking say it," I order, folding my arms across my chest. "You *are*."

"Oh, hey, Sage," Violet chirps as she glides down the stairs. She smiles, walking toward me, and then stops the second she gets a look at Alex. "Wait—what happened? What'd I miss? Today is not supposed to come with tears!"

"Adrian. He broke up with me," Alex answers, reaching up to dry her cheeks.

Violet scoffs before she mutters, "It's about time." We all look at her in shock. From the expressions on the guys' faces, I'm sure they're thinking the same thing as me. *Not* the right thing to say. Violet waves us off before she goes on to explain, "I'm serious. That dude was on a serious ego trip. I thought he was cool at first, but as soon as his girl started bruising his ego simply by being the badass that she is, he turned into a jerk. I had a hunch it would come to this, but it needed to play out naturally." She pauses, pointing a finger at Alex. "You don't need that kind of shit in your life. He should be proud of you, not threatened by you. You're better off, Zip."

Then, without missing a beat, she walks right up to Alex and takes her hand. "Come on. You leave in less than a half an hour. We have to do something about those puffy eyes. When you land in L.A., the paparazzi is only allowed to capture your badass side, not your broken heart. *That* is for your music—not for the world to gossip about, and *definitely* not for Adrian to gloat over."

Alex just stares up at her in awe, unmoving.

"Chop, chop!"

Derrick wraps his hands around her hips and lifts her ass off the couch, forcing her to find her feet. She gasps, looking back at him, and Maddox smacks her ass, making her shriek before looking over at *him*.

"Do what she says, church mouse," he demands.

When she takes her first step, Violet turns to lead her out of the room, winking at me as she passes. Just as they're starting up the stairs, JJ is racing down. He stops as they pass, eyeing them both curiously, but they don't pay him any mind. When he looks over at me and starts heading my way, I inform him, "Adrian broke up with her."

"Jealous motherfucking asshole," mumbles Maddox.

Derrick shakes his head before he reaches over and pats Maddox on the back. "She'll be all right."

"I think I've got something that'll cheer her up for sure," says JJ, holding up his phone. "Our video dropped an hour ago."

Much like with *You and Me*, Stefany and Greg thought it would be a good idea to release our song with a video. It worked well in terms of exposure in the past, so we were all over the idea. It was JJ who came up with the concept. Since *Mountain Roads* is an album made up entirely of songs written while we were on the road, he thought it would be cool to take some of the video footage from our time with Kings & Crowns—film captured while we were performing, to stupid videos we may have taken when we were messing around on the bus—putting it all together as a backdrop to our single. It turned out better than we had hoped.

"Well, what have you got?" asks Maddox impatiently.

"Ten thousand views. Two hundred and sixty-seven shares."

"Holy shit!" cries Maddox, standing to his feet.

"In an hour?" asks Derrick, right on his heels as they both come to take a look at JJ's evidence.

"What happened in an hour?" asks Knox as he descends the stairs. He drops his duffle next to mine as he makes his way toward us.

"Oh, just our single—*kicking ass!*" cries Maddox.

"Wait, what about our single?" We all turn and look up at the top of the stairs. Alex is leaning over the railing, her face still splotchy, but her expression expectant and hopeful.

"Hold that thought. Let me refresh," he says, holding up a finger to signal his request as he does what he says. He chuckles a second later before he turns to her and replies, "Ten thousand, two hundred and twenty views—three hundred shares."

"Oh, my God! That's…that's *amazing*," she gasps.

"Ali?" says Derrick, earning her attention. "Jealous motherfucking asshole. Remember that."

She pulls in a deep breath, nods once, and then hurries back to whatever it is she was doing.

TWENTY-FOUR

Sage

DYLAN'S SET IS INCREDIBLE. It's *huge*, classy, and bright. As we take our tour, I can't help but be in awe. Not to say that being on the set of *The Late Show* wasn't a big deal; or that performing on *The Late Late Show* wasn't a life changing experience. Both opportunities held their own weight—but Dylan is fucking one step down from *Oprah!* People love her, and the philanthropic work she does with the insane amount of money she makes is just one more reason for fans to adore her.

The crazy thing is, Todd told us that all he had to do was make one phone call and we were in. She'd heard us before, loved our music, and was already looking for an excuse to get us on the show. Todd's timing was perfect, the band's release was spot on, and here we are. The show we record today will air tomorrow. If that doesn't give us a fucking boost, I don't know what will.

After we've all had a chance to change and we've been to hair and make-up, we just hang out in the dressing room. It's fifteen minutes until the recording starts when there's a knock at the door. As Dylan pops her head in, we're all up on our feet in an instant.

"Hey, guys!" she greets, inviting herself inside.

She looks just as striking in person as she does on TV. I don't know how old she is, but I would put her in her late thirties. Her dark brown hair is cropped short, hanging down to her chin, leaving her long neck on display. She's thin, but curvy, and she's wearing a dress that shows off just about every one of them.

"You might not believe me, but I've been looking forward to today since we put it on the calendar, I swear."

"You're right," Maddox says with a laugh. "The people you've had on your couch? Yeah, I don't buy it."

She grins, propping her hands on her hips, and opens her mouth to say something, but then starts laughing as she waves her hands in front of her. "I was totally going to bust out the verse to *Just Tonight*, but that would just be humiliating for me and disrespectful to you. I love that song, though. Seriously. The first time I heard it, I thought—that's a sound worth following."

I clap my hand against my chest, stepping back as I murmur, "Wow."

It's not the first time someone has complimented our music. It's not even the first time someone *famous* has told us that they like our sound; but hearing someone praise my lyrics, I swear it will never get old.

She points at me, narrowing her eyes as she asks, "*You're* the song writer, right?"

"I write the lyrics, yeah."

"Color me impressed. I swear, if I wrote a song, I'd be booed right off the stage."

"Well, I appreciate the compliment," I chuckle.

"Okay, so, I have to know—the girl with the demons in her eyes?"

I smile as I think of Millie. The demons in her eyes have been scared away. Now, all I see in her pretty, dark green eyes is her *fire*. "She's my wife."

"Well—*damn*."

"At this point, I'm pretty sure half the songs we sing are about Millie," says JJ with a knowing grin.

"He's not kidding, either," chimes in Alex.

"*You!*" Dylan points at Alex, making her way across the room before she extends her hand. Alex takes it, a blush tinting her cheeks as she looks up at Dylan—who stands at least a head taller than her in those heels. "Get ready. When we're out there, we're *totally* going to talk about how a cute little thing like you became one of the *men* in Mountains & Men."

Alex takes a deep fortifying breath, but I can see the terror in her eyes as her stage fright rises up inside of her. Nevertheless, she paints on a smile and murmurs, "Yeah. Okay."

"She was a badass," says Derrick, folding his arms across his chest as he tips his chin at Alex. Dylan looks his way and he tells her, "You'll like the story."

"I'm sure I will," she replies with a smile. "Okay, let's see if I've got your names straight."

She goes around the room, naming each of us. She gets Knox and Maddox mixed up, which makes them laugh, but we don't give her any grief. Not only are they brothers, but they play the same instrument. With names all straightened out, we chat for a couple more minutes, and then one of her producers comes in and tells her it's time for her to go. She tells us she'll see us out there, and then we're left to wait for our cue.

We're slotted for the later part of the show, our performance the last act of the hour. Even still, it feels like no time at all before we're out there on the couch, in front of her live studio audience. Dylan makes all of us laugh, and even Alex seems to relax as we answer questions about the history of the band and what we have in the works for the rest of the year. Then, just before the commercial break, she announces that she has a surprise for us.

"I've actually just gotten word from my producers about the song you're about to play for us." None of us speak as we look at each other in confusion. She grins as she announces, "*In the Dark* is now sitting at number ninety on the Billboards Hot One Hundred chart."

For a moment, I think we're all in shock as the crowd erupts in applause. Then, Knox speaks up and says, "I—every thing that's going through my head right now—I don't think it's appropriate for television."

We all laugh, no doubt because we're all thinking the same fucking thing. It hasn't even been twenty-four hours since we dropped the track, and already it's hit the top one-hundred chart.

Fuck!

"I actually think I could pull a Tom Cruise right now," I mutter, pretty sure I'm not even kidding.

Dylan and the audience all laugh, and as smooth as someone who does this day in and day out, she promises the crowd a performance of our new *hit song* after the commercial break. Ten minutes later, when we're all set up, we play the fucking hell out of our single.

As soon as we got off stage, I reach into my pocket to call my girl and tell her our news. But when I power up my phone, I'm immediately distracted by the crazy number of notifications that I've got. I skip the social media alerts and find a text from Rosy and, unexpectedly, a text from Bones. I decide to open his first.

Bones: The Phoenix. I put you on the VIP list for tonight. Come chill while you're in town.

I remember him telling me about the club where he DJs locally, and his invitation has me looking forward to our night. It'll be the perfect way to celebrate the events of today. I tell the rest of the band, who are all on board with the idea, and then I step away to call Millie.

"Hey, baby," she answers on the second ring. I can tell she has me on speaker, something she's been doing for a while now. She rests her phone on her belly as she talks to me, in hopes that Jace can hear my voice, too.

"Hey, doll. What are you up to?"

"Going through your emails and updating your calendar. Oh, also, a courier just left. You got some packages. I think Stefany must have had them sent over. Probably more free stuff. I'll go through it in a bit."

I smile, wondering how I got so lucky? Millie is the most organized person I know, and the crazier my life seems to get, the more she seems to make order of it. "I love you."

"You better," she teases. "Are you still with Dylan?"

"We just finished up. We're about to head back to the hotel for a bit, and then we'll grab some dinner before we go out and celebrate. Millie—you're never going to believe this."

"Believe what?"

"We hit the billboard charts. Top one-hundred."

"Sage! Are you serious?" she gasps, making me smile.

"Yeah, baby doll, I'm serious. I swear—this day can't get any better. Our video went viral this morning."

"I know! I've been following it. It's hit over a million views now. Your Facebook likes have spiked, too. You're going to break two million today; I'm sure of it."

"Holy shit!"

"Baby, I'm so proud of you," she says softly. "Come home, and I'll show you just how much. I missed you this morning."

My dick jerks, remembering how she woke me up in the middle of the night—her mouth warm and wet as she took me deep. That's my girl. After all this time, the promise of being inside of her again still excites me. I wasn't lying when I told her I loved her pussy. Best cunt I've ever had.

"I'll see you tomorrow, Mrs. McCoy."

"I love you, too, by the way."

"You fucking better."

The Phoenix is *insane*. The line to get inside is so long, I'm sure people stand outside the whole night, just *hoping* to get in before last call. When we arrive, we head straight for the velvet ropes, where the paparazzi loiters and a huge bouncer hangs out in front of the door. With night having fallen hours ago, the flashes of cameras aimed our way is overwhelming as we're captured giving the bouncer our name. He nods, letting us in the VIP entrance without issue. The separate door opens up to a staircase that immediately leads to the second level of the club.

It's crowded, people sitting around high top tables or lounging on couches as they drink and socialize, but it's not nearly as packed as the area below. I head to the railing, looking down, and grin at the sight of the dance floor. It's like a *living, breathing* organism—bodies smashed together and moving to the pulse of the music. In the far corner of the room, I see Bones set up on a big platform. He's got his headphones on, his focus zeroed in on his instruments as he fills the place with sound.

My attention is drawn to my side when I feel someone nudge me, and I look over to see Derrick holding a glass for me. "Whiskey," he says, handing it over.

I nod my thanks, jerking my chin out at the crowd before I say, "Wild, right?"

He grins as he replies, "I could get used to staying up here."

"VIP, man—we made it."

"Sage, Derrick! Come here." We both turn to look over our shoulders and spot Alex waving at us from a nearby table. We join the rest of the band before she announces, "We need to toast, and I'd like to say something."

"Go for it, Zip," I insist, holding up my glass.

"Okay," she sighs before taking a deep breath. "To Mountains & Men, and an *amazing* release day. Seriously, guys, I don't think this day could have turned out any better. And…to you guys. You're the best, and you've helped keep my spirits up all day. So, thank you."

"And to Alex," pipes in Maddox, speaking loudly over the noisy room. "For being such a badass, she broke the curse of the bass slot for good."

"Cheers!" cries Knox, thrusting his glass in the middle of our circle. We all do the same, clinking our glasses together before we drink. I down the contents of mine in two gulps before I slam it down on the table with a shake of my head.

"*Fuck!* That shit's good."

"Let's party," says JJ, slamming his empty tumbler next to mine.

We share a grin and then head to the bar for a refill. After my second serving of whiskey, I'm feeling good, and I decide to brave the masses in order to go say hi to Bones. It takes me nearly twenty minutes to reach him, but when he spots me, he waves off his security guards and invites me up onto his platform.

"Yo, man, what's up? Glad you could make it!" he says, grabbing my extended hand before pulling me in to his shoulder, smacking my back with his other hand.

"This place is awesome. Thanks for hooking us up."

"My pleasure. I hear a big congrats is in order. Your new single is *hot!*"

A huge grin spreads across my face as I reply, "First billboard hit! We're pretty stoked."

"You know what—hold on." He puts up a finger before he turns to his computer. I watch as he does his thing, then he grabs the mic from the stand in front of him, bringing it to his mouth as he calls out, "What-up, Phoenix!" The mob on the dance floor screams in response, and I take in the room, loving the view. "This is your man Bones, here, and I'm gonna throw a little freestyle your way. Got my boy Sage McCoy up here, representin' Mountains & Men." They cheer again and I can't help but laugh as I wave. "If you haven't heard their new single, *In the Dark*, you need to get out more. Nah, nah, I'm just playin'. But really, it's hot—and I'm gonna give it to you with a little twist right now."

"*Sage!*" I hear someone shout my name as Bones puts the mic back, and I turn to see Alex and JJ standing on the other side of the security detail that blocks off the DJ platform. I look to Bones, pointing at my crew, and he waves them up. I take Alex's hand, helping her climb the stairs as JJ follows behind her. I can tell by the look in his eyes as he stands beside me that he's in love with Bones' set up.

"Y'all ain't ready for this shit," says Bones with a grin before the track to our single begins.

The room fills with the familiar sound of our latest jam, but then just as my mind settles in to the groove of the expected, Bones starts mashing it up with another beat. I look over at JJ, who is watching Bones intently, his head nodding to the beat, and then Bones transitions back to our song seamlessly.

"Oh, my gosh! That sounds amazing!" cries Alex.

For the next five minutes, he plays his remix, and everyone *loves* it. When he's finished, I shake his hand, patting him on the back before I offer him a mock bow.

"That was sick!"

"Had to hook it up for my boy," he laughs. "Hey, I've got to get back to it, but I'll be on break in about an hour. Drinks?"

"For sure. I'll see you up there."

We part ways, Alex waving her goodbye before the two of us make our descent off the platform. JJ asks if he can stay and watch for a bit, and Bones gives him the thumbs up, so we leave him behind. As we make our way through the craziness on the dance floor, Alex holds tight to my elbow until we make it to the clearing at the bottom of the stairs that leads back up to the VIP lounge. I let her walk up ahead of me, and just as I start to follow after her, I feel someone grab my wrist.

"Hey, babe! I didn't know you were back in L.A.!"

I turn toward the familiar voice, immediately shaking off her hand as I scowl at her. She's wearing a shirt that can barely be called as much, and a pair of cut-off shorts with sandals that lace up to her bare thigh. All that in front of me, and my dick doesn't even *flinch*.

"I'm not your *babe*, Nora. And where I am and when is none of your business."

"Ouch. Geez, can't a girl just say hello?"

I cough out a humorless laugh, shaking my head in disbelief. "I have to go."

"Oh, come on, don't be like that. Have a drink with me."

"And why the fuck would I want to do that?"

"Sage?"

I look back at Alex, who must have stopped once she heard Nora's voice, and offer her a chin lift. "I'm coming. Right behind you, Zip." She nods and then continues to make her ascent. When I focus my attention back on Nora, she's closer than she was before. "Seriously—step off, Nora. I don't know what the fuck your deal is, but we're not doing this."

"I don't know why you don't see it—*how* you don't see that fate has orchestrated this whole thing. I mean, what are the chances that we meet at the same place and at the same time *again*? You can't deny—"

"I'm not denying shit! Do you know how many people are here right now?" I ask, waving my hand to indicate the *thousands* of people that fill the club. "This is not fate. This is an unfortunate coincidence. And whatever the fuck you think is happening here, it's not. I'm married, in case you didn't hear," I mutter, knowing good and damn well she heard. Everybody fucking heard.

She rolls her eyes, folding her arms across her chest. "I'm not naïve. You were married, what, two days after that picture of us went viral? You were trying to cover your ass because you got that bitch knocked up. It's not going to last. Vegas marriages never do. Besides—look at you. Look who you've become. She doesn't know this life like I do. You'll see. And I'll be around when you do, babe. It's fate."

I look at her like the crazy bitch that she is, and then lean into her before I growl, "Stay the fuck away from me." Without another word, I turn and leave her ass behind, ignoring her as she shouts something at my back. No way in hell I'm going to let her ruin my night. We're here to celebrate—and that's exactly what I intend to do.

Millicent

I'M AT THE SINK, cleaning up after the lunch I just ate, when I hear Sage's key unlock the door. Maestro barks, trotting out of the kitchen in search of his master. I smile, listening to Sage greet his pup as he drops his bag and closes himself inside.

"'Sup, buddy? Miss me?"

Maestro snorts his excitement in return, and I'm putting my last dish in the dishwasher when Sage finally enters the kitchen.

"Hey, gorgeous," he says, walking straight for me.

"Hey. Welcome home."

He comes to stand behind me, circling his arms around my middle as he rests his hands on my protruding belly. At thirty and a half weeks pregnant, I'm starting to feel as big as a house. I seriously wonder how much more Jace will stretch me out.

Sage buries his face between my neck and my shoulder, breathing me in as he inches up my shirt to touch me skin to skin.

"How was your flight? Are you tired?"

He grunts before he murmurs, "Hung over."

I laugh, resting my head against his as I reply, "I think I've forgotten what gin even tastes like."

He grunts again, his hands sliding underneath my belly before the tips of his fingers slip into the waistband of my sweatpants. "I need to tell you something," he says softly.

"Okay."

At first, he doesn't say anything at all. Rather, he eases his hand into my panties, making me gasp. "Saw Nora last night." He speaks the words just as he begins to rub circles around my clit, and I suddenly feel bamboozled. "We were at the club—The Phoenix. I only saw her for a second; just long enough for me to warn her off."

I turn my head toward his, wanting to see his face. "Sage," I mutter, my voice airy. It can't be helped. He's worked me up already, and I can barely keep my focus on the conversation. He makes me wait a second longer before he gives me his eyes; and as he does, he reaches down and slides a finger inside of me.

"*Fuck*—that's my girl," he grumbles, his icy blue eyes finding mine through those new, sexy, horn-rimmed glasses. "Wet for me already."

"Um..." I whimper, trying really hard to remember what I was going to say.

"What is it, doll face?"

"God—I can't remember," I admit, spreading my legs wider. "You did this on purpose."

He chuckles, touching the tip of his nose to the tip of mine as he says, "You bet your sweet, little ass."

"I want more," I whisper, bringing my lips to his.

With a groan, he plunges his tongue into my mouth, kissing me deeply as he fingers me slowly. It's not enough, not by a long shot, but it's such sweet torture.

"What do you need, baby?" he asks, shoving two fingers inside of me.

I shake my head at him, the sound of his fingers coated in my arousal as he works them in and out of me turning me on even more. "Your cock, Sage—I need your cock."

He presses his hips against my ass, and I feel the bulge in his jeans, making me nod my head in agreement. Then, in the blink of an eye, his fingers are dislodged, his hands are on my hips, and he's spinning me to face him. I watch without protest as he yanks my sweatpants off before he reaches under my arms and lifts me up onto the counter top. Then, as soon as I'm settled, he unfastens his jeans and pulls out his glorious cock before he shoves aside my panties and slips right in.

The sound of my moan fills the room instantly. I throw my head back, reaching for his shoulders as he pounds in and out of me, fast and hard.

"This is gonna be quick, doll so hold on," he grunts, his hands grabbing each of my thighs as his fingers dig into my flesh. "Shit, you're so goddamn tight."

I whimper, not even caring in the slightest that I'm about to come all over the kitchen counter. "Mmmm, Sage, you feel so good."

He picks up his pace, one of his thumbs finding my clit, and my mouth falls open as the warmth in my core grows hotter and hotter.

"Come for me, Millicent. Soak my dick, baby doll."

"I'm close. I'm so close," I pant.

"Mouth, doll."

I don't hesitate. I right my neck before I lean forward, pressing my lips against his. The second he fills me with his tongue, my body begins to shudder. When he groans, my pussy clamps down around him. I come hard, humming into his mouth, and he follows a few hurried strokes later.

After he spills his seed inside of me, he continues to fuck me slowly—lazily—with his cock *and* his tongue. I drape my arms around his shoulders, wishing I could get him closer, but knowing I've got another ten weeks before that's possible. When he finally pulls his mouth from mine, I prop my forehead against his, closing my eyes as I breathe deeply.

Then, as if my lust-filled haze has suddenly evaporated, I remember how this whole thing came about. He was talking to me about Nora. He knew I'd be upset, probably for no reason, so he made sure I was properly distracted as he informed me that nothing happened. No photographs were taken. No lies have been spread. And, just as he promised, he told me everything I needed to know.

"Sage?" I ask softly, pulling away to look into his eyes.

"Yeah, doll?"

"Thanks for telling me."

He offers me a tired smile before smacking a kiss against my lips. "You're welcome."

TWENTY-FIVE

Nora

I RUN MY FINGERS THROUGH my hair, fluffing it up a bit. I swear, the air on that plane took all the life out of my golden crowning glory. Sweeping my bangs across my forehead, I decide this is as good as it's going to get. I then reach into my purse for a tube of lipstick. After applying a fresh coat, I blot and then pucker, winking at my reflection in the airport bathroom mirror.

God, it's been forever since I've been back to Colorado. I left with no intention of coming back. Nothing happens in this square state. Nobody goes anywhere. Nobody becomes anything. I wanted more for my life. I wanted to be on stage. I wanted to be a *star*. Now, I am. My success is just proof that I made the right decision when I packed my bags and never looked back.

If I see my family for holidays, they come to me. Though, there have been plenty of years where it just didn't work out. My job takes me all over the place at all times of the year. When I'm not choreographing for the show, I'm dancing wherever for whoever I can. I've toured with the biggest names in music, I've been in movies, and, honestly, it's only a matter of time before my name is lighting up the big screen. I've got the talent—and no one can deny that I've got the beauty. I'm in my prime, and I'm working my ass off to make sure I get what I want. Which is how I found myself *here*. In Colorado. An hour away from home.

I want Sage back.

Breaking up with him wasn't a mistake. Clearly, it gave him some perspective.

When I left, he wouldn't come with me. I tried to tell him that our future wasn't going to blossom in Colorado—that *he* wasn't going to get anywhere playing around in someone's garage. I know it broke his heart when he came to New York and found me in bed with someone else. In retrospect, I don't think I could have planned that better if I tried. It obviously took him a few years, but he left that apartment with a drive and determination that has gotten him where he is today.

He's not on top yet, but he's getting there. I know that he is. Anyone can see it. Anyone can *hear* it. Mountains & Men has arrived, and they've got the kind of talent that sticks around for a while. Sage is going to be everything I once thought he could be and more, and I want back in.

Our breakup wasn't about not loving one another. It was about the directions we were heading in life. Now that we're both back on the same track, there's no doubt in my mind that we have the talent, chemistry, and connection needed to rekindle what we once had and start anew. Together, we will make the perfect power couple. The things we could accomplish, the money we could make, the fame that we'd be able to attach to our names—it's everything that I want.

Unfortunately, there's just one little—well, actually, *not* so little—*knocked up* problem in my way. Once again, Sage is thinking with a misguided frame of mind. He thinks he can attach himself to some *nobody* and that it will in no way affect his growth or success. And a baby? At twenty-two? I can't even imagine how he thinks *that's* a good idea. Now is not the time for children. Though, I know how stubborn he can be. I know that getting him to see the error of his ways will be all but impossible. He needs to be pushed, like he was with me.

He needs to be betrayed.

I have every intention of *bumping* into Sage while I'm in town spending my vacation visiting with my parents. But while I'm around, I have plans for that woman he calls his wife. I'm sure it won't be hard to sell her on how horrible the lifestyle of the rock-n-roll legend on the rise will be for their child. The drugs, the alcohol, the *sex*, the late nights and the endless traveling. She thinks this is the life that she wants, but I'm sure I can convince her otherwise. For the sake of her child.

First things first, I have to find her. It shouldn't be too hard, what with Rosemary posting pictures all over social media with her new sister-in-law every time they get together. Fort Collins isn't nearly big enough for her to to go unnoticed. If I can run into Sage in Los Angeles, I can run into his knocked up bride here at home.

I study myself once more in the mirror before me, then slide my phone out of my back pocket as I make my way to the rental car information desk. I dial my mother as I walk, plastering on a smile when she answers.

"Hi, dear. To what do I owe the pleasure of your call?"

"I have a surprise for you," I chirp excitedly. "I've come home!"

TWENTY-SIX

Millicent

THE WEATHER ON THE first Saturday of October is perfect, and as I stroll down the street feeling pampered and loved, I think about Sage and the music video he's shooting at this very moment. He and the band are on the CSU campus filming. They got permission to use The Oval for the day, which looks *gorgeous* this time of year with the big, old trees filled with leaves that are changing hues. Unlike the other couple of videos they've made in the past, this one is scripted. I wanted to be there, but he insisted that he didn't want me on my feet all day. While he made a valid point, I just argued I could bring a chair. That's when he called in reinforcements. It didn't take long for Pepper and Rosemary to put together a girl's day unlike any I've ever had.

When they tried to plan me a baby shower, I insisted that it wasn't necessary. My circle of girlfriends has certainly grown over the past year, but it's not big enough to warrant the effort I'm sure they'd put into it. Nevertheless, Pepper wouldn't be stopped. Instead, she just came up with a different idea. Instead of a party where the presents were brought to me, she planned a day for *me* to go to the presents. Armed with her husband's credit card, and Abrielle's credit card, she led the pack, which consisted of Rose, Lindsey, Violet, and me. We hopped from store to store, buying anything and everything that I didn't have and could possibly need for my sweet boy.

I, of course, insisted on making a few purchases, and I couldn't talk Lindsey and

Violet out of contributing, too. Now, as we walk off the lunch we just ate in Old Town, I feel beyond grateful to be surrounded by such caring women. While none of today's gifts were for *me*, they mean more to me than if they had been. Not to mention, having Pepper along to help give me tips on what to buy and what not to buy helped tremendously.

"So, have you and my bro finally come up with a middle name for my newest nephew yet?"

I free a sigh, running my hands over my belly as I reply, "We're still toying with a couple. I don't know why we can't make up our minds. We've even talked about waiting until he's here before we make our final decision."

"You know, Carter was actually going to be Caleb until he came out. When he arrived, we decided he didn't look like a Caleb. I'm sure a name will come to you when the time is right."

"Lindsey is a perfectly acceptable unisex name," chimes in Lindsey teasingly. "Jace Lindsey McCoy—that has a nice ring to it, doesn't it?"

I laugh, looking over at her as I reply, "It actually kind of does—which means, you *aren't* helping."

"Sorry," she says, the mischievous grin on her face implying anything *but* an apology.

"What names are you trying to pick from?" asks Violet.

"Well, Sage likes Jace Jefferson—but, then his initials will be *JJ*." I raise my eyebrows at her and she hums, offering me a knowing smile. "I kind of like Jace Elliot, but I'm not sold."

"What about—"

"Oh, my god—*Rosy?* Is that you?"

Rose, who is walking just ahead of me, stops dead in her tracks at the sound of her name. I almost run into her, and as I stop myself, I reach my hand out to grab hold of Lindsey's arm to keep from losing my balance. When Rose whips around, her hair following in a gorgeous, heavy cape, I'm startled to see the anger in her eyes. She then steps to the side so that she can see around me, and she pops out her hip, propping her fist against it before she says, "There's only one person on the planet who is allowed to call me that—and it sure as hell is not *you!*"

Furrowing my brow in confusion, I turn to see who she's talking to. When I see her—*Nora Hampton,* in the flesh—my stomach drops. She's even more gorgeous in person than she is on the internet. Her body is perfection—lithe, athletic, and golden from the California sun. I notice as her eyes flit over me before she focuses her gaze back on Rose, and I can't help but wonder how I must look to her, just shy of eight months pregnant.

Holding her hands up in mock surrender, she replies, "Sorry, *Rosemary*. It's been a while. I forgot."

Rose scoffs, clearly not buying what Nora is selling, and my heart starts racing as she makes her way closer to the group.

"What, I can't even get a hello?"

"What are you doing here?" asks Pepper, coming to stand behind Rose.

"Hey, Pepper." She smirks and I already know whatever she's about to say next will not be good. "How's that hottie husband of yours?"

"Satisfied," Pepper retorts, her face completely straight.

Damn. I kind of want to give her a high five right now.

"God," Nora laughs. "What's with all the hostility?"

"In case you forgot, we're not friends," says Rose.

Folding her arms across her chest, Nora replies, "If Sage can forgive and forget, I don't know why we all can't be friends."

I narrow my eyes at her, not liking my husband's name on her lips. Then, Pepper informs, "I think you've got that wrong."

"Oh? So the little chat we had a couple weeks ago was an act? Hmm, maybe he didn't tell you about that." She cuts her eyes toward me, and I realize she's trying to start something.

"You're lying," I mutter.

"I'm sorry, we haven't met. Who are you, again?"

"*Bitch,*" Violet hisses under her breath.

"I'm his wife."

"Charmed, I'm sure."

"My feet are starting to hurt. Can we keep walking?" I say, turning my back to the bitch without waiting for a response.

No one stops me, and as we continue to make our way back to the car, I stifle a groan when we're stopped at a light. While we wait for the walking man to light up, I hope with everything I have in me that she isn't still following us. Then, when the signal turns and it's our chance to cross the street, I breathe a sigh of relief.

Unfortunately, just as I take a step into the street, I hear her call out, "His dick is just as big as I remember. Can't believe I ever let that thing slip away from me."

It happens so fast. I can feel it as *rage* begins to coarse through my veins, setting me on fire. When I turn around, Pepper grabs my wrist to stop me, but I shake her off, stepping back on the sidewalk to give this fucking *lying* bitch a piece of my mind.

"You're just *full* of lies, aren't you?" I grind out, standing as close to her as my belly will allow without touching her. "Sage wouldn't fuck you if you were the last piece of ass to walk this earth."

"Is that what he told you? Is that what he needed to say to keep his hormonal girlfriend in check?"

I ball my hands into fists as I cry, "I'm not his girlfriend, bitch—I'm his *wife.*

And *you?* You're nothing but the sorry *loser* who let go of the best damn thing that will probably ever happen to you. You know it, too, which is why you're trying to steal him back. Well, guess what? He has *me* now, and I guarantee you, you're not half the woman I am—you're not capable of loving him *half* as hard as I do—and you sure as hell aren't as good in bed, which is why after he ran into you and told you off, he left your sorry ass behind to come home and fuck *me*. Now, do yourself a favor, and go *fuck yourself,* because you better believe you'll *never* be fucking my husband *ever* again."

I turn my back to her once more, storming toward the crosswalk. There's still ten seconds left before the light will change, and I move as fast as my body will allow, bound and determined to put as much distance between me and that skank as possible.

I don't see the car turning the corner. I don't hear my friends shouting at me to stop. But I *do* hear the screech of the tires before I feel the impact of a vehicle.

Then I'm on the ground, everything fading to black.

Violet

"*Millie!*" Rosemary's scream is so loud and shrill, it's the only one I hear—but I know we all cry out when she hits the ground. Then, without pause, we all race into the street.

"Oh, my god—honey, Millie, open your eyes," Pepper says, kneeling down beside her head.

"Someone call nine-one-one!" Rose yells.

"Done. It's done. I—hello?" Lindsey says, speaking into her phone, her voice unsteady and her hands trembling. "There's been an accident. My friend—she was hit by a car. She's unconscious. And she's pregnant."

"Millie, honey—can you hear me?" Pepper's voice has now dropped to a whisper, tears flowing down her cheeks.

My heart is beating so fast, and my mind is racing, but my body is frozen. I don't know what to do. She's not moving!

"Pep—oh, god, Pep, she's bleeding."

My gaze follows the direction of Rose's focus, and I gasp when I see that Millie's jeans are starting to soak up the blood that leaks from between her legs.

Shit!

"The ambulance is on the way. The hospital is just up the street," Lindsey informs us, the phone still pressed to her ear.

"I'm going to call Harry. He might—he might—I'm going to call Harry," announces Pepper, digging through her purse to find her phone.

"Fuck—someone has to call Sage." Even as she speaks the words, Rose is pulling out her phone.

I reach up, burying my fingers in my hair, feeling too overwhelmed and utterly useless.

"Is—is she okay?"

My spine straightens at the sound of that voice. After a moment, I stand to my feet, turning to face Nora, who looks as white as a ghost.

"No," I reply, scrunching my face in disbelief. "No, she's not fucking okay! Does she *look* okay to you? *Go away!*"

"Oh, my god—is she—is she breathing?"

I turn again, seeing, for the first time, the driver of the vehicle that struck my friend. I'm about to open my mouth and ask him what in the hell he was doing, but Rose speaks first. Only, she's not speaking to *him*, she's speaking to *me*.

"He's not picking up. Will you call JJ?"

"Yeah. Yeah, of course," I reply, my shaky fingers pulling up his contact information before I send the call. It rings through to voicemail, so I hang up and try again. I'm afraid it's going to go to voicemail for a second time, but then he answers.

"Hey, babe. What's up?"

"Where's Sage? We need Sage. Put him on the phone."

"What? Why? What's—"

"*Put him on the phone, JJ!*" I yell, feeling frantic.

"Hello?" says Sage a second later, his voice guarded.

Just then, the sirens to the approaching ambulance can be heard, and my eyes well up, hoping that they're not too late.

"Sage—Millie's been in an accident. You have to come. Now. You have to come now."

"What are you talking about, Vi?"

I can barely hear him as the sirens draw closer, cars pulling out of the way as the lit up vehicle races toward us. When it's just on the other side of the street, getting ready to make the necessary U-turn, everyone steps away from Millie except for Rose. My heart breaks a little—knowing good and damn well that she will not leave Millie's side until someone pries her away. Sage is her best friend and he's not here. He's not here, but she is.

"Oh, shit," I whisper, my throat clogged with tears.

"Violet, what the *fuck!?*"

"Sage—she was hit by a car. We were walking. She's bleeding and unconscious, and—"

Before I can finish my sentence, the line goes dead.

Sage

I SLAP JJ'S PHONE against his chest, not even bothering to wait for him to grab hold of it before I let go, heading straight for Derrick. "Keys," I mutter, holding out my hand. He scowls at me in confusion, and I feel my hands begin to tremble before I yell, "Give me the fucking *keys!*"

"What's going on, Sage?" asks Maddox from behind me.

I don't turn to look at him as I bark, "It's Millie. I have to get out of here. Now. D—*give me the keys!*"

"No way," he states, shaking his head at me as he reaches his hand into his pocket. "You want to go somewhere, I'll drive. You—you do not need to be behind the wheel right now."

I know I don't have time to argue, so I turn away from him, hurrying across the lawn to the car. It kills me to think that I wouldn't have to rely on *anyone* had I driven here myself. "You better drive like a motherfucking bat out of hell, D! I need to be at the hospital *now!*"

"What? The hospital? Why is Millie at the hospital?" asks Alex. I can hear her feet shuffling through the dried leaves as she races to keep up with me.

"Sage, what's going on?" asks Stefany.

Every time someone asks, I feel myself being pushed closer and closer to my breaking point. I heard it. Heard the fear in Violet's voice. I heard the sirens of an ambulance. My girl was hit by a car. She was hit by a fucking car! My wife—my wife who is eight months pregnant was hit by a car! I was worried about her being on her goddamn feet all day—and instead, someway, somehow, she's now bleeding and unconscious.

"Sage! Bro—slow down. Tell us what's going on," says Knox, grabbing hold of my shoulder just as I'm about to reach for the passenger side handle to Derrick's ride.

"I don't fucking know!" I scream as I turn toward him, shoving him away from me. My chest tightens as the truth behind my words begins to take root. I don't know what's going on. I don't know what's wrong with Millie or if Jace is okay. *I don't fucking know,* and every second that goes by is a second lost. "She was hit by a car—that's all I know—I have to go. *Now!*"

"Shit," Stefany whispers as she begins to back away from us. "Go. Get on the road. I'll talk to the crew. Just go."

It takes ten seconds for all of us to pile into the car. The moment I'm in my seat, I feel like I could crawl right out of my skin. I don't want to be trapped in this cage. I want to *be* there. I want to know what's going on. I want to see my wife. Touch her. Kiss her. *Feel* that she's okay. That they're *both* okay.

"Sage, where am I going?" asks Derrick as he pulls out of the parking spot.

"Shit," I hiss, taking the phone from out of my pocket. I see that I've got two missed calls from Rosy, and I call her back right away. She answers almost immediately.

"Sage—are you coming? They're loading her into the ambulance right now."

My chest constricts again, and every muscle in my body grows taut. I feel so out of control that I can hardly stand it. Hearing Violet's fear was one thing, but Rosy's tone scares the hell out of me.

"Where?" I mutter through clenched teeth, unable to conjure up another word.

"Harry's hospital. I have to go, Sage—I'm riding with her. I'll stay with her as long as they let me, okay? Just—hurry."

She ends the call and I try and take deep breaths as I tell Derrick we're headed to Poudre Valley Hospital. He tells me that he can get us there in fifteen minutes, and I nod, rubbing my hands against the top of my legs as I try not to stare at the clock.

"Sage—she's going to be all right," JJ murmurs from the back seat. "She won't give up. Whatever happened, she won't go down without a fight."

I don't respond, afraid of his words; afraid of the truth behind them—afraid that the truth might not be enough.

TWENTY-SEVEN

Sage

IT TAKES US TWENTY minutes to get to the hospital. By the time we pull into the parking lot, I'm jittery as a crack addict in withdrawal. I barely even wait for Derrick to come to a full stop in front of the entrance to the hospital. I jump out of the car, not even bothering to close the door behind me, as I race inside. I look at the directory on the wall, spot the number for the maternity floor, and head directly to the stairs.

I'm out of breath when I reach the top of the seventh floor, but it doesn't slow me down. I burst through the door, my eyes scanning my surroundings until I see the nurse's station across the way.

"Sage!"

I hear Pepper to my right, glance her way long enough to see that she's headed toward me, and continue to my destination. We arrive at the same time as I ask the woman in front of me, "Where's my wife?"

"Her name is Millicent McCoy," Pepper adds gently, reaching out to run a comforting hand across my back.

The nurse looks between the two of us, offering Pepper a strange look I can't interpret before shifting her gaze back to me as she answers. "She has just been taken into surgery."

My heart drops.

"Surgery?"

"For the emergency C-section, sir."

I turn my attention to Pepper as I mutter, "He's—he's not ready yet. He's got six more weeks. He's not—he's not supposed to come out yet."

"I know, honey—but his chances are good, I think. I mean, babies have been born sooner."

"Is he going to be okay?" I ask the nurse, feeling even more desperate for information *now* than I was five minutes ago. "Is *she* going to be okay?"

"I'm not a doctor, sir. I cannot say for certain your wife's condition or prognosis. You'll have to wait for a doctor to come and update you as the situation evolves."

"Mommy!"

My head jerks, my attention drawn to Carter as he comes running for Pepper, a big smile on his face. She leans down to scoop him into her arms, whispering something in his ear before she grabs my hand and tips her chin back in the direction from which Carter came. Harry rounds the corner, pushing Sophia in her stroller, Henley walking by his side.

"I'm sorry," he says, shaking his head. "I got here as soon as I could."

"I called him right away," Pepper tells me, giving my fingers a squeeze.

I nod, feeling hopeful that with his position as an OBGYN at this hospital, he'll be able to get me the update I so desperately crave.

"The nurse doesn't know anything. *I* don't know anything. Somebody has to tell me something, or I… Could you, please—"

"I'm on it, Sage. Just give me a minute."

He squeezes my shoulder as he passes by me, headed behind the desk at the nurse's station. I watch as he speaks with her for a second. Then with a nod, he hurries back around the desk and disappears down another hallway. I can barely *think*, my head spinning in confusion, and the thought of *waiting* makes me sick.

"What happened?" I manage, looking to my sister for answers.

She opens her mouth to speak, then looks to Carter. Setting him back on his feet, she looks at Henley before she murmurs, "Do me a favor, little guy, take your brother and sister and go sit right over there, okay? Can you do that for mommy?"

He looks up at me, then over to his mother, nodding before he pushes Sophia the three feet between us and the nearest row of chairs. When they're out of earshot, Pepper sighs before focusing her attention on me. She's just getting ready to speak again when, out of the corner of my eye, I see someone walking toward me. As I turn my head to see who it is, my whole body jerks in surprise.

"What the fuck are you doing here?"

Nora looks from Pepper to me, squeezing her fingers anxiously before she says, "I never meant for this to happen. There's no way I—it was a freak accident, Sage. I didn't see it coming. I—"

"What are you—?" I twist my head, my eyes meeting Pepper's under a scowl as I ask, "What is she talking about? Why is she here?"

"I have no idea why she's here," she replies, glowering at Nora. "But it's her fault Millie got upset. They were arguing, and Millie—she should have already been halfway across the street, but she wasn't. And when she entered the crosswalk, this guy turned the corner hard and—"

"I'm so sorry, I—" Nora starts to apologize, but seals her lips shut tight when I pierce her with my gaze.

The blood in my veins turns to acid, and it takes everything in me not to wrap my hands around her neck and shake her as I demand to know, "Why were you even anywhere *near* her? What the *fuck* are you doing here? I told you to stay away from me, you crazy bitch!"

"Sage, I—"

I can't take the sound of her voice any longer, and I snap, closing the distance between us until I'm looking down at her and she's craning her neck up at me—her breath felt against my face. "When I say stay away from me," I start on a growl, "You stay the fuck away from me and *anyone* that matters to me—*especially* my wife. If I ever see your face again, I'll get a restraining order against your ass. Do you understand me?"

"But, it's not—"

The roar that comes from my throat is loud and unstoppable; but before I can say anything else, I feel two hands clamp down on my shoulders, pulling me back. I blink, and Rosy is standing in front of me.

"I got this," she says, reaching up to cup my cheek with her hand. "And if she doesn't listen to me, I'll make sure Derrick drags her out. *You* don't need to worry about this, okay?" She seems strangely calm, but I don't miss the tear streaks that mark her cheeks. She's forcing a level of control I can't seem to manage. "Mom and dad should be here soon. I just called them. Now we just...wait."

We wait. Fuck.

I shrug the hands off of my shoulders before I turn and see that I had a Bradley brother on either side of me. Figures. They've always had my back. Yet, right now, it doesn't bring me any comfort. I don't feel any peace, and the last thing I want to do is *wait.*

Knowing that I won't be able to sit still, I pace back and forth across the waiting room, *waiting* for Harry to come back and tell me something. *Anything.* It feels like forever before he finally returns, and all eyes look to him as he approaches me. Pepper comes to stand at my side, Sophia now resting on her hip; Rosy hurries to join us on my other side, obviously having succeeded in getting rid of Nora.

"According to her examination, the actual impact was broken by her purse. She doesn't have any broken bones—but during the fall, she hit her head, and the force of the fall caused a placenta abruption." I shake my head, signaling he's lost me, but he continues. "The placenta, the sack that Jace is in, it is detached from the uterus. She's lost a lot of blood—and until they've done a full examination of both Jace and Millie, we won't know if they've suffered any complications. But they are moving as fast as they can. You should hear something soon."

"Wait—" I clench my jaw closed tight, fighting the ache in my chest before I ask, "Something might be wrong with him?"

"He's early, Sage, and with the accident—"

"Shit," I mutter, pushing past him, heading toward the nearest wall. I press my forehead against it before I pound a couple punches. I can't believe this is happening. I've never felt so helpless in all of my life. I can do nothing. Nothing but *wait* and hope.

Fuck.

Hope seems like such an empty word right now. It's not concrete, it holds no power, it doesn't *change* anything. I need something *more,* but I'm not a praying man. I don't know what the hell to do.

My head snaps up and I turn around, my eyes scanning the waiting room until I find her. "Church mouse." I can barely get my voice to work, but she hears me. Her head pops up before she stands and hurries toward me.

"Hey."

"Need a favor."

"Yeah. Of course. Anything."

My vision grows blurry with tears as I lose control of my emotions—the pressure in my chest too much for me to bear any longer.

"Pray for them," I whisper. "If your God is real—pray for them. I can't fucking do anything else."

"Sage..." She reaches for my hand, holding it with both of hers as she gives my fingers a squeeze. "I'm going to tell you something good. My God is real. He's *very* real, and He can do anything. And the best part—even if you don't believe in Him, He still loves you. He still hears you and fights for you. It's kind of His thing. He wants you to know Him, and He's not afraid to show off in the event that you doubt that He's there, that He's good, because sometimes we all need that."

"Zip," I start to say, not really in the mood for a lecture—good intentioned or not.

"Just listen, okay? What I'm trying to say is, I've been praying for Millie and Jace since I walked in the door. I'm scared, too. But if I pray this prayer with you—if you'll hold my hand and believe that by the grace of God and the love of Christ that He can do this, He can fix it—well, there's power in unity."

I stare at her for a minute, not sure what to believe. Then I decide, I've got everything to lose right now. If I do this—pray with Alex, believing in the words that she says and the God that she prays them to—if the next news I hear is good news, then I'll know exactly who to thank when I can breathe again.

I dip my chin, offering her a nod, and she closes her eyes before she begins.

I listen to every word she says, clinging to each and every one. I don't know how long she prays, only that as she continues to call out to her God, I want nothing more than to be in this moment with her. For the first time since I heard about the accident, the waiting doesn't feel so bad. Of course, I'm ready to hear some good news—but standing here, her hand squeezing mine as she speaks, I finally feel like I'm doing something.

"In Jesus' name we pray, amen," she murmurs in closing.

When I open my eyes to find hers and thank her, I'm instantly distracted when I realize that we're surrounded. Everyone—the guys from the band, my sisters, even my nephews—they've closed us in, each of them holding hands. Rosy is the first to break the chain, rushing toward me before she wraps her arms around my middle, squeezing me hard.

"I'm choosing to believe they'll be okay, that our prayers have been heard."

I let go of Alex's hand, holding my sister as I look into Alex's warm, brown eyes. She smiles at me and I mouth *thank you*, somehow feeling like that will never be enough for the moment she just gave me.

"Sage McCoy?"

My head jerks in the direction of the unfamiliar voice, and I see a doctor in her pink scrubs, surveying the room. I let go of Rosy, walking around her as I approach the doctor.

"That's me."

"Hi, I'm Doctor Zhang. I understand Doctor Montgomery was able to tell you a little about your wife and son earlier?" she asks, just as Harry comes to stand beside me.

"Yeah. Are they okay?"

"Millie is stable. She did suffer from a concussion, and she lost a lot of blood. It may take her some time to wake up, and we won't know her condition conclusively until that time. She's currently getting sutured up, but you can see her as soon as she returns to her room."

"And my son?" I ask anxiously.

"He appears to have suffered no complications from the placenta abruption, and he seems to be able to breathe on his own. We have taken him to the NICU, as we would like to monitor him for a while. Often times, premature babies can suffer from jaundice, so we want to keep an eye on that—as well as regulate his body temperature. He's quite small—just four pounds, three ounces."

"Can I see him?" I ask, so relieved to hear that he's okay, I don't really care about the details.

She smiles then nods before she turns and instructs, "Follow me."

I turn to look at Harry who grins at me before patting me on the back, giving me a little push. My stomach tingles and my palms start to sweat, each step that leads me closer to Jace making me a little more nervous than I was the step before. Dr. Zhang guides me down a hall, then continues to lead the way into a separate wing. When we arrive, she has me pocket my wedding ring before I scrub my hands. As I dry them, I notice that I'm trembling, and I realize I've never been this anxious before. I've performed in front of thousands and thousands of people—but one little baby is about to bring me to my knees.

Once I have been deemed fit to enter the NICU, Dr. Zhang escorts me inside and takes me straight to Jace. I don't see him at first. A nurse is attending him as he lays under what Dr. Zhang refers to as a radiant warmer. I guess his body temperature is their greatest concern at this point.

"Hey, Susan. Dad's here," she says, speaking softly.

Susan turns to look at us before smiling at me. I can tell it's genuine, and the expression calms me down a little. Jace really must be okay, or she wouldn't look at me like that.

"Congratulations, dad—he's beautiful."

As she speaks the words, she steps away, and I suck in a breath at the sight of him. He's tiny. His little body is covered in wrinkles, and his eyes are closed, but his small lips are parted open and, just as Dr. Zhang told me, he's breathing all on his own. His hair is dark, like mine, and his head is covered in it.

"You can touch him gently, if you'd like, and talk to him," says Susan.

Without looking away from him, I lift my hand and stick out my finger, grazing it over his hair. "Hey, little man." His body jerks at the sound of my voice, and I smile at him in awe. He recognizes me. He *belongs* to me—a truth that humbles me and breaks me all at once. Yet, with each stroke of my finger across his hair, every crack and crevice inside of me is filled with a love that's unlike any other that I have ever experienced. "You're amazing," I murmur, unable to look anywhere but at him as he responds to my voice. "I love you so much, Jace. I can't wait for you to meet your mom."

I swallow down the knot in my throat before I ask the doctor, "How long? How long does he have to stay in here?"

"He's doing remarkably well, but we'll want to keep him close and monitor him through the night. Otherwise, it's possible that he'll be able to stay with mom by tomorrow morning."

I nod, still unable to take my eyes off of him. "Can I stay? Can I stay with him for a little while?"

"Absolutely. You can stay as long as you'd like."

I stay with Jace for an hour, admiring him, touching him, talking to him, and singing to him. He's perfect, and it sucks when I have to leave him behind, but I know I need to go check on Millie to see how she's doing. Susan finds another nurse to take me to Millie's room. When I arrive and see her lying in that bed, I feel relieved and frustrated all at once. She should be awake for this. This wasn't supposed to happen this way, and knowing *how* this all came about makes me so angry. I could have lost her today. I could have lost them both—and that *kills* me.

Standing next to her bedside, I take her hand in mine before leaning down to press a kiss against her forehead. There's a scratch on her right temple, and I'm sure her body is pumped full of drugs in order to combat the pain she must feel right now from her fall, followed by surgery, but she still looks beautiful. My gorgeous girl.

I lean down again, this time pressing a gentle kiss against her lips before I whisper, "You did good, doll face. You did good. Jace—god, I don't even—he's amazing. He's got my hair, and I think he has your nose. I don't know what color his eyes are, yet. He kept them closed while I was with him, but I'll find out soon. Maybe—maybe he's just waiting for his mom to open her eyes, too.

"I'm here, baby doll," I assure her, touching my forehead to hers. "Whenever you're ready, I'm right here. And Jace, too. He's ready to meet you, Millicent. You're going to love him so much. He's perfect. You did *so* good."

I LOSE TRACK OF time as the afternoon turns to evening.

When Harry came in to ask if I wanted any visitors to come see Millie, I remembered that I wasn't at the hospital alone. Though, with Millie still being out of it, I decide to forego the visitors and I went to talk to them instead. I told them what I knew the best that I could, Harry filling in the blanks when I couldn't, and then I told them that they should all head home—grab something to eat, get some rest, and come back tomorrow. They did, some more reluctantly than others.

Rosy had to be dragged out by our parents. Pepper left only after she went to the car and gathered a few of the things they had purchased for Jace earlier in the day. She then told me to give her the key to my apartment, assuring me that she'd be back first thing in the morning with anything else she thought we'd need. When the band left, they told me to text any updates, or if I wanted something better than hospital food to eat. The latter, Violet insisted upon, telling me she'd make JJ get up in the middle of the night and deliver it to me directly if she had to.

After they had gone, I asked Harry to take me back in to see Jace. I showed up just as the nurse on duty was getting ready to feed him, and she offered to let me hold him while he ate. Having him in my arms for the first time was scary as fuck. Not that I'd never held a newborn before—but he's so much smaller than any of Pepper's kids ever were. Nevertheless, I sat with him curled up against me while he ate a little, and I finally got to see his eyes. Pale green and stunning.

I stuck around long enough to change his next diaper, and then I came back to check on Millie. Now, as I sit at her bedside, both mentally and physically exhausted, I fight the urge to worry. Jace is doing so well, despite everything that happened today. Just like I said I would, I credit my thanks where it is due. I know that's all God. But we didn't just pray for Jace—we prayed for Millie, too; so I refuse to believe that I have anything to worry about.

"Knock, knock."

I turn at the sound of Harry's voice accompanied by the noise of wheels spinning against the tiled floor. He's brought Jace, and I stand to my feet, looking at him in surprise.

"What's he doing here? Is he allowed?"

"He's a strong kid. He's breathing, he's eating—he's just struggling with his body temperature. However, instead of having him stay in the NICU all night, I decided that the best diagnosis would be a few hours in dad's arms. You up for it?"

I look at Harry like he's crazy before I reply, "Fuck yeah."

He chuckles, nodding to me before he instructs, "Take your shirt off. He'll need skin-to-skin contact."

I reach behind my head without hesitation, grabbing the fabric of my long-sleeved t-shirt before I pull it off, discarding it at the foot of Millie's bed. As Harry lifts Jace out of the plastic bed, I take him into my arms, holding him snuggly against me. He makes a little noise that makes me smile as he burrows against me, seemingly appreciative of my warmth, and I ease my way back down into my chair.

"I'll leave you to it," says Harry softly. "If you need anything, just hit Millie's call button."

"Yeah," I mumble, my gaze locked in on the beautiful boy my wife made me, sure that—for a little while, at least—I won't need a damn thing. I have everything I need right here in this room.

TWENTY-EIGHT

Millicent

I WAKE BUT KEEP MY eyes sealed shut, furrowing my brow as I stifle a moan. My entire body hurts. Literally, from my head, all the way down to my toes, I feel sore and uncomfortable. Then I hear it—the incessant beeping beside me, marking time to the beat of my heart. I jerk my head in the direction of the machine, regretting the move immediately. I slowly start to right my head when I remember something. It's foggy at first, but then the details become more vivid, and I see the car just before it hit me.

I gasp, my hands dropping to my stomach instantly. Over the blankets that cover me, I feel nothing; it's all numb, and my heart rate starts to pick up speed. I reach my hands underneath the blankets, my eyes filling with tears as my hands touch my belly. Over my gown, I can tell that my flesh is squishy instead of firm, and I know right away that Jace is gone.

"Oh, god—oh, no. Jace!"

My eyes flit about the room, but I see nothing—my tears blurring my vision entirely. The pain I now feel is no longer physical, and I'm overwhelmed by the loss of him from inside of me. I don't remember giving birth to him, and I'm afraid of where he is. My sense of panic makes it hard for me to breathe, and the sob that crawls up my throat erupts.

"My baby! Where's my baby?" I'm cry.

"Oh—*shit!*"

I hear Sage's voice before I see his figure come stand beside the bed. I blink away the moisture in my eyes and see that he's not wearing a shirt, but he's got a little blue baby blanket draped over one of his arms. I recognize it right away. It was so fluffy and soft, I had to have it for Jace the instant I saw it. Violet purchased it for him when we were out.

"Hey, doll face. Fuck—it's good to see you awake."

"What happened? Where's Jace?" I whimper, still feeling confused and afraid.

Then Sage smiles, and it's as if a giant weight has been lifted off of my chest.

"He's right here, Millie," he says softly, turning his body as he lowers the blanket a little. There, tucked into the crook of his tattooed arm against his tatted chest, is the smallest little baby I've ever seen, his head shot with dark brown hair.

"Is he—is he—?"

"He's okay. He's better than okay. The doctors keep telling me he's doing remarkably well."

I burst into tears again; only this time, I'm not afraid. I'm relieved to know that he's here and he's alive and nothing bad has happened to my sweet boy.

"I want to hold him. Can I?"

"Yeah, baby—he's been waiting for you." He leans down and presses his lips against my forehead before he whispers, "Let me just call the nurse to come sit you up."

"'Kay," I murmur, trying to catch my breath and calm myself down.

A nurse comes rushing in a minute later, and after Sage tells her that I'd like to hold my son, she raises the bed until I'm sitting up. "Here, let me help you with your gown. Since you're awake, we'll try some breastfeeding. It's a great way for mommy to bond with baby."

I don't protest as she unfastens the tie behind my neck before pulling my gown down to my waist. Modesty is the last thing on my mind with my husband in the room, and a woman who obviously does this sort of thing every day. I'm more anxious about holding Jace for the first time. He's been in the world for hours—how many, I don't even know—and I need him.

The nurse walks around to the other side of the bed, gently lifting the blanket from around Jace before she scoops him from out of Sage's arms. I can tell right away that the loss of warmth has irritated him, and he starts to whimper, his little fists jerking as he scrunches his face. My eyes dance around his entire length as I take him in, and then I've got him in my arms.

The second his skin touches mine, I'm covered in goosebumps, and silent tears trickle down my face as I stare down at him. The nurse positions him so that he's not pressing against my belly, and then instructs me to rub my nipple against his mouth until he latches on. It takes him a second, but then he opens up and starts to suck, and my heart swells so big.

"I'll be back to check on you in a few minutes. You're doing great."

The nurse leaves, but I barely notice. As Jace feeds, I touch his hair and gently stroke his cheeks. I count his fingers and his toes, loving every inch of him more than I ever thought possible.

I'm pulled from my thoughts when I feel Sage run his hand over my hair. I look up at him and he bends down to press a kiss against my lips. "I love you. I love you so much," he mutters before kissing me again. "You scared the shit out of me today."

"I'm sorry," I whisper, sure that I can't even imagine what went through his mind when he got the call that I was in the hospital.

He shakes his head at me and then kisses me again, giving the back of my neck a squeeze before he turns to look down at our son. Our perfect, gorgeous son.

"Jace Alexander McCoy."

"Alexander?" I ask, a small smile curling my lips as I shift my gaze to admire Jace.

"After Alex. She prayed for him—she prayed for both of you. I was so scared, and then she told me that God is real and He can do anything and then—and then you both ended up being fine. You got hit by a car, baby doll, and you're both fine. So, yeah. Alexander."

"Jace Alexander McCoy," I hum. "I love it."

I WATCH AS the police officers leave after having taken my statement, wishing that I could leave, too. After one night in the hospital, I'm ready to go home. I'm ready to take my baby *home*. While I may have missed the whole child birth experience, the aftermath is no picnic either. It's not that I ever imagined it would be, but if I'm going to be so damn uncomfortable, I'd rather go through it at home. Though, I know I'll have to stay and endure at least another three days before the doctors clear me to leave.

I look down at my precious Jace, swaddled up in my arms, and remember why all of this is worth it. He's so amazing, and I love him so much. I'm in awe of how beautiful he is, and each time I find myself staring at him, I get lost in all of his little details. His long lashes, his little nose, his squishy lips, and his eyes—I love it when he gives me his eyes. They are the palest green I've ever seen, and absolutely stunning.

"One, cold, peach iced tea, and a cinnamon swirl coffee cake," announces Sage as he walks in the door, holding up a paper sack. He grins before he tells me, "Brandon gave us the whole cake and Sarah said that they'd be by later, if you were up for visitors."

"That's nice," I murmur, resting my head back against the pillows propped up behind me. "The police just left. They came for my statement."

"Shit," he mutters, setting the bag on the bedside table. "I was hoping to be here for that."

"You didn't miss much, baby," I insist, reaching out to grab a fistful of his shirt. I give him a little tug and he steps closer. "We can talk about it later. I just—I don't want to talk about it now. Kiss me and then feed me."

He chuckles, leaning down to kiss me before he replies, "Yes, ma'am." He then bends over and brushes his lips against Jace's cheek before he goes to retrieve the breakfast I requested. The second the cold, sweet tea touches my tongue, I fall in love with my husband a little bit more. Then, when he takes Jace so that I can eat, I almost forget how to chew as I watch them together. It's not the same as seeing him with Henley, or Carter, or even Sophia. It's *better*, and it fills my heart with so much joy. The love Sage has for Jace takes my breath away, and peace I've never known settles over me as I admire Sage as *daddy*. I knew that he would be a better father than I'd ever known, but this—*this*...there are no words to describe *this*.

When I'm done eating, he gives me Jace so that I can wake him and feed him. The doctor said that he needed to eat every couple of hours, even if he didn't wake up on his own crying for food. It worries me a little that he hasn't woken up in search of food by himself, but I was told that it's not unusual for premature babies. In the mean time, I take comfort in the fact that each time he latches onto me, our feeding sessions seem to grow more and more familiar and routine.

Just after I pass Jace back to Sage to be burped, there's a knock at the door. I cover myself up and then Pepper pokes her head inside.

"Hi," she coos, her eyes bright at the sight of me. "I know Sage texted and said ten, but I thought you wouldn't mind if I stopped by an hour early to help you feel like a human before everyone else showed up. I brought clothes for all three of you."

"Oh, my god—get in here," I gush, thrilled that I can take a shower and slip into something more comfortable.

When Pepper comes in, armed with the diaper bag we purchased yesterday—simple, yet practical, dark navy blue with white anchors all over—Jace's car seat, and a duffle full of clothes I assume are for Sage and me, I hold my arms out and force myself not to cry. It takes a great deal of effort, which is why I can't tell her what I want, but she doesn't need me to say a thing. She sets everything aside and hurries to my bedside, pulling me into a gentle hug.

"I'm so glad you're okay. God—I don't know what I would have done, what *any* of us would have done..." She shakes her head, her sentence trailing off before she takes a deep breath and pushes out a sigh. "I'm really glad you're okay."

"Thank you," I manage, letting my arms fall from around her.

Jace frees a little burp as she pulls away from me and I look over just in time to see the grin spread across Sage's face as he murmurs, "That's my boy. Good job, Jace."

"Oh, my goodness," Pepper whispers, her voice trembling.

"Well, don't just stand there, sis. Get over here. Come meet my son."

She frees a soft squeal as she hurries around the bed, clapping her hands before she reaches over to take Jace from Sage's arms. I watch as her expression melts whilst admiring Jace's face, and I can't help but smile. Something tells me I'll see that look a lot. My baby is handsome, and no one can deny it.

While Pepper chats with Jace, rocking him as she walks him around the room, Sage helps me gather what I need for my shower, and I go clean myself up. Twenty minutes later, when I come back out in a pair of Sage's sweatpants, a nursing bra, and a loose, V-neck t-shirt, I can honestly say I feel human again. Tired and sore, but not dingy and gross.

When I climb back in bed, Sage heads for the shower next. Pepper gives Jace back to me and then brushes and braids my hair. It feels so good, I almost fall asleep while she works. When she's finished, my long braid draped down the front of my chest, I lean back against the pillows, my sleeping Jace nestled against my chest, and I *do* drift off for a few minutes. I'm pulled from my sleep when Sage presses a kiss to my lips and tells me his parents and Rosemary have arrived.

Abrielle and Ewan stay for an hour, loving on their newest grandson and doting on me the entire time. It isn't until they have to leave that Rose gets her turn with Jace. She's instantly in love, a fact she tells us over and over again, and it makes me feel really good to know that she'll be just as fabulous an aunt to my child as she is to Pepper's. Then, when Harry shows up with Henley, Carter, and Sophia, the boys crowd around Sage as he sits in the chair at my side, introducing them to Jace, and I witness cousins becoming friends already.

When it's time for Jace to feed again, Rose offers to run out to get some food while Pepper and Harry gather up their crew to go home, promising that they'll be back tomorrow. For a couple of hours, it's quiet, and I manage to get a little sleep between feeding and doctor check-ins. It's early in the afternoon when everyone in the band comes by to meet our little one, and I spend another couple of hours watching Jace meet the rest of his family.

As evening approaches and everyone leaves for home, I'm sure I've never been so tired in all of my life. Yet, at the very same time, I'm certain I've never been this happy—my life has never felt this full. Now, as I watch Sage put Jace in the plastic basinet beside the bed, I laugh a little.

"What's funny?" Sage asks as he turns toward me, toeing his way out of his shoes.

"He hasn't been put down all day. He's gone from one pair of arms to another since the moment we got up. He's going to be so spoiled."

"Damn straight. Scoot over."

I do as he says, more than happy to make room for him in the bed next to me. When he's settled, he lifts his arm in invitation, and I prop my back against his side, resting my head on his shoulder as he drapes his arm across my chest. I reach up for his hand, lacing my fingers with his before I close my eyes and free a contented sigh.

"Today…today has been incredible, baby. He's a day old. He's a day old and he already knows more love than I knew for the first twenty-six years of my life." My throat starts to clog with tears, but I ignore them and my shaky voice as I go on to say, "You gave this to me. All of it. Our baby. Our family. This life—"

"Shh," he hushes, pressing his lips into my hair as I begin to cry. "It's okay, doll face. Don't cry."

"I'll never be able to thank you enough," I whimper.

"You don't have to thank me, Millicent. This is who we are. We're in this together. Always."

I nod, giving his fingers a squeeze, and then lift his hand so that I can kiss the back of his palm before I repeat, "Always."

TWENTY-NINE

Sage

I SIP AT MY BEER, MY thoughts drifting away from the conversation that's happening around me as I look across the room. Millie is sitting at a table with my sisters, Violet, Lindsey, and Eden—the woman Millie warned me about. I chuckle as I take another swig from the bottle, remembering how her cheeks heated as I shook her hand. It amazes me how many people get nervous around me now. I know this sort of thing comes with the success we're chasing; I even know what it feels like to be that fan, awe struck to be in the presence of someone I admire, but being on the receiving end still gets me every time.

"I'd stare too, if she was mine," says Easton, nudging me with his elbow. "Hell, I'd stare if she wasn't yours," he adds with a laugh. I look at him just in time to see his gaze flick over and scan my girl before he turns his attention back on me. "Didn't know chicks could look that hot a month after giving birth."

A smirk pulls at the side of my mouth as I shake my head at the lead guitarist from Twisted Tuesday, the band that'll be opening for us tonight. It's been a while since we've played together, our first tour a year in the past, now. It's crazy to think that it's been so long since our bands traveled with Lawful Sinners, but I'm glad him and the guys decided to come up to Fort Collins tonight to help us celebrate our album release. It was Todd's idea to host the event at The Golden Brew, a local brewery equipped with a stage and a space large enough for a decent sized gathering. *Mountain Roads* comes out in three days, and we're anxious to let it loose. Tonight, our fans will get a tease of what's in store for them.

I think about what Easton said about Millie and almost tell him that he's got it all wrong. My wife has *always* been hot. When I first met her, at every stage of her pregnancy, and now—five weeks later. But I don't tell him that. He wouldn't understand. He's still the guy he was when I first met him; the guy I used to be before Millie. He plays guitar in a rock band that's got some local clout. Chicks dig that. His dick digs that they dig it. That's all he cares about. I remember what that's like, but I sure as hell don't miss it. One day, he won't either. One day, he'll get it.

Instead of schooling him on how sexy Millie is, I just say, "Fucking right. Eyes off."

I clap a hand against his back good naturedly and start to make my way across the room as I down the rest of my beer. Rosy spots me, grinning when I'm halfway there, and Millie looks over to see me, too. I watch as her face softens and she smiles at me, her hand reaching up to rub Jace's back. She's got him tucked against her chest in his baby sling, the black fabric matching the black and white striped sweater dress she's got on. Her hair is loose down her back, and when I reach the table, I don't hesitate to bury my fingers in it, tugging until she tilts her head up so that I can press a kiss to her lips.

She hums as I lick the entrance of her mouth before smacking one more kiss against it and pulling away. When she opens her eyes to look into mine, my dick twitches at the lust I see there. Jace is a month old, and for the last five weeks, my dick has been dry. I'm not complaining. I know Millie's body has been through hell, and she has needed the chance to heal. Much like her dry spell when she was pregnant, she hasn't wanted much of my attention; but over the last couple of days, every time I kiss her, she holds on and kisses me deeper. I know she's starting to miss me as much as I miss her. Even still, we haven't gotten the all clear from the doctor to give each other what we want, so we've just been making out. A lot.

I think about the kiss we shared this morning in bed before Jace woke up and my dick jerks again.

"Okay, okay—we get it. You guys are disgustingly perfect for each other. No need to show off," teases Lindsey.

I look her way as I chuckle, and then, just to mess with her, I kiss Millie one more time. My girl laughs against my mouth, and then Jace makes a little noise, and I pull away to look down at him.

He's awake, his pale green eyes looking up at me before he yawns. He looks content, and I know he is because he's in his favorite place—curled up against Millie's chest. He loves being in the sling when it's wrapped around me, too. He likes to be kept close, which works out perfectly, because we like to have him close.

"Mom's still miffed you wouldn't leave Jace with them and my kids tonight," says Pepper.

I lean down and press my lips against Jace's forehead before I turn and remind her, "We brought his headphones. He'll be fine. Besides, he's got to get used to this. We'll be on tour again in two months."

Pepper laughs, holding up her hand as she says, "God, don't even get them *started* on *that*."

I don't say a word in response, knowing that she's not kidding. A while back, just after Millie met my parents, she told me we'd argue about my music until we found something else to argue about. Well, now we don't argue so much about my music anymore, as they've finally come around to the reality that this is how I intend to provide for my family; rather, they disagree with the decision I've made to bring my family *with* me everywhere I go. To say that they're pissed about Jace going on tour with us is an understatement, but I don't care.

Mountains & Men is headlining for the first time. We'll be gone for four months. Obviously, I can't miss that. But I sure as fuck am not going to miss four months of my son's life, either. He changes a little every day. I can't imagine only getting to see his face on the screen of my phone. I can't imagine going that long without holding him—not when I can make it happen for him to be with me. Not to mention the fact that *this* is why Millie quit her job, so we could do this. *Together*. So my parents? They're just going to have to get over it.

"He won't know any different," says Millie, her gaze trained on Jace as she gently strokes his cheek with the back of her finger. "He'll be surrounded by people who love him, and he'll be cared for. That's all that matters."

"I agree. My nephew is going to be such a badass—touring with his rock star daddy," says Rosy before she sips at her soda.

"You're next to join the crew."

She grins as she replies, "I better be!"

"Hey, Sage, Stef wants us to talk with some of the media," says Maddox, clapping a hand against my back before he wraps his arm around my shoulders. He scans the table before he murmurs, "Ladies," dipping his head in greeting. Then he looks at Jace before he says, "J-Jam, my man!"

Millie laughs, smiling over at him. Jace was all of a week old before he got his band nickname. It was Derrick who pointed out that his initials were JAM, and it took two seconds before the Bradley brothers decided he'd be affectionately dubbed J-Jam from then on.

"All right, I guess duty calls. You good?" I ask Millie, giving the back of her neck a squeeze.

"We're good, baby. Do your thing."

Fuck—I love her.

I give her neck a squeeze, bend down to kiss her lips one more time, and then follow after Maddox to join the rest of the band.

It's late when I walk into the apartment. I know Maestro must be knocked out when I don't hear him trotting to the door, and I wonder if Millie and Jace are asleep, too. They left just after we were finished performing, Millie wanting to get him into bed. The guys and I stuck around for a couple more hours, hanging out with fans, signing shit, and promoting our album. Rosy, being the greatest baby sister there is, volunteered to play DD. Now that I'm home with alcohol still coursing through me, I wonder if Millie would deny me if I woke her up for a goodnight kiss.

I hang my keys on the hook next to the door before I lock it and begin stripping out of my leather jacket. Peering through the dark, I toss it onto the couch as I make my way through the living room and down the hall. My steps slow when I see a soft light seeping through Jace's bedroom door, which is only partially opened. Quietly, I press my fingers against the nob and push the door open just enough for me to peek my head inside.

Millie is sitting with Jace in the rocking chair, her shirt lifted on one side as she nurses him. Her hair is pulled up into a messy bun on top of her head, and the make-up she wore earlier has been washed away. She looks half asleep, but she's smiling down at our boy, murmuring to him gently as he sucks. His little fist is wrapped around one of her fingers, and it's as if they only have eyes for each other.

I lean against the doorjamb and watch them, amazed that it's even possible for me to fall in love with them even more—but I do. Right here, right now, my chest expands to make room beside all that I already feel for them. It fills me with so much fucking pride to see Millie just like this. Jace does something to her; he pulls something out of her that only he has access to. It's so damn beautiful and so damn perfect. Moments like these, they're evidence that Millie was made for this. There's a reason this dream blossomed inside of her; there's a reason she was willing to give up everything to do this—because *this* is who she is. A mother. A wife. And a fucking damn fine good one, at that.

It doesn't make sense that she's here. It doesn't make sense that she knows how to love Jace in that special way that only a mother can. It doesn't make sense that she can love *me* in that way that only a wife can. It doesn't make sense because she wasn't raised like me. She wasn't loved the way she should have been. Then, when I came around and our connection was so instant, so intense, and so genuine, it scared the shit out of her. I fought for her, yeah. We worked hard to get here, yeah. But all that we have, all that we *will* have, and all that she has become—I can't take credit for that. Not completely. It's too big. Too grand. It doesn't make sense.

Except, I'm learning that with God—it makes all the sense in the world.

This was the game plan. I was meant for her, she was meant for me, and the things that left us broken made us fit together. The things that make us different make us strong. Our love gave us Jace, and Jace…he's our reward, our treasure, our *world*.

"I think daddy's spying on us," she mock-whispers, peeking over at me from beneath her lashes. "He's almost done. You can come in and burp him if you want."

"Nah," I say reluctantly, shaking my head. "Been drinkin'."

"Okay."

"See you in a few?" I ask, ready to fall into bed.

She nods and I sneak out of the doorway, quietly making my way to our room. By the time I've brushed my teeth, stripped down to my boxers, and crawled into bed, Millie is walking in.

"How was the rest of the party?" she asks, slipping between the sheets as I turn out the bedside lamp.

"It was fun. Missed you, though," I tell her, pulling her against my chest. I don't give her a chance to respond before my lips are pressed to hers. She melts in my arms instantly, opening her mouth when I seek entrance with my tongue. I kiss her deep, long, and *wet*—my erection pressed firmly against her hip. When she pushes against me lightly, we're both breathless as I pull away.

"One more week. God—I want you so badly!" she breathes, pressing her chest against mine.

"I feel your pain, doll face."

She huffs out a sigh and then turns to rest on her other side, pressing her ass into my crotch as I circle my arms around her. I grunt in response and she giggles before she starts to relax in my hold, sleep coming on fast.

"I'm proud of you, baby. Tonight was awesome."

"Thanks, doll," I murmur, tucking my nose between her shoulder and her neck.

"I love you."

"Love you, too."

I WAKE TO THE feel of his tongue between my legs, licking me lazily but *thoroughly*. My nipples pebble as I spread my thighs wider, groaning when he sucks my clit between his lips. With my eyes still closed tight, I have no idea what time it is, but I don't care. All that matters is that I don't hear Jace crying, which means Sage went to look in on him and found him fast asleep, giving him the green light to come back and do—

"Oh, *yes!*" I hiss, reaching down to bury my fingers in his hair as I buck my hips against him.

He pulls his mouth away immediately, biting the flesh of my inner thigh before he grumbles, "Millicent?"

"Mmmm," I hum in frustration, pulling my bottom lip between my teeth as I will my body to remain still. "Don't stop. Please."

"Don't move," he demands before his mouth descends on me once more.

I nod, even though I know he can't see me, and then suck in a sharp breath as he thrusts his tongue inside of me. It feels so good, and all I want to do is roll my hips in an attempt to get him deeper, but I don't move. I pant and moan and whimper, my skin breaking out in a thin layer of sweat as he brings me closer and closer to orgasm. Then, right when I feel myself reach the very edge, ready and willing to topple over, he sits up, taking the covers with him as he rests on his haunches.

"No!" I gasp, looking up at him pleadingly.

He grins down at me as he reaches for his hard cock, stroking it tauntingly.

I knit my eyebrows together as I mutter, "If you don't make me come before Jace wakes up—"

"He's not going to wake up," he chuckles. "At least not for another thirty minutes."

I look at the clock, even though I don't have to. I know that if we've got a half an hour, it's a little after seven in the morning. Jace gets up between seven-thirty and a quarter to eight every morning. He's an early riser, like his daddy—but he also enjoys his sleep, like his mommy. If I put him down at eight, he'll wake up around midnight for a feeding, which lasts about forty-five minutes to an hour, and then he'll sleep until morning. The same time *every* morning—like clockwork.

At first, I thought it was strange, like it was too good to be true and there must be something wrong with him. He preferred sleep at night over food at just four weeks. I thought babies were supposed to keep you up all night every night, but Jace has never been like that. Granted, he kept *me* up because I'd get nervous and I'd slip out to go check on him; but after the first six weeks, his doctor told me it was okay to let him sleep until he was ready to eat.

That, of course, was right around the time Sage and I were given the okay to start having sex again. Sometimes we do it at night; but more and more often, Sage wakes me to make love to me in the morning after I've had a good night's rest. And right now, I do feel rested. I also feel incredibly worked up and frustrated—and we've got at least thirty minutes.

I push myself up until I'm sitting, and then I slide one hand around Sage's back to support myself, reaching for his dick with the other. He lets himself go and I give him a squeeze before I whisper, "*Kiss me.*"

My stomach clenches as he lifts to his knees and then leans over me, forcing me down onto my back again—his cock still gripped in my hand as he brings his lips to mine. He opens his mouth wide, sweeping his tongue deep, and I taste my arousal as he devours me. He kisses me so well, I almost forget where I am, or *who* I am, and that we're on a time crunch. Then he breaks our kiss, dipping his head to lick and suck along the column of my neck. When he pulls my ear lobe between his teeth, I shiver in anticipation.

"You've got me, baby—what are you waiting for?" he whispers, his voice low and husky from sleep.

My eyes widen when I realize he's right, and I waste no time before I guide him inside of me. He stretches me open and fills me up like only he can—and as he does, I gaze up into his icy blue eyes as I arch my back and free a contented sigh. For a second, he doesn't move, and every muscle in my body begs me to take action, but I don't. I let him stay in control. I let him have this moment.

"Merry Christmas Eve, doll face," he tells me, hooking one arm under my left leg, his other under my right.

"Merry Chris—" My words are stolen from me as he bends me in half, easing out of me slowly before rolling his hips and plunging deep inside of me. He does it again, and my pussy flutters around his long, thick cock. His hips are magic. This is not news to me. Even still, I get lost in the pleasure he gives me as he takes me slow, loving me gentle, and yet owning me completely.

"And in my arms you'll find your ecstasy
When you lose yourself, I'll set you free
Baby, just let go and let it be, let it be
Tonight/ Just give me tonight."

I've heard him sing those words a hundred times, both in and out of bed, and yet I never tire of hearing them. They're mine. Each and every word. Each and every note. They belong to me. It's the first phrase he ever sang to me, the melody pouring from his lips when he was inside of me for the very first time. I'll never forget that moment. And as he makes love to me now, his rich, alluring, tenor voice washing over me, I know he never will, either.

"Every night, baby," I whimper, reaching my hands out to skim my fingers up each of his arms. I grab hold of his biceps and moan, "Always."

"Damn straight," he grunts, driving into me hard before pulling out of me slowly.

No other words are spoken as he pumps in and out of me, reaching so deep inside of my core, it's as if he's touching my very soul. He stokes the fire inside of me tenderly, building my orgasm patiently, and when it hits me, he slows his pace even more, arching his back as he rolls his hips and grazes his pelvis against my swollen clit. Before I can catch my breath from my first release, my second overtakes me, causing my whole body to tremble as my eyes well up with tears.

"*Sage—baby...*" I breathe, grabbing hold of the back of his neck.

"Shit, you feel so good. Oh, Millicent," he groans, his hips jerking as he starts to lose control.

I watch him as he unravels above me, feeling absolutely boneless as my gorgeous man comes inside of me. When he is spent, he frees my legs and lowers himself on top of me, resting his cheek against my chest. I circle my arms and legs around him, running my fingers through his hair as we both work to catch our breath. He's heavy on top of me, but I don't mind. I know that any minute now, we'll have to get up and start our day—but for now, this moment is ours.

Then, right on cue, my sweet boy calls to me.

Sage turns his head and presses a kiss against my collarbone as he asks, "You want me to bring him to you?"

"Could you?"

"Yeah," he sighs, pushing himself off of me.

"Change his diaper first," I remind him, unlocking my limbs from around him.

He nods and smacks a kiss against my lips before he reaches for his glasses. As he slides into his boxers, I force myself out of bed to clean up a little. After I've done my business in the bathroom, I slip into my robe, tying it loosely around me. By the time Sage brings Jace into the room, he's practically screaming, his arms and legs kicking in agitation.

"*Someone* is ready for breakfast," says Sage as he hands him to me.

"It's okay, baby," I coo, freeing a breast from my robe as I cradle him in my arms. "Mommy is right here. I haven't forgotten about you, my sweet boy." His mouth searches for my nipple, and when he finds it, he latches on right away, curling into my warmth. I smile down at him as he looks up at me, his lashes wet from his tears. "Is that better? Hmmm?" I hum gently, running my fingers over his dark hair.

"I'm going to take a shower," Sage tells me, kissing the top of my head before he disappears from the room.

I don't watch him go, already lost in Jace's pale green eyes.

It amazes me how much I love him. I didn't even know this much love was possible, but it is. I adore him. Sometimes, when I look at him, when I watch him look at *me*, I'm afraid that maybe he doesn't understand how much he means to me; or maybe I'll mess it all up and he'll think that I *don't* love him—but then he'll grab hold of my finger and he'll hold on with all his might. Or he'll smile at the sound of my voice. In those moments, I can't help but to hold onto hope that he not only understands my love, but he reciprocates it, too.

As hard as it is to wrap my head around the magnificent amount of love that I have for my son, it's just as hard for me to figure out how my mother could ever have fallen out of love with me; or how it's possible that she never really loved me at all. It doesn't make sense. I cannot fathom *not* loving this little boy with all my heart.

It's been a year since my mother was murdered. I had let her go so long ago, but the anniversary of her death coupled with my new reality as a mother has forced me to come to terms with my loss all over again. Not just the loss of her life, but *our* life and the bond we *never* had—the bond we can never establish. I didn't quite understand all that we didn't have until I had Jace. Now that I do, I think I treasure him more. That is a gift that she gave me. The only gift from her that I will hold onto and never let go—the truth that my relationship with Jace is not to be taken for granted. Not one second of it. Not ever.

"Time for a burp, yet?" asks Sage as he returns to the room, smelling delicious, wearing nothing but a pair of sweatpants.

"Just about," I reply, smiling at him as he joins me in bed.

When it's time, I hand Jace over to his daddy, who takes him gladly, propping him against his tatted chest as he works the air bubbles out of our boy. Jace watches me as he endures the routine, his pathetic expression telling me he wants more. I grin at him, running my finger down his nose, and he shakes his head as if my touch tickles. After he frees a loud burb, both Sage and I praise him before I take him back into my arms and offer him my other breast. As he continues to nurse, I turn my head to look at my husband, and then pucker my lips. He kisses me softly, and then pulls away to press a kiss against the top of Jace's head.

"This is exactly how I want to spend my Christmas Eve—with my two favorite guys in the whole wide world."

"Doll face, your wish is my command. We won't even get out of bed," Sage replies, waggling his eyebrows at me.

I giggle, my heart happy and full. "Promise?"

"You bet your sweet, little ass."

EPILOGUE

One Year Later

Sage

"ARE YOU NERVOUS?" asks Hugo as we ride the elevator to the Penthouse suite.

I cough out a laugh as I look at my personal security escort. While it's his job to make sure no harm comes to me, he has also fast become my friend. I call him Hugo the Hulk when I want to piss him off. He hates it, but it's fitting. He's huge. Though, definitely not green. More like a caramel brown. He's a lady's man, too. He's been with me for about six months, but it hasn't taken me that long to notice the attention he draws from the females.

I free a sigh, thinking about his question, wondering if my answer is the truth or a lie.

"No," I reply, shaking my head. "I mean, I don't know." I laugh again, the sound coming out more nervous than I anticipated. "It's a big night—big nomination—but I'm trying to go in with no expectations, you know? Besides, whether we win or not, Mountains & Men is performing at the Grammys, debuting a fresh track with *the* Ashley Hicks, and that's pretty fucking badass."

It's been quite a year for the band, and tonight will be the culminating event for all of our hard work. Three months after Jace was born, we hit the road for our first headlining tour. It was beyond anything I could have ever dreamed of. The cities we went to, the venues we performed in, they were packed full of people who wanted to see *us*. It was humbling, it was exhilarating, and it was still just the tip of the iceberg.

Traveling with Jace was amazing. We made it work, Millie and me, and Jace was great. We definitely had some hard days; days where the band needed a break from the little guy, and we were glad for a night or two in a hotel, but he settled into the craziness. And Millie—Millie was perfect, doing everything she could to keep Jace on a schedule and to make him feel comfortable even as we moved from place to place like the nomads we were for those four months.

When we got back, we hit the garage and got right to work, anxious to put out a third album. New ideas had been brewing while we were away, and we felt ready to do something different, something daring, something *more*—so we did. It wasn't easy, but we faced the challenge head on, we climbed that damn mountain together, and it was totally worth it.

Hugo smiles, flashing his white teeth as he says, "Yeah. Big night, all right."

"I should be asking you if *you're* nervous."

His smile fades immediately, and he folds his bulging arms across his chest as he scowls at me in instant irritation. "Please. It's the Grammys, not Madison Square Garden."

I chuckle but concede with a nod. He's right. Tonight's crowd will definitely be a whole lot tamer than a bunch of screaming fans. We haven't been to the Grammys before, but this isn't our first awards show. Last year, we got invited to the Billboard and the MTV Music Awards. That was pretty sick. Thinking back on it now, I imagine tonight will be a totally different feel. Then again, this isn't just *any* Grammy awards. Not for Mountains & Men, anyway.

When Hugo and I reach the top floor, we both walk to the door of my suite, but he plants himself right outside the entrance as I head inside.

"See you in a bit," I call out as the door closes behind me.

I'm hungry as a motherfucker after our sound check, and I hope Millie got my text asking her to order me some food. When I walk into the kitchen and see a plate with a domed lid waiting for me on the counter, my mouth waters. I uncover the cheeseburger and decide then and there that I'll have to thank my girl properly later. I grab the plate and pick up the burger, taking a big bite as I make my way further into the suite. I hear the soft hum of the TV, the volume turned down low, and I spot Kyle sitting on the couch.

Kyle started with the band when we first went on tour last year, before things started to get really crazy and we needed more muscle. He's a nice guy; but more than that, he's earned my trust, which is why he's now been charged to look after Millie and Jace.

"Hey," I mumble with my mouth full, tipping my chin in greeting.

"Hey." He nods toward the master bedroom before he says, "She's getting her hair done."

A smirk tugs at my lips as I mutter, "Bet she's loving that."

Kyle returns my smirk, shaking his head before he focuses his attention back on the television, and I make my way into the next room. When I open the door, I stop dead in my tracks as my jaw stops moving mid-chew.

Millie is sitting in a chair in front of the dresser and vanity mirror that shares a wall with the door. She's wrapped in a silk rob, her make-up dark and smoky across her eyes, and her hair done up in an intricate pattern of braids and shit that looks *gorgeous*. She doesn't notice me at first, and I can tell by her posture that no matter how great she looks, she's impatient to get out of the chair. This is one of the aspects of my work she wishes she could go without. She doesn't like to be done up for the camera; but she has yet to best the band's publicist, Todd, and my group of stylists. Tonight, she didn't even try arguing. She just had one request—she wanted to pick the designer of her dress. I look forward to seeing her when she's all ready. I'm sure to have the hottest date on the red carpet.

She sighs, but then looks down in her lap, a small smile playing at her lips as she runs her fingers through Jace's hair. He looks to be asleep, wrapped around her swollen belly. Even at a year and a half, he still likes to be kept close. Though, he definitely has a bit of an independent streak, which we're really hoping helps him transition in four months when his little brother arrives.

"Okay, Millie—you're finished," says Delilah, brushing her hands together.

"Thank *God*," she replies, reaching under Jace's arms to lift him up against her chest. He rests his head on her shoulder and she stands with a small grunt before she turns and sees me. "Hey. I didn't see you there."

"Yeah," I start to say, swallowing my bite. "You were busy stubbornly refusing to enjoy having your hair done."

She fights a smile and loses as she makes her way toward me, opening her mouth, indicating she'd like a bite of my food. I know without even asking that she's more interested in the fries, so I pop one in her mouth. She hums happily and then puckers her lips.

When I pull away from our quick kiss she says, "You better get in the shower. We're going to have to leave pretty soon."

"Yeah, I'm on it. How long has he been out?" I ask, reaching out to rub his back.

"'Bout an hour. I'll wake him just before I get him dressed."

"Oh—did our shoes get here?"

"Mmmhmm, just after you left."

"Cool." I take another big bite of my burger before I kiss the back of Jace's head and head for the bathroom. It's time I get my shit together so we can roll. Tonight, we definitely want to be on time.

Millicent

JACE IS STILL ASLEEP when Delilah helps me into my gown. My back is to the mirror as I face the bed, admiring my sweet boy while I patiently wait to be buttoned up. I'm sure the back of the dress is flawless, but why Violet insisted on designing this thing with fifty *real* satin buttons down the back, I will never know. Though, I shouldn't complain; rather, I should be grateful that it fits. It was made two weeks ago, and even though I've grown since then, it fits like a glove now.

When Delilah is finished, she taps my shoulder and I turn around to take a look at myself in the mirror. It must be said that while nights like these always feel over the top extravagant—with the hair, the make-up, and the agonizing over a dress choice—right now, I won't deny that I feel beautiful. Violet did an outstanding job on this gown, highlighting my newest and favorite curve, and I can't wait for her to see me in it.

"Sage's eyes are going to pop out of his head when he sees you in this."

I smile at my stylist as I giggle softly, knowing that she's right.

The body of the dress is a deep, *dark* purple satin with a fitted, black lace overlay. It has a plunging neckline that drops all the way past my breasts, stopping a couple inches above my small baby bump. It's a tight fit from chest to hips, which I appreciate. It keeps my boobs where they belong while simultaneously showcasing my progressing pregnancy. The fabric then falls freely over my legs all the way to the floor. The sleeves are made only of the black overlay and extend down to my wrists.

I've decided to keep my jewelry simple, wearing only diamond studs in my ears, my delicate, rose gold wedding band, and the gigantic engagement ring Sage bought me for Christmas. It's a five carat round solitaire diamond on another plain rose gold band. I love it, even though I choose not to wear it all the time, and will display it proudly this evening.

"Okay," I sigh, turning back to my sleeping son. "Time to rouse my little beast and get him dressed."

"I'll leave you to it. And don't forget your lipstick, hon. Apply just before you step out onto that carpet."

"Yes, Delilah," I say with a smile and a wave.

She really is a godsend. Sage is right. I am stubborn about being all done up, but she's patient with me, and I like her.

I head to the closet to grab Jace's tuxedo before I make my way back into the room. I manage to strip off the clothes that he's wearing and change his diaper before he wakes up with a whine. I then proceed to attack him with kisses, which always makes him giggle—no matter how grumpy he is—and my heart swells at the sound.

"Time to get dressed, baby. You're going to look so handsome!" He doesn't fight me as I put his clothes on, for which I am grateful, and I'm just tying his second sneaker when Sage emerges from the bathroom.

"Dadda!" cries Jace, pointing in his direction.

"Yeah. You see daddy? Are you going to go get him?" I lift him into the air, plant a kiss onto his cheek, and then set him on his feet. He then proceeds to walk across the room, arms flailing, toward his father. Sage bends down to scoop him up. When he's got him in his arms, he stands to his full height, and I take him in.

He's wearing a pair of black dress pants, a tailored, black, short-sleeved, button-up shirt, a black bow-tie, and a pair of black suspenders. The tattoos that wrap around his left arm are on display, as well as the family tree he's got inked on the inside of his right arm—a new branch filled in just a few days ago, *Dean* hidden in the bark of the wood.

His hair, which he wears a little longer these days, is parted down the side and slicked back; and his eyes, my *favorite* pair of icy blue eyes, are framed by those sexy, black, horn-rimmed glasses. Seriously—who the fuck looks good in those things?

Only my rock star.

My dream chaser.

My husband.

My love.

I watch as he exuberantly compliments Jace's attire before he holds up his hand for a high-five. Jace gives him one, grinning from ear to ear, and my heart swells again. That boy idolizes his daddy, and watching them interact never gets old.

When Sage turns his attention onto me, his smile fades as I watch his eyes take me in from head to toe. He doesn't say anything for a moment, and then he reaches down to adjust himself in his pants. That makes me laugh, but I can tell he doesn't find it amusing as he closes the distance between us. He wraps his free arm around me as soon as I'm in reach, pulling me against him before he leans down to run his nose down the length of mine.

"You're going to come tonight. *A lot*." He moves his mouth so that his lips are pressed against my ear as he whispers, "Gonna fuck you so good, you won't want to get out of bed in the morning."

A shiver runs down my spine as I grab hold of one of his suspenders. Unlike with Jace, Dean came with morning sickness that hit me everyday for two and a half months. Then, as soon as I started feeling getter, there was no dry spell. Even now, the feel of Sage's breath against my skin, his hand digging into my back, and the promise of his cock has me slick in anticipation.

He kisses me behind my ear, darting his tongue out before he pulls away, and I pull in a deep breath, holding my arms out for Jace. "I, uh—I need to do his hair."

Sage smirks as we make our exchange and then grabs Jace's foot and gives it a shake as he asks, "Where are daddy's shoes?"

"By the door," I say with a nod.

He hurries over and grabs the box, opening it right away before he pulls out one shoe. It's a custom made pair of red Converse with a mountain-scape etched onto the side. They match she sneakers Jace wears on his feet now. One day soon, I'm certain we're going to have a closet dedicated solely to his sneakers. Converse is currently his biggest endorsement deal, and they spoil him rotten.

"These are *sick!*" he beams.

I chuckle, pressing a kiss to Jace's temple before I head to the bathroom to finish getting him ready.

We all ride to the event together, the band and Violet—who smiles brilliantly every time she looks my way. As Delilah instructed, I apply a fresh coat of lipstick just before we step out of the limo, and Sage holds Jace in one arm, taking my hand in the other as we all make our way along the red carpet. When we stop for interviews and photos, we pass Jace back and forth between us for shots of just the band—as we so often do—before Sage takes him back, grabbing my hand with his free one.

Just as he promised, he doesn't let me go unless it's to keep me out of the spotlight I still try and avoid as much as possible. Even after the year we've had, the success of Mountains & Men growing leaps and bounds, I'm still getting used to all the attention. I'm sure it'll never really be my thing, but I'm content to stand on the sidelines and watch Sage shine. He still burns the brightest blue—like the hottest part of the flame. To me, I'm sure he always will.

When we're finally inside and in our seats, the guys and Alex chat with the other musicians and artists that are seated around us, meeting people they haven't met before and saying hello to the people they've had the opportunity to meet along their journey. Jace sits in my lap, taking it all in, drawing more than a little attention all on his own. He's adorable and so very handsome, his stunning pale green eyes sparkling with excitement, so it makes all the sense in the world that people are drawn to him.

As the show finally begins, everyone starts to settle, and I smile when Sage takes my hand, locking our fingers together. He tells people that he's not nervous, that he's got no expectations, and that he's simply grateful for the chance to be here and for the nomination itself—but I know otherwise. In the dark of night, while I'm in his arms, I see into the depths of him, and I know how much he wants this. I want it, too. For him—for *all* of them. They deserve it.

I give his hand a squeeze and he looks over at me, offering me a wink. I wink back, and then we both look up to the stage, where the host of tonight's show is delivering the opening monologue. We listen, and we wait.

My heart is beating so fast, and Sage is holding my hand so tight, I'm sure it'll be numb if they don't open that envelope soon. Even Jace is looking at his daddy in wonder, feeling his anxious energy. It's been hours, and the moment has finally arrived.

"And the winner for album of the year goes to… *Worthy*, by Mountains & Men."

I hear it as the Bradley brothers, who sit right behind me, stand to their feet with a victory cry. Violet, who is just beside me, squeals in delight. Out of the corner of my eye, I sense Derrick and Alex as they stand and wrap each other in an intimate embrace. But I barely pay attention to any of that—my gaze locked in on my husband.

He's staring at me, his chest heaving, and I can tell that he's shocked. He grabs both sides of my face, pulling me toward him before pressing his forehead against mine, and still, he has no words.

"You did it, baby! You won!" I murmur, my voice trembling with the rest of me.

"Fuck," he whispers before crushing his lips against mine.

When he pulls away, he smacks a quick kiss against the top of Jace's head before he stands and follows his band mates to the stage. The attendant holds out the trophy, but nobody reaches for it. Instead, they push Sage in front of them, and I watch as he graciously accepts the award and steps up to the mic. He shakes his head, and I can't help but giggle, my pride overflowing.

Violet scoots into the seat beside mine, wrapping her arm around me and holding me tight. I lean into her, but I don't tear my eyes away from Sage. Then, he takes a deep breath and opens his mouth to speak.

"Wow." He chuckles nervously, shaking his head as he looks down at the trophy. After another deep breath, he rolls his shoulders back and holds their award high above his head. "Thank you. Thank you to the God who makes all things possible. Thank you to every single person who has believed in us. Stefany Jordan, our manager, Greg Black, who took a chance on us, Tank, who works his ass off and pushes us every time we hit that studio—god, there are so many people, I can't name you all—but we love you, and we wouldn't be here without you. To every musician in this industry who has come before us, thank you for daring us to go to the next level. To our fans, you're amazing. You're why we get to do what we love to do. To our families—your support is everything."

He pauses, coughing out a laugh heavy with emotion. He lowers his arm, and when he looks right at me, my heart skips a beat. Violet squeals again, holding me tighter as he goes on to say, "And to my muse—my life—my heart—my love...Doll face, this is yours as much as it is ours. You inspire me every single day. You, my gorgeous girl, have always been worthy of more than an encore; you're my partner, and yet more than the harmony to the soundtrack that is our journey. Your belief in me has encouraged me and challenged me and picked me up more times than I can count. You're worthy of the dissonance, and you're worthy of my fight—'cause, baby, you *are* the melody. You're the whole damn song."

Other Books by R.C. Martin

The Bridgewater Case
Heartless

Savior Series
Guarded
Tethered
Severed

Tennessee Grace Series
Background Noise: A Tennessee Grace Short
Backwoods Belle

Made for Love Series
The Promises We Keep
Reckless Surrender
The O'Conners
So Much More
The Holloways
Fool For You
Chasing After Me

ABOUT THE AUTHOR

R.C.'s JOURNEY INTO THE WORLD of indie-publishing began like so many of her peers – with a big dream and a basket full of rejection. Confident that she'd one day pen a book someone would say yes to, she spent years crafting stories which became the foundation of her craft. When she'd finally written "the one," she just knew – and there was no rejection strong enough to stop her from sharing her novel with the world. In 2015 she published her debut, and the rest, as they say, is history – only far more romantic.

In a voice all her own, she strives to capture the magic of a kiss, the passion in a lovers' embrace, and even sometimes the breathtaking ache of a broken heart. A true believer in the power of love and the grace found in redemption, you can trust this hopeless romantic to take you on an emotional ride that leaves you forever changed.

www.rcmartinbooks.com

www.ingramcontent.com/pod-product-compliance
Lightning Source LLC
Chambersburg PA
CBHW060540310726
48982CB00009B/1328/J

* 9 7 8 1 7 3 2 7 8 0 2 1 7 *